Bayard Taylor (January 11, 1825 – December 19, 1878) was an American poet, literary critic, translator, travel author, and diplomat. Taylor was born on January 11, 1825, in Kennett Square in Chester County, Pennsylvania. He was the fourth son, the first to survive to maturity, of the Quaker couple, Joseph and Rebecca (née Way) Taylor. His father was a wealthy farmer. Bayard received his early instruction in an academy at West Chester, Pennsylvania, and later at nearby Unionville. At the age of seventeen, he was apprenticed to a printer in West Chester. The influential critic and editor Rufus Wilmot Griswold encouraged him to write poetry. The volume that resulted, Ximena, or the Battle of the Sierra Morena, and other Poems, was published in 1844 and dedicated to Griswold. Using the money from his poetry and an advance for travel articles, he visited parts of England, France, Germany and Italy, making largely pedestrian tours for almost two years. He sent accounts of his travels to the Tribune, The Saturday Evening Post, and The United States Gazette. (Source: Wikipedia)

Literary works:
Egypt And Iceland In The Year 1874
Boys of Other Countries:
Stories for American Boys (1876)
Echo Club and Other Literary Diversions (1876)
Picturesque Europe Part Thirty-Six (1877)
National Ode: The Memorial Freedom Poem, The
Bismarck: His Authentic Biography (1877)
"Assyrian Night-Song" (August 1877)
Prince Deukalion (1878)
Picturesque Europe (1878)
Studies in German Literature (1879)
Faust(1890)
Travels in Arabia (1892)
A school history of Germany (1882)

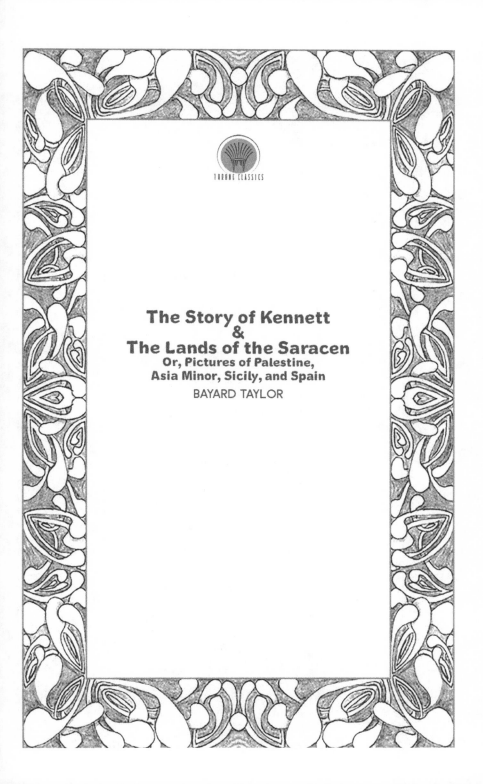

THRONE CLASSICS

The Story of Kennett
&
The Lands of the Saracen
Or, Pictures of Palestine,
Asia Minor, Sicily, and Spain

BAYARD TAYLOR

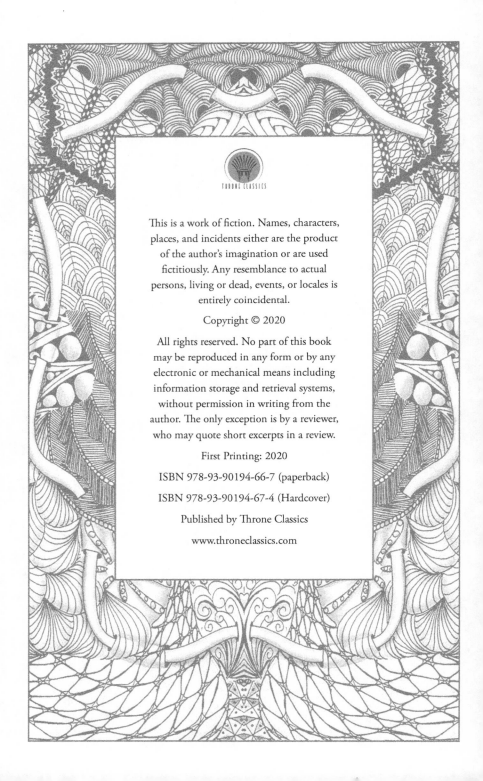

Copyright © 2020

First Printing: 2020

ISBN 978-93-90194-66-7 (paperback)

ISBN 978-93-90194-67-4 (Hardcover)

Published by Throne Classics

www.throneclassics.com

Contents

THE STORY OF KENNETT	**11**
PROLOGUE.	13
CHAPTER I. — THE CHASE.	15
CHAPTER II. — WHO SHALL HAVE THE BRUSH?	26
CHAPTER III. — MARY POTTER AND HER SON.	34
CHAPTER IV. — FORTUNE AND MISFORTUNE.	43
CHAPTER V. — GUESTS AT FAIRTHORN'S.	52
CHAPTER VI. — THE NEW GILBERT.	63
CHAPTER VII. — OLD KENNETT MEETING.	71
CHAPTER VIII. — AT DR. DEANE'S.	79
CHAPTER IX. — THE RAISING.	89
CHAPTER X. — THE RIVALS.	102
CHAPTER XI. — GUESTS AT POTTER'S.	111
CHAPTER XII. — THE EVENTS OF AN EVENING.	119
CHAPTER XIII. — TWO OLD MEN.	130
CHAPTER XIV. — DOUBTS AND SURMISES.	139
CHAPTER XV. — ALFRED BARTON BETWEEN TWO FIRES.	149
CHAPTER XVI. — MARTHA DEANE.	159
CHAPTER XVII. — CONSULTATIONS.	171
CHAPTER XVIII. — SANDY FLASH REAPPEARS.	182
CHAPTER XIX. — THE HUSKING FROLIC.	195
CHAPTER XX. — GILBERT ON THE ROAD TO CHESTER.	208
CHAPTER XXI. — ROGER REPAYS HIS MASTER.	218
CHAPTER XXII. — MARTHA DEANE TAKES A RESOLUTION.	231
CHAPTER XXIII. — A CROSS-EXAMINATION.	245
CHAPTER XXIV. — DEB. SMITH TAKES A RESOLUTION.	256
CHAPTER XXV. — TWO ATTEMPTS.	269
CHAPTER XXVI. — THE LAST OF SANDY FLASH.	281
CHAPTER XXVII. — GILBERT INDEPENDENT.	294
CHAPTER XXVIII. — MISS LAVENDER MAKES A GUESS.	305
CHAPTER XXIX. — MYSTERIOUS MOVEMENTS.	318
CHAPTER XXX. — THE FUNERAL. —	330
CHAPTER XXXI. — THE WILL. —	341
CHAPTER XXXII. — THE LOVERS.	354
CHAPTER XXXIII. — HUSBAND AND WIFE.	364
CHAPTER XXXIV. — THE WEDDING.	374

THE LANDS OF THE SARACEN, OR, PICTURES OF PALESTINE, ASIA MINOR, SICILY, AND SPAIN   389

Preface.   393

Chapter I. Life in a Syrian Quarantine.   395

Chapter II. The Coast of Palestine.   406

Chapter III. From Jaffa to Jerusalem.   418

Chapter IV. The Dead Sea and the Jordan River.   426

Chapter V. The City of Christ.   435

Chapter VI. The Hill-Country of Palestine.   447

Chapter VII. The Country of Galilee.   458

Chapter VIII. Crossing the Anti-Lebanon.   467

Chapter IX. Pictures of Damascus.   471

Chapter X. The Visions of Hasheesh.   480

Chapter XI. A Dissertation on Bathing and Bodies.   492

Chapter XII. Baalbec and Lebanon.   501

Chapter XIII. Pipes and Coffee.   513

Chapter XIV. Journey to Antioch and Aleppo.   519

Chapter XV. Life in Aleppo.   527

Chapter XVI. Through the Syrian Gates.   541

Chapter XVII. Adana and Tarsus.   549

Chapter XVIII. The Pass of Mount Taurus.   557

Chapter XIX. The Plains of Karamania. 568

Chapter XX. Scenes in Konia. 573

Chapter XXI. The Heart of Asia Minor. 579

Chapter XXII. The Forests of Phrygia. 585

Chapter XXIII. Kiutahya and the Ruins of Œzani. 596

Chapter XXIV. The Mysian Olympus. 604

Chapter XXV. Brousa and the Sea of Marmora. 613

Chapter XXVI. The Night of Predestination. 622

Chapter XXVII. The Solemnities of Bairam. 628

Chapter XXVIII. The Mosques of Constantinople. 636

Chapter XXIX. Farewell to the Orient--Malta. 645

Chapter XXX. The Festival of St. Agatha. 651

Chapter XXXI. The Eruption of Mount Etna. 660

Chapter XXXII. Gibraltar. 666

Chapter XXXIII. Cadiz And Seville. 672

Chapter XXXIV. Journey in a Spanish Diligence. 681

Chapter XXXV. Granada And The Alhambra. 689

Chapter XXXVI. The Bridle-Roads of Andalusia. 699

Chapter XXXVII. The Mountains of Ronda. 708

About Author 719

NOTABLE WORKS 725

The Story of Kennett
&
The Lands of the Saracen
Or, Pictures of Palestine,
Asia Minor, Sicily, and Spain

THE STORY OF KENNETT

PROLOGUE.

TO MY FRIENDS AND NEIGHBORS OF KENNETT:

I wish to dedicate this Story to you, not only because some of you inhabit the very houses, and till the very fields which I have given to the actors in it, but also because many of you will recognize certain of the latter, and are therefore able to judge whether they are drawn with the simple truth at which I have aimed. You are, naturally, the critics whom I have most cause to fear; but I do not inscribe these pages to you with the design of purchasing your favor. I beg you all to accept the fact as an acknowledgment of the many quiet and happy years I have spent among you; of the genial and pleasant relations into which I was born, and which have never diminished, even when I have returned to you from the farthest ends of the earth; and of the use (often unconsciously to you, I confess,) which I have drawn from your memories of former days, your habits of thought and of life.

I am aware that truth and fiction are so carefully woven together in this Story of Kennett, that you will sometimes be at a loss to disentangle them. The lovely pastoral landscapes which I know by heart, have been copied, field for field and tree for tree, and these you will immediately recognize. Many of you will have no difficulty in detecting the originals of Sandy Flash and Deb. Smith; a few will remember the noble horse which performed the service I have ascribed to Roger; and the descendants of a certain family will not have forgotten some of the pranks of Joe and Jake Fairthorn. Many more than these particulars are drawn from actual sources; but as I have employed them with a strict regard to the purposes of the Story, transferring dates and characters at my pleasure, you will often, I doubt not, attribute to invention that which I owe to family tradition. Herein, I must request that you will allow me to keep my own counsel; for the processes which led to the completed work extend through many previous years, and cannot readily be revealed. I will only say that every custom I have described is true to the time, though some of them are now obsolete; that I have used no peculiar word or phrase of the common dialect of the country which I have not myself heard; and further, that I owe the chief incidents of the last chapter, given to me on her death-bed, to the dear and noble woman whose character (not the circumstances of her life) I have endeavored to reproduce in that of Martha Deane.

The country life of our part of Pennsylvania retains more elements of its English origin than that of New England or Virginia. Until within a few years, the conservative influence of the Quakers was so powerful that it continued to shape the habits even of communities whose religious sentiment it failed to reach. Hence, whatever might be selected as incorrect of American life, in its broader sense, in these pages, is nevertheless locally true; and to this, at least, all of you, my Friends and Neighbors, can testify. In these days, when Fiction prefers to deal with abnormal characters and psychological problems more or less exceptional or morbid, the attempt to represent the elements of life in a simple, healthy, pastoral community, has been to me a source of uninterrupted enjoyment. May you read it with half the interest I have felt in writing it!

BAYARD TAYLOR.

CHAPTER I. – THE CHASE.

At noon, on the first Saturday of March, 1796, there was an unusual stir at the old Barton farm-house, just across the creek to the eastward, as you leave Kennett Square by the Philadelphia stage-road. Any gathering of the people at Barton's was a most rare occurrence; yet, on that day and at that hour, whoever stood upon the porch of the corner house, in the village, could see horsemen approaching by all the four roads which there met. Some five or six had already dismounted at the Unicorn Tavern, and were refreshing themselves with stout glasses of "Old Rye," while their horses, tethered side by side to the pegs in the long hitching-bar, pawed and stamped impatiently. An eye familiar with the ways of the neighborhood might have surmised the nature of the occasion which called so many together, from the appearance and equipment of these horses. They were not heavy animals, with the marks of plough-collars on their broad shoulders, or the hair worn off their rumps by huge breech-straps; but light and clean-limbed, one or two of them showing signs of good blood, and all more carefully groomed than usual.

Evidently, there was no "vendue" at the Barton farmhouse; neither a funeral, nor a wedding, since male guests seemed to have been exclusively bidden. To be sure, Miss Betsy Lavender had been observed to issue from Dr. Deane's door, on the opposite side of the way, and turn into the path beyond the blacksmith's, which led down through the wood and over the creek to Barton's; but then, Miss Lavender was known to be handy at all times, and capable of doing all things, from laying out a corpse to spicing a wedding-cake. Often self-invited, but always welcome, very few social or domestic events could occur in four townships (East Marlborough, Kennett, Pennsbury, and New-Garden) without her presence; while her knowledge of farms, families, and genealogies extended up to Fallowfield on one side, and over to Birmingham on the other.

It was, therefore, a matter of course, whatever the present occasion might be, that Miss Lavender put on her broad gray beaver hat, and brown stuff cloak, and took the way to Barton's. The distance could easily be walked in five minutes, and the day was remarkably pleasant for the season. A fortnight of warm, clear weather had extracted the last fang of frost, and there was already green grass in the damp hollows. Bluebirds picked the last year's berries from the cedar-trees; buds were bursting on the swamp-willows; the alders were hung with tassels, and a powdery crimson bloom began to dust the bare twigs of the maple-trees. All these signs of an early spring Miss Lavender noted as she picked her way down the wooded bank. Once, indeed, she stopped, wet her forefinger with her tongue, and held it pointed in the air. There was very little breeze, but this natural weathercock revealed from what direction it came.

"Southwest!" she said, nodding her head—"Lucky!"

Having crossed the creek on a flat log, secured with stakes at either end, a few more paces brought her to the warm, gentle knoll, upon which stood the farm-house. Here, the wood ceased, and the creek, sweeping around to the eastward, embraced a quarter of a mile of rich bottomland, before entering the rocky dell below. It was a pleasant seat, and the age of the house denoted that one of the earliest settlers had been quick to perceive its advantages. A hundred years had already elapsed since the masons had run up those walls of rusty hornblende rock, and it was even said that the leaden window-sashes, with their diamond-shaped panes of greenish glass, had been brought over from England, in the days of William Penn. In fact, the ancient aspect of the place—the tall, massive chimney at the gable, the heavy, projecting eaves, and the holly-bush in a warm nook beside the front porch, had, nineteen years before, so forcibly reminded one of Howe's soldiers of his father's homestead in mid-England, that he was numbered among the missing after the Brandywine battle, and presently turned up as a hired hand on the Barton farm, where he still lived, year in and year out.

An open, grassy space, a hundred yards in breadth, intervened between the house and the barn, which was built against the slope of the knoll, so that the bridge to the threshing-floor was nearly level, and the stables below were sheltered from the north winds, and open to the winter sun. On the other side of the lane leading from the high-road stood a wagon-house and corn-crib—the latter empty, yet evidently, in spite of its emptiness, the principal source of attraction to the visitors. A score of men and boys peeped between the upright laths, and a dozen dogs howled and sprang around the smooth corner-posts upon which the structure rested. At the door stood old Giles, the military straggler already mentioned—now a grizzly, weather-beaten man of fifty—with a jolly grin on his face, and a short leather whip in his hand.

"Want to see him, Miss Betsy?" he asked, touching his mink-skin cap, as Miss Lavender crawled through the nearest panel of the lofty picket fence.

"See him?" she repeated. "Don't care if I do, afore goin' into th' house."

"Come up, then; out o' the way, Cato! Fan, take that, you slut! Don't be afeard, Miss Betsy; if folks kept 'em in the leash, as had ought to be done, I'd have less trouble. They're mortal eager, and no wonder. There!—a'n't he a sly-lookin' divel? If I'd a hoss, Miss Betsy, I'd foller with the best of 'em, and maybe you wouldn't have the brush?"

"Have the brush. Go along, Giles! He's an old one, and knows how to take care of it. Do keep off the dreadful dogs, and let me git down!" cried Miss Lavender, gathering her narrow petticoats about her legs, and surveying the struggling animals before her with some dismay.

Giles's whip only reached the nearest, and the excited pack rushed forward again after every repulse; but at this juncture a tall, smartly-dressed man came across the lane, kicked the hounds out of the way, and extended a helping hand to the lady.

"Ho, Mr. Alfred!" said she; "Much obliged. Miss Ann's havin' her hands full, I reckon?"

Without waiting for an answer, she slipped into the yard and along the front of the house, to the kitchen entrance, at the eastern end. There we will leave her, and return to the group of gentlemen.

Any one could see at a glance that Mr. Alfred Barton was the most important person present. His character of host gave him, of course, the right to control the order of the coming chase; but his size and swaggering air of strength, his new style of hat, the gloss of his blue coat, the cut of his buckskin breeches, and above all, the splendor of his tasselled top-boots, distinguished him from his more homely apparelled guests. His features were large and heavy: the full, wide lips betrayed a fondness for indulgence, and the small, uneasy eyes a capacity for concealing this and any other quality which needed concealment. They were hard and cold, generally more than half hidden under thick lids, and avoided, rather than sought, the glance of the man to whom he spoke. His hair, a mixture of red-brown and gray, descended, without a break, into bushy whiskers of the same color, and was cut shorter at the back of the head than was then customary. Something coarse and vulgar in his nature exhaled, like a powerful odor, through the assumed shell of a gentleman, which he tried to wear, and rendered the assumption useless.

A few guests, who had come from a distance, had just finished their dinner in the farm-house. Owing to causes which will hereafter be explained, they exhibited less than the usual plethoric satisfaction after the hospitality of the country, and were the first to welcome the appearance of a square black bottle, which went the rounds, with the observation: "Whet up for a start!"

Mr. Barton drew a heavy silver watch from his fob, and carefully holding it so that the handful of glittering seals could be seen by everybody, appeared to meditate.

"Five minutes to one," he said at last. "No use in waiting much longer; 't isn't good to keep the hounds fretting. Any signs of anybody else?"

The others, in response, turned towards the lane and highway. Some, with keen eyes, fancied they could detect a horseman through the wood. Presently Giles, from his perch at the door of the corn-crib, cried out:

"There's somebody a-comin' up the meadow. I don't know the hoss; rides like Gilbert Potter. Gilbert it is, blast me! new-mounted."

"Another plough-horse!" suggested Mr. Joel Ferris, a young Pennsbury buck, who, having recently come into a legacy of four thousand pounds, wished it to be forgotten that he had never ridden any but plough-horses until within the year.

The others laughed, some contemptuously, glancing at their own well-equipped animals the while, some constrainedly, for they knew the approaching guest, and felt a slight compunction in seeming to side with Mr. Ferris. Barton began to smile stiffly, but presently bit his lip and drew his brows together.

Pressing the handle of his riding-whip against his chin, he stared vacantly up the lane, muttering "We must wait, I suppose."

His lids were lifted in wonder the next moment; he seized Ferris by the arm, and exclaimed:—

"Whom have we here?"

All eyes turned in the same direction, descried a dashing horseman in the lane.

"Upon my soul I don't know," said Ferris. "Anybody expected from the Fagg's Manor way?"

"Not of my inviting," Barton answered.

The other guests professed their entire ignorance of the stranger, who, having by this time passed the bars, rode directly up to the group. He was a short, broad-shouldered man of nearly forty, with a red, freckled face, keen, snapping gray eyes, and a close, wide mouth. Thick, jet-black whiskers, eyebrows and pig-tail made the glance of those eyes, the gleam of his teeth, and the color of his skin where it was not reddened by the wind, quite dazzling. This violent and singular contrast gave his plain, common features an air of distinction. Although his mulberry coat was somewhat faded, it had a jaunty cut, and if his breeches were worn and stained, the short, muscular thighs and strong knees they covered, told of a practised horseman.

He rode a large bay gelding, poorly groomed, and apparently not remarkable for blood, but with no marks of harness on his rough coat.

"Good-day to you, gentlemen!" said the stranger, familiarly knocking the handle of his whip against his cocked hat. "Squire Barton, how do you do?"

"How do you do, sir?" responded Mr. Barton, instantly flattered by the title, to which he had no legitimate right. "I believe," he added, "you have the advantage of me."

A broad smile, or rather grin, spread over the stranger's face. His teeth flashed, and his eyes shot forth a bright, malicious ray. He hesitated a moment, ran rapidly over the faces of the others without perceptibly moving his head, and noting the general curiosity, said, at last:—

"I hardly expected to find an acquaintance in this neighborhood, but a chase makes quick fellowship. I happened to hear of it at the Anvil Tavern,—am on my way to the Rising Sun; so, you see, if the hunt goes down Tuffkenamon, as is likely, it's so much of a lift on the way."

"All right,—glad to have you join us. What did you say your name was?" inquired Mr. Barton.

"I didn't say what; it's Fortune,—a fortune left to me by my father, ha! ha! Don't care if I do"—

With the latter words, Fortune (as we must now call him) leaned down from his saddle, took the black bottle from the unresisting hands of Mr. Ferris, inverted it against his lips, and drank so long and luxuriously as to bring water into the mouths of the spectators. Then, wiping his mouth with the back of his freckled hand, he winked and nodded his head approvingly to Mr. Barton.

Meanwhile the other horseman had arrived from the meadow, after dismounting and letting down the bars, over which his horse stepped slowly and cautiously,—a circumstance which led some of the younger guests to exchange quiet, amused glances. Gilbert Potter, however, received a hearty greeting from all, including the host, though the latter, by an increased shyness in meeting his gaze, manifested some secret constraint.

"I was afraid I should have been too late," said Gilbert; "the old break in the hedge is stopped at last, so I came over the hill above, without thinking on the swampy bit, this side."

"Breaking your horse in to rough riding, eh?" said Mr. Ferris, touching

20

a neighbor with his elbow.

Gilbert smiled good-humoredly, but said nothing, and a little laugh went around the circle. Mr. Fortune seemed to understand the matter in a flash. He looked at the brown, shaggy-maned animal, standing behind its owner, with its head down, and said, in a low, sharp tone: "I see—where did you get him?"

Gilbert returned the speaker's gaze a moment before he answered. "From a drover," he then said.

"By the Lord!"-ejaculated Mr. Barton, who had again conspicuously displayed his watch, "it's over half-past one. Look out for the hounds,—we must start, if we mean to do any riding this day!"

The owners of the hounds picked out their several animals and dragged them aside, in which operation they were uproariously assisted by the boys. The chase in Kennett, it must be confessed, was but a very faint shadow of the old English pastime. It had been kept up, in the neighborhood, from the force of habit in the Colonial times, and under the depression which the strong Quaker element among the people exercised upon all sports and recreations. The breed of hounds, not being restricted to close communion, had considerably degenerated, and few, even of the richer farmers, could afford to keep thoroughbred hunters for this exclusive object. Consequently all the features of the pastime had become rude and imperfect, and, although very respectable gentlemen still gave it their countenance, there was a growing suspicion that it was a questionable, if not demoralizing diversion. It would be more agreeable if we could invest the present occasion with a little more pomp and dignity; but we must describe the event precisely as it occurred.

The first to greet Gilbert were his old friends, Joe and Jake Fairthorn. These boys loudly lamented that their father had denied them the loan of his old gray mare, Bonnie; they could ride double on a gallop, they said; and wouldn't Gilbert take them along, one before and one behind him? But he laughed and shook his head.

"Well, we've got Watch, anyhow," said Joe, who thereupon began whispering very earnestly to Jake, as the latter seized the big family bull-dog by the collar. Gilbert foreboded mischief, and kept his eye upon the pair.

A scuffle was heard in the corn-crib, into which Giles had descended. The boys shuddered and chuckled in a state of delicious fear, which changed into a loud shout of triumph, as the soldier again made his appearance at the door, with the fox in his arms, and a fearless hand around its muzzle.

"By George! what a fine brush!" exclaimed Mr. Ferris.

A sneer, quickly disguised in a grin, ran over Fortune's face. The hounds howled and tugged; Giles stepped rapidly across the open space where the knoll sloped down to the meadow. It was a moment of intense expectation.

Just then, Joe and Jake Fairthorn let go their hold on the bull-dog's collar; but Gilbert Potter caught the animal at the second bound. The boys darted behind the corn-crib, scared less by Gilbert's brandished whip than by the wrath and astonishment in Mr. Barton's face.

"Cast him off, Giles!" the latter cried.

The fox, placed upon the ground, shot down the slope and through the fence into the meadow. Pausing then, as if first to assure himself of his liberty, he took a quick, keen survey of the ground before him, and then started off towards the left.

"He's making for the rocks!" cried Mr. Ferris; to which the stranger, who was now watching the animal with sharp interest, abruptly answered, "Hold your tongue!"

Within a hundred yards the fox turned to the right, and now, having apparently made up his mind to the course, struck away in a steady but not hurried trot. In a minute he had reached the outlying trees of the timber along the creek.

"He's a cool one, he is!" remarked Giles, admiringly.

By this time he was hidden by the barn from the sight of the hounds, and they were let loose. While they darted about in eager quest of the scent, the hunters mounted in haste. Presently an old dog gave tongue like a trumpet, the pack closed, and the horsemen followed. The boys kept pace with them over the meadow, Joe and Jake taking the lead, until the creek abruptly stopped their race, when they sat down upon the bank and cried bitterly, as the last of the hunters disappeared through the thickets on the further side.

It was not long before a high picket-fence confronted the riders. Mr. Ferris, with a look of dismay, dismounted. Fortune, Barton, and Gilbert Potter each threw off a heavy "rider," and leaped their horses over the rails. The others followed through the gaps thus made, and all swept across the field at full speed, guided by the ringing cry of the hounds.

When they reached the Wilmington road, the cry swerved again to the left, and most of the hunters, with Barton at their head, took the highway in order to reach the crossroad to New-Garden more conveniently. Gilbert and Fortune alone sprang into the opposite field, and kept a straight southwestern course for the other branch of Redley Creek. The field was divided by a stout thorn-hedge from the one beyond it, and the two horsemen, careering neck and neck, glanced at each other curiously as they approached this barrier. Their respective animals were transformed; the unkempt manes were curried by the wind, as they flew; their sleepy eyes were full of fire, and the splendid muscles, aroused to complete action, marked their hides with lines of beauty. There was no wavering in either; side by side they hung in flight above the hedge, and side by side struck the clean turf beyond.

Then Fortune turned his head, nodded approvingly to Gilbert, and muttered to himself: "He's a gallant fellow,—I'll not rob him of the brush." But he laughed a short, shrill, wicked laugh the next moment.

Before they reached the creek, the cry of the hounds ceased. They halted a moment on the bank, irresolute.

"He must have gone down towards the snuff-mill," said Gilbert, and was about to change his course.

"Stop," said the stranger; "if he has, we've lost him any way. Hark! hurrah!"

A deep bay rang from the westward, through the forest. Gilbert shouted: "The lime-quarry!" and dashed across the stream. A lane was soon reached, and as the valley opened, they saw the whole pack heading around the yellow mounds of earth which marked the locality of the quarry. At the same instant some one shouted in the rear, and they saw Mr. Alfred Barton, thundering after, and apparently bent on diminishing the distance between them.

A glance was sufficient to show that the fox had not taken refuge in the quarry, but was making a straight course up the centre of the valley. Here it was not so easy to follow. The fertile floor of Tuffkenamon, stripped of woods, was crossed by lines of compact hedge, and, moreover, the huntsmen were not free to tear and trample the springing wheat of the thrifty Quaker farmers. Nevertheless, one familiar with the ground could take advantage of a gap here and there, choose the connecting pasture-fields, and favor his course with a bit of road, when the chase swerved towards either side of the valley. Gilbert Potter soon took the lead, closely followed by Fortune. Mr. Barton was perhaps better mounted than either, but both horse and rider were heavier, and lost in the moist fields, while they gained rapidly where the turf was firm.

After a mile and a half of rather toilsome riding, all three were nearly abreast. The old tavern of the Hammer and Trowel was visible, at the foot of the northern hill; the hounds, in front, bayed in a straight line towards Avondale Woods,—but a long slip of undrained bog made its appearance. Neither gentleman spoke, for each was silently tasking his wits how to accomplish the passage most rapidly. The horses began to sink into the oozy soil: only a very practised eye could tell where the surface was firmest, and even this knowledge was but slight advantage.

Nimbly as a cat Gilbert sprang from the saddle, still holding the pummel in his right hand, touched his horse's flank with the whip, and bounded from one tussock to another. The sagacious animal seemed to understand and assist his manoeuvre. Hardly had he gained firm ground than he was in his seat again, while Mr. Barton was still plunging in the middle of the bog.

By the time he had reached the road, Gilbert shrewdly guessed where the chase would terminate. The idlers on the tavern-porch cheered him as he swept around the corner; the level highway rang to the galloping hoofs of his steed, and in fifteen minutes he had passed the long and lofty oak woods of Avondale. At the same moment, fox and hounds broke into full view, sweeping up the meadow on his left. The animal made a last desperate effort to gain a lair among the bushes and loose stones on the northern hill; but the hunter was there before him, the hounds were within reach, and one faltering moment decided his fate.

Gilbert sprang down among the frantic dogs, and saved the brush from the rapid dismemberment which had already befallen its owner. Even then, he could only assure its possession by sticking it into his hat and remounting his horse. When he looked around, no one was in sight, but the noise of hoofs was heard crashing through the wood.

Mr. Ferris, with some dozen others, either anxious to spare their horses or too timid to take the hedges in the valley, had kept the cross-road to New-Garden, whence a lane along the top of the southern hill led them into the Avondale Woods. They soon emerged, shouting and yelling, upon the meadow.

The chase was up; and Gilbert Potter, on his "plough horse," was the only huntsman in at the death.

CHAPTER II. — WHO SHALL HAVE THE BRUSH?

Mr. Barton and Fortune, who seemed to have become wonderfully intimate during the half hour in which they had ridden together, arrived at the same time. The hunters, of whom a dozen were now assembled (some five or six inferior horses being still a mile in the rear), were all astounded, and some of them highly vexed, at the result of the chase. Gilbert's friends crowded about him, asking questions as to the course he had taken, and examining the horse, which had maliciously resumed its sleepy look, and stood with drooping head. The others had not sufficient tact to disguise their ill-humor, for they belonged to that class which, in all countries, possesses the least refinement—the uncultivated rich.

"The hunt started well, but it's a poor finish," said one of these.

"Never mind!" Mr. Ferris remarked; "such things come by chance."

These words struck the company to silence. A shock, felt rather than perceived, fell upon them, and they looked at each other with an expression of pain and embarrassment. Gilbert's face faded to a sallow paleness, and his eyes were fastened upon those of the speaker with a fierce and dangerous intensity. Mr. Ferris colored, turned away, and called to his hounds.

Fortune was too sharp an observer not to remark the disturbance. He cried out, and his words produced an instant, general sense of relief:—

"It's been a fine run, friends, and we can't do better than ride back to the Hammer and Trowel, and take a 'smaller'—or a 'bigger' for that matter—at my expense. You must let me pay my footing now, for I hope to ride with you many a time to come. Faith! If I don't happen to buy that place down by the Rising Sun, I'll try to find another, somewhere about New London or Westgrove, so that we can be nearer neighbors."

With that he grinned, rather than smiled; but although his manner would have struck a cool observer as being mocking instead of cordial, the invitation was accepted with great show of satisfaction, and the horsemen fell into pairs, forming a picturesque cavalcade as they passed under the tall, leafless oaks.

Gilbert Potter speedily recovered his self-possession, but his face was stern and his manner abstracted. Even the marked and careful kindness of his friends seemed secretly to annoy him, for it constantly suggested the something by which it had been prompted. Mr. Alfred Barton, however, whether under the influence of Fortune's friendship, or from a late suspicion of his duties as host of the day, not unkindly complimented the young man, and insisted on filling his glass. Gilbert could do no less than courteously accept the attention, but he shortly afterwards stole away from the noisy company, mounted his horse, and rode slowly towards Kennett Square.

As he thus rides, with his eyes abstractedly fixed before him, we will take the opportunity to observe him more closely. Slightly under-sized, compactly built, and with strongly-marked features, his twenty-four years have the effect of thirty. His short jacket and knee-breeches of gray velveteen cover a chest broad rather than deep, and reveal the fine, narrow loins and muscular thighs of a frame matured and hardened by labor. His hands, also, are hard and strong, but not ungraceful in form. His neck, not too short, is firmly planted, and the carriage of his head indicates patience and energy. Thick, dark hair enframes his square forehead, and straight, somewhat heavy brows. His eyes of soft dark-gray, are large, clear, and steady, and only change their expression under strong excitement. His nose is straight and short, his mouth a little too wide for beauty, and less firm now than it will be ten years hence, when the yearning tenderness shall have vanished from the corners of the lips; and the chin, in its broad curve, harmonizes with the square lines of the brow. Evidently a man whose youth has not been a holiday; who is reticent rather than demonstrative; who will be strong in his loves and long in his hates; and, without being of a despondent nature, can never become heartily sanguine.

The spring-day was raw and overcast, as it drew towards its close, and the rider's musings seemed to accord with the change in the sky. His face expressed a singular mixture of impatience, determined will, and unsatisfied desire. But where most other men would have sighed, or given way to some involuntary exclamation, he merely set his teeth, and tightened the grasp on his whip-handle.

He was not destined, however, to a solitary journey. Scarcely had he made three quarters of a mile, when, on approaching the junction of a wood-road which descended to the highway from a shallow little glen on the north, the sound of hoofs and voices met his ears. Two female figures appeared, slowly guiding their horses down the rough road. One, from her closely-fitting riding-habit of drab cloth, might have been a Quakeress, but for the feather (of the same sober color) in her beaver hat, and the rosette of dark red ribbon at her throat. The other, in bluish-gray, with a black beaver and no feather, rode a heavy old horse with a blind halter on his head, and held the stout leathern reins with a hand covered with a blue woollen mitten. She rode in advance, paying little heed to her seat, but rather twisting herself out of shape in the saddle in order to chatter to her companion in the rear.

"Do look where you are going, Sally!" cried the latter as the blinded horse turned aside from the road to drink at a little brook that oozed forth from under the dead leaves.

Thus appealed to, the other lady whirled around with a half-jump, and caught sight of Gilbert Potter and of her horse's head at the same instant.

"Whoa there, Bonnie!" she cried. "Why, Gilbert, where did you come from? Hold up your head, I say! Martha, here's Gilbert, with a brush in his hat! Don't be afraid, you beast; did you never smell a fox? Here, ride in between, Gilbert, and tell us all about it! No, not on that side, Martha; you can manage a horse better than I can!"

In her efforts to arrange the order of march, she drove her horse's head into Gilbert's back, and came near losing her balance. With amused screams, and bursts of laughter, and light, rattling exclamations, she finally succeeded in placing herself at his left hand, while her adroit and self-possessed companion quietly rode up to his right Then, dropping the reins on their horses' necks, the two ladies resigned themselves to conversation, as the three slowly jogged homewards abreast.

"Now, Gilbert!" exclaimed Miss Sally Fairthorn, after waiting a moment for him to speak; "did you really earn the brush, or beg it from one of them, on the way home?"

"Begging, you know, is my usual habit," he answered, mockingly.

"I know you're as proud as Lucifer, when you've a mind to be so. There!"

Gilbert was accustomed to the rattling tongue of his left-hand neighbor, and generally returned her as good as she gave. To-day, however, he was in no mood for repartee. He drew down his brows and made no answer to her charge.

"Where was the fox earthed?" asked the other lady, after a rapid glance at his face.

Martha Deane's voice was of that quality which compels an answer, and a courteous answer, from the surliest of mankind. It was not loud, it could scarcely be called musical; but every tone seemed to exhale freshness as of dew, and brightness as of morning. It was pure, slightly resonant; and all the accumulated sorrows of life could not have veiled its inherent gladness. It could never grow harsh, never be worn thin, or sound husky from weariness; its first characteristic would always be youth, and the joy of youth, though it came from the lips of age.

Doubtless Gilbert Potter did not analyze the charm which it exercised upon him; it was enough that he felt and submitted to it. A few quiet remarks sufficed to draw from him the story of the chase, in all its particulars, and the lively interest in Martha Deane's face, the boisterous glee of Sally Fairthorn, with his own lurking sense of triumph, soon swept every gloomy line from his visage. His mouth relaxed from its set compression, and wore a winning sweetness; his eyes shone softly-bright, and a nimble spirit of gayety gave grace to his movements.

"Fairly won, I must say!" exclaimed Miss Sally Fairthorn, when the narrative was finished. "And now, Gilbert, the brush?"

"The brush?"

"Who's to have it, I mean. Did you never get one before, as you don't

29

seem to understand?"

"Yes, I understand," said he, in an indifferent tone; "it may be had for the asking."

"Then it's mine!" cried Sally, urging her heavy horse against him and making a clutch at his cap. But he leaned as suddenly away, and shot a length ahead, out of her reach. Miss Deane's horse, a light, spirited animal, kept pace with his.

"Martha!" cried the disappointed damsel, "Martha! one of us must have it; ask him, you!"

"No," answered Martha, with her clear blue eyes fixed on Gilbert's face, "I will not ask."

He returned her gaze, and his eyes seemed to say: "Will you take it, knowing what the acceptance implies?"

She read the question correctly; but of this he was not sure. Neither, if it were so, could he trust himself to interpret the answer. Sally had already resumed her place on his left, and he saw that the mock strife would be instantly renewed. With a movement so sudden as to appear almost ungracious, he snatched the brush from his cap and extended it to Martha Deane, without saying a word.

If she hesitated, it was at least no longer than would be required in order to understand the action. Gilbert might either so interpret it, or suspect that she had understood the condition in his mind, and meant to signify the rejection thereof. The language of gestures is wonderfully rapid, and all that could be said by either, in this way, was over, and the brush in Martha Deane's hand, before Sally Fairthorn became aware of the transfer.

"Well-done, Martha!" she exclaimed: "Don't let him have it again! Do you know to whom he would have given it: an A. and a W., with the look of an X,—so!"

Thereupon Sally pulled off her mittens and crossed her forefingers, an action which her companions understood—in combination with the mysterious initials—to be the rude, primitive symbol of a squint.

Gilbert looked annoyed, but before he could reply, Sally let go the rein in order to put on her mittens, and the blinded mare quickly dropping her head, the rein slipped instantly to the animal's ears. The latter perceived her advantage, and began snuffing along the edges of the road in a deliberate search for spring grass. In vain Sally called and kicked; the mare provokingly preserved her independence. Finally, a piteous appeal to Gilbert, who had pretended not to notice the dilemma, and was a hundred yards in advance, was Sally's only resource. The two halted and enjoyed her comical helplessness.

"That's enough, Gilbert," said Martha Deane, presently, "go now and pick up the rein."

He rode back, picked it up, and handed it to Sally without speaking.

"Gilbert," she said, with a sudden demure change of tone, as they rode on to where Miss Deane was waiting, "come and take supper with us, at home. Martha has promised. You've hardly been to see us in a month."

"You know how much I have to do, Sally," he answered. "It isn't only that, to-day being a Saturday; but I've promised mother to be at home by dark, and fetch a quarter of tea from the store."

"When you've once promised, I know, oxen couldn't pull you the other way."

"I don't often see your mother, Gilbert," said Martha Deane; "she is well?"

"Thank you, Martha,—too well, and yet not well enough."

"What do you mean?"

"I mean," he answered, "that she does more than she has strength to do. If she had less she would be forced to undertake less; if she had more, she would be equal to her undertaking."

"I understand you now. But you should not allow her to go on in that way; you should"—

31

What Miss Deane would have said must remain unwritten. Gilbert's eyes were upon her, and held her own; perhaps a little more color came into her face, but she did not show the slightest embarrassment. A keen observer might have supposed that either a broken or an imperfect relation existed between the two, which the gentleman was trying to restore or complete without the aid of words; and that, furthermore, while the lady was the more skilful in the use of that silent language, neither rightly understood the other.

By this time they were ascending the hill from Redley Creek to Kennett Square. Martha Deane had thus far carried the brush carelessly in her right hand; she now rolled it into a coil and thrust it into a large velvet reticule which hung from the pommel of her saddle. A few dull orange streaks in the overcast sky, behind them, denoted sunset, and a raw, gloomy twilight crept up from the east.

"You'll not go with us?" Sally asked again, as they reached the corner, and the loungers on the porch of the Unicorn Tavern beyond, perceiving Gilbert, sprang from their seats to ask for news of the chase.

"Sally, I cannot!" he answered. "Good-night!"

Joe and Jake Fairthorn rushed up with a whoop, and before Gilbert could satisfy the curiosity of the tavern-idlers, the former sat behind Sally, on the old mare, with his face to her tail, while Jake, prevented by Miss Deane's riding-whip from attempting the same performance, capered behind the horses and kept up their spirits by flinging handfuls of sand.

Gilbert found another group in "the store"—farmers or their sons who had come in for a supply of groceries, or the weekly mail, and who sat in a sweltering atmosphere around the roaring stove. They, too, had heard of the chase, and he was obliged to give them as many details as possible while his quarter of tea was being weighed, after which he left them to supply the story from the narrative of Mr. Joel Ferris, who, a new-comer announced, had just alighted at the Unicorn, a little drunk, and in a very bad humor.

"Where's Barton?" Gilbert heard some one ask of Ferris, as he mounted.

"In his skin!" was the answer, "unless he's got into that fellow Fortune's.

They're as thick as two pickpockets!"

Gilbert rode down the hill, and allowed his horse to plod leisurely across the muddy level, regardless of the deepening twilight.

He was powerfully moved by some suppressed emotion. The muscles of his lips twitched convulsively, and there was a hot surge and swell somewhere in his head, as of tears about to overrun their secret reservoir. But they failed to surprise him, this time. As the first drops fell from his dark eyelashes, he loosed the rein and gave the word to his horse. Over the ridge, along the crest, between dusky thorn-hedges, he swept at full gallop, and so, slowly sinking towards the fair valley which began to twinkle with the lights of scattered farms to the eastward, he soon reached the last steep descent, and saw the gray gleam of his own barn below him.

By this time his face was sternly set. He clinched his hands, and muttered to himself—

"It will almost kill me to ask, but I must know, and—and she must tell."

It was dark now. As he climbed again from the bottom of the hill towards the house, a figure on the summit was drawn indistinctly against the sky, unconscious that it was thus betrayed. But it vanished instantly, and then he groaned—

"God help me! I cannot ask."

CHAPTER III. — MARY POTTER AND HER SON.

While Gilbert was dismounting at the gate leading into his barn-yard, he was suddenly accosted by a boyish voice:—

"Got back, have you?"

This was Sam, the "bound-boy,"—the son of a tenant on the old Carson place, who, in consideration of three months' schooling every winter, and a "freedom suit" at the age of seventeen, if he desired then to learn a trade, was duly made over by his father to Gilbert Potter. His position was something between that of a poor relation and a servant. He was one of the family, eating at the same table, sleeping, indeed, (for economy of house-work,) in the same bed with his master, and privileged to feel his full share of interest in domestic matters; but on the other hand bound to obedience and rigid service.

"Feed's in the trough," said he, taking hold of the bridle. "I'll fix him. Better go into th' house. Tea's wanted."

Feeling as sure that all the necessary evening's work was done as if he had performed it with his own hands, Gilbert silently followed the boy's familiar advice.

The house, built like most other old farm-houses in that part of the county, of hornblende stone, stood near the bottom of a rounded knoll, overhanging the deep, winding valley. It was two stories in height, the gable looking towards the road, and showing, just under the broad double chimney, a limestone slab, upon which were rudely carved the initials of the builder and his wife, and the date "1727." A low portico, overgrown with woodbine and trumpet-flower, ran along the front. In the narrow flower-bed, under it, the crocuses and daffodils were beginning to thrust up their blunt, green points. A walk of flag-stones separated them from the vegetable garden, which was bounded at the bottom by a mill-race, carrying half the water of the creek to the saw and grist mill on the other side of the road.

Although this road was the principal thoroughfare between Kennett

Square and Wilmington, the house was so screened from the observation of travellers, both by the barn, and by some huge, spreading apple-trees which occupied the space between the garden and road, that its inmates seemed to live in absolute seclusion. Looking from the front door across a narrow green meadow, a wooded hill completely shut out all glimpse of the adjoining farms; while an angle of the valley, to the eastward, hid from sight the warm, fertile fields higher up the stream.

The place seemed lonelier than ever in the gloomy March twilight; or was it some other influence which caused Gilbert to pause on the flagged walk, and stand there, motionless, looking down into the meadow until a woman's shadow crossing the panes, was thrown upon the square of lighted earth at his feet? Then he turned and entered the kitchen.

The cloth was spread and the table set. A kettle, humming on a heap of fresh coals, and a squat little teapot of blue china, were waiting anxiously for the brown paper parcel which he placed upon the cloth. His mother was waiting also, in a high straight-backed rocking-chair, with her hands in her lap.

"You're tired waiting, mother, I suppose?" he said, as he hung his hat upon a nail over the heavy oak mantel-piece.

"No, not tired, Gilbert, but it's hungry you'll be. It won't take long for the tea to draw. Everything else has been ready this half-hour."

Gilbert threw himself upon the settle under the front window, and mechanically followed her with his eyes, as she carefully measured the precious herb, even stooping to pick up a leaf or two that had fallen from the spoon to the floor.

The resemblance between mother and son was very striking. Mary Potter had the same square forehead and level eyebrows, but her hair was darker than Gilbert's, and her eyes more deeply set. The fire of a lifelong pain smouldered in them, and the throes of some never-ending struggle had sharpened every line of cheek and brow, and taught her lips the close, hard compression, which those of her son were also beginning to learn. She

35

was about forty-five years of age, but there was even now a weariness in her motions, as if her prime of strength were already past. She wore a short gown of brown flannel, with a plain linen stomacher, and a coarse apron, which she removed when the supper had been placed upon the table. A simple cap, with a narrow frill, covered her head.

The entire work of the household devolved upon her hands alone. Gilbert would have cheerfully taken a servant to assist her, but this she positively refused, seeming to court constant labor, especially during his absence from the house. Only when he was there would she take occasion to knit or sew. The kitchen was a marvel of neatness and order. The bread-trough and dresser-shelves were scoured almost to the whiteness of a napkin, and the rows of pewter-plates upon the latter flashed like silver sconces. To Gilbert's eyes, indeed, the effect was sometimes painful. He would have been satisfied with less laborious order, a less eager and unwearied thrift. To be sure, all this was in furtherance of a mutual purpose; but he mentally determined that when the purpose had been fulfilled, he would insist upon an easier and more cheerful arrangement. The stern aspect of life from which his nature craved escape met him oftenest at home.

Sam entered the kitchen barefooted, having left his shoes at the back door. The tea was drawn, and the three sat down to their supper of bacon, bread and butter, and apple-sauce. Gilbert and his mother ate and drank in silence, but Sam's curiosity was too lively to be restrained.

"I say, how did Roger go?" he asked.

Mary Potter looked up, as if expecting the question to be answered, and Gilbert said:—

"He took the lead, and kept it."

"O cracky!" exclaimed the delighted Sam.

"Then you think it's a good bargain, Gilbert. Was it a long chase? Was he well tried?"

"All right, mother. I could sell him for twenty dollars advance—even to

Joel Ferris," he answered.

He then gave a sketch of the afternoon's adventures, to which his mother listened with a keen, steady interest. She compelled him to describe the stranger, Fortune, as minutely as possible, as if desirous of finding some form or event in her own memory to which he could be attached; but without result.

After supper Sam squatted upon a stool in the corner of the fireplace, and resumed his reading of "The Old English Baron," by the light of the burning back-log, pronouncing every word to himself in something between a whisper and a whistle. Gilbert took an account-book, a leaden inkstand, and a stumpy pen from a drawer under the window, and calculated silently and somewhat laboriously. His mother produced a clocked stocking of blue wool, and proceeded to turn the heel.

In half an hour's time, however, Sam's whispering ceased; his head nodded violently, and the book fell upon the hearth.

"I guess I'll go to bed," he said; and having thus conscientiously announced his intention, he trotted up the steep back-stairs on his hands and feet. In two minutes more, a creaking overhead announced that the act was accomplished.

Gilbert filliped the ink out of his pen into the fire, laid it in his book, and turned away from the table.

"Roger has bottom," he said at last, "and he's as strong as a lion. He and Fox will make a good team, and the roads will be solid in three days, if it don't rain."

"Why, you don't mean,"—she commenced.

"Yes, mother. You were not for buying him, I know, and you were right, inasmuch as there is always some risk. But it will make a difference of two barrels a load, besides having a horse at home. If I plough both for corn and oats next week,—and it will be all the better for corn, as the field next to Carson's is heavy,—I can begin hauling the week after, and we'll have the interest by the first of April, without borrowing a penny."

"That would be good,—very good, indeed," said she, dropping her knitting, and hesitating a moment before she continued; "only—only, Gilbert, I didn't expect you would be going so soon."

"The sooner I begin, mother, the sooner I shall finish."

"I know that, Gilbert,—I know that; but I'm always looking forward to the time when you won't be bound to go at all. Not that Sam and I can't manage awhile—but if the money was paid once"—

"There's less than six hundred now, altogether. It's a good deal to scrape together in a year's time, but if it can be done I will do it. Perhaps, then, you will let some help come into the house. I'm as anxious as you can be, mother. I'm not of a roving disposition, that you know; yet it isn't pleasant to me to see you slave as you do, and for that very reason, it's a comfort when I'm away, that you've one less to work for."

He spoke earnestly, turning his face full upon her.

"We've talked this over, often and often, but you never can make me see it in your way," he then added, in a gentler tone.

"Ay, Gilbert," she replied, somewhat bitterly, "I've had my thoughts. Maybe they were too fast; it seems so. I meant, and mean, to make a good home for you, and I'm happiest when I can do the most towards it. I want you to hold up your head and be beholden to no man. There are them in the neighborhood that were bound out as boys, and are now as good as the best."

"But they are not,"—burst from his lips, as the thought on which he so gloomily brooded sprang to the surface and took him by surprise. He checked his words by a powerful effort, and the blood forsook his face. Mary Potter placed her hand on her heart, and seemed to gasp for breath.

Gilbert could not bear to look upon her face. He turned away, placed his elbow on the table, and leaned his head upon his hand. It never occurred to him that the unfinished sentence might be otherwise completed. He knew that his thought was betrayed, and his heart was suddenly filled with a tumult of shame, pity, and fear.

For a minute there was silence. Only the long pendulum, swinging openly along the farther wall, ticked at each end of its vibration. Then Mary Potter drew a deep, weary breath, and spoke. Her voice was hollow and strange, and each word came as by a separate muscular effort.

"What are they not? What word was on your tongue, Gilbert?"

He could not answer. He could only shake his head, and bring forth a cowardly, evasive word,—"Nothing."

"But there is something! Oh, I knew it must come some time!" she cried, rather to herself than to him. "Listen to me, Gilbert! Has any one dared to say to your face that you are basely born?"

He felt, now, that no further evasion was possible; she had put into words the terrible question which he could not steel his own heart to ask. Perhaps it was better so,—better a sharp, intense pain than a dull perpetual ache. So he answered honestly now, but still kept his head turned away, as if there might be a kindness in avoiding her gaze.

"Not in so many words, mother," he said; "but there are ways, and ways of saying a thing; and the cruellest way is that which everybody understands, and I dare not. But I have long known what it meant. It is ten years, mother, since I have mentioned the word 'father' in your hearing."

Mary Potter leaned forward, hid her face in her hands, and rocked to and fro, as if tortured with insupportable pain. She stifled her sobs, but the tears gushed forth between her fingers.

"O my boy,—my boy!" she moaned. "Ten years?—and you believed it, all that time!"

He was silent. She leaned forward and grasped his arm.

"Did you,—do you believe it? Speak, Gilbert!"

When he did speak, his voice was singularly low and gentle. "Never mind, mother!" was all he could say. His head was still turned away from her, but she knew there were tears on his cheeks.

"Gilbert, it is a lie!" she exclaimed, with startling vehemence. "A lie,—A LIE! You are my lawful son, born in wedlock! There is no stain upon your name, of my giving, and I know there will be none of your own."

He turned towards her, his eyes shining and his lips parted in breathless joy and astonishment.

"Is it—is it true?" he whispered.

"True as there is a God in Heaven."

"Then, mother, give me my name! Now I ask you, for the first time, who was my father?"

She wrung her hands and moaned. The sight of her son's eager, expectant face, touched with a light which she had never before seen upon it, seemed to give her another and a different pang.

"That, too!" She murmured to herself.

"Gilbert," she then said, "have I always been a faithful mother to you? Have I been true and honest in word and deed? Have I done my best to help you in all right ways,—to make you comfortable, to spare you trouble? Have I ever,—I'll not say acted, for nobody's judgment is perfect,—but tried to act otherwise than as I thought it might be for your good?"

"You have done all that you could say, and more, mother."

"Then, my boy, is it too much for me to ask that you should believe my word,—that you should let it stand for the truth, without my giving proofs and testimonies? For, Gilbert, that I must ask of you, hard as it may seem. If you will only be content with the knowledge—: but then, you have felt the shame all this while; it was my fault, mine, and I ought to ask your forgiveness"—

"Mother—mother!" he interrupted, "don't talk that way! Yes—I believe you, without testimony. You never said, or thought, an untruth; and your explanation will be enough not only for me, but for the whole neighborhood,

40

if all witnesses are dead or gone away. If you knew of the shameful report, why didn't you deny it at once? Why let it spread and be believed in?"

"Oh," she moaned again, "if my tongue was not tied—if my tongue was not tied! There was my fault, and what a punishment! Never—never was woman punished as I have been. Gilbert, whatever you do, bind yourself by no vow, except in the sight of men!"

"I do not understand you, mother," said he.

"No, and I dare not make myself understood. Don't ask me anything more! It's hard to shut my mouth, and bear everything in silence, but it cuts my very heart in twain to speak and not tell!"

Her distress was so evident, that Gilbert, perplexed and bewildered as her words left him, felt that he dared not press her further. He could not doubt the truth of her first assertion; but, alas! it availed only for his own private consciousness,—it took no stain from him, in the eyes of the world. Yet, now that the painful theme had been opened,—not less painful, it seemed, since the suspected dishonor did not exist,—he craved and decided to ask, enlightenment on one point.

"Mother," he said, after a pause, "I do not want to speak about this thing again. I believe you, and my greatest comfort in believing is for your sake, not for mine. I see, too, that you are bound in some way which I do not understand, so that we cannot be cleared from the blame that is put upon us. I don't mind that so much, either—for my own sake, and I will not ask for an explanation, since you say you dare not give it. But tell me one thing,—will it always be so? Are you bound forever, and will I never learn anything more? I can wait; but, mother, you know that these things work in a man's mind, and there will come a time when the knowledge of the worst thing that could be will seem better than no knowledge at all."

Her face brightened a little. "Thank you, Gilbert!" she said. "Yes; there will come a day when you shall know all,—when you and me shall have justice. I do not know how soon; I cannot guess. In the Lord's good time. I have nigh out-suffered my fault, I think, and the reward cannot be far off. A few weeks, perhaps,—yet, maybe, for oh, I am not allowed even to hope for it!—maybe a few years. It will all come to the light, after so long—so long—an eternity. If I had but known!"

"Come, we will say no more now. Surely I may wait a little while, when you have waited so long. I believe you, mother. Yes, I believe you; I am your lawful son."

She rose, placed her hands on his shoulders, and kissed him. Nothing more was said.

Gilbert raked the ashes over the smouldering embers on the hearth, lighted his mother's night-lamp, and after closing the chamber-door softly behind her, stole up-stairs to his own bed.

It was long past midnight before he slept.

CHAPTER IV. — FORTUNE AND MISFORTUNE.

On the same evening, a scene of a very different character occurred, in which certain personages of this history were actors. In order to describe it, we must return to the company of sportsmen whom Gilbert Potter left at the Hammer-and-Trowel Tavern, late in the afternoon.

No sooner had he departed than the sneers of the young bucks, who felt themselves humiliated by his unexpected success, became loud and frequent. Mr. Alfred Barton, who seemed to care little for the general dissatisfaction, was finally reproached with having introduced such an unfit personage at a gentleman's hunt; whereupon he turned impatiently, and retorted:

"There were no particular invitations sent out, as all of you know. Anybody that had a horse, and knew how to manage him, was welcome. Zounds! if you fellows are afraid to take hedges, am I to blame for that? A hunter's a hunter, though he's born on the wrong side of the marriage certificate."

"That's the talk, Squire!" cried Fortune, giving his friend a hearty slap between the shoulders. "I've seen riding in my day," he continued, "both down in Loudon and on the Eastern Shore—men born with spurs on their heels, and I tell you this Potter could hold his own, even with the Lees and the Tollivers. We took the hedge together, while you were making a round of I don't know how many miles on the road; and I never saw a thing neater done. If you thought there was anything unfair about him, why didn't you head him off?"

"Yes, damme," echoed Mr. Barton, bringing down his fist upon the bar, so that the glasses jumped, "why didn't you head him off?" Mr. Barton's face was suspiciously flushed, and he was more excited than the occasion justified.

There was no answer to the question, except that which none of the young bucks dared to make.

"Well, I've had about enough of this," said Mr. Joel Ferris, turning on his heel; "who's for home?"

"Me!" answered three or four, with more readiness than grammar. Some of the steadier young farmers, who had come for an afternoon's recreation, caring little who was first in at the death, sat awhile and exchanged opinions about crops and cattle; but Barton and Fortune kept together, whispering much, and occasionally bursting into fits of uproarious laughter. The former was so captivated by his new friend, that before he knew it every guest was gone. The landlord had lighted two or three tallow candles, and now approached with the question:

"Will you have supper, gentlemen?"

"That depends on what you've got," said Fortune.

This was not language to which the host was accustomed. His guests were also his fellow-citizens: if they patronized him, he accommodated them, and the account was balanced. His meals were as good as anybody's, though he thought it that shouldn't, and people so very particular might stay away. But he was a mild, amiable man, and Fortune's keen eye and dazzling teeth had a powerful effect upon him. He answered civilly, in spite of an inward protest:

"There's ham and eggs, and frizzled beef."

"Nothing could be better!" Fortune exclaimed, jumping up. "Come 'Squire—if I stay over Sunday with you, you must at least take supper at my expense."

Mr. Barton tried to recollect whether he had invited his friend to spend Sunday with him. It must be so, of course; only, he could not remember when he had spoken, or what words he had used. It would be very pleasant, he confessed, but for one thing; and how was he to get over the difficulty?

However, here they were, at the table, Fortune heaping his plate like a bountiful host, and talking so delightfully about horses and hounds, and drinking-bouts, and all those wild experiences which have such a charm for bachelors of forty-five or fifty, that it was impossible to determine in his mind what he should do.

After the supper, they charged themselves with a few additional potations, to keep off the chill of the night air, mounted their horses, and took the New-Garden road. A good deal of confidential whispering had preceded their departure.

"They're off on a lark," the landlord remarked to himself, as they rode away, "and it's a shame, in men of their age."

After riding a mile, they reached the cross-road on the left, which the hunters had followed, and Fortune, who was a little in advance, turned into it.

"After what I told you, 'Squire," said he, "you won't wonder that I know the country so well. Let us push on; it's not more than two miles. I would be very clear of showing you one of my nests, if you were not such a good fellow. But mum's the word, you know."

"Never fear," Barton answered, somewhat thickly; "I'm an old bird, Fortune."

"That you are! Men like you and me are not made of the same stuff as those young nincompoops; we can follow a trail without giving tongue at every jump."

Highly flattered, Barton rode nearer, and gave his friend an affectionate punch in the side. Fortune answered with an arm around his waist and a tight hug, and so they rode onward through the darkness.

They had advanced for somewhat more than a mile on the cross-road, and found themselves in a hollow, with tall, and added in a low, significant tone, "If you stir from this spot in less than one hour, you are a dead man."

Then he rode on, whistling "Money Musk" as he went. Once or twice he stopped, as if to listen, and Barton's heart ceased to beat; but by degrees the sound of his horse's hoofs died away. The silence that succeeded was full of terrors. Barton's horse became restive, and he would have dismounted and held him, but for the weakness in every joint which made him think that his body was falling asunder. Now and then a leaf rustled, or the scent of some animal, unperceived by his own nostrils, caused his horse to snort and stamp. The air was raw and sent a fearful chill through his blood. Moreover, how was he to measure the hour? His watch was gone; he might have guessed by the stars, but the sky was overcast. Fortune and Sandy Flash—for there were two individuals in his bewildered brain—would surely fulfil their threat if he stirred before the appointed time. What under heaven should he do?

Wait; that was all; and he waited until it seemed that morning must be near at hand. Then, turning his horse, he rode back very slowly towards the New-Garden road, and after many panics, to the Hammer-and-Trowel. There was still light in the bar-room; should the door open, he would be seen. He put spurs to his horse and dashed past. Once in motion, it seemed that he was pursued, and along Tuffkenamon went the race, until his horse, panting and exhausted, paused to drink at Redley Creek. They had gone to bed at the Unicorn; he drew a long breath, and felt that the danger was over. In five minutes more he was at home.

Putting his horse in the stable, he stole quietly to the house, pulled off his boots in the wood-shed, and entered by a back way through the kitchen. Here he warmed his chill frame before the hot ashes, and then very gently and cautiously felt his way to bed in the dark.

The next morning, being Sunday, the whole household, servants and all, slept an hour later than usual, as was then the country custom. Giles, the old soldier, was the first to appear. He made the fire in the kitchen, put on the water to boil, and then attended to the feeding of the cattle at the barn. When this was accomplished, he returned to the house and entered a bedroom adjoining the kitchen, on the ground-floor. Here slept "Old-man Barton," as he was generally called,—Alfred's father, by name Abiah, and now eighty-five years of age. For many years he had been a paralytic, and unable to walk, but the disease had not affected his business capacity. He was the hardest, shrewdest, and cunningest miser in the county. There was not a penny of the income and expenditure of the farm, for any year, which he could not account for,—not a date of a deed, bond, or note of hand, which he had ever given or received, that was not indelibly burnt upon his memory.

No one, not even his sons, knew precisely how much he was worth. The old lawyer in Chester, who had charge of much of his investments, was as shrewd as himself, and when he made his annual visit, the first week in April, the doors were not only closed, but everybody was banished from hearing distance so long as he remained.

Giles assisted in washing and dressing the old man, then seated him in a rude arm-chair, resting on clumsy wooden castors, and poured out for him a small wine-glass full of raw brandy. Once or twice a year, usually after the payment of delayed interest, Giles received a share of the brandy; but he never learned to expect it. Then a long hickory staff was placed in the old man's hand, and his arm-chair was rolled into the kitchen, to a certain station between the fire and the southern window, where he would be out of the way of his daughter Ann, yet could measure with his eye every bit of lard she put into the frying-pan, and every spoonful of molasses that entered into the composition of her pies.

She had already set the table for breakfast. The bacon and sliced potatoes were frying in separate pans, and Ann herself was lifting the lid of the tin coffee-pot, to see whether the beverage had "come to a boil," when the old man entered, or, strictly speaking, was entered.

As his chair rolled into the light, the hideousness, not the grace and serenity of old age, was revealed. His white hair, thin and half-combed, straggled over the dark-red, purple-veined skin of his head; his cheeks were flabby bags of bristly, wrinkled leather; his mouth was a sunken, irregular slit, losing itself in the hanging folds at the corners, and even the life, gathered into his small, restless gray eyes, was half quenched under the red and heavy edges of the lids. The third and fourth fingers of his hands were crooked upon the skinny palms, beyond any power to open them.

When Ann—a gaunt spinster of fifty-five—had placed the coffee on the table, the old man looked around, and asked with a snarl: "Where's Alfred?"

"Not up yet, but you needn't wait, father."

"Wait?" was all he said, yet she understood the tone, and wheeled him

47

to the table. As soon as his plate was filled, he bent forward over it, rested his elbows on the cloth, and commenced feeding himself with hands that trembled so violently that he could with great difficulty bring the food to his mouth. But he resented all offers of assistance, which implied any weakness beyond that of the infirmity which it was impossible for him to conceal. His meals were weary tasks, but he shook and jerked through them, and would have gone away hungry rather than acknowledge the infirmity of his great age.

Breakfast was nearly over before Alfred Barton made his appearance. No truant school-boy ever dreaded the master's eye as he dreaded to appear before his father that Sunday morning. His sleep had been broken and restless; the teeth of Sandy Flash had again grinned at him in nightmare-dreams, and when he came to put on his clothes, the sense of emptiness in his breast-pocket and watch-fob impressed him like a violent physical pain. His loss was bad enough, but the inability to conceal it caused him even greater distress.

Buttoning his coat over the double void, and trying to assume his usual air, he went down to the kitchen and commenced his breakfast. Whenever he looked up, he found his father's eyes fixed upon him, and before a word had been spoken, he felt that he had already betrayed something, and that the truth would follow, sooner or later. A wicked wish crossed his mind, but was instantly suppressed, for fear lest that, also, should be discovered.

After Ann had cleared the table, and retired to her own room in order to array herself in the black cloth gown which she had worn every Sunday for the past fifteen years, the old man said, or rather wheezed out the words,—

"Kennett, meetin'?"

"Not to-day," said his son, "I've a sort of chill from yesterday." And he folded his arms and shivered very naturally.

"Did Ferris pay you?" the old man again asked.

"Y—yes."

"Where's the money?"

48

There was the question, and it must be faced. Alfred Barton worked the farm "on shares," and was held to a strict account by his father, not only for half of all the grain and produce sold, but of all the horses and cattle raised, as well as those which were bought on speculation. On his share he managed—thanks to the niggardly system enforced in the house—not only to gratify his vulgar taste for display, but even to lay aside small sums from time to time. It was a convenient arrangement, but might be annulled any time when the old man should choose, and Alfred knew that a prompt division of the profits would be his surest guarantee of permanence.

"I have not the money with me," he answered, desperately, after a pause, during which he felt his father's gaze travelling over him, from head to foot.

"Why not! You haven't spent it?" The latter question was a croaking shriek, which seemed to forebode, while it scarcely admitted, the possibility of such an enormity.

"I spent only four shillings, father, but—but—but the money's all gone!"

The crooked fingers clutched the hickory staff, as if eager to wield it; the sunken gray eyes shot forth angry fire, and the broken figure uncurved and straightened itself with a wrathful curiosity.

"Sandy Flash robbed me on the way home," said the son, and now that the truth was out, he seemed to pluck up a little courage.

"What, what, what!" chattered the old man, incredulously; "no lies, boy, no lies!"

The son unbuttoned his coat, and showed his empty watch-fob. Then he gave an account of the robbery, not strictly correct in all its details, but near enough for his father to know, without discovering inaccuracies at a later day. The hickory-stick was shaken once or twice during the recital, but it did not fall upon the culprit—though this correction (so the gossip of the neighborhood ran) had more than once been administered within the previous ten years. As Alfred Barton told his story, it was hardly a case for anger on the father's part, so he took his revenge in another way.

"This comes o' your races and your expensive company," he growled,

49

after a few incoherent sniffs and snarls; "but I don't lose my half of the horse. No, no! I'm not paid till the money's been handed over. Twenty-five dollars, remember!—and soon, that I don't lose the use of it too long. As for your money and the watch, I've nothing to do with them. I've got along without a watch for eighty-five years, and I never wore as smart a coat as that in my born days. Young men understood how to save, in my time."

Secretly, however, the old man was flattered by his son's love of display, and enjoyed his swaggering air, although nothing would have induced him to confess the fact. His own father had come to Pennsylvania as a servant of one of the first settlers, and the reverence which he had felt, as a boy, for the members of the Quaker and farmer aristocracy of the neighborhood, had now developed into a late vanity to see his own family acknowledged as the equals of the descendants of the former. Alfred had long since discovered that when he happened to return home from the society of the Falconers, or the Caswells, or the Carsons, the old man was in an unusual good-humor. At such times, the son felt sure that he was put down for a large slice of the inheritance.

After turning the stick over and over in his skinny hands, and pressing the top of it against his toothless gums, the old man again spoke.

"See here, you're old enough now to lead a steady life. You might ha' had a farm o' your own, like Elisha, if you'd done as well. A very fair bit o' money he married,—very fair,—but I don't say you couldn't do as well, or, maybe, better."

"I've been thinking of that, myself," the son replied.

"Have you? Why don't you step up to her then? Ten thousand dollars aren't to be had every day, and you needn't expect to get it without the askin'! Where molasses is dropped, you'll always find more than one fly. Others than you have got their eyes on the girl."

The son's eyes opened tolerably wide when the old man began to speak, but a spark of intelligence presently flashed into them, and an expression of cunning ran over his face.

50

"Don't be anxious, daddy!" said he, with assumed playfulness; "she's not a girl to take the first that offers. She has a mind of her own,—with her the more haste the less speed. I know what I'm about; I have my top eye open, and when there's a good chance, you won't find me sneaking behind the wood-house."

"Well, well!" muttered the old man, "we'll see,—we'll see! A good family, too,—not that I care for that. My family's as good as the next. But if you let her slip, boy"—and here he brought down the end of his stick with a significant whack, upon the floor. "This I'll tell you," he added, without finishing the broken sentence, "that whether you're a rich man or a beggar, depends on yourself. The more you have, the more you'll get; remember that! Bring me my brandy!"

Alfred Barton knew the exact value of his father's words. Having already neglected, or, at least, failed to succeed, in regard to two matches which his father had proposed, he understood the risk to his inheritance which was implied by a third failure. And yet, looking at the subject soberly, there was not the slightest prospect of success. Martha Deane was the girl in the old man's mind, and an instinct, stronger than his vanity, told him that she never would, or could, be his wife. But, in spite of that, it must be his business to create a contrary impression, and keep it alive as long as possible,—perhaps until—until—

We all know what was in his mind. Until the old man should die.

CHAPTER V. — GUESTS AT FAIRTHORN'S.

The Fairthorn farm was immediately north of Kennett Square. For the first mile towards Unionville, the rich rolling fields which any traveller may see, to this day, on either side of the road, belonged to it. The house stood on the right, in the hollow into which the road dips, on leaving the village. Originally a large cabin of hewn logs, it now rejoiced in a stately stone addition, overgrown with ivy up to the eaves, and a long porch in front, below which two mounds of box guarded the flight of stone steps leading down to the garden. The hill in the rear kept off the north wind, and this garden caught the earliest warmth of spring. Nowhere else in the neighborhood did the crocuses bloom so early, or the peas so soon appear above ground. The lack of order, the air of old neglect about the place, in nowise detracted from its warm, cosy character; it was a pleasant nook, and the relatives and friends of the family (whose name was Legion) always liked to visit there.

Several days had elapsed since the chase, and the eventful evening which followed it. It was baking-day, and the plump arms of Sally Fairthorn were floury-white up to the elbows. She was leaning over the dough-trough, plunging her fists furiously into the spongy mass, when she heard a step on the porch. Although her gown was pinned up, leaving half of her short, striped petticoat visible, and a blue and white spotted handkerchief concealed her dark hair, Sally did not stop to think of that. She rushed into the front room, just as a gaunt female figure passed the window, at the sight of which she clapped her hands so that the flour flew in a little white cloud, and two or three strips of dough peeled off her arms and fell upon the floor.

The front-door opened, and our old friend, Miss Betsy Lavender, walked into the room.

Any person, between Kildeer Hill and Hockessin, who did not know Miss Betsy, must have been an utter stranger to the country, or an idiot. She had a marvellous clairvoyant faculty for the approach of either Joy or Grief, and always turned up just at the moment when she was most wanted.

Profession had she none; neither a permanent home, but for twenty years she had wandered hither and thither, in highly independent fashion, turning her hand to whatever seemed to require its cunning. A better housekeeper never might have lived, if she could have stuck to one spot; an admirable cook, nurse, seamstress, and spinner, she refused alike the high wages of wealthy farmers and the hands of poor widowers. She had a little money of her own, but never refused payment from those who were able to give it, in order that she might now and then make a present of her services to poorer friends. Her speech was blunt and rough, her ways odd and eccentric; her name was rarely mentioned without a laugh, but those who laughed at her esteemed her none the less. In those days of weekly posts and one newspaper, she was Politics, Art, Science, and Literature to many families.

In person, Miss Betsy Lavender was peculiar rather than attractive. She was nearly, if not quite fifty years of age, rather tall, and a little stoop-shouldered. Her face, at first sight, suggested that of a horse, with its long, ridged nose, loose lips and short chin. Her eyes were dull gray, set near together, and much sharper in their operation than a stranger would suppose. Over a high, narrow forehead she wore thin bands of tan-colored hair, somewhat grizzled, and forming a coil at the back of her head, barely strong enough to hold the teeth of an enormous tortoise-shell comb. Yet her grotesqueness had nothing repellant; it was a genial caricature, at which no one could take offence. "The very person I wanted to see!" cried Sally. "Father and mother are going up to Uncle John's this afternoon; Aunt Eliza has an old woman's quilting-party, and they'll stay all night, and however am I to manage Joe and Jake by myself? Martha's half promised to come, but not till after supper. It will all go right, since you are here; come into mother's room and take off your things!"

"Well," said Miss Betsy, with a snort, "that's to be my business, eh? I'll have my hands full; a pearter couple o' lads a'n't to be found this side o' Nottin'gam. They might ha' growed up wild on the Barrens, for all the manners they've got."

Sally knew that this criticism was true; also that Miss Betsy's task was no sinecure, and she therefore thought it best to change the subject.

"There!" said she, as Miss Betsy gave the thin rope of her back hair a fierce twist, and jammed her high comb inward and outward that the teeth might catch,—"there! now you'll do! Come into the kitchen and tell me the news, while I set my loaves to rise."

"Loaves to rise," echoed Miss Betsy, seating herself on a tall, rush-bottomed chair near the window. She had an incorrigible habit of repeating the last three words of the person with whom she spoke,—a habit which was sometimes mimicked good-humoredly, even by her best friends. Many persons, however, were flattered by it, as it seemed to denote an earnest attention to what they were saying. Between the two, there it was and there it would be, to the day of her death,—Miss Lavender's "keel-mark, [Footnote: Keel, a local term for red chalk.] as the farmers said of their sheep.

"Well," she resumed, after taking breath, "no news is good news, these days. Down Whitely Creek way, towards Strickersville, there's fever, they say; Richard Rudd talks o' buildin' higher up the hill,—you know it's low and swampy about the old house,—but Sarah, she says it'll be a mortal long ways to the spring-house, and so betwixt and between them I dunno how it'll turn out. Dear me! I was up at Aunt Buffin'ton's t' other day; she's lookin' poorly; her mother, I remember, went off in a decline, the same year the Tories burnt down their barn, and I'm afeard she's goin' the same way. But, yes! I guess there's one thing you'll like to hear. Old-man Barton is goin' to put up a new wagon-house, and Mark is to have the job."

"Law!" exclaimed Sally, "what's that to me?" But there was a decided smile on her face as she put another loaf into the pan, and, although her head was turned away, a pretty flush of color came up behind her ear, and betrayed itself to Miss Lavender's quick eye.

"Nothin' much, I reckon," the latter answered, in the most matter-of-fact way, "only I thought you might like to know it, Mark bein' a neighbor, like, and a right-down smart young fellow."

"Well, I am glad of it," said Sally, with sudden candor, "he's Martha's cousin."

"Martha's cousin,—and I shouldn't wonder if he'd be something more to her, some day."

"No, indeed! What are you thinking of, Betsy?" Sally turned around and faced her visitor, regardless that her soft brunette face showed a decided tinge of scarlet. At this instant clattering feet were heard, and Joe and Jake rushed into the kitchen. They greeted their old friend with boisterous demonstrations of joy.

"Now we'll have dough-nuts," cried Joe.

"No; 'lasses-wax!" said Jake. "Sally, where's mother? Dad's out at the wall, and Bonnie's jumpin' and prancin' like anything!"

"Go along!" exclaimed Sally, with a slap which, lost its force in the air, as Jake jumped away. Then they all left the kitchen together, and escorted the mother to the garden-wall by the road, which served the purpose of a horseblock. Farmer Fairthorn—a hale, ruddy, honest figure, in broad-brimmed hat, brown coat and knee-breeches—already sat upon the old mare, and the pillion behind his saddle awaited the coming burden. Mother Fairthorn, a cheery little woman, with dark eyes and round brunette face, like her daughter, wore the scoop bonnet and drab shawl of a Quakeress, as did many in the neighborhood who did not belong to the sect. Never were people better suited to each other than these two: they took the world as they found it, and whether the crops were poor or abundant, whether money came in or had to be borrowed, whether the roof leaked, or a broken pale let the sheep into the garden, they were alike easy of heart, contented and cheerful.

The mare, after various obstinate whirls, was finally brought near the wall; the old woman took her seat on the pillion, and after a parting admonition to Sally: "Rake the coals and cover 'em up, before going to bed, whatever you do!"—they went off, deliberately, up the hill.

"Miss Betsy," said Joe, with a very grave air, as they returned to the kitchen, "I want you to tell me one thing,—whether it's true or not. Sally says I'm a monkey."

"I'm a monkey," repeated the unconscious Miss Lavender, whereupon both boys burst into shrieks of laughter, and made their escape.

"Much dough-nuts they'll get from me," muttered the ruffled spinster, as she pinned up her sleeves and proceeded to help Sally. The work went on rapidly, and by the middle of the afternoon, the kitchen wore its normal aspect of homely neatness. Then came the hour or two of quiet and rest, nowhere in the world so grateful as in a country farm-house, to its mistress and her daughters, when all the rough work of the day is over, and only the lighter task of preparing supper yet remains. Then, when the sewing or knitting has been produced, the little painted-pine work-stand placed near the window, and a pleasant neighbor drops in to enliven the softer occupation with gossip, the country wife or girl finds her life a very happy and cheerful possession. No dresses are worn with so much pleasure as those then made; no books so enjoyed as those then read, a chapter or two at a time.

Sally Fairthorn, we must confess, was not in the habit of reading much. Her education had been limited. She had ciphered as far as Compound Interest, read Murray's "Sequel," and Goldsmith's "Rome," and could write a fair letter, without misspelling many words; but very few other girls in the neighborhood possessed greater accomplishments than these, and none of them felt, or even thought of, their deficiencies. There were no "missions" in those days; it was fifty or sixty years before the formation of the "Kennett Psychological Society," and "Pamela," "Rasselas," and "Joseph Andrews," were lent and borrowed, as at present "Consuelo," Buckle, Ruskin, and "Enoch Arden."

One single work of art had Sally created, and it now hung, stately in a frame of curled maple, in the chilly parlor. It was a sampler, containing the alphabet, both large and small, the names and dates of birth of both her parents, a harp and willow-tree, the twigs whereof were represented by parallel rows of "herring-bone" stitch, a sharp zigzag spray of rose-buds, and the following stanza, placed directly underneath the harp and willow:—

> "By Babel's streams we Sat and Wept
>
> When Zion we thought on;
>
> For Grief thereof, we Hang our Harp
>
> The Willow Tree upon."

Across the bottom of the sampler was embroidered the inscription: "Done by Sarah Ann Fairthorn, May, 1792, in the 16th year of her age."

While Sally went up-stairs to her room, to put her hair into order, and tie a finer apron over her cloth gown, Miss Betsy Lavender was made the victim of a most painful experience.

Joe and Jake, who had been dodging around the house, half-coaxing and half-teasing the ancient maiden whom they both plagued and liked, had not been heard or seen for a while. Miss Betsy was knitting by the front window, waiting for Sally, when the door was hastily thrown open, and Joe appeared, panting, scared, and with an expression of horror upon his face.

"Oh, Miss Betsy!" was his breathless exclamation, "Jake! the cherry-tree!"

Dropping her work upon the floor, Miss Lavender hurried out of the house, with beating heart and trembling limbs, following Joe, who ran towards the field above the barn, where, near the fence, there stood a large and lofty cherry-tree. As she reached the fence she beheld Jake, lying motionless on his back, on the brown grass.

"The Lord have mercy!" she cried; her knees gave way, and she sank upon the ground in an angular heap. When, with a desperate groan, she lifted her head and looked through the lower rails, Jake was not to be seen. With a swift, convulsive effort she rose to her feet, just in time to catch a glimpse of the two young scamps whirling over the farther fence into the wood below.

She walked unsteadily back to the house. "It's given me such a turn," she said to Sally, after describing the trick, "that I dunno when I'll get over it."

Sally gave her some whiskey and sugar, which soon brought a vivid red to the tip of her chin and the region of her cheek-bones, after which she professed that she felt very comfortable. But the boys, frightened at the effect of their thoughtless prank, did not make their appearance. Joe, seeing Miss Betsy fall, thought she was dead, and the two hid themselves in a bed of dead leaves, beside a fallen log, not daring to venture home for supper. Sally said they should have none, and would have cleared the table; but Miss

Betsy, whose kind heart had long since relented, went forth and brought them to light, promising that she would not tell their father, provided they "would never do such a wicked thing again." Their behavior, for the rest of the evening, was irreproachable.

Just as candles were being lighted, there was another step on the porch, and the door opened on Martha Deane.

"I'm so glad!" cried Sally. "Never mind your pattens, Martha; Joe shall carry them into the kitchen. Come, let me take off your cloak and hat."

Martha's coming seemed to restore the fading daylight. Not boisterous or impulsive, like Sally, her nature burned with a bright and steady flame,— white and cold to some, golden and radiant to others. Her form was slender, and every motion expressed a calm, serene grace, which could only spring from some conscious strength of character. Her face was remarkably symmetrical, its oval outline approaching the Greek ideal; but the brow was rather high than low, and the light brown hair covered the fair temples evenly, without a ripple. Her eyes were purely blue, and a quick, soft spark was easily kindled in their depths; the cheeks round and rosy, and the mouth clearly and delicately cut, with an unusual, yet wholly feminine firmness in the lines of the upper lip. This peculiarity, again, if slightly out of harmony with the pervading gentleness of her face, was balanced by the softness and sweetness of her dimpled chin, and gave to her face a rare union of strength and tenderness. It very rarely happens that decision and power of will in a young woman are not manifested by some characteristic rather masculine than feminine; but Martha Deane knew the art of unwearied, soft assertion and resistance, and her beautiful lips could pronounce, when necessary, a final word.

Joe and Jake came forward with a half-shy delight, to welcome "Cousin Martha," as she was called in the Fairthorn household, her mother and Sally's father having been "own" cousins. There was a cheerful fire on the hearth, and the three ladies gathered in front of it, with the work-stand in the middle, while the boys took possession of the corner-nooks. The latter claimed their share of the gossip; they knew the family histories of the neighborhood much better than their school-books, and exhibited a precocious interest in this form of knowledge. The conversation, therefore, was somewhat guarded, and the knitting and sewing all the more assiduously performed, until, with great reluctance, and after repeated commands, Joe and Jake stole off to bed.

The atmosphere of the room then became infinitely more free and confidential. Sally dropped her hands in her lap, and settled herself more comfortably in her chair, while Miss Lavender, with an unobserved side-glance at her, said:—

"Mark is to put up Barton's new wagon-house, I hear, Martha."

"Yes," Martha answered; "it is not much, but Mark, of course, is very proud of his first job. There is a better one in store, though he does not know of it."

Sally pricked up her ears. "What is it?" asked Miss Betsy.

"It is not to be mentioned, you will understand. I saw Alfred Barton to-day. He seems to take quite an interest in Mark, all at once, and he told me that the Hallowells are going to build a new barn this summer. He spoke to them of Mark, and thinks the work is almost sure."

"Well, now!" Miss Betsy exclaimed, "if he gets that, after a year's journey-work, Mark is a made man. And I'll speak to Richard Rudd the next time I see him. He thinks he's beholden to me, since Sarah had the fever so bad. I don't like folks to think that, but there's times when it appears to come handy."

Sally arose, flushed and silent, and brought a plate of cakes and a basket of apples from the pantry. The work was now wholly laid aside, and the stand cleared to receive the refreshments.

"Now pare your peels in one piece, girls," Miss Betsy advised, "and then whirl 'em to find the initials o' your sweethearts' names."

"You, too, Miss Betsy!" cried Sally, "we must find out the widower's name!"

"The widower's name," Miss Betsy gravely repeated, as she took a knife.

With much mirth the parings were cut, slowly whirled three times around the head, and then let fly over the left shoulder. Miss Betsy's was first examined and pronounced to be an A.

"Who's A?" she asked.

"Alfred!" said Sally. "Now, Martha, here's yours—an S, no it's a G!"

"The curl is the wrong way," said Martha, gravely, "it's a figure 3; so, I have three of them, have I?"

"And mine," Sally continued, "is a W!"

"Yes, if you look at it upside down. The inside of the peel is uppermost: you must turn it, and then it will be an M."

Sally snatched it up in affected vexation, and threw it into the fire. "Oh, I know a new way!" she cried; "did you ever try it, Martha—with the key and the Bible!"

"Old as the hills, but awful sure," remarked Miss Lavender. "When it's done serious, it's never been known to fail."

Sally took the house-key, and brought from the old walnut cabinet a plump octavo Bible, which she opened at the Song of Solomon, eighth chapter and sixth verse. The end of the key being carefully placed therein, the halves of the book were bound together with cords, so that it could be carried by the key-handle. Then Sally and Martha, sitting face to face, placed each the end of the fore finger of the right hand under the half the ring of the key nearest to her.

"Now, Martha," said Sally, "we'll try your fortune first. Say 'A,' and then repeat the verse: 'set me as a seal upon thy heart, as a seal upon thine arm; for love is strong as death, jealousy is cruel as the grave: the coals thereof are coals of fire, which hath a most vehement flame.'"

Martha did as she was bidden, but the book hung motionless. She was thereupon directed to say B, and repeat the verse; and so on, letter by letter. The slender fingers trembled a little with the growing weight of the book, and, although Sally protested that she was holding as still "as she knew how,"

60

the trembling increased, and before the verse which followed G had been finished, the ring of the key slowly turned, and the volume fell to the floor.

Martha picked it up with a quiet smile.

"It is easy to see who was in your mind, Sally," she said. "Now let me tell your fortune: we will begin at L—it will save time."

"Save time," said Miss Lavender, rising. "Have it out betwixt and between you, girls: I'm a-goin' to bed."

The two girls soon followed her example. Hastily undressing themselves in the chilly room, they lay down side by side, to enjoy the blended warmth and rest, and the tender, delicious interchanges of confidence which precede sleep. Though so different in every fibre of their natures, they loved each other with a very true and tender affection.

"Martha," said Sally, after an interval of silence, "did you think I made the Bible turn at G?"

"I think you thought it would turn, and therefore it did. Gilbert Potter was in your mind, of course."

"And not in yours, Martha?"

"If any man was seriously in my mind, Sally, do you think I would take the Bible and the door-key in order to find out his name?"

Sally was not adroit in speech: she felt that her question had not been answered, but was unable to see precisely how the answer had been evaded.

"I certainly was beginning to think that you liked Gilbert," she said.

"So I do. Anybody may know that who cares for the information." And Martha laughed cheerfully.

"Would you say so to Gilbert himself?" Sally timidly suggested.

"Certainly; but why should he ask? I like a great many young men."

"Oh, Martha!"

"Oh, Sally!—and so do you. But there's this I will say: if I were to love a man, neither he nor any other living soul should know it, until he had told me with his own lips that his heart had chosen me."

The strength of conviction in Martha's grave, gentle voice, struck Sally dumb. Her lips were sealed on the delicious secret she was longing, and yet afraid, to disclose. He had not spoken: she hoped he loved her, she was sure she loved him. Did she speak now, she thought, she would lower herself in Martha's eyes. With a helpless impulse, she threw one arm over the latter's neck, and kissed her cheek. She did not know that with the kiss she had left a tear.

"Sally," said Martha, in a tender whisper, "I only spoke for myself. Some hearts must be silent, while it is the nature of others to speak out. You are not afraid of me: it will be womanly in you to tell me everything. Your cheek is hot: you are blushing. Don't blush, Sally dear, for I know it already."

Sally answered with an impassioned demonstration of gratitude and affection. Then she spoke; but we will not reveal the secrets of her virgin heart. It is enough that, soothed and comforted by Martha's wise counsel and sympathy, she sank into happy slumber at her side.

CHAPTER VI. — THE NEW GILBERT.

This time the weather, which so often thwarts the farmer's calculations, favored Gilbert Potter. In a week the two fields were ploughed, and what little farm-work remained to be done before the first of April, could be safely left to Sam. On the second Monday after the chase, therefore, he harnessed his four sturdy horses to the wagon, and set off before the first streak of dawn for Columbia, on the Susquehanna. Here he would take from twelve to sixteen barrels of flour (according to the state of the roads) and haul them, a two days' journey, to Newport, on the Christiana River. The freight of a dollar and a half a barrel, which he received, yielded him what in those days was considered a handsome profit for the service, and it was no unusual thing for farmers who were in possession of a suitable team, to engage in the business whenever they could spare the time from their own fields.

Since the evening when she had spoken to him, for the first time in her life, of the dismal shadow which rested upon their names, Mary Potter felt that there was an indefinable change in her relation to her son. He seemed suddenly drawn nearer to her, and yet, in some other sense which she could not clearly comprehend, thrust farther away. His manner, always kind and tender, assumed a shade of gentle respect, grateful in itself, yet disturbing, because new in her experience of him. His head was slightly lifted, and his lips, though firm as ever, less rigidly compressed. She could not tell how it was, but his voice had more authority in her ears. She had never before quite disentangled the man that he was from the child that he had been; but now the separation, sharp, sudden, and final, was impressed upon her mind. Under all the loneliness which came upon her, when the musical bells of his team tinkled into silence beyond the hill, there lurked a strange sense of relief, as if her nature would more readily adjust itself during his absence.

Instead of accepting the day with its duties, as a sufficient burden, she now deliberately reviewed the Past. It would give her pain, she knew; but what pain could she ever feel again, comparable to that which she had so recently suffered? Long she brooded over that bitter period before and immediately succeeding her son's birth, often declaring to herself how fatally she had erred, and as often shaking her head in hopeless renunciation of any present escape from the consequences of that error. She saw her position clearly, yet it seemed that she had so entangled herself in the meshes of a merciless Fate, that the only reparation she could claim, either for herself or her son, would be thrown away by forestalling—after such endless, endless submission and suffering—the Event which should set her free.

Then she recalled and understood, as never before, Gilbert's childhood and boyhood. For his sake she had accepted menial service in families where he was looked upon and treated as an incumbrance. The child, it had been her comfort to think, was too young to know or feel this,—but now, alas! the remembrance of his shyness and sadness told her a different tale. So nine years had passed, and she was then forced to part with her boy. She had bound him to Farmer Fairthorn, whose good heart, and his wife's, she well knew, and now she worked for him, alone, putting by her savings every year, and stinting herself to the utmost that she might be able to start him in life, if he should live to be his own master. Little by little, the blot upon her seemed to fade out or be forgotten, and she hoped—oh, how she had hoped!—that he might be spared the knowledge of it.

She watched him grow up, a boy of firm will, strong temper, yet great self-control; and the easy Fairthorn rule, which would have spoiled a youth of livelier spirits, was, providentially, the atmosphere in which his nature grew more serene and patient. He was steady, industrious, and faithful, and the Fairthorns loved him almost as their own son. When he reached the age of eighteen, he was allowed many important privileges: he hauled flour to Newport, having a share of the profits, and in other ways earned a sum which, with his mother's aid, enabled him to buy a team of his own, on coming of age.

Two years more of this weary, lonely labor, and the one absorbing aim of Mary Potter's life, which she had impressed upon him ever since he was old enough to understand it, drew near fulfilment. The farm upon which they now lived was sold, and Gilbert became the purchaser. There was still a debt of a thousand dollars upon the property, and she felt that until it was paid, they possessed no secure home. During the year which had elapsed since the purchase, Gilbert, by unwearied labor, had laid up about four hundred dollars, and another year, he had said, if he should prosper in his plans, would see them free at last! Then,—let the world say what it chose! They had fought their way from shame and poverty to honest independence, and the respect which follows success would at least be theirs.

This was always the consoling thought to which Mary Potter returned, from the unallayed trouble of her mind. Day by day, Gilbert's new figure became more familiar, and she was conscious that her own manner towards him must change with it. The subject of his birth, however, and the new difficulties with which it beset her, would not be thrust aside. For years she had almost ceased to think of the possible release, of which she had spoken; now it returned and filled her with a strange, restless impatience.

Gilbert, also, had ample time to review his own position, during the fortnight's absence. After passing the hills and emerging upon the long, fertile swells of Lancaster, his experienced leaders but rarely needed the guidance of his hand or voice. Often, sunk in revery, the familiar landmarks of the journey went by unheeded; often he lay awake in the crowded bedroom of a tavern, striving to clear a path for his feet a little way into the future. Only men of the profoundest culture make a deliberate study of their own natures, but those less gifted often act with an equal or even superior wisdom, because their qualities operate spontaneously, unwatched by an introverted eye. Such men may be dimly conscious of certain inconsistencies, or unsolved puzzles, in themselves, but instead of sitting down to unravel them, they seek the easiest way to pass by and leave them untouched. For them the material aspects of life are of the highest importance, and a true instinct shows them that beyond the merest superficial acquaintance with their own natures lie deep and disturbing questions, with which they are not fitted to grapple.

There comes a time, however, to every young man, even the most uncultivated, when he touches one of the primal, eternal forces of life, and is conscious of other needs and another destiny. This time had come to Gilbert Potter, forcing him to look upon the circumstances of his life from a loftier point of view. He had struggled, passionately but at random, for light,—but, fortunately, every earnest struggle is towards the light, and it now began to dawn upon him.

He first became aware of one enigma, the consideration of which was not so easy to lay aside. His mother had not been deceived: there was a change in the man since that evening. Often and often, in gloomy breedings over his supposed disgrace, he had fiercely asserted to himself that he was free from stain, and the unrespect in which he stood was an injustice to be bravely defied. The brand which he wore, and which he fancied was seen by every eye he met, existed in his own fancy; his brow was as pure, his right to esteem and honor equal, to that of any other man. But it was impossible to act upon this reasoning; still when the test came he would shrink and feel the pain, instead of trampling it under his feet.

Now that the brand was removed, the strength which he had so desperately craved, was suddenly his. So far as the world was concerned, nothing was altered; no one knew of the revelation which his mother had made to him; he was still the child of her shame, but this knowledge was no longer a torture. Now he had a right to respect, not asserted only to his own heart, but which every man would acknowledge, were it made known. He was no longer a solitary individual, protesting against prejudice and custom. Though still feeling that the protest was just, and that his new courage implied some weakness, he could not conceal from himself the knowledge that this very weakness was the practical fountain of his strength. He was a secret and unknown unit of the great majority.

There was another, more intimate subject which the new knowledge touched very nearly; and here, also, hope dawned upon a sense akin to despair. With all the force of his nature, Gilbert Potter loved Martha Deane. He had known her since he was a boy at Fairthorn's; her face had always been the brightest in his memory; but it was only since the purchase of the farm that his matured manhood had fully recognized its answering womanhood in her. He was slow to acknowledge the truth, even to his own heart, and when it could no longer be denied, he locked it up and sealed it with seven seals, determined never to betray it, to her or any one. Then arose a wild hope, that respect might come with the independence for which he was laboring, and perhaps he might dare to draw nearer,—near enough to guess if there were any answer in her heart. It was a frail support, but he clung to it as with his life, for there was none other.

Now,—although his uncertainty was as great as ever,—his approach could not humiliate her. His love brought no shadow of shame; it was proudly white and clean. Ah! he had forgotten that she did not know,—that his lips were sealed until his mother's should be opened to the world. The curse was not to be shaken off so easily.

By the time he had twice traversed the long, weary road between Columbia and Newport, Gilbert reached a desperate solution of this difficulty. The end of his meditations was: "I will see if there be love in woman as in man!—love that takes no note of birth or station, but, once having found its mate, is faithful from first to last." In love, an honest and faithful heart touches the loftiest ideal. Gilbert knew that, were the case reversed, no possible test could shake his steadfast affection, and how else could he measure the quality of hers? He said to himself: "Perhaps it is cruel, but I cannot spare her the trial." He was prouder than he knew,—but we must remember all that he endured.

It was a dry, windy March month, that year, and he made four good trips before the first of April. Returning home from Newport, by way of Wilmington, with seventy-five dollars clear profit in his pocket, his prospects seemed very cheerful. Could he accomplish two more months of hauling during the year, and the crops should be fair, the money from these sources, and the sale of his wagon and one span, would be something more than enough to discharge the remaining debt. He knew, moreover, how the farm could be more advantageously worked, having used his eyes to good purpose in passing through the rich, abundant fields of Lancaster. The land once his own,—which, like his mother, he could not yet feel,—his future, in a material sense, was assured.

Before reaching the Buck Tavern, he overtook a woman plodding slowly along the road. Her rusty beaver hat, tied down over her ears, and her faded gown, were in singular contrast to the shining new scarlet shawl upon her shoulders. As she stopped and turned, at the sound of his tinkling bells, she showed a hard red face, not devoid of a certain coarse beauty, and he recognized Deb. Smith, a lawless, irregular creature, well known about Kennett.

"Good-day, Deborah!" said he; "if you are going my way, I can give you a lift."

"He calls me 'Deborah,'" she muttered to herself; then aloud—"Ay, and thank ye, Mr. Gilbert."

Seizing the tail of the near horse with one hand, she sprang upon the wagon-tongue, and the next moment sat upon the board at his side. Then, rummaging in a deep pocket, she produced, one after the other, a short black pipe, an eel-skin tobacco-pouch, flint, tinder, and a clumsy knife. With a dexterity which could only have come from long habit, she prepared and kindled the weed, and was presently puffing forth rank streams, with an air of the deepest satisfaction.

"Which way?" asked Gilbert.

"Your'n, as far as you go,—always providin' you takes me."

"Of course, Deborah, you're welcome. I have no load, you see."

"Mighty clever in you, Mr. Gilbert; but you always was one o' the clever ones. Them as thinks themselves better born"—

"Come, Deborah, none of that!" he exclaimed.

"Ax your pardon," she said, and smoked her pipe in silence. When she had finished and knocked the ashes out against the front panel of the wagon, she spoke again, in a hard, bitter voice,—

"'Tisn't much difference what I am. I was raised on hard knocks, and now I must git my livin' by 'em. But I axes no'un's help, I'm that proud, anyways. I go my own road, and a straighter one, too, damme, than I git credit for, but I let other people go their'n. You might have wuss company than me, though I say it."

68

These words hinted at an inward experience in some respects so surprisingly like his own, that Gilbert was startled. He knew the reputation of the woman, though he would have found it difficult to tell whereupon it was based. Everybody said she was bad, and nobody knew particularly why. She lived alone, in a log-cabin in the woods; did washing and house-cleaning; worked in the harvest-fields; smoked, and took her gill of whiskey with the best of them,—but other vices, though inferred, were not proven. Involuntarily, he contrasted her position, in this respect, with his own. The world, he had recently learned, was wrong in his case; might it not also be doing her injustice? Her pride, in its coarse way, was his also, and his life, perhaps, had only unfolded into honorable success through a mother's ever-watchful care and never-wearied toil.

"Deborah," he said, after a pause, "no man or woman who makes an honest living by hard work, is bad company for me. I am trying to do the same thing that you are,—to be independent of others. It's not an easy thing for anybody, starting from nothing, but I can guess that it must be much harder for you than for me."

"Yes, you're a man!" she cried. "Would to God I'd been one, too! A man can do everything that I do, and it's all right and proper. Why did the Lord give me strength? Look at that!" She bared her right arm—hard, knitted muscle from wrist to shoulder—and clenched her fist. "What's that for?—not for a woman, I say; I could take two of 'em by the necks and pitch 'em over yon fence. I've felled an Irishman like an ox when he called me names. The anger's in me, and the boldness and the roughness, and the cursin'; I didn't put 'em there, and I can't git 'em out now, if I tried ever so much. Why did they snatch the sewin' from me when I wanted to learn women's work, and send me out to yoke th' oxen? I do believe I was a gal onc't, a six-month or so, but it's over long ago. I've been a man ever since!"

She took a bottle out of her pocket, and offered it to Gilbert. When he refused, she simply said: "You're right!" set it to her mouth, and drank long and deeply. There was a wild, painful gleam of truth in her words, which touched his sympathy. How should he dare to judge this unfortunate creature, not knowing what perverse freak of nature, and untoward circumstances of life had combined to make her what she was? His manner towards her was kind and serious, and by degrees this covert respect awoke in her a desire to deserve it. She spoke calmly and soberly, exhibiting a wonderful knowledge as they rode onwards, not only of farming, but of animals, trees, and plants.

The team, knowing that home and rest were near, marched cheerily up and down the hills along the border, and before sunset, emerging from the woods, they overlooked the little valley, the mill, and the nestling farmhouse. An Indian war-whoop rang across the meadow, and Gilbert recognized Sam's welcome therein.

"Now, Deborah," said he, "you shall stop and have some supper, before you go any farther."

"I'm obliged, all the same," said she, "but I must push on. I've to go beyond the Square, and couldn't wait. But tell your mother if she wants a man's arm in house-cleanin' time to let me know. And, Mr. Gilbert, let me say one thing: give me your hand."

The horses had stopped to drink at the creek. He gave her his right hand.

She held it in hers a moment, gazing intently on the palm. Then she bent her head and blew upon it gently, three times.

"Never mind: it's my fancy," she said. "You're born for trial and good-luck, but the trials come first, all of a heap, and the good luck afterwards. You've got a friend in Deb. Smith, if you ever need one. Good-bye to ye!"

With these words she sprang from the wagon, and trudged off silently up the hill. The horses turned of themselves into the lane leading to the barn, and Gilbert assisted Sam in unharnessing and feeding them before entering the house. By the time he was ready to greet his mother, and enjoy, without further care, his first evening at home, he knew everything that had occurred on the farm during his absence.

CHAPTER VII. — OLD KENNETT MEETING.

On the Sunday succeeding his return, Gilbert Potter proposed to his mother that they should attend the Friends' Meeting at Old Kennett.

The Quaker element, we have already stated, largely predominated in this part of the county; and even the many families who were not actually members of the sect were strongly colored with its peculiar characteristics. Though not generally using "the plain speech" among themselves, they invariably did so towards Quakers, varied but little from the latter in dress and habits, and, with very few exceptions, regularly attended their worship. In fact, no other religious attendance was possible, without a Sabbath journey too long for the well-used farm-horses. To this class belonged Gilbert and his mother, the Fairthorns, and even the Bartons. Farmer Fairthorn had a birthright, it is true, until his marriage, which having been a stolen match, and not performed according to "Friends' ceremony," occasioned his excommunication. He might have been restored to the rights of membership by admitting his sorrow for the offence, but this he stoutly refused to do. The predicament was not an unusual one in the neighborhood; but a few, among whom was Dr. Deane, Martha's father, submitted to the required humiliation. As this did not take place, however, until after her birth, Martha was still without the pale, and preferred to remain so, for two reasons: first, that a scoop bonnet was monstrous on a young woman's head; and second, that she was passionately fond of music, and saw no harm in a dance. This determination of hers was, as her father expressed himself, a "great cross" to him; but she had a habit of paralyzing his argument by turning against him the testimony of the Friends in regard to forms and ceremonies, and their reliance on the guidance of the Spirit.

Herein Martha was strictly logical, and though she, and others who belonged to the same class, were sometimes characterized, by a zealous Quaker, in moments of bitterness, as being "the world's people," they were generally regarded, not only with tolerance, but in a spirit of fraternity. The high seats in the gallery were not for them, but they were free to any other part of the meeting-house during life, and to a grave in the grassy and briery enclosure adjoining, when dead. The necessity of belonging to some organized church was recognized but faintly, if at all; provided their lives were honorable, they were considered very fair Christians.

Mary Potter but rarely attended meeting, not from any lack of the need of worship, but because she shrank with painful timidity from appearing in the presence of the assembled neighborhood. She was, nevertheless, grateful for Gilbert's success, and her heart inclined to thanksgiving; besides, he desired that they should go, and she was not able to offer any valid objection. So, after breakfast, the two best horses of the team were very carefully groomed, saddled, and—Sam having been sent off on a visit to his father, with the house-key in his pocket—the mother and son took the road up the creek.

Both were plainly, yet very respectably, dressed, in garments of the same home-made cloth, of a deep, dark brown color, but Mary Potter wore under her cloak the new crape shawl which Gilbert had brought to her from Wilmington, and his shirt of fine linen displayed a modest ruffle in front. The resemblance in their faces was even more strongly marked, in the common expression of calm, grave repose, which sprang from the nature of their journey. A stranger meeting them that morning, would have seen that they were persons of unusual force of character, and bound to each other by an unusual tie.

Up the lovely valley, or rather glen, watered by the eastern branch of Redley Creek, they rode to the main highway. It was an early spring, and the low-lying fields were already green with the young grass; the weeping-willows in front of the farm-houses seemed to spout up and fall like broad enormous geysers as the wind swayed them, and daffodils bloomed in all the warmer gardens. The dark foliage of the cedars skirting the road counteracted that indefinable gloom which the landscapes of early spring, in their grayness and incompleteness, so often inspire, and mocked the ripened summer in the close shadows which they threw. It was a pleasant ride, especially after mother and son had reached the main road, and other horsemen and horsewomen issued from the gates of farms on either side, taking their way to the meeting-house.

Only two or three families could boast vehicles,—heavy, cumbrous "chairs," as they were called, with a convex canopy resting on four stout pillars, and the bulging body swinging from side to side on huge springs of wood and leather. No healthy man or woman, however, unless he or she were very old, travelled otherwise than on horseback.

Now and then exchanging grave but kindly nods with their acquaintances, they rode slowly along the level upland, past the Anvil Tavern, through Logtown,—a cluster of primitive cabins at the junction of the Wilmington Road,—and reached the meeting-house in good season. Gilbert assisted his mother to alight at the stone platform built for that purpose near the women's end of the building, and then fastened the horses in the long, open shed in the rear. Then, as was the custom, he entered by the men's door, and quietly took a seat in the silent assembly.

The stiff, unpainted benches were filled with the congregation, young and old, wearing their hats, and with a stolid, drowsy look upon their faces. Over a high wooden partition the old women in the gallery, but not the young women on the floor of the house, could be seen. Two stoves, with interminable lengths of pipe, suspended by wires from the ceiling, created a stifling temperature. Every slight sound or motion,—the moving of a foot, the drawing forth of a pocket-handkerchief, the lifting or lowering of a head,—seemed to disturb the quiet as with a shock, and drew many of the younger eyes upon it; while in front, like the guardian statues of an Egyptian temple, sat the older members, with their hands upon their knees or clasped across their laps. Their faces were grave and severe.

After nearly an hour of this suspended animation, an old Friend rose, removed his broad-brimmed hat, and placing his hands upon the rail before him, began slowly swaying to and fro, while he spoke. As he rose into the chant peculiar to the sect, intoning alike his quotations from the Psalms and his utterances of plain, practical advice, an expression of quiet but almost luxurious satisfaction stole over the faces of his aged brethren. With half-closed eyes and motionless bodies, they drank in the sound like a rich draught, with a sense of exquisite refreshment. A close connection of ideas, a logical derivation of argument from text, would have aroused their suspicions that the speaker depended rather upon his own active, conscious intellect, than upon the moving of the Spirit; but this aimless wandering of a half-awake soul through the cadences of a language which was neither song nor speech, was, to their minds, the evidence of genuine inspiration.

When the old man sat down, a woman arose and chanted forth the suggestions which had come to her in the silence, in a voice of wonderful sweetness and strength. Here Music seemed to revenge herself for the slight done to her by the sect. The ears of the hearers were so charmed by the purity of tone, and the delicate, rhythmical cadences of the sentences, that much of the wise lessons repeated from week to week failed to reach their consciousness.

After another interval of silence, the two oldest men reached their hands to each other,—a sign which the younger members had anxiously awaited. The spell snapped in an instant; all arose and moved into the open air, where all things at first appeared to wear the same aspect of solemnity. The poplar-trees, the stone wall, the bushes in the corners of the fence, looked grave and respectful for a few minutes. Neighbors said, "How does thee do?" to each other, in subdued voices, and there was a conscientious shaking of hands all around before they dared to indulge in much conversation.

Gradually, however, all returned to the out-door world and its interests. The fences became so many posts and rails once more, the bushes so many elders and blackberries to be cut away, and the half-green fields so much sod for corn-ground. Opinions in regard to the weather and the progress of spring labor were freely interchanged, and the few unimportant items of social news, which had collected in seven days, were gravely distributed. This was at the men's end of the meeting-house; on their side, the women were similarly occupied, but we can only conjecture the subjects of their conversation. The young men—as is generally the case in religious sects of a rigid and clannish character—were by no means handsome. Their faces all bore the stamp of repression, in some form or other, and as they talked their eyes wandered with an expression of melancholy longing and timidity towards the sweet, maidenly faces, whose bloom, and pure, gentle beauty not even their hideous bonnets could obscure.

One by one the elder men came up to the stone platform with the stable old horses which their wives were to ride home; the huge chair, in which sat a privileged couple, creaked and swayed from side to side, as it rolled with ponderous dignity from the yard; and now, while the girls were waiting their turn, the grave young men plucked up courage, wandered nearer, greeted, exchanged words, and so were helped into an atmosphere of youth.

Gilbert, approaching with them, was first recognized by his old friend, Sally Fairthorn, whose voice of salutation was so loud and cheery, as to cause two or three sedate old "women-friends" to turn their heads in grave astonishment. Mother Fairthorn, with her bright, round face, followed, and then—serene and strong in her gentle, symmetrical loveliness—Martha Deane. Gilbert's hand throbbed, as he held hers a moment, gazing into the sweet blue of her eyes; yet, passionately as he felt that he loved her in that moment, perfect as was the delight of her presence, a better joy came to his heart when she turned away to speak with his mother. Mark Deane—a young giant with curly yellow locks, and a broad, laughing mouth—had just placed a hand upon his shoulder, and he could not watch the bearing of the two women to each other; but all his soul listened to their voices, and he heard in Martha Deane's the kindly courtesy and respect which he did not see.

Mother Fairthorn and Sally so cordially insisted that Mary Potter and her son should ride home with them to dinner, that no denial was possible. When the horses were brought up to the block the yard was nearly empty, and the returning procession was already winding up the hill towards Logtown.

"Come, Mary," said Mother Fairthorn, "you and I will ride together, and you shall tell me all about your ducks and turkeys. The young folks can get along without us, I guess."

Martha Deane had ridden to meeting in company with her cousin Mark and Sally, but the order of the homeward ride was fated to be different. Joe and Jake, bestriding a single horse, like two of the Haymon's-children, were growing inpatient, so they took the responsibility of dashing up to Mark and Sally, who were waiting in the road, and announcing,—

"Cousin Martha says we're to go on; she'll ride with Gilbert."

Both well knew the pranks of the boys, but perhaps they found the message well-invented if not true; for they obeyed with secret alacrity, although Sally made a becoming show of reluctance. Before they reached the bottom of the hollow, Joe and Jake, seeing two school-mates in advance, similarly mounted, dashed off in a canter, to overtake them, and the two were left alone.

Gilbert and Martha naturally followed, since not more than two could conveniently ride abreast. But their movements were so quiet and deliberate, and the accident which threw them together was accepted so simply and calmly that no one could guess what warmth of longing, of reverential tenderness, beat in every muffled throb of one of the two hearts.

Martha was an admirable horsewoman, and her slender, pliant figure never showed to greater advantage than in the saddle. Her broad beaver hat was tied down over the ears, throwing a cool gray shadow across her clear, joyous eyes and fresh cheeks. A pleasanter face never touched a young man's fancy, and every time it turned towards Gilbert it brightened away the distress of love. He caught, unconsciously, the serenity of her mood, and foretasted the peace which her being would bring to him if it were ever intrusted to his hands.

"Did you do well by your hauling, Gilbert," she asked, "and are you now home for the summer?"

"Until after corn-planting," he answered. "Then I must take two or three weeks, as the season turns out. I am not able to give up my team yet."

"But you soon will be, I hope. It must be very lonely for your mother to be on the farm without you."

These words touched him gratefully, and led him to a candid openness of speech which he would not otherwise have ventured,—not from any inherent lack of candor, but from a reluctance to speak of himself.

"That's it, Martha," he said. "It is her work that I have the farm at all, and I only go away the oftener now, that I may the sooner stay with her altogether. The thought of her makes each trip lonelier than the last."

"I like to hear you say that, Gilbert. And it must be a comfort to you, withal, to know that you are working as much for your mother's sake as your own. I think I should feel so, at least, in your place. I feel my own mother's loss more now than when she died, for I was then so young that I can only just remember her face."

"But you have a father!" he exclaimed, and the words were scarcely out of his mouth before he became aware of their significance, uttered by his lips. He had not meant so much,—only that she, like him, still enjoyed one parent's care. The blood came into his face; she saw and understood the sign, and broke a silence which would soon have become painful.

"Yes," she said, "and I am very grateful that he is spared; but we seem to belong most to our mothers."

"That is the truth," he said firmly, lifting his head with the impulse of his recovered pride, and meeting her eyes without flinching. "I belong altogether to mine. She has made me a man and set me upon my feet. From this time forward, my place is to stand between her and the world!"

Martha Deane's blood throbbed an answer to this assertion of himself. A sympathetic pride beamed in her eyes; she slightly bent her head, in answer, without speaking, and Gilbert felt that he was understood and valued. He had drawn a step nearer to the trial which he had resolved to make, and would now venture no further.

There was a glimmering spark of courage in his heart. He was surprised, in recalling the conversation afterwards, to find how much of his plans he had communicated to her during the ride, encouraged by the kindly interest she manifested, and the sensible comments she uttered. Joe and Jake, losing their mates at a cross-road, and finding Sally and Mark Deane not very lively company for them, rode back and disturbed these confidences, but not until they had drawn the two into a relation of acknowledged mutual interest.

Martha Deane had always, as she confessed to Sally, liked Gilbert Potter; she liked every young man of character and energy; but now she began to suspect that there was a rarer worth in his nature than she had guessed.

From that day he was more frequently the guest of her thoughts than ever before. Instinct, in him, had performed the same service which men of greater experience of the world would have reached through keen perception and careful tact,—in confiding to her his position, his labors and hopes, material as was the theme and seemingly unsuited to the occasion, he had in reality appreciated the serious, reflective nature underlying her girlish grace and gayety. What other young man of her acquaintance, she asked herself, would have done the same thing?

When they reached Kennett Square, Mother Fairthorn urged Martha to accompany them, and Sally impetuously seconded the invitation. Dr. Deane's horse was at his door, however, and his daughter, with her eyes on Gilbert, as if saying "for my father's sake," steadfastly declined. Mark, however, took her place, but there never had been, or could be, too many guests at the Fairthorn table.

When they reached the garden-wall, Sally sprang from her horse with such haste that her skirt caught on the pommel and left her hanging, being made of stuff too stout to tear. It was well that Gilbert was near, on the same side, and disengaged her in an instant; but her troubles did not end here. As she bustled in and out of the kitchen, preparing the dinner-table in the long sitting-room, the hooks and door-handles seemed to have an unaccountable habit of thrusting themselves in her way, and she was ready to cry at each glance of Mark's laughing eyes. She had never heard the German proverb, "who loves, teases," and was too inexperienced, as yet, to have discovered the fact for herself.

Presently they all sat down to dinner, and after the first solemn quiet,— no one venturing to eat or speak until the plates of all had been heaped with a little of everything upon the table,—the meal became very genial and pleasant. A huge brown pitcher of stinging cider added its mild stimulus to the calm country blood, and under its mellowing influence Mark announced the most important fact of his life,—he was to have the building of Hallowell's barn.

As Gilbert and his mother rode homewards, that afternoon, neither spoke much, but both felt, in some indefinite way, better prepared for the life that lay before them.

78

CHAPTER VIII. – AT DR. DEANE'S.

As she dismounted on the large flat stone outside the paling, Martha Deane saw her father's face at the window. It was sterner and graver than usual.

The Deane mansion stood opposite the Unicorn Tavern. When built, ninety years previous, it had been considered a triumph of architecture; the material was squared logs from the forest, dovetailed, and overlapping at the corners, which had the effect of rustic quoins, as contrasted with the front, which was plastered and yellow-washed. A small portico, covered with a tangled mass of eglantine and coral honeysuckle, with a bench at each end, led to the door; and the ten feet of space between it and the front paling were devoted to flowers and rose-bushes. At each corner of the front rose an old, picturesque, straggling cedar-tree.

There were two front doors, side by side,—one for the family sitting-room, the other (rarely opened, except when guests arrived) for the parlor. Martha Deane entered the former, and we will enter with her.

The room was nearly square, and lighted by two windows. On those sides the logs were roughly plastered; on the others there were partitions of panelled oak, nearly black with age and smoke, as were the heavy beams of the same wood which formed the ceiling. In the corner of the room next the kitchen there was an open Franklin stove,—an innovation at that time,— upon which two or three hickory sticks were smouldering into snowy ashes. The floor was covered with a country-made rag carpet, in which an occasional strip of red or blue listing brightened the prevailing walnut color of the woof. The furniture was simple and massive, its only unusual feature being a tall cabinet with shelves filled with glass jars, and an infinity of small drawers. A few bulky volumes on the lower shelf constituted the medical library of Dr. Deane.

This gentleman was still standing at the window, with his hands clasped across his back. His Quaker suit was of the finest drab broadcloth, and the plain cravat visible above his high, straight waistcoat, was of spotless cambric. His knee-and shoe-buckles were of the simplest pattern, but of good, solid silver, and there was not a wrinkle in the stockings of softest lamb's-wool, which covered his massive calves. There was always a faint odor of lavender, bergamot, or sweet marjoram about him, and it was a common remark in the neighborhood that the sight and smell of the Doctor helped a weak patient almost as much as his medicines.

In his face there was a curious general resemblance to his daughter, though the detached features were very differently formed. Large, unsymmetrical, and somewhat coarse,—even for a man,—they derived much of their effect from his scrupulous attire and studied air of wisdom. His long gray hair was combed back, that no portion of the moderate frontal brain might be covered; the eyes were gray rather than blue, and a habit of concealment had marked its lines in the corners, unlike the open, perfect frankness of his daughter's. The principal resemblance was in the firm, clear outline of the upper lip, which alone, in his face, had it been supported by the under one, would have made him almost handsome; but the latter was large and slightly hanging. There were marked inconsistencies in his face, but this was no disadvantage in a community unaccustomed to studying the external marks of character.

"Just home, father? How did thee leave Dinah Passmore?" asked Martha, as she untied the strings of her beaver.

"Better," he answered, turning from the window; "but, Martha, who did I see thee riding with?"

"Does thee mean Gilbert Potter?"

"I do," he said, and paused. Martha, with her cloak over her arm and bonnet in her hand, in act to leave the room, waited, saying,—

"Well, father?"

So frank and serene was her bearing, that the old man felt both relieved and softened.

"I suppose it happened so," he said. "I saw his mother with Friend

Fairthorn. I only meant thee shouldn't be seen in company with young Potter, when thee could help it; thee knows what I mean."

"I don't think, father," she slowly answered, "there is anything against Gilbert Potter's life or character, except that which is no just reproach to him."

"'The sins of the parents shall be visited upon the children, even to the third and fourth generation.' That is enough, Martha."

She went up to her room, meditating, with an earnestness almost equal to Gilbert's, upon this form of the world's injustice, which he was powerless to overcome. Her father shared it, and the fact did not surprise her; but her independent spirit had already ceased to be guided, in all things, by his views. She felt that the young man deserved the respect and admiration which he had inspired in her mind, and until a better reason could be discovered, she would continue so to regard him. The decision was reached rapidly, and then laid aside for any future necessity; she went down-stairs again in her usual quiet, cheerful mood.

During her absence another conversation had taken place.

Miss Betsy Lavender (who was a fast friend of Martha, and generally spent her Sundays at the Doctor's,) was sitting before the stove, drying her feet. She was silent until Martha left the room, when she suddenly exclaimed:

"Doctor! Judge not that ye be not judged."

"Thee may think as thee pleases, Betsy," said he, rather sharply: "it's thy nature, I believe, to take everybody's part."

"Put yourself in his place," she continued,—"remember them that's in bonds as bound with 'em,—I disremember exackly how it goes, but no matter: I say your way a'n't right, and I'd say it seven times, if need be! There's no steadier nor better-doin' young fellow in these parts than Gilbert Potter. Ferris, down in Pennsbury, or Alf Barton, here, for that matter, a'n't to be put within a mile of him. I could say something in Mary Potter's behalf, too, but I won't: for there's Scribes and Pharisees about."

Dr. Deane did not notice this thrust: it was not his habit to get angry.

"Put thyself in my place, Betsy," he said. "He's a worthy young man, in some respects, I grant thee, but would thee like thy daughter to be seen riding home beside him from Meeting? It's one thing speaking for thyself, and another for thy daughter."

"Thy daughter!" she repeated. "Old or young can't make any difference, as I see."

There was something else on her tongue, but she forcibly withheld the words. She would not exhaust her ammunition until there was both a chance and a necessity to do some execution. The next moment Martha reentered the room.

After dinner, they formed a quiet group in the front sitting-room. Dr. Deane, having no more visits to make that day, took a pipe of choice tobacco,—the present of a Virginia Friend, whose acquaintance he had made at Yearly Meeting,—and seated himself in the arm-chair beside the stove. Martha, at the west window, enjoyed a volume of Hannah More, and Miss Betsy, at the front window, labored over the Psalms. The sun shone with dim, muffled orb, but the air without was mild, and there were already brown tufts, which would soon be blossoms, on the lilac twigs.

Suddenly Miss Betsy lifted up her head and exclaimed, "Well, I never!" As she did so, there was a knock at the door.

"Come in!" said Dr. Deane, and in came Mr. Alfred Barton, resplendent in blue coat, buff waistcoat, cambric ruffles, and silver-gilt buckles. But, alas! the bunch of seals—topaz, agate, and cornelian—no longer buoyed the deep-anchored watch. The money due his father had been promptly paid, through the agency of a three-months' promissory note, and thus the most momentous result of the robbery was overcome. This security for the future, however, scarcely consoled him for the painful privation of the present. Without the watch, Alfred Barton felt that much of his dignity and importance was lacking.

Dr. Deane greeted his visitor with respect, Martha with the courtesy due to a guest, and Miss Betsy with the offhand, independent manner, under which she masked her private opinions of the persons whom she met.

"Mark isn't at home, I see," said Mr. Barton, after having taken his seat in the centre of the room: "I thought I'd have a little talk with him about the wagon-house. I suppose he told you that I got Hallowell's new barn for him?"

"Yes, and we're all greatly obliged to thee, as well as Mark," said the Doctor. "The two jobs make a fine start for a young mechanic, and I hope he'll do as well as he's been done by: there's luck in a good beginning. By the bye, has thee heard anything more of Sandy Flash's doings?"

Mr. Barton fairly started at this question. His own misfortune had been carefully kept secret, and he could not suspect that the Doctor knew it; but he nervously dreaded the sound of the terrible name.

"What is it?" he asked, in a faint voice.

"He has turned up in Bradford, this time, and they say has robbed Jesse Frame, the Collector, of between four and five hundred dollars. The Sheriff and a posse of men from the Valley hunted him for several days, but found no signs. Some think he has gone up into the Welch Mountain; but for my part, I should not be surprised if he were in this neighborhood."

"Good heavens!" exclaimed Mr. Barton, starting from his chair.

"Now's your chance," said Miss Betsy. "Git the young men together who won't feel afraid o' bein' twenty ag'in one: you know the holes and corners where he'll be likely to hide, and what's to hinder you from ketchin' him?"

"But he must have many secret friends," said Martha, "if what I have heard is true,—that he has often helped a poor man with the money which he takes only from the rich. You know he still calls himself a Tory, and many of those whose estates have been confiscated, would not scruple to harbor him, or even take his money."

"Take his money. That's a fact," remarked Miss Betsy, "and now I dunno whether I want him ketched. There's worse men goin' round, as respectable as you please, stealin' all their born days, only cunnin'ly jukin' round the law instead o' buttin' square through it. Why, old Liz Williams, o' Birmingham, herself told me with her own mouth, how she was ridin' home from Phildelphy market last winter, with six dollars, the price of her turkeys—and General Washin'ton's cook took one of 'em, but that's neither here nor there—in her pocket, and fearful as death when she come to Concord woods, and lo and behold! there she was overtook by a fresh-complected man, and she begged him to ride with her, for she had six dollars in her pocket and Sandy was known to be about. So he rode with her to her very lane-end, as kind and civil a person as she ever see, and then and there he said, 'Don't be afeard, Madam, for I, which have seen you home, is Sandy Flash himself, and here's somethin' more to remember me by,'—no sooner said than done, he put a gold guinea into her hand, and left her there as petrified as Lot's wife. Now I say, and it may be violation of the law, for all I know, but never mind, that Sandy Flash has got one corner of his heart in the right place, no matter where the others is. There's honor even among thieves, they say."

"Seriously, Alfred," said Dr. Deane, cutting Miss Betsy short before she had half expressed her sentiments, "it is time that something was done. If Flash is not caught soon, we shall be overrun with thieves, and there will be no security anywhere on the high roads, or in our houses. I wish that men of influence in the neighborhood, like thyself, would come together and plan, at least, to keep Kennett clear of him. Then other townships may do the same, and so the thing be stopped. If I were younger, and my practice were not so laborious, I would move in the matter, but thee is altogether a more suitable person."

"Do you think so?" Barton replied, with an irrepressible reluctance, around which he strove to throw an air of modesty. "That would be the proper way, certainly, but I,—I don't know,—that is, I can't flatter myself that I'm the best man to undertake it."

"It requires some courage, you know," Martha remarked, and her glance made him feel very uncomfortable, "and you are too dashing a fox-hunter not to have that. Perhaps the stranger who rode with you to Avondale—what was his name?—might be of service. If I were in your place, I should be glad of a chance to incur danger for the good of the neighborhood."

Mr. Alfred Barton was on nettles. If there were irony in her words his intellect was too muddy to detect it: her assumption of his courage could only be accepted as a compliment, but it was the last compliment he desired to have paid to himself, just at that time.

"Yes," he said, with a forced laugh, rushing desperately into the opposite extreme, "but the danger and the courage are not worth talking about. Any man ought to be able to face a robber, single-handed, and as for twenty men, why, when it's once known, Sandy Flash will only be too glad to keep away."

"Then, do thee do what I've recommended. It may be, as thee says, that the being prepared is all that is necessary," remarked Dr. Deane.

Thus caught, Mr. Barton could do no less than acquiesce, and very much to his secret dissatisfaction, the Doctor proceeded to name the young men of the neighborhood, promising to summon such as lived on the lines of his professional journeys, that they might confer with the leader of the undertaking. Martha seconded the plan with an evident interest, yet it did not escape her that neither her father nor Mr. Barton had mentioned the name of Gilbert Potter.

"Is that all?" she asked, when a list of some eighteen persons had been suggested. Involuntarily, she looked at Miss Betsy Lavender.

"No, indeed!" cried the latter. "There's Jabez Travilla, up on the ridge, and Gilbert Potter, down at the mill."

"H'm, yes; what does thee say, Alfred?" asked the Doctor.

"They're both good riders, and I think they have courage enough, but we can never tell what a man is until he's been tried. They would increase the number, and that, it seems to me, is a consideration."

"Perhaps thee had better exercise thy own judgment there," the Doctor observed, and the subject, having been as fully discussed as was possible without consultation with other persons, it was dropped, greatly to Barton's relief.

But in endeavoring to converse with Martha he only exchanged one difficulty for another. His vanity, powerful as it was, gave way before that instinct which is the curse and torment of vulgar natures,—which leaps into life at every contact of refinement, showing them the gulf between, which they know not how to cross. The impudence, the aggressive rudeness which such natures often exhibit, is either a mask to conceal their deficiency, or an angry protest against it. Where there is a drop of gentleness in the blood, it appreciates and imitates the higher nature.

This was the feeling which made Alfred Barton uncomfortable in the presence of Martha Deane,—which told him, in advance, that natures so widely sundered, never could come into near relations with each other, and thus quite neutralized the attraction of her beauty and her ten thousand dollars. His game, however, was to pay court to her, and in so pointed a way that it should be remarked and talked about in the neighborhood. Let it once come through others to the old man's ears, he would have proved his obedience and could not be reproached if the result were fruitless.

"What are you reading, Miss Martha?" he asked, after a long and somewhat awkward pause.

She handed him the book in reply.

"Ah! Hannah More,—a friend of yours? Is she one of the West-Whiteland Moores?"

Martha could not suppress a light, amused laugh, as she answered: "Oh, no, she is an English woman."

"Then it's a Tory book," said he, handing it back; "I wouldn't read it, if I was you."

"It is a story, and I should think you might."

He heard other words than those she spoke. "As Tory as—what?" he asked himself. "As I am," of course; that is what she means. "Old-man Barton" had been one of the disloyal purveyors for the British army during its occupancy of Philadelphia in the winter of 1777-8, and though the main facts of the traffic wherefrom he had drawn immense profits, never could be proved against him, the general belief hung over the family, and made a very disagreeable cloud. Whenever Alfred Barton quarrelled with any one, the taunt was sure to be flung into his teeth. That it came now, as he imagined, was as great a shock as if Martha had slapped him in the face with her own delicate hand, and his visage reddened from the blow.

Miss Betsy Lavender, bending laboriously over the Psalms, nevertheless kept her dull gray eyes in movement. She saw the misconception, and fearing that Martha did not, made haste to remark:—

"Well, Mr. Alfred, and do you think it's a harm to read a story? Why, Miss Ann herself lent me 'Alonzo and Melissa,' and 'Midnight Horrors,' and I'll be bound you've read 'em yourself on the sly. 'T a'n't much other readin' men does, save and except the weekly paper, and law enough to git a tight hold on their debtors. Come, now, let's know what you do read?"

"Not much of anything, that's a fact," he answered, recovering himself, with a shudder at the fearful mistake he had been on the point of making, "but I've nothing against women reading stories. I was rather thinking of myself when I spoke to you, Miss Martha."

"So I supposed," she quietly answered. It was provoking. Everything she said made him think there was another meaning behind the words; her composed manner, though he knew it to be habitual, more and more disconcerted him. Never did an intentional wooer find his wooing so painful and laborious. After this attempt he addressed himself to Doctor Deane, for even the question of circumventing Sandy Flash now presented itself to his mind as a relief.

There he sat, and the conversation progressed in jerks and spirts, between pauses of embarrassing silence. The sun hung on the western hill in a web of clouds; Martha and Miss Betsy rose and prepared the tea-table, and the guest, invited perforce, perforce accepted. Soon after the meal was over, however, he murmured something about cattle, took his hat and left.

Two or three horses were hitched before the Unicorn, and he saw some figures through the bar-room window. A bright thought struck him; he crossed the road and entered.

"Hallo, Alf! Where from now? Why, you're as fine as a fiddler!" cried Mr. Joel Ferris, who was fast becoming familiar, on the strength of his inheritance.

"Over the way," answered the landlord, with a wink and a jerk of his thumb.

Mr. Ferris whistled, and one of the others suggested: "He must stand a treat, on that."

"But, I say!" said the former, "how is it you're coming away so soon in the evening?"

"I went very early in the afternoon," Barton answered, with a mysterious, meaning smile, as much as to say: "It's all right; I know what I'm about." Then he added aloud,—"Step up, fellows; what'll you have?"

Many were the jests and questions to which he was forced to submit, but he knew the value of silence in creating an impression, and allowed them to enjoy their own inferences.

It is much easier to start a report, than to counteract it, when once started; but the first, only, was his business.

It was late in the evening when he returned home, and the household were in bed. Nevertheless, he did not enter by the back way, in his stockings, but called Giles down from the garret to unlock the front-door, and made as much noise as he pleased on his way to bed.

The old man heard it, and chuckled under his coverlet.

CHAPTER IX. — THE RAISING.

Steadily and serenely the Spring advanced. Old people shook their heads and said: "It will be April, this year, that comes in like a lamb and goes out like a lion,"—but it was not so. Soft, warm showers and frostless nights repaid the trustfulness of the early-expanding buds, and May came clothed completely in pale green, with a wreath of lilac and hawthorn bloom on her brow. For twenty years no such perfect spring had been known; and for twenty years afterwards the farmers looked back to it as a standard of excellence, whereby to measure the forwardness of their crops.

By the twentieth of April the young white-oak leaves were the size of a squirrel's ear,—the old Indian sign of the proper time for corn-planting, which was still accepted by the new race, and the first of May saw many fields already specked with the green points of the springing blades. A warm, silvery vapor hung over the land, mellowing the brief vistas of the interlacing valleys, touching with a sweeter pastoral beauty the irregular alternation of field and forest, and lifting the wooded slopes, far and near, to a statelier and more imposing height. The park-like region of Kennett, settled originally by emigrants from Bucks and Warwickshire, reproduced to their eyes— as it does to this day—the characteristics of their original home, and they transplanted the local names to which they were accustomed, and preserved, even long after the War of Independence, the habits of their rural ancestry. The massive stone farm-houses, the walled gardens, the bountiful orchards, and, more than all, the well-trimmed hedges of hawthorn and blackthorn dividing their fields, or bordering their roads with the living wall, over which the clematis and wild-ivy love to clamber, made the region beautiful to their eyes. Although the large original grants, mostly given by the hand of William Penn, had been divided and subdivided by three or four prolific generations, there was still enough and to spare,—and even the golden promise held out by "the Backwoods," as the new States of Ohio and Kentucky were then called, tempted very few to leave their homes.

The people, therefore, loved the soil and clung to it with a fidelity very rare in any part of our restless nation. And, truly, no one who had lived through the mild splendor of that spring, seeing, day by day, the visible deepening of the soft woodland tints, hearing the cheerful sounds of labor, far and wide, in the vapory air, and feeling at once the repose and the beauty of such a quiet, pastoral life, could have turned his back upon it, to battle with the inhospitable wilderness of the West. Gilbert Potter had had ideas of a new home, to be created by himself, and a life to which none should deny honor and respect: but now he gave them up forever. There was a battle to be fought—better here than elsewhere—here, where every scene was dear and familiar, and every object that met his eye gave a mute, gentle sense of consolation.

Restless, yet cheery labor was now the order of life on the farm. From dawn till dusk, Gilbert and Sam were stirring in field, meadow, and garden, keeping pace with the season and forecasting what was yet to come. Sam, although only fifteen, had a manly pride in being equal to the duty imposed upon him by his master's absence, and when the time came to harness the wagon-team once more, the mother and son walked over the fields together and rejoiced in the order and promise of the farm. The influences of the season had unconsciously touched them both: everything conspired to favor the fulfilment of their common plan, and, as one went forward to the repetition of his tedious journeys back and forth between Columbia and Newport, and the other to her lonely labor in the deserted farm-house, the arches of bells over the collars of the leaders chimed at once to the ears of both, an anthem of thanksgiving and a melody of hope.

So May and the beginning of June passed away, and no important event came to any character of this history. When Gilbert had delivered the last barrels at Newport, and slowly cheered homewards his weary team, he was nearly two hundred dollars richer than when he started, and—if we must confess a universal if somewhat humiliating truth—so much the more a man in courage and determination.

The country was now covered with the first fresh magnificence of summer. The snowy pyramids of dog-wood bloom had faded, but the tulip trees were tall cones of rustling green, lighted with millions of orange-colored stars, and all the underwood beneath the hemlock-forests by the courses of streams, was rosy with laurels and azaleas. The vernal-grass in the meadows was sweeter than any garden-rose, and its breath met that of the wild-grape in the thickets and struggled for preeminence of sweetness. A lush, tropical splendor of vegetation, such as England never knew, heaped the woods and hung the road-side with sprays which grew and bloomed and wantoned, as if growth were a conscious joy, rather than blind obedience to a law.

When Gilbert reached home, released from his labors abroad until October, he found his fields awaiting their owner's hand. His wheat hung already heavy-headed, though green, and the grass stood so thick and strong that it suggested the ripping music of the scythe-blade which should lay it low. Sam had taken good care of the cornfield, garden, and the cattle, and Gilbert's few words of quiet commendation were a rich reward for all his anxiety. His ambition was, to be counted "a full hand,"—this was the toga virilis, which, once entitled to wear, would make him feel that he was any man's equal.

Without a day's rest, the labor commenced again, and the passion of Gilbert's heart, though it had only strengthened during his absence, must be thrust aside until the fortune of his harvest was secured.

In the midst of the haying, however, came a message which he could not disregard,—a hasty summons from Mark Deane, who, seeing Gilbert in the upper hill-field, called from the road, bidding him to the raising of Hallowell's new barn, which was to take place on the following Saturday. "Be sure and come!" were Mark's closing words—"there's to be both dinner and supper, and the girls are to be on hand!"

It was the custom to prepare the complete frame of a barn—sills, plates, girders, posts, and stays—with all their mortices and pins, ready for erection, and then to summon all the able-bodied men of the neighborhood to assist in getting the timbers into place. This service, of course, was given gratuitously, and the farmer who received it could do no less than entertain, after the bountiful manner of the country, his helping neighbors, who therefore, although the occasion implied a certain amount of hard work, were accustomed to regard it as a sort of holiday, or merry-making. Their opportunities for recreation, indeed, were so scanty, that a barn-raising, or a husking-party by moonlight, was a thing to be welcomed.

Hallowell's farm was just half-way between Gilbert's and Kennett Square, and the site of the barn had been well-chosen on a ridge, across the road, which ran between it and the farm-house. The Hallowells were what was called "good providers," and as they belonged to the class of outside Quakers, which we have already described, the chances were that both music and dance would reward the labor of the day.

Gilbert, of course, could not refuse the invitation of so near a neighbor, and there was a hope in his heart which made it welcome. When the day came he was early on hand, heartily greeted by Mark, who exclaimed,—"Give me a dozen more such shoulders and arms as yours, and I'll make the timbers spin!"

It was a bright, breezy day, making the wheat roll and the leaves twinkle. Ranges of cumuli moved, one after the other, like heaps of silvery wool, across the keen, dark blue of the sky. "A wonderful hay-day," the old farmers remarked, with a half-stifled sense of regret; but the younger men had already stripped themselves to their shirts and knee-breeches, and set to work with a hearty good-will. Mark, as friend, half-host and commander, bore his triple responsibility with a mixture of dash and decision, which became his large frame and ruddy, laughing face. It was—really, and not in an oratorical sense,—the proudest day of his life.

There could be no finer sight than that of these lithe, vigorous specimens of a free, uncorrupted manhood, taking like sport the rude labor which was at once their destiny and their guard of safety against the assaults of the senses. As they bent to their work, prying, rolling, and lifting the huge sills to their places on the foundation-wall, they showed in every movement the firm yet elastic action of muscles equal to their task. Though Hallowell's barn did not rise, like the walls of Ilium, to music, a fine human harmony aided in its construction.

There was a plentiful supply of whiskey on hand, but Mark Deane assumed the charge of it, resolved that no accident or other disturbance should mar the success of this, his first raising. Everything went well, and by the time they were summoned to dinner, the sills and some of the uprights were in place, properly squared and tied.

It would require a Homeric catalogue to describe the dinner. To say that the table "groaned," is to give no idea of its condition. Mrs. Hallowell and six neighbors' wives moved from kitchen to dining-room, replenishing the dishes as fast as their contents diminished, and plying the double row of coatless guests with a most stern and exacting hospitality. The former would have been seriously mortified had not each man endeavored to eat twice his usual requirement.

After the slight rest which nature enforced—though far less than nature demanded, after such a meal—the work went on again with greater alacrity, since every timber showed. Rib by rib the great frame grew, and those perched aloft, pinning the posts and stays, rejoiced in the broad, bright landscape opened to their view. They watched the roads, in the intervals of their toil, and announced the approach of delayed guests, all alert for the sight of the first riding-habit.

Suddenly two ladies made their appearance, over the rise of the hill, one cantering lightly and securely, the other bouncing in her seat, from the rough trot of her horse.

"Look out! there they come!" cried a watcher.

"Who is it?" was asked from below.

"Where's Barton? He ought to be on hand,—it's Martha Deane,—and Sally with her; they always ride together."

Gilbert had one end of a handspike, helping lift a heavy piece of timber, and his face was dark with the strain; it was well that he dared not let go until the lively gossip which followed Barton's absence,—the latter having immediately gone forward to take charge of the horses,—had subsided. Leaning on the handspike, he panted,—not entirely from fatigue. A terrible possibility of loss flashed suddenly across his mind, revealing to him, in a new light, the desperate force and desire of his love.

There was no time for meditation; his help was again wanted, and he expended therein the first hot tumult of his heart. By ones and twos the girls now gathered rapidly, and erelong they came out in a body to have a look at the raising. Their coming in no wise interrupted the labor; it was rather an additional stimulus, and the young men were right. Although they were not aware of the fact, they were never so handsome in their uneasy Sunday costume and awkward social ways, as thus in their free, joyous, and graceful element of labor. Greetings were interchanged, laughter and cheerful nothings animated the company, and when Martha Deane said,—

"We may be in the way, now—shall we go in?"

Mark responded,—

"No, Martha! No, girls! I'll get twice as much work out o' my twenty-five 'jours,' if you'll only stand where you are and look at 'em."

"Indeed!" Sally Fairthorn exclaimed. "But we have work to do as well as you. If you men can't get along without admiring spectators, we girls can."

The answer which Mark would have made to this pert speech was cut short by a loud cry of pain or terror from the old half-dismantled barn on the other side of the road. All eyes were at once turned in that direction, and beheld Joe Fairthorn rushing at full speed down the bank, making for the stables below. Mark, Gilbert Potter, and Sally, being nearest, hastened to the spot.

"You're in time!" cried Joe, clapping his hands in great glee. "I was awfully afeard he'd let go before I could git down to see him fall. Look quick—he can't hold on much longer!"

Looking into the dusky depths, they saw Jake, hanging by his hands to the edges of a hole in the floor above, yelling and kicking for dear life.

"You wicked, wicked boy!" exclaimed Sally, turning to Joe, "what have you been doing?"

"Oh," he answered, jerking and twisting with fearful delight, "there was such a nice hole in the floor! I covered it all over with straw, but I had to wait ever so long before Jake stepped onto it, and then he ketched hold goin' down, and nigh spoilt the fun."

Gilbert made for the barn-floor, to succor the helpless victim; but just as his step was heard on the boards, Jake's strength gave way. His fingers slipped, and with a last howl down he dropped, eight or ten feet, upon a bed of dry manure. Then his terror was instantly changed to wrath; he bounced upon his feet, seized a piece of rotten board, and made after Joe, who, anticipating the result, was already showing his heels down the road.

Meanwhile the other young ladies had followed, and so, after discussing the incident with a mixture of amusement and horror, they betook themselves to the house, to assist in the preparations for supper. Martha Deane's eyes took in the situation, and immediately perceived that it was capable of a picturesque improvement. In front of the house stood a superb sycamore, beyond which a trellis of grape-vines divided the yard from the kitchen-garden. Here, on the cool green turf, under shade, in the bright summer air, she proposed that the tables should be set, and found little difficulty in carrying her point. It was quite convenient to the outer kitchen door, and her ready invention found means of overcoming all other technical objections. Erelong the tables were transported to the spot, the cloth laid, and the aspect of the coming entertainment grew so pleasant to the eye, that there was a special satisfaction in the labor.

An hour before sundown the frame was completed; the skeleton of the great barn rose sharp against the sky, its fresh white-oak timber gilded by the sunshine. Mark drove in the last pin, gave a joyous shout, which was answered by an irregular cheer from below, and lightly clambered down by one of the stays. Then the black jugs were produced, and passed from mouth to mouth, and the ruddy, glowing young fellows drew their shirt-sleeves across their faces, and breathed the free, full breath of rest.

Gilbert Potter, sitting beside Mark,—the two were mutually drawn towards each other, without knowing or considering why,—had gradually worked himself into a resolution to be cool, and to watch the movements of his presumed rival. More than once, during the afternoon, he had detected Barton's eyes, fixed upon him with a more than accidental interest; looking up now, he met them again, but they were quickly withdrawn, with a shy, uneasy expression, which he could not comprehend. Was it possible that Barton conjectured the carefully hidden secret of his heart? Or had the country gossip been free with his name, in some way, during his absence? Whatever it was, the dearer interests at stake prevented him from dismissing it from his mind. He was preternaturally alert, suspicious, and sensitive.

He was therefore a little startled, when, as they were all rising in obedience to Farmer Hallowell's summons to supper, Barton suddenly took hold of his arm.

"Gilbert," said he, "we want your name in a list of young men we are getting together, for the protection of our neighborhood. There are suspicions, you know, that Sandy Flash has some friends hereabouts, though nobody seems to know exactly who they are; and our only safety is in clubbing together, to smoke him out and hunt him down, if he ever comes near us. Now, you're a good hunter"—

"Put me down, of course!" Gilbert interrupted, immensely relieved to find how wide his suspicions had fallen from the mark. "That would be a more stirring chase than our last; it is a shame and a disgrace that he is still at large."

"How many have we now?" asked Mark, who was walking on the other side of Barton.

"Twenty-one, with Gilbert," the latter replied.

"Well, as Sandy is said to count equal to twenty, we can meet him evenly, and have one to spare," laughed Mark.

"Has any one here ever seen the fellow?" asked Gilbert. "We ought to know his marks."

"He's short, thick-set, with a red face, jet-black hair, add heavy whiskers," said Barton.

"Jet-black hair!" Mark exclaimed; "why, it's red as brick-dust! And I never heard that he wore whiskers."

"Pshaw! what was I thinking of? Red, of course—I meant red, all the time," Barton hastily assented, inwardly cursing himself for a fool. It was evident that the less he conversed about Sandy Flash, the better.

Loud exclamations of surprise and admiration interrupted them. In the shade of the sycamore, on the bright green floor of the silken turf, stood the long supper-table, snowily draped, and heaped with the richest products of cellar, kitchen, and dairy. Twelve chickens, stewed in cream, filled huge dishes at the head and foot, while hams and rounds of cold roast-beef accentuated the space between. The interstices were filled with pickles, pies, jars of marmalade, bowls of honey, and plates of cheese. Four coffee-pots steamed in readiness on a separate table, and the young ladies, doubly charming in their fresh white aprons, stood waiting to serve the tired laborers. Clumps of crown-roses, in blossom, peered over the garden-paling, the woodbine filled the air with its nutmeg odors, and a broad sheet of sunshine struck the upper boughs of the arching sycamore, and turned them into a gilded canopy for the banquet. It might have been truly said of Martha Deane, that she touched nothing which she did not adorn.

In the midst of her duties as directress of the festival, she caught a glimpse of the three men, as they approached together, somewhat in the rear of the others. The embarrassed flush had not quite faded from Barton's face, and Gilbert's was touched by a lingering sign of his new trouble. Mark, light-hearted and laughing, precluded the least idea of mystery, but Gilbert's eye met hers with what she felt to be a painfully earnest, questioning expression. The next moment they were seated at the table, and her services were required on behalf of all.

Unfortunately for the social enjoyments of Kennett, eating had come to be regarded as a part of labor; silence and rapidity were its principal features. Board and platter were cleared in a marvellously short time, the plates changed, the dishes replenished, and then the wives and maidens took the places of the young men, who lounged off to the road-side, some to smoke their pipes, and all to gossip.

Before dusk, Giles made his appearance, with an old green bag under his arm. Barton, of course, had the credit of this arrangement, and it made him, for the time, very popular. After a pull at the bottle, Giles began to screw his fiddle, drawing now and then unearthly shrieks from its strings. The more eager of the young men thereupon stole to the house, assisted in carrying in the tables and benches, and in other ways busied themselves to bring about the moment when the aprons of the maidens could be laid aside, and their lively feet given to the dance. The moon already hung over the eastern wood, and a light breeze blew the dew-mist from the hill.

Finally, they were all gathered on the open bit of lawn between the house and the road. There was much hesitation at first, ardent coaxing and bashful withdrawal, until Martha broke the ice by boldly choosing Mark as her partner, apportioning Sally to Gilbert, and taking her place for a Scotch reel. She danced well and lightly, though in a more subdued manner than was then customary. In this respect, Gilbert resembled her; his steps, gravely measured, though sufficiently elastic, differed widely from Mark's springs, pigeon-wings, and curvets. Giles played with a will, swaying head and fiddle up and down and beating time with his foot; and the reel went off so successfully that there was no hesitation in getting up the next dance.

Mark was alert, and secured Sally this time. Perhaps Gilbert would have made the like exchange, but Mr. Alfred Barton stepped before him, and bore off Martha. There was no appearance of design about the matter, but Gilbert felt a hot tingle in his blood, and drew back a little to watch the pair. Martha moved through the dance as if but half conscious of her partner's presence, and he seemed more intent on making the proper steps and flourishes than on improving the few brief chances for a confidential word. When he spoke, it was with the unnecessary laugh, which is meant to show ease of manner, and betrays the want of it. Gilbert was puzzled; either the two were unconscious of the gossip which linked their names so intimately, (which seemed scarcely possible,) or they were studiedly concealing an actual tender relation. Among those simple-hearted people, the shyness of love rivalled the secrecy of crime, and the ways by which the lover sought to assure himself of his fortune were

98

made very difficult by the shrinking caution with which he concealed the evidence of his passion. Gilbert knew how well the secret of his own heart was guarded, and the reflection, that others might be equally inscrutable, smote him with sudden pain.

The figures moved before him in the splendid moonlight, and with every motion of Martha's slender form the glow of his passion and the torment of his uncertainty increased. Then the dance dissolved, and while he still stood with folded arms, Sally Fairthorn's voice whispered eagerly in his ear,—

"Gilbert—Gilbert! now is your chance to engage Martha for the Virginia reel!"

"Let me choose my own partners, Sally!" he said, so sternly, that she opened wide her black eyes.

Martha, fanning herself with her handkerchief spread over a bent willow-twig, suddenly passed before him, like an angel in the moonlight. A soft, tender star sparkled in each shaded eye, a faint rose-tint flushed her cheeks, and her lips, slightly parted to inhale the clover-scented air, were touched with a sweet, consenting smile.

"Martha!"

The word passed Gilbert's lips almost before he knew he had uttered it. Almost a whisper, but she heard, and, pausing, turned towards him.

"Will you dance with me now?"

"Am I your choice, or Sally's, Gilbert? I overheard your very independent remark."

"Mine!" he said, with only half truth. A deep color, shot into his face, and he knew the moonlight revealed it, but he forced his eyes to meet hers. Her face lost its playful expression, and she said, gently,—

"Then I accept."

They took their places, and the interminable Virginia reel—under which name the old-fashioned Sir Roger de Coverley was known—commenced. It so happened that Gilbert and Mr. Alfred Barton had changed their recent places. The latter stood outside the space allotted to the dance, and appeared to watch Martha Deane and her new partner. The reviving warmth in Gilbert's bosom instantly died, and gave way to a crowd of torturing conjectures. He went through his part in the dance so abstractedly, that when they reached the bottom of the line, Martha, out of friendly consideration for him, professed fatigue and asked his permission to withdraw from the company. He gave her his arm, and they moved to one of the benches.

"You, also, seem tired, Gilbert," she said.

"Yes—no!" he answered, confusedly, feeling that he was beginning to tremble. He stood before her as she sat, moved irresolutely, as if to leave, and then, facing her with a powerful effort, he exclaimed,—"Martha, do you know what people say about Alfred Barton and yourself?"

"It would make no difference if I did," she answered; "people will say anything."

"But is it—is it true?"

"Is what true?" she quietly asked.

"That he is to marry you!" The words were said, and he would have given his life to recall them. He dropped his head, not daring to meet her eyes.

Martha Deane rose to her feet, and stood before him. Then he lifted his head; the moon shone full upon it, while her face was in shadow, but he saw the fuller light of her eye, the firmer curve of her lip.

"Gilbert Potter," she said, "what right have you to ask me such a question?"

"I have no right—none," he answered, in a voice whose suppressed, husky tones were not needed to interpret the pain and bitterness of his face. Then he quickly turned away and left her.

Martha Deane remained a minute, motionless, standing as he left her. Her heart was beating fast, and she could not immediately trust herself to rejoin the gay company. But now the dance was over, and the inseparable Sally hastened forward.

"Martha!" cried the latter, hot and indignant, "what is the matter with Gilbert? He is behaving shamefully; I saw him just now turn away from you as if you were a—a shock of corn. And the way he snapped me up—it is really outrageous!"

"It seems so, truly," said Martha. But she knew that Gilbert Potter loved her, and with what a love.

CHAPTER X. — THE RIVALS.

Due to the abundant harvest of that year, and the universal need of extra labor for a time, Gilbert Potter would have found his burden too heavy, but for welcome help from an unexpected quarter. On the very morning that he first thrust his sickle into the ripened wheat, Deb Smith made her appearance, in a short-armed chemise and skirt of tow-cloth.

"I knowed ye'd want a hand," she said, "without sendin' to ask. I'll reap ag'inst the best man in Chester County, and you won't begrudge me my bushel o' wheat a day, when the harvest's in."

With this exordium, and a pull at the black jug under the elder-bushes in the fence-corner, she took her sickle and bent to work. It was her boast that she could beat both men and women on their own ground. She had spun her twenty-four cuts of yarn, in a day, and husked her fifty shocks of heavy corn. For Gilbert she did her best, amazing him each day with a fresh performance, and was well worth the additional daily quart of whiskey which she consumed.

In this pressing, sweltering labor, Gilbert dulled, though he could not conquer, his unhappy mood. Mary Potter, with a true mother's instinct, surmised a trouble, but the indications were too indefinite for conjecture. She could only hope that her son had not been called upon to suffer a fresh reproach, from the unremoved stain hanging over his birth.

Miss Betsy Lavender's company at this time was her greatest relief, in a double sense. No ten persons in Kennett possessed half the amount of confidences which were intrusted to this single lady; there was that in her face which said: "I only blab what I choose, and what's locked up, is locked up." This was true; she was the greatest distributor of news, and the closest receptacle of secrets—anomalous as the two characters may seem—that ever blessed a country community.

Miss Betsy, like Deb Smith, knew that she could be of service on the

Potter farm, and, although her stay was perforce short, on account of an approaching house-warming near Doe-Run, her willing arms helped to tide Mary Potter over the heaviest labor of harvest. There were thus hours of afternoon rest, even in the midst of the busy season, and during one of these the mother opened her heart in relation to her son's silent, gloomy moods.

"You'll perhaps say it's all my fancy, Betsy," she said, "and indeed I hope it is; but I know you see more than most people, and two heads are better than one. How does Gilbert seem to you?"

Miss Betsy mused awhile, with an unusual gravity on her long face. "I dunno," she remarked, at length; "I've noticed that some men have their vapors and tantrums, jist as some women have, and Gilbert's of an age to—well, Mary, has the thought of his marryin' ever come into your head?"

"No!" exclaimed Mary Potter, with almost a frightened air.

"I'll be bound! Some women are lookin' out for daughter-in-laws before their sons have a beard, and others think theirs is only fit to wear short jackets when they ought to be raisin' up families. I dunno but what it'll be a cross to you, Mary,—you set so much store by Gilbert, and it's natural, like, that you should want to have him all to y'rself,—but a man shall leave his father and mother and cleave unto his wife,—or somethin' like it. Yes, I say it, although nobody clove unto me."

Mary Potter said nothing. Her face grew very pale, and such an expression of pain came into it that Miss Betsy, who saw everything without seeming to look at anything, made haste to add a consoling word.

"Indeed, Mary," she said, "now I come to consider upon it, you won't have so much of a cross. You a'n't the mother you've showed yourself to be, if you're not anxious to see Gilbert happy, and as for leavin' his mother, there'll be no leavin' needful, in his case, but on the contrary, quite the reverse, namely, a comin' to you. And it's no bad fortin', though I can't say it of my own experience; but never mind, all the same, I've seen the likes—to have a brisk, cheerful daughter-in-law keepin' house, and you a-settin' by the window, knittin' and restin' from mornin' till night, and maybe little caps and clothes to make, and lots o' things to teach, that young wives don't know o' theirselves. And then, after awhile you'll be called 'Granny,' but you won't mind it, for grandchildren's a mighty comfort, and no responsibility like your own. Why, I've knowed women that never seen what rest or comfort was, till they'd got to be grandmothers!"

Something in this homely speech touched Mary Potter's heart, and gave her the relief of tears. "Betsy," she said at last, "I have had a heavy burden to bear, and it has made me weak."

"Made me weak," Miss Betsy repeated. "And no wonder. Don't think I can't guess that, Mary."

Here two tears trickled down the ridge of her nose, and she furtively wiped them off while adjusting her high comb. Mary Potter's face was turned towards her with a wistful, appealing expression, which she understood.

"Mary," she said, "I don't measure people with a two-foot rule. I take a ten-foot pole, and let it cover all that comes under it. Them that does their dooty to Man, I guess you won't have much trouble in squarin' accounts with the Lord. You know how I feel towards you without my tellin' of it, and them that's quick o' the tongue are always full o' the heart. Now, Mary, I know as plain as if you 'd said it, that there's somethin' on your mind, and you dunno whether to share it with me or not. What I say is, don't hurry yourself; I 'd rather show fellow-feelin' than cur'osity; so, see your way clear first, and when the tellin' me anything can help, tell it—not before."

"It wouldn't help now," Mary Potter responded.

"Wouldn't help now. Then wait awhile. Nothin' 's so dangerous as speakin' before the time, whomsoever and wheresoever. Folks talk o' bridlin' the tongue; let 'em git a blind halter, say I, and a curb-bit, and a martingale! Not that I set an example, Goodness knows, for mine runs like a mill-clapper, rickety-rick, rickety-rick; but never mind, it may be fast, but it isn't loose!"

In her own mysterious way, Miss Betsy succeeded in imparting a good deal of comfort to Mary Potter. She promised "to keep Gilbert under her eyes,"—which, indeed, she did, quite unconsciously to himself, during the last two days of her stay. At table she engaged him in conversation, bringing in references, in the most wonderfully innocent and random manner, to most of the families in the neighborhood. So skilfully did she operate that even Mary Potter failed to perceive her strategy. Deb Smith, sitting bare-armed on the other side of the table, and eating like six dragoons, was the ostensible target of her speech, and Gilbert was thus stealthily approached in flank. When she tied her bonnet-strings to leave, and the mother accompanied her to the gate, she left this indefinite consolation behind her:

"Keep up your sperrits, Mary. I think I'm on the right scent about Gilbert, but these young men are shy foxes. Let me alone, awhile yet, and whatever you do, let him alone. There's no danger—not even a snarl, I guess. Nothin' to bother your head about. You weren't his mother. Good lack! if I'm right, you'll see no more o' his tantrums in two months' time—and so, good-bye to you!"

The oats followed close upon the wheat harvest, and there was no respite from labor until the last load was hauled into the barn, filling its ample bays to the very rafters. Then Gilbert, mounted on his favorite Roger, rode up to Kennett Square one Saturday afternoon, in obedience to a message from Mr. Alfred Barton, informing him that the other gentlemen would there meet to consult measures for mutual protection against highwaymen in general and Sandy Flash in particular. As every young man in the neighborhood owned his horse and musket, nothing more was necessary than to adopt a system of action.

The meeting was held in the bar-room of the Unicorn, and as every second man had his own particular scheme to advocate, it was both long and noisy. Many thought the action unnecessary, but were willing, for the sake of the community, to give their services. The simplest plan—to choose a competent leader, and submit to his management—never occurred to these free and independent volunteers, until all other means of unity had failed. Then Alfred Barton, as the originator of the measure, was chosen, and presented the rude but sufficient plan which had been suggested to him by Dr. Deane. The men were to meet every Saturday evening at the Unicorn, and exchange intelligence; but they could be called together at any time by a summons from Barton. The landlord of the Unicorn was highly satisfied with this arrangement, but no one noticed the interest with which the ostler, an Irishman named Dougherty, listened to the discussion.

Barton's horse was hitched beside Gilbert's, and as the two were mounting, the former said,—

"If you're going home, Gilbert, why not come down our lane, and go through by Carson's. We can talk the matter over a little; if there's any running to do, I depend a good deal on your horse."

Gilbert saw no reason for declining this invitation, and the two rode side by side down the lane to the Barton farm-house. The sun was still an hour high, but a fragrant odor of broiled herring drifted out of the open kitchen-window. Barton thereupon urged him to stop and take supper, with a cordiality which we can only explain by hinting at his secret intention to become the purchaser of Gilbert's horse.

"Old-man Barton" was sitting in his arm-chair by the window, feebly brandishing his stick at the flies, and watching his daughter Ann, as she transferred the herrings from the gridiron to a pewter platter.

"Father, this is Gilbert Potter," said Mr. Alfred, introducing his guest.

The bent head was lifted with an effort, and the keen eyes were fixed on the young man, who came forward to take the crooked, half-extended hand.

"What Gilbert Potter?" he croaked.

Mr. Alfred bit his lips, and looked both embarrassed and annoyed. But he could do no less than say,—

"Mary Potter's son."

Gilbert straightened himself proudly, as if to face a coming insult. After a long, steady gaze, the old man gave one of his hieroglyphic snorts, and then muttered to himself,—"Looks like her."

During the meal, he was so occupied with the labor of feeding himself, that he seemed to forget Gilbert's presence. Bending his head sideways, from time to time, he jerked out a croaking question, which his son, whatever annoyance he might feel, was forced to answer according to the old man's humor.

"In at the Doctor's, boy?"

"A few minutes, daddy, before we came together."

"See her? Was she at home?"

"Yes," came very shortly from Mr. Alfred's lips; he clenched his fists under the table-cloth.

"That's right, boy; stick up to her!" and he chuckled and munched together in a way which it made Gilbert sick to hear. The tail of the lean herring on his plate remained untasted; he swallowed the thin tea which Miss Ann poured out, and the heavy "half-Indian" bread with a choking sensation. He had but one desire,—to get away from the room, out of human sight and hearing.

Barton, ill at ease, and avoiding Gilbert's eye, accompanied him to the lane. He felt that the old man's garrulity ought to be explained, but knew not what to say. Gilbert spared him the trouble—

"When are we to wish you joy, Barton?" he asked, in a cold, hard voice.

Barton laughed in a forced way, clutched at his tawny whisker, and with something like a flush on his heavy face, answered in what was meant to be an indifferent tone:

"Oh, it's a joke of the old man's—don't mean anything."

"It seems to be a joke of the whole neighborhood, then; I have heard it from others."

"Have you?" Barton eagerly asked. "Do people talk about it much? What do they say?"

This exhibition of vulgar vanity, as he considered it, was so repulsive to Gilbert, in his desperate, excited condition, that for a moment he did not trust

107

himself to speak. Holding the bridle of his horse, he walked mechanically down the slope, Barton following him.

Suddenly he stopped, faced the latter, and said, in a stern voice: "I must know, first, whether you are betrothed to Martha Deane."

His manner was so unexpectedly solemn and peremptory that Barton, startled from his self-possession, stammered,—

"N-no: that is, not yet."

Another pause. Barton, curious to know how far gossip had already gone, repeated the question:

"Well, what do people say?"

"Some, that you and she will be married," Gilbert answered, speaking slowly and with difficulty, "and some that you won't. Which are right?"

"Damme, if I know!" Barton exclaimed, returning to his customary swagger. It was quite enough that the matter was generally talked about, and he had said nothing to settle it, in either way. But his manner, more than his words, convinced Gilbert that there was no betrothal as yet, and that the vanity of being regarded as the successful suitor of a lovely girl had a more prominent place than love, in his rival's heart. By so much was his torture lightened, and the passion of the moment subsided, after having so nearly betrayed itself.

"I say, Gilbert," Barton presently remarked, walking on towards the bars which led into the meadow-field; "it's time you were looking around in that way, hey?"

"It will be time enough when I am out of debt."

"But you ought, now, to have a wife in your house."

"I have a mother, Barton."

"That's true, Gilbert. Just as I have a father. The old man's queer, as you saw—kept me out of marrying; when I was young, and now drives me to it.

I might ha' had children grown"—

He paused, laying his hand on the young man's shoulder. Gilbert fancied that he saw on Barton's coarse, dull face the fleeting stamp of some long-buried regret, and a little of the recent bitterness died out of his heart.

"Good-bye!" he said, offering his hand with greater ease than he would have thought possible, fifteen minutes sooner.

"Good-bye, Gilbert! Take care of Roger. Sandy Flash has a fine piece of horse-flesh, but you beat him once—Damnation! You could beat him, I mean. If he comes within ten miles of us, I'll have the summonses out in no time."

Gilbert cantered lightly down the meadow. The soft breath of the summer evening fanned his face, and something of the peace expressed in the rich repose of the landscape fell upon his heart. But peace, he felt, could only come to him through love. The shame upon his name—the slow result of labor—even the painful store of memories which the years had crowded in his brain—might all be lightly borne, or forgotten, could his arms once clasp the now uncertain treasure. A tender mist came over his deep, dark eyes, a passionate longing breathed in his softened lips, and he said to himself,—

"I would lie down and die at her feet, if that could make her happy; but how to live, and live without her?" This was a darkness which his mind refused to entertain. Love sees no justice on Earth or in Heaven, that includes not its own fulfilled desire.

Before reaching home, he tried to review the situation calmly. Barton's true relation to Martha Deane he partially suspected, so far as regarded the former's vanity and his slavish subservience to his father's will; but he was equally avaricious, and it was well known in Kennett that Martha possessed, or would possess, a handsome property in her own right. Gilbert, therefore, saw every reason to believe that Barton was an actual, if not a very passionate wooer.

That fact, however, was in itself of no great importance, unless Dr. Deane favored the suit. The result depended on Martha herself; she was called an "independent girl," which she certainly was, by contrast with other girls of the same age. It was this free, firm, independent, yet wholly womanly spirit which Gilbert honored in her, and which (unless her father's influence were too powerful) would yet save her to him, if she but loved him. Then he felt that his nervous, inflammable fear of Barton was incompatible with true honor for her, with trust in her pure and lofty nature. If she were so easily swayed, how could she stand the test which he was still resolved—nay, forced by circumstances—to apply?

With something like shame of his past excitement, yet with strength which had grown out of it, his reflections were terminated by Roger stopping at the barn-yard gate.

CHAPTER XI. — GUESTS AT POTTER'S.

A week or two later, there was trouble, but not of a very unusual kind, in the Fairthorn household. It was Sunday, the dinner was on the table, but Joe and Jake were not to be found. The garden, the corn-crib, the barn, and the grove below the house, were searched, without detecting the least sign of the truants. Finally Sally's eyes descried a remarkable object moving over the edge of the hill, from the direction of the Philadelphia road. It was a huge round creature, something like a cylindrical tortoise, slowly advancing upon four short, dark legs.

"What upon earth is that?" she cried.

All eyes were brought to bear upon this phenomenon, which gradually advanced until it reached the fence. Then it suddenly separated into three parts, the round back falling off, whereupon it was seized by two figures and lifted upon the fence.

"It's the best wash-tub, I do declare!" said Sally; "whatever have they been doing with it?"

Having crossed the fence, the boys lifted the inverted tub over their heads, and resumed their march. When they came near enough, it could be seen that their breeches and stockings were not only dripping wet, but streaked with black swamp-mud. This accounted for the unsteady, hesitating course of the tub, which at times seemed inclined to approach the house, and then tacked away towards the corner of the barn-yard wall. A few vigorous calls, however, appeared to convince it that the direct course was the best, for it set out with a grotesque bobbing trot, which brought it speedily to the kitchen-door.

Then Joe and Jake crept out, dripping to the very crowns of their heads, with their Sunday shirts and jackets in a horrible plight. The truth, slowly gathered from their mutual accusations, was this: they had resolved to have a boating excursion on Redley Creek, and had abstracted the tub that morning when nobody was in the kitchen. Slipping down through the wood, they had launched it in a piece of still water. Joe got in first, and when Jake let go of the tub, it tilted over; then he held it for Jake, who squatted in the centre, and floated successfully down the stream until Joe pushed him with a pole, and made the tub lose its balance. Jake fell into the mud, and the tub drifted away; they had chased it nearly to the road before they recovered it.

"You bad boys, what shall I do with you?" cried Mother Fairthorn. "Put on your every-day clothes, and go to the garret. Sally, you can ride down to Potter's with the pears; they won't keep, and I expect Gilbert has no time to come for any, this summer."

"I'll go," said Sally, "but Gilbert don't deserve it. The way he snapped me up at Hallowell's—and he hasn't been here since!"

"Don't be hard on him, Sally!" said the kindly old woman; nor was Sally's more than a surface grudge. She had quite a sisterly affection for Gilbert, and was rather hurt than angered by what he had said in the fret of a mood which she could not comprehend.

The old mare rejoiced in a new bridle, with a head-stall of scarlet morocco, and Sally would have made a stately appearance, but for the pears, which, stowed in the two ends of a grain-bag, and hung over the saddle, would not quite be covered by her riding-skirt. She trudged on slowly, down the lonely road, but had barely crossed the level below Kennett Square, when there came a quick sound of hoofs behind her.

It was Mark and Martha Deane, who presently drew rein, one on either side of her.

"Don't ride fast, please," Sally begged; "I can't, for fear of smashing the pears. Where are you going?"

"To Falconer's," Martha replied; "Fanny promised to lend me some new patterns; but I had great trouble in getting Mark to ride with me."

"Not, if you will ride along, Sally," Mark rejoined. "We'll go with you first, and then you'll come with us. What do you say, Martha?"

112

"I'll answer for Martha!" cried Sally; "I am going to Potter's, and it's directly on your way."

"Just the thing," said Mark; "I have a little business with Gilbert."

It was all settled before Martha's vote had been taken, and she accepted the decision without remark. She was glad, for Sally's sake, that they had fallen in with her, for she had shrewdly watched Mark, and found that, little by little, a serious liking for her friend was sending its roots down through the gay indifference of his surface mood. Perhaps she was not altogether calm in spirit at the prospect of meeting Gilbert Potter; but, if so, no sign of the agitation betrayed itself in her face.

Gilbert, sitting on the porch, half-hidden behind a mass of blossoming trumpet-flower, was aroused from his Sabbath reverie by the sound of hoofs. Sally Fairthorn's voice followed, reaching even the ears of Mary Potter, who thereupon issued from the house to greet the unexpected guest. Mark had already dismounted, and although Sally protested that she would remain in the saddle, the strong arms held out to her proved too much of a temptation; it was so charming to put her hands on his shoulders, and to have his take her by the waist, and lift her to the ground so lightly!

While Mark was performing this service, (and evidently with as much deliberation as possible,) Gilbert could do no less than offer his aid to Martha Deane, whose sudden apparition he had almost incredulously realized. A bright, absorbing joy kindled his sad, strong features into beauty, and Martha felt her cheeks grow warm, in spite of herself, as their eyes met. The hands that touched her waist were firm, but no hands had ever before conveyed to her heart such a sense of gentleness and tenderness, and though her own gloved hand rested but a moment on his shoulder, the action seemed to her almost like a caress.

"How kind of you—all—to come!" said Gilbert, feeling that his voice expressed too much, and his words too little.

"The credit of coming is not mine, Gilbert," she answered. "We overtook Sally, and gave her our company for the sake of hers, afterwards. But I shall like to take a look at your place; how pleasant you are making it!"

"You are the first to say so; I shall always remember that!"

Mary Potter now advanced, with grave yet friendly welcome, and would have opened her best room to the guests, but the bowery porch, with its swinging scarlet bloom, haunted by humming-birds and hawk-moths, wooed them "o take their seats in its shade. The noise of a plunging cascade, which restored the idle mill-water to its parted stream, made a mellow, continuous music in the air. The high road was visible at one point, across the meadow, just where it entered the wood; otherwise, the seclusion of the place was complete.

"You could not have found a lovelier home, M—Mary," said Martha, terrified to think how near the words "Mrs. Potter" had been to her lips. But she had recovered herself so promptly that the hesitation was not noticed.

"Many people think the house ought to be upon the road," Mary Potter replied, "but Gilbert and I like it as it is. Yes, I hope it will be a good home, when we can call it our own."

"Mother is a little impatient," said Gilbert, "and perhaps I am also. But if we have health, it won't be very long to wait."

"That's a thing soon learned!" cried Mark. "I mean to be impatient. Why, when I was doing journey-work, I was as careless as the day's long, and so from hand to mouth didn't trouble me a bit; but now, I ha'n't been undertaking six months, and it seems that I feel worried if I don't get all the jobs going!"

Martha smiled, well pleased at this confession of the change, which she knew better how to interpret than Mark himself. But Sally, in her innocence, remarked:

"Oh Mark! that isn't right."

"I suppose it isn't. But maybe you've got to wish for more than you get, in order to get what you do. I guess I take things pretty easy, on the whole, for it's nobody's nature to be entirely satisfied. Gilbert, will you be satisfied when

114

your farm's paid for?"

"No!" answered Gilbert with an emphasis, the sound of which, as soon as uttered, smote him to the heart. He had not thought of his mother. She clasped her hands convulsively, and looked at him, but his face was turned away.

"Why, Gilbert!" exclaimed Sally.

"I mean," he said, striving to collect his thoughts, "that there is something more than property"—but how should he go on? Could he speak of the family relation, then and there? Of honor in the community, the respect of his neighbors, without seeming to refer to the brand upon his and his mother's name? No; of none of these things. With sudden energy, he turned upon himself, and continued:

"I shall not feel satisfied until I am cured of my own impatience—until I can better control my temper, and get the weeds and rocks and stumps out of myself as well as out of my farm."

"Then you've got a job!" Mark laughed. "I think your fields are pretty tolerable clean, what I've seen of 'em. Nobody can say they're not well fenced in. Why, compared with you, I'm an open common, like the Wastelands, down on Whitely Creek, and everybody's cattle run over me!"

Mark's thoughtlessness was as good as tact. They all laughed heartily at his odd continuation of the simile, and Martha hastened to say:

"For my part, I don't think you are quite such an open common, Mark, or Gilbert so well fenced in. But even if you are, a great many things may be hidden in a clearing, and some people are tall enough to look over a high hedge. Betsy Lavender says some men tell all about themselves without saying a word, while others talk till Doomsday and tell nothing."

"And tell nothing," gravely repeated Mark, whereat no one could repress a smile, and Sally laughed outright.

Mary Potter had not mingled much in the society of Kennett, and did not know that this imitation of good Miss Betsy was a very common thing, and had long ceased to mean any harm. It annoyed her, and she felt it her duty to say a word for her friend.

"There is not a better or kinder-hearted woman in the county," she said, "than just Betsy Lavender. With all her odd ways of speech, she talks the best of sense and wisdom, and I don't know who I'd sooner take for a guide in times of trouble."

"You could not give Betsy a higher place than she deserves," Martha answered. "We all esteem her as a dear friend, and as the best helper where help is needed. She has been almost a mother to me."

Sally felt rebuked, and exclaimed tearfully, with her usual impetuous candor,—"Now you know I meant no harm; it was all Mark's doing!"

"If you've anything against me, Sally, I forgive you for it. It isn't in my nature to bear malice," said Mark, with so serious an air, that poor Sally was more bewildered than ever. Gilbert and Martha, however, could not restrain their laughter at the fellow's odd, reckless humor, whereupon Sally, suddenly comprehending the joke, sprang from her seat. Mark leaped from the porch, and darted around the house, followed by Sally with mock-angry cries and brandishings of her riding-whip.

The scene was instantly changed to Gilbert's eyes. It was wonderful! There, on the porch of the home he so soon hoped to call his own, sat his mother, Martha Deane, and himself. The two former had turned towards each other, and were talking pleasantly; the hum of the hawk-moths, the mellow plunge of the water, and the stir of the soft summer breeze in the leaves, made a sweet accompaniment to their voices. His brain grew dizzy with yearning to fix that chance companionship, and make it the boundless fortune of his life. Under his habit of repression, his love for her had swelled and gathered to such an intensity, that it seemed he must either speak or die.

Presently the rollicking couple made their appearance. Sally's foot had caught in her riding-skirt as she ran, throwing her at full length on the sward, and Mark, in picking her up, had possessed himself of the whip. She was not hurt in the least, (her life having been a succession of tears and tumbles,) but

116

Mark's arm found it necessary to encircle her waist, and she did not withdraw from the support until they came within sight of the porch.

It was now time for the guests to leave, but Mary Potter must first produce her cakes and currant-wine,—the latter an old and highly superior article, for there had been, alas! too few occasions which called for its use.

"Gilbert," said Mark, as they moved towards the gate, "why can't you catch and saddle Roger, and ride with us? You have nothing to do?"

"No; I would like—but where are you going?"

"To Falconer's; that is, the girls; but we won't stay for supper—I don't fancy quality company."

"Nor I," said Gilbert, with a gloomy face. "I have never visited Falconer's, and they might not thank you for introducing me."

He looked at Martha, as he spoke. She understood him, and gave him her entire sympathy and pity,—yet it was impossible for her to propose giving up the visit, solely for his sake. It was not want of independence, but a maidenly shrinking from the inference of the act, which kept her silent.

Mark, however, cut through the embarrassment. "I'll tell you what, Gilbert!" he exclaimed, "you go and get Roger from the field, while we ride on to Falconer's. If the girls will promise not to be too long about their patterns and their gossip, and what not, we can be back to the lane-end by the time you get there; then we'll ride up t' other branch o' Redley Creek, to the cross-road, and out by Hallowell's. I want to have a squint at the houses and barns down that way; nothing like business, you know!"

Mark thought he was very cunning in thus disposing of Martha during the ride, unconscious of the service he was offering to Gilbert. The latter's eagerness shone from his eyes, but still he looked at Martha, trembling for a sign that should decide his hesitation. Her lids fell before his gaze, and a faint color came into her face, yet she did not turn away. This time it was Sally Fairthorn who spoke.

"Five minutes will be enough for us, Mark," she said. "I'm not much acquainted with Fanny Falconer. So, Gilbert, hoist Martha into her saddle, and go for Roger."

He opened the gate for them, and then climbed over the fence into the hill-field above his house. Having reached the crest, he stopped to watch the three riding abreast, on a smart trot, down the glen. Sally looked back, saw him, and waved her hand; then Mark and Martha turned, giving no sign, yet to his eyes there seemed a certain expectancy in the movement.

Roger came from the farthest corner of the field at his call, and followed him down the hill to the bars, with the obedient attachment of a dog. When he had carefully brushed and then saddled the horse, he went to seek his mother, who was already making preparations for their early supper.

"Mother," he said, "I am going to ride a little way."

She looked at him wistfully and questioningly, as if she would fain have asked more; but only said,—

"Won't you be home to supper, Gilbert?"

"I can't tell, but don't wait a minute, if I'm not here when it's ready."

He turned quickly, as if fearful of a further question, and the next moment was in the saddle.

The trouble in Mary Potter's face increased. Sighing sorely, she followed to the bridge of the barn, and presently descried him, beyond the mill, cantering lightly down the road. Then, lifting her arms, as in a blind appeal for help, she let them fall again, and walked slowly back to the house.

CHAPTER XII. — THE EVENTS OF AN EVENING.

At the first winding of the creek, Gilbert drew rein, with a vague, half-conscious sense of escape. The eye which had followed him thus far was turned away at last.

For half a mile the road lay through a lovely solitude of shade and tangled bowery thickets, beside the stream. The air was soft and tempered, and filled the glen like the breath of some utterly peaceful and happy creature; yet over Gilbert's heart there brooded another atmosphere than this. The sultriness that precedes an emotional crisis weighed heavily upon him.

No man, to whom Nature has granted her highest gift,—that of expression,—can understand the pain endured by one of strong feelings, to whom not only this gift has been denied, but who must also wrestle with an inherited reticence. It is well that in such cases a kindly law exists, to aid the helpless heart. The least portion of the love which lights the world has been told in words; it works, attracts, and binds in silence. The eye never knows its own desire, the hand its warmth, the voice its tenderness, nor the heart its unconscious speech through these, and a thousand other vehicles. Every endeavor to hide the special fact betrays the feeling from which it sprang.

Like all men of limited culture, Gilbert felt his helplessness keenly. His mind, usually clear in its operations, if somewhat slow and cautious, refused to assist him here; it lay dead or apathetic in an air surcharged with passion. An anxious expectancy enclosed him with stifling pressure; he felt that it must be loosened, but knew not how. His craving for words—words swift, clear, and hot as lightning, through which his heart might discharge itself— haunted him like a furious hunger.

The road, rising out of the glen, passed around the brow of a grassy hill, whence he could look across a lateral valley to the Falconer farm-house. Pausing here, he plainly descried a stately "chair" leaning on its thills, in the shade of the weeping-willow, three horses hitched side by side to the lane-fence, and a faint glimmer of color between the mounds of box which almost hid the porch. It was very evident to his mind that the Falconers had other visitors, and that neither Mark nor Sally, (whatever might be Martha Deane's inclination,) would be likely to prolong their stay; so he slowly rode on, past the lane-end, and awaited them at the ford beyond.

It was not long—though the wood on the western hill already threw its shadow into the glen—before the sound of voices and hoofs emerged from the lane. Sally's remark reached him first:

"They may be nice people enough, for aught I know, but their ways are not my ways, and there's no use in trying to mix them."

"That's a fact!" said Mark. "Hallo, here's Gilbert, ahead of us!"

They rode into the stream together, and let their horses drink from the clear, swift-flowing water. In Mark's and Sally's eyes, Gilbert was as grave and impassive as usual, but Martha Deane was conscious of a strange, warm, subtle power, which seemed to envelop her as she drew near him. Her face glowed with a sweet, unaccustomed flush; his was pale, and the shadow of his brows lay heavier upon his eyes. Fate was already taking up the invisible, floating filaments of these two existences, and weaving them together.

Of course it happened, and of course by the purest accident, that Mark and Sally first reached the opposite bank, and took the narrow wood-road, where the loose, briery sprays of the thickets brushed them on either side. Sally's hat, and probably her head, would have been carried off by a projecting branch, had not Mark thrown his arm around her neck and forcibly bent her forwards. Then she shrieked and struck at him with her riding-whip, while Mark's laugh woke all the echoes of the woods.

"I say, Gilbert!" he cried, turning back in his saddle, "I'll hold you responsible for Martha's head; it's as much as I can do to keep Sally's on her shoulders."

Gilbert looked at his companion, as she rode slowly by his side, through the cool, mottled dusk of the woods. She had drawn the strings of her beaver through a buttonhole of her riding-habit, and allowed it to hang upon her back. The motion of the horse gave a gentle, undulating grace to her erect, self-reliant figure, and her lips, slightly parted, breathed maidenly trust and consent. She turned her face towards him and smiled, at Mark's words.

"The warning is unnecessary," he said. "You will give me no chance to take care of you, Martha."

"Is it not better so?" she asked.

He hesitated; he would have said "No," but finally evaded a direct answer.

"I would be glad enough to do you a service—even so little as that," were his words, and the tender tone in which they were spoken made itself evident to his own ears.

"I don't doubt it, Gilbert," she answered, so kindly and cordially that he was smitten to the heart. Had she faltered in her reply,—had she blushed and kept silence,—his hope would have seized the evidence and rushed to the trial; but this was the frankness of friendship, not the timidity of love. She could not, then, suspect his passion, and ah, how the risks of its utterance were multiplied!

Meanwhile, the wonderful glamour of her presence—that irresistible influence which at once takes hold of body and spirit—had entered into every cell of his blood. Thought and memory were blurred into nothingness by this one overmastering sensation. Riding through the lonely woods, out of shade into yellow, level sunshine, in the odors of minty meadows and moist spices of the creekside, they twain seemed to him to be alone in the world. If they loved not each other, why should not the leaves shrivel and fall, the hills split asunder, and the sky rain death upon them? Here she moved at his side—he could stretch out his hand and touch her; his heart sprang towards her, his arms ached for very yearning to clasp her,—his double nature demanded her with the will and entreated for her with the affection! Under all, felt though not suspected, glowed the vast primal instinct upon which the strength of manhood and of womanhood is based.

Sally and Mark, a hundred yards in advance, now thrown into sight

121

and now hidden by the windings of the road, were so pleasantly occupied with each other that they took no heed of the pair behind them. Gilbert was silent; speech was mockery, unless it gave the words which he did not dare to pronounce. His manner was sullen and churlish in Martha's eyes, he suspected; but so it must be, unless a miracle were sent to aid him. She, riding as quietly, seemed to meditate, apparently unconscious of his presence; how could he know that she had never before been so vitally conscious of it?

The long rays of sunset withdrew to the tree-tops, and a deeper hush fell upon the land. The road which had mounted along the slope of a stubble-field, now dropped again into a wooded hollow, where a tree, awkwardly felled, lay across it. Roger pricked up his ears and leaped lightly over. Martha's horse followed, taking the log easily, but she reined him up the next moment, uttering a slight exclamation, and stretched out her hand wistfully towards Gilbert.

To seize it and bring Roger to a stand was the work of an instant. "What is the matter, Martha?" he cried.

"I think the girth is broken," said she. "The saddle is loose, and I was nigh losing my balance. Thank you, I can sit steadily now."

Gilbert sprang to the ground and hastened to her assistance.

"Yes, it is broken," he said, "but I can give you mine. You had better dismount, though; see, I will hold the pommel firm with one hand, while I lift you down with the other. Not too fast, I am strong; place your hands on my shoulders—so!"

She bent forward and laid her hands upon his shoulders. Then, as she slid gently down, his right arm crept around her waist, holding her so firmly and securely that she had left the saddle and hung in its support while her feet had not yet touched the earth. Her warm breath was on Gilbert's forehead; her bosom swept his breast, and the arm that until then had supported, now swiftly, tenderly, irresistibly embraced her. Trembling, thrilling from head to foot, utterly unable to control the mad impulse of the moment, he drew her to his heart and laid his lips to hers. All that he would have said—all, and more than all, that words could have expressed—was now said, without words. His kiss clung as if it were the last this side of death—clung until he felt that Martha feebly strove to be released.

The next minute they stood side by side, and Gilbert, by a revulsion equally swift and overpowering, burst into a passion of tears.

He turned and leaned his head against Roger's neck. Presently a light touch came upon his shoulder.

"Gilbert!"

He faced her then, and saw that her own cheeks were wet. "Martha!" he cried, "unless you love me with a love like mine for you, you can never forgive me!"

She came nearer; she laid her arms around him, and lifted her face to his. Then she said, in a tender, tremulous whisper,—

"Gilbert—Gilbert! I forgive you."

A pang of wonderful, incredulous joy shot through his heart. Exalted by his emotion above the constraints of his past and present life, he arose and stood free and strong in his full stature as a man. He held her softly and tenderly embraced, and a purer bliss than the physical delight of her warm, caressing presence shone upon his face as he asked,—

"Forever, Martha?"

"Forever."

"Knowing what I am?"

"Because I know what you are, Gilbert!"

He bowed his head upon her shoulder, and she felt softer tears—tears which came this time without sound or pang—upon her neck. It was infinitely touching to see this strong nature so moved, and the best bliss that a true woman's heart can feel—the knowledge of the boundless bounty which her love brings with it—opened upon her consciousness. A swift instinct revealed to her the painful struggles of Gilbert's life,—the stern, reticent strength they had developed,—the anxiety and the torture of his long-suppressed passion, and the power and purity of that devotion with which his heart had sought and claimed her. She now saw him in his true character,—firm as steel, yet gentle as dew, patient and passionate, and purposely cold only to guard the sanctity of his emotions.

The twilight deepened in the wood, and Roger, stretching and shaking himself, called the lovers to themselves. Gilbert lifted his head and looked into Martha's sweet, unshrinking eyes.

"May the Lord bless you, as you have blessed me!" he said, solemnly. "Martha, did you guess this before?"

"Yes," she answered, "I felt that it must be so."

"And you did not draw back from me—you did not shun the thought of me! You were"—

He paused; was there not blessing enough, or must he curiously question its growth?

Martha, however, understood the thought in his mind. "No, Gilbert!" she said, "I cannot truly say that I loved you at the time when I first discovered your feeling towards me. I had always esteemed and trusted you, and you were much in my mind; but when I asked myself if I could look upon you as my husband, my heart hesitated with the answer. I did not deserve your affection then, because I could not repay it in the same measure. But, although the knowledge seemed to disturb me, sometimes, yet it was very grateful, and therefore I could not quite make up my mind to discourage you. Indeed, I knew not what was right to do, but I found myself more and more strongly drawn towards you; a power came from you when we met, that touched and yet strengthened me, and then I thought, 'Perhaps I do love him.' To-day, when I first saw your face, I knew that I did. I felt your heart calling to me like one that cries for help, and mine answered. It has been slow to speak, Gilbert, but I know it has spoken truly at last!"

He replaced the broken girth, lifted her into the saddle, mounted his

124

own horse, and they resumed their ride along the dusky valley. But how otherwise their companionship now!

"Martha," said Gilbert, leaning towards her and touching her softly as he spoke, as if fearful that some power in his words might drive them apart,— "Martha, have you considered what I am called? That the family name I bear is in itself a disgrace? Have you imagined what it is to love one so dishonored as I am?"

The delicate line of her upper lip grew clear and firm again, temporarily losing its relaxed gentleness. "I have thought of it," she answered, "but not in that way. Gilbert, I honored you before I loved you. I will not say that this thing makes no difference, for it does—a difference in the name men give you, a difference in your work through life (for you must deserve more esteem to gain as much as other men)—and a difference in my duty towards you. They call me 'independent,' Gilbert, because, though a woman, I dare to think for myself; I know not whether they mean praise by the word, or no; but I think it would frighten away the thought of love from many men. It has not frightened you; and you, however you were born, are the faithfullest and best man I know. I love you with my whole heart, and I will be true to you!"

With these words, Martha stretched out her hand. Gilbert took and held it, bowing his head fondly over it, and inwardly thanking God that the test which his pride had exacted was over at last. He could reward her truth, spare her the willing sacrifice,—and he would.

"Martha," he said, "if I sometimes doubted whether you could share my disgrace, it was because I had bitter cause to feel how heavy it is to bear. God knows I would have come to you with a clean and honorable name, if I could have been patient to wait longer in uncertainty. But I could not tell how long the time might be,—I could not urge my mother, nor even ask her to explain"—

"No, no, Gilbert! Spare her!" Martha interrupted.

"I have, Martha,—God bless you for the words!—and I will; it would be the worst wickedness not to be patient, now! But I have not yet told you"—

A loud halloo rang through the dusk.

"It is Mark's voice," said Martha; "answer him!"

Gilbert shouted, and a double cry instantly replied. They had reached the cross-road from New-Garden, and Mark and Sally, who had been waiting impatiently for a quarter of an hour, rode to meet them. "Did you lose the road?" "Whatever kept you so long?" were the simultaneous questions.

"My girth broke in jumping over the tree," Martha answered, in her clear, untroubled voice. "I should have been thrown off, but for Gilbert's help. He had to give me his own girth, and so we have ridden slowly, since he has none."

"Take my breast-strap," said Mark.

"No," said Gilbert, "I can ride Roger bareback, if need be, with the saddle on my shoulder."

Something in his voice struck Mark and Sally singularly. It was grave and subdued, yet sweet in its tones as never before; he had not yet descended from the solemn exaltation of his recent mood. But the dusk sheltered his face, and its new brightness was visible only to Martha's eyes.

Mark and Sally again led the way, and the lovers followed in silence up the hill, until they struck the Wilmington road, below Hallowell's. Here Gilbert felt that it was best to leave them.

"Well, you two are cheerful company!" exclaimed Sally, as they checked their horses. "Martha, how many words has Gilbert spoken to you this evening?"

"As many as I have spoken to him," Martha answered; "but I will say three more,—Good-night, Gilbert!"

"Good-night!" was all he dared say, in return, but the pressure of his hand burned long upon her fingers.

He rode homewards in the starlight, transformed by love and gratitude, proud, tender, strong to encounter any fate. His mother sat in the lonely kitchen, with the New Testament in her lap; she had tried to read, but her thoughts wandered from the consoling text. The table was but half-cleared, and the little old teapot still squatted beside the coals.

Gilbert strove hard to assume his ordinary manner, but he could not hide the radiant happiness that shone from his eyes and sat upon his lips.

"You've not had supper?" Mary Potter asked.

"No, mother! but I'm sorry you kept things waiting; I can do well enough without."

"It's not right to go without your regular meals, Gilbert. Sit up to the table!"

She poured out the tea, and Gilbert ate and drank in silence. His mother said nothing, but he knew that her eye was upon him, and that he was the subject of her thoughts. Once or twice he detected a wistful, questioning expression, which, in his softened mood, touched him almost like a reproach.

When the table had been cleared and everything put away, she resumed her seat, breathing an unconscious sigh as she dropped her hands into her lap. Gilbert felt that he must now speak, and only hesitated while he considered how he could best do so, without touching her secret and mysterious trouble.

"Mother!" he said at last, "I have something to tell you."

"Ay, Gilbert?"

"Maybe it'll seem good news to you; but maybe not. I have asked Martha Deane to be my wife!"

He paused, and looked at her. She clasped her hands, leaned forward, and fixed her dark, mournful eyes intently upon his face.

"I have been drawn towards her for a long time," Gilbert continued. "It has been a great trouble to me, because she is so pretty, and withal so proud in the way a girl should be,—I liked her pride, even while it made me afraid,—and they say she is rich also. It might seem like looking too high, mother, but I couldn't help it."

"There's no woman too high for you, Gilbert!" Mary Potter exclaimed. Then she went on, in a hurried, unsteady voice: "It isn't that—I mistrusted it would come so, some day, but I hoped—only for your good, my boy, only for that—I hoped not so soon. You're still young—not twenty-five, and there's debt on the farm;—couldn't you ha' waited a little, Gilbert?"

"I have waited, mother," he said, slightly turning away his head, that he might not see the tender reproach in her face, which her question seemed to imply. "I did wait—and for that reason. I wanted first to be independent, at least; and I doubt that I would have spoken so soon, but there were others after Martha, and that put the thought of losing her into my head. It seemed like a matter of life or death. Alfred Barton tried to keep company with her—he didn't deny it to my face; the people talked of it. Folks always say more than they know, to be sure, but then, the chances were so much against me, mother! I was nigh crazy, sometimes. I tried my best and bravest to be patient, but to-day we were riding alone,—Mark and Sally gone ahead,—and—and then it came from my mouth, I don't know how; I didn't expect it. But I shouldn't have doubted Martha; she let me speak; she answered me—I can't tell you her words, mother, though I'll never forget one single one of 'em to my dying day. She gave me her hand and said she would be true to me forever."

Gilbert waited, as if his mother might here speak, but she remained silent.

"Do you understand, mother?" he continued. "She pledged herself to me—she will be my wife. And I asked her—you won't be hurt, for I felt it to be my duty—whether she knew how disgraced I was in the eyes of the people,—whether my name would not be a shame for her to bear? She couldn't know what we know: she took me even with the shame,—and she looked prouder than ever when she stood by me in the thought of it! She would despise me, now, if I should offer to give her up on account of it, but she may know as much as I do, mother? She deserves it."

There was no answer. Gilbert looked up.

Mary Potter sat perfectly still in her high rocking-chair. Her arms hung

128

passively at her sides, and her head leaned back and was turned to one side, as if she were utterly exhausted. But in the pale face, the closed eyes, and the blue shade about the parted lips, he saw that she was unconscious of his words. She had fainted.

CHAPTER XIII. — TWO OLD MEN.

Shortly after Martha Deane left home for her eventful ride to Falconer's, the Doctor also mounted his horse and rode out of the village in the opposite direction. Two days before, he had been summoned to bleed "Old-man Barton," on account of a troublesome buzzing in the head, and, although not bidden to make a second professional visit, there was sufficient occasion for him to call upon his patient in the capacity of a neighbor.

Dr. Deane never made a step outside the usual routine of his business without a special and carefully considered reason. Various causes combined to inspire his movement in the present instance. The neighborhood was healthy; the village was so nearly deserted that no curious observers lounged upon the tavern-porch, or sat upon the horse-block at the corner-store; and Mr. Alfred Barton had been seen riding towards Avondale. There would have been safety in a much more unusual proceeding; this, therefore, might be undertaken in that secure, easy frame of mind which the Doctor both cultivated and recommended to the little world around him.

The Barton farm-house was not often molested by the presence of guests, and he found it as quiet and lifeless as an uninhabited island of the sea. Leaving his horse hitched in the shade of the corn-crib, he first came upon Giles, stretched out under the holly-bush, and fast asleep, with his head upon his jacket. The door and window of the family-room were open, and Dr. Deane, walking softly upon the thick grass, saw that Old-man Barton was in his accustomed seat. His daughter Ann was not visible; she was at that moment occupied in taking out of the drawers of her queer old bureau, in her narrow bedroom up-stairs, various bits of lace and ribbon, done up in lavender, and perchance (for we must not be too curious) a broken sixpence or a lock of dead hair.

The old man's back was towards the window, but the Doctor could hear that papers were rustling and crackling in his trembling hands, and could see that an old casket of very solid oak, bound with iron, stood on the table at his elbow. Thereupon he stealthily retraced his steps to the gate, shut it with a sharp snap, cleared his throat, and mounted the porch with slow, loud, deliberate steps. When he reached the open door, he knocked upon the jamb without looking into the room. There was a jerking, dragging sound for a moment, and then the old man's snarl was heard:

"Who's there?"

Dr. Deane entered, smiling, and redolent of sweet-marjoram. "Well, Friend Barton," he said, "let's have a look at thee now!"

Thereupon he took a chair, placed it in front of the old man, and sat down upon it, with his legs spread wide apart, and his ivory-headed cane (which he also used as a riding-whip) bolt upright between them. He was very careful not to seem to see that a short quilt, which the old man usually wore over his knees, now lay in a somewhat angular heap upon the table.

"Better, I should say,—yes, decidedly better," he remarked, nodding his head gravely. "I had nothing to do this afternoon,—the neighborhood is very healthy,—and thought I would ride down and see how thee's getting on. Only a friendly visit, thee knows."

The old man had laid one shaking arm and crooked hand upon the edge of the quilt, while with the other he grasped his hickory staff. His face had a strange, ashy color, through which the dark, corded veins on his temples showed with singular distinctness. But his eye was unusually bright and keen, and its cunning, suspicious expression did not escape the Doctor's notice.

"A friendly visit—ay!" he growled—"not like Doctors' visits generally, eh? Better?—of course I'm better. It's no harm to tap one of a full-blooded breed. At our age, Doctor, a little blood goes a great way."

"No doubt, no doubt!" the Doctor assented. "Especially in thy case. I often speak of thy wonderful constitution."

"Neighborly, you say, Doctor—only neighborly?" asked the old man. The Doctor smiled, nodded, and seemed to exhale a more powerful herbaceous odor.

"Mayhap, then, you'll take a bit of a dram?—a thimble-full won't come amiss. You know the shelf where it's kep'—reach to, and help yourself, and then help me to a drop."

Dr. Deane rose and took down the square black bottle and the diminutive wine-glass beside it. Half-filling the latter,—a thimble-full in verity,—he drank it in two or three delicate little sips, puckering his large under-lip to receive them.

"It's right to have the best, Friend Barton," he said, "there's more life in it!" as he filled the glass to the brim and held it to the slit in the old man's face.

The latter eagerly drew off the top fulness, and then seized the glass in his shaky hand. "Can help myself," he croaked—"don't need waitin' on; not so bad as that!"

His color presently grew, and his neck assumed a partial steadiness. "What news, what news?" he asked. "You gather up a plenty in your goin's-around. It's little I get, except the bones, after they've been gnawed over by the whole neighborhood."

"There is not much now, I believe," Dr. Deane observed.

"Jacob and Leah Gilpin have another boy, but thee hardly knows them, I think. William Byerly died last week in Birmingham; thee's heard of him,—he had a wonderful gift of preaching. They say Maryland cattle will be cheap, this fall: does Alfred intend to fatten many? I saw him riding towards New-Garden."

"I guess he will," the old man answered,—"must make somethin' out o' the farm. That pastur'-bottom ought to bring more than it does."

"Alfred doesn't look to want for much," the Doctor continued. "It's a fine farm he has."

"Me, I say!" old Barton exclaimed, bringing down the end of his stick upon the floor. "The farm's mine!"

"But it's the same thing, isn't it?" asked Dr. Deane, in his cheeriest voice and with his pleasantest smile.

The old man looked at him for a moment, gave an incoherent grunt, the meaning of which the Doctor found it impossible to decipher, and presently, with a cunning leer, said.—

"Is all your property the same thing as your daughter's?"

"Well—well," replied the Doctor, softly rubbing his hands, "I should hope so—yes, I should hope so."

"Besides what she has in her own right?"

"Oh, thee knows that will be hers without my disposal. What I should do for her would be apart from that. I am not likely, at my time of life, to marry again—but we are led by the Spirit, thee knows; we cannot say, I will do thus and so, and these and such things shall happen, and those and such other shall not."

"Ay, that's my rule, too, Doctor," said the old man, after a pause, during which he had intently watched his visitor, from under his wrinkled eyelids.

"I thought," the Doctor resumed, "thee was pretty safe against another marriage, at any rate, and thee had perhaps made up thy mind about providing for thy children.

"It's better for us old men to have our houses set in order, that we may spare ourselves worry and anxiety of mind. Elisha is already established in his own independence, and I suppose Ann will give thee no particular trouble; but if Alfred, now, should take a notion to marry, he couldn't, thee sees, be expected to commit himself without having some idea of what thee intends to do for him."

Dr. Deane, having at last taken up his position and uncovered his front of attack, waited for the next movement of his adversary. He was even aware of a slight professional curiosity to know how far the old man's keen, shrewd, wary faculties had survived the wreck of his body.

The latter nodded his head, and pressed the top of his hickory stick against his gums several times, before he answered. He enjoyed the encounter, though not so sure of its issue as he would have been ten years earlier.

"I'd do the fair thing, Doctor!" he finally exclaimed; "whatever it might be, it'd be fair. Come, isn't that enough?"

"In a general sense, it is. But we are talking now as neighbors. We are both old men, Friend Barton, and I think we know how to keep our own counsel. Let us suppose a case—just to illustrate the matter, thee understands. Let us say that Friend Paxson—a widower, thee knows—had a daughter Mary, who had—well, a nice little penny in her own right,—and that thy son Alfred desired her in marriage. Friend Paxson, as a prudent father, knowing his daughter's portion, both what it is and what it will be,—he would naturally wish, in Mary's interest, to know that Alfred would not be dependent on her means, but that the children they might have would inherit equally from both. Now, it strikes me that Friend Paxson would only be right in asking thee what thee would do for thy son—nay, that, to be safe, he would want to see some evidence that would hold in law. Things are so uncertain, and a wise man guardeth his own household."

The old man laughed until his watery eyes twinkled. "Friend Paxson is a mighty close and cautious one to deal with," he said. "Mayhap he'd like to manage to have me bound, and himself go free?"

"Thee's mistaken, indeed!" Dr. Deane protested. "He's not that kind of a man. He only means to do what's right, and to ask the same security from thee, which thee—I'm sure of it, Friend Barton!—would expect him to furnish."

The old man began to find this illustration uncomfortable; it was altogether one-sided. Dr. Deane could shelter himself behind Friend Paxson and the imaginary daughter, but the applications came personally home to him. His old patience had been weakened by his isolation from the world, and his habits of arbitrary rule. He knew, moreover, the probable amount of Martha's fortune, and could make a shrewd guess at the Doctor's circumstances; but if the settlements were to be equal, each must give his share its highest valuation in order to secure more from the other. It was a difficult game, because these men viewed it in the light of a business transaction, and each considered that any advantage over the other would be equivalent to a pecuniary gain on his own part.

"No use beatin' about the bush, Doctor," the old man suddenly said. "You don't care for Paxson's daughter, that never was; why not put your Martha in her place. She has a good penny, I hear—five thousand, some say."

"Ten, every cent of it!" exclaimed Dr. Deane, very nearly thrown off his guard. "That is, she will have it, at twenty-five; and sooner, if she marries with my consent. But why does thee wish particularly to speak of her?"

"For the same reason you talk about Alfred. He hasn't been about your house lately, I s'pose, hey?"

The Doctor smiled, dropping his eyelids in a very sagacious way. "He does seem drawn a little our way, I must confess to thee," he said, "but we can't always tell how much is meant. Perhaps thee knows his mind better than I do?"

"Mayhap I do—know what it will be, if I choose! But I don't begrudge sayin' that he likes your girl, and I shouldn't wonder if he'd showed it."

"Then thee sees, Friend Barton," Dr. Deane continued, "that the case is precisely like the one I supposed; and what I would consider right for Friend Paxson, would even be right for myself. I've no doubt thee could do more for Alfred than I can do for Martha, and without wrong to thy other children,—Elisha, as I said, being independent, and Ann not requiring a great deal,—and the two properties joined together would be a credit to us, and to the neighborhood. Only, thee knows, there must be some legal assurance beforehand. There is nothing certain,—even thy mind is liable to change,— ah, the mind of man is an unstable thing!"

The Doctor delivered these words in his most impressive manner, uplifting both eyes and hands.

The old man, however, seemed to pay but little attention to it. Turning his head on one side, he said, in a quick, sharp voice: "Time enough for that

135

when we come to it How's the girl inclined? Is the money hers, anyhow, at twenty-five,—how old now? Sure to be a couple, hey?—settle that first!"

Dr. Deane crossed his legs carefully, so as not to crease the cloth too much, laid his cane upon them, and leaned back a little in his chair. "Of course I've not spoken to Martha," he presently said; "I can only say that she hasn't set her mind upon anybody else, and that is the main thing. She has followed my will in all, except as to joining the Friends, and there I felt that I couldn't rightly command, where the Spirit had not spoken. Yes, the money will be hers at twenty-five,—she is twenty-one now,—but I hardly think it necessary to take that into consideration. If thee can answer for Alfred, I think I can answer for her."

"The boy's close about his money," broke in the old man, with a sly, husky chuckle. "What he has, Doctor, you understand, goes toward balancin' what she has, afore you come onto me, at all. Yes, yes, I know what I'm about. A good deal, off and on, has been got out o' this farm, and it hasn't all gone into my pockets. I've a trifle put out, but you can't expect me to strip myself naked, in my old days. But I'll do what's fair—I'll do what's fair!"

"There's only this," the Doctor added, meditatively, "and I want thee to understand, since we've, somehow or other, come to mention the matter, that we'd better have another talk, after we've had more time to think of it. Thee can make up thy mind, and let me know about what thee'll do; and I the same. Thee has a starting-point on my side, knowing the amount of Martha's fortune—that, of course, thee must come up to first, and then we'll see about the rest!"

Old-man Barton felt that he was here brought up to the rack. He recognized Dr. Deane's advantage, and could only evade it by accepting his proposition for delay. True, he had already gone over the subject, in his lonely, restless broodings beside the window, but this encounter had freshened and resuscitated many points. He knew that the business would be finally arranged, but nothing would have induced him to hasten it. There was a great luxury in this preliminary skirmishing.

"Well, well!" said he, "we needn't hurry. You're right there, Doctor. I s'pose you won't do anything to keep the young ones apart?"

"I think I've shown my own wishes very plainly, Friend Barton. It is necessary that Alfred should speak for himself, though, and after all we've said, perhaps it might be well if thee should give him a hint. Thee must remember that he has never yet mentioned the subject to me."

Dr. Deane thereupon arose, smoothed his garments, and shook out, not only sweet marjoram, but lavender, cloves, and calamus. His broad-brimmed drab hat had never left his head during the interview. There were steps on the creaking floor overhead, and the Doctor perceived that the private conference must now close. It was nearly a drawn game, so far; but the chance of advantage was on his side.

"Suppose I look at thy arm,—in a neighborly way, of course," he said, approaching the old man's chair.

"Never mind—took the bean off this mornin'—old blood, you know, but lively yet. Gad, Doctor! I've not felt so brisk for a year." His eyes twinkled so, under their puffy lids, the flabby folds in which his mouth terminated worked so curiously,—like those of a bellows, where they run together towards the nozzle,—and the two movable fingers on each hand opened and shut with such a menacing, clutching motion, that for one moment the Doctor felt a chill, uncanny creep run over his nerves.

"Brandy!" the old man commanded. "I've not talked so much at once't for months. You might take a little more, maybe. No? well, you hardly need it. Good brandy's powerful dear, these times."

Dr. Deane had too much tact to accept the grudging invitation. After the old man had drunk, he carefully replaced the bottle and glass on their accustomed shelf, and disposed himself to leave. On the whole, he was well satisfied with the afternoon's work, not doubting but that he had acted the part of a tender and most considerate parent towards his daughter.

Before they met, she also had disposed of her future, but in a very different way.

Miss Ann descended the stairs in time to greet the Doctor before his departure. She would have gladly retained him to tea, as a little relief to the loneliness and weariness of the day; but she never dared to give an invitation except when it seconded her father's, which, in the present case, was wanting.

CHAPTER XIV. — DOUBTS AND SURMISES.

Gilbert's voice, sharpened by his sudden and mortal fear, recalled Mary Potter to consciousness. After she had drunk of the cup of water which he brought, she looked slowly and wearily around the kitchen, as if some instinct taught her to fix her thoughts on the signs and appliances of her every-day life, rather than allow them to return to the pang which had overpowered her. Little by little she recovered her calmness and a portion of her strength, and at last, noticing her son's anxious face, she spoke.

"I have frightened you, Gilbert; but there is no occasion for it. I wasn't rightly prepared for what you had to say—and—and—but, please, don't let us talk any more about it to-night. Give me a little time to think—if I can think. I'm afraid it's but a sad home I'm making for you, and sure it's a sad load I've put upon you, my poor boy! But oh, try, Gilbert, try to be patient a little while longer,—it can't be for long,—for I begin to see now that I've worked out my fault, and that the Lord in Heaven owes me justice!"

She clenched her hands wildly, and rose to her feet. Her steps tottered, and he sprang to her support.

"Mother," he said, "let me help you to your room. I'll not speak of this again; I wouldn't have spoken to-night, if I had mistrusted that it could give you trouble. Have no fear that I can ever be impatient again; patience is easy to me now!"

He spoke kindly and cheerfully, registering a vow in his heart that his lips should henceforth be closed upon the painful theme, until his mother's release (whatever it was and whenever it might come) should open them.

But competent as he felt in that moment to bear the delay cheerfully, and determined as he was to cast no additional weight on his mother's heart, it was not so easy to compose his thoughts, as he lay in the dusky, starlit bedroom up-stairs. The events of the day, and their recent consequences, had moved his strong nature to its very foundations. A chaos of joy, wonder, doubt, and dread surged through him. Over and over he recalled the sweet pressure of Martha Deane's lip, the warm curve of her bosom, the dainty, delicate firmness of her hand. Was this—could this possession really be his? In his mother's mysterious secret there lay an element of terror. He could not guess why the revelation of his fortunate love should agitate her so fearfully, unless—and the suspicion gave him a shock—her history were in some way involved with that of Martha Deane.

This thought haunted and perplexed him, continually returning to disturb the memory of those holy moments in the twilight dell, and to ruffle the bright current of joy which seemed to gather up and sweep away with it all the forces of his life. Any fate but to lose her, he said to himself; let the shadow fall anywhere, except between them! There would be other troubles, he foresaw,—the opposition of her father; the rage and hostility of Alfred Barton; possibly, when the story became known (as it must be in the end), the ill-will or aversion of the neighborhood. Against all these definite and positive evils, he felt strong and tolerably courageous, but the Something which evidently menaced him through his mother made him shrink with a sense of cowardice.

Hand in hand with this dread he went into the world of sleep. He stood upon the summit of the hill behind Falconer's farm-house, and saw Martha beckoning to him from the hill on the other side of the valley. They stretched and clasped hands through the intervening space; the hills sank away, and they found themselves suddenly below, on the banks of the creek. He threw his arms around her, but she drew back, and then he saw that it was Betsy Lavender, who said: "I am your father—did you never guess it before?" Down the road came Dr. Deane and his mother, walking arm in arm; their eyes were fixed on him, but they did not speak. Then he heard Martha's voice, saying: "Gilbert, why did you tell Alfred Barton? Nobody must know that I am engaged to both of you." Betsy Lavender said: "He can only marry with my consent—Mary Potter has nothing to do with it." Martha then came towards him smiling, and said: "I will not send back your saddle-girth—see, I am wearing it as a belt!" He took hold of the buckle and drew her nearer; she began to weep, and they were suddenly standing side by side, in a dark room, before his dead mother, in her coffin.

This dream, absurd and incoherent as it was, made a strange impression upon Gilbert's mind. He was not superstitious, but in spite of himself the idea became rooted in his thoughts that the truth of his own parentage affected, in some way, some member of the Deane family. He taxed his memory in vain for words or incidents which might help him to solve this doubt. Something told him that his obligation to his mother involved the understanding that he would not even attempt to discover her secret; but he could not prevent his thoughts from wandering around it, and making blind guesses as to the vulnerable point.

Among these guesses came one which caused him to shudder; he called it impossible, incredible, and resolutely barred it from his mind. But with all his resolution, it only seemed to wait at a little distance, as if constantly seeking an opportunity to return. What if Dr. Deane were his own father? In that case Martha would be his half-sister, and the stain of illegitimacy would rest on her, not on him! There was ruin and despair in the supposition; but, on the other hand, he asked himself why should the fact of his love throw his mother into a swoon? Among the healthy, strong-nerved people of Kennett such a thing as a swoon was of the rarest occurrence, and it suggested some terrible cause to Gilbert's mind. It was sometimes hard for him to preserve his predetermined patient, cheerful demeanor in his mother's presence, but he tried bravely, and succeeded.

Although the harvest was well over, there was still much work to do on the farm, in order that the month of October might be appropriated to hauling,—the last time, Gilbert hoped, that he should be obliged to resort to this source of profit. Though the price of grain was sure to decline, on account of the extraordinary harvest, the quantity would make up for this deficiency. So far, his estimates had been verified. A good portion of the money was already on hand, and his coveted freedom from debt in the following spring became now tolerably secure. His course, in this respect, was in strict accordance with the cautious, plodding, conscientious habits of the community in which he lived. They were satisfied to advance steadily and slowly, never establishing a new mark until the old one had been reached.

Gilbert was impatient to see Martha again, not so much for the delight of love, as from a sense of the duty which he owed to her. His mother had not answered his question,—possibly not even heard it,—and he did not dare to approach her with it again. But so much as he knew might be revealed to the wife of his heart; of that he was sure. If she could but share his confidence in his mother's words, and be equally patient to await the solution, it would give their relation a new sweetness, an added sanctity and trust.

He made an errand to Fairthorn's at the close of the week, hoping that chance might befriend him, but almost determined, in any case, to force an interview. The dread he had trampled down still hung around him, and it seemed that Martha's presence might dissipate it. Something, at least, he might learn concerning Dr. Deane's family, and here his thoughts at once reverted to Miss Betsy Lavender. In her he had the true friend, the close mouth, the brain crammed with family intelligence!

The Fairthorns were glad to see their "boy," as the old woman still called him. Joe and Jake threw their brown legs over the barn-yard fence and clamored for a ride upon Roger. "Only along the level, t'other side o' the big hill, Gilbert!" said Joe, whereupon the two boys punched each other in the sides and nearly smothered with wicked laughter. Gilbert understood them; he shook his head, and said: "You rascals, I think I see you doing that again!" But he turned away his face, to conceal a smile at the recollection.

It was, truly, a wicked trick. The boys had been in the habit of taking the farm-horses out of the field and riding them up and down the Unionville road. It was their habit, as soon as they had climbed "the big hill," to use stick and voice with great energy, force the animals into a gallop, and so dash along the level. Very soon, the horses knew what was expected of them, and whenever they came abreast of the great chestnut-tree on the top of the hill, they would start off as if possessed. If any business called Farmer Fairthorn to the Street Road, or up Marlborough way, Joe and Jake, dancing with delight, would dart around the barn, gain the wooded hollow, climb the big hill behind the lime-kiln, and hide themselves under the hedge, at the commencement of the level road. Here they could watch their father, as his benign, unsuspecting face came in sight, mounting the hill, either upon the gray mare, Bonnie, or

142

the brown gelding, Peter. As the horse neared the chestnut-tree, they fairly shook with eager expectancy—then came the start, the astonishment of the old man, his frantic "Whoa, there, whoa!" his hat soaring off on the wind, his short, stout body bouncing in the saddle, as, half-unseated, he clung with one hand to the mane and the other to the bridle!—while the wicked boys, after breathlessly watching him out of sight, rolled over and over on the grass, shrieking and yelling in a perfect luxury of fun.

Then they knew that a test would come, and prepared themselves to meet it. When, at dinner, Farmer Fairthorn turned to his wife and said: "Mammy," (so he always addressed her) "I don't know what's the matter with Bonnie; why, she came nigh runnin' off with me!"—Joe, being the oldest and boldest, would look up in well-affected surprise, and ask, "Why, how, Daddy?" while Jake would bend down his head and whimper,—"Somethin' 's got into my eye." Yet the boys were very good-hearted fellows, at bottom, and we are sorry that we must chronicle so many things to their discredit.

Sally Fairthorn met Gilbert in her usual impetuous way. She was glad to see him, but she could not help saying: "Well, have you got your tongue yet, Gilbert? Why, you're growing to be as queer as Dick's hat-band! I don't know any more where to find you, or how to place you; whatever is the matter?"

"Nothing, Sally," he answered, with something of his old playfulness, "nothing except that the pears were very good. How's Mark?"

"Mark!" she exclaimed with a very well assumed sneer. "As if I kept an account of Mark's comings and goings!" But she could not prevent an extra color from rising into her face.

"I wish you did, Sally," Gilbert gravely remarked. "Mark is a fine fellow, and one of my best friends, and he'd be all the better, if a smart, sensible girl like yourself would care a little for him."

There was no answer to this, and Sally, with a hasty "I'll tell mother you're here!" darted into the house.

Gilbert was careful not to ask many questions during his visit; but Sally's rattling tongue supplied him with all he would have been likely to learn, in any case. She had found Martha at home the day before, and had talked about him, Gilbert. Martha hadn't noticed anything "queer" in his manner, whereupon she, Sally, had said that Martha was growing "queer" too; then Martha remarked that—but here Sally found that she had been talking altogether too fast, so she bit her tongue and blushed a little. The most important piece of news, however, was that Miss Lavender was then staying at Dr. Deane's.

On his way to the village, Gilbert chose the readiest and simplest way of accomplishing his purpose. He would call on Betsy Lavender, and ask her to arrange her time so that she could visit his mother during his approaching absence from home. Leaving his horse at the hitching-post in front of the store, he walked boldly across the road and knocked at Dr. Deane's door.

The Doctor was absent. Martha and Miss Lavender were in the sitting-room, and a keen, sweet throb in his blood responded to the voice that bade him enter.

"Gilbert Potter, I'll be snaked!" exclaimed Miss Lavender, jumping up with a start that overturned her footstool.

"Well, Gilbert!" and "Well, Martha!" were the only words the lovers exchanged, on meeting, but their hands were quick to clasp and loath to loose. Martha Deane was too clear-headed to be often surprised by an impulse of the heart, but when the latter experience came to her, she never thought of doubting its justness. She had not been fully, vitally aware of her love for Gilbert until the day when he declared it, and now, in memory, the two circumstances seemed to make but one fact. The warmth, the beauty, the spiritual expansion which accompany love had since then dawned upon her nature in their true significance. Proudly and cautiously as she would have guarded her secret from an intrusive eye, just as frank, tender, and brave was she to reveal every emotion of her heart to her lover. She was thoroughly penetrated with the conviction of his truth, of the integral nobility of his manhood; and these, she felt, were the qualities her heart had unconsciously craved. Her mind was made up inflexibly; it rejoiced in his companionship, it trusted in his fidelity, and if she considered conventional difficulties, it was only to estimate how they could most speedily be overthrown. Martha Deane was in advance of her age,—or, at least, of the community in which she lived.

They could only exchange common-places, of course, in Miss Lavender's presence; and perhaps they were not aware of the gentle, affectionate way in which they spoke of the weather and similar topics. Miss Lavender was; her eyes opened widely, then nearly closed with an expression of superhuman wisdom; she looked out of the window and nodded to the lilac-bush, then exclaiming in desperate awkwardness: "Goodness me, I must have a bit o' sage!" made for the garden, with long strides.

Gilbert was too innocent to suspect the artifice—not so Martha. But while she would have foiled the inference of any other woman, she accepted Betsy's without the least embarrassment, and took Gilbert's hand again in her own before the door had fairly closed.

"O Martha!" he cried, "if I could but see you oftener—but for a minute, every day! But there—I won't be impatient. I've thought of you ever since, and I ask myself, the first thing when I wake, morning after morning, is it really true?"

"And I say to myself, every morning, it is true," she answered. Her lovely blue eyes smiled upon him with a blissful consent, so gentle and so perfect, that he would fain have stood thus and spoken no word more.

"Martha," he said, returning to the thought of his duty, "I have something to say. You can hear it now. My mother declares that I am her lawful son, born in wedlock—she gave me her solemn word—but more than that she will not allow me to ask, saying she's bound for a time, and something, I don't know what, must happen before she can set herself right in the eyes of the world. I believe her, Martha, and I want that you should believe her, for her sake and for mine. I can't make things clear to you, now, because they're not clear to myself; only, what she has declared is and must be true! I am not base-born, and it'll be made manifest, I'm sure; the Lord will open her mouth in his own good time—and until then, we must wait! Will you wait with me?"

He spoke earnestly and hurriedly, and his communication was so

145

unexpected that she scarcely comprehended its full import. But for his sake, she dared not hesitate to answer.

"Can you ask it, Gilbert? Whatever your mother declares to you, must be true; yet I scarcely understand it."

"Nor can I! I've wearied my brains, trying to guess why she can't speak, and what it is that'll give her the liberty at last. I daren't ask her more—she fainted dead away, the last time."

"Strange things sometimes happen in this world," said Martha, with a grave tenderness, laying her hand upon his arm, "and this seems to be one of the strangest. I am glad you have told me, Gilbert,—it will make so much difference to you!"

"So it don't take you from me, Martha," he groaned, in a return of his terrible dread.

"Only Death can do that—and then but for a little while."

Here Miss Betsy Lavender made her appearance, but without the sage.

"How far a body can see, Martha," she exclaimed, "since the big gum-tree's been cut down. It lays open the sight o' the road across the creek, and I seen your father ridin' down the hill, as plain as could be!"

"Betsy," said Gilbert, "I wanted to ask you about coming down our way."

"Our way. Did you? I see your horse hitched over at the store. I've an arrand,—sewin'-thread and pearl buttons,—and so I'll git my bonnet and you can tell me on the way."

The lovers said farewell, and Betsy Lavender accompanied Gilbert, proposing to walk a little way with him and get the articles on her return.

"Gilbert Potter," she said, when they were out of sight and ear-shot of the village, "I want you to know that I've got eyes in my head. I'm a safe body, as you can see, though it mayn't seem the proper thing in me to say it, but all other folks isn't, so look out!"

146

"Betsy!" he exclaimed, "you seem to know everything about everybody— at least, you know what I am, perhaps better than I do myself; now suppose I grant you're right, what do you think of it?"

"Think of it? Go 'long!—you know what you want me to say, that there never was such a pair o' lovyers under the firmament! Let my deeds prove what I think, say I—for here's a case where deeds is wanted!"

"You can help me, Betsy—you can help me now! Do you know—can you guess—who was my father?"

"Good Lord!" was her surprised exclamation—"No, I don't, and that's the fact."

"Who was Martha Deane's mother?"

"A Blake—Naomi, one o' the Birmingham Blakes, and a nice woman she was, too. I was at her weddin', and I helped nuss her when Martha was born." "Had Dr. Deane been married before?"

"Married before? Well—no!" Here Miss Betsy seemed to be suddenly put upon her guard. "Not to that extent, I should say. However, it's neither here nor there. Good lack, boy!" she cried, noticing a deadly paleness on Gilbert's face—"a-h-h-h, I begin to understand now. Look here, Gilbert! Git that nonsense out o' y'r head, jist as soon as you can. There's enough o' trouble ahead, without borrowin' any more out o' y'r wanderin' wits. I don't deny but what I was holdin' back somethin', but it's another thing as ever was. I'll speak you clear o' your misdoubtin's, if that's y'r present bother. You don't feel quite as much like a live corpse, now, I reckon, hey?"

"O, Betsy!" he said, "if you knew how I have been perplexed, you wouldn't wonder at my fancies!"

"I can fancy all that, my boy," she gently answered, "and I'll tell you another thing, Gilbert—your mother has a heavy secret on her mind, and I rather guess it concerns your father. No—don't look so eager-like—I don't know it. All I do know is that you were born in Phildelphy."

"In Philadelphia! I never heard that."

"Well—it's neither here nor there. I've had my hands too full to spy out other people's affairs, but many a thing has come to me in a nateral way, or half-unbeknown. You can't do better than leave all sich wild guesses and misdoubtin's to me, that's better able to handle 'em. Not that I'm a-goin' to preach and declare anything until I know the rights of it, whatever and wherever. Well, as I was sayin'—for there's Beulah Green comin' up the road, and you must git your usual face onto you, though Goodness knows, mine's so crooked, I've often said nothin' short o' Death'll ever make much change in it—but never mind, I'll go down a few days to your mother, when you're off, though I don't promise to do much, except, maybe, cheer her up a bit; but we'll see, and so remember me to her, and good-bye!"

With these words and a sharp, bony wring of his hand. Bliss Betsy strode rapidly back to the village. It did not escape Gilbert's eye that, strongly as she had pronounced against his secret fear, the detection of it had agitated her. She had spoken hurriedly, and hastened away as if desiring to avoid further questions. He could not banish the suspicion that she knew something which might affect his fortune; but she had not forbidden his love for Martha—she had promised to help him, and that was a great consolation. His cheerfulness, thenceforth, was not assumed, and he rejoiced to see a very faint, shadowy reflection of it, at times, in his mother's face.

CHAPTER XV. — ALFRED BARTON BETWEEN TWO FIRES.

For some days after Dr. Deane's visit, Old-man Barton was a continual source of astonishment to his son Alfred and his daughter Ann. The signs of gradual decay which one of them, at least, had watched with the keenest interest, had suddenly disappeared; he was brighter, sharper, more talkative than at any time within the previous five years. The almost worn-out machinery of his life seemed to have been mysteriously repaired, whether by Dr. Deane's tinkering, or by one of those freaks of Nature which sometimes bring new teeth and hair to an aged head, neither the son nor the daughter could guess. To the former this awakened activity of the old man's brain was not a little annoying. He had been obliged to renew his note for the money borrowed to replace that which had been transferred to Sandy Flash, and in the mean time was concocting an ingenious device by which the loss should not entirely fall on his own half-share of the farm-profits. He could not have endured his father's tyranny without the delight of the cautious and wary revenges of this kind which he sometimes allowed himself to take. Another circumstance, which gave him great uneasiness, was this: the old man endeavored in various ways, both direct and indirect, to obtain knowledge of the small investments which he had made from time to time. The most of these had been, through the agency of the old lawyer at Chester, consolidated into a first-class mortgage; but it was Alfred's interest to keep his father in ignorance of the other sums, not because of their importance, but because of their insignificance. He knew that the old man's declaration was true,—"The more you have, the more you'll get!"

The following Sunday, as he was shaving himself at the back kitchen-window,—Ann being up-stairs, at her threadbare toilet,—Old Barton, who had been silent during breakfast, suddenly addressed him:

"Well, boy, how stands the matter now?"

The son knew very well what was meant, but he thought it best to ask, with an air of indifference,—

"What matter, Daddy?"

"What matter, eh? The colt's lame leg, or the farrow o' the big sow? Gad, boy! don't you ever think about the gal, except when I put it into your head?"

"Oh, that!" exclaimed Alfred, with a smirk of well-assumed satisfaction—"that, indeed! Well, I think I may say, Daddy, that all's right in that quarter."

"Spoken to her yet?"

"N-no, not right out, that is; but since other folks have found out what I'm after, I guess it's plain enough to her. And a good sign is, that she plays a little shy."

"Shouldn't wonder," growled the old man. "Seems to me you play a little shy, too. Have to take it in my own hands, if it ever comes to anything."

"Oh, it isn't at all necessary; I can do my own courting," Alfred replied, as he wiped his razor and laid it away.

"Do it, then, boy, in short order! You're too old to stand in need o' much billin' and cooin'—but the gal's rayther young, and may expect it—and I s'pose it's the way. But I'd sooner you'd step up to the Doctor, bein' as I can only take him when he comes here to me loaded and primed. He's mighty cute and sharp, but if you've got any gumption, we'll be even with him."

Alfred turned around quickly and looked at his father.

"Ay, boy, I've had one bout with him, last Sunday, and there's more to come."

"What was it?"

"Set yourself down on that cheer, and keep your head straight a bit, so that what goes into one ear, don't fly out at the t'other."

While Alfred, with a singular expression of curiosity and distrust, obeyed this command, the old man deliberated, for the last time, on the peculiar tactics to be adopted, so that his son should be made an ally, as against Dr. Deane, and yet be prevented from becoming a second foe, as against his own property. For it was very evident that while it was the father's interest to exaggerate the son's presumed wealth, it was the latter's interest to underrate it. Thus a third element came into play, making this a triangular game of avarice. If Alfred could have understood his true position, he would have been more courageous; but his father had him at a decided advantage.

"Hark ye, boy!" said he, "I've waited e'en about long enough, and it's time this thing was either a hit or a flash in the pan. The Doctor's ready for 't; for all his cunnin' he couldn't help lettin' me see that; but he tries to cover both pockets with one hand while he stretches out the t'other. The gal's money's safe, ten thousand of it, and we've agreed that it'll be share and share; only, your'n bein' more than her'n, why, of course he must make up the difference."

The son was far from being as shrewd as the father, or he would have instantly chosen the proper tack; but he was like a vessel caught in stays, and experienced considerable internal pitching and jostling. In one sense it was a relief that the old man supposed him to be worth much more than was actually the case, but long experience hinted that a favorable assumption of this kind often led to a damaging result. So with a wink and grin, the miserable hypocrisy of which was evident to his own mind, he said:

"Of course he must make up the difference, and more too! I know what's fair and square."

"Shut your mouth, boy, till I give you leave to open it. Do you hear?— the gal's ten thousand dollars must be put ag'inst the ten thousand you've saved off the profits o' the farm; then, the rest you've made bein' properly accounted for, he must come down with the same amount. Then, you must find out to a hair what he's worth of his own—not that it concerns you, but I must know. What you've got to do is about as much as you've wits for. Now, open your mouth!"

"Ten thousand!" exclaimed Alfred, beginning to comprehend the matter more clearly; "why, it's hardly quite ten thousand altogether, let alone anything over!"

"No lies, no lies! I've got it all in my head, if you haven't. Twenty years on shares—first year, one hundred and thirty-seven dollars—that was the year the big flood swep' off half the corn on the bottom; second year, two hundred and fifteen, with interest on the first, say six on a hundred, allowin' the thirty-seven for your squanderin's, two hundred and twenty-one; third year, three hundred and five, with interest, seventeen, makes three hundred and twenty-two, and twenty, your half of the bay horse sold to Sam Falconer, forty-two; fourth year"—

"Never mind, Daddy!" Alfred interrupted; "I've got it all down in my books; you needn't go over it."

The old man struck his hickory staff violently upon the floor. "I will go over it!" he croaked, hoarsely. "I mean to show you, boy, to your own eyes and your own ears, that you're now worth thirteen thousand two hundred and forty-nine dollars and fifteen cents! And ten thousand of it balances the gal's ten thousand, leavin' three thousand two hundred and forty-nine and fifteen cents, for the Doctor to make up to you! And you'll show him your papers, for you're no son of mine if you've put out your money without securin' it. I don't mind your goin' your own road with what you've arned, though, for your proper good, you needn't ha' been so close; but now you've got to show what's in your hand, if you mean to git it double!"

Alfred Barton was overwhelmed by the terrors of this unexpected dilemma. His superficial powers of dissimulation forsook him; he could only suggest, in a weak voice:

"Suppose my papers don't show that much?"

"You've made that, or nigh onto it, and your papers must show it! If money can't stick to your fingers, do you s'pose I'm goin' to put more into 'em? Fix it any way you like with the Doctor, so you square accounts. Then, afterwards, let him come to me—ay, let him come!"

Here the old man chuckled until he brought on a fit of coughing, which drove the dark purple blood into his head. His son hastened to restore him with a glass of brandy.

"There, that'll do," he said, presently; "now you know what's what. Go

152

up to the Doctor's this afternoon, and have it out before you come home. I can't dance at your weddin', but I wouldn't mind help nuss another grandchild or two—eh, boy?"

"Damme, and so you shall, Dad!" the son exclaimed, relapsing into his customary swagger, as the readiest means of flattering the old man's more amiable mood. It was an easier matter to encounter Dr. Deane—to procrastinate and prolong the settlement of terms, or shift the responsibility of the final result from his own shoulders. Of course the present command must be obeyed, and it was by no means an agreeable one; but Alfred Barton had courage enough for any emergency not yet arrived. So he began to talk and joke very comfortably about his possible marriage, until Ann, descending to the kitchen in her solemn black gown, interrupted the conference.

That afternoon, as Alfred took his way by the foot-path to the village, he seated himself in the shade, on one end of the log which spanned the creek, in order to examine his position, before venturing on a further step. We will not probe the depths of his meditations; probably they were not very deep, even when most serious; but we may readily conjecture those considerations which were chiefly obvious to his mind. The affair, which he had so long delayed, through a powerful and perhaps a natural dread, was now brought to a crisis. He could not retreat without extreme risk to his prospects of inheritance; since his father and Dr. Deane had come to an actual conference, he was forced to assume the part which was appropriate to him. Sentiment, he was aware, would not be exacted, but a certain amount of masculine anticipation belonged to his character of lover; should he assume this, also, or meet Dr. Deane on a hard business ground?

It is a matter of doubt whether any vulgar man suspects the full extent of his vulgarity; but there are few who are not conscious, now and then, of a very uncomfortable difference between themselves and the refined natures with whom they come in contact. Alfred Barton had never been so troubled by this consciousness as when in the presence of Martha Deane. He was afraid of her; he foresaw that she, as his wife, would place him in a more painful subjection than that which his father now enforced. He was weary of bondage, and longed to draw a free, unworried breath. With all his swagger, his life had not always been easy or agreeable. A year or two more might see him, in fact and in truth, his own master. He was fifty years old; his habits of life were fixed; he would have shrunk from the semi-servitude of marriage, though with a woman after his own heart, and there was nothing in this (except the money) to attract him.

"I see no way!" he suddenly exclaimed, after a fit of long and unsatisfactory musing.

"Nor I neither, unless you make room for me!" answered a shrill voice at his side.

He started as if shot, becoming aware of Miss Betsy Lavender, who had just emerged from the thicket.

"Skeered ye, have I?" said she. "Why, how you do color up, to be sure! I never was that red, even in my blushin' days; but never mind, what's said to nobody is nobody's business."

He laughed a forced laugh. "I was thinking, Miss Betsy," he said, "how to get the grain threshed and sent to the mills before prices come down. Which way are you going?"

She had been observing him through half-closed eyes, with her head a little thrown back. First slightly nodding to herself, as if assenting to some mental remark, she asked,—

"Which way are you goin'? For my part I rather think we're changin' places,—me to see Miss Ann, and you to see Miss Martha."

"You're wrong!" he exclaimed. "I was only going to make a little neighborly call on the Doctor."

"On the Doctor! Ah-ha! it's come to that, has it? Well, I won't be in the way."

"Confound the witch!" he muttered to himself, as she sprang upon the log and hurried over.

Mr. Alfred Barton was not acquainted with the Greek drama, or he

154

would have had a very real sense of what is meant by Fate. As it was, he submitted to circumstances, climbed the hill, and never halted until he found himself in Dr. Deane's sitting-room.

Of course, the Doctor was alone and unoccupied; it always happens so. Moreover he knew, and Alfred Barton knew that he knew, the subject to be discussed; but it was not the custom of the neighborhood to approach an important interest except in a very gradual and roundabout manner. Therefore the Doctor said, after the first greeting,—

"Thee'll be getting thy crops to market soon, I imagine?"

"I'd like to," Barton replied, "but there's not force enough on our place, and the threshers are wanted everywhere at once. What would you do,— hurry off the grain now, or wait to see how it may stand in the spring?"

Dr. Deane meditated a moment, and then answered with great deliberation: "I never like to advise, where the chances are about even. It depends, thee knows, on the prospect of next year's crops. But, which ever way thee decides, it will make less difference to thee than to them that depend altogether upon their yearly earnings."

Barton understood this stealthy approach to the important subject, and met it in the same way. "I don't know," he said; "it's slow saving on half-profits. I have to look mighty close, to make anything decent."

"Well," said the Doctor, "what isn't laid up by thee, is laid up for thee, I should judge."

"I should hope so, Doctor; but I guess you know the old man as well as I do. If anybody could tell what's in his mind, it's Lawyer Stacy, and he's as close as a steel-trap. I've hardly had a fair chance, and it ought to be made up to me."

"It will be, no doubt." And then the Doctor, resting his chin upon his cane, relapsed into a grave, silent, expectant mood, which his guest well understood.

"Doctor," he said at last, with an awkward attempt at a gay, confidential manner, "you know what I come for today. Perhaps I'm rather an old boy to be here on such an errand; I've been a bit afraid lest you might think me so; and for that reason I haven't spoken to Martha at all, (though I think she's smart enough to guess how my mind turns,) and won't speak, till I first have your leave. I'm not so young as to be light-headed in such matters; and, most likely, I'm not everything that Martha would like; but—but—there's other things to be considered—not that I mind 'em much, only the old man, you know, is very particular about 'em, and so I've come up to see if we can't agree without much trouble."

Dr. Deane took a small pinch of Rappee, and then touched his nose lightly with his lavendered handkerchief. He drew up his hanging under-lip until it nearly covered the upper, and lifted his nostrils with an air at once of reticence and wisdom. "I don't deny," he said slowly, "that I've suspected something of what is in thy mind, and I will further say that thee's done right in coming first to me. Martha being an only d—child, I have her welfare much at heart, and if I had known anything seriously to thy discredit, I would not have permitted thy attentions. So far as that goes, thee may feel easy. I did hope, however, that thee would have some assurance of what thy father intends to do for thee—and perhaps thee has,—Elisha being established in his own independence, and Ann not requiring a great deal, thee would inherit considerable, besides the farm. And it seems to me that I might justly, in Martha's interest, ask for some such assurance."

If Alfred Barton's secret thought had been expressed in words, it would have been: "Curse the old fool—he knows what the old man is, as well as I do!" But he twisted a respectful hypocrisy out of his whisker, and said,—

"Ye-e-es, that seems only fair. How am I to get at it, though? I daren't touch the subject with a ten-foot pole, and yet it stands both to law and reason that I should come in for a handsome slice o' the property. You might take it for granted, Doctor?"

"So I might, if thy father would take for granted what I might be able to do. I can see, however, that it's hardly thy place to ask him; that might be left to me."

156

This was an idea which had not occurred to Alfred Barton. A thrill of greedy curiosity shot through his heart; he saw that, with Dr. Deane's help, he might be able to ascertain the amount of the inheritance which must so soon fall to him. This feeling, fed by the impatience of his long subjection, took complete possession of him, and he resolved to further his father's desires, without regard to present results.

"Yes, that might be left to me," the Doctor repeated, "after the other matter is settled. Thee knows what I mean. Martha will have ten thousand dollars in her own right, at twenty-five,—and sooner, if she marries with my approbation. Now, thee or thy father must bring an equal sum; that is understood between us—and I think thy father mentioned that thee could do it without calling upon him. Is that the case?"

"Not quite—but, yes, very nearly. That is, the old man's been so close with me, that I'm a little close with him, Doctor, you see! He doesn't know exactly how much I have got, and as he threatens to leave me according to what I've saved, why, I rather let him have his own way about the matter."

A keen, shrewd smile flitted over the Doctor's face.

"But if it isn't quite altogether ten thousand, Doctor," Barton continued, "I don't say but what it could be easily made up to that figure. You and I could arrange all that between our two selves, without consulting the old man,— and, indeed, it's not his business, in any way,—and so, you might go straight to the other matter at once."

"H'm," mused the Doctor, with his chin again upon his stick, "I should perhaps be working in thy interest, as much as in mine. Then thee can afford to come up fair and square to the mark. Of course, thee has all the papers to show for thy own property?"

"I guess there'll be no trouble about that," Barton answered, carelessly. "I lend on none but the best security. 'T will take a little time—must go to Chester—so we needn't wait for that; 't will be all right!"

"Oh, no doubt; but hasn't thee overlooked one thing?"

"What?"

"That Martha should first know thy mind towards her."

It was true, he had overlooked that important fact, and the suggestion came to him very like an attack of cramp. He laughed, however, took out a red silk handkerchief, and tried to wipe a little eagerness into his face.

"No, Doctor!" he exclaimed, "not forgot, only keeping the best for the last. I wasn't sure but you might want to speak to her yourself, first; but she knows, doesn't she?"

"Not to my direct knowledge; and I wouldn't like to venture to speak in her name."

"Then, I'll—that is, you think I'd better have a talk with her. A little tough, at my time of life, ha! ha!—but faint heart never won fair lady; and I hadn't thought of going that far to-day, though of course, I'm anxious,—been in my thoughts so long,—and perhaps—perhaps"—

"I'll tell thee," said the Doctor, seeming not to notice Barton's visible embarrassment, which he found very natural; "do thee come up again next First-day afternoon prepared to speak thy mind. I will give Martha a hint of thy purpose beforehand, but only a hint, mind thee; the girl has a smart head of her own, and thee'll come on faster with her if thee pleads thy own cause with thy own mouth."

"Yes, I'll come then!" cried Barton, so relieved at his present escape that his relief took the expression of joy. Dr. Deane was a fair judge of character; he knew all of Alfred Barton's prominent traits, and imagined that he was now reading him like an open book; but it was like reading one of those Latin sentences which, to the ear, are made up of English words. The signs were all correct, only they belonged to another language.

The heavy wooer shortly took his departure. While on the return path, he caught sight of Miss Betsy Lavender's beaver, bobbing along behind the pickets of the hill-fence, and, rather than encounter its wearer in his present mood, he stole into the shelter of one of the cross-hedges, and made his way into the timbered bottom below.

158

CHAPTER XVI. — MARTHA DEANE.

Little did Dr. Deane suspect the nature of the conversation which had that morning been held in his daughter's room, between herself and Betsy Lavender.

When the latter returned from her interview with Gilbert Potter, the previous evening, she found the Doctor already arrived. Mark came home at supper-time, and the evening was so prolonged by his rattling tongue that no room was left for any confidential talk with Martha, although Miss Betsy felt that something ought to be said, and it properly fell to her lot to broach the delicate subject.

After breakfast on Sunday morning, therefore, she slipped up to Martha's room, on the transparent pretence of looking again at a new dress, which had been bought some days before. She held the stuff to the light, turned it this way and that, and regarded it with an importance altogether out of proportion to its value.

"It seems as if I couldn't git the color rightly set in my head," she remarked; "'t a'n't quiet laylock, nor yit vi'let, and there ought, by rights, to be quilled ribbon round the neck, though the Doctor might consider it too gay; but never mind, he'd dress you in drab or slate if he could, and I dunno, after all"—

"Betsy!" exclaimed Martha, with an impetuousness quite unusual to her calm nature, "throw down the dress! Why won't you speak of what is in your mind; don't you see I'm waiting for it?"

"You're right, child!" Miss Betsy cried, flinging the stuff to the farthest corner of the room; "I'm an awkward old fool, with all my exper'ence. Of course I seen it with half a wink; there! don't be so trembly now. I know how you feel, Martha; you wouldn't think it, but I do. I can tell the real signs from the passin' fancies, and if ever I see true-love in my born days, I see it in you, child, and in him."

Martha's face glowed in spite of herself. The recollection of Gilbert's embrace in the dusky glen came to her, already for the thousandth time, but warmer, sweeter at each recurrence. She felt that her hand trembled in that of the spinster, as they sat knee to knee, and that a tender dew was creeping into her eyes; leaning forward, she laid her face a moment on her friend's shoulder, and whispered,—

"It is all very new and strange, Betsy; but I am happy."

Miss Lavender did not answer immediately. With her hand on Martha's soft, smooth hair, she was occupied in twisting her arm so that the sleeve might catch and conceal two troublesome tears which were at that moment trickling down her nose. Besides, she was not at all sure of her voice, until something like a dry crust of bread in her throat had been forcibly swallowed down.

Martha, however, presently lifted her head with a firm, courageous expression, though the rosy flush still suffused her cheeks. "I'm not as independent as people think," she said, "for I couldn't help myself when the time came, and I seem to belong to him, ever since."

"Ever since. Of course you do!" remarked Miss Betsy, with her head down and her hands busy at her high comb and thin twist of hair; "every woman, savin' and exceptin' myself, and no fault o' mine, must play Jill to somebody's Jack; it's man's way and the Lord's way, but worked out with a mighty variety, though I say it, but why not, my eyes bein' as good as anybody else's! Come now, you're lookin' again after your own brave fashion; and so, you're sure o' your heart, Martha?"

"Betsy, my heart speaks once and for all," said Martha, with kindling eyes.

"Once and for all. I knowed it—and so the Lord help us! For here I smell wagon-loads o' trouble; and if you weren't a girl to know her own mind and stick to it, come weal, come woe, and he with a bull-dog's jaw that'll never let go, and I mean no runnin' of him down, but on the contrary, quite the reverse, I'd say to both, git over it somehow for it won't be, and no matter

160

if no use, it's my dooty,—well, it's t'other way, and I've got to give a lift where I can, and pull this way, and shove that way, and hold back everybody, maybe, and fit things to things, and unfit other things,—Good Lord, child, you've made an awful job for me!"

Therewith Miss Betsy laughed, with a dry, crisp, cheerfulness which quite covered up and concealed her forebodings. Nothing pleased her better than to see realized in life her own views of what ought to be, and the possibility of becoming one of the shaping and regulating powers to that end stirred her nature to its highest and most joyous activity.

Martha Deane, equally brave, was more sanguine. The joy of her expanding love foretold its fulfilment to her heart. "I know, Betsy," she said, "that father would not hear of it now; but we are both young and can wait, at least until I come into my property—ours, I ought to say, for I think of it already as being as much Gilbert's as mine. What other trouble can there be?"

"Is there none on his side, Martha?"

"His birth? Yes, there is—or was, though not to me—never to me! I am so glad, for his sake,—but, Betsy, perhaps you do not know"—

"If there's anything I need to know, I'll find it out, soon or late. He's worried, that I see, and no wonder, poor boy! But as you say, there's time enough, and my single and solitary advice to both o' you, is, don't look at one another before folks, if you can't keep your eyes from blabbin'. Not a soul suspicions anything now, and if you two'll only fix it betwixt and between you to keep quiet, and patient, and as forbearin' in showin' feelin' as people that hate each other like snakes, why, who knows but somethin' may turn up, all unexpected, to make the way as smooth for ye as a pitch-pine plank!"

"Patient!" Martha murmured to herself. A bright smile broke over her face, as she thought how sweet it would be to match, as best a woman might, Gilbert's incomparable patience and energy of purpose. The tender humility of her love, so beautifully interwoven with the texture of its pride and courage, filled her heart with a balmy softness and peace. She was already prepared to lay her firm, independent spirit at his feet, or exercise it only as her new, eternal duty to him might require. Betsy Lavender's warning could not ripple the bright surface of her happiness; she knew that no one (hardly even Gilbert, as yet) suspected that in her heart the love of a strong and faithful and noble man outweighed all other gifts or consequences of life—that, to keep it, she would give up home, friends, father, the conventional respect of every one she knew!

"Well, child!" exclaimed Miss Lavender, after a long lapse of silence; "the words is said that can't be taken back, accordin' to my views o' things, though, Goodness knows, there's enough and enough thinks different, and you must abide by 'em; and what I think of it all I'll tell you when the end comes, not before, so don't ask me now; but one thing more, there's another sort of a gust brewin', and goin' to break soon, if ever, and that is, Alf. Barton,—though you won't believe it,—he's after you in his stupid way, and your father favors him. And my advice is, hold him off as much as you please, but say nothin' o' Gilbert!"

This warning made no particular impression upon Martha. She playfully tapped Miss Betsy's high comb, and said: "Now, if you are going to be so much worried about me, I shall be sorry that you found it out."

"Well I won't!—and now let me hook your gownd."

Often, after that, however, did Martha detect Miss Betsy's eyes fixed upon her with a look of wistful, tender interest, and she knew, though the spinster would not say it, that the latter was alive with sympathy, and happy in the new confidence between them. With each day, her own passion grew and deepened, until it seemed that the true knowledge of love came after its confession. A sweet, warm yearning for Gilbert's presence took its permanent seat in her heart; not only his sterling manly qualities, but his form, his face—the broad, square brow; the large, sad, deep-set gray eyes; the firm, yet impassioned lips—haunted her fancy. Slowly and almost unconsciously as her affection had been developed, it now took the full stature and wore the radiant form of her maiden dream of love.

If Dr. Deane noticed the physical bloom and grace which those days brought to his daughter, he was utterly innocent of the true cause. Perhaps he imagined that his own eyes were first fairly opened to her beauty by the prospect of soon losing her. Certainly she had never seemed more obedient and attractive. He had not forgotten his promise to Alfred Barton; but no very convenient opportunity for speaking to her on the subject occurred until the following Sunday morning. Mark was not at home, and he rode with her to Old Kennett Meeting.

As they reached the top of the long hill beyond the creek, Martha reined in her horse to enjoy the pleasant westward view over the fair September landscape. The few houses of the village crowned the opposite hill; but on this side the winding, wooded vale meandered away, to lose itself among the swelling slopes of clover and stubble-field; and beyond, over the blue level of Tuffkenamon, the oak-woods of Avondale slept on the horizon. It was a landscape such as one may see, in a more cultured form, on the road from Warwick to Stratford. Every one in Kennett enjoyed the view, but none so much as Martha Deane, upon whom its harmonious, pastoral aspect exercised an indescribable charm.

To the left, on the knoll below, rose the chimneys of the Barton farm-house, over the round tops of the apple-trees, and in the nearest field Mr. Alfred's Maryland cattle were fattening on the second growth of clover.

"A nice place, Martha!" said Dr. Deane, with a wave of his arm, and a whiff of sweet herbs.

"Here, in this first field, is the true place for the house," she answered, thinking only of the landscape beauty of the farm.

"Does thee mean so?" the Doctor eagerly asked, deliberating with himself how much of his plan it was safe to reveal. "Thee may be right, and perhaps thee might bring Alfred to thy way of thinking."

She laughed. "It's hardly worth the trouble."

"I've noticed, of late," her father continued, "that Alfred seems to set a good deal of store by thee. He visits us pretty often."

"Why, father!" she exclaimed, as they, rode onward, "it's rather thee that attracts him, and cattle, and crops, and the plans for catching Sandy Flash! He looks frightened whenever I speak to him."

"A little nervous, perhaps. Young men are often so, in the company of young women, I've observed."

Martha laughed so cheerily that her father said to himself: "Well, it doesn't displease her, at any rate." On the other hand, is was possible that she might have failed to see Barton in the light of a wooer, and therefore a further hint would be required.

"Now that we happen to speak of him, Martha," he said, "I might as well tell thee that, in my judgment, he seems to be drawn towards thee in the way of marriage. He may be a little awkward in showing it, but that's a common case. When he was at our house, last First-day, he spoke of thee frequently, and said that he would like to—well, to see thee soon. I believe he intends coming up this afternoon."

Martha became grave, as Betsy Lavender's warning took so suddenly a positive form. However, she had thought of this contingency as a possible thing, and must prepare herself to meet it with firmness.

"What does thee say?" the Doctor asked, after waiting a few minutes for an answer.

"Father, I hope thee's mistaken. Alfred Barton is not overstocked with wit, I know, but he can hardly be that foolish. He is almost as old as thee."

She spoke quietly, but with that tone of decision which Dr. Deane so well knew. He set his teeth and drew up his under-lip to a grim pout. If there was to be resistance, he thought, she would not find him so yielding as on other points; but he would first try a middle course.

"Understand me, Martha," he said; "I do not mean to declare what Alfred Barton's sentiments really are, but what, in my judgment, they might be. And thee had better wait and learn, before setting thy mind either for or against him: It's hardly putting much value upon thyself, to call him foolish."

"It is a humiliation to me, if thee is right, father," she said.

164

"I don't see that. Many young women would be proud of it. I'll only say one thing, Martha; if he seeks thee, and does speak his mind, do thee treat him kindly and respectfully."

"Have I ever treated thy friends otherwise?" she asked.

"My friends! thee's right—he is my friend."

She made no reply, but her soul was already courageously arming itself for battle. Her father's face was stern and cold, and she saw, at once, that he was on the side of the enemy. This struggle safely over, there would come another and a severer one. It was well that she had given herself time, setting the fulfilment of her love so far in advance.

Nothing more was said on this theme, either during the ride to Old Kennett, or on the return. Martha's plan was very simple: she would quietly wait until Alfred Barton should declare his sentiments, and then reject him once and forever. She would speak clearly, and finally; there should be no possibility of misconception. It was not a pleasant task; none but a vain and heartless woman would be eager to assume it; and Martha Deane hoped that it might be spared her.

But she, no less than her irresolute lover, (if we can apply that word to Alfred Barton,) was an instrument in the hands of an uncomfortable Fate. Soon after dinner a hesitating knock was heard at the door, and Barton entered with a more uneasy air than ever before. Erelong, Dr. Deane affected to have an engagement with an invalid on the New-Garden road; Betsy Lavender had gone to Fairthorn's for the afternoon, and the two were alone.

For a few moments, Martha was tempted to follow her father's example, and leave Alfred Barton to his own devices. Then she reflected that this was a cowardly feeling; it would only postpone her task. He had taken his seat, as usual, in the very centre of the room; so she came forward and seated herself at the front window, with her back to the light, thus, woman-like, giving herself all the advantages of position.

Having his large, heavy face before her, in full light, she was at first a little surprised on finding that it expressed not even the fond anxiety, much less the eagerness, of an aspiring wooer. The hair and whiskers, it is true, were so smoothly combed back that they made long lappets on either side of his face; unusual care had been taken with his cambric cravat and shirt-ruffles, and he wore his best blue coat, which was entirely too warm for the season. In strong contrast to this external preparation, were his restless eyes which darted hither and thither in avoidance of her gaze, the fidgety movements of his thick fingers, creeping around buttons and in and out of button-holes, and finally the silly, embarrassed half-smile which now and then came to his mouth, and made the platitudes of his speech almost idiotic.

Martha Deane felt her courage rise as she contemplated this picture. In spite of the disgust which his gross physical appearance, and the contempt which his awkward helplessness inspired, she was conscious of a lurking sense of amusement. Even a curiosity, which we cannot reprehend, to know by what steps and in what manner he would come to the declaration, began to steal into her mind, now that it was evident her answer could not possibly wound any other feeling than vanity.

In this mood, she left the burden of the conversation to him. He might flounder, or be completely stalled, as often as he pleased; it was no part of her business to help him.

In about three minutes after she had taken her seat by the window, he remarked, with a convulsive smile,—

"Apples are going to be good, this year."

"Are they?" she said.

"Yes; do you like 'em? Most girls do."

"I believe I do,—except Russets," Martha replied, with her hands clasped in her lap, and her eyes full upon his face.

He twisted the smoothness out of one whisker, very much disconcerted at her remark, because he could not tell—he never could, when speaking with her—whether or not she was making fun of him. But he could think of nothing to say, except his own preferences in the matter of apples,—a theme which he pursued until Martha was very tired of it.

He next asked after Mark Deane, expressing at great length his favorable opinion of the young, carpenter, and relating what pains he had taken to procure for him the building of Hallowell's barn. But to each observation Martha made the briefest possible replies, so that in a short time he was forced to start another topic.

Nearly an hour had passed, and Martha's sense of the humorous had long since vanished under the dreary monotony of the conversation, when Alfred Barton seemed to have come to a desperate resolution to end his embarrassment. Grasping his knees with both hands, and dropping his head forward so that the arrows of her eyes might glance from his fat forehead, he said,—

"I suppose you know why I come here to-day, Miss Martha?"

All her powers were awake and alert in a moment. She scrutinized his face keenly, and, although his eyes were hidden, there were lines enough visible, especially about the mouth, to show that the bitter predominated over the sweet, in his emotions.

"To see my father, wasn't it? I'm sorry he was obliged to leave home," she answered.

"No, Miss Martha, I come to see you. I have some thing to say to you, and I 'in sure you know what I mean by this time, don't you?"

"No. How should I?" she coolly replied. It was not true; but the truest-hearted woman that ever lived could have given no other answer.

Alfred Barton felt the sensation of a groan pass through him, and it very nearly came out of his mouth. Then he pushed on, in a last wild effort to perform the remainder of his exacted task in one piece:

"I want you to be—to be—my—wife! That is, my father and yours are agreed about it, and they think I ought to speak to you. I'm a good deal older, and—and perhaps you mightn't fancy me in all things, but they say it'll make little difference; and if you haven't thought about it much, why, there's no hurry as to making up your mind. I've told you now, and to be sure you ought to know, while the old folks are trying to arrange property matters, and it's my place, like, to speak to you first."

Here he paused; his face was very red, and the perspiration was oozing in great drops from every pore. He drew forth the huge red silk handkerchief, and mopped his cheeks, his nose, and his forehead; then lifted his head and stole a quick glance at Martha. Something in his face puzzled her, and yet a sudden presentiment of his true state of feeling flashed across her mind. She still sat, looking steadily at him, and for a few moments did not speak.

"Well?" he stammered.

"Alfred Barton," she said, "I must ask you one question, do you love me?"

He seemed to feel a sharp sting. The muscles of his mouth twitched; he bit his lip, sank his head again, and murmured,—

"Y-yes."

"He does not," she said to herself. "I am spared this humiliation. It is a mean, low nature, and fears mine—fears, and would soon hate. He shall not see even so much of me as would be revealed by a frank, respectful rejection. I must punish him a little for the deceit, and I now see how to do it."

While these thoughts passed rapidly through her brain, she waited until he should again venture to meet her eye. When he lifted his head, she exclaimed,—

"You have told an untruth! Don't turn your head away; look me in the face, and hear me tell you that you do not love me—that you have not come to me of your own desire, and that you would rather ten thousand times I should say No, if it were not for a little property of mine! But suppose I, too, were of a similar nature; suppose I cared not for what is called love, but only for money and lands such as you will inherit; suppose I found the plans of my father and your father very shrewd and reasonable, and were disposed to enter into them—what then?"

Alfred Barton was surprised out of the last remnant of his hypocrisy. His face, so red up to this moment, suddenly became sallow; his chin dropped, and an expression of amazement and fright came into the eyes fixed on Martha's.

The game she was playing assumed a deeper interest; here was something which she could not yet fathom. She saw what influence had driven him to her, against his inclination, but his motive for seeming to obey, while dreading success, was a puzzle. Singularly enough, a slight feeling of commiseration began to soften her previous contempt, and hastened her final answer.

"I see that these suppositions would not please you," she said, "and thank you for the fact. Your face is more candid than your speech. I am now ready to say, Alfred Barton,—because I am sure the knowledge will be agreeable to you,—that no lands, no money, no command of my father, no degree of want, or misery, or disgrace, could ever make me your wife!"

She had risen from her chair while speaking, and he also started to his feet. Her words, though such an astounding relief in one sense, had nevertheless given him pain; there was a sting in them which cruelly galled his self-conceit. It was enough to be rejected; she need not have put an eternal gulf between their natures.

"Well," said he, sliding the rim of his beaver backwards and forwards between his fingers, "I suppose I'll have to be going. You're very plain-spoken, as I might ha' known. I doubt whether we two would make a good team, and no offence to you, Miss Martha. Only, it'll be a mortal disappointment to the old man, and—look here, it a'n't worth while to say anything about it, is it?"

Alfred Barton was strongly tempted to betray the secret reason which Martha had not yet discovered. After the strong words he had taken from her, she owed him a kindness, he thought; if she would only allow the impression that the matter was still undecided—that more time (which a coy young maiden might reasonably demand) had been granted! On the other hand, he feared that her clear, firm integrity of character would be repelled by the nature of his motive. He was beginning to feel, greatly to his own surprise, a profound respect for her.

"If my father questions me about your visit," she said, "I shall tell him simply that I have declined your offer. No one else is likely to ask me."

"I don't deny," he continued, still lingering near the door, "that I've been urged by my father—yours, too, for that matter—to make the offer. But I don't want you to think hard of me. I've not had an easy time of it, and if you knew everything, you'd see that a good deal isn't rightly to be laid to my account."

He spoke sadly, and so genuine a stamp of unhappiness was impressed upon his face, that Martha's feeling of commiseration rose to the surface.

"You'll speak to me, when we happen to meet?" he said.

"If I did not," she answered, "every one would suspect that something had occurred. That would be unpleasant for both of us. Do not think that I shall bear malice against you; on the contrary, I wish you well."

He stooped, kissed her hand, and then swiftly, silently, and with averted head, left the room.

CHAPTER XVII. – CONSULTATIONS.

When Dr. Deane returned home, in season for supper, he found Martha and Betsy Lavender employed about their little household matters. The former showed no lack of cheerfulness or composure, nor, on the other hand, any such nervous unrest as would be natural to a maiden whose hand had just been asked in marriage. The Doctor could not at all guess, from her demeanor, whether anything had happened during his absence. That Alfred Barton had not remained was rather an unfavorable circumstance; but then, possibly, he had not found courage to speak. All things being considered, it seemed best that he should say nothing to Martha, until he had had another interview with his prospective son-in-law.

At this time Gilbert Potter, in ignorance of the cunning plans which were laid by the old men, was working early and late to accomplish all necessary farm-labor by the first of October. That month he had resolved to devote to the road between Columbia and Newport, and if but average success attended his hauling, the earnings of six round trips, with the result of his bountiful harvest, would at last place in his hands the sum necessary to defray the remaining debt upon the farm. His next year's wheat-crop was already sowed, the seed-clover cut, and the fortnight which still intervened was to be devoted to threshing. In this emergency, as at reaping-time, when it was difficult to obtain extra hands, he depended on Deb. Smith, and she did not fail him.

Her principal home, when she was not employed on farm-work, was a log-hut, on the edge of a wood, belonging to the next farm north of Fairthorn's. This farm—the "Woodrow property," as it was called—had been stripped of its stock and otherwise pillaged by the British troops, (Howe and Cornwallis having had their headquarters at Kennett Square), the day previous to the Battle of Brandywine, and the proprietor had never since recovered from his losses. The place presented a ruined and desolated appearance, and Deb. Smith, for that reason perhaps, had settled herself in the original log-cabin of the first settler, beside a swampy bit of ground, near the road. The Woodrow farm-house was on a ridge beyond the wood, and no other dwelling was in sight.

The mysterious manner of life of this woman had no doubt given rise to the bad name which she bore in the neighborhood. She would often disappear for a week or two at a time, and her return seemed to take place invariably in the night. Sometimes a belated farmer would see the single front window of her cabin lighted at midnight, and hear the dulled sound of voices in the stillness. But no one cared to play the spy upon her movements very closely; her great strength and fierce, reckless temper made her dangerous, and her hostility would have been worse than the itching of ungratified curiosity. So they let her alone, taking their revenge in the character they ascribed to her, and the epithets they attached to her name.

When Gilbert, after hitching his horse in a corner of the zigzag picket-fence, climbed over and approached the cabin, Deb. Smith issued from it to meet him, closing the heavy plank door carefully behind her.

"So, Mr. Gilbert!" she cried, stretching out her hard, red hand, "I reckon you want me ag'in: I've been holdin off from many jobs o' thrashin', this week, because I suspicioned ye'd be comin' for me."

"Thank you, Deborah!" said he, "you're a friend in need."

"Am I? There you speak the truth. Wait till you see me thump the Devil's tattoo with my old flail on your thrashin'-floor! But you look as cheery as an Easter-mornin' sun; you've not much for to complain of, these days, I guess?"

Gilbert smiled.

"Take care!" she cried, a kindly softness spreading over her rough face, "good luck's deceitful! If I had the strands o' your fortin' in my hands, may be I wouldn't twist 'em even; but I ha'n't, and my fingers is too thick to manage anything smaller 'n a rope-knot. You're goin'? Well, look out for me bright and early o' Monday, and my sarvice to your mother!"

As he rode over the second hill, on his way to the village, Gilbert's heart leaped, as he beheld Betsy Lavender just turning into Fairthorn's gate. Except his mother, she was the only person who knew of his love, and he had great need of her kind and cautious assistance.

He had not allowed his heart simply to revel in the ecstasy of its wonderful fortune, or to yearn with inexpressible warmth for Martha's dearest presence, though these emotions haunted him constantly; he had also endeavored to survey the position in which he stood, and to choose the course which would fulfil both his duty towards her and towards his mother. His coming independence would have made the prospect hopefully bright, but for the secret which lay across it like a threatening shadow. Betsy Lavender's assurances had only partially allayed his dread; something hasty and uncertain in her manner still lingered uneasily in his memory, and he felt sure that she knew more than she was willing to tell. Moreover, he craved with all the strength of his heart for another interview with Martha, and he knew of no way to obtain it without Betsy's help.

Her hand was on the gate-latch when his call reached her ears. Looking up the road, she saw that he had stopped his horse between the high, bushy banks, and was beckoning earnestly. Darting a hasty glance at the ivy-draped windows nearest the road, and finding that she was not observed, she hurried to meet him.

"Betsy," he whispered, "I must see Martha again before I leave, and you must tell me how."

"Tell me how. Folks say that lovyers' wits are sharp," said she, "but I wouldn't give much for either o' your'n. I don't like underhanded goin's-on, for my part, for things done in darkness'll come to light, or somethin' like it; but never mind, if they're crooked everyway they won't run in straight tracks, all't once't. This I see, and you see, and she sees, that we must all keep as dark as sin."

"But there must be some way," Gilbert insisted. "Do you never walk out together? And couldn't we arrange a time—you, too, Betsy, I want you as well!"

"I'm afeard I'd be like the fifth wheel to a wagon."

"No, no! You must be there—you must hear a good part of what I have to say."

"A good part—that'll do; thought you didn't mean the whole. Don't fret so, lad; you'll have Roger trampin' me down, next thing. Martha and me talk o' walkin' over to Polly Withers's. She promised Martha a pa'tridge-breasted aloe, and they say you've got to plant it in pewter sand, and only water it once't a month, and how it can grow I can't see; but never mind, all the same—s'pose we say Friday afternoon about three o'clock, goin' through the big woods between the Square and Witherses, and you might have a gun, for the squirls is plenty, and so accidental-like, if anybody should come along"—

"That's it, Betsy!" Gilbert cried, his face flashing, "thank you, a thousand times!"

"A thousand times," she repeated. "Once't is enough."

Gilbert rode homewards, after a pleasant call at Fairthorn's, in a very joyous mood. Not daring to converse with his mother on the one subject which filled his heart, he showed her the calculations which positively assured his independence in a short time. She was never weary of going over the figures, and although her sad, cautious nature always led her to anticipate disappointments, there was now so much already in hand that she was forced to share her son's sanguine views. Gilbert could not help noticing that this idea of independence, for which she had labored so strenuously, seemed to be regarded, in her mind, as the first step towards her mysterious and long-delayed justification; she was so impatient for its accomplishment, her sad brow lightened so, her breath came so much freer as she admitted that his calculations were correct!

Nevertheless, as he frequently referred to the matter on the following days, she at last said,—

"Please, Gilbert, don't always talk so certainly of what isn't over and settled! It makes me fearsome, so to take Providence for granted beforehand. I don't think the Lord likes it, for I've often noticed that it brings disappointment; and I'd rather be humble and submissive in heart, the better to deserve our

174

good fortune when it comes."

"You may be right, mother," he answered; "but it's pleasant to me to see you looking a little more hopeful."

"Ay, lad, I'd never look otherwise, for your sake, if I could." And nothing more was said.

Before sunrise on Monday morning, the rapid, alternate beats of three flails, on Gilbert's threshing-floor, made the autumnal music which the farmer loves to hear. Two of these—Gilbert's and Sam's—kept time with each other, one falling as the other rose; but the third, quick, loud, and filling all the pauses with thundering taps, was wielded by the arm of Deb. Smith. Day by day, the pile of wheat-sheaves lessened in the great bay, and the cone of golden straw rose higher in the barn-yard. If a certain black jug, behind the barn-door, needed frequent replenishing, Gilbert knew that the strength of its contents passed into the red, bare, muscular arms which shamed his own, and that Deb., while she was under his roof, would allow herself no coarse excess, either of manner or speech. The fierce, defiant look left her face, and when she sat, of an evening, with her pipe in the chimney-corner, both mother and son found her very entertaining company. In Sam she inspired at once admiration and despair. She could take him by the slack of the waist-band and lift him at arm's-length, and he felt that he should never be "a full hand," if he were obliged to equal her performances with the flail.

Thus, his arm keeping time to the rhythm of joy in his heart, and tasting the satisfaction of labor as never before in his life, the days passed to Gilbert Potter. Then came the important Friday, hazy with "the smoke of burning summer," and softly colored with the drifts of golden-rods and crimson sumac leaves along the edges of the yet green forests. Easily feigning an errand to the village, he walked rapidly up the road in the warm afternoon, taking the cross-road to New-Garden just before reaching Hallowell's, and then struck to the right across the fields.

After passing the crest of the hill, the land sloped gradually down to the eastern end of Tuffkenamon valley, which terminates at the ridge upon which Kennett Square stands. Below him, on the right, lay the field and hedge, across which he and Fortune (he wondered what had become of the man) had followed the chase; and before him, on the level, rose the stately trees of the wood which was to be his trysting-place. It was a sweet, peaceful scene, and but for the under-current of trouble upon which all his sensations floated, he could have recognized the beauty and the bliss of human life, which such golden days suggest.

It was scarcely yet two o'clock, and he watched the smooth field nearest the village for full three-quarters of an hour, before his sharp eyes could detect any moving form upon its surface. To impatience succeeded doubt, to doubt, at its most cruel height, a shock of certainty. Betsy Lavender and Martha Deane had entered the field at the bottom, and, concealed behind the hedge of black-thorn, had walked half-way to the wood before he discovered them, by means of a lucky break in the hedge. With breathless haste he descended the slope, entered the wood at its lower edge, and traversed the tangled thickets of dogwood and haw, until he gained the foot-path, winding through the very heart of the shade.

It was not many minutes before the two advancing forms glimmered among the leaves. As he sprang forward to meet them, Miss Betsy Lavender suddenly exclaimed,—"Well, I never, Martha! here's wintergreen!" and was down on her knees, on the dead leaves, with her long nose nearly touching the plants.

When the lovers saw each other's eyes, one impulse drew them heart to heart. Each felt the clasp of the other's arms, and the sweetness of that perfect kiss, which is mutually given, as mutually taken,—the ripe fruit of love, which having once tasted, all its first timid tokens seem ever afterwards immature and unsatisfactory. The hearts of both had unconsciously grown in warmth, in grace and tenderness; and they now felt, for the first time, the utter, reciprocal surrender of their natures which truly gave them to each other.

As they slowly unwound the blissful embrace, and, holding each other's hands, drew their faces apart until either's eyes could receive the other's beloved countenance, no words were spoken,—and none were needed.

176

Thenceforward, neither would ever say to the other,—"Do you love me as well as ever?" or "Are you sure you can never change?"—for theirs were natures to which such tender doubt and curiosity were foreign. It was not the age of introversion or analytical love; they were sound, simple, fervent natures, and believed forever in the great truth which had come to them.

"Gilbert," said Martha, presently, "it was right that we should meet before you leave home. I have much to tell you—for now you must know everything that concerns me; it is your right."

Her words were very grateful. To hear her say "It is your right," sent a thrill of purely unselfish pride through his breast. He admitted an equal right, on her part; the moments were precious, and he hastened to answer her declaration by one as frank and confiding.

"And I," he said, "could not take another step until I had seen you. Do not fear, Martha, to test my patience or my faith in you, for anything you may put upon me will be easy to bear. I have turned our love over and over in my mind; tried to look at it—as we both must, sooner or later—as something which, though it don't in any wise belong to others, yet with which others have the power to interfere. The world isn't made quite right, Martha, and we're living in it."

Martha's lip took a firmer curve. "Our love is right, Gilbert," she exclaimed, "and the world must give way!"

"It must—I've sworn it! Now let us try to see what are the mountains in our path, and how we can best get around or over them. First, this is my position."

Thereupon Gilbert clearly and rapidly explained to her his precise situation. He set forth his favorable prospects of speedy independence, the obstacle which his mother's secret threw in their way, and his inability to guess any means which might unravel the mystery, and hasten his and her deliverance. The disgrace once removed, he thought, all other impediments to their union would be of trifling importance.

"I see all that clearly," said Martha, when he had finished; "now, this is my position."

She told him frankly her father's plans concerning her and gave him, with conscientious minuteness, all the details of Alfred Barton's interview. At first his face grew dark, but at the close he was able to view the subject in its true character, and to contemplate it with as careless a merriment as her own.

"You see, Gilbert," were Martha's final words, "how we are situated. If I marry, against my father's consent, before I am twenty-five"—

"Don't speak of your property, Martha!" he cried; "I never took that into mind!"

"I know you didn't. Gilbert, but I do! It is mine, and must be mine, to be yours; here you must let me have my own way—I will obey you in everything else. Four years is not long for us to wait, having faith in each other; and in that time, I doubt not, your mother's secret will be revealed. You cannot, must not, press her further; in the meantime we will see each other as often as possible"—

"Four years!" Gilbert interrupted, in a tone almost of despair.

"Well—not quite," said Martha, smiling archly; "since you must know my exact age, Gilbert, I was twenty-one on the second of last February; so that the time is really three years, four months, and eleven days."

"I'd serve seven years, as Jacob served, if need be," he said. "It's not alone the waiting; it's the anxiety, the uncertainty, the terrible fear of that which I don't know. I'm sure that Betsy Lavender guesses something about it; have you told her what my mother says?"

"It was your secret, Gilbert."

"I didn't think," he answered, softly. "But it's well she should know. She is the best friend we have. Betsy!"

"A mortal long time afore I'm wanted!" exclaimed Miss Lavender, with assumed grimness, as she obeyed the call. "I s'pose you thought there was no watch needed, and both ends o' the path open to all the world. Well—what

178

am I to do?—move mountains like a grain o' mustard seed (or however it runs), dip out th' ocean with a pint-pot, or ketch old birds with chaff, eh?"

Gilbert, aware that she was familiar with the particular difficulties on Martha's side, now made her acquainted with his own. At the mention of his mother's declaration in regard to his birth, she lifted her hands and nodded her head, listening, thenceforth to the end, with half-closed eyes and her loose lips drawn up in a curious pucker.

"What do you think of it?" he asked, as she remained silent.

"Think of it? About as pretty a snarl as ever I see. I can't say as I'm so over and above taken aback by what your mother says. I've all along had a hankerin' suspicion of it in my bones. Some things seems to me like the smell o' water-melons, that I've knowed to come with fresh snow; you know there is no water-melons, but then, there's the smell of 'em! But it won't do to hurry a matter o' this kind—long-sufferin' and slow to anger, though that don't quite suit, but never mind, all the same—my opinion is, ye've both o' ye got to wait!"

"Betsy, do you know nothing about it? Can you guess nothing?" Gilbert persisted.

She stole a quick glance at Martha, which he detected, and a chill ran through his blood. His face grew pale.

"Nothin' that fits your case," said Miss Lavender, presently. She saw the renewal of Gilbert's suspicion, and was casting about in her mind how to allay it without indicating something else which she wished to conceal. "This I'll say," she exclaimed at last, with desperate frankness, "that I do know somethin' that may be o' use, when things comes to the wust, as I hope they won't, but it's neither here nor there so far as you two are concerned; so don't ask me, for I won't tell, and if it's to be done, I'm the only one to do it! If I've got my little secrets, I'm keepin' 'em in your interest, remember that!"

There was the glimmer of a tear in each of Miss Lavender's eyes before she knew it.

"Betsy, my dear friend!" cried Gilbert, "we know you and trust you.

179

Only say this, for my sake—that you think my mother's secret is nothing which will part Martha and me!"

"Martha and me. I do think so—am I a dragon, or a—what's that Job talks about?—a behemoth? It's no use; we must all wait and see what'll turn up. But, Martha, I've rather a bright thought, for a wonder; what if we could bring Alf. Barton into the plot, and git him to help us for the sake o' his bein' helped?"

Martha looked surprised, but Gilbert flushed up to the roots of his hair, and set his lips firmly together.

"I dunno as it'll do," continued Miss Betsy, with perfect indifference to these signs, "but then it might. First and foremost, we must try to find out what he wants, for it isn't you, Martha; so you, Gilbert, might as well be a little more of a cowcumber than you are at this present moment. But if it's nothin' ag'inst the law, and not likely, for he's too cute, we might even use a vessel—well, not exackly o' wrath, but somethin' like it. There's more 'n one concern at work in all this, it strikes me, and it's wuth while to know 'em all."

Gilbert was ashamed of his sensitiveness in regard to Barton, especially after Martha's frank and merry confession; so he declared himself entirely willing to abide by her judgment.

"It would not be pleasant to have Alfred Barton associated with us, even in the way of help," she said. "I have a woman's curiosity to know what he means, I confess, but, unless Betsy could make the discovery without me, I would not take any steps towards it."

"Much would be fittin' to me, child," said Miss Lavender, "that wouldn't pass for you, at all. We've got six weeks till Gilbert comes back, and no need o' hurry, except our arrand to Polly Withers's, which'll come to nothin', unless you each take leave of other mighty quick, while I'm lookin' for some more wintergreen."

With these words she turned short around and strode away.

"It had best be our own secret yet, Martha?" he asked.

"Yes, Gilbert, and all the more precious."

They clasped hands and kissed, once, twice, thrice, and then the underwood slowly deepened between them, and the shadows of the forest separated them from each other.

CHAPTER XVIII. — SANDY FLASH REAPPEARS.

During the month of October, while Gilbert Potter was occupied with his lonely and monotonous task, he had ample leisure to evolve a clear, calm, happy purpose from the tumult of his excited feelings. This was, first, to accomplish his own independence, which now seemed inevitably necessary, for his mother's sake, and its possible consequences to her; then, strong in the knowledge of Martha Deane's fidelity, to wait with her.

With the exception of a few days of rainy weather, his hauling prospered, and he returned home after five weeks' absence, to count up the gains of the year and find that very little was lacking of the entire amount to be paid.

Mary Potter, as the prospect of release drew so near, became suddenly anxious and restless. The knowledge that a very large sum of money (as she considered it) was in the house, filled her with a thousand new fears. There were again rumors of Sandy Flash lurking around Marlborough, and she shuddered and trembled whenever his name was mentioned. Her uneasiness became at last so great that Gilbert finally proposed writing to the conveyancer in Chester who held the mortgage, and asking whether the money might not as well be paid at once, since he had it in hand, as wait until the following spring.

"It's not the regular way," said she, "but then, I suppose it'll hold in law. You can ask Mr. Trainer about that. O Gilbert, if it can be done, it'll take a great load off my mind!"

"Whatever puts the mortgage into my hands, mother," said he, "is legal enough for us. I needn't even wait to sell the grain; Mark Deane will lend me the seventy-five dollars still to be made up, if he has them—or, if he can't, somebody else will. I was going to the Square this evening; so I'll write the letter at once, and put it in the office."

The first thing Gilbert did, on reaching the village, was to post the letter in season for the mail-rider, who went once a week to and fro between

Chester and Peach-bottom Ferry, on the Susquehanna. Then he crossed the street to Dr. Deane's, in order to inquire for Mark, but with the chief hope of seeing Martha for one sweet moment, at least. In this, however, he was disappointed; as he reached the gate, Mark issued from the door.

"Why, Gilbert, old boy!" he shouted; "the sight o' you's good for sore eyes! What have you been about since that Sunday evening we rode up the west branch? I was jist steppin' over to the tavern to see the fellows—come along, and have a glass o' Rye!"

He threw his heavy arm over Gilbert's shoulder, and drew him along.

"In a minute, Mark; wait a bit—I've a little matter of business with you. I need to borrow seventy-five dollars for a month or six weeks, until my wheat is sold. Have you that much that you're not using?"

"That and more comin' to me soon," said Mark, "and of course you can have it. Want it right away?"

"Very likely in ten or twelve days."

"Oh, well, never fear—I'll have some accounts squared by that time! Come along!" And therewith the good-natured fellow hurried his friend into the bar-room of the Unicorn.

"Done pretty well, haulin', this time?" asked Mark, as they touched glasses.

"Very well," answered Gilbert, "seeing it's the last time. I'm at an end with hauling now."

"You don't say so? Here's to your good luck!" exclaimed Mark, emptying his glass.

A man, who had been tilting his chair against the wall, in the farther corner of the room, now arose and came forward. It was Alfred Barton.

During Gilbert's absence, neither this gentleman's plan nor that of his father, had made much progress. It was tolerably easy, to be sure, to give the old man the impression that the preliminary arrangements with regard to money were going on harmoniously; but it was not so easy to procure Dr. Deane's acceptance of the part marked out for him. Alfred had sought an interview with the latter soon after that which he had had with Martha, and the result was not at all satisfactory. The wooer had been obliged to declare that his suit was unsuccessful; but, he believed, only temporarily so. Martha had been taken by surprise; the question had come upon her so suddenly that she could scarcely be said to know her own mind, and time must be allowed her. Although this statement seemed probable to Dr. Deane, as it coincided with his own experience in previously sounding his daughter's mind, yet Alfred's evident anxiety that nothing should be said to Martha upon the subject, and that the Doctor should assume to his father that the question of balancing her legacy was as good as settled, (then proceed at once to the discussion of the second and more important question,) excited the Doctor's suspicions. He could not well avoid giving the required promise in relation to Martha, but he insisted on seeing the legal evidences of Alfred Barton's property, before going a step further.

The latter was therefore in a state of great perplexity. The game he was playing seemed safe enough, so far, but nothing had come of it, and beyond this point it could not be carried, without great increase of risk. He was more than once tempted to drop it entirely, confessing his complete and final rejection, and allowing his father to take what course he pleased; but presently the itching of his avaricious curiosity returned in full force, and suggested new expedients.

No suspicion of Gilbert Potter's relation to Martha Deane had ever entered his mind. He had always had a liking for the young man, and would, no doubt, have done him any good service which did not require the use of money. He now came forward very cordially and shook-hands with the two.

Gilbert had self-possession enough to control his first impulse, and to meet his rival with his former manner. Secure in his own fortune, he even felt that he could afford to be magnanimous, and thus, by degrees, the dislike wore off which Martha's confession had excited.

"What is all this talk about Sandy Flash?" he asked.

184

"He's been seen up above," said Barton; "some say, about Marlborough, and some, along the Strasburg road. He'll hardly come this way; he's too cunning to go where the people are prepared to receive him."

If either of the three had happened to look steadily at the back window of the bar-room, they might have detected, in the dusk, the face of Dougherty, the Irish ostler of the Unicorn Tavern. It disappeared instantly, but there was a crack nearly half an inch wide between the bottom of the back-door and the sill under it, and to that crack a large, flat ear was laid.

"If he comes any nearer, you must send word around at once," said Gilbert,—"not wait until he's already among us."

"Let me alone for that!" Barton exclaimed; "Damn him, I only wish he had pluck enough to come!"

Mark was indignant "What's the sheriff and constables good for?" he cried. "It's a burnin' shame that the whole country has been plundered so long, and the fellow still runnin' at large. Much he cares for the five hundred dollars on his head."

"It's a thousand, now," said Barton. "They've doubled it."

"Come, that'd be a good haul for us. We're not bound to keep inside of our township; I'm for an up and down chase all over the country, as soon as the fall work's over!"

"And I, too," said Gilbert

"You 're fellows after my own heart, both o' you!" Barton asserted, slapping them upon the back. "What'll you take to drink?"

By this time several others had assembled, and the conversation became general. While the flying rumors about Sandy Flash were being produced and discussed, Barton drew Gilbert aside.

"Suppose we step out on the back-porch," he said, "I want to have a word with you."

The door closed between them and the noisy bar-room. There was a rustling noise under the porch, as of a fowl disturbed on its roost, and then everything was still.

"Your speaking of your having done well by hauling put it into my head, Gilbert," Barton continued. "I wanted to borrow a little money for a while, and there's reasons why I shouldn't call upon anybody who'd tell of it. Now, as you've got it, lying idle"—

"It happens to be just the other way, Barton," said Gilbert, interrupting him. "I came here to-night to borrow."

"How's that?" Barton could not help asking, with a momentary sense of chagrin. But the next moment he added, in a milder tone, "I don't mean to pry into your business."

"I shall very likely have to use my money soon," Gilbert explained, "and must at least wait until I hear from Chester. That will be another week, and then, if the money should not be wanted, I can accommodate you. But, to tell you the truth, I don't think there's much chance of that."

"Shall you have to go down to Chester?"

"I hope so."

"When?"

"In ten or twelve days from now."

"Then," said Barton, "I 'll fix it this way. 'Tisn't only the money I want, but to have it paid in Chester, without the old man or Stacy knowing anything of the matter. If I was to go myself, Stacy'd never rest till he found out my business—Faith! I believe if I was hid in the hayloft o' the William Penn Tavern, he'd scent me out. Now, I can get the money of another fellow I know, if you'll take it down and hand it over for me. Would you be that obliging?"

"Of course," Gilbert answered. "If I go it will be no additional trouble."

"All right," said Barton, "between ourselves, you understand."

A week later, a letter, with the following address was brought to the post-office by the mail-rider,—

"To Mr. Gilbert Potter, Esq. Kennett Square P. O. These, with Care and Speed."

Gilbert, having carefully cut around the wafer and unfolded the sheet of strong yellowish paper, read this missive,—

"Sir: Yr respd favour of ye [Footnote: This form of the article, though in general disuse at the time, was still frequently employed in epistolary writing, in that part of Pennsylvania. [ed note: The r in Yr and e in ye, etc. are superscripted.]] 11th came duly to hand, and ye proposition wh it contains has been submitted to Mr. Jones, ye present houlder of ye mortgage. He wishes me to inform you that he did not anticipate ye payment before ye first day of April, 1797, wh was ye term agreed upon at ye payment of ye first note; nevertheless, being required to accept full and lawful payment, whensoever tendered, he hath impowered me to receive ye moneys at yr convenience, providing ye settlement be full and compleat, as aforesaid, and not merely ye payment of a part or portion thereof.

"Yr obt servt,

"ISAAC TRAINER."

Gilbert, with his limited experience of business matters, had entirely overlooked the fact, that the permission of the creditor is not necessary to the payment of a debt. He had a profound respect for all legal forms, and his indebtedness carried with it a sense of stern and perpetual responsibility, which, alas! has not always been inherited by the descendants of that simple and primitive period.

Mary Potter received the news with a sigh of relief. The money was again counted, the interest which would be due somewhat laboriously computed, and finally nothing remained but the sum which Mark Deane had promised to furnish. This Mark expected to receive on the following Wednesday, and Gilbert and his mother agreed that the journey to Chester should be made at the close of the same week.

They went over these calculations in the quiet of the Sabbath afternoon, sitting alone in the neat, old-fashioned kitchen, with the dim light of an Indian-summer sun striking through the leafless trumpet-vines, and making a quaint network of light and shade on the whitewashed window-frame. The pendulum ticked drowsily along the opposite wall, and the hickory back-log on the hearth hummed a lamentable song through all its simmering pores of sap. Peaceful as the happy landscape without, dozing in dreams of the departed summer, cheery as the tidy household signs within, seemed at last the lives of the two inmates. Mary Potter had not asked how her son's wooing had further sped, but she felt that he was contented of heart; she, too, indulging finally in the near consummation of her hopes,—which touched her like the pitying sympathy of the Power that had dealt so singularly with her life,—was nearer the feeling of happiness than she had been for long and weary years.

Gilbert was moved by the serenity of her face, and the trouble, which he knew it concealed, seemed, to his mind, to be wearing away. Carefully securing the doors, they walked over the fields together, pausing on the hilltop to listen to the caw of the gathering crows, or to watch the ruby disc of the beamless sun stooping to touch the western rim of the valley. Many a time had they thus gone over the farm together, but never before with such a sense of peace and security. The day was removed, mysteriously, from the circle of its fellows, and set apart by a peculiar influence which prevented either from ever forgetting it, during all the years that came after.

They were not aware that at the very moment this influence was profoundest in their hearts, new rumors of Sandy Flash's movements had reached Kennett Square, and were being excitedly discussed at the Unicorn Tavern. He had been met on the Street Road, riding towards the Red Lion, that very afternoon, by a man who knew his face; and, later in the evening came a second report, that an individual of his build had crossed the Philadelphia Road, this side of the Anvil, and gone southward into the woods. Many were the surmises, and even detailed accounts, of robberies that either had been or might be committed, but no one could say precisely how much was true.

Mark Deane was not at home, and the blacksmith was commissioned to summon Alfred Barton, who had ridden over to Pennsbury, on a friendly visit to Mr. Joel Ferris. When he finally made his appearance, towards ten o'clock, he was secretly horror-stricken at the great danger he had escaped; but it gave him an admirable opportunity to swagger. He could do no less than promise to summon the volunteers in the morning, and provision was made accordingly, for despatching as many messengers as the village could afford.

Since the British occupation, nearly twenty years before, Kennett Square had not known as lively a day as that which followed. The men and boys were in the street, grouped in front of the tavern, the women at the windows, watching, some with alarmed, but many with amused faces. Sally Fairthorn, although it was washing-day, stole up through Dr. Deane's garden and into Martha's room, for at least half an hour, but Joe and Jake left their overturned shocks of corn unhusked for the whole day.

Some of the young farmers to whom the message had been sent, returned answer that they were very busy and could not leave their work; the horses of others were lame; the guns of others broken. By ten o'clock, however, there were nine volunteers, very irregularly armed and mounted, in attendance; by eleven o'clock, thirteen, and Alfred Barton, whose place as leader was anything but comfortable, began to swell with an air of importance, and set about examining the guns of his command. Neither he nor any one else noticed particularly that the Irish ostler appeared to be a great connoisseur in muskets, and was especially interested in the structure of the flints and pans.

"Let's look over the roll, and see how many are true blue," said Barton, drawing a paper from his pocket. "There's failing nine or ten, among 'em some I fully counted on—Withers, he may come yet; Ferris, hardly time to get word; but Carson, Potter, and Travilla ought to turn up curst soon, or we'll have the sport without 'em!"

"Give me a horse, Mr. Barton, and I'll ride down for Gilbert!" cried Joe Fairthorn.

"No use,—Giles went this morning," growled Barton.

"It's time we were starting; which road would be best to take?" asked one of the volunteers.

"All roads lead to Rome, but all don't lead to Sandy Flash, ha! ha!" said another, laughing at his own smartness.

"Who knows where he was seen last?" Barton asked, but it was not easy to get a coherent answer. One had heard one report, and another another; he had been seen from the Street Road on the north all the way around eastward by the Red Lion and the Anvil, and in the rocky glen below the Barton farm, to the lime-quarries of Tuffkenamon on the west.

"Unless we scatter, it'll be like looking for a needle in a haystack," remarked one of the more courageous volunteers.

"If they'd all had spunk enough to come," said Barton, "we might ha' made four parties, and gone out on each road. As it is, we're only strong enough for two."

"Seven to one?—that's too much odds in Sandy's favor!" cried a light-headed youth, whereat the others all laughed, and some of them blushed a little.

Barton bit his lip, and with a withering glance at the young man, replied,—"Then we'll make three parties, and you shall be the third."

Another quarter of an hour having elapsed, without any accession to the troop, Barton reluctantly advised the men to get their arms, which had been carelessly placed along the tavern-porch, and to mount for the chase.

Just then Joe and Jake Fairthorn, who had been dodging back and forth through the village, watching the roads, made their appearance with the announcement,—

"Hurray—there's another—comin' up from below, but it a'n't Gilbert. He's stuck full o' pistols, but he's a-foot, and you must git him a horse. I tell you, he looks like a real buster!"

"Who can it be?" asked Barton.

"We'll see, in a minute," said the nearest volunteers, taking up their muskets.

190

"There he is,—there he is!" cried Joe.

All eyes, turned towards the crossing of the roads, beheld, just rounding the corner-house, fifty paces distant, a short, broad-shouldered, determined figure, making directly for the tavern. His face was red and freckled, his thin lips half-parted with a grin which showed the flash of white teeth between them, and his eyes sparkled with the light of a cold, fierce courage. He had a double-barrelled musket on his shoulder, and there were four pistols in the tight leathern belt about his waist.

Barton turned deadly pale as he beheld this man. An astonished silence fell upon the group, but, the next moment, some voice exclaimed, in an undertone, which, nevertheless, every one heard,—

"By the living Lord! Sandy Flash himself!"

There was a general confused movement, of which Alfred Barton took advantage to partly cover his heavy body by one of the porch-pillars. Some of the volunteers started back, others pressed closer together. The pert youth, alone, who was to form the third party, brought his musket to his shoulder.

Quick as lightning Sandy Flash drew a pistol from his belt and levelled it at the young man's breast.

"Ground arms!" he cried, "or you are a dead man."

He was obeyed, although slowly and with grinding teeth.

"Stand aside!" he then commanded. "You have pluck, and I should hate to shoot you. Make way, the rest o' ye! I've saved ye the trouble o' ridin' far to find me. Whoever puts finger to trigger, falls. Back, back, I say, and open the door for me!"

Still advancing as he spoke, and shifting his pistol so as to cover now one, now another of the group, he reached the tavern-porch. Some one opened the door of the barroom, which swung inwards. The highwayman strode directly to the bar, and there stood, facing the open door, while he cried to the trembling bar-keeper,—

"A glass o' Rye, good and strong!"

It was set before him. Holding the musket in his arm, he took the glass, drank, wiped his mouth with the back of his hand, and then, spinning a silver dollar into the air, said, as it rang upon the floor,—

"I stand treat to-day; let the rest o' the gentlemen drink at my expense!"

He then walked out, and slowly retreated backwards towards the corner-house, covering his retreat with the levelled pistol, and the flash of his dauntless eye.

He had nearly reached the corner, when Gilbert Potter dashed up behind him, with Roger all in a foam. Joe Fairthorn, seized with deadly terror when he heard the terrible name, had set off at full speed for home; but descrying Gilbert approaching on a gallop, changed his course, met the latter, and gasped out the astounding intelligence. All this was the work of a minute, and when Gilbert reached the corner, a single glance showed him the true state of affairs. The confused group in front of the tavern, some faces sallow with cowardice, some red with indignation and shame; the solitary, retreating figure, alive in every nerve with splendid courage, told him the whole story, which Joe's broken words had only half hinted.

Flinging himself from his horse, he levelled his musket, and cried out,—

"Surrender!"

Sandy Flash, with a sudden spring, placed his back against the house, pointed his pistol at Gilbert, and said: "Drop your gun, or I fire!"

For answer, Gilbert drew the trigger; the crack of the explosion rang sharp and clear, and a little shower of mortar covered Sandy Flash's cocked hat. The ball had struck the wall about four inches above his head.

He leaped forward; Gilbert clubbed his musket and awaited him. They were scarcely two yards apart; the highwayman's pistol-barrel was opposite Gilbert's heart, and the two men were looking into each other's eyes. The group in front of the tavern stood as if paralyzed, every man holding his breath.

"Halt!" said Sandy Flash. "Halt! I hate bloodshed, and besides that, young Potter, you're not the man that'll take me prisoner. I could blow your brains out by movin' this finger, but you're safe from any bullet o' mine, whoever a'n't!"

At the last words a bright, mocking, malicious grin stole over his face. Gilbert, amazed to find himself known to the highwayman, and puzzled with certain familiar marks in the latter's countenance, was swiftly enlightened by this grin. It was Fortune's face before him, without the black hair and whiskers,—and Fortune's voice that spoke!

Sandy Flash saw the recognition. He grinned again. "You'll know your friend, another time," he said, sprang five feet backward, whirled, gained the cover of the house, and was mounting his horse among the bushes at the bottom of the garden, before any of the others reached Gilbert, who was still standing as if thunder-struck.

By this time Sandy Flash had leaped the hedge and was careering like lightning towards the shelter of the woods. The interest now turned upon Gilbert Potter, who was very taciturn and thoughtful, and had little to relate. They noticed, however, that his eyes were turned often and inquiringly upon Alfred Barton, and that the latter as steadily avoided meeting them.

When Gilbert went to bring Roger, who had quietly waited at the crossing of the roads, Deb. Smith suddenly made her appearance.

"I seen it all," she said. "I was a bit up the road, but I seen it. You shouldn't ha' shot, Mr. Gilbert, though it isn't him that's born to be hit with a bullet; but you're safe enough from his bullets, anyhow—whatever happens, you're safe!"

"What do you mean, Deborah?" he exclaimed, as she almost repeated to him Sandy Flash's very words.

"I mean what I say," she answered. "You wouldn't be afeard, but it'll be a comfort to your mother. I must have a drink o' whiskey after that sight."

With these words she elbowed her way into the barroom. Most of the Kennett Volunteers were there engaged in carrying out a similar resolution.

They would gladly have kept the whole occurrence secret, but that was impossible. It was known all over the country, in three days, and the story of it has not yet died out of the local annals.

CHAPTER XIX. — THE HUSKING FROLIC.

Jake Fairthorn rushed into Dr. Deane's door with a howl of terror.

"Cousin Martha! Betsy!" he cried; "he's goin' to shoot Gilbert!"

"None o' your tricks, boy!" Betsy Lavender exclaimed, in her most savage tone, as she saw the paleness of Martha's face. "I'm up to 'em. Who'd shoot Gilbert Potter? Not Alf Barton, I'll be bound; he'd be afeard to shoot even Sandy Flash!"

"It's Sandy Flash,—he's there! Gilbert shot his hat off!" cried Jake.

"The Lord have mercy!" And the next minute Miss Betsy found herself, she scarcely knew how, in the road.

Both had heard the shot, but supposed that it was some volunteer discharging an old load from his musket; they knew nothing of Sandy's visit to the Unicorn, and Jake's announcement seemed simply incredible.

"O you wicked boy! What'll become o' you?" cried Miss Lavender, as she beheld Gilbert Potter approaching, leading Roger by the bridle. But at the same instant she saw, from the faces of the crowd, that something unusual had happened. While the others instantly surrounded Gilbert, the young volunteer who alone had made any show of fight, told the story to the two ladies. Martha Deane's momentary shock of terror disappeared under the rush of mingled pride and scorn which the narrative called up in her heart.

"What a pack of cowards!" she exclaimed, her cheeks flushing,—"to stand still and see the life of the only man that dares to face a robber at the mercy of the robber's pistol!"

Gilbert approached. His face was grave and thoughtful, but his eye brightened as it met hers. No two hands ever conveyed so many and such swift messages as theirs, in the single moment when they touched each other. The other women of the village crowded around, and he was obliged, though with evident reluctance, to relate his share in the event.

In the mean time the volunteers had issued from the tavern, and were loudly discussing what course to pursue. The most of them were in favor of instant pursuit. To their credit it must be said that very few of them were actual cowards; they had been both surprised by the incredible daring of the highwayman, and betrayed by the cowardly inefficiency of their own leader. Barton, restored to his usual complexion by two glasses of whiskey, was nearly ready to head a chase which he suspected would come to nothing; but the pert young volunteer, who had been whispering with some of the younger men, suddenly cried out,—

"I say, fellows, we've had about enough o' Barton's command; and I, for one, am a-goin' to enlist under Captain Potter."

"Good!" "Agreed!" responded a number of others, and some eight or ten stepped to one side. The few remaining around Alfred Barton began to look doubtful, and all eyes were turned curiously upon him.

Gilbert, however, stepped forward and said: "It's bad policy to divide our forces just now, when we ought to be off on the hunt. Mr. Barton, we all know, got up the company, and I am willing to serve under him, if he'll order us to mount at once! If not, rather than lose more time, I'll head as many as are ready to go."

Barton saw how the tide was turning, and suddenly determined to cover up his shame, if possible, with a mantle of magnanimity.

"The fellows are right, Gilbert!" he said. "You deserve to take the lead to-day, so go ahead; I'll follow you!"

"Mount, then, all of you!" Gilbert cried, without further hesitation. In a second he was on Roger's back. "You, Barton," he ordered, "take three with you and make for the New-Garden cross-road as fast as you can. Pratt, you and three more towards the Hammer-and-Trowel; while I, with the rest, follow the direct trail."

No more time was wasted in talking. The men took their guns and mounted, the two detached commands were told off, and in five minutes the village was left to its own inhabitants.

Gilbert had a long and perplexing chase, but very little came of it. The trail of Sandy Flash's horse was followed without much difficulty until it struck the west branch of Redley Creek. There it suddenly ceased, and more than an hour elapsed before some one discovered it, near the road, a quarter of a mile further up the stream. Thence it turned towards the Hammer-and-Trowel, but no one at the farm-houses on the road had seen any one pass except a Quaker, wearing the usual broad-brimmed hat and drab coat, and mounted on a large, sleepy-looking horse.

About the middle of the afternoon, Gilbert detected, in one of the lanes leading across to the Street Road, the marks of a galloping steed, and those who had a little lingering knowledge of wood-craft noticed that the gallop often ceased suddenly, changed to a walk, and was then as suddenly resumed. Along the Street Road no one had been seen except a Quaker, apparently the same person. Gilbert and his hunters now suspected the disguise, but the difficulty of following the trail had increased with every hour of lost time; and after scouring along the Brandywine and then crossing into the Pocopsin valley, they finally gave up the chase, late in the day. It was the general opinion that Sandy had struck northward, and was probably safe in one of his lairs among the Welch Mountains.

When they reached the Unicorn tavern at dusk, Gilbert found Joe Fairthorn impatiently waiting for him. Sally had been "tearin' around like mad," (so Joe described his sister's excitement,) having twice visited the village during the afternoon in the hope of seeing the hero of the day—after Sandy Flash, of course, who had, and deserved, the first place.

"And, Gilbert," said Joe, "I wasn't to forgit to tell you that we're a-goin' to have a huskin' frolic o' Wednesday night,—day after to-morrow, you know. Dad's behindhand with huskin', and the moon's goin' to be full, and Mark he said Let's have a frolic, and I'm comin' home to meet Gilbert anyhow, and so I'll be there. And Sally she said I'll have Martha and lots o' girls, only we shan't come out into the field till you're nigh about done. Then Mark he said That won't take long, and if you don't help me with my shocks I won't come, and Sally she hit him, and so it's all agreed. And you'll come, Gilbert, won't you?"

"Yes, yes, Joe," Gilbert answered, a little impatiently; "tell Sally I'll come." Then he turned Roger's head towards home.

He was glad of the solitary ride which allowed him to collect his thoughts. Fearless as was his nature, the danger he had escaped might well have been cause for grave self-congratulation; but the thought of it scarcely lingered beyond the moment of the encounter. The astonishing discovery that the stranger, Fortune, and the redoubtable Sandy Flash were one and the same person; the mysterious words which this person had addressed to him; the repetition of the same words by Deb. Smith,—all these facts, suggesting, as their common solution, some secret which concerned himself, perplexed his mind, already more than sufficiently occupied with mystery.

It suddenly flashed across his memory, as he rode homeward, that on the evening when he returned from the fox-chase, his mother had manifested an unusual interest in the strange huntsman, questioning him minutely as to the latter's appearance. Was she—or, rather, had she been, at one time of her life—acquainted with Sandy Flash? And if so—

"No!" he cried aloud, "it is impossible! It could not—cannot be!" The new possibility which assailed him was even more terrible than his previous belief in the dishonor of his birth. Better, a thousand times, he thought, be basely born than the son of an outlaw! It seemed that every attempt he made to probe his mother's secret threatened to overwhelm him with a knowledge far worse than the fret of his ignorance. Why not be patient, therefore, leaving the solution to her and to time?

Nevertheless, a burning curiosity led him to relate to his mother, that evening, the events of the day. He watched her closely as he described his encounter with the highwayman, and repeated the latter's words. It was quite natural that Mary Potter should shudder and turn pale during the recital— quite natural that a quick expression of relief should shine from her face at the close; but Gilbert could not be sure that her interest extended to any one except himself. She suggested no explanation of Sandy Flash's words, and he asked none.

"I shall know no peace, child," she said, "until the money has been paid, and the mortgage is in your hands."

"You won't have long to wait, now, mother," he answered cheerily. "I shall see Mark on Wednesday evening, and therefore can start for Chester on Friday, come rain or shine. As for Sandy Flash, he's no doubt up on the Welch Mountain by this time. It isn't his way to turn up twice in succession, in the same place."

"You don't know him, Gilbert. He won't soon forget that you shot at him."

"I seem to be safe enough, if he tells the truth." Gilbert could not help remarking.

Mary Potter shook her head, and said nothing.

Two more lovely Indian-summer days went by, and as the wine-red sun slowly quenched his lower limb in the denser smoke along the horizon, the great bronzed moon struggled out of it, on the opposite rim of the sky. It was a weird light and a weird atmosphere, such as we might imagine overspreading Babylonian ruins, on the lone plains of the Euphrates; but no such fancies either charmed or tormented the lusty, wide-awake, practical lads and lasses, whom the brightening moon beheld on their way to the Fairthorn farm. "The best night for huskin' that ever was," comprised the sum of their appreciation.

At the old farm-house there was great stir of preparation. Sally, with her gown pinned up, dodged in and out of kitchen and sitting-room, catching herself on every door-handle, while Mother Fairthorn, beaming with quiet content, stood by the fire, and inspected the great kettles which were to contain the materials for the midnight supper. Both were relieved when Betsy Lavender made her appearance, saying,—

"Let down your gownd, Sally, and give me that ladle. What'd be a mighty heap o' work for you, in that flustered condition, is child's-play to the likes o' me, that's as steady as a cart-horse,—not that self-praise, as the sayin' is, is any recommendation,—but my kickin' and prancin' days is over, and high time, too."

"No, Betsy, I'll not allow it!" cried Sally. "You must enjoy yourself, too." But she had parted with the ladle, while speaking, and Miss Lavender, repeating the words "Enjoy yourself, too!" quietly took her place in the kitchen.

The young men, as they arrived, took their way to the corn-field, piloted by Joe and Jake Fairthorn. These boys each carried a wallet over his shoulders, the jug in the front end balancing that behind, and the only casualty that occurred was when Jake, jumping down from a fence, allowed his jugs to smite together, breaking one of them to shivers.

"There, that'll come out o' your pig-money," said Joe.

"I don't care," Jake retorted, "if daddy only pays me the rest."

The boys, it must be known, received every year the two smallest pigs of the old sow's litter, with the understanding that these were to be their separate property, on condition of their properly feeding and fostering the whole herd. This duty they performed with great zeal and enthusiasm, and numberless and splendid were the castles which they built with the coming money; yet, alas! when the pigs were sold, it always happened that Farmer Fairthorn found some inconvenient debt pressing him, and the boys' pig-money was therefore taken as a loan,—only as a loan,—and permanently invested.

There were between three and four hundred shocks to husk, and the young men, armed with husking-pegs of hickory, fastened by a leathern strap over the two middle fingers, went bravely to work. Mark Deane, who had reached home that afternoon, wore the seventy-five dollars in a buckskin belt around his waist, and anxiously awaited the arrival of Gilbert Potter, of whose adventure he had already heard. Mark's presumed obligations to Alfred Barton prevented him from expressing his overpowering contempt for that gentleman's conduct, but he was not obliged to hold his tongue about Gilbert's pluck and decision, and he did not.

The latter, detained at the house by Mother Fairthorn and Sally,—both of whom looked upon him as one arisen from the dead,—did not reach the field until the others had selected their rows, overturned the shocks, and were seated in a rustling line, in the moonlight.

"Gilbert!" shouted Mark, "come here! I've kep' the row next to mine, for

200

you! And I want to get a grip o' your hand, my bold boy!"

He sprang up, flinging an armful of stalks behind him, and with difficulty restrained an impulse to clasp Gilbert to his broad breast. It was not the custom of the neighborhood; the noblest masculine friendship would have been described by the people in no other terms than "They are very thick," and men who loved each other were accustomed to be satisfied with the knowledge. The strong moonlight revealed to Gilbert Potter the honest heart which looked out of Mark's blue eyes, as the latter held his hand like a vice, and said,—

"I've heard all about it."

"More than there was occasion for, very likely," Gilbert replied. "I'll tell you my story some day, Mark; but tonight we must work and not talk."

"All right, Gilbert. I say, though, I've got the money you wanted; we'll fix the matter after supper."

The rustling of the corn-stalks recommenced, and the tented lines of shocks slowly fell as the huskers worked their way over the brow of the hill, whence the ground sloped down into a broad belt of shade, cast by the woods in the bottom. Two or three dogs which had accompanied their masters coursed about the field, or darted into the woods in search of an opossum-trail. Joe and Jake Fairthorn would gladly have followed them, but were afraid of venturing into the mysterious gloom; so they amused themselves with putting on the coats which the men had thrown aside, and gravely marched up and down the line, commending the rapid and threatening the tardy workers.

Erelong, the silence was broken by many a shout of exultation or banter, many a merry sound of jest or fun, as the back of the night's task was fairly broken. One husker mimicked the hoot of an owl in the thickets below; another sang a melody popular at the time, the refrain of which was,—

"Be it late or early, be it late or soon,

It's I will enjoy the sweet rose in June!"

201

"Sing out, boys!" shouted Mark, "so the girls can hear you! It's time they were comin' to look after us."

"Sing, yourself!" some one replied. "You can out-bellow the whole raft."

Without more ado, Mark opened his mouth and began chanting, in a ponderous voice,—

> *"On yonder mountain summit*
>
> *My castle you will find,*
>
> *Renown'd in ann-cient historee,—*
>
> *My name it's Rinardine!"*

Presently, from the upper edge of the wood, several feminine voices were heard, singing another part of the same song:—

> *"Beware of meeting Rinar,*
>
> *All on the mountains high!"*

Such a shout of fun ran over the field, that the frighted owl ceased his hooting in the thicket. The moon stood high, and turned the night-haze into diffused silver. Though the hollows were chill with gathering frost, the air was still mild and dry on the hills, and the young ladies, in their warm gowns of home-made flannel, enjoyed both the splendor of the night and the lively emulation of the scattered laborers.

"Turn to, and give us a lift, girls," said Mark.

"Beware of meeting Rinar!" Sally laughed.

"Because you know what you promised him, Sally," he retorted. "Come, a bargain's a bargain; there's the outside row standin'—not enough of us to stretch all the way acrost the field—so let's you and me take that and bring it down square with th' others. The rest may keep my row a-goin', if they can."

Two or three of the other maidens had cut the supporting stalks of the next shock, and overturned it with much laughing. "I can't husk, Mark," said

202

Martha Deane, "but I'll promise to superintend these, if you will keep Sally to her word."

There was a little running hither and thither, a show of fight, a mock scramble, and it ended by Sally tumbling over a pumpkin, and then being carried off by Mark to the end of the outside row of shocks, some distance in the rear of the line of work. Here he laid the stalks straight for her, doubled his coat and placed it on the ground for a seat, and then took his place on the other side of the shock.

Sally husked a few ears in silence, but presently found it more agreeable to watch her partner, as he bent to the labor, ripping the covering from each ear with one or two rapid motions, snapping the cob, and flinging the ear over his shoulder into the very centre of the heap, without turning his head. When the shock was finished, there were five stalks on her side, and fifty on Mark's.

He laughed at the extent of her help, but, seeing how bright and beautiful her face looked in the moonlight, how round and supple her form, contrasted with his own rough proportions, he added, in a lower tone,—

"Never mind the work, Sally—I only wanted to have you with me."

Sally was silent, but happy, and Mark proceeded to overthrow the next shock.

When they were again seated face to face, he no longer bent so steadily over the stalks, but lifted his head now and then to watch the gloss of the moon on her black hair, and the mellow gleam that seemed to slide along her cheek and chin, playing with the shadows, as she moved.

"Sally!" he said at last, "you must ha' seen, over and over ag'in, that I like to be with you. Do you care for me, at all?"

She flushed and trembled a little as she answered,—"Yes, Mark, I do."

He husked half a dozen ears rapidly, then looked up again and asked,—

"Do you care enough for me, Sally, to take me for good and all? I can't put it into fine speech, but I love you dearly and honestly; will you marry me?"

Sally bent down her head, so choked with the long-delayed joy that she found it impossible to speak. Mark finished the few remaining stalks and put them behind him; he sat upon the ground at her feet.

"There's my hand, Sally; will you take it, and me with it?"

Her hand slowly made its way into his broad, hard palm. Once the surrender expressed, her confusion vanished; she lifted her head for his kiss, then leaned it on his shoulder and whispered,—

"Oh, Mark, I've loved you for ever and ever so long a time!"

"Why, Sally, deary," said he, "that's my case, too; and I seemed to feel it in my bones that we was to be a pair; only, you know, I had to get a foothold first. I couldn't come to you with empty hands—though, faith! there's not much to speak of in 'em!"

"Never mind that, Mark,—I'm so glad you want me!"

And indeed she was; why should she not, therefore, say so?

"There's no need o' broken sixpences, or true-lovers' knots, I guess," said Mark, giving her another kiss. "I'm a plain-spoken fellow, and when I say I want you for my wife, Sally, I mean it. But we mustn't be settin' here, with the row unhusked; that'll never do. See if I don't make the ears spin! And I guess you can help me a little now, can't you?"

With a jolly laugh, Mark picked up the corn-cutter and swung it above the next shock. In another instant it would have fallen, but a loud shriek burst out from the bundled stalks, and Joe Fairthorn crept forth on his hands and knees.

The lovers stood petrified. "Why, you young devil!" exclaimed Mark, while the single word "JOE!" which came from Sally's lips, contained the concentrated essence of a thousand slaps.

"Don't—don't!" whimpered Joe. "I'll not tell anybody, indeed I wont!"

204

"If you do," threatened Mark, brandishing the corn-cutter, "it isn't your legs I shall cut off, but your head, even with the shoulders. What were you doin' in that shock?"

"I wanted to hear what you and Sally were sayin' to each other. Folks said you two was a-courtin'," Joe answered.

The comical aspect of the matter suddenly struck Mark, and he burst into a roar of laughter.

"Mark, how can you?" said Sally, bridling a little.

"Well,—it's all in the fam'ly, after all. Joe, tarnation scamp as he is, is long-headed enough to keep his mouth shut, rather than have people laugh at his relations—eh, Joe?"

"I said I'd never say a word," Joe affirmed, "and I won't. You see if I even tell Jake. But I say, Mark, when you and Sally get married, will you be my uncle?"

"It depends on your behavior," Mark gravely answered, seating himself to husk. Joe magnanimously left the lovers, and pitched over the third shock ahead, upon which he began to husk with might and main, in order to help them out with their task.

By the time the outside row was squared, the line had reached the bottom of the slope, where the air was chill, although the shadows of the forest had shifted from the field. Then there was a race among the huskers for the fence, the girls promising that he whose row was first husked out, should sit at the head of the table, and be called King of the Corn-field. The stalks rustled, the cobs snapped, the ears fell like a shower of golden cones, and amid much noise and merriment, not only the victor's row but all the others were finished, and Farmer Fairthorn's field stood husked from end to end.

Gilbert Potter had done his share of the work steadily, and as silently as the curiosity of the girls, still excited by his recent adventure, would allow. It was enough for him that he caught a chance word, now and then, from Martha. The emulation of the race with which the husking closed favored them, and he gladly lost a very fair chance of becoming King of the Corn-field for the opportunity of asking her to assist him in contriving a brief interview, on the way to the house.

Where two work together to the same end, there is no doubt about the result, especially as, in this case, the company preferred returning through the wood instead of crossing the open, high-fenced fields. When they found themselves together, out of ear-shot of the others, Gilbert lost no time in relating the particulars of his encounter with Sandy Flash, the discovery he had made, and the mysterious assurance of Deb. Smith.

Martha listened with the keenest interest. "It is very, very strange," she said, "and the strangest of all is that he should be that man, Fortune. As for his words, I do not find them so singular. He has certainly the grandest courage, robber as he is, and he admires the same quality in you; no doubt you made a favorable impression upon him on the day of the fox-chase; and so, although you are hunting him down, he will not injure you, if he can help it. I find all that very natural, in a man of his nature."

"But Deb. Smith?" Gilbert asked.

"That," said Martha, "is rather a curious coincidence, but nothing more, I think. She is said to be a superstitious creature, and if you have ever befriended her,—and you may have done so, Gilbert, without your good heart being aware of it,—she thinks that her spells, or charms, or what not, will save you from harm. No, I was wrong; it is not so very strange, except Fortune's intimacy with Alfred Barton, which everybody was talking about at the time."

Gilbert drew a deep breath of relief. How the darkness of his new fear vanished, in the light of Martha's calm, sensible words! "How wonderfully you have guessed the truth!". he cried. "So it is; Deb. Smith thinks she is beholden to me for kind treatment; she blew upon my palm, in a mysterious way, and said she would stand by me in time of need! But that about Fortune puzzles me. I can see that Barton is very shy of me since he thinks I've made the discovery."

"We must ask Betsy Lavender's counsel, there," said Martha. "It is beyond my depth."

The supper smoked upon the table when they reached the farm-house. It had been well earned, and it was enjoyed, both in a physical and a social sense, to the very extent of the guests' capacities. The King sat at the head of the table, and Gilbert Potter—forced into that position by Mark—at the foot. Sally Fairthorn insisted on performing her duty as handmaiden, although, as Betsy Lavender again and again declared, her room was better than her help. Sally's dark eyes fairly danced and sparkled; her full, soft lips shone with a scarlet bloom; she laughed with a wild, nervous joyousness, and yet rushed about haunted with a fearful dread of suddenly bursting into tears. Her ways were so well known, however, that a little extra impulsiveness excited no surprise. Martha Deane was the only person who discovered what had taken place. As the girls were putting on their hats and cloaks in the bedroom, Sally drew her into the passage, kissed her a number of times with passionate vehemence, and then darted off without saying a word.

Gilbert rode home through the splendid moonlight, in the small hours of the morning, with a light heart, and Mark's money-belt buckled around his waist.

CHAPTER XX. — GILBERT ON THE ROAD TO CHESTER.

Being now fully prepared to undertake his journey to Chester, Gilbert remembered his promise to Alfred Barton. As the subject had not again been mentioned between them,—probably owing to the excitement produced by Sandy Flash's visit to Kennett Square, and its consequences,—he felt bound to inform Barton of his speedy departure, and to renew his offer of service.

He found the latter in the field, assisting Giles, who was hauling home the sheaves of corn-fodder in a harvest-wagon. The first meeting of the two men did not seem to be quite agreeable to either. Gilbert's suspicions had been aroused, although he could give them no definite form, and Barton shrank from any reference to what had now become a very sore topic.

"Giles," said the latter, after a moment of evident embarrassment, "I guess you may drive home with that load, and pitch it off; I'll wait for you here."

When the rustling wain had reached a convenient distance, Gilbert began,—

"I only wanted to say that I'm going to Chester tomorrow."

"Oh, yes!" Barton exclaimed, "about that money? I suppose you want all o' yours?"

"It's as I expected. But you said you could borrow elsewhere, and send it by me."

"The fact is," said Barton, "that I've both borrowed and sent. I'm obliged to you, all the same, Gilbert; the will's as good as the deed, you know; but I got the money from—well, from a friend, who was about going down on his own business, and so that stone killed both my birds. I ought to ha' sent you word, by rights."

"Is your friend," Gilbert asked, "a safe and trusty man?"

"Safe enough, I guess—a little wild, at times, maybe; but he's not such a fool as to lose what he'd never have a chance of getting again."

"Then," said Gilbert, "it's hardly likely that he's the same friend you took such a fancy to, at the Hammer-and-Trowel, last spring?"

Alfred Barton started as if he had been shot, and a deep color spread over his face. His lower jaw slackened and his eyes moved uneasily from side to side.

"Who—who do you mean?" he stammered.

The more evident his embarrassment became, the more Gilbert was confirmed in his suspicion that there was some secret understanding between the two men. The thing seemed incredible, but the same point, he remembered had occurred to Martha Deane's mind, when she so readily explained the other circumstances.

"Barton," he said, sternly, "you know very well whom I mean. What became of your friend Fortune? Didn't you see him at the tavern, last Monday morning?"

"Y-yes—oh, yes! I know who he is now, the damned scoundrel! I'd give a hundred dollars to see him dance upon nothing!"

He clenched his fists, and uttered a number of other oaths, which need not be repeated. His rage seemed so real that Gilbert was again staggered. Looking at the heavy, vulgar face before him,—the small, restless eyes, the large sensuous mouth, the forehead whose very extent, in contradiction to ordinary laws, expressed imbecility rather than intellect, it was impossible to associate great cunning and shrewdness with such a physiognomy. Every line, at that moment, expressed pain and exasperation. But Gilbert felt bound to go a step further.

"Barton," he said, "didn't you know who Fortune was, on that day?"

"N-no—no! On that day—NO! Blast me if I did!"

"Not before you left him?"

"Well, I'll admit that a suspicion of it came to me at the very last moment—too late to be of any use. But come, damme! that's all over, and what's the good o' talking? You tried your best to catch the fellow, too, but he was too much for you! 'T isn't such an easy job, eh?"

This sort of swagger was Alfred Barton's only refuge, when he was driven into a corner. Though some color still lingered in his face, he spread his shoulders with a bold, almost defiant air, and met Gilbert's eye with a steady gaze. The latter was not prepared to carry his examination further, although he was still far from being satisfied.

"Come, come, Gilbert!" Barton presently resumed, "I mean no offence. You showed yourself to be true blue, and you led the hunt as well as any man could ha' done; but the very thought o' the fellow makes me mad, and I'll know no peace till he's strung up. If I was your age, now! A man seems to lose his spirit as he gets on in years, and I'm only sorry you weren't made captain at the start, instead o' me. You shall be, from this time on; I won't take it again!"

"One thing I'll promise you," said Gilbert, with a meaning look, "that I won't let him walk into the bar-room of the Unicorn, without hindrance."

"I'll bet you won't!" Barton exclaimed. "All I'm afraid of is, that he won't try it again."

"We'll see; this highway-robbery must have an end. I must now be going. Good-bye!"

"Good-bye, Gilbert; take care o' yourself!" said Barton, in a very good humor, now that the uncomfortable interview was over. "And, I say," he added, "remember that I stand ready to do you a good turn, whenever I can!"

"Thank you!" responded Gilbert, as he turned Roger's head; but he said to himself,—"when all other friends fail, I may come to you, not sooner."

The next morning showed signs that the Indian Summer had reached its close. All night long the wind had moaned and lamented in the chimneys, and the sense of dread in the outer atmosphere crept into the house and weighed upon the slumbering inmates. There was a sound in the forest as of sobbing Dryads, waiting for the swift death and the frosty tomb. The blue haze of dreams which had overspread the land changed into an ashy, livid mist, dragging low, and clinging to the features of the landscape like a shroud to the limbs of a corpse.

The time, indeed, had come for a change. It was the 2nd of November; and after a summer and autumn beautiful almost beyond parallel, a sudden and severe winter was generally anticipated. In this way, even the most ignorant field-hand recognized the eternal balance of Nature.

Mary Potter, although the day had arrived for which she had so long and fervently prayed, could not shake off the depressing influence of the weather. After breakfast, when Gilbert began to make preparations for the journey, she found herself so agitated that it was with difficulty she could give him the usual assistance. The money, which was mostly in silver coin, had been sewed into tight rolls, and was now to be carefully packed in the saddle-bags: the priming of the pistols was to be renewed, and the old, shrivelled covers of the holsters so greased, hammered out, and padded that they would keep the weapons dry in case of rain. Although Gilbert would reach Chester that evening,—the distance being not more than twenty-four miles,—the preparations, principally on account of his errand, were conducted with a grave and solemn sense of their importance.

When, finally, everything was in readiness,—the saddle-bags so packed that the precious rolls could not rub or jingle; the dinner of sliced bread and pork placed over them, in a folded napkin; the pistols, intended more for show than use, thrust into the antiquated holsters; and all these deposited and secured on Roger's back,—Gilbert took his mother's hand, and said,—

"Good-bye, mother! Don't worry, now, if I shouldn't get back until late to-morrow evening; I can't tell exactly how long the business will take."

He had never looked more strong and cheerful. The tears came to Mary Potter's eyes, but she held them hack by a powerful effort. All she could say—and her voice trembled in spite of herself—was,—

"Good-bye, my boy! Remember that I've worked, and thought, and prayed, for you alone,—and that I'd do more—I'd do all, if I only could!"

His look said, "I do not forget!" He sat already in the saddle, and was straightening the folds of his heavy cloak, so that it might protect his knees. The wind had arisen, and the damp mist was driving down the glen, mixed with scattered drops of a coming rain-storm. As he rode slowly away, Mary Potter lifted her eyes to the dense gray of the sky, darkening from moment to moment, listened to the murmur of the wind over the wooded hills opposite, and clasped her hands with the appealing gesture which had now become habitual to her.

"Two days more!" she sighed, as she entered the house,—"two days more of fear and prayer! Lord forgive me that I am so weak of faith—that I make myself trouble where I ought to be humble and thankful!"

Gilbert rode slowly, because he feared the contents of his saddle-bags would be disturbed by much jolting. Proof against wind and weather, he was not troubled by the atmospheric signs, but rather experienced a healthy glow and exhilaration of the blood as the mist grew thicker and beat upon his face like the blown spray of a waterfall. By the time he had reached the Carson farm, the sky contracted to a low, dark arch of solid wet, in which there was no positive outline of cloud, and a dull, universal roar, shorn of all windy sharpness, hummed over the land.

From the hill behind the farm-house, whence he could overlook the bottom-lands of Redley Creek, and easily descry, on a clear day, the yellow front of Dr. Deane's house in Kennett Square, he now beheld a dim twilight chaos, wherein more and more of the distance was blotted out. Yet still some spell held up the suspended rain, and the drops that fell seemed to be only the leakage of the airy cisterns before they burst. The fields on either hand were deserted. The cattle huddled behind the stacks or crouched disconsolately in fence-corners. Here and there a farmer made haste to cut and split a supply of wood for his kitchen-fire, or mended the rude roof on which his pigs depended for shelter; but all these signs showed how soon he intended to be snugly housed, to bide out the storm.

It was a day of no uncertain promise. Gilbert confessed to himself, before he reached the Philadelphia road, that he would rather have chosen another day for the journey; yet the thought of returning was farthest from his mind. Even when the rain, having created its little pools and sluices in every hollow of the ground, took courage, and multiplied its careering drops, and when the wet gusts tore open his cloak and tugged at his dripping hat, he cheerily shook the moisture from his cheeks and eyelashes, patted Roger's streaming neck, and whistled a bar or two of an old carol.

There were pleasant hopes enough to occupy his mind, without dwelling on these slight external annoyances. He still tried to believe that his mother's release would be hastened by the independence which lay folded in his saddlebags, and the thud of the wet leather against Roger's hide was a sound to cheer away any momentary foreboding. Then, Martha—dear, noble girl! She was his; it was but to wait, and waiting must be easy when the end was certain. He felt, moreover, that in spite of his unexplained disgrace, he had grown in the respect of his neighbors; that his persevering integrity was beginning to bring its reward, and he thanked God very gratefully that he had been saved from adding to his name any stain of his own making.

In an hour or more the force of the wind somewhat abated, but the sky seemed to dissolve into a massy flood. The rain rushed down, not in drops, but in sheets, and in spite of his cloak, he was wet to the skin. For half an hour he was obliged to halt in the wood between Old Kennett and Chadd's Ford, and here he made the discovery that with all his care the holsters were nearly full of water. Brown streams careered down the long, meadowy hollow on his left, wherein many Hessian soldiers lay buried. There was money buried with them, the people believed, but no one cared to dig among the dead at midnight, and many a wild tale of frighted treasure-seekers recurred to his mind.

At the bottom of the long hill flowed the Brandywine, now rolling swift and turbid, level with its banks. Roger bravely breasted the flood, and after a little struggle, reached the opposite side. Then across the battle-meadow, in the teeth of the storm, along the foot of the low hill, around the brow of which the entrenchments of the American army made a clayey streak, until the ill-fated field, sown with grape-shot and bullets which the farmers turned up every spring with their furrows, lay behind him. The story of the day was familiar to him, from the narratives of scores of eye-witnesses, and he thought to himself, as he rode onward, wet, lashed by the furious rain, yet still of good cheer,—"Though the fight was lost, the cause was won."

After leaving the lovely lateral valley which stretches eastward for two miles, at right angles to the course of the Brandywine, he entered a rougher and wilder region, more thickly wooded and deeply indented with abrupt glens. Thus far he had not met with a living soul. Chester was now not more than eight or ten miles distant, and, as nearly as he could guess, it was about two o'clock in the afternoon. With the best luck, he could barely reach his destination by nightfall, for the rain showed no signs of abating, and there were still several streams to be crossed.

His blood leaped no more so nimbly along his veins; the continued exposure had at last chilled and benumbed him. Letting the reins fall upon Roger's neck, he folded himself closely in his wet cloak, and bore the weather with a grim, patient endurance. The road dropped into a rough glen, crossed a stony brook, and then wound along the side of a thickly wooded hill. On his right the bank had been cut away like a wall; on the left a steep slope of tangled thicket descended to the stream.

One moment, Gilbert knew that he was riding along this road, Roger pressing close to the bank for shelter from the wind and rain; the next, there was a swift and tremendous grip on his collar, Roger slid from under him, and he was hurled backwards, with great force, upon the ground. Yet even in the act of falling, he seemed to be conscious that a figure sprang down upon the road from the bank above.

It was some seconds before the shock, which sent a crash through his brain and a thousand fiery sparkles into his eyes, passed away. Then a voice, keen, sharp, and determined, which it seemed that he knew, exclaimed,—

"Damn the beast! I'll have to shoot him."

Lifting his head with some difficulty, for he felt weak and giddy, and propping himself on his arm, he saw Sandy Flash in the road, three or four

214

paces off, fronting Roger, who had whirled around, and with levelled ears and fiery eyes, seemed to be meditating an attack.

The robber wore a short overcoat, made entirely of musk-rat skins, which completely protected the arms in his belt. He had a large hunting-knife in his left hand, and appeared to be feeling with his right for the stock of a pistol. It seemed to Gilbert that nothing but the singular force of his eye held back the horse from rushing upon him.

"Keep as you are, young man!" he cried, without turning his head, "or a bullet goes into your horse's brain. I know the beast, and don't want to see him slaughtered. If you don't, order him to be quiet!"

Gilbert, although he knew every trait of the noble animal's nature better than those of many a human acquaintance, was both surprised and touched at the instinct with which he had recognized an enemy, and the fierce courage with which he stood on the defensive. In that moment of bewilderment, he thought only of Roger, whose life hung by a thread, which his silence would instantly snap. He might have seen—had there been time for reflection—that nothing would have been gained, in any case, by the animal's death; for, stunned and unarmed as he was, he was no match for the powerful, wary highwayman.

Obeying the feeling which entirely possessed him, he cried,—"Roger! Roger, old boy!"

The horse neighed a shrill, glad neigh of recognition, and pricked up his ears. Sandy Flash stood motionless; he had let go of his pistol, and concealed the knife in a fold of his coat.

"Quiet, Roger, quiet!" Gilbert again commanded.

The animal understood the tone, if not the words. He seemed completely reassured, and advanced a step or two nearer. With the utmost swiftness and dexterity, combined with an astonishing gentleness,—making no gesture which might excite Roger's suspicion,—Sandy Flash thrust his hand into the holsters, smiled mockingly, cut the straps of the saddle-bags with a single movement of his keen-edged knife, tested the weight of the bags, nodded, grinned, and then, stepping aside, he allowed the horse to pass him. But he watched every motion of the head and ears, as he did so.

Roger, however, seemed to think only of his master. Bending down his head, he snorted warmly into Gilbert's pale face, and then swelled his sides with a deep breath of satisfaction. Tears of shame, grief, and rage swam in Gilbert's eyes. "Roger," he said, "I've lost everything but you!"

He staggered to his feet and leaned against the bank. The extent of his loss—the hopelessness of its recovery—the impotence of his burning desire to avenge the outrage—overwhelmed him. The highwayman still stood, a few paces off, watching him with a grim curiosity.

With a desperate effort, Gilbert turned towards him. "Sandy Flash," he cried, "do you know what you are doing?"

"I rather guess so,"—and the highwayman grinned. "I've done it before, but never quite so neatly as this time."

"I've heard it said, to your credit," Gilbert continued, "that, though you rob the rich, you sometimes give to the poor. This time you've robbed a poor man."

"I've only borrowed a little from one able to spare a good deal more than I've got,—and the grudge I owe him isn't paid off yet."

"It is not so!" Gilbert cried. "Every cent has been earned by my own and my mother's hard work. I was taking it to Chester, to pay off a debt upon the farm; and the loss and the disappointment will well nigh break my mother's heart. According to your views of things, you owe me a grudge, but you are outside of the law, and I did my duty as a lawful man by trying to shoot you!"

"And I, bein" outside o' the law, as you say, have let you off mighty easy, young man!" exclaimed Sandy Flash, his eyes shining angrily and his teeth glittering. "I took you for a fellow o' pluck, not for one that'd lie, even to the robber they call me! What's all this pitiful story about Barton's money?"

"Barton's money!"

"Oh—ay! You didn't agree to take some o' his money to Chester?" The mocking expression on the highwayman's face was perfectly diabolical. He slung the saddle-bags over his shoulders, and turned to leave.

Gilbert was so amazed that for a moment he knew not what to say. Sandy Flash took three strides up the road, and then sprang down into the thicket.

"It is not Barton's money!" Gilbert cried, with a last desperate appeal,— "it is mine, mine and my mother's!"

A short, insulting laugh was the only answer.

"Sandy Flash!" he cried again, raising his voice almost to a shout, as the crashing of the robber's steps through the brushwood sounded farther and farther down the glen, "Sandy Flash! You have plundered a widow's honest earnings to-day, and a curse goes with such plunder! Hark you! if never before, you are cursed from this hour forth! I call upon God, in my mother's name, to mark you!"

There was no sound in reply, except the dull, dreary hum of the wind and the steady lashing of the rain. The growing darkness of the sky told of approaching night, and the wild glen, bleak enough before, was now a scene of utter and hopeless desolation to Gilbert's eyes. He was almost unmanned, not only by the cruel loss, but also by the stinging sense of outrage which it had left behind. A mixed feeling of wretched despondency and shame filled his heart, as he leaned, chill, weary, and still weak from the shock of his fall, upon Roger's neck.

The faithful animal turned his head from time to time, as if to question his master's unusual demeanor. There was a look of almost human sympathy in his large eyes; he was hungry and restless, yet would not move until the word of command had been given.

"Poor fellow!" said Gilbert, patting his cheek, "we've both fared ill to-day. But you mustn't suffer any longer for my sake."

He then mounted and rode onward through the storm.

CHAPTER XXI. — ROGER REPAYS HIS MASTER.

A mile or more beyond the spot where Gilbert Potter had been waylaid, there was a lonely tavern, called the "Drovers' Inn." Here he dismounted, more for his horse's sake than his own, although he was sore, weary, and sick of heart. After having carefully groomed Roger with his own hands, and commended him to the special attentions of the ostler, he entered the warm public room, wherein three or four storm-bound drovers were gathered around the roaring fire of hickory logs.

The men kindly made way for the pale, dripping, wretched-looking stranger; and the landlord, with a shrewd glance and a suggestion of "Something hot, I reckon?" began mixing a compound proper for the occasion. Laying aside his wet cloak, which was sent to the kitchen to be more speedily dried, Gilbert presently sat in a cloud of his own steaming garments, and felt the warmth of the potent liquor in his chilly blood.

All at once, it occurred to him that the highwayman had not touched his person. There was not only some loose silver in his pockets, but Mark Deane's money-belt was still around his waist. So much, at least, was rescued, and he began to pluck up a little courage. Should he continue his journey to Chester, explain the misfortune to the holder of his mortgage, and give notice to the County Sheriff of this new act of robbery? Then the thought came into his mind that in that case he might be detained a day or two, in order to make depositions, or comply with some unknown legal form. In the mean time the news would spread over the country, no doubt with many exaggerations, and might possibly reach Kennett—even the ears of his mother. That reflection decided his course. She must first hear the truth from his mouth; he would try to give her cheer and encouragement, though he felt none himself; then, calling his friends together, he would hunt Sandy Flash like a wild beast until they had tracked him to his lair.

"Unlucky weather for ye, it seems?" remarked the curious landlord, who, seated in a corner of the fireplace, had for full ten minutes been watching

Gilbert's knitted brows, gloomy, brooding eyes, and compressed lips.

"Weather?" he exclaimed, bitterly. "It's not the weather. Landlord, will you have a chance of sending to Chester to-morrow?"

"I'm going, if it clears up," said one of the drovers.

"Then, my friend," Gilbert continued, "will you take a letter from me to the Sheriff?"

"If it's nothing out of the way," the man replied.

"It's in the proper course of law—if there is any law to protect us. Not a mile and a half from here, landlord, I have been waylaid and robbed on the public road!"

There was a general exclamation of surprise, and Gilbert's story, which he had suddenly decided to relate, in order that the people of the neighborhood might be put upon their guard, was listened to with an interest only less than the terror which it inspired. The landlady rushed into the bar-room, followed by the red-faced kitchen wench, and both interrupted the recital with cries of "Dear, dear!" and "Lord save us!" The landlord, meanwhile, had prepared another tumbler of hot and hot, and brought it forward, saying,—

"You need it, the Lord knows, and it shall cost you nothing."

"What I most need now," Gilbert said, "is pen, ink, and paper, to write out my account. Then I suppose you can get me up a cold check, [Footnote: A local term, in use at the time, signifying a "lunch."] for I must start homewards soon."

"Not 'a cold check' after all that drenching and mishandling!" the landlord exclaimed. "We'll have a hot supper in half an hour, and you shall stay, and welcome. Wife, bring down one of Liddy's pens, the schoolmaster made for her, and put a little vinegar into th' ink-bottle; it's most dried up!"

In a few minutes the necessary materials for a letter, all of the rudest kind, were supplied, and the landlord and drovers hovered around as Gilbert began to write, assisting him with the most extraordinary suggestions.

"I'd threaten," said a drover, "to write straight to General Washington, unless they promise to catch the scoundrel in no time!"

"And don't forget the knife and pistol!" cried the landlord.

"And say the Tory farmers' houses ought to be searched!"

"And give his marks, to a hair!"

Amid all this confusion, Gilbert managed to write a brief, but sufficiently circumstantial account of the robbery, calling upon the County authorities to do their part in effecting the capture of Sandy Flash. He offered his services and those of the Kennett troop, announcing that he should immediately start upon the hunt, and expected to be seconded by the law.

When the letter had been sealed and addressed, the drovers—some of whom carried money with them, and had agreed to travel in company, for better protection—eagerly took charge of it, promising to back the delivery with very energetic demands for assistance.

Night had fallen, and the rain fell with it, in renewed torrents. The dreary, universal hum of the storm rose again, making all accidental sounds of life impertinent, in contrast with its deep, tremendous monotone. The windows shivered, the walls sweat and streamed, and the wild wet blew in under the doors, as if besieging that refuge of warm, red fire-light.

"This beats the Lammas flood o' '68," said the landlord, as he led the way to supper. "I was a young man at the time, and remember it well. Half the dams on Brandywine went that night."

After a bountiful meal, Gilbert completely dried his garments and prepared to set out on his return, resisting the kindly persuasion of the host and hostess that he should stay all night. A restless, feverish energy filled his frame. He felt that he could not sleep, that to wait idly would be simple misery, and that only in motion towards the set aim of his fierce, excited desires, could he bear his disappointment and shame. But the rain still came down with a volume which threatened soon to exhaust the cisterns of the air, and in that hope he compelled himself to wait a little.

Towards nine o'clock the great deluge seemed to slacken. The wind arose, and there were signs of its shifting, erelong, to the northwest, which would bring clear weather in a few hours. The night was dark, but not pitchy; a dull phosphoric gleam overspread the under surface of the sky. The woods were full of noises, and every gully at the roadside gave token, by its stony rattle, of the rain-born streams.

With his face towards home and his back to the storm, Gilbert rode into the night. The highway was but a streak of less palpable darkness; the hills on either hand scarcely detached themselves from the low, black ceiling of sky behind them. Sometimes the light of a farm-house window sparkled faintly, like a glow-worm, but whether far or near, he could not tell; he only knew how blest must be the owner, sitting with wife and children around his secure hearthstone,—how wretched his own life, cast adrift in the darkness,—wife, home, and future, things of doubt!

He had lost more than money; and his wretchedness will not seem unmanly when we remember the steady strain and struggle of his previous life. As there is nothing more stimulating to human patience, and courage, and energy, than the certain prospect of relief at the end, so there is nothing more depressing than to see that relief suddenly snatched away, and the same round of toil thrust again under one's feet! This is the fate of Tantalus and Sisyphus in one.

Not alone the money; a year, or two years, of labor would no doubt replace what he had lost. But he had seen, in imagination, his mother's feverish anxiety at an end; household help procured, to lighten her over-heavy toil; the possibility of her release from some terrible obligation brought nearer, as he hoped and trusted, and with it the strongest barrier broken down which rose between him and Martha Deane. All these things which he had, as it were, held in his hand, had been stolen from him, and the loss was bitter because it struck down to the roots of the sweetest and strongest fibres of his heart. The night veiled his face, but if some hotter drops than those of the storm were shaken from his cheek, they left no stain upon his manhood.

The sense of outrage, of personal indignity, which no man can appreciate

221

who has not himself been violently plundered, added its sting to his miserable mood. He thirsted to avenge the wrong; Barton's words involuntarily came back to him,—"I'll know no peace till the villain has been strung up!" Barton! How came Sandy Flash to know that Barton intended to send money by him? Had not Barton himself declared that the matter should be kept secret? Was there some complicity between the latter and Sandy Flash? Yet, on the other hand, it seemed that the highwayman believed that he was robbing Gilbert of Barton's money. Here was an enigma which he could not solve.

All at once, a hideous solution presented itself. Was it possible that Barton's money was to be only apparently stolen—in reality returned to him privately, afterwards? Possibly the rest of the plunder divided between the two confederates? Gilbert was not in a charitable mood; the human race was much more depraved, in his view, than twelve hours before; and the inference which he would have rejected as monstrous, that very morning, now assumed a possible existence. One thing, at least, was certain; he would exact an explanation, and if none should be furnished, he would make public the evidence in his hands.

The black, dreary night seemed interminable. He could only guess, here and there, at a landmark, and was forced to rely more upon Roger's instinct of the road than upon the guidance of his senses. Towards midnight, as he judged, by the solitary crow of a cock, the rain almost entirely ceased. The wind began to blow, sharp and keen, and the hard vault of the sky to lift a little. He fancied that the hills on his right had fallen away, and that the horizon was suddenly depressed towards the north. Roger's feet began to splash in constantly deepening water, and presently a roar, distinct from that of the wind, filled the air.

It was the Brandywine. The stream had overflowed its broad meadow-bottoms, and was running high and fierce beyond its main channel. The turbid waters made a dim, dusky gleam around him; soon the fences disappeared, and the flood reached to his horse's belly. But he knew that the ford could be distinguished by the break in the fringe of timber; moreover, that the creek-bank was a little higher than the meadows behind it, and so far, at least, he might venture. The ford was not more than twenty yards across, and he could trust Roger to swim that distance.

The faithful animal pressed bravely on, but Gilbert soon noticed that he seemed at fault. The swift water had forced him out of the road, and he stopped, from time to time, as if anxious and uneasy. The timber could now be discerned, only a short distance in advance, and in a few minutes they would gain the bank.

What was that? A strange rustling, hissing sound, as of cattle trampling through dry reeds,—a sound which quivered and shook, even in the breath of the hurrying wind! Roger snorted, stood still, and trembled in every limb; and a sensation of awe and terror struck a chill through Gilbert's heart. The sound drew swiftly nearer, and became a wild, seething roar, filling the whole breadth of the valley.

"Great God!" cried Gilbert, "the dam!—the dam has given way!" He turned Roger's head, gave him the rein, struck, spurred, cheered, and shouted. The brave beast struggled through the impeding flood, but the advance wave of the coming inundation already touched his side. He staggered; a line of churning foam bore down upon them, the terrible roar was all around and over them, and horse and rider were whirled away.

What happened during the first few seconds, Gilbert could never distinctly recall. Now they were whelmed in the water, now riding its careering tide, torn through the tops of brushwood, jostled by floating logs and timbers of the dam-breast, but always, as it seemed, remorselessly held in the heart of the tumult and the ruin.

He saw, at last, that they had fallen behind the furious onset of the flood, but Roger was still swimming with it, desperately throwing up his head from time to time, and snorting the water from his nostrils. All his efforts to gain a foothold failed; his strength was nearly spent, and unless some help should come in a few minutes, it would come in vain. And in the darkness, and the rapidity with which they were borne along, how should help come?

All at once, Roger's course stopped. He became an obstacle to the flood, which pressed him against some other obstacle below, and rushed over horse and rider. Thrusting out his hand, Gilbert felt the rough bark of a tree. Leaning towards it and clasping the log in his arms, he drew himself from the saddle, while Roger, freed from his burden, struggled into the current and instantly disappeared.

As nearly as Gilbert could ascertain, several timbers, thrown over each other, had lodged, probably upon a rocky islet in the stream, the uppermost one projecting slantingly out of the flood. It required all his strength to resist the current which sucked, and whirled, and tugged at his body, and to climb high enough to escape its force, without overbalancing his support. At last, though still half immerged, he found himself comparatively safe for a time, yet as far as ever from a final rescue.

He must await the dawn, and an eternity of endurance lay in those few hours. Meantime, perhaps, the creek would fall, for the rain had ceased, and there were outlines of moving cloud in the sky. It was the night which made his situation so terrible, by concealing the chances of escape. At first, he thought most of Roger. Was his brave horse drowned, or had he safely gained the bank below? Then, as the desperate moments went by, and the chill of exposure and the fatigue of exertion began to creep over him, his mind reverted, with a bitter sweetness, a mixture of bliss and agony, to the two beloved women to whom his life belonged,—the life which, alas! he could not now call his own, to give.

He tried to fix his thoughts on Death, to commend his soul to Divine Mercy; but every prayer shaped itself into an appeal that he might once more see the dear faces and bear the dear voices. In the great shadow of the fate which hung over him, the loss of his property became as dust in the balance, and his recent despair smote him with shame. He no longer fiercely protested against the injuries of fortune, but entreated pardon and pity for the sake of his love.

The clouds rolled into distincter masses, and the northwest wind still hunted them across the sky, until there came, first a tiny rift for a star, then a gap for a whole constellation, and finally a broad burst of moonlight. Gilbert now saw that the timber to which he clung was lodged nearly in the centre of the channel, as the water swept with equal force on either side of him. Beyond the banks there was a wooded hill on the left; on the right an overflowed meadow. He was too weak and benumbed to trust himself to the flood, but he imagined that it was beginning to subside, and therein lay his only hope.

Yet a new danger now assailed him, from the increasing cold. There was already a sting of frost, a breath of ice, in the wind. In another hour the sky was nearly swept bare of clouds, and he could note the lapse of the night by the sinking of the moon. But he was by this time hardly in a condition to note anything more. He had thrown himself, face downwards, on the top of the log, his arms mechanically clasping it, while his mind sank into a state of torpid, passive suffering, growing nearer to the dreamy indifference which precedes death. His cloak had been torn away in the first rush of the inundation, and the wet coat began to stiffen in the wind, from the ice gathering over it.

The moon was low in the west, and there was a pale glimmer of the coming dawn in the sky, when Gilbert Potter suddenly raised his head. Above the noise of the water and the whistle of the wind, he heard a familiar sound,—the shrill, sharp neigh of a horse. Lifting himself, with great exertion, to a sitting posture, he saw two men, on horseback, in the flooded meadow, a little below him. They stopped, seemed to consult, and presently drew nearer.

Gilbert tried to shout, but the muscles of his throat were stiff, and his lungs refused to act. The horse neighed again. This time there was no mistake; it was Roger that he heard! Voice came to him, and he cried aloud,—a hoarse, strange, unnatural cry.

The horsemen heard it, and rapidly pushed up the bank, until they reached a point directly opposite to him. The prospect of escape brought a thrill of life to his frame; he looked around and saw that the flood had indeed fallen.

"We have no rope," he heard one of the men say. "How shall we reach him?"

"There is no time to get one, now," the other answered. "My horse is stronger than yours. I'll go into the creek just below, where it's broader and not so deep, and work my way up to him."

"But one horse can't carry both."

"His will follow, be sure, when it sees me."

As the last speaker moved away, Gilbert saw a led horse plunging through the water, beside the other. It was a difficult and dangerous undertaking. The horseman and the loose horse entered the main stream below, where its divided channel met and broadened, but it was still above the saddle-girths, and very swift. Sometimes the animals plunged, losing their foothold; nevertheless, they gallantly breasted the current, and inch by inch worked their way to a point about six feet below Gilbert. It seemed impossible to approach nearer.

"Can you swim?" asked the man.

Gilbert shook his head. "Throw me the end of Roger's bridle!" he then cried.

The man unbuckled the bridle and threw it, keeping the end of the rein in his hand. Gilbert tried to grasp it, but his hands were too numb. He managed, however, to get one arm and his head through the opening, and relaxed his hold on the log.

A plunge, and the man had him by the collar. He felt himself lifted by a strong arm and laid across Roger's saddle. With his failing strength and stiff limbs, it was no slight task to get into place, and the return, though less laborious to the horses, was equally dangerous, because Gilbert was scarcely able to support himself without help.

"You're safe now," said the man, when they reached the bank, "but it's a downright mercy of God that you're alive!"

The other horseman joined them, and they rode slowly across the flooded meadow. They had both thrown their cloaks around Gilbert, and carefully steadied him in the saddle, one on each side. He was too much exhausted to ask how they had found him, or whither they were taking him,—too numb for curiosity, almost for gratitude.

226

"Here's your saviour!" said one of the men, patting Roger's shoulder. "It was all along of him that we found you. Want to know how? Well—about three o'clock it was, maybe a little earlier, maybe a little later, my wife woke me up. 'Do you hear that?' she says. I listened and heard a horse in the lane before the door, neighing,—I can't tell you exactly how it was,—like as if he'd call up the house. 'T was rather queer, I thought, so I got up and looked out of window, and it seemed to me he had a saddle on. He stamped, and pawed, and then he gave another yell, and stamped again. Says I to my wife, 'There's something wrong here,' and I dressed and went out. When he saw me, he acted the strangest you ever saw; thinks I, if ever an animal wanted to speak, that animal does. When I tried to catch him, he shot off, run down the lane a bit, and then came back as strangely acting as ever. I went into the house and woke up my brother, here, and we saddled our horses and started. Away went yours ahead, stopping every minute to look round and see if we followed. When we came to the water, I kind o' hesitated, but 't was no use; the horse would have us go on, and on, till we found you. I never heard tell of the like of it, in my born days!"

Gilbert did not speak, but two large tears slowly gathered in his eyes, and rolled down his cheeks. The men saw his emotion, and respected it.

In the light of the cold, keen dawn, they reached a snug farm-house, a mile from the Brandywine. The men lifted Gilbert from the saddle, and would have carried him immediately into the house, but he first leaned upon Roger's neck, took the faithful creature's head in his arms, and kissed it.

The good housewife was already up, and anxiously awaiting the return of her husband and his brother. A cheery fire crackled on the hearth, and the coffee-pot was simmering beside it. When Gilbert had been partially revived by the warmth, the men conducted him into an adjoining bed-room, undressed him, and rubbed his limbs with whiskey. Then, a large bowl of coffee having been administered, he was placed in bed, covered with half a dozen blankets, and the curtains were drawn over the windows. In a few minutes he was plunged in a slumber almost as profound as that of the death from which he had been so miraculously delivered.

It was two hours past noon when he awoke, and he no sooner fully comprehended the situation and learned how the time had sped, than he insisted on rising, although still sore, weak, and feverish. The good farmer's wife had kept a huge portion of dinner hot before the fire, and he knew that without compelling a show of appetite, he would not be considered sufficiently recovered to leave. He had but one desire,—to return home. So recently plucked from the jaws of Death, his life still seemed to be an uncertain possession.

Finally Roger was led forth, quiet and submissive as of old,—having forgotten his good deed as soon as it had been accomplished,—and Gilbert, wrapped in the farmer's cloak, retraced his way to the main road. As he looked across the meadow, which told of the inundation in its sweep of bent, muddy grass, and saw, between the creekbank trees, the lodged timber to which he had clung, the recollection of the night impressed him like a frightful dream. It was a bright, sharp, wintry day,—the most violent contrast to that which had preceded it. The hills on either side, whose outlines he could barely guess in the darkness, now stood out from the air with a hard, painful distinctness; the sky was an arch of cold, steel-tinted crystal; and the north wind blew with a shrill, endless whistle through the naked woods.

As he climbed the long hill west of Chadd's Ford, Gilbert noticed how the meadow on his right had been torn by the flood gathered from the fields above. In one place a Hessian skull had been snapped from the buried skeleton, and was rolled to light, among the mud and pebbles. Not far off, something was moving among the bushes, and he involuntarily drew rein.

The form stopped, appeared to crouch down for a moment, then suddenly rose and strode forth upon the grass. It was a woman, wearing a man's flannel jacket, and carrying a long, pointed staff in her hand. As she approached with rapid strides, he recognized Deb. Smith.

"Deborah!" he cried, "what are you doing here?"

She set her pole to the ground and vaulted over the high picket-fence, like an athlete.

"Well," she said, "if I'd ha' been shy o' you, Mr. Gilbert, you wouldn't ha' seen me. I'm not one of them as goes prowlin' around among dead bodies' bones at midnight; what I want, I looks for in the daytime."

"Bones?" he asked. "You're surely not digging up the Hessians?"

"Not exackly; but, you see, the rain's turned out a few, and some on 'em, folks says, was buried with lots o' goold platted up in their pig-tails. I know o' one man that dug up two or three to git their teeth, (to sell to the tooth-doctors, you know,) and when he took hold o' the pig-tail to lift the head by, the hair come off in his hand, and out rattled ten good goolden guineas. Now, if any money's washed out, there's no harm in a body's pickin' of it up, as I see."

"What luck have you had?" asked Gilbert.

"Nothin' to speak of; a few buttons, and a thing or two. But I say, Mr. Gilbert, what luck ha' you had?" She had been keenly and curiously inspecting his face.

"Deborah!" he exclaimed, "you're a false prophet! You told me that, whatever happened, I was safe from Sandy Flash."

"Eh?"

There was a shrill tone of surprise and curiosity in this exclamation.

"You ought to know Sandy Flash better, before you prophesy in his name," Gilbert repeated, in a stern voice.

"Oh, Mr. Gilbert, tell me what you mean?" She grasped his leg with one hand, while she twisted the other in Roger's mane, as if to hold both horse and rider until the words were explained.

Thereupon he related to her in a brief, fierce way, all that had befallen him. Her face grew red and her eyes flashed; she shook her fist and swore under her breath, from time to time, while he spoke.

"You'll be righted, Mr. Gilbert!" she then cried, "you'll be righted, never fear! Leave it to me! Haven't I always kep' my word to you? You're believin' I lied the last time, and no wonder; but I'll prove the truth o' my words yet—

may the Devil git my soul, if I don't!"

"Don't think that I blame you, Deborah," he said. "You were too sure of my good luck, because you wished me to have it—that's all."

"Thank ye for that! But it isn't enough for me. When I promise a thing, I have power to keep my promise. Ax me no more questions; bide quiet awhile, and if the money isn't back in your pocket by New-Year, I give ye leave to curse me, and kick me, and spit upon me!"

Gilbert smiled sadly and incredulously, and rode onward. He made haste to reach home, for a dull pain began to throb in his head, and chill shudders ran over his body. He longed to have the worst over which yet awaited him, and gain a little rest for body, brain, and heart.

CHAPTER XXII. — MARTHA DEANE TAKES A RESOLUTION.

Mary Potter had scarcely slept during the night of her son's absence. A painful unrest, such as she never remembered to have felt before, took complete possession of her. Whenever the monotony of the drenching rain outside lulled her into slumber for a few minutes, she was sure to start up in bed with a vague, singular impression that some one had called her name. After midnight, when the storm fell, the shrill wailing of the rising wind seemed to forebode disaster. Although she believed Gilbert to be safely housed in Chester, the fact constantly slipped from her memory, and she shuddered at every change in the wild weather as if he were really exposed to it.

The next day, she counted the hours with a feverish impatience. It seemed like tempting Providence, but she determined to surprise her son with a supper of unusual luxury for their simple habits, after so important and so toilsome a journey. Sam had killed a fowl; it was picked and dressed, but she had not courage to put it into the pot, until the fortune of the day had been assured.

Towards sunset she saw, through the back-kitchen-window, a horseman approaching from the direction of Carson's. It seemed to be Roger, but could that rider, in the faded brown cloak, be Gilbert? His cloak was blue; he always rode with his head erect, not hanging like this man's, whose features she could not see. Opposite the house, he lifted his head—it was Gilbert, but how old and haggard was his face!

She met him at the gate. His cheeks were suddenly flushed, his eyes bright, and the smile with which he looked at her seemed to be joyous; yet it gave her a sense of pain and terror.

"Oh, Gilbert!" she cried; "what has happened?"

He slid slowly and wearily off the horse, whose neck he fondled a moment before answering her.

"Mother," he said at last, "you have to thank Roger that I am here tonight. I have come back to you from the gates of death; will you be satisfied with that for a while?"

"I don't understand you, my boy! You frighten me; haven't you been at Chester?"

"No," he answered, "there was no use of going."

A presentiment of the truth came to her, but before she could question him further, he spoke again.

"Mother, let us go into the house. I'm cold and tired; I want to sit in your old rocking-chair, where I can rest my head. Then I'll tell you everything; I wish I had an easier task!"

She noticed that his steps were weak and slow, felt that his hands were like ice, and saw his blue lips and chattering teeth. She removed the strange cloak, placed her chair in front of the fire, seated him in it, and then knelt upon the floor to draw off his stiff, sodden top-boots. He was passive as a child in her hands. Her care for him overcame all other dread, and not until she had placed his feet upon a stool, in the full warmth of the blaze, given him a glass of hot wine and lavender, and placed a pillow under his head, did she sit down at his side to hear the story.

"I thought of this, last night," he said, with a faint smile; "not that I ever expected to see it. The man was right; it's a mercy of God that I ever got out alive!"

"Then be grateful to God, my boy!" she replied, "and let me be grateful, too. It will balance misfortune,—for that there it misfortune in store for us. I see plainly."

Gilbert then spoke. The narrative was long and painful, and he told it wearily and brokenly, yet with entire truth, disguising nothing of the evil that had come upon them. His mother sat beside him, pale, stony, stifling the sobs that rose in her throat, until he reached the period of his marvellous rescue, when she bent her head upon his arm and wept aloud.

"That's all, mother!" he said at the close; "it's hard to bear, but I'm more troubled on your account than on my own."

"Oh, I feared we were over-sure!" she cried. "I claimed payment before it was ready. The Lord chooses His own time, and punishes them that can't wait for His ways to be manifest! It's terribly hard; and yet, while His left hand smites, His right hand gives mercy! He might ha' taken you, my boy, but He makes a miracle to save you for me!"

When she had outwept her passionate tumult of feeling, she grew composed and serene. "Haven't I yet learned to be patient, in all these years?" she said. "Haven't I sworn to work out with open eyes the work I took in blindness? And after waiting twenty-five years, am I to murmur at another year or two? No, Gilbert! It's to be done; I will deserve my justice! Keep your courage, my boy; be brave and patient, and the sight of you will hold me from breaking down!"

She arose, felt his hands and feet, set his pillow aright, and then stooped and kissed him. His chills had ceased; a feeling of heavy, helpless languor crept over him.

"Let Sam see to Roger, mother!" he murmured. "Tell him not to spare the oats."

"I'd feed him with my own hands, Gilbert, if I could leave you. I'd put fine wheat-bread into his manger, and wrap him in blankets off my own bed! To think that Roger,—that I didn't want you to buy,—Lord forgive me, I was advising your own death!"

It was fortunate for Mary Potter that she saw a mysterious Providence, which, to her mind, warned and yet promised while it chastised, in all that had occurred. This feeling helped her to bear a disappointment, which would otherwise have been very grievous. The idea of an atoning ordeal, which she must endure in order to be crowned with the final justice, and so behold her life redeemed, had become rooted in her nature. To Gilbert much of this feeling was inexplicable, because he was ignorant of the circumstances which had called it into existence. But he saw that his mother was not yet hopeless, that she did not seem to consider her deliverance as materially postponed, and a glimmer of hope was added to the relief of having told his tale.

He was still feverish, dozing and muttering in uneasy dreams, as he lay back in the old rocking-chair, and Mary Potter, with Sam's help, got him to bed, after administering a potion which she was accustomed to use in all complaints, from mumps to typhus fever.

As for Roger, he stood knee-deep in clean litter, with half a bushel of oats before him.

The next morning Gilbert did not arise, and as he complained of great soreness in every part of his body, Sam was dispatched for Dr. Deane.

It was the first time this gentleman had ever been summoned to the Potter farm-house. Mary Potter felt considerable trepidation at his arrival, both on account of the awe which his imposing presence inspired, and the knowledge of her son's love for his daughter,—a fact which, she rightly conjectured, he did not suspect. As he brought his ivory-headed cane, his sleek drab broadcloth, and his herbaceous fragrance into the kitchen, she was almost overpowered.

"How is thy son ailing?" he asked. "He always seemed to me to be a very healthy young man."

She described the symptoms with a conscientious minuteness.

"How was it brought on?" he asked again.

She had not intended to relate the whole story, but only so much of it as was necessary for the Doctor's purposes; but the commencement excited his curiosity, and he knew so skilfully how to draw one word after another, suggesting further explanations without directly asking them, that Mary Potter was led on and on, until she had communicated all the particulars of her son's misfortune.

"This is a wonderful tale thee tells me," said the Doctor—"wonderful! Sandy Flash, no doubt, has reason to remember thy son, who, I'm told, faced him very boldly on Second-day morning. It is really time the country was aroused; we shall hardly be safe in our own houses. And all night in the

234

Brandywine flood—I don't wonder thy son is unwell. Let me go up to him."

Dr. Deane's prescriptions usually conformed to the practice of his day,—bleeding and big doses,—and he would undoubtedly have applied both of these in Gilbert's case, but for the latter's great anxiety to be in the saddle and on the hunt of his enemy. He stoutly refused to be bled, and the Doctor had learned, from long observation, that patients of a certain class must be humored rather than coerced. So he administered a double dose of Dover's Powders, and prohibited the drinking of cold water. His report was, on the whole, reassuring to Mary Potter. Provided his directions were strictly followed, he said, her son would be up in two or three days; but there might be a turn for the worse, as the shock to the system had been very great, and she ought to have assistance.

"There's no one I can call upon," said she, "without it's Betsy Lavender, and I must ask you to tell her for me, if you think she can come."

"I'll oblige thee, certainly," the Doctor answered. "Betsy is with us, just now, and I don't doubt but she can spare a day or two. She may be a little headstrong in her ways, but thee'll find her a safe nurse."

It was really not necessary, as the event proved. Rest and warmth were what Gilbert most needed. But Dr. Deane always exaggerated his patient's condition a little, in order that the credit of the latter's recovery might be greater. The present case was a very welcome one, not only because it enabled him to recite a most astonishing narrative at second-hand, but also because it suggested a condition far more dangerous than that which the patient actually suffered. He was the first person to bear the news to Kennett Square, where it threw the village into a state of great excitement, which rapidly spread over the neighborhood.

He related it at his own tea-table that evening, to Martha and Miss Betsy Lavender. The former could with difficulty conceal her agitation; she turned red and pale, until the Doctor finally remarked,—

"Why, child, thee needn't be so frightened."

"Never mind!" exclaimed Miss Betsy, promptly coming to the rescue, "it's enough to frighten anybody. It fairly makes me shiver in my shoes. If Alf. Barton had ha' done his dooty like a man, this wouldn't ha' happened!"

"I've no doubt Alfred did the best he could, under the circumstances," the Doctor sternly remarked.

"Fiddle-de-dee!" was Miss Betsy's contemptuous answer. "He's no more gizzard than a rabbit. But that's neither here nor there; Mary Potter wants me to go down and help, and go I will!"

"Yes, I think thee might as well go down to-morrow morning, though I'm in hopes the young man may be better, if he minds my directions," said the Doctor.

"To-morrow mornin'? Why not next week? When help's wanted, give it right away; don't let the grass grow under your feet, say I! Good luck that I gev up Mendenhall's home-comin' over t' the Lion, or I wouldn't ha' been here; so another cup o' tea, Martha, and I'm off!"

Martha left the table at the same time, and followed Miss Betsy up-stairs. Her eyes were full of tears, but she did not tremble, and her voice came firm and clear.

"I am going with you," she said.

Miss Lavender whirled around and looked at her a minute, without saying a word.

"I see you mean it, child. Don't think me hard or cruel, for I know your feelin's as well as if they was mine; but all the same, I've got to look ahead, and back'ards, and on this side and that, and so lookin', and so judgin', accordin' to my light, which a'n't all tied up in a napkin, what I've got to say is, and ag'in don't think me hard, it won't do!"

"Betsy," Martha Deane persisted, "a misfortune like this brings my duty with it. Besides, he may be in great danger; he may have got his death,"—

"Don't begin talkin' that way," Miss Lavender interrupted, "or you'll put me out o' patience. I'll say that for your father, he's always mortal concerned for a bad case, Gilbert Potter or not; and I can mostly tell the heft of a sickness by the way he talks about it,—so that's settled; and as to dooties, it's very well and right, I don't deny it, but never mind, all the same, I said before, the whole thing's a snarl, and I say it ag'in, and unless you've got the end o' the ravellin's in your hand, the harder you pull, the wuss you'll make it!"

There was good sense in these words, and Martha Deane felt it. Her resolution began to waver, in spite of the tender instinct which told her that Gilbert Potter now needed precisely the help and encouragement which she alone could give.

"Oh, Betsy," she murmured, her tears falling without restraint, "it's hard for me to seem so strange to him, at such a time!"

"Yes," answered the spinster, setting her comb tight with a fierce thrust, "it's hard every one of us can't have our own ways in this world! But don't take on now, Martha dear; we only have your father's word, and not to be called a friend's, but I'll see how the land lays, and tomorrow evenin', or next day at th' outside, you'll know everything fair and square. Neither you nor Gilbert is inclined to do things rash, and what you both agree on, after a proper understanding I guess'll be pretty nigh right. There! where's my knittin'-basket?"

Miss Lavender trudged off, utterly fearless of the night walk of two miles, down the lonely road. In less than an hour she knocked at the door of the farm-house, and was received with open arms by Mary Potter. Gilbert had slept the greater part of the day, but was now awake, and so restless, from the desire to leave his bed, that his mother could with difficulty restrain him.

"Set down and rest yourself, Mary!" Miss Betsy exclaimed. "I'll go up and put him to rights."

She took a lamp and mounted to the bed-room. Gilbert, drenched in perspiration, and tossing uneasily under a huge pile of blankets, sprang up as her gaunt figure entered the door. She placed the lamp on a table, pressed him down on the pillow by main force, and covered him up to the chin.

"Martha?" he whispered, his face full of intense, piteous eagerness.

"Will you promise to lay still and sweat, as you're told

"Yes, yes!"

"Now let me feel your pulse. That'll do; now for your tongue! Tut, tut! the boy's not so bad. I give you my word you may get up and dress yourself to-morrow mornin', if you'll only hold out to-night. And as for thorough-stem tea, and what not, I guess you've had enough of 'em; but you can't jump out of a sick-spell into downright peartness, at one jump!"

"Martha, Martha!" Gilbert urged.

"You're both of a piece, I declare! There was she, this very night, dead set on comin' down with me, and mortal hard it was to persuade her to be reasonable!"

Miss Lavender had not a great deal to relate, but Gilbert compelled her to make up by repetition what she lacked in quantity. And at every repetition the soreness seemed to decrease in his body, and the weakness in his muscles, and hope and courage to increase in his heart.

"Tell her," he exclaimed, "it was enough that she wanted to come. That alone has put new life into me!"

"I see it has," said Miss Lavender, "and now, maybe, you've got life enough to tell me all the ups and downs o' this affair, for I can't say as I rightly understand it."

The conference was long and important. Gilbert related every circumstance of his adventure, including the mysterious allusion to Alfred Barton, which he had concealed from his mother. He was determined, as his first course, to call the volunteers together and organize a thorough hunt for the highwayman. Until that had been tried, he would postpone all further plans of action. Miss Lavender did not say much, except to encourage him in this determination. She felt that there was grave matter for reflection in what had happened. The threads of mystery seemed to increase, and she imagined it possible that they might all converge to one unknown point.

"Mary," she said, when she descended to the kitchen, "I don't see but what the boy's goin' on finely. Go to bed, you, and sleep quietly; I'll take the settle, here, and I promise you I'll go up every hour through the night, to see whether he's kicked his coverin's off."

Which promise she faithfully kept, and in the morning Gilbert came down to breakfast, a little haggard, but apparently as sound as ever. Even the Doctor, when he arrived, was slightly surprised at the rapid improvement.

"A fine constitution for medicines to work on," he remarked. "I wouldn't wish thee to be sick, but when thee is, it's a pleasure to see how thy system obeys the treatment."

Martha Deane, during Miss Lavender's absence, had again discussed, in her heart, her duty to Gilbert. Her conscience was hardly satisfied with the relinquishment of her first impulse. She felt that there was, there must be, something for her to do in this emergency. She knew that he had toiled, and dared, and suffered for her sake, while she had done nothing. It was not pride,—at least not the haughty quality which bears an obligation uneasily,— but rather the impulse, at once brave and tender, to stand side by side with him in the struggle, and win an equal right to the final blessing.

In the afternoon Miss Lavender returned, and her first business was to give a faithful report of Gilbert's condition and the true story of his misfortune, which she repeated, almost word for word, as it came from his lips. It did not differ materially from that which Martha had already heard, and the direction which her thoughts had taken, in the mean time, seemed to be confirmed. The gentle, steady strength of purpose that looked from her clear blue eyes, and expressed itself in the firm, sharp curve of her lip, was never more distinct than when she said,—

"Now, Betsy, all is clear to me. You were right before, and I am right now. I must see Gilbert when he calls the men together, and after that I shall know how to act."

Three days afterwards, there was another assemblage of the Kennett Volunteers at the Unicorn Tavern. This time, however, Mark Deane was on hand, and Alfred Barton did not make his appearance. That Gilbert Potter should take the command was an understood matter. The preliminary consultation was secretly held, and when Dougherty, the Irish ostler, mixed himself, as by accident, among the troop, Gilbert sharply ordered him away. Whatever the plan of the chase was, it was not communicated to the crowd of country idlers; and there was, in consequence, some grumbling at, and a great deal of respect for, the new arrangement.

Miss Betsy Lavender had managed to speak to Gilbert before the others arrived; therefore, after they had left, to meet the next day, equipped for a possible absence of a week, he crossed the road and entered Dr. Deane's house.

This time the two met, not so much as lovers, but rather as husband and wife might meet after long absence and escape from imminent danger. Martha Deane knew how cruel and bitter Gilbert's fate must seem to his own heart, and she resolved that all the cheer which lay in her buoyant, courageous nature should be given to him. Never did a woman more sweetly blend the tones of regret and faith, sympathy and encouragement.

"The time has come, Gilbert," she said at last, "when our love for each other must no longer be kept a secret—at least from the few who, under other circumstances, would have a right to know it. We must still wait, though no longer (remember that!) than we were already agreed to wait; but we should betray ourselves, sooner or later, and then the secret, discovered by others, would seem to hint at a sense of shame. We shall gain respect and sympathy, and perhaps help, if we reveal it ourselves. Even if you do not take the same view, Gilbert, think of this, that it is my place to stand beside you in your hour of difficulty and trial; that other losses, other dangers, may come, and you could not, you must not, hold me apart when my heart tells me we should be together!"

She laid her arms caressingly over his shoulders, and looked in his face. A wonderful softness and tenderness touched his pale, worn countenance. "Martha," he said, "remember that my disgrace will cover you, yet awhile."

"Gilbert!"

That one word, proud, passionate, reproachful, yet forgiving, sealed his lips.

"So be it!" he cried. "God knows, I think but of you. If I selfishly considered myself, do you think I would hold back my own honor?"

"A poor honor," she said, "that I sit comfortably at home and love you, while you are face to face with death!"

Martha Deane's resolution was inflexibly taken. That same evening she went into the sitting-room, where her father was smoking a pipe before the open stove, and placed her chair opposite to his.

"Father," she said, "thee has never asked any questions concerning Alfred Barton's visit."

The Doctor started, and looked at her keenly, before replying. Her voice had its simple, natural tone, her manner was calm and self-possessed; yet something in her firm, erect posture and steady eye impressed him with the idea that she had determined on a full and final discussion of the question.

"No, child," he answered, after a pause. "I saw Alfred, and he said thee was rather taken by surprise. He thought, perhaps, thee didn't rightly know thy own mind, and it would be better to wait a little. That is the chief reason why I haven't spoken to thee."

"If Alfred Barton said that, he told thee false," said she. "I knew my own mind, as well then as now. I said to him that nothing could ever make me his wife."

"Martha!" the Doctor exclaimed, "don't be hasty! If Alfred is a little older"—

"Father!" she interrupted, "never mention this thing again! Thee can neither give me away, nor sell me; though I am a woman, I belong to myself. Thee knows I'm not hasty in anything. It was a long time before I rightly knew my own heart; but when I did know it and found that it had chosen truly, I gave it freely, and it is gone from me forever!"

"Martha, Martha!" cried Dr. Deane, starting from his seat, "what does all this mean?"

"It means something which it is thy right to know, and therefore I have made up my mind to tell thee, even at the risk of incurring thy lasting displeasure. It means that I have followed the guidance of my own heart and bestowed it on a man a thousand times better and nobler than Alfred Barton ever was, and, if the Lord spares us to each other, I shall one day be his wife!"

The Doctor glared at his daughter in speechless amazement. But she met his gaze steadily, although her face grew a shade paler, and the expression of the pain she could not entirely suppress, with the knowledge of the struggle before her, trembled a little about the corners of her lips.

"Who is this man?" he asked.

"Gilbert Potter."

Dr. Deane's pipe dropped from his hand and smashed upon the iron hearth.

"Martha Deane!" he cried. "Does the d—— what possesses thee? Wasn't it enough that thee should drive away the man I had picked out for thee, with a single view to thy own interest and happiness; but must thee take up, as a wicked spite to thy father, with almost the only man in the neighborhood who brings thee nothing but poverty and disgrace? It shall not be—it shall never be!"

"It must be, father," she said gently. "God hath joined our hearts and our lives, and no man—not even thee—shall put them asunder. If there were disgrace, in the eyes of the world,—which I now know there is not,—Gilbert has wiped it out by his courage, his integrity, and his sufferings. If he is poor, I am well to do."

"Thee forgets," the Doctor interrupted, in a stern voice, "the time isn't up!"

"I know that unless thee gives thy consent, we must wait three years; but I hope, father, when thee comes to know Gilbert better, thee will not be so hard. I am thy only child, and my happiness cannot be indifferent to thee. I

242

have tried to obey thee in all things"—

He interrupted her again. "Thee's adding another cross to them I bear for thee already! Am I not, in a manner, thy keeper, and responsible for thee, before the world and in the sight of the Lord? But thee hardened thy heart against the direction of the Spirit, and what wonder, then, that it's hardened against me?"

"No, father," said Martha, rising and laying her hand softly upon his arm, "I obeyed the Spirit in that other matter, as I obey my conscience in this. I took my duty into my own hands, and considered it in a humble, and, I hope, a pious spirit. I saw that there were innocent needs of nature, pleasant enjoyments of life, which did not conflict with sincere devotion, and that I was not called upon to renounce them because others happened to see the world in a different light. In this sense, thee is not my keeper; I must render an account, not to thee, but to Him who gave me my soul. Neither is thee the keeper of my heart and its affections. In the one case and the other my right is equal,—nay, it stands as far above thine as Heaven is above the earth!"

In the midst of his wrath, Dr. Deane could not help admiring his daughter. Foiled and exasperated as he was by the sweet, serene, lofty power of her words, they excited a wondering respect which he found it difficult to hide.

"Ah, Martha!" he said, "thee has a wonderful power, if it were only directed by the true Light! But now, it only makes the cross heavier. Don't think that I'll ever consent to see thee carry out thy strange and wicked fancies! Thee must learn to forget this man, Potter, and the sooner thee begins the easier it will be!"

"Father," she answered, with a sad smile, "I'm sorry thee knows so little of my nature. The wickedness would be in forgetting. It is very painful to me that we must differ. Where my duty was wholly owed to thee, I have never delayed to give it; but here it is owed to Gilbert Potter,—owed, and will be given."

"Enough, Martha!" cried the Doctor, trembling with anger; "don't

243

mention his name again!"

"I will not, except when the same duty requires it to be mentioned. But, father, try to think less harshly of the name; it will one day be mine!"

She spoke gently and imploringly, with tears in her eyes. The conflict had been, as she said, very painful; but her course was plain, and she dared not flinch a step at the outset. The difficulties must be met face to face, and resolutely assailed, if they were ever to be overcome.

Dr. Deane strode up and down the room in silence, with his hands behind his back. Martha stood by the fire, waiting his further speech, but he did not look at her, and at the end of half an hour, commanded shortly and sharply, without turning his head,—

"Go to bed!"

"Good-night, father," she said, in her usual clear sweet voice, and quietly left the room.

CHAPTER XXIII. — A CROSS-EXAMINATION.

The story of Gilbert Potter's robbery and marvellous escape from death ran rapidly through the neighborhood, and coming, as it did, upon the heels of his former adventure, created a great excitement. He became almost a hero in the minds of the people. It was not their habit to allow any man to quite assume so lofty a character as that, but they granted to Gilbert fully as much interest as, in their estimation, any human being ought properly to receive. Dr. Deane was eagerly questioned, wherever he went; and if his garments could have exhaled the odors of his feelings, his questioners would have smelled aloes and asafoetida instead of sweet-marjoram and bergamot. But—in justice to him be it said—he told and retold the story very correctly; the tide of sympathy ran so high and strong, that he did not venture to stem it on grounds which could not be publicly explained.

The supposed disgrace of Gilbert's birth seemed to be quite forgotten for the time; and there was no young man of spirit in the four townships who was not willing to serve under his command. More volunteers offered, in fact, than could be profitably employed. Sandy Flash was not the game to be unearthed by a loud, numerous, sweeping hunt; traps, pitfalls, secret and unwearied following of his many trails, were what was needed. So much time had elapsed that the beginning must be a conjectural beating of the bushes, and to this end several small companies were organized, and the country between the Octorara and the Delaware very effectually scoured.

When the various parties reunited, after several days, neither of them brought any positive intelligence, but all the greater store of guesses and rumors. Three or four suspicious individuals had been followed and made to give an account of themselves; certain hiding-places, especially the rocky lairs along the Brandywine and the North Valley-Hill, were carefully examined, and some traces of occupation, though none very recent, were discovered. Such evidence as there was seemed to indicate that part of the eastern branch of the Brandywine, between the forks of the stream and the great Chester Valley, as being the probable retreat of the highwayman, and a second expedition was at once organized. The Sheriff, with a posse of men from the lower part of the county, undertook to watch the avenues of escape towards the river.

This new attempt was not more successful, so far as its main object was concerned, but it actually stumbled upon Sandy Flash's trail, and only failed by giving tongue too soon and following too impetuously. Gilbert and his men had a tantalizing impression (which later intelligence proved to have been correct) that the robber was somewhere near them,—buried in the depths of the very wood they were approaching, dodging behind the next barn as it came into view, or hidden under dead leaves in some rain-washed gulley. Had they but known, one gloomy afternoon in late December, that they were riding under the cedar-tree in whose close, cloudy foliage he was coiled, just above their heads! Had they but guessed who the deaf old woman was, with her face muffled from the cold, and six cuts of blue yarn in her basket! But detection had not then become a science, and they were far from suspecting the extent of Sandy Flash's devices and disguises.

Many of the volunteers finally grew tired of the fruitless chase, and returned home; others could only spare a few days from their winter labors; but Gilbert Potter, with three or four faithful and courageous young fellows,— one of whom was Mark Deane,—returned again and again to the search, and not until the end of December did he confess himself baffled. By this time all traces of the highwayman were again lost; he seemed to have disappeared from the country.

"I believe Pratt's right," said Mark, as the two issued from the Marlborough woods, on their return to Kennett Square. "Chester County is too hot to hold him."

"Perhaps so," Gilbert answered, with a gloomy face. He was more keenly disappointed at the failure than he would then confess, even to Mark. The outrage committed upon him was still unavenged, and thus his loss, to his proud, sensitive nature, carried a certain shame with it. Moreover, the loss itself must speedily be replaced. He had half flattered himself with the hope of capturing not only Sandy Flash, but his plunder; it was hard to forget that, for a day or two, he had been independent,—hard to stoop again to be a borrower and a debtor!

"What are the county authorities good for?" Mark exclaimed. "Between you and me, the Sheriff's a reg'lar puddin'-head. I wish you was in his place."

"If Sandy is safe in Jersey, or down on the Eastern Shore, that would do no good. It isn't enough that he leaves us alone, from this time on; he has a heavy back-score to settle."

"Come to think on it, Gilbert," Mark continued, "isn't it rather queer that you and him should be thrown together in such ways? There was Barton's fox-chase last spring; then your shootin' at other, at the Square; and then the robbery on the road. It seems to me as if he picked you out to follow you, and yet I don't know why."

Gilbert started. Mark's words reawakened the dark, incredible suspicion which Martha Deane had removed. Again he declared to himself that he would not entertain the thought, but he could not reject the evidence that there was something more than accident in all these encounters. If any one besides Sandy Flash were responsible for the last meeting, it must be Alfred Barton. The latter, therefore, owed him an explanation, and he would demand it.

When they reached the top of the "big hill" north of the Fairthorn farm-house, whence they looked eastward down the sloping corn-field which had been the scene of the husking-frolic, Mark turned to Gilbert with an honest blush all over his face, and said,—

"I don't see why you shouldn't know it, Gilbert. I'm sure Sally wouldn't care; you're almost like a brother to her."

"What?" Gilbert asked, yet with a quick suspicion of the coming intelligence.

"Oh, I guess you know, well enough, old fellow. I asked her that night, and it's all right between us. What do you say to it, now?"

"Mark, I'm glad of it; I wish you joy, with all my heart!" Gilbert stretched out his hand, and as he turned and looked squarely into Mark's half-bashful yet wholly happy face, he remembered Martha's words, at their last interview.

"You are like a brother to me, Mark," he said, "and you shall have my secret. What would you say if I had done the same thing?"

"No?" Mark exclaimed; "who?"

"Guess!"

"Not—not Martha?"

Gilbert smiled.

"By the Lord! It's the best day's work you've ever done! Gi' me y'r hand ag'in; we'll stand by each other faster than ever, now!"

When they stopped at Fairthorn's, the significant pressure of Gilbert's hand brought a blush into Sally's cheek; but when Mark met Martha with his tell-tale face, she answered with a proud and tender smile.

Gilbert's first business, after his return, was to have a consultation with Miss Betsy Lavender, who alone knew of the suspicions attaching to Alfred Barton. The spinster had, in the mean time, made the matter the subject of profound and somewhat painful cogitation. She had ransacked her richly stored memory of persons and events, until her brain was like a drawer of tumbled clothes; had spent hours in laborious mental research, becoming so absorbed that she sometimes gave crooked answers when spoken to, and was haunted with a terrible dread of having thought aloud; and had questioned the oldest gossips right and left, coming as near the hidden subject as she dared. When they met, she communicated the result to Gilbert in this wise:

"'T a'n't agreeable for a body to allow they're flummuxed, but if I a'n't, this time, I'm mighty near onto it. It's like lookin' for a set o' buttons that'll match, in a box full o' tail-ends o' things. This'n 'd do, and that'n 'd do; but you can't put this'n and that'n together; and here's got to be square work, everything fittin' tight and hangin' plumb, or it'll be throwed back onto your hands, and all to be done over ag'in. I dunno when I've done so much head-work and to no purpose, follerin' here and guessin' there, and nosin' into everything that's past and gone; and so my opinion is, whether you like it or not, but never mind, all the same, I can't do no more than give it, that we'd better drop what's past and gone, and look a little more into these present times!"

"Well, Betsy," said Gilbert, with a stern, determined face, "this is what I shall do. I am satisfied that Barton is connected, in some way, with Sandy Flash. What it is, or whether the knowledge will help us, I can't guess; but I shall force Barton to tell me!"

"To tell me. That might do, as far as it goes," she remarked, after a moment's reflection. "It won't be easy; you'll have to threaten as well as coax, but I guess you can git it out of him in the long run, and maybe I can help you here, two bein' better than one, if one is but a sheep's-head."

"I don't see, Betsy, that I need to call on you."

"This way, Gilbert. It's a strong p'int o' law, I've heerd tell, not that I know much o' law, Goodness knows, nor ever want to, but never mind, it's a strong p'int when there's two witnesses to a thing,—one to clinch what the t'other drives in; and you must have a show o' law to work on Alf. Barton, or I'm much mistaken!"

Gilbert reflected a moment. "It can do no harm," he then said; "can you go with me, now?"

"Now's the time! If we only git the light of a farden-candle out o' him, it'll do me a mortal heap o' good; for with all this rakin' and scrapin' for nothin', I'm like a heart pantin' after the water-brooks, though a mouth would be more like it, to my thinkin', when a body's so awful dry as that comes to!"

The two thereupon took the foot-path down through the frozen fields and the dreary timber of the creek-side, to the Barton farm-house. As they approached the barn, they saw Alfred Barton sitting on a pile of straw and watching Giles, who was threshing wheat. He seemed a little surprised at their appearance; but as Gilbert and he had not met since their interview in the corn-field before the former's departure for Chester, he had no special cause for embarrassment.

"Come into the house," he said, leading the way.

"No," Gilbert answered, "I came here to speak with you privately. Will you walk down the lane?"

"No objection, of course," said Barton, looking from Gilbert to Miss Lavender, with a mixture of curiosity and uneasiness. "Good news, I hope; got hold of Sandy's tracks, at last?"

"One of them."

"Ah, you don't say so! Where?"

"Here!"

Gilbert stopped and faced Barton. They were below the barn, and out of Giles's hearing.

"Barton," he resumed, "you know what interest I have in the arrest of that man, and you won't deny my right to demand of you an account of your dealings with him. When did you first make his acquaintance?"

"I've told you that, already; the matter has been fully talked over between us," Barton answered, in a petulant tone.

"It has not been fully talked over. I require to know, first of all, precisely when, and under what circumstances, you and Sandy Flash came together. There is more to come, so let us begin at the beginning."

"Damme, Gilbert, you were there, and saw as much as I did. How could I know who the cursed black-whiskered fellow was?"

"But you found it out," Gilbert persisted, "and the manner of your finding it out must be explained."

Barton assumed a bold, insolent manner. "I don't see as that follows," he said. "It has nothing in the world to do with his robbery of you; and as for Sandy Flash, I wish to the Lord you'd get hold of him, yourself, instead of trying to make me accountable for his comings and goings!"

"He's tryin' to fly off the handle," Miss Lavender remarked. "I'd drop that part o' the business a bit, if I was you, and come to the t'other proof."

"What the devil have you to do here?" asked Barton.

"Miss Betsy is here because I asked her," Gilbert said. "Because all that passes between us may have to be repeated in a court of justice, and two witnesses are better than one!"

He took advantage of the shock which these words produced upon Barton, and repeated to him the highwayman's declarations, with the inference they might bear if not satisfactorily explained. "I kept my promise," he added, "and said nothing to any living soul of your request that I should carry money for you to Chester. Sandy Flash's information, therefore, must have come, either directly or indirectly, from you."

Barton had listened with open mouth and amazed eyes.

"Why, the man is a devil!" he cried. "I, neither, never said a word of the matter to any living soul!"

"Did you really send any money?" Gilbert asked.

"That I did! I got it of Joel Ferris, and it happened he was bound for Chester, the very next day, on his own business; and so, instead of turning it over to me, he just paid it there, according to my directions. You'll understand, this is between ourselves?"

He darted a sharp, suspicious glance at Miss Betsy Lavender, who gravely nodded her head.

"The difficulty is not yet explained," said Gilbert, "and perhaps you'll now not deny my right to know something more of your first acquaintance with Sandy Flash?"

"Have it then!" Barton exclaimed, desperately—"and much good may it do you! I thought his name was Fortune, as much as you did, till nine o'clock that night, when he put a pistol to my breast in the woods! If you think I'm colloguing with him, why did he rob me under threat of murder,—money, watch, and everything?"

"Ah-ha!" said Miss Lavender, "and so that's the way your watch has been gittin' mended all this while? Mainspring broke, as I've heerd say; well, I don't wonder! Gilbert, I guess this much is true. Alf. Barton'd never live so long without that watch, and that half-peck o' seals, if he could help it!"

"This, too, may as well be kept to ourselves," Barton suggested. "It isn't agreeable to a man to have it known that he's been so taken in as I was, and that's just the reason why I kept it to myself; and, of course, I shouldn't like it to get around."

Gilbert could do no less than accept this part of the story, and it rendered his later surmises untenable. But the solution which he sought was as far off as ever.

"Barton," he said, after a long pause, "will you do your best to help me in finding out how Sandy Flash got the knowledge?"

"Only show me a way! The best would be to catch him and get it from his own mouth."

He looked so earnest, so eager, and—as far as the traces of cunning in his face would permit—so honest, that Gilbert yielded to a sudden impulse, and said,—

"I believe you, Barton. I've done you wrong in my thoughts,—not willingly, for I don't want to think badly of you or any one else,—but because circumstances seemed to drive me to it. It would have been better if you had told me of your robbery at the start."

"You're right there, Gilbert! I believe I was an outspoken fellow enough, when I was young, and all the better for it, but the old man's driven me into a curst way of keeping dark about everything, and so I go on heaping up trouble for myself."

"Trouble for myself, Alf. Barton," said Miss Lavender, "that's the truest word you've said this many a day. Murder will out, you know, and so will robbery, and so will—other things. More o' your doin's is known, not that they're agreeabler, but on the contrary, quite the reverse, and as full need to be explained, though it don't seem to matter much, yet it may, who can tell? And now look here, Gilbert; my crow is to be picked, and you've seen the color of it, but never mind, all the same, since Martha's told the Doctor, it can't make much difference to you. And this is all between ourselves, you understand?"

The last words were addressed to Barton, with a comical, unconscious imitation of his own manner. He guessed something of what was coming, though not the whole of it, and again became visibly uneasy; but he stammered out,—"Yes; oh, yes! of course."

Gilbert could form a tolerably correct idea of the shape and size of Miss Lavender's crow. He did not feel sure that this was the proper time to have it picked, or even that it should be picked at all; but he imagined that Miss Lavender had either consulted Martha Deane, or that she had wise reasons of her own for speaking. He therefore remained silent.

"First and foremost," she resumed, "I'll tell you, Alf. Barton, what we know o' your doin's, and then it's for you to judge whether we'll know any more. Well, you've been tryin' to git Martha Deane for a wife, without wantin' her in your heart, but rather the contrary, though it seems queer enough when a body comes to think of it, but never mind; and your father's druv you to it; and you were of a cold shiver for fear she'd take you, and yet you want to let on it a'n't settled betwixt and between you—oh, you needn't chaw your lips and look yaller about the jaws, it's the Lord's truth; and now answer me this, what do you mean? and maybe you'll say what right have I got to ask, but never mind, all the same, if I haven't, Gilbert Potter has, for it's him that Martha Deane has promised to take for a husband!"

It was a day of surprises for Barton. In his astonishment at the last announcement, he took refuge from the horror of Miss Lavender's first revelations. One thing was settled,—all the fruits of his painful and laborious plotting were scattered to the winds. Denial was of no use, but neither could an honest explanation, even if he should force himself to give it, be of any possible service.

"Gilbert," he asked, "is this true?—about you, I mean."

"Martha Deane and I are engaged, and were already at the time when you addressed her," Gilbert answered.

"Good heavens! I hadn't the slightest suspicion of it. Well—I don't begrudge you your luck, and of course I'll draw back, and never say another word, now or ever."

"You wouldn't ha' been comfortable with Martha Deane, anyhow," Miss Lavender grimly remarked. "'T isn't good to hitch a colt-horse and an old spavined critter in one team. But that's neither here nor there; you ha'n't told us why you made up to her for a purpose, and kep' on pretendin' she didn't know her own mind."

"I've promised Gilbert that I won't interfere, and that's enough," said Barton, doggedly.

Miss Lavender was foiled for a moment, but she presently returned to the attack. "I dunno as it's enough, after what's gone before," she said. "Couldn't you go a step furder, and lend Gilbert a helpin' hand, whenever and whatever?"

"Betsy!" Gilbert exclaimed.

"Let me alone, lad! I don't speak in Gilbert's name, nor yet in Martha's; only out o' my own mind. I don't ask you to do anything, but I want to know how it stands with your willin'ness."

"I've offered, more than once, to do him a good turn, if I could; but I guess my help wouldn't be welcome," Barton answered. The sting of the suspicion rankled in his mind, and Gilbert's evident aversion sorely wounded his vanity.

"Wouldn't be welcome. Then I'll only say this; maybe I've got it in my power, and 't isn't sayin' much, for the mouse gnawed the mashes o' the lion's net, to help you to what you're after, bein' as it isn't Martha, and can't be her money. S'pose I did it o' my own accord, leavin' you to feel beholden to me, or not, after all's said and done?"

But Alfred Barton was proof against even this assault. He was too dejected to enter, at once, into a new plot, the issue of which would probably

254

be as fruitless as the others. He had already accepted a sufficiency of shame, for one day. This last confession, if made, would place his character in a still grosser and meaner light; while, if withheld, the unexplained motive might be presented as a partial justification of his course. He had been surprised into damaging admissions; but here he would take a firm stand.

"You're right so far, Betsy," he said, "that I had a reason—a good reason, it seemed to me, but I may be mistaken—for what I did. It concerns no one under Heaven but my own self; and though I don't doubt your willingness to do me a good turn, it would make no difference—you couldn't help one bit. I've given the thing up, and so let it be!"

There was nothing more to be said, and the two cross-examiners took their departure. As they descended to the creek, Miss Lavender remarked, as if to herself,—

"No use—it can't be screwed out of him! So there's one cur'osity the less; not that I'm glad of it, for not knowin' worries more than knowin', whatsoever and whosoever. And I dunno as I think any the wuss of him for shuttin' his teeth so tight onto it."

Alfred Barton waited until the two had disappeared behind the timber in the bottom. Then he slowly followed, stealing across the fields and around the stables, to the back-door of the Unicorn bar-room. It was noticed that, although he drank a good deal that afternoon, his ill-humor was not, as usual, diminished thereby.

CHAPTER XXIV. — DEB. SMITH TAKES A RESOLUTION.

It was a raw, overcast evening in the early part of January. Away to the west there was a brownish glimmer in the dark-gray sky, denoting sunset, and from that point there came barely sufficient light to disclose the prominent features of a wild, dreary, uneven landscape.

The foreground was a rugged clearing in the forest, just where the crest of a high hill began to slope rapidly down to the Brandywine. The dark meadows, dotted with irregular lakes of ice, and long, dirty drifts of unmelted snow, but not the stream itself, could be seen. Across the narrow valley rose a cape, or foreland, of the hills beyond, timbered nearly to the top, and falling, on either side, into deep lateral glens,—those warm nooks which the first settlers loved to choose, both from their snug aspect of shelter, and from the cold, sparkling springs of water which every one of them held in its lap. Back of the summits of all the hills stretched a rich, rolling upland, cleared and mapped into spacious fields, but showing everywhere an edge of dark, wintry woods against the darkening sky.

In the midst of this clearing stood a rough cabin, or rather half-cabin, of logs; for the back of it was formed by a ledge of slaty rocks, some ten or twelve feet in height, which here cropped out of the hill-side. The raw clay with which the crevices between the logs had been stopped, had fallen out in many places; the roof of long strips of peeled bark was shrivelled by wind and sun, and held in its place by stones and heavy branches of trees, and a square tower of plastered sticks in one corner very imperfectly suggested a chimney. There was no inclosed patch of vegetable-ground near, no stable, improvised of corn-shocks, for the shelter of cow or pig, and the habitation seemed not only to be untenanted, but to have been forsaken years before.

Yet a thin, cautious thread of smoke stole above the rocks, and just as the starless dusk began to deepen into night, a step was heard, slowly climbing upward through the rustling leaves and snapping sticks of the forest. A woman's figure, wearily scaling the hill under a load which almost concealed the upper part of her body, for it consisted of a huge wallet, a rattling collection of articles tied in a blanket, and two or three bundles slung over her shoulders with a rope. When at last, panting from the strain, she stood beside the cabin, she shook herself, and the articles, with the exception of the wallet, tumbled to the ground. The latter she set down carefully, thrust her arm into one of the ends and drew forth a heavy jug, which she raised to her mouth. The wind was rising, but its voice among the trees was dull and muffled; now and then a flake of snow dropped out of the gloom, as if some cowardly, insulting creature of the air were spitting at the world under cover of the night.

"It's likely to be a good night," the woman muttered, "and he'll be on the way by this time. I must put things to rights."

She entered the cabin by a narrow door in the southern end. Her first care was to rekindle the smouldering fire from a store of boughs and dry brushwood piled in one corner. When a little flame leaped up from the ashes, it revealed an interior bare and dismal enough, yet very cheery in contrast with the threatening weather outside. The walls were naked logs and rock, the floor of irregular flat stones, and no furniture remained except some part of a cupboard or dresser, near the chimney. Two or three short saw-cuts of logs formed as many seats, and the only sign of a bed was a mass of dry leaves, upon which a blanket had been thrown, in a hollow under the overhanging base of the rock.

Untying the blanket, the woman drew forth three or four rude cooking utensils, some dried beef and smoked sausages, and two huge round loaves of bread, and arranged them upon the one or two remaining shelves of the dresser. Then she seated herself in front of the fire, staring into the crackling blaze, which she mechanically fed from time to time, muttering brokenly to herself in the manner of one accustomed to be much alone.

"It was a mean thing, after what I'd said,—my word used to be wuth somethin', but times seems to ha' changed. If they have, why shouldn't I change with 'em, as well's anybody else? Well, why need it matter? I've got a bad name.... No, that'll never do! Stick to what you're about, or you'll be

257

wuthlesser, even, than they says you are!"

She shook her hard fist, and took another pull at the jug.

"It's well I laid in a good lot o' that," she said. "No better company for a lonesome night, and it'll stop his cussin', I reckon, anyhow. Eh? What's that?"

From the wood came a short, quick yelp, as from some stray dog. She rose, slipped out the door, and peered into the darkness, which was full of gathering snow. After listening a moment, she gave a low whistle. It was not answered, but a stealthy step presently approached, and a form, dividing itself from the gloom, stood at her side.

"All right, Deb?"

"Right as I can make it. I've got meat and drink, and I come straight from the Turk's Head, and Jim says the Sheriff's gone back to Chester, and there's been nobody out these three days. Come in and take bite and sup, and then tell me everything."

They entered the cabin. The door was carefully barred, and then Sandy Flash, throwing off a heavy overcoat, such as the drovers were accustomed to wear, sat down by the fire. His face was redder than its wont, from cold and exposure, and all its keen, fierce lines were sharp and hard. As he warmed his feet and hands at the blaze, and watched Deb. Smith while she set the meat upon the coals, and cut the bread with a heavy hunting-knife, the wary, defiant look of a hunted animal gradually relaxed, and he said,—

"Faith, Deb., this is better than hidin' in the frost. I believe I'd ha' froze last night, if I hadn't got down beside an ox for a couple o' hours. It's a dog's life they've led me, and I've had just about enough of it."

"Then why not give it up, Sandy, for good and all? I'll go out with you to the Backwoods, after—after things is settled."

"And let 'em brag they frightened me away!" he exclaimed, with an oath. "Not by a long shot, Deb. I owe 'em a score for this last chase—I'll make the rich men o' Chester County shake in their shoes, and the officers o' the law, and the Volunteers, damme! before I've done with 'em. When I go away for

258

good, I'll leave somethin' behind me for them to remember me by!"

"Well, never mind; eat a bit—the meat's ready, and see here, Sandy! I carried this all the way."

He seized the jug and took a long draught. "You're a good 'un, Deb.," he said. "A man isn't half a man when his belly's cold and empty."

He fell to, and ate long and ravenously. Warmed at last, both by fire and fare, and still more by his frequent potations, he commenced the story of his disguises and escapes, laughing at times with boisterous self-admiration, swearing brutally and bitterly at others, over the relentless energy with which he had been pursued. Deb. Smith listened with eager interest, slapping him upon the back with a force of approval which would have felled an ordinary man, but which Sandy Flash cheerfully accepted as a caress.

"You see," he said at the close, "after I sneaked between Potter's troop and the Sheriff's, and got down into the lower corner o' the county, I managed to jump aboard a grain-sloop bound for Newport, but they were froze in at the mouth o' Christeen; so I went ashore, dodged around Wilmington, (where I'm rather too well known,) and come up Whitely Creek as a drover from Mar'land. But from Grove up to here, I've had to look out mighty sharp, takin' nigh onto two days for what I could go straight through in half a day."

"Well, I guess you're safe here, Sandy," she said; "they'll never think o' lookin' for you twice't in the same place. Why didn't you send word for me before? You've kep' me a mortal long time a-waitin', and down on the Woodrow farm would ha' done as well as here."

"It's a little too near that Potter. He'd smell me out as quick as if I was a skunk to windward of him. Besides, it's time I was pitchin' on a few new holes; we must talk it over together, Deb."

He lifted the jug again to his mouth. Deb. Smith, although she had kept nearly even pace with him, was not so sensible to the potency of the liquor, and was watching for the proper degree of mellowness, in order to broach the subject over which she had been secretly brooding since his arrival.

"First of all, Sandy," she now said, "I want to talk to you about Gilbert

Potter. The man's my friend, and I thought you cared enough about me to let my friends alone."

"So I do, Deb., when they let me alone. I had a right to shoot the fellow, but I let him off easy, as much for your sake as because he was carryin' another man's money."

"That's not true!" she cried. "It was his own money, every cent of it,—hard-earned money, meant to pay off his debts; and I can say it because I helped him earn it, mowin' and reapin' beside him in the harvest-field, thrashin' beside him in the barn, eatin' at his table, and sleepin' under his roof. I gev him my word he was safe from you, but you've made me out a liar, with no more thought o' me than if I'd been a stranger or an enemy!"

"Come, Deb., don't get into your tantrums. Potter may be a decent fellow, as men go, for anything I know, but you're not beholden to him because he treated you like a Christian as you are. You seem to forgit that he tried to take my life,—that he's hardly yet giv' up huntin' me like a wild beast! Damn him, if the money was his, which I don't believe, it wouldn't square accounts between us. You think more o' his money than o' my life, you huzzy!"

"No I don't, Sandy!" she protested, "no I don't. You know me better'n that. What am I here for, to-night? Have I never helped you, and hid you, and tramped the country for you back and forth, by day and by night,—and for what? Not for money, but because I'm your wife, whether or not priest or 'squire has said it. I thought you cared for me, I did, indeed; I thought you might do one thing to please me!"

There was a quivering motion in the muscles of her hard face; her lips were drawn convulsively, with an expression which denoted weeping, although no tears came to her eyes.

"Don't be a fool!" Sandy exclaimed. "S'pose you have served me, isn't it somethin' to have a man to serve? What other husband is there for you in the world, than me,—the only man that isn't afeard o' your fist? You've done your duty by me, I'll allow, and so have I done mine by you!"

260

"Then," she begged, "do this one thing over and above your duty. Do it, Sandy, as a bit o' kindness to me, and put upon me what work you please, till I've made it up to you! You dunno what it is, maybe, to have one person in the world as shows a sort o' respect for you—that gives you his hand honestly, like a gentleman, and your full Chris'en name. It does good when a body's been banged about as I've been, and more used to curses than kind words, and not a friend to look after me if I was layin' at Death's door—and I don't say you wouldn't come, Sandy, but you can't. And there's no denyin' that he had the law on his side, and isn't more an enemy than any other man. Maybe he'd even be a friend in need, as far as he dared, if you'd only do it"—

"Do what? What in the Devil's name is the woman drivin' at?" yelled Sandy Flash.

"Give back the money; it's his'n, not Barton's,—I know it. Tell me where it is, and I'll manage the whole thing for you. It's got to be paid in a month or two, folks says, and they'll come on him for it, maybe take and sell his farm—sell th' only house, Sandy, where I git my rights, th' only house where I git a bit o' peace an' comfort! You wouldn't be that hard on me?"

The highwayman took another deep drink and rose to his feet. His face was stern and threatening. "I've had enough o' this foolery," he said. "Once and for all, Deb., don't you poke your nose into my affairs! Give back the money? Tell you where it is? Pay him for huntin' me down? I could take you by the hair and knock your head ag'in the wall, for them words!"

She arose also and confronted him. The convulsive twitching of her mouth ceased, and her face became as hard and defiant as his. "Sandy Flash, mark my words!" she exclaimed. "You're a-goin' the wrong way, when you stop takin' only from the Collectors and the proud rich men, and sparin' the poor. Instead o' doin' good to balance the bad, it'll soon be all bad, and you no better 'n a common thief! You needn't show your teeth; it's true, and I say it square to y'r face!"

She saw the cruel intensity of his anger, but did not flinch. They had had many previous quarrels, in which neither could claim any very great advantage over the other; but the highwayman was now in an impatient and exasperated mood, and she dared more than she suspected in defying him.

"You ———!" (the epithet he used cannot be written,) "will you stop your jaw, or shall I stop it for you? I'm your master, and I give you your orders, and the first order is, Not another word, now and never, about Potter or his money!"

He had never before outraged her by such a word, never before so brutally asserted his claim to her obedience. All the hot, indignant force of her fierce, coarse nature rose in resistance. She was thoroughly aroused and fearless. The moment had come, she felt, when the independence which had been her compensation amid all the hardships and wrongs of her life, was threatened,—when she must either preserve it by a desperate effort, or be trampled under foot by this man, whom she both loved and feared, and in that moment, hated.

"I'll not hold my jaw!" she cried, with flashing eyes. "Not even at your biddin', Sandy Flash! I'll not rest till I have the money out o' you; there's no law ag'inst stealin' from a thief!"

The answer was a swift, tremendous blow of the highwayman's fist, delivered between her eyes. She fell, and lay for a moment stunned, the blood streaming from her face. Then with a rapid movement, she seized the hunting-knife which lay beside the fire, and sprang to her feet.

The knife was raised in her right hand, and her impulse was to plunge it into his heart. But she could not avoid his eyes; they caught and held her own, as if by some diabolical fascination. He stood motionless, apparently awaiting the blow. Nothing in his face or attitude expressed fear; only all the power of the man seemed to be concentrated in his gaze, and to hold her back. The impulse once arrested, he knew, it would not return. The eyes of each were fixed on the other's, and several minutes of awful silence thus passed.

Finally, Deb. Smith slightly shuddered, as if with cold, her hand slowly fell, and without a word she turned away to wash her bloody face.

Sandy Flash grinned, took another drink of whiskey, resumed his seat before the fire, and then proceeded to fill his pipe. He lit and smoked it to the end, without turning his head, or seeming to pay the least attention to her movements. She, meanwhile, had stopped the flow of blood from her face, bound a rag around her forehead, and lighted her own pipe, without speaking. The highwayman first broke the silence.

"As I was a-sayin'," he remarked, in his ordinary tone, "we've got to look out for new holes, where the scent isn't so strong as about these. What do you think o' th' Octorara?"

"Where?" she asked. Her voice was hoarse and strange, but he took no notice of it, gazing steadily into the fire as he puffed out a huge cloud of smoke.

"Well, pretty well down," he said. "There's a big bit o' woodland, nigh onto two thousand acres, belongin' to somebody in Baltimore that doesn't look at it once't in ten years, and my thinkin' is, it'd be as safe as the Backwoods. I must go to—it's no difference where—to-morrow mornin', but I'll be back day after to-morrow night, and you needn't stir from here till I come. You've grub enough for that long, eh?"

"It'll do," she muttered.

"Then, that's enough. I must be off an hour before day, and I'm devilish fagged and sleepy, so here goes!"

With these words he rose, knocked the ashes out of his pipe, and stretched himself on the bed of leaves. She continued to smoke her pipe.

"Deb.," he said, five minutes afterwards, "I'm not sure o' wakin'. You look out for me,—do you hear?"

"I hear," she answered, in the same low, hoarse voice, without turning her head. In a short time Sandy Flash's deep breathing announced that he slept. Then she turned and looked at him with a grim, singular smile, as the wavering fire-light drew clear pictures of his face which the darkness as constantly wiped out again. By-and-by she noiselessly moved her seat nearer to the wall, leaned her head against the rough logs, and seemed to sleep. But, even if it were sleep, she was conscious of his least movement, and started into alert wakefulness, if he turned, muttered in dreams, or crooked a finger among the dead leaves. From time to time she rose, stole out of the cabin and looked at the sky. Thus the night passed away.

There was no sign of approaching dawn in the dull, overcast, snowy air; but a blind, animal instinct of time belonged to her nature, and about two hours before sunrise, she set about preparing a meal. When all was ready, she bent over Sandy Flash, seized him by the shoulder, and shook his eyes open.

"Time!" was all she said.

He sprang up, hastily devoured the bread and meat, and emptied the jug of its last remaining contents.

"Hark ye, Deb.," he exclaimed, when he had finished, "you may as well trudge over to the Turk's Head and fill this while I'm gone. We'll need all of it, and more, tomorrow night. Here's a dollar, to pay for't. Now I must be on the tramp, but you may look for me to-morrow, an hour after sun."

He examined his pistols, stuck them in his belt, threw his drover's cloak over his shoulders, and strode out of the cabin. She waited until the sound of his footsteps had died away in the cold, dreary gloom, and then threw herself upon the pallet which he had vacated. This time she slept soundly, until hours after the gray winter day had come up the sky.

Her eyes were nearly closed by the swollen flesh, and she laid handfuls of snow upon her face, to cool the inflamation. At first, her movements were uncertain, expressing a fierce conflict, a painful irresolution of feeling; she picked up the hunting-knife, looked at it with a ghastly smile, and then threw it from her. Suddenly, however, her features changed, and every trace of her former hesitation vanished. After hurriedly eating the fragments left from Sandy's breakfast, she issued from the cabin and took a straight and rapid course eastward, up and over the hill.

During the rest of that day and the greater part of the next, the cabin was deserted.

It was almost sunset, and not more than an hour before Sandy Flash's promised return, when Deb. Smith again made her appearance. Her face was pale, (except for the dark blotches around the eyes,) worn, and haggard; she seemed to have grown ten years older in the interval.

Her first care was to rekindle the fire and place the replenished jug in its accustomed place. Then she arranged and rearranged the rude blocks which served for seats, the few dishes and the articles of food on the shelf, and, when all had been done, paced back and forth along the narrow floor, as if pushed by some invisible, tormenting power.

Finally a whistle was heard, and in a minute afterwards Sandy Flash entered the door. The bright blaze of the hearth shone upon his bold, daring, triumphant face.

"That's right, Deb.," he said. "I'm dry and hungry, and here's a rabbit you can skin and set to broil in no time. Let's look at you, old gal! The devil!—I didn't mean to mark you like that. Well, bygones is bygones, and better times is a-comin'."

"Sandy!" she cried, with a sudden, appealing energy, "Sandy—once't more! Won't you do for me what I want o' you?"

His face darkened in an instant. "Deb!" was all the word he uttered, but she understood the tone. He took off his pistol-belt and laid it on the shelf. "Lay there, pets!" he said; "I won't want you to-night. A long tramp it was, and I'm glad it's over. Deb., I guess I've nigh tore off one o' my knee-buckles, comin' through the woods."

Placing his foot upon one of the logs, he bent down to examine the buckle. Quick as lightning, Deb., who was standing behind him, seized each of his arms, just above the elbows, with her powerful hands, and drew them towards each other upon his back. At the same time she uttered a shrill, wild cry,—a scream so strange and unearthly in its character that Sandy Flash's blood chilled to hear it.

"Curse you, Deb., what are you doing? Are you clean mad?" he ejaculated, struggling violently to free his arms.

"Which is strongest now?" she asked; "my arms, or your'n? I've got you,

265

I'll hold you, and I'll only let go when I please!"

He swore and struggled, but he was powerless in her iron grip. In another minute the door of the cabin was suddenly burst open, and two armed men sprang upon him. More rapidly than the fact can be related, they snapped a pair of heavy steel handcuffs upon his wrists, pinioned his arms at his sides, and bound his knees together. Then, and not till then, Deb. Smith relaxed her hold.

Sandy Flash made one tremendous muscular effort, to test the strength of his bonds, and then stood motionless. His white teeth flashed between his parted lips, and there was a dull, hard glare in his eyes which told that though struck dumb with astonishment and impotent rage, he was still fearless, still unsubdued. Deb. Smith, behind him, leaned against the wall, pale and panting.

"A good night's work!" remarked Chaffey, the constable, as he possessed himself of the musket, pistol-belt, and hunting-knife. "I guess this pitcher won't go to the well any more."

"We'll see," Sandy exclaimed, with a sneer. "You've got me, not through any pluck o' your'n, but through black, underhanded treachery. You'd better double chain and handcuff me, or I may be too much for you yet!"

"I guess you'll do," said the constable, examining the cords by the light of a lantern which his assistant had in the mean time fetched from without. "I'll even untie your knees, for you've to walk over the hill to the next farm-house, where we'll find a wagon to carry you to Chester jail. I promise you more comfortable quarters than these, by daylight."

The constable then turned to Deb. Smith, who had neither moved nor spoken.

"You needn't come with us without you want to," he said. "You can get your share of the money at any time; but you must remember to be ready to appear and testify, when Court meets."

"Must I do that?" she gasped.

"Why, to be sure! It's a reg'lar part of the trial, and can't be left out, though there's enough to hang the fellow ten times over, without you."

The two unbound Sandy Flash's knees and placed themselves on each side of him, the constable holding a cocked pistol in his right hand.

"March is the word, is it?" said the highwayman. "Well, I'm ready. Potter was right, after all; he said there'd be a curse on the money, and there is; but I never guessed the curse'd come upon me through you, Deb!"

"Oh, Sandy!" she cried, starting forward, "you druv me to it! The curse was o' your own makin'—and I gev you a last chance to-night, but you throwed it from you!"

"Very well, Deb," he answered, "if I've got my curse, don't think you'll not have your'n! Go down to Chester and git your blood-money, and see what'll come of it, and what'll come to you!"

He turned towards her as he spoke, and the expression of his face seemed so frightful that she shuddered and covered her eyes. The next moment, the old cabin door creaked open, fell back with a crash, and she was alone.

She stared around at the dreary walls. The sound of their footsteps had died away, and only the winter night-wind wailed through the crannies of the hut. Accustomed as she was to solitary life and rudest shelter, and to the companionship of her superstitious fancies, she had never before felt such fearful loneliness, such overpowering dread. She heaped sticks upon the fire, sat down before it, and drank from the jug. Its mouth was still wet from his lips, and it seemed that she was already drinking down the commencement of the curse.

Her face worked, and hard, painful groans burst from her lips. She threw herself upon the floor and grovelled there, until the woman's relief which she had almost unlearned forced its forgotten way, through cramps and agonies, to her eyes. In the violent passion of her weeping and moaning, God saw and pitied, that night, the struggles of a dumb, ignorant, yet not wholly darkened nature.

Two hours afterwards she arose, sad, stern, and determined, packed together the things she had brought with her, quenched the fire (never again to be relighted) upon the hearth, and took her way, through cold and darkness, down the valley.

CHAPTER XXV. — TWO ATTEMPTS.

The news of Sandy Flash's capture ran like wildfire through the county. As the details became more correctly known, there was great rejoicing but greater surprise, for Deb. Smith's relation to the robber, though possibly surmised by a few, was unsuspected by the community at large. In spite of the service which she had rendered by betraying her paramour into the hands of justice, a bitter feeling of hostility towards her was developed among the people, and she was generally looked upon as an accomplice to Sandy Flash's crimes, who had turned upon him only when she had ceased to profit by them.

The public attention was thus suddenly drawn away from Gilbert Potter, and he was left to struggle, as he best might, against the difficulties entailed by his loss. He had corresponded with Mr. Trainer, the conveyancer in Chester, and had learned that the money still due must not only be forthcoming on the first of April, but that it probably could not be obtained there. The excitement for buying lands along the Alleghany, Ohio, and Beaver rivers, in western Pennsylvania, had seized upon the few capitalists of the place, and Gilbert's creditor had already been subjected to inconvenience and possible loss, as one result of the robbery. Mr. Trainer therefore suggested that he should make a new loan in his own neighborhood, where the spirit of speculation had not yet reached.

The advice was prudent and not unfriendly, although of a kind more easy to give than to carry into execution. Mark's money-belt had been restored, greatly against the will of the good-hearted fellow (who would have cheerfully lent Gilbert the whole amount had he possessed it), and there was enough grain yet to be threshed and sold, to yield something more than a hundred dollars; but this was all which Gilbert could count upon from his own resources. He might sell the wagon and one span of horses, reducing by their value the sum which he would be obliged to borrow; yet his hope of recovering the money in another year could only be realized by retaining them, to continue, from time to time, his occupation of hauling flour.

Although the sympathy felt for him was general and very hearty, it never took the practical form of an offer of assistance, and he was far too proud to accept that plan of relief which a farmer, whose barn had been struck by lightning and consumed, had adopted, the previous year,—going about the neighborhood with a subscription-list, and soliciting contributions. His nearest friends were as poor as, or poorer than, himself, and those able to aid him felt no call to tender their services.

Martha Deane knew of this approaching trouble, not from Gilbert's own lips, for she had seen him but once and very briefly since his return from the chase of Sandy Flash. It was her cousin Mark, who, having entered into an alliance, offensive and defensive, with her lover, betrayed (considering that the end sanctioned the means) the confidence reposed in him.

The thought that her own coming fortune lay idle, while Gilbert might be saved by the use of a twentieth part of it, gave Martha Deane no peace. The whole belonged to him prospectively, yet would probably be of less service when it should be legally her own to give, than the fragment which now would lift him above anxiety and humiliation. The money had been bequeathed to her by a maternal aunt, whose name she bore, and the provisions by which the bequest was accompanied, so light and reasonable be fore, now seemed harsh and unkind. The payment of the whole sum, or any part of it, she saw, could not be anticipated. But she imagined there must be a way to obtain a loan of the necessary amount, with the bequest as security. With her ignorance of business matters, she felt the need of counsel in this emergency; yet her father was her guardian, and there seemed to be no one else to whom she could properly apply. Not Gilbert, for she fancied he might reject the assistance she designed, and therefore she meant to pay the debt before it became due, without his knowledge; nor Mark, nor Farmer Fairthorn. Betsy Lavender, when appealed to, shook her head, and remarked,—

"Lord bless you, child! a wuss snarl than ever. I'm gittin' a bit skeary, when you talk o' law and money matters, and that's the fact. Not that I find fault with your wishin' to do it, but the contrary, and there might be ways,

270

as you say, only I'm not lawyer enough to find 'em, and as to advisin' where I don't see my way clear, Defend me from it!"

Thus thrown back upon herself, Martha was forced to take the alternative which she would gladly have avoided, and from which, indeed, she hoped nothing,—an appeal to her father. Gilbert Potter's name had not again been mentioned between them. She, for her part, had striven to maintain her usual gentle, cheerful demeanor, and it is probable that Dr. Deane made a similar attempt; but he could not conceal a certain coldness and stiffness, which made an uncomfortable atmosphere in their little household.

"Well, Betsy," Martha said (they were in her room, upstairs), "Father has just come in from the stable, I see. Since there is no other way, I will go down and ask his advice."

"You don't mean it, child!" cried the spinster.

Martha left the room, without answer.

"She's got that from him, anyhow," Miss Betsy remarked, "and which o' the two is stubbornest, I couldn't undertake to say. If he's dead-set on the wrong side, why, she's jist as dead-set on the right side, and that makes a mortal difference. I don't see why I should be all of a trimble, that only sets here and waits, while she's stickin' her head into the lion's mouth; but so it is! Isn't about time for you to be doin' somethin', Betsy Lavender!"

Martha Deane entered the front sitting-room with a grave, deliberate step. The Doctor sat at his desk, with a pair of heavy silver-rimmed spectacles on his nose, looking over an antiquated "Materia Medica." His upper lip seemed to have become harder and thinner, at the expense of the under one, which pouted in a way that expressed vexation and ill-temper. He was, in fact, more annoyed than he would have confessed to any human being. Alfred Barton's visits had discontinued, and he could easily guess the reason. Moreover, a suspicion of Gilbert Potter's relation to his daughter was slowly beginning to permeate the neighborhood; and more than once, within the last few days, all his peculiar diplomacy had been required to parry a direct question. He foresaw that the subject would soon come to the notice of his elder brethren among the Friends, who felt self-privileged to rebuke and remonstrate, even in family matters of so delicate a nature.

It was useless, the Doctor knew, to attempt coercion with Martha. If any measure could succeed in averting the threatened shame, it must be kindly persuasion, coupled with a calm, dispassionate appeal to her understanding. The quiet, gentle way in which she had met his anger, he now saw, had left the advantage of the first encounter on her side. His male nature and long habit of rule made an equal self-control very difficult, on his part, and he resolved to postpone a recurrence to the subject until he should feel able to meet his daughter with her own weapons. Probably some reflection of the kind then occupied his mind, in spite of the "Materia Medica" before him.

"Father," said Martha, seating herself with a bit of sewing in her hand, "I want to ask thee a few questions about business matters."

The Doctor looked at her. "Well, thee's taking a new turn," he remarked. "Is it anything very important?"

"Very important," she answered; "it's about my own fortune."

"I thought thee understood, Martha, that that matter was all fixed and settled, until thee's twenty-five, unless—unless"—

Here the Doctor hesitated. He did not wish to introduce the sore subject of his daughter's marriage.

"I know what thee means, father. Unless I should sooner marry, with thy consent. But I do not expect to marry now, and therefore do not ask thy permission. What I want to know is, whether I could not obtain a loan of a small sum of money, on the security of the legacy?"

"That depends on circumstances," said the Doctor, slowly, and after a long pause, during which he endeavored to guess his daughter's design. "It might be,—yes, it might be; but, Martha, surely thee doesn't want for money? Why should thee borrow?"

"Couldn't thee suppose, father, that I need it for some good purpose? I've always had plenty, it is true; but I don't think thee can say I ever squandered it foolishly or thoughtlessly. This is a case where I wish to make an investment,—a permanent investment."

"Ah, indeed? I always fancied thee cared less for money than a prudent woman ought. How much might this investment be?"

"About six hundred dollars," she answered.

"Six hundred!" exclaimed the Doctor; "that's a large sum to venture, a large sum! Since thee can only raise it with my help, thee'll certainly admit my right, as thy legal guardian, if not as thy father, to ask where, how, and on what security the money will be invested?"

Martha hesitated only long enough to reflect that her father's assertion was probably true, and without his aid she could do nothing. "Father," she then said, "I am the security."

"I don't understand thee, child."

"I mean that my whole legacy will be responsible to the lender for its repayment in three years from this time. The security I ask, I have in advance; it is the happiness of my life!"

"Martha! thee doesn't mean to say that thee would"—

Dr. Deane could get no further. Martha, with a sorrowful half-smile, took up his word.

"Yes, father, I would. Lest thee should not have understood me right, I repeat that I would, and will, lift the mortgage on Gilbert Potter's farm. He has been very unfortunate, and there is a call for help which nobody heeds as he deserves. If I give it now, I simply give a part in advance. The whole will be given afterwards."

Dr. Deane's face grew white, and his lip trembled, in spite of himself. It was a minute or two before he ventured to say, in a tolerably steady voice,—

"Thee still sets up thy right (as thee calls it) against mine, but mine is older built and will stand. To help thee to this money would only be to encourage thy wicked fancy for the man. Of course, I can't do it; I wonder thee should expect it of me. I wonder, indeed, thee should think of taking as a husband one who borrows money of thee almost as soon as he has spoken his mind!"

For an instant Martha Deane's eyes flashed. "Father!" she cried, "it is not so! Gilbert doesn't even know my desire to help him. I must ask this of thee, to speak no evil of him in my hearing. It would only give me unnecessary pain, not shake my faith in his honesty and goodness. I see thee will not assist me, and so I must endeavor to find whether the thing cannot be done without thy assistance. In three years more the legacy will be mine, I shall go to Chester, and consult a lawyer, whether my own note for that time could not be accepted!"

"I can spare thee the trouble," the Doctor said. "In case of thy death before the three years are out, who is to pay the note? Half the money falls to me, and half to thy uncle Richard. Thy aunt Martha was wise. It truly seems as if she had foreseen just what has happened, and meant to baulk thy present rashness. Thee may go to Chester, and welcome, if thee doubts my word; but unless thee can give positive assurance that thee will be alive in three years' time, I don't know of any one foolish enough to advance thee money."

The Doctor's words were cruel enough; he might have spared his triumphant, mocking smile. Martha's heart sank within her, as she recognized her utter helplessness. Not yet, however, would she give up the sweet hope of bringing aid; for Gilbert's sake she would make another appeal.

"I won't charge thee, father, with being intentionally unkind. It would almost seem, from thy words, that thee is rather glad than otherwise, because my life is uncertain. If I should die, would thee not care enough for my memory to pay a debt, the incurring of which brought me peace and happiness during life? Then, surely, thee would forgive; thy heart is not so hard as thee would have me believe; thee wishes me happiness, I cannot doubt, but thinks it will come in thy way, not in mine. Is it not possible to grant me this—only this—and leave everything else to time?"

Dr. Deane was touched and softened by his daughter's words. Perhaps he might even have yielded to her entreaty at once, had not a harsh and selfish condition presented itself in a very tempting form to his mind.

"Martha," he said, "I fancy that thee looks upon this matter of the loan in the light of a duty, and will allow that thy motives may be weighty to thy own mind. I ask thee to calm thyself, and consider things clearly. If I grant thy request, I do so against my own judgment, yea,—since it concerns thy interests,—against my own conscience. This is not a thing to be lightly done, and if I should yield, I might reasonably expect some little sacrifice of present inclination—yet all for thy future good—on thy part. I would cheerfully borrow the six hundred dollars for thee, or make it up from my own means, if need be, to know that the prospect of thy disgrace was averted. Thee sees no disgrace, I am aware, and pity that it is so; but if thy feeling for the young man is entirely pure and unselfish, it should be enough to know that thee had saved him from ruin, without considering thyself bound to him for life."

The Doctor sharply watched his daughter's face while he spoke. She looked up, at first, with an eager, wondering light of hope in her eyes,—a light that soon died away, and gave place to a cloudy, troubled expression. Then the blood rose to her cheeks, and her lips assumed the clear, firm curve which always reflected the decisions of her mind.

"Father," she said, "I see thee has learned how to tempt, as well as threaten. For the sake of doing a present good, thee would have me bind myself to do a life-long injustice. Thee would have me take an external duty to balance a violation of the most sacred conscience of my heart. How little thee knows me! It is not alone that I am necessary to Gilbert Potter's happiness, but also that he is necessary to mine. Perhaps it is the will of Heaven that so great a bounty should not come to me too easily, and I must bear, without murmuring, that my own father is set against me. Thee may try me, if thee desires, for the coming three years, but I can tell thee as well, now, what the end will be. Why not rather tempt me by offering the money Gilbert needs, on the condition of my giving up the rest of the legacy to thee? That would be a temptation, I confess."

"No!" he exclaimed, with rising exasperation, "if thee has hardened thy heart against all my counsels for thy good, I will at least keep my own conscience free. I will not help thee by so much as the moving of a finger. All I can do is, to pray that thy stubborn mind may be bent, and gradually led back to the Light!"

He put away the book, took his cane and broad-brimmed hat, and turned to leave the room. Martha rose, with a sad but resolute face, and went up-stairs to her chamber.

Miss Betsy Lavender, when she learned all that had been said, on both sides, was thrown into a state of great agitation and perplexity of mind. She stared at Martha Deane, without seeming to see her, and muttered from time to time such fragmentary phrases as,—"If I was right-down sure," or, "It'd only be another weepon tried and throwed away, at the wust."

"What are you thinking of, Betsy?" Martha finally asked.

"Thinkin' of? Well, I can't rightly tell you. It's a bit o' knowledge that come in my way, once't upon a time, never meanin' to make use of it in all my born days, and I wouldn't now, only for your two sakes; not that it concerns you a mite; but never mind, there's ten thousand ways o' workin' on men's minds, and I can't do no more than try my way."

Thereupon Miss Lavender arose, and would have descended to the encounter at once, had not Martha wisely entreated her to wait a day or two, until the irritation arising from her own interview had had time to subside in her father's mind.

"It's puttin' me on nettles, now that I mean fast and firm to do it; but you're quite right, Martha," the spinster said.

Three or four days afterwards she judged the proper time had arrived, and boldly entered the Doctor's awful presence. "Doctor," she began, "I've come to have a little talk, and it's no use beatin' about the bush, plainness o' speech bein' one o' my ways; not that folks always thinks it a virtue, but oftentimes the contrary, and so may you, maybe; but when there's a worry in a house, it's better, whatsoever and whosoever, to have it come to a head than go on achin' and achin', like a blind bile!"

"H'm," snorted the Doctor, "I see what thee's driving at, and I may as well tell thee at once, that if thee comes to me from Martha, I've heard enough from her, and more than enough."

"More 'n enough," repeated Miss Lavender. "But you're wrong. I come neither from Martha, nor yet from Gilbert Potter; but I've been thinkin' that you and me, bein' old,—in a measure, that is,—and not so direckly concerned, might talk the thing over betwixt and between us, and maybe come to a better understandin' for both sides."

Dr. Deane was not altogether disinclined to accept this proposition. Although Miss Lavender sometimes annoyed him, as she rightly conjectured, by her plainness of speech, he had great respect for her shrewdness and her practical wisdom. If he could but even partially win her to his views, she would be a most valuable ally.

"Then say thy say, Betsy," he assented.

"Thy say, Betsy. Well, first and foremost, I guess we may look upon Alf. Barton's courtin' o' Martha as broke off for good, the fact bein' that he never wanted to have her, as he's told me since with his own mouth."

"What?" Dr. Deane exclaimed.

"With his own mouth." Miss Lavender repeated. "And as to his reasons for lettin' on, I don't know 'em. Maybe you can guess 'em, as you seem to ha' had everything cut and dried betwixt and between you; but that's neither here nor there—Alf. Barton bein' out o' the way, why, the coast's clear, and so Gilbert's case is to be considered by itself; and let's come to the p'int, namely, what you've got ag'in him?"

"I wonder thee can ask, Betsy! He's poor, he's base-born, without position or influence in the neighborhood,—in no way a husband for Martha Deane! If her head's turned because he has been robbed, and marvellously saved, and talked about, I suppose I must wait till she comes to her right senses."

"I rather expect," Miss Lavender gravely remarked, "that they were bespoke before all that happened, and it's not a case o' sudden fancy, but somethin' bred in the bone and not to be cured by plasters. We won't talk o' that now, but come back to Gilbert Potter, and I dunno as you're quite right in any way about his bein's and doin's. With that farm o' his'n, he can't be called poor, and I shouldn't wonder, though I can't give no proofs, but never mind, wait awhile and you'll see, that he's not base-born, after all; and as for respect in the neighborhood, there's not a man more respected nor looked up to,—so the last p'int's settled, and we'll take the t' other two; and I s'pose you mean his farm isn't enough?"

"Thee's right," Dr. Deane said. "As Martha's guardian, I am bound to watch over her interests, and every prudent man will agree with me that her husband ought at least to be as well off as herself."

"Well, all I've got to say, is, it's lucky for you that Naomi Blake didn't think as you do, when she married you. What's sass for the goose ought to be sass for the gander (meanin' you and Gilbert), and every prudent man will agree with me."

This was a home-thrust, which Dr. Deane was not able to parry. Miss Lavender had full knowledge whereof she affirmed, and the Doctor knew it.

"I admit that there might be other advantages," he said, rather pompously, covering his annoyance with a pinch of snuff,—"advantages which partly balance the want of property. Perhaps Naomi Blake thought so too. But here, I think, it would be hard for thee to find such. Or does thee mean that the man's disgraceful birth is a recommendation?"

"Recommendation? No!" Miss Lavender curtly replied.

"We need go no further, then. Admitting thee's right in all other respects, here is cause enough for me. I put it to thee, as a sensible woman, whether I would not cover both myself and Martha with shame, by allowing her marriage with Gilbert Potter?"

Miss Lavender sat silently in her chair and appeared to meditate.

"Thee doesn't answer," the Doctor remarked, after a pause.

"I dunno how it come about," she said, lifting her head and fixing her dull eyes on vacancy; "I was thinkin' o' the time I was up at Strasburg, while your brother was livin', more 'n twenty year ago."

With all his habitual self-control and gravity of deportment, Dr. Deane could not repress a violent start of surprise. He darted a keen, fierce glance at Miss Betsy's face, but she was staring at the opposite wall, apparently unconscious of the effect of her words.

"I don't see what that has to do with Gilbert Potter," he presently said, collecting himself with an effort.

"Nor I, neither," Miss Lavender absently replied, "only it happened that I knowed Eliza Little,—her that used to live at the Gap, you know,—and just afore she died, that fall the fever was so bad, and I nussin' her, and not another soul awake in the house, she told me a secret about your brother's boy, and I must say few men would ha' acted as Henry done, and there's more 'n one mighty beholden to him."

Dr. Deane stretched out his hand as if he would close her mouth. His face was like fire, and a wild expression of fear and pain shot from his eyes.

"Betsy Lavender," he said, in a hollow voice, "thee is a terrible woman. Thee forces even the secrets of the dying from them, and brings up knowledge that should be hidden forever. What can all this avail thee? Why does thee threaten me with appearances, that cannot now be explained, all the witnesses being dead?"

"Witnesses bein' dead," she repeated. "Are you sorry for that?"

He stared at her in silent consternation.

"Doctor," she said, turning towards him for the first time, "there's no livin' soul that knows, except you and me, and if I seem hard, I'm no harder than the knowledge in your own heart. What's the difference, in the sight o' the Lord, between the one that has a bad name and the one that has a good name? Come, you set yourself up for a Chris'en, and so I ask you whether you're the one that ought to fling the first stone; whether repentance—and there's that, of course, for you a'n't a nateral bad man, Doctor, but rather the contrary—oughtn't to be showed in deeds, to be wuth much! You're set ag'in

Martha, and your pride's touched, which I can't say as I wonder at, all folks havin' pride, me among the rest, not that I've much to be proud of, Goodness knows; but never mind, don't you talk about Gilbert Potter in that style, leastways before me!"

During this speech, Dr. Deane had time to reflect. Although aghast at the unexpected revelation, he had not wholly lost his cunning. It was easy to perceive what Miss Lavender intended to do with the weapon in her hands, and his aim was to render it powerless.

"Betsy," he said, "there's one thing thee won't deny,—that, if there was a fault, (which I don't allow), it has been expiated. To make known thy suspicions would bring sorrow and trouble upon two persons for whom thee professes to feel some attachment; if thee could prove what thee thinks, it would be a still greater misfortune for them than for me. They are young, and my time is nearly spent. We all have serious burdens which we must bear alone, and thee mustn't forget that the same consideration for the opinion of men which keeps thee silent, keeps me from consenting to Martha's marriage with Gilbert Potter. We are bound alike."

"We're not!" she cried, rising from her seat. "But I see it's no use to talk any more, now. Perhaps since you know that there's a window in you, and me lookin' in, you'll try and keep th' inside o' your house in better order. Whether I'll act accordin' to my knowledge or not, depends on how things turns out, and so sufficient unto the day is the evil thereof, or however it goes!"

With these words she left the room, though foiled, not entirely hopeless.

"It's like buttin' over an old stone-wall," she said to Martha. "The first hit with a rammer seems to come back onto you, and jars y'r own bones, and may be the next, and the next; and then little stones git out o' place, and then the wall shakes, and comes down,—and so we've been a-doin'. I guess I made a crack to-day, but we'll see."

CHAPTER XXVI. – THE LAST OF SANDY FLASH.

The winter crept on, February was drawing to a close, and still Gilbert Potter had not ascertained whence the money was to be drawn which would relieve him from embarrassment. The few applications he had made were failures; some of the persons really had no money to invest, and others were too cautious to trust a man who, as everybody knew, had been unfortunate. In five weeks more the sum must be made up, or the mortgage would be foreclosed.

Both Mary Potter and her son, in this emergency, seemed to have adopted, by accident or sympathy, the same policy towards each other,— to cheer and encourage, in every possible way. Gilbert carefully concealed his humiliation, on returning home from an unsuccessful appeal for a loan, and his mother veiled her renewed sinking of the heart, as she heard of his failure, under a cheerful hope of final success, which she did not feel. Both had, in fact, one great consolation to fall back upon,—she that he had been mercifully saved to her, he that he was beloved by a noble woman.

All the grain that could be spared and sold placed but little more than a hundred dollars in Gilbert's hands, and he began seriously to consider whether he should not be obliged to sell his wagon and team. He had been offered a hundred and fifty dollars, (a very large sum, in those days,) for Roger, but he would as soon have sold his own right arm. Not even to save the farm would he have parted with the faithful animal. Mark Deane persisted in increasing his seventy-five dollars to a hundred, and forcing the loan upon his friend; so one third of the amount was secure, and there was still hope for the rest.

It is not precisely true that there had been no offer of assistance. There was one, which Gilbert half-suspected had been instigated by Betsy Lavender. On a Saturday afternoon, as he visited Kennett Square to have Roger's fore-feet shod, he encountered Alfred Barton at the blacksmith's shop, on the same errand.

"The man I wanted to see!" cried the latter, as Gilbert dismounted.

"Ferris was in Chester last week, and he saw Chaffey, the constable, you know, that helped catch Sandy; and Chaffey told him he was sure, from something Sandy let fall, that Deb. Smith had betrayed him out of revenge, because he robbed you. I want to know how it all hangs together."

Gilbert suddenly recalled Deb. Smith's words, on the day after his escape from the inundation, and a suspicion of the truth entered his mind for the first time.

"It must have been so!" he exclaimed. "She has been a better friend to me than many people of better name."

Barton noticed the bitterness of the remark, and possibly drew his own inference from it. He looked annoyed for a moment, but presently beckoned Gilbert to one side, and said,—

"I don't know whether you've given up your foolish suspicions about me and Sandy; but the trial comes off next week, and you'll have to be there as a witness, of course, and can satisfy yourself, if you please, that my explanation was nothing but the truth. I've not felt so jolly in twenty years, as when I heard that the fellow was really in the jug!"

"I told you I believed your words," Gilbert answered, "and that settles the matter. Perhaps I shall find out how Sandy learned what you said to me that evening, on the back-porch of the Unicorn, and if so, I am bound to let you know it."

"See here, Gilbert!" Barton resumed. "Folks say you must borrow the money you lost, or the mortgage on your farm will be foreclosed. Is that so? and how much money might it be, altogether, if you don't mind telling?"

"Not so much, if those who have it to lend, had a little faith in me,— some four or five hundred dollars."

"That ought to be got, without trouble," said Barton. "If I had it by me, I'd lend it to you in a minute; but you know I borrowed from Ferris myself, and all o' my own is so tied up that I couldn't move it without the old man getting on my track. I'll tell you what I'll do, though; I'll indorse your note for a year, if it can be kept a matter between ourselves and the lender. On account of the old man, you understand."

The offer was evidently made in good faith, and Gilbert hesitated, reluctant to accept it, and yet unwilling to reject it in a manner that might seem unfriendly.

"Barton," he said at last, "I've never yet failed to meet a money obligation. All my debts, except this last, have been paid on the day I promised, and it seems a little hard that my own name, alone, shouldn't be good for as much as I need. Old Fairthorn would give me his indorsement, but I won't ask for it; and I mean no offence when I say that I'd rather get along without yours, if I can. It's kind in you to make the offer, and to show that I'm not ungrateful, I'll beg you to look round among your rich friends and help me to find the loan."

"You're a mighty independent, fellow, Gilbert, but I can't say as I blame you for it. Yes, I'll look round in a few days, and maybe I'll stumble on the right man by the time I see you again."

When Gilbert returned home, he communicated this slight prospect of relief to his mother. "Perhaps I am a little too proud," he said; "but you've always taught me, mother, to be beholden to no man, if I could help it; and I should feel more uneasy under an obligation to Barton than to most other men. You know I must go to Chester in a few days, and must wait till I'm called to testify. There will then be time to look around, and perhaps Mr. Trainer may help me yet."

"You're right, boy!" Mary Potter cried, with flashing eyes. "Keep your pride; it's not of the mean kind! Don't ask for or take any man's indorsement!"

Two days before the time when Gilbert was summoned to Chester, Deb. Smith made her appearance at the farm. She entered the barn early one morning, with a bundle in her hand, and dispatched Sam, whom she found in the stables, to summon his master. She looked old, weather-beaten, and haggard, and her defiant show of strength was gone.

In betraying Sandy Flash into the hands of justice, she had acted from a fierce impulse, without reflecting upon the inevitable consequences of the step. Perhaps she did not suspect that she was also betraying herself, and more than confirming all the worst rumors in regard to her character. In the universal execration which followed the knowledge of her lawless connection with Sandy Flash, and her presumed complicity in his crimes, the merit of her service to the county was lost. The popular mind, knowing nothing of her temptations, struggles, and sufferings, was harsh, cold, and cruel, and she felt the weight of its verdict as never before. A few persons of her own ignorant class, who admired her strength and courage in their coarse way, advised her to hide until the first fury of the storm should be blown over. Thus she exaggerated the danger, and even felt uncertain of her reception by the very man for whose sake she had done the deed and accepted the curse.

Gilbert, however, when he saw her worn, anxious face, the eyes, like those of a dumb animal, lifted to his with an appeal which she knew not how to speak, felt a pang of compassionate sympathy.

"Deborah!" he said, "you don't look well; come into the house and warm yourself!"

"No!" she cried, "I won't darken your door till you've heerd what I've got to say. Go 'way, Sam; I want to speak to Mr. Gilbert, alone."

Gilbert made a sign, and Sam sprang down the ladder, to the stables under the threshing-floor.

"Mayhap you've heerd already," she said. "A blotch on a body's name spreads fast and far. Mine was black enough before, God knows, but they've blackened it more."

"If all I hear is true," Gilbert exclaimed, "you've blackened it for my sake, Deborah. I'm afraid you thought I blamed you, in some way, for not preventing my loss; but I'm sure you did what you could to save me from it!"

"Ay, lad, that I did! But the devil seemed to ha' got into him. Awful words passed between us, and then—the devil got into me, and—you know what follered. He wouldn't believe the money was your'n, or I don't think he'd ha' took it; he wasn't a bad man at heart, Sandy wasn't, only stubborn at the wrong times, and brung it onto himself by that. But you know what folks says about me?"

"I don't care what they say, Deborah!" Gilbert cried. "I know that you are a true and faithful friend to me, and I've not had so many such in my life that I'm likely to forget what you've tried to do!"

Her hard, melancholy face became at once eager and tender. She stepped forward, put her hand on Gilbert's arm, and said, in a hoarse, earnest, excited whisper,—

"Then maybe you'll take it? I was almost afeard to ax you,—I thought you might push me away, like the rest of 'em; but you'll take it, and that'll seem like a liftin' of the curse! You won't mind how it was got, will you? I had to git it in that way, because no other was left to me!"

"What do you mean, Deborah?"

"The money, Mr. Gilbert! They allowed me half, though the constables was for thirds, but the Judge said I'd arned the full half,—God knows, ten thousand times wouldn't pay me!—and I've got it here, tied up safe. It's your'n, you know, and maybe there a'n't quite enough, but as fur as it goes; and I'll work out the amount o' the rest, from time to time, if you'll let me come onto your place!"

Gilbert was powerfully and yet painfully moved. He forgot his detestation of the relation in which Deb. Smith had stood to the highwayman, in his gratitude for her devotion to himself. He felt an invincible repugnance towards accepting her share of the reward, even as a loan; it was "blood-money," and to touch it in any way was to be stained with its color; yet how should he put aside her kindness without inflicting pain upon her rude nature, made sensitive at last by abuse, persecution, and remorse?

His face spoke in advance of his lips, and she read its language with wonderful quickness.

"Ah!" she cried, "I mistrusted how it'd be; you don't want to say it right out, but I'll say it for you! You think the money'd bring you no luck,—maybe a downright curse,—and how can I say it won't? Ha'n't it cursed me? Sandy said it would, even as your'n follered him. What's it good for, then? It burns my hands, and them that's clean, won't touch it. There, you damned devil's-bait,—my arm's sore, and my heart's sore, wi' the weight o' you!"

With these words she flung the cloth, with its bunch of hard silver coins, upon the threshing-floor. It clashed like the sound of chains. Gilbert saw that she was sorely hurt. Tears of disappointment, which she vainly strove to hold back, rose to her eyes, as she grimly folded her arms, and facing him, said,—

"Now, what am I to do?"

"Stay here for the present, Deborah," he answered.

"Eh? A'n't I summonsed? The job I undertook isn't done yet; the wust part's to come! Maybe they'll let me off from puttin' the rope round his neck, but I a'n't sure o' that!"

"Then come to me afterwards," he said, gently, striving to allay her fierce, self-accusing mood. "Remember that you always have a home and a shelter with me, whenever you need them. And I'll take your money," he added, picking it up from the floor,—"take it in trust for you, until the time shall come when you will be willing to use it. Now go in to my mother."

The woman was softened and consoled by his words. But she still hesitated.

"Maybe she won't—she won't"—

"She will!" Gilbert exclaimed. "But if you doubt, wait here until I come back."

Mary Potter earnestly approved of his decision, to take charge of the money, without making use of it. A strong, semi-superstitious influence had so entwined itself with her fate, that she even shrank from help, unless it came in an obviously pure and honorable form. She measured the fulness of her coming justification by the strict integrity of the means whereby she sought to deserve it. Deb. Smith, in her new light, was no welcome guest, and with all her coarse male strength, she was still woman enough to guess the fact;

286

but Mary Potter resolved to think only that her son had been served and befriended. Keeping that service steadily before her eyes, she was able to take the outcast's hand, to give her shelter and food, and, better still, to soothe her with that sweet, unobtrusive consolation which only a woman can bestow,— which steals by avenues of benevolent cunning into a nature that would repel a direct expression of sympathy.

The next morning, however, Deb. Smith left the house, saying to Gilbert,—"You won't see me ag'in, without it may be in Court, till after all's over; and then I may have to ask you to hide me for awhile. Don't mind what I've said; I've no larnin', and can't always make out the rights o' things,—and sometimes it seems there's two Sandys, a good 'un and a bad 'un, and meanin' to punish one, I've ruined 'em both!"

When Gilbert reached Chester, the trial was just about to commence. The little old town on the Delaware was crowded with curious strangers, not only from all parts of the county, but even from Philadelphia and the opposite New-Jersey shore. Every one who had been summoned to testify was beset by an inquisitive circle, and none more so than himself. The Court-house was packed to suffocation; and the Sheriff, heavily armed, could with difficulty force a way through the mass. When the clanking of the prisoner's irons was heard, all the pushing, struggling, murmuring sounds ceased until the redoubtable highwayman stood in the dock.

He looked around the Court-room with his usual defiant air, and no one observed any change of expression, as his eyes passed rapidly over Deb. Smith's face, or Gilbert Potter's. His hard red complexion was already beginning to fade in confinement, and his thick hair, formerly close-cropped for the convenience of disguises, had grown out in not ungraceful locks. He was decidedly a handsome man, and his bearing seemed to show that he was conscious of the fact.

The trial commenced. To the astonishment of all, and, as it was afterwards reported, against the advice of his counsel, the prisoner plead guilty to some of the specifications of the indictment, while he denied others. The Collectors whom he had plundered were then called to the witness-stand, but the public seemed to manifest less interest in the loss of its own money, than in the few cases where private individuals had suffered, and waited impatiently for the latter.

Deb. Smith had so long borne the curious gaze of hundreds of eyes, whenever she lifted her head, that when her turn came, she was able to rise and walk forward without betraying any emotion. Only when she was confronted with Sandy Flash, and he met her with a wonderfully strange, serious smile, did she shudder for a moment and hastily turn away. She gave her testimony in a hard, firm voice, making her statements as brief as possible, and volunteering nothing beyond what was demanded.

On being dismissed from the stand, she appeared to hesitate. Her eyes wandered over the faces of the lawyers, the judges, and the jurymen, as if with a dumb appeal, but she did not speak. Then she turned towards the prisoner, and some words passed between them, which, in the general movement of curiosity, were only heard by the two or three persons who stood nearest.

"Sandy!" she was reported to have said, "I couldn't help myself; take the curse off o' me!"

"Deb., it's too late," he answered. "It's begun to work, and it'll work itself out!"

Gilbert noticed the feeling of hostility with which Deb. Smith was regarded by the spectators,—a feeling that threatened to manifest itself in some violent way, when the restraints of the place should be removed. He therefore took advantage of the great interest with which his own testimony was heard, to present her character in the light which her services to him shed upon it. This was a new phase of the story, and produced a general movement of surprise. Sandy Flash, it was noticed, sitting with his fettered hands upon the rail before him, leaned forward and listened intently, while an unusual flush deepened upon his cheeks.

The statements, though not strictly in evidence, were permitted by the Court, and they produced the effect which Gilbert intended. The excitement reached its height when Deb. Smith, ignorant of rule, suddenly rose and cried out,—

"It's true as Gospel, every word of it! Sandy, do you hear?"

She was removed by the constable, but the people, as they made way, uttered no word of threat or insult. On the contrary, many eyes rested on her hard, violent, wretched face with an expression of very genuine compassion.

The trial took its course, and terminated with the result which everybody—even the prisoner himself—knew to be inevitable. He was pronounced guilty, and duly sentenced to be hanged by the neck until he was dead.

Gilbert employed the time which he could spare from his attendance at the Court, in endeavoring to make a new loan, but with no positive success. The most he accomplished was an agreement, on the part of his creditor, that the foreclosure might be delayed two or three weeks, provided there was a good prospect of the money being obtained. In ordinary times he would have had no difficulty; but, as Mr. Trainer had written, the speculation in western lands had seized upon capitalists, and the amount of money for permanent investment was already greatly diminished.

He was preparing to return home, when Chaffey, the constable, came to him with a message from Sandy Flash. The latter begged for an interview, and both Judge and Sheriff were anxious that Gilbert should comply with his wishes, in the hope that a full and complete confession might be obtained. It was evident that the highwayman had accomplices, but he steadfastly refused to name them, even with the prospect of having his sentence commuted to imprisonment for life.

Gilbert did not hesitate a moment. There were doubts of his own to be solved,—questions to be asked, which Sandy Flash could alone answer. He followed the constable to the gloomy, high-walled jail-building, and was promptly admitted by the Sheriff into the low, dark, heavily barred cell, wherein the prisoner sat upon a wooden stool, the links of his leg-fetters passed through a ring in the floor.

Sandy Flash lifted his face to the light, and grinned, but not with his

289

old, mocking expression. He stretched out his hand which Gilbert took,—hard and cold as the rattling chain at his wrist. Then, seating himself with a clash upon the floor, he pushed the stool towards his visitor, and said,—

"Set down, Potter. Limited accommodations, you see. Sheriff, you needn't wait; it's private business."

The Sheriff locked the iron door behind him, and they were alone.

"Potter," the highwayman began, "you see I'm trapped and done for, and all, it seems, on account o' that little affair o' your'n. You won't think it means much, now, when I say I was in the wrong there; but I swear I was! I had no particular spite ag'in Barton, but he's a swell, and I like to take such fellows down; and I was dead sure you were carryin' his money, as you promised to."

"Tell me one thing," Gilbert interrupted; "how did you know I promised to take money for him?"

"I knowed it, that's enough; I can give you, word for word, what both o' you said, if you doubt me."

"Then, as I thought, it was Barton himself!" Gilbert cried.

Sandy Flash burst into a roaring laugh. "Him! Ah-ha! you think we go snacks, eh? Do I look like a fool? Barton'd give his eye-teeth to put the halter round my neck with his own hands! No, no, young man; I have ways and ways o' learnin' things that you nor him'll never guess."

His manner, even more than his words, convinced Gilbert Barton was absolved, but the mystery remained. "You won't deny that you have friends?" he said.

"Maybe," Sandy replied, in a short, rough tone. "That's nothin' to you," he continued; "but what I've got to say is, whether or no you're a friend to Deb., she thinks you are. Do you mean to look after her, once't in a while, or are you one o' them that forgits a good turn?"

"I have told her," said Gilbert, "that she shall always have a home and a shelter in my house. If it's any satisfaction to you, here's my hand on it!"

"I believe you, Potter. Deb.'s done ill by me; she shouldn't ha' bullied me when I was sore and tetchy, and fagged out with your curst huntin' of me up and down! But I'll do that much for her and for you. Here; bend your head down; I've got to whisper."

Gilbert leaned his ear to the highwayman's mouth.

"You'll only tell her, you understand?"

Gilbert assented.

"Say to her these words,—don't forgit a single one of 'em!—Thirty steps from the place she knowed about, behind the two big chestnut-trees, goin' towards the first cedar, and a forked sassyfrack growin' right over it. What she finds, is your'n."

"Sandy!" Gilbert exclaimed, starting from his listening posture.

"Hush, I say! You know what I mean her to do,—give you your money back. I took a curse with it, as you said. Maybe that's off o' me, now!"

"It is!" said Gilbert, in a low tone, "and forgiveness—mine and my mother's—in the place of it. Have you any"—he hesitated to say the words— "any last messages, to her or anybody else, or anything you would like to have done?"

"Thank ye, no!—unless Deb. can find my black hair and whiskers. Then you may give 'em to Barton, with my dutiful service."

He laughed at the idea, until his chains rattled.

Gilbert's mind was haunted with the other and darker doubt, and he resolved, in this last interview, to secure himself against its recurrence. In such an hour he could trust the prisoner's words.

"Sandy," he asked, "have you any children?"

"Not to my knowledge; and I'm glad of it."

"You must know," Gilbert continued, "what the people say about my birth. My mother is bound from telling me who my father was, and I dare

291

not ask her any questions. Did you ever happen to know her, in your younger days, or can you remember anything that will help me to discover his name?"

The highwayman sat silent, meditating, and Gilbert felt that his heart was beginning to beat painfully fast, as he waited for the answer.

"Yes," said Sandy, at last, "I did know Mary Potter when I was a boy, and she knowed me, under another name. I may say I liked her, too, in a boy's way, but she was older by three or four years, and never thought o' lookin' at me. But I can't remember anything more; if I was out o' this, I'd soon find out for you!"

He looked up with an eager, questioning glance, which Gilbert totally misunderstood.

"What was your other name?" he asked, in a barely audible voice.

"I dunno as I need tell it," Sandy answered; "what'd be the good? There's some yet livin', o' the same name, and they wouldn't thank me."

"Sandy!" Gilbert cried desperately, "answer this one question,—don't go out of the world with a false word in your mouth!—You are not my father?"

The highwayman looked at him a moment, in blank amazement. "No, so help me God!" he then said.

Gilbert's face brightened so suddenly and vividly that Sandy muttered to himself,—"I never thought I was that bad."

"I hear the Sheriff at the outside gate," he whispered again. "Don't forgit—thirty steps from the place she knowed about—behind the two big chestnut-trees, goin' towards the first cedar—and a forked sassyfrack growin' right over it! Good-bye, and good-luck to the whole o' your life!"

The two clasped hands with a warmth and earnestness which surprised the Sheriff. Then Gilbert went out from his old antagonist.

That night Sandy Flash made an attempt to escape from the jail, and very nearly succeeded. It appeared, from some mysterious words which he afterwards let fall, and which Gilbert alone could have understood, that he had a superstitious belief that something he had done would bring him a new turn of fortune. The only result of the attempt was to hasten his execution. Within ten days from that time he was transformed from a living terror into a romantic name.

CHAPTER XXVII. — GILBERT INDEPENDENT.

Gilbert Potter felt such an implicit trust in Sandy Flash's promise of restitution, that, before leaving Chester, he announced the forthcoming payment of the mortgage to its holder. His homeward ride was like a triumphal march, to which his heart beat the music. The chill March winds turned into May-breezes as they touched him; the brown meadows were quick with ambushed bloom. Within three or four months his life had touched such extremes of experience, that the fate yet to come seemed to evolve itself speedily and naturally from that which was over and gone. Only one obstacle yet remained in his path,—his mother's secret. Towards that he was powerless; to meet all others he was brimming with strength and courage.

Mary Potter recognized, even more keenly and with profounder faith than her son, the guidance of some inscrutable Power. She did not dare to express so uncertain a hope, but something in her heart whispered that the day of her own deliverance was not far off, and she took strength from it.

It was nearly a week before Deb. Smith made her appearance. Gilbert, in the mean time, had visited her cabin on the Woodrow farm, to find it deserted, and he was burning with impatience to secure, through her, the restoration of his independence. He would not announce his changed prospects, even to Martha Deane, until they were put beyond further risk. The money once in his hands, he determined to carry it to Chester without loss of time.

When Deb. arrived, she had a weary, hunted look, but she was unusually grave and silent, and avoided further reference to the late tragical episode in her life. Nevertheless, Gilbert led her aside and narrated to her the particulars of his interview with Sandy Flash. Perhaps he softened, with pardonable equivocation, the latter's words in regard to her; perhaps he conveyed a sense of forgiveness which had not been expressed; for Deb. more than once drew the corners of her hard palms across her eyes. When he gave the marks by which she was to recognize a certain spot, she exclaimed,—

"It was hid the night I dreamt of him! I knowed he must ha' been nigh, by that token. O, Mr. Gilbert, he said true! I know the place; it's not so far away; this very night you'll have y'r money back!"

After it was dark she set out, with a spade upon her shoulder, forbidding him to follow, or even to look after her. Both mother and son were too excited to sleep. They sat by the kitchen-fire, with one absorbing thought in their minds, and speech presently became easier than silence.

"Mother," said Gilbert, "when—I mean if—she brings the money, all that has happened will have been for good. It has proved to us that we have true friends (and I count my Roger among them), and I think that our independence will be worth all the more, since we came so nigh losing it again."

"Ay, my boy," she replied; "I was over-hasty, and have been lessoned. When I bend my mind to submit, I make more headway than when I try to take the Lord's work into my own hands. I'm fearsome still, but it seems there's a light coming from somewhere,—I don't know where."

"Do you feel that way, mother?" he exclaimed. "Do you think—let me mention it this once!—that the day is near when you will be free to speak? Will there be anything more you can tell me, when we stand free upon our own property?"

Mary Potter looked upon his bright, wistful, anxious face, and sighed. "I can't tell—I can't tell," she said. "Ah, my boy, you would understand it, if I dared say one thing, but that might lead you to guess what mustn't be told; and I will be faithful to the spirit as well as the letter. It must come soon, but nothing you or I can do would hasten it a minute."

"One word more, mother," he persisted, "will our independence be no help to you?"

"A great help," she answered, "or, maybe, a great comfort would be the true word. Without it, I might be tempted to—but see, Gilbert, how can I talk? Everything you say pulls at the one thing that cuts my mouth like a knife, because it's shut tight on it! And the more because I owe it to you,— because I'm held back from my duty to my child,—maybe, every day putting a fresh sorrow into his heart! Oh, it's not easy, Gilbert; it don't grow lighter from use, only my faith is the stronger and surer, and that helps me to bear it."

"Mother, I meant never to have spoken of this again," he said. "But you're mistaken; it is no sorrow; I never knew what it was to have a light heart, until you told me your trouble, and the question came to my mouth to-night because I shall soon feel strong in my own right as a man, and able to do more than you might guess. If, as you say, no man can help you, I will wait and be patient with you."

"That's all we can do now, my child. I wasn't reproaching you for speaking, for you've held your peace a long while, when I know you've been fretting; but this isn't one of the troubles that's lightened by speech, because all talking must go around the outside, and never touch the thing itself."

"I understand," he said, and gazed for a long time into the fire, without speaking.

Mary Potter watched his face, in the wavering light of the flame. She marked the growing decision of the features, the forward, fearless glance of the large, deep-set eye, the fuller firmness and sweetness of the mouth, and the general expression, not only of self-reliance, but of authority, which was spread over the entire countenance. Both her pride in her son, and her respect for him, increased as she gazed. Heretofore, she had rather considered her secret as her own property, her right to which he should not question; but now it seemed as if she were forced to withhold something that of right belonged to him. Yet no thought that the mysterious obligation might be broken ever entered her mind.

Gilbert was thinking of Martha Deane. He had passed that first timidity of love which shrinks from the knowledge of others, and longed to tell his mother what noble fidelity and courage Martha had exhibited. Only the recollection of the fearful swoon into which she had fallen bound his tongue; he felt that the first return to the subject must come from her. She lay back in her chair and seemed to sleep; he rose from time to time, went out into the lane and listened,—and so the hours passed away.

Towards midnight a heavy step was heard, and Deb. Smith, hot, panting, her arms daubed with earth, and a wild light in her eyes, entered the kitchen. With one hand she grasped the ends of her strong tow-linen apron, with the other she still shouldered the spade. She knelt upon the floor between the two, set the apron in the light of the fire, unrolled the end of a leathern saddle-bag, and disclosed the recovered treasure.

"See if it's all right!" she said.

Mary Potter and Gilbert bent over the rolls and counted them. It was the entire sum, untouched.

"Have you got a sup o' whiskey, Mr. Gilbert?" Deb. Smith asked. "Ugh! I'm hot and out o' breath, and yet I feel mortal cold. There was a screech-owl hootin' in the cedar; and I dunno how't is, but there always seems to be things around, where money's buried. You can't see 'em, but you hear 'em. I thought I'd ha' dropped when I turned up the sassyfrack bush, and got hold on it; and all the way back I feared a big arm'd come out o' every fence-corner, and snatch it from me!" [Footnote: It does not seem to have been generally known in the neighborhood that the money was unearthed. A tradition of that and other treasure buried by Sandy Flash, is still kept alive; and during the past ten years two midnight attempts have been made to find it, within a hundred yards of the spot indicated in the narrative.]

Mary Potter set the kettle on the fire, and Deb. Smith was soon refreshed with a glass of hot grog. Then she lighted her pipe and watched the two as they made preparations for the journey to Chester on the morrow, now and then nodding her head with an expression which chased away the haggard sorrow from her features.

This time the journey was performed without incident. The road was safe, the skies were propitious, and Gilbert Potter returned from Chester an independent man, with the redeemed mortgage in his pocket. His first care was to assure his mother of the joyous fact; his next to seek Martha Deane, and consult with her about their brightening future.

On the way to Kennett Square, he fell in with Mark, who was radiant with the promise of Richard Rudd's new house, secured to him by the shrewd assistance of Miss Betsy Lavender.

"I tell you what it is, Gilbert," said he; "don't you think I might as well speak to Daddy Fairthorn about Sally? I'm gettin' into good business now, and I guess th' old folks might spare her pretty soon."

"The sooner, Mark, the better for you; and you can buy the wedding-suit at once, for I have your hundred dollars ready."

"You don't mean that you wont use it, Gilbert?"

Who so delighted as Mark, when he heard Gilbert's unexpected story? "Oh, glory!" he exclaimed; "the tide's turnin', old fellow! What'll you bet you're not married before I am? It's got all over the country that you and Martha are engaged, and that the Doctor's full o' gall and wormwood about it; I hear it wherever I go, and there's more for you than there is against you, I tell you that!"

The fact was as Mark had stated. No one was positively known to have spread the rumor, but it was afloat and generally believed. The result was to invest Gilbert with a fresh interest. His courage in confronting Sandy Flash, his robbery, his wonderful preservation from death, and his singular connection, through Deb. Smith, with Sandy Flash's capture, had thrown a romantic halo around his name, which was now softly brightened by the report of his love. The stain of his birth and the uncertainty of his parentage did not lessen this interest, but rather increased it; and as any man who is much talked about in a country community will speedily find two parties created, one enthusiastically admiring, the other contemptuously depreciating him, so now it happened in this case.

The admirers, however, were in a large majority, and they possessed a great advantage over the detractors, being supported by a multitude of facts, while the latter were unable to point to any act of Gilbert Potter's life that was not upright and honorable. Even his love of Martha Deane was shorn of its presumption by her reciprocal affection. The rumor that she had openly defied her father's will created great sympathy, for herself and for Gilbert, among the young people of both sexes,—a sympathy which frequently was made manifest to Dr. Deane, and annoyed him not a little. His stubborn opposition to his daughter's attachment increased, in proportion as his power to prevent it diminished.

We may therefore conceive his sensations when Gilbert Potter himself boldly entered his presence. The latter, after Mark's description, very imperfect though it was, of Martha's courageous assertion of the rights of her heart, had swiftly made up his mind to stand beside her in the struggle, with equal firmness and equal pride. He would openly seek an interview with her, and if he should find her father at home, as was probable at that hour, would frankly and respectfully acknowledge his love, and defend it against any attack.

On entering the room, he quietly stepped forward with extended hand, and saluted the Doctor, who was so taken by surprise that he mechanically answered the greeting before he could reflect what manner to adopt towards the unwelcome visitor.

"What might be thy business with me?" he asked, stiffly, recovering from the first shock.

"I called to see Martha," Gilbert answered. "I have some news which she will be glad to hear."

"Young man," said the Doctor, with his sternest face and voice, "I may as well come to the point with thee, at once. If thee had had decency enough to apply to me before speaking thy mind to Martha, it would have saved us all a great deal of trouble. I could have told thee then, as I tell thee now, that I will never consent to her marriage with thee. Thee must give up all thought of such a thing."

"I will do so," Gilbert replied, "when Martha tells me with her own mouth that such is her will. I am not one of the men who manage their hearts according to circumstances. I wish, indeed, I were more worthy of Martha; but I am trying to deserve her, and I know no better way than to be faithful as she is faithful. I mean no disrespect to you, Dr. Deane. You are her father; you have every right to care for her happiness, and I will admit that you honestly think I am not the man who could make her happy. All I ask is, that you should wait a little and know me better. Martha and I have both decided that we must wait, and there is time enough for you to watch my conduct, examine my character, and perhaps come to a more favorable judgment of me."

Dr. Deane saw that it would be harder to deal with Gilbert Potter than he had imagined. The young man stood before him so honestly and fearlessly, meeting his angry gaze with such calm, frank eyes, and braving his despotic will with such a modest, respectful opposal, that he was forced to withdraw from his haughty position, and to set forth the same reasons which he had presented to his daughter.

"I see," he said, with a tone slightly less arrogant, "that thee is sensible, in some respects, and therefore I put the case to thy understanding. It's too plain to be argued. Martha is a rich bait for a poor man, and perhaps I oughtn't to wonder—knowing the heart of man as I do—that thee was tempted to turn her head to favor thee; but the money is not yet hers, and I, as her father, can never allow that thy poverty shall stand for three years between her and some honorable man to whom her money would be no temptation! Why, if all I hear be true, thee hasn't even any certain roof to shelter a wife; thy property, such as it is, may be taken out of thy hands!"

Gilbert could not calmly hear these insinuations. All his independent pride of character was aroused; a dark flush came into his face, the blood was pulsing hotly through his veins, and indignant speech was rising to his lips, when the inner door unexpectedly opened, and Martha entered the room.

She instantly guessed what was taking place, and summoned up all her self-possession, to stand by Gilbert, without increasing her father's exasperation. To the former, her apparition was like oil on troubled waters. His quick blood struck into warm channels of joy, as he met her glowing eyes, and felt the throb of her soft, elastic palm against his own. Dr. Deane set his teeth, drew up his under lip, and handled his cane with restless fingers.

"Father," said Martha, "if you are talking of me, it is better that I should be present. I am sure there is nothing that either thee or Gilbert would wish to conceal from me."

300

"No, Martha!" Gilbert exclaimed; "I came to bring you good news. The mortgage on my farm is lifted, and I am an independent man!"

"Without my help! Does thee hear that, father?"

Gilbert did not understand her remark; without heeding it, he continued,—

"Sandy Flash, after his sentence, sent for me and told me where the money he took from me was to be found. I carried it to Chester, and have paid off all my remaining debt. Martha, your father has just charged me with being tempted by your property. I say to you, in his presence, put it beyond my reach,—give it away, forfeit the conditions of the legacy,—let me show truly whether I ever thought of money in seeking you!"

"Gilbert," she said, gently, "father doesn't yet know you as I do. Others will no doubt say the same thing, and we must both make up our minds to have it said; yet I cannot, for that, relinquish what is mine of right. We are not called upon to sacrifice to the mistaken opinions of men; your life and mine will show, and manifest to others in time, whether it is a selfish tie that binds us together."

"Martha!" Dr. Deane exclaimed, feeling that he should lose ground, unless this turn of the conversation were interrupted; "thee compels me to show thee how impossible the thing is, even if this man were of the richest. Admitting that he is able to support a family, admitting that thee waits three years, comes into thy property, and is still of a mind to marry him against my will, can thee forget—or has he so little consideration for thee as to forget—that he bears his mother's name?"

"Father!"

"Let me speak, Martha," said Gilbert, lifting his head, which had drooped for a moment. His voice was earnest and sorrowful, yet firm. "It is true that I bear my mother's name. It is the name of a good, an honest, an honorable, and a God-fearing woman. I wish I could be certain that the name which legally belongs to me will be as honorable and as welcome. But Martha knows, and you, her father, have a right to know, that I shall have another.

I have not been inconsiderate. I trampled down my love for her, as long as I believed it would bring disgrace. I will not say that now, knowing her as I do, I could ever give her up, even if the disgrace was not removed,"—

"Thank you, Gilbert!" Martha interrupted.

"But there is none, Dr. Deane," he continued, "and when the time comes, my birth will be shown to be as honorable as your own, or Mark's."

Dr. Deane was strangely excited at these words. His face colored, and he darted a piercing, suspicious glance at Gilbert. The latter, however, stood quietly before him, too possessed by what he had said to notice the Doctor's peculiar expression; but it returned to his memory afterwards.

"Why," the Doctor at last stammered, "I never heard of this before!"

"No," Gilbert answered, "and I must ask of you not to mention it further, at present. I must beg you to be patient until my mother is able to declare the truth."

"What keeps her from it?"

"I don't know," Gilbert sadly replied.

"Come!" cried the Doctor, as sternly as ever, "this is rather a likely story! If Potter isn't thy name, what is?"

"I don't know," Gilbert repeated.

"No; nor no one else! How dare thee address my daughter,—talk of marriage with her,—when thee don't know thy real name? What name would thee offer to her in exchange for her own? Young man, I don't believe thee!"

"I do," said Martha, rising and moving to Gilbert's side.

"Martha, go to thy room!" the Doctor cried. "And as for thee, Gilbert Potter, or Gilbert Anything, I tell thee, once and for all, never speak of this thing again,—at least, until thee can show a legal name and an honorable birth! Thee has not prejudiced me in thy favor by thy devices, and it stands to reason that I should forbid thee to see my daughter,—to enter my doors!"

"Dr. Deane," said Gilbert, with sad yet inflexible dignity, "it is impossible, after what you have said, that I should seek to enter your door, until my words are proved true, and I am justified in your eyes. The day may come sooner than you think. But I will do nothing secretly; I won't promise anything to you that I can't promise to myself; and so I tell you, honestly and above-board, that while I shall not ask Martha to share my life until I can offer her my true name, I must see her from time to time. I'm not fairly called upon to give up that."

"No, Gilbert," said Martha, who had not yet moved from her place by his side, "it is as necessary to my happiness as to yours. I will not ask you to come here again; you cannot, and must not, even for my sake; but when I need your counsel and your sympathy, and there is no other way left, I will go to you."

"Martha!" Dr. Deane exclaimed; but the word conveys no idea of his wrath and amazement.

"Father," she said, "this is thy house, and it is for thee to direct, here. Within its walls, I will conduct myself according to thy wishes; I will receive no guest whom thee forbids, and will even respect thy views in regard to my intercourse with our friends; but unless thee wants to deprive me of all liberty, and set aside every right of mine as an accountable being, thee must allow me sometimes to do what both my heart and my conscience command!"

"Is it a woman's place," he angrily asked, "to visit a man?"

"When the two have need of each other, and God has joined their hearts in love and in truth, and the man is held back from reaching the woman, then it is her place to go to him!"

Never before had Dr. Deane beheld upon his daughter's sweet, gentle face such an expression of lofty spiritual authority. While her determination really outraged his conventional nature, he felt that it came from a higher source than his prohibition. He knew that nothing which he could urge at that moment would have the slightest weight in her mind, and moreover, that the liberal, independent customs of the neighborhood, as well as the respect of his sect for professed spiritual guidance, withheld him from any harsh attempt at coercion. He was powerless, but still inflexible.

As for Martha, what she had said was simply included in what she was resolved to do; the greater embraced the less. It was a defiance of her father's authority, very painful from the necessity of its assertion, but rendered inevitable by his course. She knew with what tenacity he would seize and hold every inch of relinquished ground; she felt, as keenly as Gilbert himself, the implied insult which he could not resent; and her pride, her sense of justice, and the strong fidelity of her woman's heart, alike impelled her to stand firm.

"Good-bye, Martha!" Gilbert said, taking her hand "I must wait."

"We wait together, Gilbert!"

CHAPTER XXVIII. — MISS LAVENDER MAKES A GUESS.

There were signs of spring all over the land, and Gilbert resumed his farm-work with the fresh zest which the sense of complete ownership gave. He found a purchaser for his wagon, sold one span of horses, and thus had money in hand for all the coming expenses of the year. His days of hauling, of anxiety, of painful economy, were over; he rejoiced in his fully developed and recognized manhood, and was cheered by the respect and kindly sympathy of his neighbors.

Meanwhile, the gossip, not only of Kennett, but of Marlborough, Pennsbury, and New-Garden, was as busy as ever. No subject of country talk equalled in interest the loves of Gilbert Potter and Martha Deane. Mark, too open-hearted to be intrusted with any secret, was drawn upon wherever he went, and he revealed more (although he was by no means Martha's confidant) than the public had any right to know. The idlers at the Unicorn had seen Gilbert enter Dr. Deane's house, watched his return therefrom, made shrewd notes of the Doctor's manner when he came forth that evening, and guessed the result of the interview almost as well as if they had been present.

The restoration of Gilbert's plundered money, and his hardly acquired independence as a landholder, greatly strengthened the hands of his friends. There is no logic so convincing as that of good luck; in proportion as a man is fortunate (so seems to run the law of the world), he attracts fortune to him. A good deed would not have helped Gilbert so much in popular estimation, as this sudden and unexpected release from his threatened difficulties. The blot upon his name was already growing fainter, and a careful moral arithmetician might have calculated the point of prosperity at which it would cease to be seen.

Nowhere was the subject discussed with greater interest and excitement than in the Fairthorn household. Sally, when she first heard the news, loudly protested her unbelief; why, the two would scarcely speak to each other, she said; she had seen Gilbert turn his back on Martha, as if he couldn't bear the sight of her; it ought to be, and she would be glad if it was, but it wasn't!

When, therefore, Mark confirmed the report, and was led on, by degrees, to repeat Gilbert's own words, Sally rushed out into the kitchen with a vehemence which left half her apron hanging on the door-handle, torn off from top to bottom in her whirling flight, and announced the fact to her mother.

Joe, who was present, immediately cried out,—

"O, Sally! now I may tell about Mark, mayn't I?"

Sally seized him by the collar, and pitched him out the kitchen-door. Her face was the color of fire.

"My gracious, Sally!" exclaimed Mother Fairthorn, in amazement; "what's that for?"

But Sally had already disappeared, and was relating her trouble to Mark, who roared with wicked laughter, whereupon she nearly cried with vexation.

"Never mind," said he; "the boy's right. I told Gilbert this very afternoon that it was about time to speak to the old man; and he allowed it was. Come out with me and don't be afeard—I'll do the talkin'."

Hand in hand they went into the kitchen, Sally blushing and hanging back a little. Farmer Fairthorn had just come in from the barn, and was warming his hands at the fire. Mother Fairthorn might have had her suspicions, but it was her nature to wait cheerfully, and say nothing.

"See here, Daddy and Mammy!" said Mark, "have either o' you any objections to Sally and me bein' a pair?"

Farmer Fairthorn smiled, rubbed his hands together, and turning to his wife, asked,—"What has Mammy to say to it?"

She looked up at Mark with her kindly eyes, in which twinkled something like a tear, and said,—"I was guessin' it might turn out so between you two, and if I'd had anything against you, Mark, I wouldn't ha' let it run on. Be a steady boy, and you'll make Sally a steady woman. She's had pretty much her own way."

Thereupon Farmer Fairthorn, still rubbing his hands, ventured to remark,—"The girl might ha' done worse." This was equivalent to a hearty commendation of the match, and Mark so understood it. Sally kissed her mother, cried a little, caught her gown on a corner of the kitchen-table, and thus the betrothal was accepted as a family fact. Joe and Jake somewhat disturbed the bliss of the evening, it is true, by bursting into the room from time to time, staring significantly at the lovers, and then rushing out again with loud whoops and laughter.

Sally could scarcely await the coming of the next day, to visit Martha Deane. At first she felt a little piqued that she had not received the news from Martha's own lips, but this feeling speedily vanished in the sympathy with her friend's trials. She was therefore all the more astonished at the quiet, composed bearing of the latter. The tears she had expected to shed were not once drawn upon.

"O, Martha!" she cried, after the first impetuous outburst of feeling,— "to think that it has all turned out just as I wanted! No, I don't quite mean that; you know I couldn't wish you to have crosses; but about Gilbert! And it's too bad—Mark has told me dreadful things, but I hope they're not all true; you don't look like it; and I'm so glad, you can't think!"

Martha smiled, readily untangling Sally's thoughts, and said,—"I mustn't complain, Sally. Nothing has come to pass that I had not prepared my mind to meet. We will only have to wait a little longer than you and Mark."

"No you won't!" Sally exclaimed. "I'll make Mark wait, too! And everything must be set right—somebody must do something! Where's Betsy Lavender?"

"Here!" answered the veritable voice of the spinster, through the open door of the small adjoining room.

"Gracious, how you frightened me!" cried Sally. "But, Betsy, you seem to be able to help everybody; why can't you do something for Martha and Gilbert?"

"Martha and Gilbert. That's what I ask myself, nigh onto a hundred times a day, child. But there's things that takes the finest kind o' wit to see through, and you can't make a bead-purse out of a sow's-ear, neither jerk Time by the forelock, when there a'n't a hair, as you can see, to hang on to. I dunno as you'll rightly take my meanin'; but never mind, all the same, I'm flummuxed, and it's the longest and hardest flummux o' my life!"

Miss Betsy Lavender, it must here be explained, was more profoundly worried than she was willing to admit. Towards Martha she concealed the real trouble of her mind under the garb of her quaint, jocular speech, which meant much or little, as one might take it. She had just returned from one of her social pilgrimages, during which she had heard nothing but the absorbing subject of gossip. She had been questioned and cross-questioned, entreated by many, as Sally had done, to do something (for all had great faith in her powers), and warned by a few not to meddle with what did not concern her. Thus she had come back that morning, annoyed, discomposed, and more dissatisfied with herself than ever before, to hear Martha's recital of what had taken place during her absence.

In spite of Martha's steady patience and cheerfulness, Miss Lavender knew that the painful relation in which she stood to her father would not be assuaged by the lapse of time. She understood Dr. Deane's nature quite as well as his daughter, and was convinced that, for the present, neither threats nor persuasions would move his stubborn resistance. According to the judgment of the world (the older part of it, at least), he had still right on his side. Facts were wanted; or, rather, the one fact upon which resistance was based must be removed.

With all this trouble, Miss Lavender had a presentiment that there was work for her to do, if she could only discover what it was. Her faith in her own powers of assistance was somewhat shaken, and she therefore resolved to say nothing, promise nothing, until she had both hit upon a plan and carried it into execution.

Two or three days after Sally's visit, on a mild, sunny morning in the beginning of April, she suddenly announced her intention of visiting the

Potter farm-house.

"I ha'n't seen Mary since last fall, you know, Martha," she said; "and I've a mortal longin' to wish Gilbert joy o' his good luck, and maybe say a word to keep him in good heart about you. Have you got no message to send by me?"

"Only my love," Martha answered; "and tell him how you left me. He knows I will keep my word; when I need his counsel, I will go to him."

"If more girls talked and thought that way, us women'd have fairer shakes," Miss Lavender remarked, as she put on her cloak and pattens.

When she reached the top of the hill overlooking the glen, she noticed fresh furrows in the field on her left. Clambering through the fence, she waited until the heads of a pair of horses made their appearance, rising over the verge of the hill. As she conjectured, Gilbert Potter was behind them, guiding the plough-handle. He was heartily glad to see her, and halted his team at the corner of the "land."

"I didn't know as you'd speak to me," said she, with assumed grimness. "Maybe you wouldn't, if I didn't come direct from her. Ah, you needn't look wild; it's only her love, and what's the use, for you had it already; but never mind, lovyers is never satisfied; and she's chipper and peart enough, seein' what she has to bear for your sake, but she don't mind that, on the contrary, quite the reverse, and I'm sure you don't deserve it!"

"Did she tell you what passed between us, the last time?" Gilbert asked.

"The last time. Yes. And jokin' aside, which often means the contrary in my crooked ways o' talkin', a'n't it about time somethin' was done?"

"What can be done?"

"I dunno," said Miss Lavender, gravely. "You know as well as I do what's in the way, or rather none of us knows what it is, only where it is; and a thing unbeknown may be big or little; who can tell? And latterly I've thought, Gilbert, that maybe your mother is in the fix of a man I've heerd tell on, that fell into a pit, and ketched by the last bush, and hung on, and hung on, till he could hold on no longer; so he gev himself up to death, shet his eyes and let go, and lo and behold! the bottom was a matter o' six inches under his feet! Leastways, everything p'ints to a sort o' skeary fancy bein' mixed up with it, not a thing to laugh at, I can tell you, but as earnest as sin, for I've seen the likes, and maybe easy to make straight if you could only look into it yourself; but you think there's no chance o' that?"

"No," said Gilbert. "I've tried once too often, already; I shall not try again."

"Try again," Miss Lavender repeated. "Then why not?"—but here she paused, and seemed to meditate. The fact was, she had been tempted to ask Gilbert's advice in regard to the plan she was revolving in her brain. The tone of his voice, however, was discouraging; she saw that he had taken a firm and gloomy resolution to be silent,—his uneasy air hinted that he desired to avoid further talk on this point. So, with a mental reprimand of the indiscretion into which her sympathy with him had nearly betrayed her, she shut her teeth and slightly bit her tongue.

"Well, well," she said; "I hope it'll come out before you're both old and sour with waitin', that's all! I don't want such true-love as your'n to be like firkin-butter at th' end; for as fresh, and firm, and well-kep' as you please, it ha'n't got the taste o' the clover and the sweet-grass; but who knows? I may dance at your weddin', after all, sooner'n I mistrust; and so I'm goin' down to spend the day with y'r mother!"

She strode over the furrow and across the weedy sod, and Gilbert resumed his ploughing. As she approached the house, Miss Lavender noticed that the secured ownership of the property was beginning to express itself in various slight improvements and adornments. The space in front of the porch was enlarged, and new flower-borders set along the garden-paling; the barn had received a fresh coat of whitewash, as well as the trunks of the apple-trees, which shone like white pillars; and there was a bench with bright straw bee-hives under the lilac-bush. Mary Potter was at work in the garden, sowing her early seeds.

"Well, I do declare!" exclaimed Miss Lavender, after the first cordial greetings were over. "Seems almost like a different place, things is so snugged up and put to rights."

"Yes," said Mary Potter; "I had hardly the heart, before, to make it everything that we wanted; and you can't think what a satisfaction I have in it now."

"Yes, I can! Give me the redishes, while you stick in them beets. I've got a good forefinger for plantin' 'em,—long and stiff; and I can't stand by and see you workin' alone, without fidgets."

Miss Lavender threw off her cloak and worked with a will. When the gardening was finished, she continued her assistance in the house, and fully earned her dinner before she sat down to it. Then she insisted on Mary Potter bringing out her sewing, and giving her something more to do; it was one of her working-days, she said; she had spent rather an idle winter; and moreover, she was in such spirits at Gilbert's good fortune, that she couldn't be satisfied without doing something for him, and to sew up the seams of his new breeches was the very thing! Never had she been so kind, so cheerful, and so helpful, and Mary Potter's nature warmed into happy content in her society.

No one should rashly accuse Miss Lavender if there was a little design in this. The task she had set herself to attempt was both difficult and delicate. She had divided it into two portions, requiring very different tactics, and was shrewd enough to mask, in every possible way, the one from which she had most hopes of obtaining a result. She made no reference, at first, to Gilbert's attachment to Martha Deane, but seemed to be wholly absorbed in the subject of the farm; then, taking wide sweeps through all varieties of random gossip, preserving a careless, thoughtless, rattling manner, she stealthily laid her pitfalls for the unsuspecting prey.

"I was over't Warren's t' other day," she said, biting off a thread, "and Becky had jist come home from Phildelphy. There's new-fashioned bonnets comin' up, she says. She stayed with Allen's, but who they are I don't know. Laws! now I think on it, Mary, you stayed at Allen's, too, when you were there!"

"No," said Mary Potter, "it was at—Treadwell's."

"Treadwell's? I thought you told me Allen's. All the same to me, Allen or Treadwell; I don't know either of 'em. It's a long while since I've been in Phildelphy, and never likely to go ag'in. I don't fancy trampin' over them hard bricks, though, to be sure, a body sees the fashions; but what with boxes tumbled in and out o' the stores, and bar'ls rollin', and carts always goin' by, you're never sure o' y'r neck; and I was sewin' for Clarissa Lee, Jackson that was, that married a dry goods man, the noisiest place that ever was; you could hardly hear yourself talk; but a body gets used to it, in Second Street, close't to Market, and were you anywheres near there?"

"I was in Fourth Street," Mary Potter answered, with a little hesitation. Miss Lavender secretly noticed her uneasiness, which, she also remarked, arose not from suspicion, but from memory.

"What kind o' buttons are you goin' to have, Mary?" she asked. "Horn splits, and brass cuts the stuff, and mother o' pearl wears to eternity, but they're so awful dear. Fourth Street, you said? One street's like another to me, after you get past the corners. I'd always know Second, though, by the tobacco-shop, with the wild Injun at the door, liftin' his tommyhawk to skulp you—ugh!—but never mind, all the same, skulp away for what I care, for I a'n't likely ever to lay eyes on you ag'in!"

Having thus, with perhaps more volubility than was required, covered up the traces of her design, Miss Lavender cast about how to commence the second and more hopeless attack. It was but scant intelligence which she had gained, but in that direction she dared not venture further. What she now proposed to do required more courage and less cunning.

Her manner gradually changed; she allowed lapses of silence to occur, and restricted her gossip to a much narrower sweep. She dwelt, finally, upon the singular circumstances of Sandy Flash's robbery of Gilbert, and the restoration of the money.

"Talkin' o' Deb. Smith," she then said, "Mary, do you mind when I was here last harvest, and the talk we had about Gilbert? I've often thought on it since, and how I guessed right for once't, for I know the ways o' men, if I am an old maid, and so it's come out as I said, and a finer couple than they'll make can't be found in the county!"

Mary Potter looked up, with a shadow of the old trouble on her face. "You know all about it, Betsy, then?" she asked.

"Bless your soul, Mary, everybody knows about it! There's been nothin' else talked about in the neighborhood for the last three weeks; why, ha'n't Gilbert told you o' what passed between him and Dr. Deane, and how Martha stood by him as no woman ever stood by a man?"

An expression of painful curiosity, such as shrinks from the knowledge it craves, came into Mary Potter's eyes. "Gilbert has told me nothing," she said, "since—since that time."

"That time. I won't ask you what time; it's neither here nor there; but you ought to know the run o' things, when it's common talk." And therewith Miss Lavender began at the beginning, and never ceased until she had brought the history, in all its particulars, down to that very day. She did not fail to enlarge on the lively and universal Interest in the fortunes of the lovers which was manifested by the whole community. Mary Potter's face grew paler and paler as she spoke, but the tears which some parts of the recital called forth were quenched again, as it seemed, by flashes of aroused pride.

"Now," Miss Lavender concluded, "you see just how the matter stands. I'm not hard on you, savin' and exceptin' that facts is hard, which they sometimes are I don't deny; but here we're all alone with our two selves, and you'll grant I'm a friend, though I may have queer ways o' showin' it; and why shouldn't I say that all the trouble comes o' Gilbert bearin' your name?"

"Don't I know it!" Mary Potter cried. "Isn't my load heaped up heavier as it comes towards the end? What can I do but wait till the day when I can give Gilbert his father's name?"

"His father's name! Then you can do it, some day? I suspicioned as much. And you've been bound up from doin' it, all this while,—and that's what's been layin' so heavy on your mind, wasn't it?"

"Betsy," said Mary Potter, with sudden energy, "I'll say as much as I dare, so that I may keep my senses. I fear, sometimes, I'll break together for want of a friend like you, to steady me while I walk the last steps of my hard road. Gilbert was born in wedlock; I'm not bound to deny that; but I committed a sin,—not the sin people charge me with,—and the one that persuaded me to it has to answer for more than I have. I bound myself not to tell the name of Gilbert's father,—not to say where or when I was married, not to do or say anything to put others On the track, until—but there's the sin and the trouble and the punishment all in one. If I told that, you might guess the rest. You know what a name I've had to bear, but I've taken my cross and fought my way, and put up with all things, that I might deserve the fullest justification the Lord has in His hands. If I had known all beforehand, Betsy,—but I expected the release in a month or two, and it hasn't come in twenty-five years!"

"Twenty-five years!" repeated Miss Lavender, heedless of the drops running down her thin face. "If there was a sin, Mary, even as big as a yearlin' calf, you've worked off the cost of it, years ago! If you break your word now, you'll stand justified in the sight o' the Lord, and of all men, and even if you think a scrimption of it's left, remember your dooty to Gilbert, and take a less justification for his sake!"

"I've been tempted that way, Betsy, but the end I wanted has been set in my mind so long I can't get it out. I've seen the Lord's hand so manifest in these past days, that I'm fearsome to hurry His judgments. And then, though I try not to, I'm waiting from day to day,—almost from hour to hour,—and it seems that if I was to give up and break my vow, He would break it for me the next minute afterwards, to punish my impatience!"

"Why," Miss Lavender exclaimed, "it must be your husband's death you're waitin' for!"

Mary Potter started up with a wild look of alarm. "No—no—not his death!" she cried. "I should want him to—be living! Ask me no more questions; forget what I've said, if it don't incline you to encourage me! That's why I've told you so much!"

Miss Lavender instantly desisted from further appeal. She rose, put her

314

arm around Mary Potter's waist, and said,—"I didn't mean to frighten or to worry you, deary. I may think your conscience has worked on itself, like, till it's ground a bit too sharp; but I see just how you're fixed, and won't say another word, without it's to give comfort. An open confession's good for the soul, they say, and half a loaf's better than no bread, and you haven't violated your word a bit, and so let it do you good!"

In fact, when Mary Potter grew calm, she was conscious of a relief the more welcome because it was so rare in her experience. Miss Lavender, moreover, hastened to place Gilbert's position in a more cheerful light, and the same story, repeated for a different purpose, now assumed quite another aspect. She succeeded so well, that she left behind her only gratitude for the visit.

Late in the afternoon she came forth from the farmhouse, and commenced slowly ascending the hill. She stopped frequently and looked about her; her narrow forehead was wrinkled, and the base of her long nose was set between two deep furrows. Her lips were twisted in a pucker of great perplexity, and her eyes were nearly closed in a desperate endeavor to solve some haunting, puzzling question.

"It's queer," she muttered to herself, when she had nearly reached the top of the hill,—"it's mortal queer! Like a whip-poor-will on a moonlight night: you hear it whistlin' on the next fence-rail, it doesn't seem a yard off; you step up to ketch it, and there's nothin' there; then you step back ag'in, and 'whip-poor-will! whip-poor-will!' whistles louder 'n ever,—and so on, the whole night, and some folks says they can throw their voices outside o' their bodies, but that's neither here nor there.

"Now why can't I ketch hold o' this thing? It isn't a yard off me, I'll be snaked! And I dunno what ever she said that makes me think so, but I feel it in my bones, and no use o' callin' up words; it's one o' them things that comes without callin', when they come at all, and I'm so near guessin' I'll have no peace day or night."

With many similar observations she resumed her walk, and presently reached the border of the ploughed land. Gilbert's back was towards her; he was on the descending furrow. She looked at him, started, suddenly lost her breath, and stood with open mouth and wide, fixed eyes.

"HA-HA-A! HA-HA-A-A!"

Loud and shrill her cry rang across the valley. It was like the yell of a war-horse, scenting the battle afar off. All the force of her lungs and muscles expended itself in the sound.

The next instant she dropped upon the moist, ploughed earth, and sat there, regardless of gown and petticoat. "Good Lord!" she repeated to herself, over and over again. Then, seeing Gilbert approaching, startled by the cry, she slowly arose to her feet.

"A good guess," she said to herself, "and what's more, there's ways o' provin' it. He's comin', and he mustn't know; you're a fool, Betsy Lavender, not to keep your wits better about you, and go rousin' up the whole neighborhood; good look that your face is crooked and don't show much o' what's goin' on inside!"

"What's the matter, Betsy?" asked Gilbert.

"Nothin'—one o' my crazy notions," she said. "I used to holler like a kildeer when I was a girl and got out on the Brandywine hills alone, and I s'pose I must ha' thought about it, and the yell sort o' come of itself, for it just jerked me off o' my feet; but you needn't tell anybody that I cut such capers in my old days, not that folks'd much wonder, but the contrary, for they're used to me."

Gilbert laughed heartily, but he hardly seemed satisfied with the explanation. "You're all of a tremble," he said.

"Am I? Well, it's likely,—and my gownd all over mud; but there's one favor I want to ask o' you, and no common one, neither, namely, the loan of a horse for a week or so."

"A horse?" Gilbert repeated.

"A horse. Not Roger, by no means; I couldn't ask that, and he don't know me, anyhow; but the least rough-pacin' o' them two, for I've got considerable

316

ridin' over the country to do, and I wouldn't ask you, but it's a busy time o' year, and all folks isn't so friendly."

"You shall have whatever you want, Betsy," he said. "But you've heard nothing?"—

"Nothin' o' one sort or t'other. Make yourself easy, lad."

Gilbert, however, had been haunted by new surmises in regard to Dr. Deane. Certain trifles had returned to his memory since the interview, and rather than be longer annoyed with them, he now opened his heart to Miss Lavender.

A curious expression came over her face. "You've got sharp eyes and ears Gilbert," she said. "Now supposin' I wanted your horse o' purpose to clear up your doubts in a way to satisfy you, would you mind lettin' me have it?"

"Take even Roger!" he exclaimed.

"No, that bay'll do. Keep thinkin' that's what I'm after, and ask me no more questions."

She crossed the ploughed land, crept through the fence, and trudged up the road. When a clump of bushes on the bank had hid Gilbert from her sight, she stopped, took breath, and chuckled with luxurious satisfaction.

"Betsy Lavender," she said, with marked approval, "you're a cuter old thing than I took you to be!"

CHAPTER XXIX. — MYSTERIOUS MOVEMENTS.

The next morning Sam took Gilbert's bay horse to Kennett Square, and hitched him in front of Dr. Deane's door. Miss Lavender, who was on the look-out, summoned the boy into the house, to bring her own side-saddle down from the garret, and then proceeded to pack a small valise, with straps corresponding to certain buckles behind the saddle. Martha Deane looked on with some surprise at this proceeding, but as Miss Lavender continued silent, she asked no questions.

"There!" exclaimed the spinster, when everything was ready, "now I'm good for a week's travel, if need be! You want to know where I'm goin', child, I see, and you might as well out with the words, though not much use, for I hardly know myself."

"Betsy," said Martha, "you seem so strange, so unlike yourself, ever since you came home last evening. What is it?"

"I remembered somethin', on the way up; my head's been so bothered that I forgot things, never mind what, for I must have some business o' my own or I wouldn't seem to belong to myself; and so I've got to trapes round considerable,—money matters and the likes,—and folks a'n't always ready for you to the minute; therefore count on more time than what's needful, say I."

"And you can't guess when you will be back?" Martha asked.

"Hardly under a week. I want to finish up everything and come home for a good long spell."

With these words she descended to the road, valise in hand, buckled it to the saddle, and mounted the horse. Then she said good-bye to Martha, and rode briskly away, down the Philadelphia road.

Several days passed and nothing was heard of her. Gilbert Potter remained on his farm, busy with the labor of the opening spring; Mark Deane was absent, taking measurements and making estimates for the new house, and Sally Fairthorn spent all her spare time in spinning flax for a store of sheets and table-cloths, to be marked "S. A. F." in red silk, when duly woven, hemmed, and bleached.

One afternoon, during Miss Lavender's absence, Dr. Deane was again called upon to attend Old-man Barton. It was not an agreeable duty, for the Doctor suspected that something more than medical advice was in question. He had not visited the farm-house since his discovery of Martha's attachment to Gilbert Potter,—had even avoided intercourse with Alfred Barton, towards whom his manner became cold and constrained. It was a sore subject in his thoughts, and both the Bartons seemed to be, in some manner, accessory to his disappointment.

The old man complained of an attack of "buzzing in the head," which molested him at times, and for which bleeding was the Doctor's usual remedy. His face had a flushed, congested, purple hue, and there was an unnatural glare in his eyes; but the blood flowed thickly and sluggishly from his skinny arm, and a much longer time than usual elapsed before he felt relieved.

"Gad, Doctor!" he said, when the vein had been closed, "the spring weather brings me as much fulness as a young buck o' twenty. I'd be frisky yet, if 't wasn't for them legs. Set down, there; you've news to tell me!"

"I think, Friend Barton," Dr. Deane answered, "thee'd better be quiet a spell. Talking isn't exactly good for thee."

"Eh?" the old man growled; "maybe you'd like to think so, Doctor. If I am house-bound, I pick up some things as they go around. And I know why you let our little matter drop so sudden."

He broke off with a short, malicious laugh, which excited the Doctor's ire. The latter seated himself, smoothed his garments and his face, became odorous of bergamot and wintergreen, and secretly determined to repay the old man for this thrust.

"I don't know what thee may have heard, Friend Barton," he remarked, in his blandest voice. "There is always plenty of gossip in this neighborhood, and some persons, no doubt, have been too free with my name,—mine and my daughter's, I may say. But I want thee to know that that has nothing to do with the relinquishment of my visits to thee. If thee's curious to learn the reason, perhaps thy son Alfred may be able to give it more circumstantially than I can."

"What, what, what!" exclaimed the old man. "The boy told you not to come, eh?"

"Not in so many words, mind thee; but he made it unnecessary,—quite unnecessary. In the first place, he gave me no legal evidence of any property, and until that was done, my hands were tied. Further, he seemed very loath to address Martha at all, which was not so singular, considering that he never took any steps, from the first, to gain her favor; and then he deceived me into imagining that she wanted time, after she had positively refused his addresses. He is mistaken, and thee too, if you think that I am very anxious to have a man of no spirit and little property for my son-in-law!"

The Doctor's words expressed more than he intended. They not only stung, but betrayed his own sting. Old-man Barton crooked his claws around his hickory staff, and shook with senile anger; while his small, keen eyes glared on his antagonist's face. Yet he had force enough to wait until the first heat of his feeling subsided.

"Doctor," he then said, "mayhap my boy's better than a man o' no name and no property. He's worth, anyways, what I choose to make him worth. Have you made up y'r mind to take the t'other, that you've begun to run him down, eh?"

They were equally matched, this time. The color came into Dr. Deane's face, and then faded, leaving him slightly livid about the mouth. He preserved his external calmness, by a strong effort, but there was a barely perceptible tremor in his voice, as he replied,—

"It is not pleasant to a man of my years to be made a fool of, as I have every reason to believe thy son has attempted. If I had yielded to his persuasions, I should have spent much time—all to no purpose, I doubt not—in endeavoring to ascertain what thee means to do for him in thy will.

It was, indeed, the only thing he seemed to think or care much about. If he has so much money of his own, as thee says, it is certainly not creditable that he should be so anxious for thy decease."

The Doctor had been watching the old man as he spoke, and the increasing effect of his words was so perceptible that he succeeded in closing with an agreeable smile and a most luxurious pinch of snuff. He had not intended to say so much, at the commencement of the conversation, but he had been sorely provoked, and the temptation was irresistible.

The effect was greater than he had imagined. Old Barton's face was so convulsed, that, for a few minutes, the Doctor feared an attack of complete paralysis. He became the physician again, undid his work as much as possible, and called Miss Ann into the room, to prevent any renewal of the discussion. He produced his stores of entertaining gossip, and prolonged his stay until all threatening symptoms of the excitement seemed to be allayed. The old man returned to his ordinary mood, and listened, and made his gruff comments, but with temporary fits of abstraction. After the Doctor's departure, he scarcely spoke at all, for the remainder of the evening.

A day or two afterwards, when Alfred Barton returned in the evening from a sale in the neighborhood, he was aware of a peculiar change in his father's manner. His first impression was that the old man, contrary to Dr. Deane's orders, had resumed his rations of brandy, and exceeded the usual allowance. There was a vivid color on his flabby cheeks; he was alert, talkative, and frequently chuckled to himself, shifting the hickory staff from hand to hand, or rubbing his gums backward and forward on its rounded end.

He suddenly asked, as Alfred was smoking his pipe before the fire,—

"Know what I've been thinkin' of, to-day, boy?"

"No, daddy; anything about the crops?"

"Ha! ha! a pretty good crop for somebody it'll be! Nearly time for me to make my will, eh? I'm so old and weak—no life left in me—can't last many days!"

He laughed with a hideous irony, as he pronounced these words. His son stared at him, and the fire died out in the pipe between his teeth. Was the old man getting childish? he asked himself. But no; he had never looked more diabolically cunning and watchful.

"Why, daddy," Alfred said at last, "I thought—I fancied, at least, you'd done that, long ago."

"Maybe I have, boy; but maybe I want to change it. I had a talk with the Doctor when he came down to bleed me, and since there's to be no match between you and the girl"—

He paused, keeping his eyes on his son's face, which lengthened and grew vacant with a vague alarm.

"Why, then," he presently resumed, "you're so much poorer by the amount o' her money. Would it be fair, do you think, if I was to put that much to what I might ha' meant for you before? Don't you allow you ought to have a little more, on account o' your disapp'intment?

"If you think so, dad, it's all right," said the son, relighting his pipe. "I don't know, though what Elisha'd say to it; but then, he's no right to complain, for he married full as much as I'd ha' got."

"That he did, boy; and when all's said and done, the money's my own to do with it what I please. There's no law o' the oldest takin' all. Yes, yes, I'll have to make a new will!"

A serene joy diffused itself through Alfred Barton's breast. He became frank, affectionate, and confidential.

"To tell you the truth, dad," he said, "I was mighty afraid you'd play the deuce with me, because all's over between me and Martha Deane. You seemed so set on it."

"So I was—so I was," croaked the old man, "but I've got over it since I saw the Doctor. After all I've heerd, she's not the wife for you; it's better as it is. You'd rayther have the money without her, tell the truth now, you dog, ha! ha!"

"Damme, dad, you've guessed it!" Alfred cried, joining in the laugh.

"She's too high-flown for me. I never fancied a woman that's ready to take you down, every other word you say; and I'll tell you now, that I hadn't much stomach for the match, at any time; but you wanted it, you know, and I've done what I could, to please you."

"You're a good boy, Alfred,—a mighty good boy."

There was nothing very amusing in this opinion, but the old man laughed over it, by fits and starts, for a long time.

"Take a drop o' brandy, boy!" he said. "You may as well have my share, till I'm ready to begin ag'in."

This was the very climax of favor. Alfred arose with a broad beam of triumph on his face, filled the glass, and saying,—"Here's long life to you, dad!" turned it into his mouth.

"Long life?" the old man muttered. "It's pretty long as it is,—eighty-six and over; but it may be ninety-six, or a hundred and six; who knows? Anyhow, boy, long or short, I'll make a new will."

Giles was now summoned, to wheel him into the adjoining room and put him to bed. Alfred Barton took a second glass of brandy (after the door was closed), lighted a fresh pipe, and seated himself again before the embers to enjoy the surprise and exultation of his fortune. To think that he had worried himself so long for that which finally came of itself! Half his fear of the old man, he reflected, had been needless; in many things he had acted like the veriest fool! Well, it was a consolation to know that all his anxieties were over. The day that should make him a rich and important man might be delayed (his father's strength and vitality were marvellous), but it was certain to come.

Another day or two passed by, and the old man's quick, garrulous, cheerful mood continued, although he made no further reference to the subject of the will. Alfred Barton deliberated whether he should suggest sending for Lawyer Stacy, but finally decided not to hazard his prospects by a show of impatience. He was therefore not a little surprised when his sister Ann suddenly made her appearance in the barn, where he and Giles were

323

mending some dilapidated plough-harness, and announced that the lawyer was even then closeted with their father. Moreover, for the first time in his knowledge, Ann herself had been banished from the house. She clambered into the hay-mow, sat down in a comfortable spot, and deliberately plied her knitting-needles.

Ann seemed to take the matter as coolly as if it were an every-day occurrence, but Alfred could not easily recover from his astonishment. There was more than accident here, he surmised. Mr. Stacy had made his usual visit, not a fortnight before; his father's determination had evidently been the result of his conversation with Dr. Deane; and in the mean time no messenger had been sent to Chester, neither was there time for a letter to reach there. Unless Dr. Deane himself were concerned in secretly bringing about the visit,—a most unlikely circumstance,—Alfred Barton could not understand how it happened.

"How did th' old man seem, when you left the house?" he asked.

"'Pears to me I ha'n't seen him so chipper these twenty years," said Ann.

"And how long are they to be left alone?"

"No tellin'," she answered, rattling her needles. "Mr. Stacy'll come, when all's done; and not a soul is to go any nearer the house till he gives the word."

Two hours, three hours, four hours passed away, before the summons came. Alfred Barton found himself so curiously excited that he was fain to leave the harness to Giles, and quiet himself with a pipe or two in the meadow. He would have gone up to the Unicorn for a little stronger refreshment, but did not dare to venture out of sight of the house. Miss Ann was the perfect image of Patience in a hay-mow, smiling at his anxiety. The motion of her needles never ceased, except when she counted the stitches in narrowing.

Towards sunset, Mr. Stacy made his appearance at the barn-door, but his face was a sealed book.

On the morning of that very day, another mysterious incident occurred. Jake Fairthorn had been sent to Carson's on the old gray mare, on some farm-errand,—perhaps to borrow a pick-axe or a post-spade. He had returned as far as the Philadelphia road, and was entering the thick wood on the level before descending to Redley Creek, when he perceived Betsy Lavender leading Gilbert Potter's bay horse through a gap in the fence, after which she commenced putting up the rails behind her.

"Why, Miss Betsy! what are you doin'?" cried Jake, spurring up to the spot.

"Boys should speak when they're spoken to, and not come where they're not wanted," she answered, in a savage tone. "Maybe I'm goin' to hunt bears."

"Oh, please, let me go along!" eagerly cried Jake, who believed in bears.

"Go along! Yes, and be eat up." Miss Lavender looked very much annoyed. Presently, however, her face became amiable; she took a buckskin purse out of her pocket, selected a small silver coin, and leaning over the fence, held it out to Jake.

"Here!" she said, "here's a 'levenpenny-bit for you, if you'll be a good boy, and do exackly as I bid you. Can you keep from gabblin', for two days? Can you hold your tongue and not tell anybody till day after to-morrow that you seen me here, goin' into the woods?"

"Why, that's easy as nothin'!" cried Jake, pocketing the coin. Miss Lavender, leading the horse, disappeared among the trees.

But it was not quite so easy as Jake supposed. He had not been at home ten minutes, before the precious piece of silver, transferred back and forth between his pocket and his hand in the restless ecstasy of possession, was perceived by Joe. Then, as Jake stoutly refused to tell where it came from, Joe rushed into the kitchen, exclaiming,—

"Mammy, Jake's stole a levy!"

This brought out Mother Fairthorn and Sally, and the unfortunate Jake, pressed and threatened on all sides, began to cry lamentably.

"She'll take it from me ag'in, if I tell," he whimpered.

"She? Who?" cried both at once, their curiosity now fully excited; and the end of it was that Jake told the whole story, and was made wretched.

"Well!" Sally exclaimed, "this beats all! Gilbert Potter's bay horse, too! Whatever could she be after? I'll have no peace till I tell Martha, and so I may as well go up at once, for there's something in the wind, and if she don't know already, she ought to!"

Thereupon Sally put on her bonnet, leaving her pewters half scoured, and ran rather than walked to the village. Martha Deane could give no explanation of the circumstance, but endeavored, for Miss Lavender's sake, to conceal her extreme surprise.

"We shall know what it means," she said, "when Betsy comes home, and if it's anything that concerns me, I promise, Sally, to tell you. It may, however, relate to some business of her own, and so, I think, we had better quietly wait and say nothing about it."

Nevertheless, after Sally's departure, Martha meditated long and uneasily upon what she had heard. The fact that Miss Lavender had come back from the Potter farmhouse in so unusual a frame of mind, borrowed Gilbert's horse, and set forth on some mysterious errand, had already disquieted her. More than the predicted week of absence had passed, and now Miss Lavender, instead of returning home, appeared to be hiding in the woods, anxious that her presence in the neighborhood should not be made known. Moreover she had been seen by the landlord of the Unicorn, three days before, near Logtown, riding towards Kennett Square.

These mysterious movements filled Martha Deane with a sense of anxious foreboding. She felt sure that they were connected, in some way, with Gilbert's interests, and Miss Lavender's reticence now seemed to indicate a coming misfortune which she was endeavoring to avert. If these fears were correct, Gilbert needed her help also. He could not come to her; was she not called upon to go to him?

Her resolution was soon taken, and she only waited until her father had left on a visit to two or three patients along the Street Road. His questions, she knew, would bring on another painful conflict of will, and she would save her strength for Gilbert's necessities. To avoid the inferences of the tavern loungers, she chose the longer way, eastward out of the village to the cross-road running past the Carson place.

All the sweet, faint tokens of Spring cheered her eyes and calmed the unrest of her heart, as she rode. Among the dead leaves of the woods, the snowy blossoms of the blood-root had already burst forth in starry clusters; the anemones trembled between the sheltering knees of the old oaks, and here and there a single buttercup dropped its gold on the meadows. These things were so many presentiments of brighter days in Nature, and they awoke a corresponding faith in her own heart.

As she approached the Potter farm she slackened her horse's pace, and deliberated whether she should ride directly to the house or seek for Gilbert in the fields. She had not seen Mary Potter since that eventful Sunday, the previous summer, and felt that Gilbert ought to be consulted before a visit which might possibly give pain. Her doubts were suddenly terminated by his appearance, with Sam and an ox-cart, in the road before her.

Gilbert could with difficulty wait until the slow oxen had removed Sam out of hearing.

"Martha! were you coming to me?" he asked.

"As I promised, Gilbert," she said. "But do not look so anxious. If there really is any trouble, I must learn it of you."

She then related to him what she had noticed in Miss Lavender's manner, and learned of her movements. He stood before her, listening, with his hand on the mane of her horse, and his eyes intently fixed on her face. She saw the agitation her words produced, and her own vague fears returned.

"Can you guess her business, Gilbert?" she asked.

"Martha," he answered, "I only know that there is something in her mind, and I believe it concerns me. I am afraid to guess anything more, because I have only my own wild fancies to go upon, and it won't do to give 'em play!"

"What are those fancies, Gilbert? May I not know?"

"Can you trust me a little, Martha?" he implored. "Whatever I know, you shall know; but if I sometimes seek useless trouble for myself, why should I seek it for you? I'll tell you now one fear I've kept from you, and you'll see what I mean."

He related to her his dread that Sandy Flash might prove to be his father, and the solution of it in the highwayman's cell. "Have I not done right?" he asked.

"I am not sure, Gilbert," she replied, with a brave smile; "you might have tested my truth, once more, if you had spoken your fears."

"I need no test, Martha; and you won't press me for another, now. I'll only say, and you'll be satisfied with it, that Betsy seemed to guess what was in my mind, and promised, or rather expected, to come back with good news."

"Then," said Martha, "I must wait until she makes her appearance."

She had hardly spoken the words, before a figure became visible between the shock-headed willows, where the road crosses the stream. A bay horse— and then Betsy Lavender herself!

Martha turned her horse's head, and Gilbert hastened forward with her, both silent and keenly excited.

"Well!" exclaimed Miss Betsy, "what are you two a-doin' here?"

There was news in her face, both saw; yet they also remarked that the meeting did not seem to be entirely welcome to her.

"I came," said Martha, "to see whether Gilbert could tell me why you were hiding in the woods, instead of coming home."

"It's that—that good-for-nothin' serpent, Jake Fairthorn!" cried Miss Lavender. "I see it all now. Much Gilbert could tell you, howsever, or you him, o' my business, and haven't I a right to it, as well as other folks; but never

328

mind, fine as it's spun it'll come to the sun, as they say o' flax and sinful doin's; not that such is mine, but you may think so if you like, and you'll know in a day or two, anyhow!"

Martha saw that Miss Lavender's lean hands were trembling, and guessed that her news must be of vital importance. "Betsy," she said, "I see you don't mean to tell us; but one word you can't refuse—is it good or bad?"

"Good or bad?" Miss Lavender repeated, growing more and more nervous, as she looked at the two anxious faces. "Well, it isn't bad, so peart yourselves up, and ask me no more questions, this day, nor yet to-morrow, maybe; because if you do, I'll just screech with all my might; I'll holler, Gilbert, wuss 'n you heerd, and much good that'll do you, givin' me a crazy name all over the country. I'm in dead earnest; if you try to worm anything more out o' me, I'll screech; and so I was goin' to bring your horse home, Gilbert, and have a talk with your mother, but you've made me mortal weak betwixt and between you; and I'll ride back with Martha, by your leave, and you may send Sam right away for the horse. No; let Sam come now, and walk alongside, to save me from Martha's cur'osity."

Miss Lavender would not rest until this arrangement was made. The two ladies then rode away through the pale, hazy sunset, leaving Gilbert Potter in a fever of impatience, dread, and hope.

CHAPTER XXX. – THE FUNERAL. –

The next morning, at daybreak, Dr. Deane was summoned in haste to the Barton farm-house. Miss Betsy Lavender, whose secrets, whatever they were, had interfered with her sleep, heard Giles's first knock, and thrust her night-cap out the window before he could repeat it. The old man, so Giles announced, had a bad spell,—a 'plectic fit, Lawyer Stacy called it, and they didn't know as he'd live from one hour to another.

Miss Lavender aroused the Doctor, then dressed herself in haste, and prepared to accompany him. Martha, awakened by the noise, came into the spinster's room in her night-dress.

"Must you go, Betsy?" she asked.

"Child, it's a matter o' life and death, more likely death; and Ann's a dooless critter at best, hardly ever off the place, and need o' Chris'en help, if there ever was such; so don't ask me to stay, for I won't, and all the better for me, for I daresn't open my lips to livin' soul till I've spoke with Mary Potter!"

Miss Lavender took the foot-path across the fields, accompanied by Giles, who gave up his saddled horse to Dr. Deane. The dawn was brightening in the sky as they reached the farm-house, where they found Alfred Barton restlessly walking backwards and forwards in the kitchen, while Ann and Mr. Stacy were endeavoring to apply such scanty restoratives—consisting principally of lavender and hot bricks—as the place afforded.

An examination of the eyes and the pulse, and a last abortive attempt at phlebotomy, convinced Dr. Deane that his services were no longer needed. Death, which so many years before had lamed half the body, now asserted his claim to the whole. A wonderfully persistent principle of vitality struggled against the clogged functions, for two or three hours, then yielded, and the small fragment of soul in the old man was cast adrift, with little chance of finding a comfortable lodging in any other world.

Ann wandered about the kitchen in a dazed state, dropping tears everywhere, and now and then moaning,—"O Betsy, how'll I ever get up the funeral dinner?" while Alfred, after emptying the square bottle of brandy, threw himself upon the settle and went to sleep. Mr. Stacy and Miss Lavender, who seemed to know each other thoroughly at the first sight, took charge of all the necessary arrangements; and as Alfred had said,—"I can't look after anything; do as you two like, and don't spare expense!" they ordered the coffin, dispatched messengers to the relatives and neighbors, and soothed Ann's unquiet soul by selecting the material for the dinner, and engaging the Unicorn's cook.

When all was done, late in the day, Miss Lavender called Giles and said,—"Saddle me a horse, and if no side-saddle, a man's'll do, for go I must; it's business o' my own, Mr. Stacy, and won't wait for me; not that I want to do more this day than what I've done. Goodness knows; but I'll have a fit, myself, if I don't!"

She reached the Potter farm-house at dark, and both mother and son were struck with her flushed, excited, and yet weary air. Their supper was over, but she refused to take anything more than a cup of tea; her speech was forced, and more rambling and disconnected than ever. When Mary Potter left the kitchen to bring some fresh cream from the spring-house, Miss Lavender hastily approached Gilbert, laid her hand on his shoulder, and said,—

"Lad, be good this once't, and do what I tell you. Make a reason for goin' to bed as soon as you can; for I've been workin' in your interest all this while, only I've got that to tell your mother, first of all, which you mustn't hear; and you may hope as much as you please, for the news isn't bad, as'll soon be made manifest!"

Gilbert was strangely impressed by her solemn, earnest manner, and promised to obey. He guessed, and yet feared to believe, that the long release of which his mother had spoken bad come at last; how else, he asked himself, should Miss Lavender become possessed of knowledge which seemed so important? As early as possible he went up to his bedroom, leaving the two women alone. The sound of voices, now high and hurried, now, apparently, low and broken, came to his ears. He resisted the temptation to listen,

331

smothered his head in the pillow to further muffle the sounds, and after a long, restless struggle with his own mind, fell asleep. Deep in the night he was awakened by the noise of a shutting door, and then all was still.

It was very evident, in the morning, that he had not miscalculated the importance of Miss Lavender's communication. Was this woman, whose face shone with such a mingled light of awe and triumph, his mother? Were these features, where the deep lines of patience were softened into curves of rejoicing, the dark, smouldering gleam of sorrow kindled into a flashing light of pride, those he had known from childhood? As he looked at her, in wonder renewed with every one of her movements and glances, she took him by the hand and said,—

"Gilbert, wait a little!"

Miss Lavender insisted on having breakfast by sunrise, and as soon as the meal was over demanded her horse. Then first she announced the fact of Old-man Barton's death, and that the funeral was to be on the following day.

"Mary, you must be sure and come," she said, as she took leave; "I know Ann expects it of you. Ten o'clock, remember!"

Gilbert noticed that his mother laid aside her sewing, and when the ordinary household labor had been performed, seated herself near the window with a small old Bible, which he had never before seen in her hands. There was a strange fixedness in her gaze, as if only her eyes, not her thoughts, were directed upon its pages. The new expression of her face remained; it seemed already to have acquired as permanent a stamp as the old. Against his will he was infected by its power, and moved about in barn and field all day with a sense of the unreality of things, which was very painful to his strong, practical nature.

The day of the old man's funeral came. Sam led up the horses, and waited at the gate with them to receive his master's parting instructions. Gilbert remarked with surprise that his mother placed a folded paper between the leaves of the Bible, tied the book carefully in a linen handkerchief, and carried it with her. She was ready, but still hesitated, looking around the kitchen with the manner of one who had forgotten something. Then she returned to her own room, and after some minutes, came forth, paler than before, but proud, composed, and firm.

"Gilbert," she said, almost in a whisper, "I have tried you sorely, and you have been wonderfully kind and patient. I have no right to ask anything more; I could tell you everything now, but this is not the place nor the time I had thought of, for so many years past. Will you let me finish the work in the way pointed out to me?"

"Mother," he answered, "I cannot judge in this matter, knowing nothing. I must be led by you; but, pray, do not let it be long?"

"It will not be long, my boy, or I wouldn't ask it. I have one more duty to perform, to myself, to you, and to the Lord, and it must be done in the sight of men. Will you stand by me, not question my words, not interfere with my actions, however strange they may seem, but simply believe and obey?"

"I will, mother," he said, "because you make me feel that I must."

They mounted, and side by side rode up the glen. Mary Potter was silent; now and then her lips moved, not, as once, in some desperate appeal of the heart for pity and help, but as with a thanksgiving so profound that it must needs be constantly renewed, to be credited.

After passing Carson's, they took the shorter way across the fields, and approached the Barton farm-house from below. A large concourse of people was already assembled; and the rude black hearse, awaiting its burden in the lane, spread the awe and the gloom of death over the scene. The visitors were grouped around the doors, silent or speaking cautiously in subdued tones; and all new-comers passed into the house to take their last look at the face, of the dead.

The best room, in which the corpse lay, was scarcely used once in a year, and many of the neighbors had never before had occasion to enter it. The shabby, antiquated furniture looked cold and dreary from disuse, and the smell of camphor in the air hardly kept down the musty, mouldy odors which exhaled from the walls. The head and foot of the coffin rested on two chairs placed in the centre of the room; and several women, one of whom was Miss Betsy Lavender, conducted the visitors back and forth, as they came. The members of the bereaved family were stiffly ranged around the walls, the chief mourners consisting of the old man's eldest son, Elisha, with his wife and three married sons, Alfred, and Ann.

Mary Potter took her son's arm, and they passed through the throng at the door, and entered the house. Gilbert silently returned the nods of greeting; his mother neither met nor avoided the eyes of others. Her step was firm, her head erect, her bearing full of pride and decision. Miss Lavender, who met her with a questioning glance at the door, walked beside her to the room of death, and then—what was remarkable in her—became very pale.

They stood by the coffin. It was not a peaceful, solemn sight, that yellow face, with its wrinkles and creases and dark blotches of congealed blood, made more pronounced and ugly by the white shroud and cravat, yet a tear rolled down Mary Potter's cheek as she gazed upon it. Other visitors came, and Gilbert gently drew her away, to leave the room; but with a quick pressure upon his arm, as if to remind him of his promise, she quietly took her seat near the mourners, and by a slight motion indicated that he should seat himself at her side.

It was an unexpected and painful position; but her face, firm and calm, shamed his own embarrassment. He saw, nevertheless, that the grief of the mourners was not so profound as to suppress the surprise, if not indignation, which the act called forth. The women had their handkerchiefs to their eyes, and were weeping in a slow, silent, mechanical way; the men had handkerchiefs in their hands, but their faces were hard, apathetic, and constrained.

By-and-by the visitors ceased; the attending women exchanged glances with each other and with the mourners, and one of the former stepped up to Mary Potter and said gently,—

"It is only the family, now."

This was according to custom, which required that just before the coffin was closed, the members of the family of the deceased should be left alone with him for a few minutes, and take their farewell of his face, undisturbed by other eyes. Gilbert would have risen, but his mother, with her hand on his arm, quietly replied,—

"We belong to the family."

The woman withdrew, though with apparent doubt and hesitation, and they were left alone with the mourners.

Gilbert could scarcely trust his senses. A swift suspicion of his mother's insanity crossed his mind; but when he looked around the room and beheld Alfred Barton gazing upon her with a face more livid than that of the dead man, this suspicion was followed by another, no less overwhelming. For a few minutes everything seemed to whirl and spin before his eyes; a light broke upon him, but so unexpected, so incredible, that it came with the force of a blow.

The undertaker entered the room and screwed down the lid of the coffin; the pall-bearers followed and carried it to the hearse. Then the mourners rose and prepared to set forth, in the order of their relation to the deceased. Elisha Barton led the way, with his wife; then Ann, clad in her Sunday black, stepped forward to take Alfred's arm.

"Ann," said Mary Potter, in a low voice, which yet was heard by every person in the room, "that is my place."

She left Gilbert and moved to Alfred Barton's side. Then, slightly turning, she said,—"Gilbert, give your arm to your aunt."

For a full minute no other word was said. Alfred Barton stood motionless, with Mary Potter's hand on his arm. A fiery flush succeeded to his pallor; his jaw fell, and his eyes were fixed upon the floor. Ann took Gilbert's arm in a helpless, bewildered way.

"Alfred, what does all this mean?" Elisha finally asked.

He said nothing; Mary Potter answered for him,—"It is right that he should walk with his wife rather than his sister."

The horses and chairs were waiting in the lane, and helping neighbors were at the door; but the solemn occasion was forgotten, in the shock produced by this announcement. Gilbert started and almost reeled; Ann clung to him with helpless terror; and only Elisha, whose face grew dark and threatening, answered.

"Woman," he said, "you are out of your senses! Leave us; you have no business here!"

She met him with a proud, a serene and steady countenance. "Elisha," she answered, "we are here to bury your father and my father-in-law. Let be until the grave has closed over him; then ask Alfred whether I could dare to take my rightful place before to-day."

The solemn decision of her face and voice struck him dumb. His wife whispered a few words in his ear, and he turned away with her, to take his place in the funeral procession.

It was Alfred Barton's duty to follow, and if it was not grief which impelled him to bury his face in his handkerchief as they issued from the door, it was a torture keener than was ever mingled with grief,—the torture of a mean nature, pilloried in its meanest aspect for the public gaze. Mary, (we must not call her Potter, and cannot yet call her Barton,) rather led him than was led by him, and lifted her face to the eyes of men. The shame which she might have felt, as his wife, was lost in the one overpowering sense of the justification for which she had so long waited and suffered.

When the pair appeared in the yard, and Gilbert followed with Miss Ann Barton on his arm, most of the funeral guests looked on in stupid wonder, unable to conceive the reason of the two thus appearing among the mourners. But when they had mounted and were moving off, a rumor of the startling truth ran from lip to lip. The proper order of the procession was forgotten; some untied their horses in haste and pushed forward to convince themselves of the astonishing fact; others gathered into groups and discussed it earnestly. Some had suspected a relation of the kind, all along, so they said; others scouted at the story, and were ready with explanations of their own. But not a soul had another thought to spare for Old-man Barton that day.

Dr. Deane and Martha heard what had happened as they were

mounting their horses. When they took their places in the line, the singular companionship, behind the hearse, was plainly visible. Neither spoke a word, but Martha felt that her heart was beating fast, and that her thoughts were unsteady.

Presently Miss Lavender rode up and took her place at her side. Tears were streaming from her eyes, and she was using her handkerchief freely. It was sometime before she could command her feelings enough to say, in a husky whisper,—

"I never thought to ha' had a hand in such wonderful doin's, and how I held up through it, I can't tell. Glory to the Lord, the end has come; but, no—not yet—not quite; only enough for one day, Martha; isn't it?"

"Betsy," said Martha, "please ride a little closer, and explain to me how it came about. Give me one or two points for my mind to rest on, for I don't seem to believe even what I see."

"What I see. No wonder, who could? Well, it's enough that Mary was married to Alf. Barton a matter o' twenty-six year ago, and that he swore her to keep it secret till th' old man died, and he's been her husband all this while, and knowed it!"

"Father!" Martha exclaimed in a low, solemn voice, turning to Dr. Deane, "think, now, what it was thee would have had me do!"

The Doctor was already aware of his terrible mistake. "Thee was led, child," he answered, "thee was led! It was a merciful Providence."

"Then might thee not also admit that I have been led in that other respect, which has been so great a trial to thee?"

He made no reply.

The road to Old Kennett never seemed so long; never was a corpse so impatiently followed. A sense of decency restrained those who were not relatives from pushing in advance of those who were; yet it was, very tantalizing to look upon the backs of Alfred Barton and Mary, Gilbert and Ann, when their faces must be such a sight to see!

These four, however, rode in silence. Each, it may be guessed, was sufficiently occupied with his or her own sensations,—except, perhaps, Ann Barton, who had been thrown so violently out of her quiet, passive round of life by her father's death, that she was incapable of any great surprise. Her thoughts were more occupied with the funeral-dinner, yet to come, than with the relationship of the young man at her side.

Gilbert slowly admitted the fact into his mind, but he was so unprepared for it by anything in his mother's life or his own intercourse with Alfred Barton, that he was lost in a maze of baffled conjectures. While this confusion lasted, he scarcely thought of his restoration to honor, or the breaking down of that fatal barrier between him and Martha Deane. His first sensation was one of humiliation and disappointment. How often had he been disgusted with Alfred Barton's meanness and swagger! How much superior, in many of the qualities of manhood, was even the highwayman, whose paternity he had so feared! As he looked at the broad, heavy form before him, in which even the lines of the back expressed cowardice and abject shame, he almost doubted whether his former disgrace was not preferable to his present claim to respect.

Then his eyes turned to his mother's figure, and a sweet, proud joy swept away the previous emotion. Whatever the acknowledged relationship might be to him, to her it was honor—yea, more than honor; for by so much and so cruelly as she had fallen below the rights of her pure name as a woman, the higher would she now be set, not only in respect, but in the reverence earned by her saintly patience and self-denial. The wonderful transformation of her face showed him what this day was to her life, and he resolved that no disappointment of his own should come between her and her triumph.

To Gilbert the way was not too long, nor the progress too slow. It gave him time to grow familiar, not only with the fact, but with his duty. He forcibly postponed his wandering conjectures, and compelled his mind to dwell upon that which lay immediately before him.

It was nearly noon before the hearse reached Old Kennett meeting-house. The people of the neighborhood, who had collected to await its arrival, came forward and assisted the mourners to alight. Alfred Barton mechanically took his place beside his wife, but again buried his face in his handkerchief. As the wondering, impatient crowd gathered around, Gilbert felt that all was known, and that all eyes were fixed upon himself and his mother, and his face reflected her own firmness and strength. From neither could the spectators guess what might be passing in their hearts. They were both paler than usual, and their resemblance to each other became very striking. Gilbert, in fact, seemed to have nothing of his father except the peculiar turn of his shoulders and the strong build of his chest.

They walked over the grassy, briery, unmarked mounds of old graves to the spot where a pile of yellow earth denoted Old Barton's resting-place. When the coffin had been lowered, his children, in accordance with custom, drew near, one after the other, to bend over and look into the narrow pit. Gilbert led up his trembling aunt, who might have fallen in, had he not carefully supported her. As he was withdrawing, his eyes suddenly encountered those of Martha Deane, who was standing opposite, in the circle of hushed spectators. In spite of himself a light color shot into his face, and his lips trembled. The eager gossips, who had not missed even the wink of an eyelid, saw this fleeting touch of emotion, and whence it came. Thenceforth Martha shared their inspection; but from the sweet gravity of her face, the untroubled calm of her eyes, they learned nothing more.

When the grave had been filled, and the yellow mound ridged and patted with the spade, the family returned to the grassy space in front of the meeting-house, and now their more familiar acquaintances, and many who were not, gathered around to greet them and offer words of condolence. An overpowering feeling of curiosity was visible upon every face; those who did not venture to use their tongues, used their eyes the more.

Alfred Barton was forced to remove the handkerchief from his face, and its haggard wretchedness (which no one attributed to grief for his father's death), could no longer be hidden. He appeared to have suddenly become an old man, with deeper wrinkles, slacker muscles, and a helpless, tottering air of weakness. The corners of his mouth drooped, hollowing his cheeks, and his eyes seemed unable to bear up the weight of the lids; they darted rapidly from side to side, or sought the ground, not daring to encounter, for more than an instant, those of others.

There was no very delicate sense of propriety among the people, and very soon an inquisitive old Quaker remarked,—

"Why, Mary, is this true that I hear? Are you two man and wife?"

"We are," she said.

"Bless us! how did it happen?"

The bystanders became still as death, and all ears were stretched to catch the answer. But she, with proud, impenetrable calmness, replied,—

"It will be made known."

And with these words the people were forced, that day to be satisfied.

CHAPTER XXXI. — THE WILL. —

During the homeward journey from the grave, Gilbert and his mother were still the central figures of interest. That the members of the Barton family were annoyed and humiliated, was evident to all eyes; but it was a pitiful, undignified position, which drew no sympathy towards them, while the proud, composed gravity of the former commanded respect. The young men and women, especially, were unanimously of the opinion that Gilbert had conducted himself like a man. They were disappointed, it was true, that he and Martha Deane had not met, in the sight of all. It was impossible to guess whether she had been already aware of the secret, or how the knowledge of it would affect their romantic relation to each other.

Could the hearts of the lovers have been laid bare, the people would have seen that never had each felt such need of the other,—never had they been possessed with such restless yearning. To the very last, Gilbert's eyes wandered from time to time towards the slender figure in the cavalcade before him, hoping for the chance of a word or look; but Martha's finer instinct told her that she must yet hold herself aloof. She appreciated the solemnity of the revelation, saw that much was yet unexplained, and could have guessed, even without Miss Lavender's mysterious hints, that the day would bring forth other and more important disclosures.

As the procession drew nearer Kennett Square, the curiosity of the funeral guests, baulked and yet constantly stimulated, began to grow disorderly. Sally Fairthorn was in such a flutter that she scarcely knew what she said or did; Mark's authority alone prevented her from dashing up to Gilbert, regardless of appearances. The old men, especially those in plain coats and broad-brimmed hats, took every opportunity to press near the mourners; and but for Miss Betsy Lavender, who hovered around the latter like a watchful dragon, both Gilbert and his mother would have been seriously annoyed. Finally the gate at the lane-end closed upon them, and the discomfited public rode on to the village, tormented by keen envy of the few who had been bidden to the funeral-dinner.

When Mary alighted from her horse, the old lawyer approached her.

"My name is Stacy, Mrs. Barton," he said, "and Miss Lavender will have told you who I am. Will you let me have a word with you in private?"

She slightly started at the name he had given her; it was the first symptom of agitation she had exhibited. He took her aside, and began talking earnestly in a low tone. Elisha Barton looked on with an amazed, troubled air, and presently turned to his brother.

"Alfred," he said, "it is quite time all this was explained."

But Miss Lavender interfered.

"It's your right, Mr. Elisha, no denyin' that, and the right of all the fam'ly; so we've agreed to have it done afore all together, in the lawful way, Mr. Stacy bein' a lawyer; but dinner first, if you please, for eatin' 's good both for grief and cur'osity, and it's hard tellin' which is uppermost in this case. Gilbert, come here!"

He was standing alone, beside the paling. He obeyed her call.

"Gilbert, shake hands with your uncle and aunt Mr. Elisha, this is your nephew, Gilbert Barton, Mr. Alfred's son."

They looked at each other for a moment. There was that in Gilbert's face which enforced respect. Contrasted with his father, who stood on one side, darting stealthy glances at the group from the corners of his eyes, his bearing was doubly brave and noble. He offered his hand in silence, and both Elisha Barton and his wife felt themselves compelled to take it. Then the three sons, who knew the name of Gilbert Potter, and were more astonished than shocked at the new relationship, came up and greeted their cousin in a grave but not unfriendly way.

"That's right!" exclaimed Miss Lavender. "And now come in to dinner, all o' ye! I gev orders to have the meats dished as soon as the first horse was seen over the rise o' the hill, and it'll all be smokin' on the table."

Though the meal was such as no one had ever before seen in the Barton farm-house, it was enjoyed by very few of the company. The sense of something to come after it made them silent and uncomfortable. Mr. Stacy, Miss Lavender, and the sons of Elisha Barton, with their wives, carried on a scattering, forced conversation, and there was a general feeling of relief when the pies, marmalade, and cheese had been consumed, and the knives and forks laid crosswise over the plates.

When they arose from the table, Mr. Stacy led the way into the parlor. A fire, in the mean time, had been made in the chill, open fireplace, but it scarcely relieved the dreary, frosty aspect of the apartment. The presence of the corpse seemed to linger there, attaching itself with ghastly distinctness to the chair and hickory staff in a corner.

The few dinner-guests who were not relatives understood that this meeting excluded them, and Elisha Barton was therefore surprised to notice, after they had taken their seats, that Miss Lavender was one of the company.

"I thought," he said, with a significant look, "that it was to be the family only."

"Miss Lavender is one of the witnesses to the will," Mr. Stacy answered, "and her presence is necessary, moreover, as an important testimony in regard to some of its provisions."

Alfred Barton and Gilbert both started at these words, but from very different feelings. The former, released from public scrutiny, already experienced a comparative degree of comfort, and held up his head with an air of courage; yet now the lawyer's announcement threw him into an agitation which it was not possible to conceal. Miss Lavender looked around the circle, coolly nodded her head to Elisha Barton, and said nothing.

Mr. Stacy arose, unlocked a small niche let into the wall of the house, and produced the heavy oaken casket in which the old man kept the documents relating to his property. This he placed upon a small table beside his chair, opened it, and took out the topmost paper. He was completely master of the situation, and the deliberation with which he surveyed the circle of excited faces around him seemed to indicate that he enjoyed the fact.

"The last will and testament of Abiah Barton, made the day before his death," he said, "revokes all former wills, which were destroyed by his order, in the presence of myself and Miss Elizabeth Lavender."

All eyes were turned upon the spinster, who again nodded, with a face of preternatural solemnity.

"In order that you, his children and grandchildren," Mr. Stacy continued, "may rightly understand the deceased's intention in making this last will, when the time comes for me to read it, I must first inform you that he was acquainted with the fact of his son Alfred's marriage with Mary Potter."

Alfred Barton half sprang from his seat, and then fell back with the same startled, livid face, which Gilbert already knew. The others held their breath in suspense,—except Mary, who sat near the lawyer, firm, cold, and unmoved.

"The marriage of Alfred Barton and Mary Potter must therefore be established, to your satisfaction," Mr. Stacy resumed, turning towards Elisha. "Alfred Barton, I ask you to declare whether this woman is your lawfully wedded wife?"

A sound almost like a groan came from his throat, but it formed the syllable,—"Yes."

"Further, I ask you to declare whether Gilbert Barton, who has until this day borne his mother's name of Potter, is your lawfully begotten son?"

"Yes."

"To complete the evidence," said the lawyer, "Mary Barton, give me the paper in your hands."

She untied the handkerchief, opened the Bible, and handed Mr. Stacy the slip of paper which Gilbert had seen her place between the leaves that morning. The lawyer gave it to Elisha Barton, with the request that he would read it aloud.

344

It was the certificate of a magistrate at Burlington, in the Colony of New Jersey, setting forth that he had united in wedlock Alfred Barton and Mary Potter. The date was in the month of June, 1771.

"This paper," said Elisha, when he had finished reading, "appears to be genuine. The evidence must have been satisfactory to you, Mr. Stacy, and to my father, since it appears to have been the cause of his making a new will; but as this new will probably concerns me and my children, I demand to know why; if the marriage was legal, it has been kept secret so long? The fact of the marriage does not explain what has happened to-day."

Mr. Stacy turned towards Gilbert's mother, and made a sign.

"Shall I explain it in my way, Alfred?" she asked, "or will you, in yours?"

"There's but one story," he answered, "and I guess it falls to your place to tell it."

"It does!" she exclaimed. "You, Elisha and Ann, and you, Gilbert, my child, take notice that every word of what I shall say is the plain God's truth. Twenty-seven years ago, when I was a young woman of twenty, I came to this farm to help Ann with the house-work. You remember it, Ann; it was just after your mother's death. I was poor; I had neither father nor mother, but I was as proud as the proudest, and the people called me good-looking. You were vexed with me, Ann, because the young men came now and then, of a Sunday afternoon; but I put up with your hard words. You did not know that I understood what Alfred's eyes meant when he looked at me; I put up with you because I believed I could be mistress of the house, in your place. You have had your revenge of me since, if you felt the want of it—so let that rest!"

She paused. Ann, with her handkerchief to her eyes, sobbed out,— "Mary, I always liked you better 'n you thought."

"I can believe it," she continued, "for I have been forced to look into my heart and learn how vain and mistaken I then was. But I liked Alfred, in those days; he was a gay young man, and accounted good-looking, and there were merry times just before the war, and he used to dress bravely, and was talked about as likely to marry this girl or that. My head was full of him, and

345

I believed my heart was. I let him see from the first that it must be honest love between us, or not at all; and the more I held back, the more eager was he, till others began to notice, and the matter was brought to his father's ears."

"I remember that!" cried Elisha, suddenly.

"Yet it was kept close," she resumed. "Alfred told me that the old man had threatened to cut him out of his will if he should marry me, and I saw that I must leave the farm; but I gave out that I was tired of the country, and wanted to find service in Philadelphia. I believed that Alfred would follow me in a week or two, and he did. He brought news I didn't expect, and it turned my head upside down. His father had had a paralytic stroke, and nobody believed he'd live more than a few weeks. It was in the beginning of June, and the doctors said he couldn't get over the hot weather. Alfred said to me, Why wait?—you'll be taking up with some city fellow, and I want you to be my wife at once. On my side I thought, Let him be made rich and free by his father's death, and wives will be thrown in his way; he'll lose his liking for me, by little and little, and somebody else will be mistress of the farm. So I agreed, and we went to Burlington together, as being more out of the way and easier to be kept secret; but just before we came to the Squire's, he seemed to grow fearsome all at once, lest it should be found out, and he bought a Bible and swore me by my soul's salvation never to say I was married to him until after his father died. Here's the Bible, Alfred! Do you remember it? Here, here's the place where I kissed it when I took the oath!"

She rose from her seat, and held it towards him. No one could doubt the solemn truth of her words. He nodded his head mechanically, unable to speak. Still standing, she turned towards Elisha Barton, and exclaimed,—

"He took the same oath, but what did it mean to him! What does it mean to a man? I was young and vain; I thought only of holding fast to my good luck! I never thought of—of"—(here her faced flushed, and her voice began to tremble)—"of you, Gilbert! I fed my pride by hoping for a man's death, and never dreamed I was bringing a curse on a life that was yet to come! Perhaps he didn't then, either; the Lord pardon me if I judge him too hard. What I charge him with, is that he held me to my oath, when—when

346

the fall went by and the winter, and his father lived, and his son was to be born! It was always the same,—Wait a little, a month or so, maybe; the old man couldn't live, and it was the difference between riches and poverty for us. Then I begged for poverty and my good name, and after that he kept away from me. Before Gilbert was born, I hoped I might die in giving him life; then I felt that I must live for his sake. I saw my sin, and what punishment the Lord had measured out to me, and that I must earn His forgiveness; and He mercifully hid from my sight the long path that leads to this day; for if the release hadn't seemed so near, I never could have borne to wait!"

All the past agony of her life seemed to discharge itself in these words. They saw what the woman had suffered, what wonderful virtues of patience and faith had been developed from the vice of her pride, and there was no heart in the company so stubborn as to refuse her honor. Gilbert's eyes were fixed on her face with an absorbing expression of reverence; he neither knew nor heeded that there were tears on his cheeks. The women wept in genuine emotion, and even the old lawyer was obliged to wipe his dimmed spectacles.

Elisha rose, and approaching Alfred, asked, in a voice which he strove to make steady,—"Is all this true?"

Alfred sank his head; his reply was barely audible,—

"She has said no more than the truth."

"Then," said Elisha, taking her hand, "I accept you, Mary Barton, and acknowledge your place in our family."

Elisha's wife followed, and embraced her with many tears, and lastly Ann, who hung totteringly upon her shoulder as she cried,—

"Indeed, Mary, indeed I always liked you; I never wished you any harm!"

Thus encouraged, Alfred Barton made a powerful effort. There seemed but one course for him to take; it was a hard one, but he took it.

"Mary," he said, "you have full right and justice on your side. I've acted meanly towards you—meaner, I'm afraid, than any man before ever acted towards his wife. Not only to you, but to Gilbert; but I always meant to do my duty in the end. I waited from month to month, and year to year, as you did; and then things got set in their way, and it was harder and harder to let out the truth. I comforted myself—that wasn't right, either, I know,—but I comforted myself with the thought that you were doing well; I never lost sight of you, and I've been proud of Gilbert, though I didn't dare show it, and always wanted to lend him a helping hand, if he'd let me."

She drew herself up and faced him with flashing eyes.

"How did you mean to do your duty by me? How did you mean to lend Gilbert a helping hand? Was it by trying to take a second wife during my lifetime, and that wife the girl whom Gilbert loves?"

Her questions cut to the quick, and the shallow protestations he would have set up were stripped off in a moment, leaving bare every cowardly shift of his life. Nothing was left but the amplest confession.

"You won't believe me, Mary," he stammered, feebly weeping with pity of his own miserable plight, "and I can't ask to—but it's the truth! Give me your Bible! I'll kiss the place you kissed, and swear before God that I never meant to marry Martha Deane! I let the old man think so, because he hinted it'd make a difference in his will, and he drove me—he and Dr. Deane together—to speak to her. I was a coward and a fool that I let myself be driven that far, but I couldn't and wouldn't have married her!"

"The whole snarl's comin' undone," interrupted Miss Lavender. "I see the end on't. Do you mind that day, Alf. Barton, when I come upon you sudden, settin' on the log and sayin' 'I can't see the way,'—the very day, I'll be snaked, that you spoke to the Doctor about Martha Deane!—and then you so mortal glad that she wouldn't have you! You have acted meaner 'n dirt; I don't excuse him, Mary; but never mind, justice is justice, and he's told the truth this once't."

"Sit down, friends!" said Mr. Stacy. "Before the will is read, I want Miss Lavender to relate how it was that Abiah Barton and myself became acquainted with the fact of the marriage."

The reading of the will had been almost forgotten in the powerful

348

interest excited by Mary Barton's narrative. The curiosity to know its contents instantly revived, but was still subordinate to that which the lawyer's statement occasioned. The whole story was so singular, that it seemed as yet but half explained.

"Well, to begin at the beginnin'," said Miss Lavender, "it all come o' my wishin' to help two true-lovyers, and maybe you'll think I'm as foolish as I'm old, but never mind, I'll allow that; and I saw that nothin' could be done till Gilbert got his lawful name, and how to get it was the trouble, bein' as Mary was swore to keep secret. The long and the short of it is, I tried to worm it out o' her, but no use; she set her teeth as tight as sin, and all I did learn was, that when she was in Phildelphy—I knowed Gilbert was born there, but didn't let on—she lived at Treadwells, in Fourth Street Then turnin' over everything in my mind, I suspicioned that she must be waitin' for somebody to die, and that's what held her bound; it seemed to me I must guess right away, but I couldn't and couldn't, and so goin' up the hill, nigh puzzled to death, Gilbert ploughin' away from me, bendin' his head for'ard a little—there! turn round, Gilbert! turn round, Alf. Barton I Look at them two sets o' shoulders!"

Miss Lavender's words were scarcely comprehensible, but all saw the resemblance between father and son, in the outline of the shoulders, and managed to guess her meaning.

"Well," she continued, "it struck me then and there, like a streak o' lightnin'; I screeched and tumbled like a shot hawk, and so betwixt the saddle and the ground, as the sayin' is, it come to me—not mercy, but knowledge, all the same, you know what I mean; and I saw them was Alf. Barton's shoulders, and I remembered the old man was struck with palsy the year afore Gilbert was born, and I dunno how many other things come to me all of a heap; and now you know, Gilbert, what made me holler. I borrowed the loan o' his bay horse and put off for Phildelphy the very next day, and a mortal job it was; what with bar'ls and boxes pitched hither and yon, and people laughin' at y'r odd looks,—don't talk o' Phildelphy manners to me, for I've had enough of 'em!—and old Treadwell dead when I did find him, and the daughter married to Greenfield in the brass and tin-ware business, it's a mercy I ever found out anything."

"Come to the point, Betsy," said Elisha, impatiently.

"The point, Betsy. The p'int 's this: I made out from the Greenfield woman that the man who used to come to see Mary Potter was the perfect pictur' o' young Alf. Barton; then to where she went next, away down to the t'other end o' Third Street, boardin', he payin' the board till just afore Gilbert was born—and that's enough, thinks I, let me get out o' this rackety place. So home I posted, but not all the way, for no use to tell Mary Potter, and why not go right to Old-man Barton, and let him know who his daughter-in-law and son is, and see what'll come of it? Th' old man, you must know, always could abide me better 'n most women, and I wasn't a bit afeard of him, not lookin' for legacies, and wouldn't have 'em at any such price; but never mind. I hid my horse in the woods and sneaked into the house across the fields, the back way, and good luck that nobody was at home but Ann, here; and so I up and told the old man the whole story."

"The devil!" Alfred Barton could not help exclaiming, as he recalled his father's singular manner on the evening of the day in question.

"Devil!" Miss Lavender repeated. "More like an angel put it into my head. But I see Mr. Elisha's fidgetty, so I'll make short work o' the rest. He curst and swore awful, callin' Mr. Alfred a mean pup, and I dunno what all, but he hadn't so much to say ag'in Mary Potter; he allowed she was a smart lass, and he'd heerd o' Gilbert's doin's, and the lad had grit in him. 'Then,' says I, 'here's a mighty wrong been done, and it's for you to set it right afore you die, and if you manage as I tell you, you can be even with Mr. Alfred;' and he perks up his head and asks how, and says I 'This way'—but what I said'll be made manifest by Mr. Stacy, without my jumpin' ahead o' the proper time. The end of it was, he wound up by sayin',—'Gad, if Stacy was only here!' 'I'll bring him!' says I, and it was fixed betwixt and between us two, Ann knowin' nothin' o' the matter; and off I trapesed back to Chester, and brung Mr. Stacy, and if that good-for-nothin' Jake Fairthorn hadn't ha' seen me"—

"That will do, Miss Lavender," said Mr. Stacy, interrupting her. "I have only to add that Abiah Barton was so well convinced of the truth of the marriage, that his new will only requires the proof which has to-day been furnished, in order to express his intentions fully and completely. It was his wish that I should visit Mary Barton on the very morning afterwards; but his sudden death prevented it, and Miss Lavender ascertained, the same evening, that Mary, in view of the neglect and disgrace which she had suffered, demanded to take her justification into her own hands. My opinion coincided with that of Miss Lavender, that she alone had the right to decide in the matter, and that we must give no explanation until she had asserted, in her own way, her release from a most shameful and cruel bond."

It was a proud moment of Miss Lavender's life, when, in addition to her services, the full extent of which would presently be known, a lawyer of Mr. Stacy's reputation so respectfully acknowledged the wisdom of her judgment.

"If further information upon any point is required," observed the lawyer, "it may be asked for now; otherwise, I will proceed to the reading of the will."

"Was—was my father of sound mind,—that is, competent to dispose of his property?" asked Elisha Barton, with a little hesitation.

"I hope the question will not be raised," said Mr. Stacy, gravely; "but if it is I must testify that he was in as full possession of his faculties as at any time since his first attack, twenty-six years ago."

He then read the will, amid the breathless silence of the company. The old man first devised to his elder son, Elisha Barton, the sum of twenty thousand dollars, investments secured by mortgages on real estate; an equal amount to his daughter-in-law, Mary, provided she was able to furnish legal proof of her marriage to his son, Alfred Barton; five thousand dollars each to his four grand-children, the three sons of Elisha, and Gilbert Barton; ten thousand dollars to his daughter Ann; and to his son Alfred the occupancy and use of the farm during his life, the property, at his death, to pass into the hands of Gilbert Barton. There was also a small bequest to Giles, and the reversions of the estate were to be divided equally among all the heirs. The witnesses to the will were James Stacy and Elizabeth Lavender.

Gilbert and his mother now recognized, for the first time, what they owed to the latter. A sense of propriety kept them silent; the fortune which had thus unexpectedly fallen into their hands was the least and poorest part of their justification. Miss Lavender, also, was held to silence, but it went hard with her. The reading of the will gave her such an exquisite sense of enjoyment that she felt quite choked in the hush which followed it.

"As the marriage is now proven," Mr. Stacy said, folding up the paper, "there is nothing to prevent the will from being carried into effect."

"No, I suppose not," said Elisha; "it is as fair as could be expected."

"Mother, what do you say?" asked Gilbert, suddenly.

"Your grandfather wanted to do me justice, my boy," said she. "Twenty thousand dollars will not pay me for twenty-five years of shame; no money could; but it was the only payment he had to offer. I accept this as I accepted my trials. The Lord sees fit to make my worldly path smooth to my feet, and I have learned neither to reject mercy nor wrath."

She was not elated; she would not, on that solemn day, even express gratification in the legacy, for her son's sake. Though her exalted mood was but dimly understood by the others, they felt its influence. If any thought of disputing the will, on the ground of his father's incompetency, had ever entered Elisha Barton's mind, he did not dare, then or afterwards, to express it.

The day was drawing to a close, and Elisha Barton, with his sons, who lived in the adjoining township of Pennsbury, made preparations to leave. They promised soon to visit Gilbert and his mother. Miss Lavender, taking Gilbert aside, announced that she was going to return to Dr. Deane's.

"I s'pose I may tell her," she said, trying to hide her feelings under a veil of clumsy irony, "that it's all up betwixt and between you, now you're a rich man; and of course as she wouldn't have the father, she can't think o' takin' the son."

"Betsy," he whispered, "tell her that I never yet needed her love so much as now, and that I shall come to her tomorrow."

"Well, you know the door stands open, even accordin' to the Doctor's words."

As Gilbert went forth to look after the horses, Alfred Barton followed him. The two had not spoken directly to each other during the whole day.

"Gilbert," said the father, putting his hand on the son's shoulder, "you know, now, why it always cut me, to have you think ill of me. I deserve it, for I've been no father to you; and after what you've heard to-day, I may never have a chance to be one. But if you could give me a chance—if you could"—

Here his voice seemed to fail. Gilbert quietly withdrew his shoulder from the hand, hesitated a moment, and then said,—"Don't ask me anything now, if you please. I can only think of my mother to-day."

Alfred Barton walked to the garden-fence, leaned his arms upon it, and his head upon them. He was still leaning there, when mother and son rode by in the twilight, on their way home.

CHAPTER XXXII. — THE LOVERS.

Both mother and son made the homeward ride in silence. A wide space, a deep gulf of time, separated them from the morning. The events of the day had been so startling, so pregnant with compressed fate, the emotions they had undergone had been so profound, so mixed of the keenest elements of wonder, pain, and pride, that a feeling of exhaustion succeeded. The old basis of their lives seemed to have shifted, and the new foundations were not yet firm under their feet.

Yet, as they sat together before the hearth-fire that evening, and the stern, proud calm of Gilbert's face slowly melted into a gentler and tenderer expression, his mother was moved to speak.

"This has been my day," she said; "it was appointed and set apart for me from the first; it belonged to me, and I have used it, in my right, from sun to sun. But I feel now, that it was not my own strength alone that held me up. I am weak and weary, and it almost seems that I fail in thanksgiving. Is it, Gilbert, because you do not rejoice as I had hoped you would?"

"Mother," he answered, "whatever may happen in my life, I can never feel so proud of myself, as I felt to-day, to be your son. I do rejoice for your sake, as I shall for my own, no doubt, when I get better used to the truth. You could not expect me, at once, to be satisfied with a father who has not only acted so cruelly towards you, but whom I have suspected of being my own rival and enemy. I don't think I shall ever like the new name as well as the old, but it is enough for me that the name brings honor and independence to you!"

"Perhaps I ought to ha' told you this morning, Gilbert I thought only of the justification, not of the trial; and it seemed easier to speak in actions, to you and to all men at once, as I did, than to tell the story quietly to you alone. I feared it might take away my strength, if I didn't follow, step by step, the course marked out for me."

"You were right, mother!" he exclaimed. "What trial had I, compared with yours? What tale had I to tell—what pain to feel, except that if I had not been born, you would have been saved twenty-five years of suffering!"

"No, Gilbert!—never say, never think that! I see already the suffering and the sorrow dying away as if they'd never been, and you left to me for the rest of life the Lord grants; to me a son has been more than a husband!"

"Then," he asked in an anxious, hesitating tone, "would you consider that I was not quite so much a son—that any part of my duty to you was lost—if I wished to bring you a daughter, also?".

"I know what you mean, Gilbert Betsy Lavender has told me all. I am glad you spoke of it, this day; it will put the right feeling of thanksgiving into my heart and yours. Martha Deane never stood between us, my boy; it was I that stood between you and her!"

"Mother!" he cried, a joyous light shining from his face, "you love her? You are willing that she should be my wife?"

"Ay, Gilbert; willing, and thankful, and proud."

"But the very name of her struck you down! You fell into a deadly faint when I told you I had spoken my mind to her!"

"I see, my boy," she said; "I see now why you never mentioned her name, from that time. It was not Martha Deane, but the name of the one you thought wanted to win her away from you,—your father's name, Gilbert,— that seemed to put a stop to my life. The last trial was the hardest of all, but don't you see it was only the bit of darkness that comes before the daylight?"

While this new happiness brought the coveted sense of thanksgiving to mother and son, and spread an unexpected warmth and peace over the close of the fateful day, there was the liveliest excitement in Kennett Square, over Miss Lavender's intelligence. That lady had been waylaid by a dozen impatient questioners before she could reach the shelter of Dr. Deane's roof; and could only purchase release by a hurried statement of the main facts, in which Alfred Barton's cruelty, and his wife's wonderful fidelity to her oath, and the justice done to her and Gilbert by the old man's will, were set forth with an energy that multiplied itself as the gossip spread.

In the adjoining townships, it was reported and believed, the very next day, that Alfred Barton had tried to murder his wife and poison his father—that Mary had saved the latter, and inherited, as her reward, the entire property.

Once safely housed, Miss Lavender enjoyed another triumph. She related the whole story, in every particular, to Martha Deane, in the Doctor's presence, taking especial care not to omit Alfred's words in relation to his enforced wooing.

"And there's one thing I mustn't forgit, Martha," she declared, at the close of her narrative. "Gilbert sends word to you that he needs your true-love more 'n ever, and he's comin' up to see you to-morrow; and says I to him, The door's open, even accordin' to the Doctor's words; and so it is, for he's got his true name, and free to come. You're a man o' your word, Doctor, and nothin' 's been said or done, thank Goodness, that can't be easy mended!"

What impression this announcement made upon Dr. Deane could not be guessed by either of the women. He rose, went to the window, looked into the night for a long time without saying a word, and finally betook himself to his bed.

The next morning, although there were no dangerous cases on his hands, he rode away, remarking that he should not be home again until the evening. Martha knew what this meant, and also what Miss Lavender meant in hurrying down to Fairthorn's, soon after the Doctor's departure. She became restless with tender expectation; her cheeks burned, and her fingers trembled so that she was forced to lay aside her needle-work. It seemed very long since she had even seen Gilbert; it was a long time (in the calendar of lovers) since the two had spoken to each other. She tried to compare the man he had been with the man he now was,—Gilbert poor, disgraced and in trouble, with Gilbert rich and honorably born; and it almost seemed as if the latter had impoverished her heart by taking from it the need of that faithful, passionate sympathy which she had bestowed upon the former.

The long hour of waiting came to an end. Roger was once more tethered at the gate, and Gilbert was in the room. It was not danger, this time, beyond the brink of which they met, but rather a sudden visitation of security; yet both were deeply and powerfully agitated. Martha was the first to recover her composure. Withdrawing herself from Gilbert's arms, she said,—

"It was not right that the tests should be all on my side. Now it is my turn to try you, Gilbert!"

Even her arch, happy smile did not enlighten him. "How, Martha?" he asked.

"Since you don't know, you are already tested. But how grave you look! Have I not yet learned all of this wonderful, wonderful history? Did Betsy Lavender keep something back?"

"Martha!" he cried, "you shame me out of the words I had meant to say. But they were doubts of my own position, not of you. Is my new name better or worse in your ears, than my old one?"

"To me you are only Gilbert," she answered, "as I am Martha to you. What does it matter whether we write Potter or Barton? Either is good in itself, and so would any other name be; but Barton means something, as the world goes, and therefore we will take it. Gilbert, I have put myself in your place, since I learned the whole truth. I guessed you would come to me with a strange, uncertain feeling,—not a doubt, but rather a wonder; and I endeavored to make your new circumstances clear to my mind. Our duty to your mother is plain; she is a woman beside whom all other women we know seem weak and insignificant. It is not that which troubled you, I am sure, when you thought of me. Let me say, then, that so far as our relation to your father is concerned, I will be guided entirely by your wishes."

"Martha," he said, "that is my trouble,—or, rather, my disappointment,—that with my true name I must bring to you and fasten upon you the whole mean and shameful story! One parent must always be honored at the expense of the other, and my name still belongs to the one that is disgraced."

"I foresaw your feeling, Gilbert. You were on the point of making another test for me; that is not fair. The truth has come too suddenly,—the waters of your life have been stirred too deeply; you must wait until they clear. Leave that to Alfred Barton and your mother. To me, I confess, he seems very weak rather than very bad. I can now understand the pains which his addresses to me must have cost him. If I ever saw fear on a man's face, it was on his when he thought I might take him at his word. But, to a man like you, a mean nature is no better than a bad one. Perhaps I feel your disappointment as deeply as you can; yet it is our duty to keep this feeling to ourselves. For your mother's sake, Gilbert; you must not let the value of her justification be lessened in her eyes. She deserves all the happiness you and I can give her, and if she is willing to receive me, some day, as a daughter"—

Gilbert interrupted her words by clasping her in his arms. "Martha!" he exclaimed, "your heart points out the true way because it is true to the core! In these things a woman sees clearer than a man; when I am with you only, I seem to have proper courage and independence—I am twice myself! Won't you let me claim you—take you—soon? My mother loves you; she will welcome you as my wife, and will your father still stand between us?"

Martha smiled. "My father is a man of strong will," she said, "and it is hard for him to admit that his judgment was wrong. We must give him a little time,—not urge, not seem to triumph, spare his pride, and trust to his returning sense of what is right. You might claim reparation, Gilbert, for his cruel words; I could not forbid you; but after so much strife let there be peace, if possible."

"It is at least beyond his power," Gilbert replied, "to accuse me of sordid motives. As I said before, Martha, give up your legacy, if need be, but come to me!"

"As I said before, Gilbert, the legacy is honestly mine, and I will come to you with it in my hands."

Then they both began to smile, but it was a conflict of purpose which drew them nearer together, in both senses,—an emulation of unselfish love, which was compromised by clasping arms and silent lips.

There was a sudden noise in the back part of the house. A shrill voice

358

was heard, exclaiming,—"I will—I will! don't hold me!"—the door burst open, and Sally Fairthorn whirled into the room, with the skirt of her gown torn loose, on one side, from the body. Behind her followed Miss Lavender, in a state of mingled amusement and anger.

Sally kissed Martha, then Gilbert, then threw an arm around the neck of each, crying and laughing hysterically: "O Martha! O Gilbert! you'll be married first,—I said it,—but Mark and I must be your bridesmaids; don't laugh, you know what I mean; and Betsy wouldn't have me break in upon you; but I waited half an hour, and then off, up here, she after me, and we're both out o' breath! Did ever, ever such a thing happen!"

"You crazy thing!" cried Miss Lavender. "No, such a thing never happened, and wouldn't ha' happened this time, if I'd ha' been a little quicker on my legs; but never mind, it serves me right; you two are to blame, for why need I trouble my head furder about ye? There's cases, they say, where two's company, and three's overmuch; but you may fix it for yourselves next time, and welcome; and there's one bit o' wisdom I've got by it,—foller true-lovyers, and they'll wear your feet off, and then want you to go on the stumps!"

"We won't relieve you yet, Betsy," said Gilbert; "will we, Martha? The good work you've done for us isn't finished."

"Isn't finished. Well, you'll gi' me time to make my will, first. How long d' ye expect me to last, at this rate? Is my bones brass and my flesh locus'-wood? Am I like a tortle, that goes around the fields a hundred years?"

"No," Gilbert answered, "but you shall be like an angel, dressed all in white, with roses in your hair. Sally and Mark, you know, want to be the first bridesmaids"—

Sally interrupted him with a slap, but it was not very violent, and he did not even attempt to dodge it.

"Do you hear, Betsy?" said Martha. "It must be as Gilbert says."

"A pretty fool you'd make o' me," Miss Lavender remarked, screwing up her face to conceal her happy emotion.

Gilbert soon afterwards left for home, but returned towards evening, determined, before all things, to ascertain his present standing with Dr. Deane. He did not anticipate that the task had been made easy for him; but this was really the case. Wherever Dr. Deane had been that day, whoever he had seen, the current of talk all ran one way. When the first surprise of the news had been exhausted, and the Doctor had corrected various monstrous rumors from his own sources of positive knowledge, one inference was sure to follow,—that now there could be no objection to his daughter becoming Gilbert Barton's wife. He was sounded, urged, almost threatened, and finally returned home with the conviction that any further opposition must result in an immense sacrifice of popularity.

Still, he was not ready to act upon that conviction, at once. He met Gilbert with a bland condescension, and when the latter, after the first greeting, asked,—

"Have I now the right to enter your house?"

The Doctor answered,—

"Certainly. Thee has kept thy word, and I will willingly admit that I did thee wrong in suspecting thee of unworthy devices. I may say, also, that so far as I was able to judge, I approved of thy behavior on the day of thy grandfather's funeral. In all that has happened heretofore, I have endeavored to act cautiously and prudently; and thee will grant, I doubt not, that thy family history is so very far out of the common way, as that no man could be called upon to believe it without the strongest evidence. Of course, all that I brought forward against thee now falls to the ground."

"I trust, then," Gilbert said, "that you have no further cause to forbid my engagement with Martha. My mother has given her consent, and we both hope for yours."

Dr. Deane appeared to reflect, leaning back in his chair, with his cane across his knees. "It is a very serious thing," he said, at last,—"very serious, indeed. Not a subject for hasty decision. Thee offered, if I remember rightly, to give me time to know thee better; therefore thee cannot complain if I were now disposed to accept thy offer."

Gilbert fortunately remembered Martha's words, and restrained his impatience.

"I will readily give you time, Dr. Deane," he replied, "provided you will give me opportunities. You are free to question all who know me, of course, and I suppose you have done so. I will not ask you to take the trouble to come to me, in order that we may become better acquainted, but only that you will allow me to come to you."

"It would hardly be fair to deny thee that much," said the Doctor.

"I will ask no more now. I never meant, from the first, to question your interest in Martha's happiness, or your right to advise her. It may be too soon to expect your consent, but at least you'll hold back your refusal?"

"Thee's a reasonable young man, Gilbert," the Doctor remarked, after a pause which was quite unnecessary. "I like that in thee. We are both agreed, then, that while I shall be glad to see thee in my house, and am willing to allow to Martha and thee the intercourse proper to a young man and woman, it is not yet to be taken for granted that I sanction your desired marriage. Remember me kindly to thy mother, and say, if thee pleases, that I shall soon call to see her."

Gilbert had scarcely reached home that evening, before Deb. Smith, who had left the farm-house on the day following the recovery of the money, suddenly made her appearance. She slipped into the kitchen without knocking, and crouched down in a corner of the wide chimney-place, before she spoke. Both mother and son were struck by the singular mixture of shyness and fear in her manner.

"I heerd all about it, to-day," she presently said, "and I wouldn't ha' come here, if I'd ha' knowed where else to go to. They're after me, this time, Sandy's friends, in dead earnest; they'll have my blood, if they can git it; but you said once't you'd shelter me, Mr. Gilbert!"

"So I will, Deborah!" he exclaimed; "do you doubt my word?"

"No, I don't; but I dunno how't is—you're rich now, and as well-born as the best of 'em, and Mary's lawful-married and got her lawful name; and you both seem to be set among the folks that can't feel for a body like me; not that your hearts is changed, only it comes different to me, somehow."

"Stay here, Deborah, until you feel sure you're safe," said Mary. "If Gilbert or I should refuse to protect you, your blood would be upon our heads. I won't blame you for doubting us; I know how easy it is to lose faith in others; but if you think I was a friend to you while my name was disgraced, you must also remember that I knew the truth then as well as the world knows it now."

"Bless you for sayin' that, Mary! There wasn't much o' my name at any time; but what little I might ha' had is clean gone—nothin' o' me left but the strong arm! I'm not a coward, as you know, Mr. Gilbert; I'll meet any man, face to face, in a fair and open fight. Let 'em come in broad day, and on the high road!—not lay in wait in bushes and behind fences, to shoot me down unawares."

They strove to quiet her fears, and little by little she grew composed. The desperate recklessness of her mood contrasted strangely with her morbid fear of an ambushed enemy. Gilbert suspected that it might be a temporary insanity, growing out of her remorse for having betrayed Sandy Flash. When she had been fed, and had smoked a pipe or two, she seemed quite to forget it, and was almost her own self when she went up to her bed in the western room.

The moon, three quarters full, was hanging over the barn, and made a peaceful, snowy light about the house. She went to the window, opened it, and breathed the cool air of the April night. The "herring-frogs" were keeping up an incessant, birdlike chirp down the glen, and nearer at hand the plunging water of the mill-race made a soothing noise. It really seemed that the poor creature had found a quiet refuge at last.

Suddenly, something rustled and moved behind the mass of budding lilacs, at the farther corner of the garden-paling. She leaned forward; the next moment there was a flash, the crack of a musket rang sharp and loud through the dell, followed by a whiz and thud at her very ear. A thin drift of smoke rose above the bushes, and she saw a man's figure springing to the cover of the nearest apple-tree. In another minute, Gilbert made his appearance, gun in hand.

"Shoot him, Gilbert!" cried Deb. Smith; "it's Dougherty!"

Whoever it was, the man escaped; but by a singular coincidence, the Irish ostler disappeared that night from the Unicorn tavern, and was never again seen in the neighborhood.

The bullet had buried itself in the window-frame, after having passed within an inch or two of Deb. Smith's head. [Footnote: The hole made by the bullet still remains in the window-frame of the old farm-house.] To Gilbert's surprise, all her fear was gone; she was again fierce and defiant, and boldly came and went, from that night forth, saying that no bullet was or would be cast, to take her life.

Therein she was right; but it was a dreary life and a miserable death which awaited her. For twenty-five years she wandered about the neighborhood, achieving wonders in spinning, reaping and threshing, by the undiminished force of her arm, though her face grew haggard and her hair gray; sometimes plunging into wild drinking-bouts with the rough male companions of her younger days; sometimes telling a new generation, with weeping and violent self-accusation, the story of her treachery; but always with the fearful conviction of a yet unfulfilled curse hanging over her life. Whether it was ever made manifest, no man could tell; but when she was found lying dead on the floor of her lonely cabin on the Woodrow farm, with staring, stony eyes, and the lines of unspeakable horror on her white face, there were those who recalled her own superstitious forebodings, and believed them.

CHAPTER XXXIII. — HUSBAND AND WIFE.

It may readily be guessed that such extraordinary developments as those revealed in the preceding chapters produced more than a superficial impression upon a quiet community like that of Kennett and the adjoining townships. People secluded from the active movements of the world are drawn to take the greater interest in their own little family histories,—a feeling which by-and-by amounts to a partial sense of ownership, justifying not only any degree of advice or comment, but sometimes even actual interference.

The Quakers, who formed a majority of the population, and generally controlled public sentiment in domestic matters, through the purity of their own domestic life, at once pronounced in favor of Mary Barton. The fact of her having taken an oath was a slight stumbling-block to some; but her patience, her fortitude, her submission to what she felt to be the Divine Will, and the solemn strength which had upborne her on the last trying day, were qualities which none could better appreciate. The fresh, warm sympathies of the younger people, already given to Gilbert and Martha, now also embraced her; far and wide went the wonderful story, carrying with it a wave of pity and respect for her, of contempt and denunciation for her husband.

The old Friends and their wives came to visit her, in their stately chairs; almost daily, for a week or two, the quiet of the farm was invaded, either by them, or by the few friends who had not forsaken her in her long disgrace, and were doubly welcome now. She received them all with the same grave, simple dignity of manner, gratefully accepting their expressions of sympathy, and quietly turning aside the inconsiderate questions that would have probed too deeply and painfully.

To an aged Friend,—a preacher of the sect,—who plumply asked her what course she intended to pursue towards her husband, she replied,—

"I will not trouble my season of thanksgiving. What is right for me to do will be made manifest when the occasion comes."

This reply was so entirely in the Quaker spirit that the old man was silenced. Dr. Deane, who was present, looked upon her with admiration.

Whatever conjectures Alfred Barton might have made in advance, of the consequences which would follow the disclosure of his secret marriage, they could have borne no resemblance to the reality. It was not in his nature to imagine the changes which the years had produced in his wife. He looked forward to wealth, to importance in the community, and probably supposed that she would only be too glad to share the proud position with him. There would be a little embarrassment at first, of course; but his money would soon make everything smooth.

Now, he was utterly defeated, crushed, overwhelmed. The public judgment, so much the more terrible where there is no escape from it, rolled down upon him. Avoided or coldly ignored by the staid, respectable farmers, openly insulted by his swaggering comrades of the fox-hunt and the bar-room, jeered at and tortured by the poor and idle hangers-on of the community, who took a malicious pleasure in thus repaying him for his former haughtiness and their own humility, he found himself a moral outcast. His situation became intolerable. He no longer dared to show himself in the village, or upon the highways, but slunk about the house and farm, cursing himself, his father and the miserable luck of his life.

When, finally, Giles begged to know how soon his legacy would be paid, and hinted that he couldn't stay any longer than to get possession of the money, for, hard as it might be to leave an old home, he must stop going to the mill, or getting the horses shod, or sitting in the Unicorn bar-room of a Saturday night, and a man might as well be in jail at once, and be done with it—when Alfred Barton heard all this, he deliberated, for a few minutes, whether it would not be a good thing to cut his own throat.

Either that, or beg for mercy; no other course was left.

That evening he stole up to the village, fearful, at every step, of being seen and recognized, and knocked timidly at Dr. Deane's door. Martha and her father were sitting together, when he came into the room, and they were equally startled at his appearance. His large frame seemed to have fallen in, his head was bent, and his bushy whiskers had become quite gray; deep wrinkles seamed his face; his eyes were hollow, and the corners of his mouth drooped with an expression of intolerable misery.

"I wanted to say a word to Miss Martha, if she'll let me," he said, looking from one to the other.

"I allowed thee to speak to my daughter once too often," Dr. Deane sternly replied. "What thee has to say now, must be said in my presence."

He hesitated a moment, then took a chair and sat down, turning towards Martha. "It's come to this," he said, "that I must have a little mercy, or lay hands on my own life. I haven't a word to say for myself; I deserve it all. I'll do anything that's wanted of me—whatever Mary says, or people think is her right that she hasn't yet got, if it's mine to give. You said you wished me well, Miss Martha, even at the time I acted so shamefully; I remember that, and so I ask you to help me."

She saw that he spoke truth, at last, and all her contempt and disgust could not keep down the quick sensation of pity which his wretchedness inspired. But she was unprepared for his appeal, and uncertain how to answer it.

"What would you have me do?" she asked.

"Go to Mary on my behalf! Ask her to pardon me, if she can, or say what I can do to earn her pardon—that the people may know it. They won't be so hard on me, if they know she's done that. Everything depends on her, and if it's true, as they say, that she's going to sue for a divorce and take back her own name for herself and Gilbert, and cut loose from me forever, why, it'll just"—

He paused, and buried his face in his hands.

"I have not heard of that," said Martha.

"Haven't you?" he asked. "But it's too likely to be true."

"Why not go directly to Mary, yourself?"

"I will, Miss Martha, if you'll go with me, and maybe say a kind word now and then,—that is, if you think it isn't too soon for mercy!"

"It is never too soon to ask for mercy," she said, coming to a sudden decision. "I will go with you; let it be tomorrow."

"Martha," warned Dr. Deane, "isn't thee a little hasty?"

"Father, I decide nothing. It is in Mary's hands. He thinks my presence will give him courage, and that I cannot refuse."

The next morning, the people of Kennett Square were again startled out of their proprieties by the sight of Alfred Barton, pale, agitated, and avoiding the gaze of every one, waiting at Dr. Deane's gate, and then riding side by side with Martha down the Wilmington road. An hour before, she had dispatched Joe Fairthorn with a note to Gilbert, informing him of the impending visit. Once on the way, she feared lest she had ventured too far; it might be, as her father had said, too hasty; and the coming meeting with Gilbert and his mother disquieted her not a little. It was a silent, anxious ride for both.

When they readied the gate, Gilbert was on hand to receive them. His face always brightened at the sight of Martha, and his hands lifted her as tenderly as ever from the saddle. "Have I done right?" she anxiously whispered.

"It is for mother to say," he whispered back.

Alfred Barton advanced, offering his hand. Gilbert looked upon his father's haggard, imploring face, a moment; a recollection of his own disgrace shot into his heart, to soften, not to exasperate; and he accepted the hand. Then he led the way into the house.

Mary Barton had simply said to her son,—"I felt that he would come, sooner or later, and that I must give him a hearing—better now, perhaps, since you and Martha will be with me."

They found her awaiting them, pale and resolute.

Gilbert and Martha moved a little to one side, leaving the husband and wife facing each other. Alfred Barton was too desperately moved to shrink from Mary's eyes; he strove to read something in her face, which might spare

367

him the pain of words; but it was a strange face he looked upon. Not that of the black-eyed, bright-cheeked girl, with the proud carriage of her head and the charming scorn of her red lip, who had mocked, fascinated, and bewildered him. The eyes were there, but they had sunk into the shade of the brows, and looked upon him with an impenetrable expression; the cheeks were pale, the mouth firm and rigid, and out of the beauty which seduced had grown a power to resist and command.

"Will you shake hands with me, Mary?" he faltered.

She said nothing, but moved her right hand slightly towards him. It lay in his own a moment, cold and passive.

"Mary!" he cried, falling on his knees at her feet, "I'm a ruined, wretched man! No one speaks to me but to curse; I've no friend left in the world; the very farmhand leaves me! I don't know what'll become of me, unless you feel a little pity—not that I deserve any, but I ask it of you, in the name of God!"

Martha clung to Gilbert's arm, trembling, and more deeply moved than she was willing to show. Mary Barton's face was convulsed by some passing struggle, and when she spoke, her voice was hoarse and broken.

"You know what it is, then," she said, "to be disgraced in the eyes of the world. If you have suffered so much in these two weeks, you may guess what I have borne for twenty-five years!"

"I see it now, Mary!" he cried, "as I never saw it before. Try me! Tell me what to do!"

"The Lord has done it, already; there is nothing left."

He groaned; his head dropped hopelessly upon his breast.

Gilbert felt that Martha's agitation ceased. She quietly released her hold of his arm, lifted her head, and spoke,—

"Mother, forgive me if I speak when I should hold my peace; I would only remind you that there is yet one thing left. It is true, as you say; the Lord has justified you in His own way, and at His own time, and has revenged the wrong done to you by branding the sin committed towards Himself. Now He leaves the rest to your own heart. Think that He holds back and waits for the words that shall declare whether you understand the spirit in which He deals towards His children!"

"Martha, my dear child!" Mary Barton exclaimed,—"what can I do?"

"It is not for me to advise you, mother. You, who put my impatient pride to shame, and make my love for Gilbert seem selfish by contrast with your long self-sacrifice! What right have I, who have done nothing, to speak to you, who have done so much that we never can reckon it? But, remember that in the Lord's government of the world pardon follows repentance, and it is not for us to exact like for like, to the uttermost farthing!"

Mary Barton sank into a chair, covered her face with her hands, and wept aloud.

There were tears in Martha's eyes; her voice trembled, and her words came with a softness and tenderness that soothed while they pierced:

"Mother, I am a woman like yourself; and, as a woman, I feel the terrible wrong that has been done to you. It may be as hard for you now to forget, as then to bear; but it is certainly greater and nobler to forgive than to await justice! Because I reverence you as a strong and pure and great-hearted woman—because I want to see the last and best and sweetest grace of our sex added to your name—and lastly, for Gilbert's sake, who can feel nothing but pain in seeing his father execrated and shunned—I ask your forgiveness for your husband!"

"Mary!" Alfred Barton cried, lifting up his head in a last appeal, "Mary, this much, at least! Don't go to the courts for a divorce! Don't get back your own name for yourself and Gilbert! Keep mine, and make it more respectable for me! And I won't ask you to pardon me, for I see you can't!"

"It is all clear to me, at last!" said Mary Barton. "I thank you, Martha, my child, for putting me in the right path. Alfred, don't kneel to me; if the Lord can pardon, who am I that I should be unforgiving? I fear me I was nigh to forfeit His mercy. Gilbert, yours was half the shame; yours is half the wrong; can you join me in pardoning your father and my husband?"

Gilbert was powerfully moved by the conflict of equally balanced emotions, and but for the indication which Martha had given, he might not at once have been able to decide. But it seemed now that his course was also clear. He said,—

"Mother, since you have asked the question, I know how it should be answered. If you forgive your husband, I forgive my—my father."

He stepped forward, seized Alfred Barton gently by the shoulder, and raised him to his feet Mary Barton then took her husband's hand in hers, and said, in a solemn voice,—

"I forgive you, Alfred, and will try to forget I know not what you may have heard said, but I never meant to go before the court for a divorce. Your name is a part of my right, a part of Gilbert's—our son's—right; it is true that you have debased the name, but we will keep it and make it honorable! We will not do that to the name of Barton which you have done to the name of Potter!"

It was very evident that though she had forgiven, she had not yet forgotten. The settled endurance of years could not be unlearned in a moment. Alfred Barton felt that her forgiveness implied no returning tenderness, not even an increase of respect; but it was more than he had dared to hope, and he felt humbly grateful. He saw that a consideration for Gilbert's position had been the chief element to which he owed his wife's relenting mood, and this knowledge was perhaps his greatest encouragement.

"Mary," he said, "you are kinder than I deserve. I wish I could make you and Gilbert understand all that I have felt. Don't think my place was easy; it wasn't. It was a hell of another kind. I have been punished in my way, and will be now to the end o' my life, while you two will be looked up to, and respected beyond any in the neighborhood; and if I'm not treated like a dog, it'll only be for your sakes! Will you let me say to the people that you have pardoned me? Will you say it yourselves?"

Martha, and perhaps Gilbert also, felt that it was the reflected image

370

of Alfred Barton's meanness, as it came back to him in the treatment he had experienced, rather than his own internal consciousness of it, which occasioned his misery. But his words were true thus far; his life was branded by it, and the pardon of those he had wronged could not make that life more than tolerable.

"Why not?" said Gilbert, replying to him. "There has been enough of secrets. I am not ashamed of forgiveness—my shame is, that forgiveness is necessary."

Alfred Barton looked from mother to son with a singular, wistful expression. He seemed uncertain whether to speak or how to select his words. His vain, arrogant spirit was completely broken, but no finer moral instinct came in its place to guide him; his impulses were still coarse, and took, from habit, the selfish color of his nature. There are some persons whom even humiliation clothes with a certain dignity; but he was not one of them. There are others whose tact, in such emergencies, assumes the features of principle, and sets up a feeble claim to respect; but this quality is a result of culture, which he did not possess. He simply saw what would relieve him from the insupportable load of obloquy under which he groaned, and awkwardly hazarded the pity he had excited, in asking for it.

"Mary," he stammered, "I—I hardly know how to say the words, but you'll understand me; I want to make good to you all the wrong I did, and there seems no way but this,—if you'll let me care for you, slave for you, anything you please; you shall have your own say in house and farm; Ann'll give up everything to you. She always liked you, she says, and she's lonely since th' old man died and nobody comes near us—not just at once, I mean, but after awhile, when you've had time to think of it, and Gilbert's married. You're independent in your own right, I know, and needn't do it; but, see! it'd give me a chance, and maybe Gilbert wouldn't feel quite so hard towards me, and"—

He stopped, chilled by the increasing coldness of his wife's face. She did not immediately reply; to Martha's eye she seemed to be battling with some proud, vindictive instinct. But she spoke at last, and calmly:

371

"Alfred, you should not have gone so far. I have pardoned you, and that means more than the words. It means that I must try to overcome the bitterness of my recollections, that I must curb the tongues of others when they are raised against you, must greet you when we meet, and in all proper ways show the truth of my forgiveness to the world. Anger and reproach may be taken from the heart, and yet love be as far off as ever. If anything ever could lead me back to you it would not be love, but duty to my son, and his desire; but I cannot see the duty now. I may never see it. Do not propose this thing again. I will only say, if it be any comfort to you, that if you try to show your repentance as I my pardon, try to clean your name from the stain you have cast upon it, my respect shall keep pace with that of your neighbors, and I shall in this way, and in no other, be drawn nearer to you!"

"Gilbert," said Alfred Barton, "I never knew your mother before to-day. What she says gives me some hope, and yet it makes me afraid. I'll try to bring her nearer, I will, indeed; but I've been governed so long by th' old man that I don't seem to have any right strength o' my own. I must have some help, and you're the only one I can ask it of; will you come and see me sometimes? I've been so proud of you, all to myself, my boy! and if I thought you could once call me 'father' before I die"—

Gilbert was not proof against these words and the honest tears by which they were accompanied. Many shy hesitating tokens of affection in his former intercourse with Alfred Barton, suddenly recurred to his mind, with their true interpretation. His load had been light, compared to his mother's; he had only learned the true wrong in the hour of reparation; and moreover, in assuming his father's name he became sensitive to the prominence of its shame.

"Father," he answered, "if you have forfeited a son's obedience, you have still a man's claim to be helped. Mother is right; it is in your power to come nearer to us. She must stand aside and wait; but I can cross the line which separates you, and from this time on I shall never cross it to remind you of what is past and pardoned, but to help you, and all of us, to forget it!"

Martha laid her hand upon Gilbert's shoulder, leaned up and kissed him upon the cheek.

"Rest here!" she said. "Let a good word close the subject! Gilbert, take your father out and show him your farm. Mother, it is near dinner-time; I will help you set the table. After dinner, Mr. Barton, you and I will ride home together."

Her words were obeyed; each one felt that no more should be said at that time. Gilbert showed the barn, the stables, the cattle in the meadow, and the fields rejoicing in the soft May weather; Martha busied herself in kitchen and cellar, filling up the pauses of her labor with cheerful talk; and when the four met at the table, so much of the constraint in their relation to each other had been conquered, that a stranger would never have dreamed of the gulf which had separated them a few hours before. Martha shrewdly judged that when Alfred Barton had eaten at his wife's table, they would both meet more easily in the future. She did not expect that the breach could ever be quite filled; but she wished, for Gilbert's sake, to make it as narrow as possible.

After dinner, while the horses were being saddled, the lovers walked down the garden-path, between the borders of blue iris and mountain-pink.

"Gilbert," said Martha, "are you satisfied with what has happened?"

"Yes," he answered, "but it has shown to me that something more must be done."

"What?"

"Martha, are these the only two who should be brought nearer?"

She looked at him with a puzzled face. There was a laughing light in his eyes, which brought a new lustre to here, and a delicate blush to her fair cheeks.

"Is it not too soon for me to come?" she whispered.

"You have come," he answered; "you were in your place; and it will be empty—the house will be lonely, the farm without its mistress—until you return to us!"

CHAPTER XXXIV. — THE WEDDING.

The neighborhood had decreed it There was but one just, proper, and satisfactory conclusion to all these events. The decision of Kennett was unanimous that its story should be speedily completed. New-Garden, Marlborough, and Pennsbury, so far as heard from, gave their hearty consent; and the people would have been seriously disappointed—the tide of sympathy might even have been checked—had not Gilbert Barton and Martha Deane prepared to fulfil the parts assigned to them.

Dr. Deane, of course, floated with the current. He was too shrewd to stand forth as a conspicuous obstacle to the consummation of the popular sense of justice. He gave, at once, his full consent to the nuptials, and took the necessary steps, in advance, for the transfer of his daughter's fortune into her own hands. In short, as Miss Lavender observed, there was an end of snarls. The lives of the lovers were taken up, as by a skilful hand, and evenly reeled together.

Gilbert now might have satisfied his ambition (and the people, under the peculiar circumstances of the case, would have sanctioned it) by buying the finest farm in the neighborhood; but Martha had said,—

"No other farm can be so much yours, and none so welcome a home to me. Let us be satisfied with it, at least for the first years."

And therein she spoke wisely.

It was now the middle of May, and the land was clothed in tender green, and filled with the sweet breath of sap and bud and blossom. The vivid emerald of the willow-trees, the blush of orchards, and the cones of snowy bloom along the wood-sides, shone through and illumined even the days of rain. The Month of Marriage wooed them in every sunny morning, in every twilight fading under the torch of the lovers' star.

In spite of Miss Lavender's outcries, and Martha's grave doubts, a fortnight's delay was all that Gilbert would allow. He would have dispensed with bridal costumes and merrymakings,—so little do men understand of these matters; but he was hooted down, overruled, ignored, and made to feel his proper insignificance. Martha almost disappeared from his sight during the interval. She was sitting upstairs in a confusion of lutestring, whalebone, silk, and cambric; and when she came down to him for a moment, the kiss had scarcely left her lips before she began to speak of the make of his new coat, and the fashion of the articles he was still expected to furnish.

If he visited Fairthorn's, it was even worse. The sight of him threw Sally into such a flutter that she sewed the right side of one breadth to the wrong side of another, attempted to clear-starch a woollen stocking, or even, on one occasion, put a fowl into the pot, unpicked and undressed. It was known all over the country that Sally and Mark Deane were to be bridesmaid and groomsman, and they both determined to make a brave appearance.

But there was another feature of the coming nuptials which the people did not know. Gilbert and Martha had determined that Miss Betsy Lavender should be second bridesmaid, and Martha had sent to Wilmington for a purple silk, and a stomacher of the finest cambric, in which to array her. A groomsman of her age was not so easy to find; but young Pratt, who had stood so faithfully by Gilbert during the chase of Sandy Flash, merrily avowed his willingness to play the part; and so it was settled without Miss Lavender's knowledge.

The appointed morning came, bringing a fair sky, mottled with gentle, lingering clouds, and a light wind from the west. The wedding company were to meet at Kennett Square, and then ride to Squire Sinclair's, where the ceremony would be performed by that magistrate; and before ten o'clock, the hour appointed for starting, all the surrounding neighborhood poured into the village. The hitching-bar in front of the Unicorn, and every post of fence or garden-paling, was occupied by the tethered horses. The wedding-guests, comprising some ten or fifteen persons, assembled at Dr. Deane's, and each couple, as they arrived, produced an increasing excitement among the spectators.

The fact that Alfred Barton had been formally pardoned by his wife and

375

son, did not lessen the feeling with which he was regarded, but it produced a certain amount of forbearance. The people were curious to know whether he had been bidden to the wedding, and the conviction was general that he had no business to be there. The truth is, it had been left free to him whether to come or not, and he had very prudently chosen to be absent.

Dr. Deane had set up a "chair," which was to be used for the first time on this occasion. It was a ponderous machine, with drab body and wheels, and curtains of drab camlet looped up under its stately canopy. When it appeared at the gate, the Doctor came forth, spotless in attire, bland, smiling, a figure of sober gloss and agreeable odors. He led Mary Barton by the hand; and her steel-colored silk and white crape shawl so well harmonized with his appearance, that the two might have been taken for man and wife. Her face was calm, serene, and full of quiet gratitude. They took their places in the chair, the lines were handed to the Doctor, and he drove away, nodding right and left to the crowd.

Now the horses were brought up in pairs, and the younger guests began to mount. The people gathered closer and closer; and when Sam appeared, leading the well-known and beloved Roger, there was a murmur which, in a more demonstrative community, would have been a cheer. Somebody had arranged a wreath of lilac and snowy viburnum, and fastened it around Roger's forehead; and he seemed to wear it consciously and proudly. Many a hand was stretched forth to pat and stroke the noble animal, and everybody smiled when he laid his head caressingly over the neck of Martha's gray.

Finally, only six horses remained unmounted; then there seemed to be a little delay in-doors. It was explained when young Pratt appeared, bold and bright, leading the reluctant Miss Lavender, rustling in purple splendor, and blushing—actually blushing—as she encountered the eyes of the crowd. The latter were delighted. There was no irony in the voice that cried,—"Hurrah for Betsy Lavender!" and the cheer that followed was the expression of a downright, hearty good will. She looked around from her saddle, blushing, smiling, and on the point of bursting into tears; and it was a godsend, as she afterwards remarked, that Mark Deane and Sally Fairthorn appeared at that moment.

376

Mark, in sky-blue coat and breeches, suggested, with his rosy face and yellow locks, a son of the morning; while Sally's white muslin and cherry-colored scarf heightened the rich beauty of her dark hair and eyes, and her full, pouting lips. They were a buxom pair, and both were too happy in each other and in the occasion, to conceal the least expression of it.

There now only remained our hero and heroine, who immediately followed. No cheer greeted them, for the wonderful chain of circumstances which had finally brought them together, made the joy of the day solemn, and the sympathy of the people reverential. Mark and Sally represented the delight of betrothal; these two the earnest sanctity of wedlock.

Gilbert was plainly yet richly dressed in a bottle-green coat, with white waistcoat and breeches; his ruffles, gloves, hat, and boots were irreproachable. So manly looking a bridegroom had not been seen in Kennett for many a day. Martha's dress of heavy pearl-gray satin was looped up over a petticoat of white dimity, and she wore a short cloak of white crape. Her hat, of the latest style, was adorned with a bunch of roses and a white, drooping feather. In the saddle, she was charming; and as the bridal pair slowly rode forward, followed by their attendants in the proper order, a murmur of admiration, in which there was no envy and no ill-natured qualification, went after them.

A soft glitter of sunshine, crossed by the shadows of slow-moving clouds, lay upon the landscape. Westward, the valley opened in quiet beauty, the wooded hills on either side sheltering, like protecting arms, the white farmhouses, the gardens, and rosy orchards scattered along its floor. On their left, the tall grove rang with the music of birds, and was gay, through all its light-green depths, with the pink blossoms of the wild azalea. The hedges, on either side, were purple with young sprays, and a bright, breathing mass of sweet-brier and wild grape crowned the overhanging banks, between which the road ascended the hill beyond.

At first the company were silent; but the enlivening motion of the horses, the joy of the coming summer, the affectionate sympathy of Nature, soon disposed them to a lighter mood. At Hallowell's, the men left their hoes in the corn-field, and the women their household duties, to greet them by the roadside. Mark looked up at the new barn, and exclaimed,—

"Not quite a year ago! Do you mind it, Gilbert?"

Martha pointed to the green turf in front of the house, and said with an arch voice,—

"Gilbert, do you remember the question you put to me, that evening?"

And finally Sally burst out, in mock indignation,—

"Gilbert, there's where you snapped me up, because I wanted you to dance with Martha; what do you think of yourself now?"

"You all forget," he answered, "that you are speaking of somebody else."

"How? somebody else?" asked Sally.

"Yes; I mean Gilbert Potter."

"Not a bad turn-off," remarked Miss Lavender. "He's too much for you. But I'm glad, anyhow, you've got your tongues, for it was too much like a buryin' before, and me fixed up like King Solomon, what for, I'd like to know? and the day made o' purpose for a weddin', and true-love all right for once't—I'd like just to holler and sing and make merry to my heart's content, with a nice young man alongside o' me, too, a thing that don't often happen!"

They were heartily, but not boisterously, merry after this; but as they reached the New-Garden road, there came a wild yell from the rear, and the noise of galloping hoofs. Before the first shock of surprise had subsided, the Fairthorn gray mare thundered up, with Joe and Jake upon her back, the scarlet lining of their blue cloaks flying to the wind, their breeches covered with white hair from the mare's hide, and their faces wild with delight. They yelled again as they drew rein at the head of the procession.

"Why, what upon earth"—began Sally; but Joe saved her the necessity of a question.

"Daddy said we shouldn't go!" he cried. "But we would,—we got Bonnie out o' the field, and put off! Cousin Martha, you'll let us go along and see you get married; won't you, now? Maybe we'll never have another chance!"

This incident produced great amusement. The boys received the permission they coveted, but were ordered to the rear Mark reminding them that as he was soon to be their uncle, they must learn, betimes, to give heed to his authority.

"Be quiet, Mark!" exclaimed Sally, with a gentle slap.

"Well, I don't begrudge it to 'em," said Miss Lavender. "It's somethin' for 'em to remember when they're men-grown; and they belong to the fam'ly, which I don't; but never mind, all the same, no more do you, Mr. Pratt; and I wish I was younger, to do credit to you!"

Merrily trotted the horses along the bit of level upland; and then, as the land began to fall towards the western branch of Redley Creek, they saw the Squire's house on a green knoll to the north, and Dr. Deane's new chair already resting in the shade of the gigantic sycamore at the door. The lane-gates were open, the Squire's parlor was arranged for their reception; and after the ladies had put themselves to rights, in the upper rooms, the company gathered together for the ceremony.

Sunshine, and hum of bees, and murmur of winds, and scent of flowers, came in through the open windows, and the bridal pair seemed to stand in the heart of the perfect spring-time. Yet tears were shed by all the women except the bride; and Sally Fairthorn was so absorbed by the rush of her emotions, that she came within an ace of saying "I will!" when the Squire put the question to Martha. The ceremony was brief and plain, but the previous history of the parties made it very impressive. When they had been pronounced man and wife, and the certificate of marriage had been duly signed and witnessed by all present, Mary Barton stepped forward and kissed her son and daughter with a solemn tenderness. Then the pent-up feelings of all the others broke loose, and the amount of embracing which followed was something quite unusual for Kennett. Betsy Lavender was not cheated out of her due share; on the contrary, it was ever afterwards reported that she received more salutes than even the bride. She was kissed by Gilbert, by Mark, by her young partner, by Dr. Deane, and lastly by the jolly Squire himself,—to say nothing of the feminine kisses, which, indeed, being very imperfect gifts, hardly deserve to be recorded.

"Well!" she exclaimed, pushing her ruffled hair behind her ears, and smoothing down her purple skirt, "to think o' my bein' kissed by so many men, in my old days!—but why not?—it may be my last chance, as Joe Fairthorn says, and laugh if you please, I've got the best of it; and I don't belie my natur', for twistin' your head away and screechin' is only make-believe, and the more some screeches the more they want to be kissed; but fair and square, say I,—if you want it take it, and that's just what I've done!"

There was a fresh rush for Miss Lavender after this, and she stood her ground with commendable patience, until Mark ventured to fold her in a good-natured hug, when she pushed him away, saying,—

"For the Lord's sake, don't spile my new things! There—go 'way, now! I've had enough to last me ten year!"

Dr. Deane soon set out with Mary Barton, in the chair, and the rest of the company mounted their horses, to ride back to Kennett Square by the other road, past the quarries and across Tuffkenamon.

As they halted in the broad, shallow bed of the creek, letting their horses drink from the sparkling water, while the wind rollicked among the meadow bloom of golden saxifrage and scarlet painted-cup and blue spiderwort before them, the only accident of the day occurred; but it was not of a character to disturb their joyous mood.

The old Fairthorn mare stretched her neck to its utmost length before she bent it to drink, obliging Joe to lean forwards over her shoulder, to retain his hold of the short rein. Jake, holding on to Joe, leaned with him, and they waited in this painful posture till the mare slowly filled herself from the stream. Finally she seemed to be satisfied; she paused, snorted, and then, with wide nostrils, drank an equal amount of air. Her old sides swelled; the saddle-girth, broken in two places long before, and mended with tow-strings, suddenly parted, and Joe, Jake, saddle and all, tumbled down her neck into the water. They scrambled out in a lamentable plight, soused and dripping, amid the endless laughter of the company, and were glad to keep to the rear for the remainder of the ride.

In Dr. Deane's house, meanwhile, there were great preparations for the wedding-dinner. A cook had been brought from Wilmington, at an unheard-of expense, and the village was filled with rumors of the marvellous dishes she was to produce. There were pippins encased in orange-peel and baked; a roasted peacock, with tail spread; a stuffed rock-fish; a whole ham enveloped in dough, like a loaf of bread, and set in the oven; and a wilderness of the richest and rarest pies, tarts, and custards.

Whether all these rumors were justified by the dinner, we will not undertake to say; it is certain that the meal, which was spread in the large sitting-room, was most bountiful. No one was then shocked by the decanters of Port and Canary wine upon the sideboard, or refused to partake of the glasses of foamy egg-nog offered to them from time to time, through the afternoon. The bride-cake was considered a miracle of art, and the fact that Martha divided it with a steady hand, making the neatest and cleanest of cuts, was considered a good omen for her married life. Bits of the cake were afterwards in great demand throughout the neighborhood, not so much to eat, as to dream upon.

The afternoon passed away rapidly, with mirth and noise, in the adjoining parlor. Sally Fairthorn found a peculiar pleasure in calling her friend "Martha Barton!" whereupon Mark said,—

"Wait a bit, Martha, and you can pay her back. Daddy Fairthorn promised this morning to give me a buildin' lot off the field back o' the corner, and just as soon as Rudd's house is up, I'm goin' to work at mine."

"Mark, do hush!" Sally exclaimed, reddening, "and before everybody!"

Miss Lavender sat in the midst, stately, purple, and so transformed that she professed she no longer knew her own self. She was, nevertheless, the life of the company; the sense of what she had done to bring on the marriage was a continual source of inspiration. Therefore, when songs were proposed and sung, and Mark finally called upon her, uproariously seconded by all the rest, she was moved, for the last time in her life, to comply.

"I dunno what you mean, expectin' such a thing o' me," she said. "Tears to me I'm fool enough already, settin' here in purple and fine linen, like the Queen o' Rome,—not that I don't like singin', but the contrary, quite the reverse; but with me it'd be a squawk and nothin' else; and fine feathers may make fine birds for what I care, more like a poll-parrot than a nightingale, and they say you must stick thorns into 'em to make 'em sing; but I guess it'll be t' other way, and my singin'll stick thorns into you!"

They would take no denial; she could and must sing them a song. She held out until Martha said, "for my wedding-day, Betsy!" and Gilbert added, "and mine, too." Then she declared, "Well, if I must, I s'pose I must But as for weddin'-songs, such as I've heerd in my younger days, I dunno one of 'em, and my head's pretty much cleared o' such things, savin' and exceptin' one that might be a sort o' warnin' for Mark Deane, who knows?—not that there's sea-farin' men about these parts; but never mind, all the same; if you don't like it, Mark, you've brung it onto yourself!"

Thereupon, after shaking herself, gravely composing her face, and clearing her throat, she began, in a high, shrill, piercing voice, rocking her head to the peculiar lilt of the words, and interpolating short explanatory remarks, to sing—

THE BALLAD OF THE HOUSE-CARPENTER.

"'Well-met, well-met, my own true-love!'

"*She* says,—

"'Well-met, well-met, cried he;

For't is I have returned from the salt, salt sea,

And it's all for the love of thee!'

"'It's I might ha' married a king's daughter fair,'

"He goes on sayin',—

"'And fain would she ha' married me,

But it's I have refused those crowns of gold,

And it's all for the love of thee!'

"Then *she,*—

"'If you might ha' married a king's daughter fair,'

I think you are for to blame;

For it's I have married a house-carpentèr,

And I think he's a fine young man!'

"So look out, Mark! and remember, all o' you, that they're talkin' turn about; and he begins—

"'If you'll forsake your house-carpentèr

And go along with me,

I'll take you to where the grass grows green

On the banks of the sweet Wil-lee!'

"'If I forsake my house-carpentèr,

And go along with thee,

It's what have you got for to maintain me upon,

And to keep me from slave-ree?'

"'It's I have sixteen ships at sea,

All sailing for dry land,

And four-and-twenty sailors all on board

Shall be at your command!'

"She then took up her lovely little babe,

And she gave it kisses three;

'Lie still, lie still, my lovely little babe,

And keep thy father compa-nee!'

"She dressed herself in rich array,

And she walked in high degree,

And the four-and-twenty sailors took 'em on board.

And they sailed for the open sea!

"They had not been at sea two weeks,

And I'm sure it was not three,

Before this maid she began for to weep,

And she wept most bitter-lee.

"'It's do you weep for your gold?' cries he;

'Or do you weep for your store,

Or do you weep for your house-carpenter

You never shall see any more?'

"'I do not weep for my gold,' cries she,

'Nor I do not weep for my store,

But it's I do weep for my lovely little babe,

I never shall see any more!'

"They had not been at sea three weeks,

And I'm sure it was not four,

When the vessel it did spring a leak,

And it sank to rise no more!"

"Now, Mark, here comes the Moral:

"Oh, cruel be ye, sea-farin' men,

Oh, cruel be your lives,—

A-robbing of the house-carpenters,

And a-taking of their wives!"

The shouts and laughter which greeted the conclusion of Miss Lavender's song brought Dr. Deane into the room. He was a little alarmed lest his standing in the Society might be damaged by so much and such unrestrained merriment under his roof. Still he had scarcely the courage to reprimand the bright, joyous faces before him; he only smiled, shook his head, and turned to leave.

"I'm a-goin', too," said Miss Lavender, rising. "The sun's not an hour high, and the Doctor, or somebody, must take Mary Barton home; and it's about time the rest o' you was makin' ready; though they've gone on with the supper, there's enough to do when you get there!"

The chair rolled away again, and the bridal party remounted their horses in the warm, level light of the sinking sun. They were all in their saddles except Gilbert and Martha.

"Go on!" he cried, in answer to their calls; "we will follow."

"It won't be half a home-comin', without you're along," said Mark; "but I see you want it so. Come on, boys and girls!"

Gilbert returned to the house and met Martha, descending the stairs in her plain riding-dress. She descended into his open arms, and rested there, silent, peaceful, filled with happy rest.

"My wife at last, and forever!" he whispered.

They mounted and rode out of the village. The fields were already beginning to grow gray under the rosy amber of the western sky. The breeze had died away, but the odors it had winnowed from orchard and meadow still hung in the air. Faint cheeps and chirps of nestling life came from the hedges and grassy nooks of bank and thicket, but they deepened, not disturbed, the delicious repose settling upon the land. Husband and wife rode slowly, and their friendly horses pressed nearer to each other, and there was none to see how their eyes grew deeper and darker with perfect tenderness, their lips more sweetly soft and warm, with the unspoken, because unspeakable, fortune of love. In the breath of that happy twilight all the pangs of the Past melted away; disgrace, danger, poverty, trial, were behind them; and before them, nestling yet unseen in the green dell which divided the glimmering landscape, lay the peace, the shelter, the life-long blessing of Home.

THE LANDS OF THE SARACEN, OR, PICTURES OF PALESTINE, ASIA MINOR, SICILY, AND SPAIN

TO WASHINGTON IRVING,

This book--the chronicle of my travels through lands once occupied by the Saracens--naturally dedicates itself to you, who, more than any other American author, have revived the traditions, restored the history, and illustrated the character of that brilliant and heroic people. Your cordial encouragement confirmed me in my design of visiting the East, and making myself familiar with Oriental life; and though I bring you now but imperfect returns, I can at least unite with you in admiration of a field so rich in romantic interest, and indulge the hope that I may one day pluck from it fruit instead of blossoms. In Spain, I came upon your track, and I should hesitate to exhibit my own gleanings where you have harvested, were it not for the belief that the rapid sketches I have given will but enhance, by the contrast, the charm of your finished picture.

Bayard Taylor.

PREFACE.

This volume comprises the second portion of a series of travels, of which the "Journey to Central Africa," already published, is the first part. I left home, intending to spend a winter in Africa, and to return during the following summer; but circumstances afterwards occurred, which prolonged my wanderings to nearly two years and a half, and led me to visit many remote and unexplored portions of the globe. To describe this journey in a single work, would embrace too many incongruous elements, to say nothing of its great length, and as it falls naturally into three parts, or episodes, of very distinct character, I have judged it best to group my experiences under three separate heads, merely indicating the links which connect them. This work includes my travels in Palestine, Syria, Asia Minor, Sicily and Spain, and will be followed by a third and concluding volume, containing my adventures in India, China, the Loo-Choo Islands, and Japan. Although many of the letters, contained in this volume, describe beaten tracks of travel, I have always given my own individual impressions, and may claim for them the merit of entire sincerity. The journey from Aleppo to Constantinople, through the heart of Asia Minor, illustrates regions rarely traversed by tourists, and will, no doubt, be new to most of my readers. My aim, throughout the work, has been to give correct pictures of Oriental life and scenery, leaving antiquarian research and speculation to abler hands. The scholar, or the man of science, may complain with reason that I have neglected valuable opportunities for adding something to the stock of human knowledge: but if a few of the many thousands, who can only travel by their firesides, should find my pages answer the purpose of a series of cosmoramic views--should in them behold with a clearer inward eye the hills of Palestine, the sun-gilded minarets of Damascus, or the lonely pine-forests of Phrygia--should feel, by turns, something of the inspiration and the indolence of the Orient--I shall have achieved all I designed, and more than I can justly hope.

New York, *October*, 1854.

Chapter I. Life in a Syrian Quarantine.

Voyage from Alexandria to Beyrout--Landing at Quarantine--The Guardiano--Our Quarters--Our Companions--Famine and Feasting--The Morning--The Holy Man of Timbuctoo--Sunday in Quarantine--Islamism--We are Registered--Love through a Grating--Trumpets--The Mystery Explained--Delights of Quarantine--Oriental vs. American Exaggeration--A Discussion of Politics--Our Release--Beyrout--Preparations for the Pilgrimage.

"The mountains look on Quarantine, And Quarantine looks on the sea."

Quarantine MS.

In Quarantine, Beyrout, *Saturday, April* 17, 1852.

Everybody has heard of Quarantine, but in our favored country there are many untravelled persons who do not precisely know what it is, and who no doubt wonder why it should be such a bugbear to travellers in the Orient. I confess I am still somewhat in the same predicament myself, although I have already been twenty-four hours in Quarantine. But, as a peculiarity of the place is, that one can do nothing, however good a will he has, I propose to set down my experiences each day, hoping that I and my readers may obtain some insight into the nature of Quarantine, before the term of my probation is over.

I left Alexandria on the afternoon of the 14th inst., in company with Mr. Carter Harrison, a fellow-countryman, who had joined me in Cairo, for the tour through Palestine. We had a head wind, and rough sea, and I remained in a torpid state during most of the voyage. There was rain the second night; but, when the clouds cleared away yesterday morning, we were gladdened by the sight of Lebanon, whose summits glittered with streaks of snow. The lower slopes of the mountains were green with fields and forests, and Beyrout, when we ran up to it, seemed buried almost out of sight, in the foliage of its mulberry groves. The town is built along the northern side of a peninsula, which projects about two miles from the main line of the coast, forming a road for vessels. In half an hour after our arrival, several large boats came alongside, and we were told to get our baggage in order and embark for Quarantine. The time necessary to purify a traveller arriving from Egypt from suspicion of the plague, is five days, but the days of arrival and departure are counted, so that the durance amounts to but three full days. The captain of the Osiris mustered the passengers together, and informed them that each one would be obliged to pay six piastres for the transportation of himself and his baggage. Two heavy lighters are now drawn up to the foot of the gangway, but as soon as the first box tumbles into them, the men tumble out. They attach the craft by cables to two smaller boats, in which they sit, to tow the infected loads. We are all sent down together, Jews, Turks, and Christians--a confused pile of men, women, children, and goods. A little boat from the city, in which there are representatives from the two hotels, hovers around us, and cards are thrown to us. The zealous agents wish to supply us immediately with tables, beds, and all other household appliances; but we decline their help until we arrive at the mysterious spot. At last we float off--two lighters full of infected, though respectable, material, towed by oarsmen of most scurvy appearance, but free from every suspicion of taint.

The sea is still rough, the sun is hot, and a fat Jewess becomes sea-sick. An Italian Jew rails at the boatmen ahead, in the Neapolitan patois, for the distance is long, the Quarantine being on the land-side of Beyrout. We see the rows of little yellow houses on the cliff, and with great apparent risk of being swept upon the breakers, are tugged into a small cove, where there is a landing-place. Nobody is there to receive us; the boatmen jump into the water and push the lighters against the stone stairs, while we unload our own baggage. A tin cup filled with sea-water is placed before us, and we each drop six piastres into it--for money, strange as it may seem, is infectious. By this time, the guardianos have had notice of our arrival, and we go up with them to choose our habitations. There are several rows of one-story houses overlooking the sea, each containing two empty rooms, to be had for a hundred piastres; but a square two-story dwelling stands apart from them, and the whole of it may be had for thrice that sum. There are seven Frank prisoners, and we take it for ourselves. But the rooms are bare, the kitchen empty, and we learn the important fact, that Quarantine is durance vile, without even the bread and water. The guardiano says the agents of the hotel are at the gate, and we can order from them whatever we want. Certainly; but at their own price, for we are wholly at their mercy. However, we go down stairs, and the chief officer, who accompanies us, gets into a corner as we pass, and holds a stick before him to keep us off. He is now clean, but if his garments brush against ours, he is lost. The people we meet in the grounds step aside with great respect to let us pass, but if we offer them our hands, no one would dare to touch a finger's tip.

Here is the gate: a double screen of wire, with an interval between, so that contact is impossible. There is a crowd of individuals outside, all anxious to execute commissions. Among them is the agent of the hotel, who proposes to fill our bare rooms with furniture, send us a servant and cook, and charge us the same as if we lodged with him. The bargain is closed at once, and he hurries off to make the arrangements. It is now four o'clock, and the bracing air of the headland gives a terrible appetite to those of us who, like me, have been sea-sick and fasting for forty-eight hours. But there is no food within the Quarantine except a patch of green wheat, and a well in the limestone rock. We two Americans join company with our room-mate, an Alexandrian of Italian parentage, who has come to Beyrout to be married, and make the tour of our territory. There is a path along the cliffs overhanging the sea, with glorious views of Lebanon, up to his snowy top, the pine-forests at his base, and the long cape whereon the city lies at full length, reposing beside the waves. The Mahommedans and Jews, in companies of ten (to save expense), are lodged in the smaller dwellings, where they have already aroused millions of fleas from their state of torpid expectancy. We return, and take a survey of our companions in the pavilion: a French woman, with two ugly and peevish children (one at the breast), in the next room, and three French gentlemen in the other--a merchant, a young man with hair of extraordinary length, and a filateur, or silk-manufacturer, middle-aged and cynical. The first is a gentleman in every sense of the word, the latter endurable, but the young Absalom is my aversion, I am subject to involuntary likings and dislikings, for which I can give no reason, and though the man may be in every way amiable, his presence is very distasteful to me.

We take a pipe of consolation, but it only whets our appetites. We give up our promenade, for exercise is still worse; and at last the sun goes down, and yet no sign of dinner. Our pavilion becomes a Tower of Famine, and the Italian recites Dante. Finally a strange face appears at the door. By Apicius! it is a servant from the hotel, with iron bedsteads, camp-tables, and some large chests, which breathe an odor of the Commissary Department. We go stealthily down to the kitchen, and watch the unpacking. Our dinner is there, sure enough, but alas! it is not yet cooked. Patience is no more; my companion manages to filch a raw onion and a crust of bread, which we share, and roll under our tongues as a sweet morsel, and it gives us strength for another hour. The Greek dragoman and cook, who are sent into Quarantine for our sakes, take compassion on us; the fires are kindled in the cold furnaces; savory steams creep up the stairs; the preparations increase, and finally climax in the rapturous announcement: "Messieurs, dinner is ready." The soup is liquified bliss; the cotelettes d'agneau are cotelettes de bonheur; and as for that broad dish of Syrian larks--Heaven forgive us the regret, that more songs had not been silenced for our sake! The meal is all nectar and ambrosia, and now, filled and contented, we subside into sleep on comfortable couches. So closes the first day of our incarceration.

This morning dawned clear and beautiful. Lebanon, except his snowy crest, was wrapped in the early shadows, but the Mediterranean gleamed like a shield of sapphire, and Beyrout, sculptured against the background of its mulberry groves, was glorified beyond all other cities. The turf around our pavilion fairly blazed with the splendor of the yellow daisies and crimson poppies that stud it. I was satisfied with what I saw, and felt no wish to leave Quarantine to-day. Our Italian friend, however, is more impatient. His betrothed came early to see him, and we were edified by the great alacrity with which he hastened to the grate, to renew his vows at two yards' distance from her. In the meantime, I went down to the Turkish houses, to cultivate the acquaintance of a singular character I met on board the steamer. He is a negro of six feet four, dressed in a long scarlet robe. His name is Mahommed Senoosee, and he is a fakeer, or holy man, from Timbuctoo. He has been two years absent from home, on a pilgrimage to Mecca and Medina, and is now on his way to Jerusalem and Damascus. He has travelled extensively in all parts of Central Africa, from Dar-Fur to Ashantee, and professes to be on good terms with the Sultans of Houssa and Bornou. He has even been in the great kingdom of Waday, which has never been explored by Europeans, and as far south as Iola, the capital of Adamowa. Of the correctness of his narrations I have not the least doubt, as they correspond geographically with all that we know of the interior of Africa. In answer to my question whether a European might safely make the same tour, he replied that there would be no difficulty, provided he was accompanied by a native, and he offered to take me even to Timbuctoo, if I would return with him. He was very curious to obtain information about America, and made notes of all that I told him, in the quaint character used by the Mughrebbins, or Arabs of the West, which has considerable resemblance to the ancient Cufic. He wishes to join company with me for the journey to Jerusalem, and perhaps I shall accept him.

Sunday, April 18.

As Quarantine is a sort of limbo, without the pale of civilized society, we have no church service to-day. We have done the best we could, however, in sending one of the outside dragomen to purchase a Bible, in which we succeeded. He brought us a very handsome copy, printed by the American Bible Society in New York. I tried vainly in Cairo and Alexandria to find a missionary who would supply my heathenish destitution of the Sacred Writings; for I had reached the East through Austria, where they are prohibited, and to travel through Palestine without them, would be like sailing without pilot or compass. It gives a most impressive reality to Solomon's "house of the forest of Lebanon," when you can look up from the page to those very forests and those grand mountains, "excellent with the cedars." Seeing the holy man of Timbuctoo praying with his face towards Mecca, I went down to him, and we conversed for a long time on religious matters. He is tolerably well informed, having read the Books of Moses and the Psalms of David, but, like all Mahommedans, his ideas of religion consist mainly of forms, and its reward is a sensual paradise. The more intelligent of the Moslems give a spiritual interpretation to the nature of the Heaven promised by the Prophet, and I have heard several openly confess their disbelief in the seventy houries and the palaces of pearl and emerald. Shekh Mahommed Senoosee scarcely ever utters a sentence in which is not the word "Allah," and "La illah il' Allah" is repeated at least every five minutes. Those of his class consider that there is a peculiar merit in the repetition of the names and attributes of God. They utterly reject the doctrine of the Trinity, which they believe implies a sort of partnership, or God-firm (to use their own words), and declare that all who accept it are hopelessly damned. To deny Mahomet's prophetship would excite a violent antagonism, and I content myself with making them acknowledge that God is greater than all Prophets or Apostles, and that there is but one God for all the human race. I have never yet encountered that bitter spirit of bigotry which is so frequently ascribed to them; but on the contrary, fully as great a tolerance as they would find exhibited towards them by most of the Christian sects.

This morning a paper was sent to us, on which we were requested to write our names, ages, professions, and places of nativity. We conjectured that we were subjected to the suspicion of political as well as physical taint, but happily this was not the case. I registered myself as a voyageur, the French as negocians and when it came to the woman's turn, Absalom, who is a partisan of female progress, wished to give her the same profession as her husband--a machinist. But she declared that her only profession was that of a "married woman," and she was so inscribed. Her peevish boy rejoiced in the title of "pleuricheur," or "weeper," and the infant as "titeuse," or "sucker." While this was going on, the guardiano of our room came in very mysteriously, and beckoned to my companion, saying that "Mademoiselle was at the gate." But it was the Italian who was wanted, and again, from the little window of our pavilion, we watched his hurried progress over the lawn. No sooner had she departed, than he took his pocket telescope, slowly sweeping the circuit of the bay as she drew nearer and nearer Beyrout. He has succeeded in distinguishing, among the mass of buildings, the top of the house in which she lives, but alas! it is one story too low, and his patient espial has only been rewarded by the sight of some cats promenading on the roof.

I have succeeded in obtaining some further particulars in relation to Quarantine. On the night of our arrival, as we were about getting into our beds, a sudden and horrible gush of brimstone vapor came up stairs, and we all fell to coughing like patients in a pulmonary hospital. The odor increased

400

till we were obliged to open the windows and sit beside them in order to breathe comfortably. This was the preparatory fumigation, in order to remove the ranker seeds of plague, after which the milder symptoms will of themselves vanish in the pure air of the place. Several times a day we are stunned and overwhelmed with the cracked brays of three discordant trumpets, as grating and doleful as the last gasps of a dying donkey. At first I supposed the object of this was to give a greater agitation to the air, and separate and shake down the noxious exhalations we emit; but since I was informed that the soldiers outside would shoot us in case we attempted to escape, I have concluded that the sound is meant to alarm us, and prevent our approaching too near the walls. On inquiring of our guardiano whether the wheat growing within the grounds was subject to Quarantine, he informed me that it did not ecovey infection, and that three old geese, who walked out past the guard with impunity, were free to go and come, as they had never been known to have the plague. Yesterday evening the medical attendant, a Polish physician, came in to inspect us, but he made a very hasty review, looking down on us from the top of a high horse.

Monday, April 19.

Eureka! the whole thing is explained. Talking to day with the guardiano, he happened to mention that he had been three years in Quarantine, keeping watch over infected travellers. "What!" said I, "you have been sick three years." "Oh no," he replied; "I have never been sick at all." "But are not people sick in Quarantine?" "Stafferillah!" he exclaimed; "they are always in better health than the people outside." "What is Quarantine for, then?" I persisted. "What is it for?" he repeated, with a pause of blank amazement at my ignorance, "why, to get money from the travellers!" Indiscreet guardiano! It were better to suppose ourselves under suspicion of the plague, than to have such an explanation of the mystery. Yet, in spite of the unpalatable knowledge, I almost regret that this is our last day in the establishment. The air is so pure and bracing, the views from our windows so magnificent, the colonized branch of the Beyrout Hotel so comfortable, that I am content to enjoy this pleasant idleness--the more pleasant since, being involuntary, it is no weight on the conscience. I look up to the Maronite villages, perched on the slopes of Lebanon, with scarce a wish to climb to them, or turning to the

401

sparkling Mediterranean, view

"The speronara's sail of snowy hue

Whitening and brightening on that field of blue,"

and have none of that unrest which the sight of a vessel in motion suggests.

To-day my friend from Timbuctoo came up to have another talk. He was curious to know the object of my travels, and as he would not have comprehended the exact truth, I was obliged to convey it to him through the medium of fiction. I informed him that I had been dispatched by the Sultan of my country to obtain information of the countries of Africa; that I wrote in a book accounts of everything I saw, and on my return, would present this book to the Sultan, who would reward me with a high rank--perhaps even that of Grand Vizier. The Orientals deal largely in hyperbole, and scatter numbers and values with the most reckless profusion. The Arabic, like the Hebrew, its sister tongue, and other old original tongues of Man, is a language of roots, and abounds with the boldest metaphors. Now, exaggeration is but the imperfect form of metaphor. The expression is always a splendid amplification of the simple fact. Like skilful archers, in order to hit the mark, they aim above it. When you have once learned his standard of truth, you can readily gauge an Arab's expressions, and regulate your own accordingly. But whenever I have attempted to strike the key-note myself, I generally found that it was below, rather than above, the Oriental pitch.

The Shekh had already informed me that the King of Ashantee, whom he had visited, possessed twenty-four houses full of gold, and that the Sultan of Houssa had seventy thousand horses always standing saddled before his palace, in order that he might take his choice, when he wished to ride out. By this he did not mean that the facts were precisely so, but only that the King was very rich, and the Sultan had a great many horses. In order to give the Shekh an idea of the great wealth and power of the American Nation, I was obliged to adopt the same plan. I told him, therefore, that our country was two years' journey in extent, that the Treasury consisted of four thousand houses filled to the roof with gold, and that two hundred thousand soldiers on horseback kept continual guard around Sultan Fillmore's palace. He received these tremendous statements with the utmost serenity and satisfaction, carefully writing them in his book, together with the name of Sultan Fillmore, whose fame has ere this reached the remote regions of Timbuctoo. The Shekh, moreover, had the desire of visiting England, and wished me to give him a letter to the English Sultan. This rather exceeded my powers, but I wrote a simple certificate explaining who he was, and whence he came, which I sealed with an immense display of wax, and gave him. In return, he wrote his name in my book, in the Mughrebbin character, adding the sentence: "There is no God but God."

This evening the forbidden subject of politics crept into our quiet community, and the result was an explosive contention which drowned even the braying of the agonizing trumpets outside. The gentlemanly Frenchman is a sensible and consistent republican, the old filateur a violent monarchist, while Absalom, as I might have foreseen, is a Red, of the schools of Proudhon and Considerant. The first predicted a Republic in France, the second a Monarchy in America, and the last was in favor of a general and total demolition of all existing systems. Of course, with such elements, anything like a serious discussion was impossible; and, as in most French debates, it ended in a bewildering confusion of cries and gesticulations. In the midst of it, I was struck by the cordiality with which the Monarchist and the Socialist united in their denunciations of England and the English laws. As they sat side by side, pouring out anathemas against "perfide Albion," I could not help exclaiming: "Voilà, comme les extrêmes se rencontrent!" This turned the whole current of their wrath against me, and I was glad to make a hasty retreat.

The physician again visited us to-night, to promise a release to-morrow morning. He looked us all in the faces, to be certain that there were no signs of pestilence, and politely regretted that he could not offer us his hand. The husband of the "married woman" also came, and relieved the other gentlemen from the charge of the "weeper." He was a stout, ruddy Provençal, in a white blouse, and I commiserated him sincerely for having such a disagreeable wife.

To-day, being the last of our imprisonment, we have received many tokens of attention from dragomen, who have sent their papers through the grate to us, to be returned to-morrow after our liberation. They are not very prepossessing specimens of their class, with the exception of Yusef Badra, who brings a recommendation from my friend, Ross Browne. Yusef is a handsome, dashing fellow, with something of the dandy in his dress and air, but he has a fine, clear, sparkling eye, with just enough of the devil in it to make him attractive. I think, however, that, the Greek dragoman, who has been our companion in Quarantine, will carry the day. He is by birth a Boeotian, but now a citizen of Athens, and calls himself François Vitalis. He speaks French, German, and Italian, besides Arabic and Turkish, and as he has been for twelve or fifteen years vibrating between Europe and the East, he must by this time have amassed sufficient experience to answer the needs of rough-and-tumble travellers like ourselves. He has not asked us for the place, which displays so much penetration on his part, that we shall end by offering it to him. Perhaps he is content to rest his claims upon the memory of our first Quarantine dinner. If so, the odors of the cutlets and larks--even of the raw onion, which we remember with tears--shall not plead his cause in vain.

Beyrout (out of Quarantine), *Wednesday, May* 21.

The handsome Greek, Diamanti, one of the proprietors of the "Hotel de Belle Vue," was on hand bright and early yesterday morning, to welcome us out of Quarantine. The gates were thrown wide, and forth we issued between two files of soldiers, rejoicing in our purification. We walked through mulberry orchards to the town, and through its steep and crooked streets to the hotel, which stands beyond, near the extremity of the Cape, or Ras Beyrout. The town is small, but has an active population, and a larger commerce than any other port in Syria. The anchorage, however, is an open road, and in stormy weather it is impossible for a boat to land. There are two picturesque old castles on some rocks near the shore, but they were almost destroyed by the English bombardment in 1841. I noticed two or three granite columns, now used as the lintels of some of the arched ways in the streets, and other fragments of old masonry, the only remains of the ancient Berytus.

Our time, since our release, has been occupied by preparations for the journey to Jerusalem. We have taken François as dragoman, and our mukkairee, or muleteers, are engaged to be in readiness to-morrow morning. I learn that the Druses are in revolt in Djebel Hauaran and parts of the Anti-Lebanon, which will prevent my forming any settled plan for the tour through Palestine and Syria. Up to this time, the country has been considered quite safe, the only robbery this winter having been that of the party of Mr. Degen, of New York, which was plundered near Tiberias. Dr. Robinson left here two weeks ago for Jerusalem, in company with Dr. Eli Smith, of the American Mission at this place.

Chapter II. The Coast of Palestine.

The Pilgrimage Commences--The Muleteers--The Mules--The Donkey--Journey to Sidon--The Foot of Lebanon--Pictures--The Ruins of Tyre--A Wild Morning--The Tyrian Surges--Climbing the Ladder of Tyre--Panorama of the Bay of Acre--The Plain of Esdraelon--Camp in a Garden--Acre--the Shore of the Bay--Haifa--Mount Carmel and its Monastery--A Deserted Coast--The Ruins of Cæsarea--The Scenery of Palestine--We become Robbers--El Haram--Wrecks--the Harbor and Town of Jaffa.

"Along the line of foam, the jewelled chain, The largesse of the ever-giving main."

R. H. Stoddard.

Ramleh, *April* 27, 1852.

We left Beyrout on the morning of the 22d. Our caravan consisted of three horses, three mules, and a donkey, in charge of two men--Dervish, an erect, black-bearded, and most impassive Mussulman, and Mustapha, who is the very picture of patience and good-nature. He was born with a smile on his face, and has never been able to change the expression. They are both masters of their art, and can load a mule with a speed and skill which I would defy any Santa Fé trader to excel. The animals are not less interesting than their masters. Our horses, to be sure, are slow, plodding beasts, with considerable endurance, but little spirit; but the two baggage mules deserve gold medals from the Society for the Promotion of Industry. I can overlook any amount of waywardness in the creatures, in consideration of the steady, persevering energy, the cheerfulness and even enthusiasm with which they perform their duties. They seem to be conscious that they are doing well, and to take a delight in the consciousness. One of them has a band of white shells around his neck, fastened with a tassel and two large blue beads; and you need but look at him to see that he is aware how becoming it is. He thinks it was given to him for good conduct, and is doing his best to merit another. The little donkey is a still more original animal. He is a practical humorist, full of perverse tricks, but all intended for effect, and without a particle of malice. He generally walks behind, running off to one side or the other to crop a mouthful of grass, but no sooner does Dervish attempt to mount him, than he sets off at full gallop, and takes the lead of the caravan. After having performed one of his feats, he turns around with a droll glance at us, as much as to say: "Did you see that?" If we had not been present, most assuredly he would never have done it. I can imagine him, after his return to Beyrout, relating his adventures to a company of fellow-donkeys, who every now and then burst into tremendous brays at some of his irresistible dry sayings.

I persuaded Mr. Harrison to adopt the Oriental costume, which, from five months' wear in Africa, I greatly preferred to the Frank. We therefore rode out of Beyrout as a pair of Syrian Beys, while François, with his belt, sabre, and pistols had much the aspect of a Greek brigand. The road crosses the hill behind the city, between the Forest of Pines and a long tract of red sand-hills next the sea. It was a lovely morning, not too bright and hot, for light, fleecy vapors hung along the sides of Lebanon. Beyond the mulberry orchards, we entered on wild, half-cultivated tracts, covered with a bewildering maze of blossoms. The hill-side and stony shelves of soil overhanging the sea fairly blazed with the brilliant dots of color which were rained upon them. The pink, the broom, the poppy, the speedwell, the lupin, that beautiful variety of the cyclamen, called by the Syrians "deek e-djebel" (cock o' the mountain), and a number of unknown plants dazzled the eye with their profusion, and loaded the air with fragrance as rare as it was unfailing. Here and there, clear, swift rivulets came down from Lebanon, coursing their way between thickets of blooming oleanders. Just before crossing the little river Damoor, François pointed out, on one of the distant heights, the residence of the late Lady Hester Stanhope. During the afternoon we crossed several offshoots of the Lebanon, by paths incredibly steep and stony, and towards evening reached Saïda, the ancient Sidon, where we obtained permission to pitch our tent in a garden. The town is built on a narrow point of land, jutting out from the centre of a bay, or curve in the coast, and contains about five thousand inhabitants. It is a quiet, sleepy sort of a place, and contains nothing of the old Sidon except a few stones and the fragments of a mole, extending into the sea. The fortress in the water, and the Citadel, are remnants of Venitian sway. The clouds gathered after nightfall, and occasionally there was a dash of rain on our tent. But I heard it with the same quiet happiness, as when, in boyhood, sleeping beneath the rafters, I have heard the rain beating all night upon the roof. I breathed the sweet breath of the grasses whereon my carpet was spread, and old Mother Earth, welcoming me back to her bosom, cradled me into calm and refreshing sleep. There is no rest more grateful than that which we take on the turf or the sand, except the rest below it.

We rose in a dark and cloudy morning, and continued our way between fields of barley, completely stained with the bloody hue of the poppy, and meadows turned into golden mosaic by a brilliant yellow daisy. Until noon our road was over a region of alternate meadow land and gentle though stony elevations, making out from Lebanon. We met continually with indications of ancient power and prosperity. The ground was strewn with hewn blocks, and the foundations of buildings remain in many places. Broken sarcophagi lie half-buried in grass, and the gray rocks of the hills are pierced with tombs. The soil, though stony, appeared to be naturally fertile, and the crops of wheat, barley, and lentils were very flourishing. After rounding the promontory which forms the southern boundary of the Gulf of Sidon, we rode for an hour or two over a plain near the sea, and then came down to a valley which ran up among the hills, terminating in a natural amphitheatre. An ancient barrow, or tumulus, nobody knows of whom, stands near the sea. During the day I noticed two charming little pictures. One, a fountain gushing into a broad square basin of masonry, shaded by three branching cypresses. Two Turks sat on its edge, eating their bread and curdled milk, while their horses drank out of the stone trough below. The other, an old Mahommedan, with a green turban and white robe, seated at the foot of a majestic sycamore, over the high bank of a stream that tumbled down its bed of white marble rock to the sea.

The plain back of the narrow, sandy promontory on which the modern Soor is built, is a rich black loam, which a little proper culture would turn into a very garden. It helped me to account for the wealth of ancient Tyre. The approach to the town, along a beach on which the surf broke with a continuous roar, with the wreck of a Greek vessel in the foreground, and a stormy sky behind, was very striking. It was a wild, bleak picture, the white minarets of the town standing out spectrally against the clouds. We rode up the sand-hills, back of the town, and selected a good camping-place among the ruins of Tyre. Near us there was an ancient square building, now used as a cistern, and filled with excellent fresh water. The surf roared tremendously on the rocks, on either hand, and the boom of the more distant breakers came to my ear like the wind in a pine forest. The remains of the ancient sea-wall are still to be traced for the entire circuit of the city, and the heavy surf breaks upon piles of shattered granite columns. Along a sort of mole, protecting an inner harbor on the north side, are great numbers of these columns. I counted fifteen in one group, some of them fine red granite, and some of the marble of Lebanon. The remains of the pharos and the fortresses strengthening the sea-wall, were pointed out by the Syrian who accompanied us as a guide, but his faith was a little stronger than mine. He even showed us the ruins of the jetty built by Alexander, by means of which the ancient city, then insulated by the sea, was taken. The remains of the causeway gradually formed the promontory by which the place is now connected with the main land. These are the principal indications of Tyre above ground, but the guide informed us that the Arabs, in digging among the sand-hills for the stones of the old buildings, which they quarry out and ship to Beyrout, come upon chambers, pillars, arches, and other objects. The Tyrian purple is still furnished by a muscle found upon the coast, but Tyre is now only noted for its tobacco and mill-stones. I saw many of the latter lying in the streets of the town, and an Arab was selling a quantity at auction in the square, as we passed. They are cut out from a species of dark volcanic rock, by the Bedouins of the mountains. There were half a dozen small coasting vessels lying in the road, but the old harbors are entirely destroyed. Isaiah's prophecy is literally fulfilled: "Howl, ye ships of Tarshish; for it is laid waste, so that there is no house, no entering in."

On returning from our ramble we passed the house of the Governor, Daood Agha, who was dispensing justice in regard to a lawsuit then before him. He asked us to stop and take coffee, and received us with much grace and dignity. As we rose to leave, a slave brought me a large bunch of choice flowers from his garden.

We set out from Tyre at an early hour, and rode along the beach around the head of the bay to the Ras-el-Abiad, the ancient Promontorium Album. The morning was wild and cloudy, with gleams of sunshine that flashed out over the dark violet gloom of the sea. The surf was magnificent, rolling up in grand billows, which broke and formed again, till the last of the long, falling fringes of snow slid seething up the sand. Something of ancient power was in their shock and roar, and every great wave that plunged and drew back again, called in its solemn bass: "Where are the ships of Tyre? where are the ships of Tyre?" I looked back on the city, which stood advanced far into the sea, her feet bathed in thunderous spray. By and by the clouds cleared away, the sun came out bold and bright, and our road left the beach for a meadowy plain, crossed by fresh streams, and sown with an inexhaustible wealth of flowers. Through thickets of myrtle and mastic, around which the rue and lavender grew in dense clusters, we reached the foot of the mountain, and began ascending the celebrated Ladder of Tyre. The road is so steep as to resemble a staircase, and climbs along the side of the promontory, hanging over precipices of naked white rock, in some places three hundred feet in height. The mountain is a mass of magnesian limestone, with occasional beds of marble. The surf has worn its foot into hollow caverns, into which the sea rushes with a dull, heavy boom, like distant thunder. The sides are covered with thickets of broom, myrtle, arbutus, ilex, mastic and laurel, overgrown with woodbine, and interspersed with patches of sage, lavender, hyssop, wild thyme, and rue. The whole mountain is a heap of balm; a bundle of sweet spices.

Our horses' hoofs clattered up and down the rounds of the ladder, and we looked our last on Tyre, fading away behind the white hem of the breakers, as we turned the point of the promontory. Another cove of the mountain-coast followed, terminated by the Cape of Nakhura, the northern point of the Bay of Acre. We rode along a stony way between fields of wheat and barley, blotted almost out of sight by showers of scarlet poppies and yellow chrysanthemums. There were frequent ruins: fragments of sarcophagi, foundations of houses, and about half way between the two capes, the mounds of Alexandro-Schœnæ. We stopped at a khan, and breakfasted under a magnificent olive tree, while two boys tended our horses to see that they ate only the edges of the wheat field. Below the house were two large cypresses,

410

and on a little tongue of land the ruins of one of those square towers of the corsairs, which line all this coast. The intense blue of the sea, seen close at hand over a broad field of goldening wheat, formed a dazzling and superb contrast of color. Early in the afternoon we climbed the Ras Nakhura, not so bold and grand, though quite as flowery a steep as the Promontorium Album. We had been jogging half an hour over its uneven summit, when the side suddenly fell away below us, and we saw the whole of the great gulf and plain of Acre, backed by the long ridge of Mount Carmel. Behind the sea, which makes a deep indentation in the line of the coast, extended the plain, bounded on the east, at two leagues' distance, by a range of hills covered with luxuriant olive groves, and still higher, by the distant mountains of Galilee. The fortifications of Acre were visible on a slight promontory near the middle of the Gulf. From our feet the line of foamy surf extended for miles along the red sand-beach, till it finally became like a chalk-mark on the edge of the field of blue.

We rode down the mountain and continued our journey over the plain of Esdraelon--a picture of summer luxuriance and bloom. The waves of wheat and barley rolled away from our path to the distant olive orchards; here the water gushed from a stone fountain and flowed into a turf-girdled pool, around which the Syrian women were washing their garments; there, a garden of orange, lemon, fig, and pomegranate trees in blossom, was a spring of sweet odors, which overflowed the whole land. We rode into some of these forests, for they were no less, and finally pitched our tent in one of them, belonging to the palace of the former Abdallah Pasha, within a mile of Acre. The old Saracen aqueduct, which still conveys water to the town, overhung our tent. For an hour before reaching our destination, we had seen it on the left, crossing the hollows on light stone arches. In one place I counted fifty-eight, and in another one hundred and three of these arches, some of which were fifty feet high. Our camp was a charming place: a nest of deep herbage, under two enormous fig-trees, and surrounded by a balmy grove of orange and citron. It was doubly beautiful when the long line of the aqueduct was lit up by the moon, and the orange trees became mounds of ambrosial darkness.

In the morning we rode to Acre, the fortifications of which have been

411

restored on the land-side. A ponderous double gateway of stone admitted us into the city, through what was once, apparently, the court-yard of a fortress. The streets of the town are narrow, terribly rough, and very dirty, but the bazaars are extensive and well stocked. The principal mosque, whose heavy dome is visible at some distance from the city, is surrounded with a garden, enclosed by a pillared corridor, paved with marble. All the houses of the city are built in the most massive style, of hard gray limestone or marble, and this circumstance alone prevented their complete destruction during the English bombardment in 1841. The marks of the shells are everywhere seen, and the upper parts of the lofty buildings are completely riddled with cannon-balls, some of which remain embedded in the stone. We made a rapid tour of the town on horseback, followed by the curious glances of the people, who were in doubt whether to consider us Turks or Franks. There were a dozen vessels in the harbor, which is considered the best in Syria.

The baggage-mules had gone on, so we galloped after them along the hard beach, around the head of the bay. It was a brilliant morning; a delicious south-eastern breeze came to us over the flowery plain of Esdraelon; the sea on our right shone blue, and purple, and violet-green, and black, as the shadows or sunshine crossed it, and only the long lines of roaring foam, for ever changing in form, did not vary in hue. A fisherman stood on the beach in a statuesque attitude, his handsome bare legs bathed in the frothy swells, a bag of fish hanging from his shoulder, and the large square net, with its sinkers of lead in his right hand, ready for a cast. He had good luck, for the waves brought up plenty of large fish, and cast them at our feet, leaving them to struggle back into the treacherous brine. Between Acre and Haifa we passed six or eight wrecks, mostly of small trading vessels. Some were half buried in sand, some so old and mossy that they were fast rotting away, while a few had been recently hurled there. As we rounded the deep curve of the bay, and approached the line of palm-trees girding the foot of Mount Carmel, Haifa, with its wall and Saracenic town in ruin on the hill above, grew more clear and bright in the sun, while Acre dipped into the blue of the Mediterranean. The town of Haifa, the ancient Caiapha, is small, dirty, and beggarly looking; but it has some commerce, sharing the trade of Acre in the productions of Syria. It was Sunday, and all the Consular flags were flying.

It was an unexpected delight to find the American colors in this little Syrian town, flying from one of the tallest poles. The people stared at us as we passed, and I noticed among them many bright Frankish faces, with eyes too clear and gray for Syria. O ye kind brothers of the monastery of Carmel! forgive me if I look to you for an explanation of this phenomenon.

We ascended to Mount Carmel. The path led through a grove of carob trees, from which the beans, known in Germany as St. John's bread, are produced. After this we came into an olive grove at the foot of the mountain, from which long fields of wheat, giving forth a ripe summer smell, flowed down to the shore of the bay. The olive trees were of immense size, and I can well believe, as Fra Carlo informed us, that they were probably planted by the Roman colonists, established there by Titus. The gnarled, veteran boles still send forth vigorous and blossoming boughs. There were all manner of lovely lights and shades chequered over the turf and the winding path we rode. At last we reached the foot of an ascent, steeper than the Ladder of Tyre. As our horses slowly climbed to the Convent of St. Elijah, whence we already saw the French flag floating over the shoulder of the mountain, the view opened grandly to the north and east, revealing the bay and plain of Acre, and the coast as far as Ras Nakhura, from which we first saw Mount Carmel the day previous. The two views are very similar in character, one being the obverse of the other. We reached the Convent--Dayr Mar Elias, as the Arabs call it--at noon, just in time to partake of a bountiful dinner, to which the monks had treated themselves. Fra Carlo, the good Franciscan who receives strangers, showed us the building, and the Grotto of Elijah, which is under the altar of the Convent Church, a small but very handsome structure of Italian marble. The sanctity of the Grotto depends on tradition entirely, as there is no mention in the Bible of Elijah having resided on Carmel, though it was from this mountain that he saw the cloud, "like a man's hand," rising from the sea. The Convent, which is quite new--not yet completed, in fact--is a large, massive building, and has the aspect of a fortress.

As we were to sleep at Tantura, five hours distant, we were obliged to make a short visit, in spite of the invitation of the hospitable Fra Carlo to spend the night there. In the afternoon we passed the ruins of Athlit, a town

413

of the Middle Ages, and the Castel Pellegrino of the Crusaders. Our road now followed the beach, nearly the whole distance to Jaffa, and was in many places, for leagues in extent, a solid layer of white, brown, purple and rosy shells, which cracked and rattled under our horses' feet. Tantura is a poor Arab village, and we had some difficulty in procuring provisions. The people lived in small huts of mud and stones, near the sea. The place had a thievish look, and we deemed it best to be careful in the disposal of our baggage for the night.

In the morning we took the coast again, riding over millions of shells. A line of sandy hills, covered with thickets of myrtle and mastic, shut off the view of the plain and meadows between the sea and the hills of Samaria. After three hours' ride we saw the ruins of ancient Cæsarea, near a small promontory. The road turned away from the sea, and took the wild plain behind, which is completely overgrown with camomile, chrysanthemum and wild shrubs. The ruins of the town are visible at a considerable distance along the coast. The principal remains consist of a massive wall, flanked with pyramidal bastions at regular intervals, and with the traces of gateways, draw-bridges and towers. It was formerly surrounded by a deep moat. Within this space, which may be a quarter of a mile square, are a few fragments of buildings, and toward the sea, some high arches and masses of masonry. The plain around abounds with traces of houses, streets, and court-yards. Cæsarea was one of the Roman colonies, but owed its prosperity principally to Herod. St. Paul passed through it on his way from Macedon to Jerusalem, by the very road we were travelling.

During the day the path struck inland over a vast rolling plain, covered with sage, lavender and other sweet-smelling shrubs, and tenanted by herds of gazelles and flocks of large storks. As we advanced further, the landscape became singularly beautiful. It was a broad, shallow valley, swelling away towards the east into low, rolling hills, far back of which rose the blue line of the mountains--the hill-country of Judea. The soil, where it was ploughed, was the richest vegetable loam. Where it lay fallow it was entirely hidden by a bed of grass and camomile. Here and there great herds of sheep and goats browsed on the herbage. There was a quiet pastoral air about the landscape, a soft serenity in its forms and colors, as if the Hebrew patriarchs still made it their abode. The district is famous for robbers, and we kept our arms in readiness, never suffering the baggage to be out of our sight.

Towards evening, as Mr. H. and myself, with François, were riding in advance of the baggage mules, the former with his gun in his hand, I with a pair of pistols thrust through the folds of my shawl, and François with his long Turkish sabre, we came suddenly upon a lonely Englishman, whose companions were somewhere in the rear. He appeared to be struck with terror on seeing us making towards him, and, turning his horse's head, made an attempt to fly. The animal, however, was restive, and, after a few plunges, refused to move. The traveller gave himself up for lost; his arms dropped by his side; he stared wildly at us, with pale face and eyes opened wide with a look of helpless fright. Restraining with difficulty a shout of laughter, I said to him: "Did you leave Jaffa to-day?" but so completely was his ear the fool of his imagination, that he thought I was speaking Arabic, and made a faint attempt to get out the only word or two of that language which he knew. I then repeated, with as much distinctness as I could command: "Did--you--leave--Jaffa--to-day?" He stammered mechanically, through his chattering teeth, "Y-y-yes!" and we immediately dashed off at a gallop through the bushes. When we last saw him, he was standing as we left him, apparently not yet recovered from the shock.

At the little village of El Haram, where we spent the night, I visited the tomb of Sultan Ali ebn-Aleym, who is now revered as a saint. It is enclosed in a mosque, crowning the top of a hill. I was admitted into the court-yard without hesitation, though, from the porter styling me "Effendi," he probably took me for a Turk. At the entrance to the inner court, I took off my slippers and walked to the tomb of the Sultan--a square heap of white marble, in a small marble enclosure. In one of the niches in the wall, near the tomb, there is a very old iron box, with a slit in the top. The porter informed me that it contained a charm, belonging to Sultan Ali, which was of great use in producing rain in times of drouth.

In the morning we sent our baggage by a short road across the country to this place, and then rode down the beach towards Jaffa. The sun came out bright and hot as we paced along the line of spray, our horses' feet sinking above the fetlocks in pink and purple shells, while the droll sea-crabs scampered away from our path, and the blue gelatinous sea-nettles were tossed before us by the surge. Our view was confined to the sand-hills--sometimes covered with a flood of scarlet poppies--on one hand; and to the blue, surf-fringed sea on the other. The terrible coast was still lined with wrecks, and just before reaching the town, we passed a vessel of some two hundred tons, recently cast ashore, with her strong hull still unbroken. We forded the rapid stream of El Anjeh, which comes down from the Plain of Sharon, the water rising to our saddles. The low promontory in front now broke into towers and white domes, and great masses of heavy walls. The aspect of Jaffa is exceedingly picturesque. It is built on a hill, and the land for many miles around it being low and flat, its topmost houses overlook all the fields of Sharon. The old harbor, protected by a reef of rocks, is on the north side of the town, but is now so sanded up that large vessels cannot enter. A number of small craft were lying close to the shore. The port presented a different scene when the ships of Hiram, King of Tyre, came in with the materials for the Temple of Solomon. There is but one gate on the land side, which is rather strongly fortified. Outside of this there is an open space, which we found filled with venders of oranges and vegetables, camel-men and the like, some vociferating in loud dispute, some given up to silence and smoke, under the shade of the sycamores.

We rode under the heavily arched and towered gateway, and entered the bazaar. The street was crowded, and there was such a confusion of camels, donkeys, and men, that we made our way with difficulty along the only practicable street in the city, to the sea-side, where François pointed out a hole in the wall as the veritable spot where Jonah was cast ashore by the whale. This part of the harbor is the receptacle of all the offal of the town; and I do not wonder that the whale's stomach should have turned on approaching it. The sea-street was filled with merchants and traders, and we were obliged to pick our way between bars of iron, skins of oil, heaps of oranges, and piles of building timber. At last we reached the end, and, as there was no other thoroughfare, returned the same way we went, passed out the gate, and took the road to Ramleh and Jerusalem.

But I hear the voice of François, announcing, "Messieurs, le diner est prêt." We are encamped just beside the pool of Ramleh, and the mongrel children of the town are making a great noise in the meadow below it. Our horses are enjoying their barley; and Mustapha stands at the tent-door tying up his sacks. Dogs are barking and donkeys braying all along the borders of the town, whose filth and dilapidation are happily concealed by the fig and olive gardens which surround it. I have not curiosity enough to visit the Greek and Latin Convents embedded in its foul purlieus, but content myself with gazing from my door upon the blue hills of Palestine, which we must cross to-morrow, on our way to Jerusalem.

Chapter III. From Jaffa to Jerusalem.

The Garden of Jaffa--Breakfast at a Fountain--The Plain of Sharon--The Ruined Mosque of Ramleh--A Judean Landscape--The Streets of Ramleh--Am I in Palestine?--A Heavenly Morning--The Land of Milk and Honey--Entering the Hill-Country--The Pilgrim's Breakfast--The Father of Lies--A Church of the Crusaders--The Agriculture of the Hills--The Valley of Elah--Day-Dreams--The Wilderness--The Approach--We see the Holy City.

--"Through the air sublime,

Over the wilderness and o'er the plain;

Till underneath them fair Jerusalem,

The Holy City, lifted high her towers."

Paradise Regained.

Jerusalem, *Thursday, April* 29, 1852.

Leaving the gate of Jaffa, we rode eastward between delightful gardens of fig, citron, orange, pomegranate and palm. The country for several miles around the city is a complete level--part of the great plain of Sharon--and the gray mass of building crowning the little promontory, is the only landmark seen above the green garden-land, on looking towards the sea. The road was lined with hedges of giant cactus, now in blossom, and shaded occasionally with broad-armed sycamores. The orange trees were in bloom, and at the same time laden down with ripe fruit. The oranges of Jaffa are the finest in Syria, and great numbers of them are sent to Beyrout and other ports further north. The dark foliage of the pomegranate fairly blazed with its heavy scarlet blossoms, and here and there a cluster of roses made good the Scriptural renown of those of Sharon. The road was filled with people, passing to and fro, and several families of Jaffa Jews were having a sort of pic-nic in the choice shady spots.

Ere long we came to a fountain, at a point where two roads met. It was a large square structure of limestone and marble, with a stone trough in front, and a delightful open chamber at the side. The space in front was shaded with immense sycamore trees, to which we tied our horses, and then took our seats in the window above the fountain, where the Greek brought us our breakfast. The water was cool and delicious, as were our Jaffa oranges. It was a charming spot, for as we sat we could look under the boughs of the great trees, and down between the gardens to Jaffa and the Mediterranean. After leaving the gardens, we came upon the great plain of Sharon, on which we could see the husbandmen at work far and near, ploughing and sowing their grain. In some instances, the two operations were made simultaneously, by having a sort of funnel attached to the plough-handle, running into a tube which entered the earth just behind the share. The man held the plough with one hand, while with the other he dropped the requisite quantity of seed through the tube into the furrow. The people are ploughing now for their summer crops, and the wheat and barley which they sowed last winter are already in full head. On other parts of the plain, there were large flocks of sheep and goats, with their attendant shepherds. So ran the rich landscape, broken only by belts of olive trees, to the far hills of Judea.

Riding on over the long, low swells, fragrant with wild thyme and camomile, we saw at last the tower of Ramleh, and down the valley, an hour's ride to the north-east, the minaret of Ludd, the ancient Lydda. Still further, I could see the houses of the village of Sharon, embowered in olives. Ramleh is built along the crest and on the eastern slope of a low hill, and at a distance appears like a stately place, but this impression is immediately dissipated on entering it. West of the town is a large square tower, between eighty and ninety feet in height. We rode up to it through an orchard of ancient olive trees, and over a field of beans. The tower is evidently a minaret, as it is built in the purest Saracenic style, and is surrounded by the ruins of a mosque. I have rarely seen anything more graceful than the ornamental arches of the upper portions. Over the door is a lintel of white marble, with an Arabic inscription. The mosque to which the tower is attached is almost entirely destroyed, and only part of the arches of a corridor around three sides of a court-yard, with the fountain in the centre, still remain. The subterranean cisterns, under the court-yard, amazed me with their extent and magnitude.

They are no less than twenty-four feet deep, and covered by twenty-four vaulted ceilings, each twelve feet square, and resting on massive pillars. The mosque, when entire, must have been one of the finest in Syria.

We clambered over the broken stones cumbering the entrance, and mounted the steps to the very summit. The view reached from Jaffa and the sea to the mountains near Jerusalem, and southward to the plain of Ascalon--a great expanse of grain and grazing land, all blossoming as the rose, and dotted, especially near the mountains, with dark, luxuriant olive-groves. The landscape had something of the green, pastoral beauty of England, except the mountains, which were wholly of Palestine. The shadows of fleecy clouds, drifting slowly from east to west, moved across the landscape, which became every moment softer and fairer in the light of the declining sun.

I did not tarry in Ramleh. The streets are narrow, crooked, and filthy as only an Oriental town can be. The houses have either flat roofs or domes, out of the crevices in which springs a plentiful crop of weeds. Some yellow dogs barked at us as we passed, children in tattered garments stared, and old turbaned heads were raised from the pipe, to guess who the two brown individuals might be, and why they were attended by such a fierce cawass. Passing through the eastern gate, we were gladdened by the sight of our tents, already pitched in the meadow beside the cistern. Dervish had arrived an hour before us, and had everything ready for the sweet lounge of an hour, to which we treat ourselves after a day's ride. I watched the evening fade away over the blue hills before us, and tried to convince myself that I should reach Jerusalem on the morrow. Reason said: "You certainly will!"---but to Faith the Holy City was as far off as ever. Was it possible that I was in Judea? Was this the Holy Land of the Crusades, the soil hallowed by the feet of Christ and his Apostles? I must believe it. Yet it seemed once that if I ever trod that earth, then beneath my feet, there would be thenceforth a consecration in my life, a holy essence, a purer inspiration on the lips, a surer faith in the heart. And because I was not other than I had been, I half doubted whether it was the Palestine of my dreams.

A number of Arab cameleers, who had come with travellers across the Desert from Egypt, were encamped near us. François was suspicious of some of them, and therefore divided the night into three watches, which were kept by himself and our two men. Mustapha was the last, and kept not only himself, but myself, wide awake by his dolorous chants of love and religion. I fell sound asleep at dawn, but was roused before sunrise by François, who wished to start betimes, on account of the rugged road we had to travel. The morning was mild, clear, and balmy, and we were soon packed and in motion. Leaving the baggage to follow, we rode ahead over the fertile fields. The wheat and poppies were glistening with dew, birds sang among the fig-trees, a cool breeze came down from the hollows of the hills, and my blood leaped as nimbly and joyously as a young hart on the mountains of Bether.

Between Ramleh and the hill-country, a distance of about eight miles, is the rolling plain of Arimathea, and this, as well as the greater part of the plain of Sharon, is one of the richest districts in the world. The soil is a dark-brown loam, and, without manure, produces annually superb crops of wheat and barley. We rode for miles through a sea of wheat, waving far and wide over the swells of land. The tobacco in the fields about Ramleh was the most luxuriant I ever saw, and the olive and fig attain a size and lusty strength wholly unknown in Italy. Judea cursed of God! what a misconception, not only of God's mercy and beneficence, but of the actual fact! Give Palestine into Christian hands, and it will again flow with milk and honey. Except some parts of Asia Minor, no portion of the Levant is capable of yielding such a harvest of grain, silk, wool, fruits, oil, and wine. The great disadvantage under which the country labors, is its frequent drouths, but were the soil more generally cultivated, and the old orchards replanted, these would neither be so frequent nor so severe.

We gradually ascended the hills, passing one or two villages, imbedded in groves of olives. In the little valleys, slanting down to the plains, the Arabs were still ploughing and sowing, singing the while an old love-song, with its chorus of "ya, ghazalee! ya, ghazalee!" (oh, gazelle! oh, gazelle!) The valley narrowed, the lowlands behind us spread out broader, and in half an hour more we were threading a narrow pass, between stony hills, overgrown with ilex, myrtle, and dwarf oak. The wild purple rose of Palestine blossomed on all sides, and a fragrant white honeysuckle in some places hung from the rocks. The path was terribly rough, and barely wide enough for two persons on horseback to pass each other. We met a few pilgrims returning from Jerusalem, and a straggling company of armed Turks, who had such a piratical air, that without the solemn asseveration of François that the road was quite safe, I should have felt uneasy about our baggage. Most of the persons we passed were Mussulmen, few of whom gave the customary "Peace be with you!" but once a Syrian Christian saluted me with, "God go with you, O Pilgrim!" For two hours after entering the mountains, there was scarcely a sign of cultivation. The rock was limestone, or marble, lying in horizontal strata, the broken edges of which rose like terraces to the summits. These shelves were so covered with wild shrubs--in some places even with rows of olive trees---that to me they had not the least appearance of that desolation so generally ascribed to them.

In a little dell among the hills there is a small ruined mosque, or chapel (I could not decide which), shaded by a group of magnificent terebinth trees. Several Arabs were resting in its shade, and we hoped to find there the water we were looking for, in order to make breakfast. But it was not to be found, and we climbed nearly to the summit of the first chain of hills, where in a small olive orchard, there was a cistern, filled by the late rains. It belonged to two ragged boys, who brought us an earthen vessel of the water, and then asked, "Shall we bring you milk, O Pilgrims!" I assented, and received a small jug of thick buttermilk, not remarkably clean, but very refreshing. My companion, who had not recovered from his horror at finding that the inhabitants of Ramleh washed themselves in the pool which supplied us and them, refused to touch it. We made but a short rest, for it was now nearly noon, and there were yet many rough miles between us and Jerusalem. We crossed the first chain of mountains, rode a short distance over a stony upland, and then descended into a long cultivated valley, running to the eastward. At the end nearest us appeared the village of Aboo 'l Ghosh (the Father of Lies), which takes its name from a noted Bedouin shekh, who distinguished himself a few years ago by levying contributions on travellers. He obtained a large sum of money in this way, but as he added murder to robbery, and fell upon Turks as well as Christians, he was finally captured, and is now expiating his offences in some mine on the coast of the Black Sea.

Near the bottom of the village there is a large ruined building, now used as a stable by the inhabitants. The interior is divided into a nave and two side-aisles by rows of square pillars, from which spring pointed arches. The door-way is at the side, and is Gothic, with a dash of Saracenic in the ornamental mouldings above it. The large window at the extremity of the nave is remarkable for having round arches, which circumstance, together with the traces of arabesque painted ornaments on the columns, led me to think it might have been a mosque; but Dr. Robinson, who is now here, considers it a Christian church, of the time of the Crusaders. The village of Aboo 'l Ghosh is said to be the site of the birth-place of the Prophet Jeremiah, and I can well imagine it to have been the case. The aspect of the mountain-country to the east and north-east would explain the savage dreariness of his lamentations. The whole valley in which the village stands, as well as another which joins it on the east, is most assiduously cultivated. The stony mountain sides are wrought into terraces, where, in spite of soil which resembles an American turnpike, patches of wheat are growing luxuriantly, and olive trees, centuries old, hold on to the rocks with a clutch as hard and bony as the hand of Death. In the bed of the valley the fig tree thrives, and sometimes the vine and fig grow together, forming the patriarchal arbor of shade familiar to us all. The shoots of the tree are still young and green, but the blossoms of the grape do not yet give forth their goodly savor. I did not hear the voice of the turtle, but a nightingale sang in the briery thickets by the brook side, as we passed along.

Climbing out of this valley, we descended by a stony staircase, as rugged as the Ladder of Tyre, into the Wady Beit-Hanineh. Here were gardens of oranges in blossom, with orchards of quince and apple, overgrown with vines, and the fragrant hawthorn tree, snowy with its bloom. A stone bridge, the only one on the road, crosses the dry bed of a winter stream, and, looking up the glen, I saw the Arab village of Kulonieh, at the entrance of the valley of Elah, glorious with the memories of the shepherd-boy, David. Our road turned off to the right, and commenced ascending a long, dry glen between mountains which grew more sterile the further we went. It was nearly two hours past noon, the sun fiercely hot, and our horses were nigh jaded out with the rough road and our impatient spurring. I began to fancy we could see Jerusalem from the top of the pass, and tried to think of the ancient days of

Judea. But it was in vain. A newer picture shut them out, and banished even the diviner images of Our Saviour and His Disciples. Heathen that I was, I could only think of Godfrey and the Crusaders, toiling up the same path, and the ringing lines of Tasso vibrated constantly in my ear:

"Ecco apparir Gierusalemm' si vede;

Ecco additar Gierusalemm' si scorge;

Ecco da mille voci unitamente,

Gierusalemme salutar si sente!"

The Palestine of the Bible--the Land of Promise to the Israelites, the land of Miracle and Sacrifice to the Apostles and their followers--still slept in the unattainable distance, under a sky of bluer and more tranquil loveliness than that to whose cloudless vault I looked up. It lay as far and beautiful as it once seemed to the eye of childhood, and the swords of Seraphim kept profane feet from its sacred hills. But these rough rocks around me, these dry, fiery hollows, these thickets of ancient oak and ilex, had heard the trumpets of the Middle Ages, and the clang and clatter of European armor--I could feel and believe that. I entered the ranks; I followed the trumpets and the holy hymns, and waited breathlessly for the moment when every mailed knee should drop in the dust, and every bearded and sunburned cheek be wet with devotional tears.

But when I climbed the last ridge, and looked ahead with a sort of painful suspense, Jerusalem did not appear. We were two thousand feet above the Mediterranean, whose blue we could dimly see far to the west, through notches in the chain of hills. To the north, the mountains were gray, desolate, and awful. Not a shrub or a tree relieved their frightful barrenness. An upland tract, covered with white volcanic rock, lay before us. We met peasants with asses, who looked (to my eyes) as if they had just left Jerusalem. Still forward we urged our horses, and reached a ruined garden, surrounded with hedges of cactus, over which I saw domes and walls in the distance. I drew a long breath and looked at François. He was jogging along without turning his head; he could not have been so indifferent if that was really the city. Presently, we reached another slight rise in the rocky plain. He began to urge his panting horse, and at the same instant we both lashed the spirit into ours, dashed on at a break-neck gallop, round the corner of an old wall on the top of the hill, and lo! the Holy City! Our Greek jerked both pistols from his holsters, and fired them into the air, as we reined up on the steep.

From the descriptions of travellers, I had expected to see in Jerusalem an ordinary modern Turkish town; but that before me, with its walls, fortresses, and domes, was it not still the City of David? I saw the Jerusalem of the New Testament, as I had imagined it. Long lines of walls crowned with a notched parapet and strengthened by towers; a few domes and spires above them; clusters of cypress here and there; this was all that was visible of the city. On either side the hill sloped down to the two deep valleys over which it hangs. On the east, the Mount of Olives, crowned with a chapel and mosque, rose high and steep, but in front, the eye passed directly over the city, to rest far away upon the lofty mountains of Moab, beyond the Dead Sea. The scene was grand in its simplicity. The prominent colors were the purple of those distant mountains, and the hoary gray of the nearer hills. The walls were of the dull yellow of weather-stained marble, and the only trees, the dark cypress and moonlit olive. Now, indeed, for one brief moment, I knew that I was in Palestine; that I saw Mount Olivet and Mount Zion; and--I know not how it was--my sight grew weak, and all objects trembled and wavered in a watery film. Since we arrived, I have looked down upon the city from the Mount of Olives, and up to it from the Valley of Jehosaphat; but I cannot restore the illusion of that first view.

We allowed our horses to walk slowly down the remaining half-mile to the Jaffa gate. An Englishman, with a red silk shawl over his head, was sketching the city, while an Arab held an umbrella over him. Inside the gate we stumbled upon an Italian shop with an Italian sign, and after threading a number of intricate passages under dark archways, and being turned off from one hotel, which was full of travellers, reached another, kept by a converted German Jew, where we found Dr. Robinson and Dr. Ely Smith, who both arrived yesterday. It sounds strange to talk of a hotel in Jerusalem, but the world is progressing, and there are already three. I leave to-morrow for Jericho, the Jordan, and the Dead Sea, and shall have more to say of Jerusalem on my return.

425

Chapter IV. The Dead Sea and the Jordan River.

Bargaining for a Guard--Departure from Jerusalem--The Hill of Offence--Bethany--The Grotto of Lazarus--The Valley of Fire--Scenery of the Wilderness--The Hills of Engaddi--The shore of the Dead Sea--A Bituminous Bath--Gallop to the Jordan--A watch for Robbers--The Jordan--Baptism--The Plains of Jericho--The Fountain of Elisha--The Mount of Temptation--Return to Jerusalem.

"And the spoiler shall come upon every city, and no city shall escape; the valley also shall perish and the plain shall be destroyed, as the Lord hath spoken."

--Jeremiah, xlviii. 8.

Jerusalem, *May* 1, 1852.

I returned this after noon from an excursion to the Dead Sea, the River Jordan, and the site of Jericho. Owing to the approaching heats, an early visit was deemed desirable, and the shekhs, who have charge of the road, were summoned to meet us on the day after we arrived. There are two of these gentlemen, the Shekh el-Aràb (of the Bedouins), and the Shekh el-Fellaheen (of the peasants, or husbandmen), to whom each traveller is obliged to pay one hundred piastres for an escort. It is, in fact, a sort of compromise, by which the shekhs agree not to rob the traveller, and to protect him against other shekhs. If the road is not actually safe, the Turkish garrison here is a mere farce, but the arrangement is winked at by the Pasha, who, of course, gets his share of the 100,000 piastres which the two scamps yearly levy upon travellers. The shekhs came to our rooms, and after trying to postpone our departure, in order to attach other tourists to the same escort, and thus save a little expense, took half the pay and agreed to be ready the next morning. Unfortunately for my original plan, the Convent of San Saba has been closed within two or three weeks, and no stranger is now admitted. This unusual step was caused by the disorderly conduct of some Frenchmen who visited San Saba. We sent to the Bishop of the Greek Church, asking a simple permission to view the interior of the Convent; but without effect.

We left the city yesterday morning by St. Stephen's Gate, descended to the Valley of Jehosaphat, rode under the stone wall which encloses the supposed Gethsemane, and took a path leading along the Mount of Olives, towards the Hill of Offence, which stands over against the southern end of the city, opposite the mouth of the Vale of Hinnon. Neither of the shekhs made his appearance, but sent in their stead three Arabs, two of whom were mounted and armed with sabres and long guns. Our man, Mustapha, had charge of the baggage-mule, carrying our tent and the provisions for the trip. It was a dull, sultry morning; a dark, leaden haze hung over Jerusalem, and the khamseen, or sirocco-wind, came from the south-west, out of the Arabian Desert. We had again resumed the Oriental costume, but in spite of an ample turban, my face soon began to scorch in the dry heat. From the crest of the Hill of Offence there is a wide view over the heights on both sides of the valley of the Brook Kedron. Their sides are worked into terraces, now green with springing grain, and near the bottom planted with olive and fig trees. The upland ridge or watershed of Palestine is cultivated for a considerable distance around Jerusalem. The soil is light and stony, yet appears to yield a good return for the little labor bestowed upon it.

Crossing the southern flank of Mount Olivet, in half an hour we reached the village of Bethany, hanging on the side of the hill. It is a miserable cluster of Arab huts, with not a building which appears to be more than a century old. The Grotto of Lazarus is here shown, and, of course, we stopped to see it. It belongs to an old Mussulman, who came out of his house with a piece of waxed rope, to light us down. An aperture opens from the roadside into the hill, and there is barely room enough for a person to enter. Descending about twenty steps at a sharp angle, we landed in a small, damp vault, with an opening in the floor, communicating with a short passage below. The vault was undoubtedly excavated for sepulchral purposes, and the bodies were probably deposited (as in many Egyptian tombs) in the pit under it. Our guide, however, pointed to a square mass of masonry in one corner as the tomb of Lazarus, whose body, he informed us, was still walled up there. There was an arch in the side of the vault, once leading to other chambers, but now closed up, and the guide stated that seventy-four Prophets were interred therein. There seems to be no doubt that the present Arab village occupies the site of Bethany; and if it could be proved that this pit existed at the beginning of the Christian Era, and there never had been any other, we might accept it as the tomb of Lazarus. On the crest of a high hill, over against Bethany, is an Arab village on the site of Bethpage.

We descended into the valley of a winter stream, now filled with patches of sparse wheat, just beginning to ripen. The mountains grew more bleak and desolate as we advanced, and as there is a regular descent in the several ranges over which one must pass, the distant hills of the lands of Moab and Ammon were always in sight, rising like a high, blue wall against the sky. The Dead Sea is 4,000 feet below Jerusalem, but the general slope of the intervening district is so regular that from the spires of the city, and the Mount of Olives, one can look down directly upon its waters. This deceived me as to the actual distance, and I could scarcely credit the assertion of our Arab escort, that it would require six hours to reach it. After we had ridden nearly two hours, we left the Jericho road, sending Mustapha and a staunch old Arab direct to our resting-place for the night, in the Valley of the Jordan. The two mounted Bedouins accompanied us across the rugged mountains lying between us and the Dead Sea.

At first, we took the way to the Convent of Mar Saba, following the course of the Brook Kedron down the Wady en-Nar (Valley of Fire). In half an hour more we reached two large tanks, hewn out under the base of a limestone cliff, and nearly filled with rain. The surface was covered with a greenish vegetable scum, and three wild and dirty Arabs of the hills were washing themselves in the principal one. Our Bedouins immediately dismounted and followed their example, and after we had taken some refreshment, we had the satisfaction of filling our water-jug from the same sweet pool. After this, we left the San Saba road, and mounted the height east of the valley. From that point, all signs of cultivation and habitation disappeared. The mountains were grim, bare, and frightfully rugged. The scanty grass, coaxed into life by the winter rains, was already scorched out of all greenness; some bunches of wild sage, gnaphalium, and other hardy aromatic herbs spotted the yellow soil, and in sheltered places the scarlet poppies burned like coals of fire among the rifts of the gray limestone rock. Our track kept along the higher ridges and crests of the hills, between the glens and gorges which sank on either hand to a dizzy depth below, and were so steep as to be almost inaccessible. The region is so scarred, gashed and torn, that no work of man's hand can save it from perpetual desolation. It is a wilderness more hopeless than the Desert. If I were left alone in the midst of it, I should lie down and await death, without thought or hope of rescue.

The character of the day was peculiarly suited to enhance the impression of such scenery. Though there were no clouds, the sun was invisible: as far as we could see, beyond the Jordan, and away southward to the mountains of Moab and the cliffs of Engaddi, the whole country was covered as with the smoke of a furnace; and the furious sirocco, that threatened to topple us down the gulfs yawning on either hand, had no coolness on its wings. The horses were sure-footed, but now and then a gust would come that made them and us strain against it, to avoid being dashed against the rock on one side, or hurled off the brink on the other. The atmosphere was painfully oppressive, and by and by a dogged silence took possession of our party. After passing a lofty peak which François called Djebel Nuttar, the Mountain of Rain, we came to a large Moslem building, situated on a bleak eminence, overlooking part of the valley of the Jordan. This is the tomb called Nebbee Moussa by the Arabs, and believed by them to stand upon the spot where Moses died. We halted at the gate, but no one came to admit us, though my companion thought he saw a man's head at one of the apertures in the wall. Arab tradition here is as much at fault as Christian tradition in many other places. The true Nebo is somewhere in the chain of Pisgah; and though, probably, I saw it, and all see it who go down to the Jordan, yet "no man knoweth its place unto this day."

Beyond Nebbee Moussa, we came out upon the last heights overlooking the Dead Sea, though several miles of low hills remained to be passed. The head of the sea was visible as far as the Ras-el-Feshka on the west; and the hot fountains of Callirhoë on the eastern shore. Farther than this, all was vapor and darkness. The water was a soft, deep purple hue, brightening into blue.

Our road led down what seemed a vast sloping causeway from the mountains, between two ravines, walled by cliffs several hundred feet in height. It gradually flattened into a plain, covered with a white, saline incrustation, and grown with clumps of sour willow, tamarisk, and other shrubs, among which I looked in vain for the osher, or Dead Sea apple. The plants appeared as if smitten with leprosy; but there were some flowers growing almost to the margin of the sea. We reached the shore about 2 P.M. The heat by this time was most severe, and the air so dense as to occasion pains in my ears. The Dead Sea is 1,300 feet below the Mediterranean, and without doubt the lowest part of the earth's surface. I attribute the oppression I felt to this fact and to the sultriness of the day, rather than to any exhalation from the sea itself. François remarked, however, that had the wind--which by this time was veering round to the north-east--blown from the south, we could scarcely have endured it. The sea resembles a great cauldron, sunk between mountains from three to four thousand feet in height; and probably we did not experience more than a tithe of the summer heat.

I proposed a bath, for the sake of experiment, but François endeavored to dissuade us. He had tried it, and nothing could be more disagreeable; we risked getting a fever, and, besides, there were four hours of dangerous travel yet before us. But by this time we were half undressed, and soon were floating on the clear bituminous waves. The beach was fine gravel and shelved gradually down. I kept my turban on my head, and was careful to avoid touching the water with my face. The sea was moderately warm and gratefully soft and soothing to the skin. It was impossible to sink; and even while swimming, the body rose half out of the water. I should think it possible to dive for a short distance, but prefer that some one else would try the experiment. With a log of wood for a pillow, one might sleep as on one of the patent mattresses. The taste of the water is salty and pungent, and stings the tongue like saltpetre. We were obliged to dress in all haste, without even wiping off the detestable liquid; yet I experienced very little of that discomfort which most travellers have remarked. Where the skin had been previously bruised, there was a slight smarting sensation, and my body felt clammy and glutinous, but the bath was rather refreshing than otherwise.

We turned our horses' heads towards the Jordan, and rode on over

430

a dry, barren plain. The two Bedouins at first dashed ahead at full gallop, uttering cries, and whirling their long guns in the air. The dust they raised was blown in our faces, and contained so much salt that my eyes began to smart painfully. Thereupon I followed them at an equal rate of speed, and we left a long cloud of the accursed soil whirling behind us. Presently, however, they fell to the rear, and continued to keep at some distance from us. The reason of this was soon explained. The path turned eastward, and we already saw a line of dusky green winding through the wilderness. This was the Jordan, and the mountains beyond, the home of robber Arabs, were close at hand. Those robbers frequently cross the river and conceal themselves behind the sand-hills on this side. Our brave escort was, therefore, inclined to put us forward as a forlorn-hope, and secure their own retreat in case of an attack. But as we were all well armed, and had never considered their attendance as anything more than a genteel way of buying them off from robbing us, we allowed them to lag as much as they chose. Finally, as we approached the Pilgrims' Ford, one of them took his station at some distance from the river, on the top of a mound, while the other got behind some trees near at hand; in order, as they said, to watch the opposite hills, and alarm us whenever they should see any of the Beni Sukrs, or the Beni Adwams, or the Tyakh, coming down upon us.

The Jordan at this point will not average more than ten yards in breadth. It flows at the bottom of a gully about fifteen feet deep, which traverses the broad valley in a most tortuous course. The water has a white, clayey hue, and is very swift. The changes of the current have formed islands and beds of soil here and there, which are covered with a dense growth of ash, poplar, willow, and tamarisk trees. The banks of the river are bordered with thickets, now overgrown with wild vines, and fragrant with flowering plants. Birds sing continually in the cool, dark coverts of the trees. I found a singular charm in the wild, lonely, luxuriant banks, the tangled undergrowth, and the rapid, brawling course of the sacred stream, as it slipped in sight and out of sight among the trees. It is almost impossible to reach the water at any other point than the Ford of the Pilgrims, the supposed locality of the passage of the Israelites and the baptism of Christ. The plain near it is still blackened by the camp-fires of the ten thousand pilgrims who went down from Jerusalem three weeks ago, to bathe. We tied our horses to the trees, and prepared to follow their example, which was necessary, if only to wash off the iniquitous slime of the Dead Sea. François, in the meantime, filled two tin flasks from the stream and stowed them in the saddle-bags. The current was so swift, that one could not venture far without the risk of being carried away; but I succeeded in obtaining a complete and most refreshing immersion. The taint of Gomorrah was not entirely washed away, but I rode off with as great a sense of relief as if the baptism had been a moral one, as well, and had purified me from sin.

We rode for nearly two hours, in a north-west direction, to the Bedouin village of Rihah, near the site of ancient Jericho. Before reaching it, the gray salt waste vanishes, and the soil is covered with grass and herbs. The barren character of the first region is evidently owing to deposits from the vapors of the Dead Sea, as they are blown over the plain by the south wind. The channels of streams around Jericho are filled with nebbuk trees, the fruit of which is just ripening. It is apparently indigenous, and grows more luxuriantly than on the White Nile. It is a variety of the rhamnus, and is set down by botanists as the Spina Christi, of which the Saviour's mock crown of thorns was made. I see no reason to doubt this, as the twigs are long and pliant, and armed with small, though most cruel, thorns. I had to pay for gathering some of the fruit, with a torn dress and bleeding fingers. The little apples which it bears are slightly acid and excellent for alleviating thirst. I also noticed on the plain a variety of the nightshade with large berries of a golden color. The spring flowers, so plentiful now in all other parts of Palestine, have already disappeared from the Valley of the Jordan.

Rihah is a vile little village of tents and mud-huts, and the only relic of antiquity near it is a square tower, which may possibly be of the time of Herod. There are a few gardens in the place, and a grove of superb fig-trees. We found our tent already pitched beside a rill which issues from the Fountain of Elisha. The evening was very sultry, and the musquitoes gave us no rest. We purchased some milk from an old man who came to the tent, but such was his mistrust of us that he refused to let us keep the earthen vessel containing it until morning. As we had already paid the money to his son, we would not let him take the milk away until he had brought the money

432

back. He then took a dagger from his waist and threw it before us as security, while he carried off the vessel and returned the price. I have frequently seen the same mistrustful spirit exhibited in Egypt. Our two Bedouins, to whom I gave some tobacco in the evening, manifested their gratitude by stealing the remainder of our stock during the night.

This morning we followed the stream to its source, the Fountain of Elisha, so called as being probably that healed by the Prophet. If so, the healing was scarcely complete. The water, which gushes up strong and free at the foot of a rocky mound, is warm and slightly brackish. It spreads into a shallow pool, shaded by a fine sycamore tree. Just below, there are some remains of old walls on both sides, and the stream goes roaring away through a rank jungle of canes fifteen feet in height. The precise site of Jericho, I believe, has not been fixed, but "the city of the palm trees," as it was called, was probably on the plain, near some mounds which rise behind the Fountain. Here there are occasional traces of foundation walls, but so ruined as to give no clue to the date of their erection. Further towards the mountain there are some arches, which appear to be Saracenic. As we ascended again into the hill-country, I observed several traces of cisterns in the bottoms of ravines, which collect the rains. Herod, as is well known, built many such cisterns near Jericho, where he had a palace. On the first crest, to which we climbed, there is part of a Roman tower yet standing. The view, looking back over the valley of Jordan, is magnificent, extending from the Dead Sea to the mountains of Gilead, beyond the country of Ammon. I thought I could trace the point where the River Yabbok comes down from Mizpeh of Gilead to join the Jordan.

The wilderness we now entered was fully as barren, but less rugged than that through which we passed yesterday. The path ascended along the brink of a deep gorge, at the bottom of which a little stream foamed over the rocks. The high, bleak summits towards which we were climbing, are considered by some Biblical geographers to be Mount Quarantana, the scene of Christ's fasting and temptation. After two hours we reached the ruins of a large khan or hostlery, under one of the peaks, which François stated to be the veritable "high mountain" whence the Devil pointed out all the kingdoms of the earth. There is a cave in the rock beside the road, which the superstitious look upon as the orifice out of which his Satanic Majesty issued. We met large numbers of Arab families, with their flocks, descending from the mountains to take up their summer residence near the Jordan. They were all on foot, except the young children and goats, which were stowed together on the backs of donkeys. The men were armed, and appeared to be of the same tribe as our escort, with whom they had a good understanding.

The morning was cold and cloudy, and we hurried on over the hills to a fountain in the valley of the Brook Kedron, where we breakfasted. Before we had reached Bethany a rain came down, and the sky hung dark and lowering over Jerusalem, as we passed the crest of Mount Olivet. It still rains, and the filthy condition of the city exceeds anything I have seen, even in the Orient.

Chapter V. The City of Christ.

Modern Jerusalem--The Site of the City--Mount Zion--Mount Moriah--The Temple--the Valley of Jehosaphat--The Olives of Gethsemane--The Mount of Olives--Moslem Tradition--Panorama from the Summit--The Interior of the City--The Population--Missions and Missionaries--Christianity in Jerusalem--Intolerance--The Jews of Jerusalem--The Face of Christ--The Church of the Holy Sepulchre--The Holy of Holies--The Sacred Localities--Visions of Christ--The Mosque of Omar--The Holy Man of Timbuctoo--Preparations for Departure.

"Cut off thy hair, O Jerusalem, and cast it away, and take up a lamentation in high places; for the Lord hath rejected and forsaken the generation of his wrath."--Jeremiah vii. 29.

"Here pilgrims roam, that strayed so far to seek

In Golgotha him dead, who lives in Heaven."

Milton.

Jerusalem, *Monday, May* 3, 1852.

Since travel is becoming a necessary part of education, and a journey through the East is no longer attended with personal risk, Jerusalem will soon be as familiar a station on the grand tour as Paris or Naples. The task of describing it is already next to superfluous, so thoroughly has the topography of the city been laid down by the surveys of Robinson and the drawings of Roberts. There is little more left for Biblical research. The few places which can be authenticated are now generally accepted, and the many doubtful ones must always be the subjects of speculation and conjecture. There is no new light which can remove the cloud of uncertainties wherein one continually wanders. Yet, even rejecting all these with the most skeptical spirit, there still remains enough to make the place sacred in the eyes of every follower of Christ. The city stands on the ancient site; the Mount of Olives looks down upon it; the foundations of the Temple of Solomon are on Mount

Moriah; the Pool of Siloam has still a cup of water for those who at noontide go down to the Valley of Jehosaphat; the ancient gate yet looketh towards Damascus, and of the Palace of Herod, there is a tower which Time and Turk and Crusader have spared.

Jerusalem is built on the summit ridge of the hill-country of Palestine, just where it begins to slope eastward. Not half a mile from the Jaffa Gate, the waters run towards the Mediterranean. It is about 2,700 feet above the latter, and 4,000 feet above the Dead Sea, to which the descent is much more abrupt. The hill, or rather group of small mounts, on which Jerusalem stands, slants eastward to the brink of the Valley of Jehosaphat, and the Mount of Olives rises opposite, from the sides and summit of which, one sees the entire city spread out like a map before him. The Valley of Hinnon, the bed of which is on a much higher level than that of Jehosaphat, skirts the south-western and southern part of the walls, and drops into the latter valley at the foot of Mount Zion, the most southern of the mounts. The steep slope at the junction of the two valleys is the site of the city of the Jebusites, the most ancient part of Jerusalem. It is now covered with garden-terraces, the present wall crossing from Mount Zion on the south to Mount Moriah on the east. A little glen, anciently called the Tyropeon, divides the mounts, and winds through to the Damascus Gate, on the north, though from the height of the walls and the position of the city, the depression which it causes in the mass of buildings is not very perceptible, except from the latter point, Moriah is the lowest of the mounts, and hangs directly over the Valley of Jehosaphat. Its summit was built up by Solomon so as to form a quadrangular terrace, five hundred by three hundred yards in dimension. The lower courses of the grand wall, composed of huge blocks of gray conglomerate limestone, still remain, and there seems to be no doubt that they are of the time of Solomon. Some of the stones are of enormous size; I noticed several which were fifteen, and one twenty-two feet in length. The upper part of the wall was restored by Sultan Selim, the conqueror of Egypt, and the level of the terrace now supports the great Mosque of Omar, which stands on the very site of the temple. Except these foundation walls, the Damascus Gate and the Tower of Hippicus, there is nothing left of the ancient city. The length of the present wall of circumference is about two miles, but the circuit of Jerusalem, in the time of Herod, was probably double that distance.

The best views of the city are from the Mount of Olives, and the hill north of it, whence Titus directed the siege which resulted in its total destruction. The Crusaders under Godfrey of Bouillon encamped on the same hill. My first walk after reaching here, was to the summit of the Mount of Olives. Not far from the hotel we came upon the Via Dolorosa, up which, according to Catholic tradition, Christ toiled with the cross upon his shoulders. I found it utterly impossible to imagine that I was walking in the same path, and preferred doubting the tradition. An arch is built across the street at the spot where they say he was shown to the populace. (Ecce Homo.) The passage is steep and rough, descending to St. Stephen's Gate by the Governor's Palace, which stands on the site of the house of Pontius Pilate. Here, in the wall forming the northern part of the foundation of the temple, there are some very fine remains of ancient workmanship. From the city wall, the ground descends abruptly to the Valley of Jehosaphat. The Turkish residents have their tombs on the city side, just under the terrace of the mosque, while thousands of Jews find a peculiar beatitude in having themselves interred on the opposite slope of the Mount of Olives, which is in some places quite covered with their crumbling tombstones. The bed of the Brook Kedron is now dry and stony. A sort of chapel, built in the bottom of the valley, is supposed by the Greeks to cover the tomb of the Virgin--a claim which the Latins consider absurd. Near this, at the very foot of the Mount of Olives, the latter sect have lately built a high stone wall around the Garden of Gethsemane, for the purpose, apparently, of protecting the five aged olives. I am ignorant of the grounds wherefore Gethsemane is placed here. Most travellers have given their faith to the spot, but Dr. Robinson, who is more reliable than any amount of mere tradition, does not coincide with them. The trees do not appear as ancient as some of those at the foot of Mount Carmel, which are supposed to date from the Roman colony established by Titus. Moreover, it is well known that at the time of the taking of Jerusalem by that Emperor, all the trees, for many miles around, were destroyed. The olive-trees, therefore, cannot be those under which Christ rested, even supposing this to be the true site of Gethseniane.

The Mount of Olives is a steep and rugged hill, dominating over the city and the surrounding heights. It is still covered with olive orchards, and planted with patches of grain, which do not thrive well on the stony soil. On the summit is a mosque, with a minaret attached, which affords a grand panoramic view. As we reached it, the Chief of the College of Dervishes, in the court of the Mosque of Omar, came out with a number of attendants. He saluted us courteously, which would not have been the case had he been the Superior of the Latin Convent, and we Greek Monks. There were some Turkish ladies in the interior of the mosque, so that we could not gain admittance, and therefore did not see the rock containing the foot-prints of Christ, who, according to Moslem tradition, ascended to heaven from this spot. The Mohammedans, it may not be generally known, accept the history of Christ, except his crucifixion, believing that he passed to heaven without death, another person being crucified in his stead. They call him the Roh-Allah, or Spirit of God, and consider him, after Mahomet, as the holiest of the Prophets.

We ascended to the gallery of the minaret. The city lay opposite, so fairly spread out to our view that almost every house might be separately distinguished. It is a mass of gray buildings, with dome-roofs, and but for the mosques of Omar and El Aksa, with the courts and galleries around them, would be exceedingly tame in appearance. The only other prominent points are the towers of the Holy Sepulchre, the citadel, enclosing Herod's Tower, and the mosque on mount Zion. The Turkish wall, with its sharp angles, its square bastions, and the long, embrasured lines of its parapet, is the most striking feature of the view. Stony hills stretch away from the city on all sides, at present cheered with tracts of springing wheat, but later in the season, brown and desolate. In the south, the convent of St. Elias is visible, and part of the little town of Bethlehem. I passed to the eastern side of the gallery, and looking thence, deep down among the sterile mountains, beheld a long sheet of blue water, its southern extremity vanishing in a hot, sulphury haze. The mountains of Ammon and Moab, which formed the background of my first view of Jerusalem, leaned like a vast wall against the sky, beyond the mysterious sea and the broad valley of the Jordan. The great depression of this valley below the level of the Mediterranean gives it a most remarkable character. It appears even deeper than is actually the case, and resembles an enormous chasm or moat, separating two different regions of the earth. The khamseen was blowing from the south, from out the deserts of Edom, and threw its veil of fiery vapor over the landscape. The muezzin pointed out to me the location of Jericho, of Kerak in Moab, and Es-Salt in the country of Ammon. Ere long the shadow of the minaret denoted noon, and, placing his hands on both sides of his mouth, he cried out, first on the South side, towards Mecca, and then to the West, and North, and East: "God is great: there is no God but God, and Mohammed is His Prophet! Let us prostrate ourselves before Him: and to Him alone be the glory!"

Jerusalem, internally, gives no impression but that of filth, ruin, poverty, and degradation. There are two or three streets in the western or higher portion of the city which are tolerably clean, but all the others, to the very gates of the Holy Sepulchre, are channels of pestilence. The Jewish Quarter, which is the largest, so sickened and disgusted me, that I should rather go the whole round of the city walls than pass through it a second time. The bazaars are poor, compared with those of other Oriental cities of the same size, and the principal trade seems to be in rosaries, both Turkish and Christian, crosses, seals, amulets, and pieces of the Holy Sepulchre. The population, which may possibly reach 20,000, is apparently Jewish, for the most part; at least, I have been principally struck with the Hebrew face, in my walks. The number of Jews has increased considerably within a few years, and there is also quite a number who, having been converted to Protestantism, were brought hither at the expense of English missionary societies for the purpose of forming a Protestant community. Two of the hotels are kept by families of this class. It is estimated that each member of the community has cost the Mission about £4,500: a sum which would have Christianized tenfold the number of English heathen. The Mission, however, is kept up by its patrons, as a sort of religious luxury. The English have lately built a very handsome church within the walls, and the Rev. Dr. Gobat, well known by his missionary labors in Abyssinia, now has the title of Bishop of Jerusalem. A friend of his in Central Africa gave me a letter of introduction for him, and I am quite disappointed in finding him absent. Dr. Barclay, of Virginia, a most worthy man in every respect, is at the head of the American Mission here. There is, besides, what is called the "American Colony," at the village of Artos, near Bethlehem: a little community of religious enthusiasts, whose experiments in cultivation have met with remarkable success, and are much spoken of at present.

Whatever good the various missions here may, in time, accomplish (at present, it does not amount to much), Jerusalem is the last place in the world where an intelligent heathen would be converted to Christianity. Were I cast here, ignorant of any religion, and were I to compare the lives and practices of the different sects as the means of making my choice--in short, to judge of each faith by the conduct of its professors--I should at once turn Mussulman. When you consider that in the Holy Sepulchre there are nineteen chapels, each belonging to a different sect, calling itself Christian, and that a Turkish police is always stationed there to prevent the bloody quarrels which often ensue between them, you may judge how those who call themselves followers of the Prince of Peace practice the pure faith he sought to establish. Between the Greek and Latin churches, especially, there is a deadly feud, and their contentions are a scandal, not only to the few Christians here, but to the Moslems themselves. I believe there is a sort of truce at present, owing to the settlement of some of the disputes--as, for instance, the restoration of the silver star, which the Greeks stole from the shrine of the Nativity, at Bethlehem. The Latins, however, not long since, demolished, vi et armis, a chapel which the Greeks commenced building on Mount Zion. But, if the employment of material weapons has been abandoned for the time, there is none the less a war of words and of sounds still going on. Go into the Holy Sepulchre, when mass is being celebrated, and you can scarcely endure the din. No sooner does the Greek choir begin its shrill chant, than the Latins fly to the assault. They have an organ, and terribly does that organ strain its bellows and labor its pipes to drown the rival singing. You think the Latins will carry the day, when suddenly the cymbals of the Abyssinians strike in with harsh brazen clang, and, for the moment, triumph. Then there are Copts, and Maronites, and Armenians, and I know not how many other sects, who must have their share; and the service that should be a many-toned harmony pervaded by one grand spirit of devotion, becomes a discordant orgie, befitting the rites of Belial.

A long time ago--I do not know the precise number of years--the Sultan granted a firman, in answer to the application of both Jews and Christians, allowing the members of each sect to put to death any person belonging to the other sect, who should be found inside of their churches or synagogues. The firman has never been recalled, though in every place but Jerusalem it remains a dead letter. Here, although the Jews freely permit Christians to enter their synagogue, a Jew who should enter the Holy Sepulchre would be lucky if he escaped with his life. Not long since, an English gentleman, who was taken by the monks for a Jew, was so severely beaten that he was confined to his bed for two months. What worse than scandal, what abomination, that the spot looked upon by so many Christians as the most awfully sacred on earth, should be the scene of such brutish intolerance! I never pass the group of Turkish officers, quietly smoking their long pipes and sipping their coffee within the vestibule of the Church, without a feeling of humiliation. Worse than the money-changers whom Christ scourged out of the Temple, the guardians of this edifice make use of His crucifixion and resurrection as a means of gain. You may buy a piece of the stone covering the Holy Sepulchre, duly certified by the Greek Patriarch of Jerusalem, for about $7. At Bethlehem, which I visited this morning, the Latin monk who showed us the manger, the pit where 12,000 innocents were buried, and other things, had much less to say of the sacredness or authenticity of the place, than of the injustice of allowing the Greeks a share in its possession.

The native Jewish families in Jerusalem, as well as those in other parts of Palestine, present a marked difference to the Jews of Europe and America. They possess the same physical characteristics--the dark, oblong eye, the prominent nose, the strongly-marked cheek and jaw--but in the latter, these traits have become harsh and coarse. Centuries devoted to the lowest and most debasing forms of traffic, with the endurance of persecution and contumely, have greatly changed and vulgarized the appearance of the race. But the Jews of the Holy City still retain a noble beauty, which proved to my mind their descent from the ancient princely houses of Israel The forehead is loftier, the eye larger and more frank in its expression, the nose more delicate in its prominence, and the face a purer oval. I have remarked the same distinction in the countenances of those Jewish families of Europe, whose members have devoted themselves to Art or Literature. Mendelssohn's was a face that might have belonged to the House of David.

On the evening of my arrival in the city, as I set out to walk through the bazaars, I encountered a native Jew, whose face will haunt me for the rest of my life. I was sauntering slowly along, asking myself "Is this Jerusalem?" when, lifting my eyes, they met those of Christ! It was the very face which Raphael has painted--the traditional features of the Saviour, as they are recognised and accepted by all Christendom. The waving brown hair, partly hidden by a Jewish cap, fell clustering about the ears; the face was the most perfect oval, and almost feminine in the purity of its outline; the serene, child-like mouth was shaded with a light moustache, and a silky brown beard clothed the chin; but the eyes--shall I ever look into such orbs again? Large, dark, unfathomable, they beamed with an expression of divine love and divine sorrow, such as I never before saw in human face. The man had just emerged from a dark archway, and the golden glow of the sunset, reflected from a white wall above, fell upon his face. Perhaps it was this transfiguration which made his beauty so unearthly; but, during the moment that I saw him, he was to me a revelation of the Saviour. There are still miracles in the Land of Judah. As the dusk gathered in the deep streets, I could see nothing but the ineffable sweetness and benignity of that countenance, and my friend was not a little astonished, if not shocked, when I said to him, with the earnestness of belief, on my return: "I have just seen Christ."

I made the round of the Holy Sepulchre on Sunday, while the monks were celebrating the festival of the Invention of the Cross, in the chapel of the Empress Helena. As the finding of the cross by the Empress is almost the only authority for the places inclosed within the Holy Sepulchre, I went there inclined to doubt their authenticity, and came away with my doubt vastly strengthened. The building is a confused labyrinth of chapels, choirs, shrines, staircases, and vaults--without any definite plan or any architectural beauty, though very rich in parts and full of picturesque effects. Golden lamps continually burn before the sacred places, and you rarely visit the church without seeing some procession of monks, with crosses, censers, and tapers, threading the shadowy passages, from shrine to shrine It is astonishing how many localities are assembled under one roof. At first, you are shown, the stone on which Christ rested from the burden of the cross; then, the place where the soldiers cast lots for His garments, both of them adjoining the

Sepulchre. After seeing this, you are taken to the Pillar of Flagellation; the stocks; the place of crowning with thorns; the spot where He met His mother; the cave where the Empress Helena found the cross; and, lastly, the summit of Mount Calvary. The Sepulchre is a small marble building in the centre of the church. We removed our shoes at the entrance, and were taken by a Greek monk, first into a sort of ante-chamber, lighted with golden lamps, and having in the centre, inclosed in a case of marble, the stone on which the angel sat. Stooping through a low door, we entered the Sepulchre itself. Forty lamps of gold burn unceasingly above the white marble slab, which, as the monks say, protects the stone whereon the body of Christ was laid. As we again emerged, our guide led us up a flight of steps to a second story, in which stood a shrine, literally blazing with gold. Kneeling on the marble floor, he removed a golden shield, and showed us the hole in the rock of Calvary, where the cross was planted. Close beside it was the fissure produced by the earthquake which followed the Crucifixion. But, to my eyes, aided by the light of the dim wax taper, it was no violent rupture, such as an earthquake would produce, and the rock did not appear to be the same as that of which Jerusalem is built. As we turned to leave, a monk appeared with a bowl of sacred rose-water, which he sprinkled on our hands, bestowing a double portion on a rosary of sandal-wood which I carried But it was a Mohammedan rosary, brought from Mecca, and containing the sacred number of ninety-nine beads.

I have not space here to state all the arguments for and against the localities in the Holy Sepulchre, I came to the conclusion that none of them were authentic, and am glad to have the concurrence of such distinguished authority as Dr. Robinson. So far from this being a matter of regret, I, for one, rejoice that those sacred spots are lost to the world. Christianity does not need them, and they are spared a daily profanation in the name of religion. We know that Christ has walked on the Mount of Olives, and gone down to the Pool of Siloam, and tarried in Bethany; we know that here, within the circuit of our vision, He has suffered agony and death, and that from this little point went out all the light that has made the world greater and happier and better in its later than in its earlier days.

Yet, I must frankly confess, in wandering through this city--revered alike by Christians, Jews and Turks as one of the holiest in the world--I have been reminded of Christ, the Man, rather, than of Christ, the God. In the glory which overhangs Palestine afar off, we imagine emotions which never come, when we tread the soil and walk over the hallowed sites. As I toiled up the Mount of Olives, in the very footsteps of Christ, panting with the heat and the difficult ascent, I found it utterly impossible to conceive that the Deity, in human form, had walked there before me. And even at night, as I walk on the terraced roof, while the moon, "the balmy moon of blessed Israel," restores the Jerusalem of olden days to my imagination, the Saviour who then haunts my thoughts is the Man Jesus, in those moments of trial when He felt the weaknesses of our common humanity; in that agony of struggle in the garden of Gethsemane, in that still more bitter cry of human doubt and human appeal from the cross: "My God, my God, why hast Thou forsaken me!" Yet there is no reproach for this conception of the character of Christ. Better the divinely-inspired Man, the purest and most perfect of His race, the pattern and type of all that is good and holy in Humanity, than the Deity for whose intercession we pray, while we trample His teachings under our feet. It would be well for many Christian sects, did they keep more constantly before their eyes the sublime humanity of Christ. How much bitter intolerance and persecution might be spared the world, if, instead of simply adoring Him as a Divine Mediator, they would strive to walk the ways He trod on earth. But Christianity is still undeveloped, and there is yet no sect which represents its fall and perfect spirit.

It is my misfortune if I give offence by these remarks. I cannot assume emotions I do not feel, and must describe Jerusalem as I found it. Since being here, I have read the accounts of several travellers, and in many cases the devotional rhapsodies--the ecstacies of awe and reverence--in which they indulge, strike me as forced and affected. The pious writers have described what was expected of them, not what they found. It was partly from reading such accounts that my anticipations were raised too high, for the view of the city from the Jaffa road and the panorama from the Mount of Olives are the only things wherein I have been pleasantly disappointed.

By far the most interesting relic left to the city is the foundation wall

444

of Solomon's Temple. The Mosque of Omar, according to the accounts of the Turks, and Mr. Gather wood's examination, rests on immense vaults, which are believed to be the substructions of the Temple itself. Under the dome of the mosque there is a large mass of natural rock, revered by the Moslems as that from which Mahomet mounted the beast Borak when he visited the Seven Heavens, and believed by Mr. Catherwood to have served as part of the foundation of the Holy of Holies. No Christian is allowed to enter the mosque, or even its enclosure, on penalty of death, and even the firman of the Sultan has failed to obtain admission for a Frank. I have been strongly tempted to make the attempt in my Egyptian dress, which happens to resemble that of a mollah or Moslem priest, but the Dervishes in the adjoining college have sharp eyes, and my pronunciation of Arabic would betray me in case I was accosted. I even went so far as to buy a string of the large beads usually carried by a mollah, but unluckily I do not know the Moslem form of prayer, or I might carry out the plan under the guise of religious abstraction. This morning we succeeded in getting a nearer view of the mosque from the roof of the Governor's palace. François, by assuming the character of a Turkish cawass, gained us admission. The roof overlooks the entire enclosure of the Haram, and gives a complete view of the exterior of the mosque and the paved court surrounding it. There is no regularity in the style of the buildings in the enclosure, but the general effect is highly picturesque. The great dome of the mosque is the grandest in all the Orient, but the body of the edifice, made to resemble an octagonal tent, and covered with blue and white tiles, is not high enough to do it justice. The first court is paved with marble, and has four porticoes, each of five light Saracenic arches, opening into the green park, which occupies the rest of the terrace. This park is studded with cypress and fig trees, and dotted all over with the tombs of shekhs. As we were looking down on the spacious area, behold! who should come along but Shekh Mohammed Senoosee, the holy man of Timbuctoo, who had laid off his scarlet robe and donned a green one. I called down to him, whereupon he looked up and recognised us. For this reason I regret our departure from Jerusalem, as I am sure a little persuasion would induce the holy man to accompany me within the mosque.

We leave to-morrow for Damascus, by way of Nazareth and Tiberius.

445

My original plan was to have gone to Djerash, the ancient Geraza, in the land of Gilead, and thence to Bozrah, in Djebel Hauaran. But Djebel Adjeloun, as the country about Djerash is called, is under a powerful Bedouin shekh, named Abd-el Azeez, and without an escort from him, which involves considerable delay and a fee of $150, it would be impossible to make the journey. We are therefore restricted to the ordinary route, and in case we should meet with any difficulty by the way, Mr. Smith, the American Consul, who is now here, has kindly procured us a firman from the Pasha of Jerusalem. All the travellers here are making preparations to leave, but there are still two parties in the Desert.

Chapter VI. The Hill-Country of Palestine.

Leaving Jerusalem--The Tombs of the Kings--El Bireh--The Hill-Country--First View of Mount Hermon--The Tomb of Joseph--Ebal and Gerizim--The Gardens of Nablous--The Samaritans--The Sacred Book--A Scene in the Synagogue--Mentoi and Telemachus--Ride to Samaria--The Ruins of Sebaste--Scriptural Landscapes--Halt at Genin--The Plain of Esdraelon--Palestine and California--The Hills of Nazareth--Accident--Fra Joachim--The Church of the Virgin--The Shrine of the Annunciation--The Holy Places.

"Blest land of Judea! thrice hallowed of song,

Where the holiest of memories pilgrim-like throng:

In the shade of thy palms, by the shores of thy sea,

On the hills of thy beauty, my heart is with thee!"

J. G. Whittier.

Latin Convent, Nazareth, *Friday May* 7, 1852.

We left Jerusalem by the Jaffa Gate, because within a few months neither travellers nor baggage are allowed to pass the Damascus Gate, on account of smuggling operations having been carried on there. Not far from the city wall there is a superb terebinth tree, now in the full glory of its shining green leaves. It appears to be bathed in a perpetual dew; the rounded masses of foliage sparkle and glitter in the light, and the great spreading boughs flood the turf below with a deluge of delicious shade. A number of persons were reclining on the grass under it, and one of them, a very handsome Christian boy, spoke to us in Italian and English. I scarcely remember a brighter and purer day than that of our departure. The sky was a sheet of spotless blue; every rift and scar of the distant hills was retouched with a firmer pencil, and all the outlines, blurred away by the haze of the previous few days, were restored with wonderful distinctness. The temperature was hot, but not sultry, and the air we breathed was an elixir of immortality.

Through a luxuriant olive grove we reached the Tombs of the Kings, situated in a small valley to the north of the city. Part of the valley, if not the whole of it, has been formed by quarrying away the crags of marble and conglomerate limestone for building the city. Near the edge of the low cliffs overhanging it, there are some illustrations of the ancient mode of cutting stone, which, as well as the custom of excavating tombs in the rock, was evidently borrowed from Egypt. The upper surface of the rocks, was first made smooth, after which the blocks were mapped out and cut apart by grooves chiselled between them. I visited four or five tombs, each of which had a sort of vestibule or open portico in front. The door was low, and the chambers which I entered, small and black, without sculptures of any kind. The tombs bear some resemblance in their general plan to those of Thebes, except that they are without ornaments, either sculptured or painted. There are fragments of sarcophagi in some of them. On the southern side of the valley is a large quarry, evidently worked for marble, as the blocks have been cut out from below, leaving a large overhanging mass, part of which has broken off and fallen down. Some pieces which I picked up were of a very fine white marble, somewhat resembling that of Carrara. The opening of the quarry made a striking picture, the soft pink hue of the weather-stained rock contrasting exquisitely with the vivid green of the vines festooning the entrance.

From the long hill beyond the Tombs, we took our last view of Jerusalem, far beyond whose walls I saw the Church of the Nativity, at Bethlehem. The Jewish synagogue on the top of the mountain called Nebbee Samwil, the highest peak in Palestine, was visible at some distance to the west. Notwithstanding its sanctity, I felt little regret at leaving Jerusalem, and cheerfully took the rough road northward, over the stony hills. There were few habitations in sight, yet the hill-sides were cultivated, wherever it was possible for anything to grow. The wheat was just coming into head, and the people were at work, planting maize. After four hours' ride, we reached El Bireh, a little village on a hill, with the ruins of a convent and a large khan. The place takes its name from a fountain of excellent water, beside which we

448

found our tents already pitched. In the evening, two Englishmen, an ancient Mentor, with a wild young Telemachus in charge, arrived, and camped near us. The night was calm and cool, and the full moon poured a flood of light over the bare and silent hills.

We rose long before sunrise, and rode off in the brilliant morning-- the sky unstained by a speck of vapor. In the valley, beyond El Bireh, the husbandmen were already at their ploughs, and the village boys were on their way to the uncultured parts of the hills, with their flocks of sheep and goats. The valley terminated in a deep gorge, with perpendicular walls of rock on either side. Our road mounted the hill on the eastern side, and followed the brink of the precipice through the pass, where an enchanting landscape opened upon us. The village of Yebrood crowned a hill which rose opposite, and the mountain slopes leaning towards it on all sides were covered with orchards of fig trees; and either rustling with wheat or cleanly ploughed for maize. The soil was a dark brown loam, and very rich. The stones have been laboriously built into terraces; and, even where heavy rocky boulders almost hid the soil, young fig and olive trees were planted in the crevices between them. I have never seen more thorough and patient cultivation. In the crystal of the morning air, the very hills laughed with plenty, and the whole landscape beamed with the signs of gladness on its countenance.

The site of ancient Bethel was not far to the right of our road. Over hills laden with the olive, fig, and vine, we passed to Ain el-Haramiyeh, or the Fountain of the Robbers. Here there are tombs cut in the rock on both sides of the valley. Over another ridge, we descended to a large, bowl-shaped valley, entirely covered with wheat, and opening eastward towards the Jordan. Thence to Nablous (the Shechem of the Old and Sychar of the New Testament) is four hours through a winding dell of the richest harvest land; On the way, we first caught sight of the snowy top of Mount Hermon, distant at least eighty miles in a straight line. Before reaching Nablous, I stopped to drink at a fountain of clear and sweet water, beside a square pile of masonry, upon which sat two Moslem dervishes. This, we were told, was the Tomb of Joseph, whose body, after having accompanied the Israelites in all their wanderings, was at last deposited near Shechem. There is less reason to doubt

449

this spot than most of the sacred places of Palestine, for the reason that it rests, not on Christian, but on Jewish tradition. The wonderful tenacity with which the Jews cling to every record or memento of their early history, and the fact that from the time of Joseph a portion of them have always lingered near the spot, render it highly probable that the locality of a spot so sacred should have been preserved from generation to generation to the present time. It has been recently proposed to open this tomb, by digging under it from the side. If the body of Joseph was actually deposited here, there are, no doubt, some traces of it remaining. It must have been embalmed, according to the Egyptian custom, and placed in a coffin of the Indian sycamore, the wood of which is so nearly incorruptible, that thirty-five centuries would not suffice for its decomposition. The singular interest of such a discovery would certainly justify the experiment. Not far from the tomb is Jacob's Well, where Christ met the Woman of Samaria. This place is also considered as authentic, for the same reasons. If not wholly convincing to all, there is, at least, so much probability in them that one is freed from that painful coldness and incredulity with which he beholds the sacred shows of Jerusalem.

Leaving the Tomb of Joseph, the road turned to the west, and entered the narrow pass between Mounts Ebal and Gerizim. The former is a steep, barren peak, clothed with terraces of cactus, standing on the northern side of the pass. Mount Gerizim is cultivated nearly to the top, and is truly a mountain of blessing, compared with its neighbor. Through an orchard of grand old olive-trees, we reached Nablous, which presented a charming picture, with its long mass of white, dome-topped stone houses, stretching along the foot of Gerizim through a sea of bowery orchards. The bottom of the valley resembles some old garden run to waste. Abundant streams, poured from the generous heart of the Mount of Blessing, leap and gurgle with pleasant noises through thickets of orange, fig, and pomegranate, through bowers of roses and tangled masses of briars and wild vines. We halted in a grove of olives, and, after our tent was pitched, walked upward through the orchards to the Ras-el-Ain (Promontory of the Fountain), on the side of Mount Gerizim. A multitude of beggars sat at the city gate; and, as they continued to clamor after I had given sufficient alms, I paid them with "Allah deelek!"--(God give it to you!)--the Moslem's reply to such importunity--and

450

they ceased in an instant. This exclamation, it seems, takes away from them the power of demanding a second time.

From under the Ras-el-Ain gushes forth the Fountain of Honey, so called from the sweetness and purity of the water. We drank of it, and I found the taste very agreeable, but my companion declared that it had an unpleasant woolly flavor. When we climbed a little higher, we found that the true source from which the fountain is supplied was above, and that an Arab was washing a flock of sheep in it! We continued our walk along the side of the mountain to the other end of the city, through gardens of almond, apricot, prune, and walnut-trees, bound each to each by great vines, whose heavy arms they seemed barely able to support. The interior of the town is dark and filthy; but it has a long, busy bazaar extending its whole length, and a café, where we procured the best coffee in Syria.

Nablous is noted for the existence of a small remnant of the ancient Samaritans. The stock has gradually dwindled away, and amounts to only forty families, containing little more than a hundred and fifty individuals. They live in a particular quarter of the city, and are easily distinguished from the other inhabitants by the cast of their features. After our guide, a native of Nablous, had pointed out three or four, I had no difficulty in recognising all the others we met. They have long, but not prominent noses, like the Jews; small, oblong eyes, narrow lips, and fair complexions, most of them having brown hair. They appear to be held in considerable obloquy by the Moslems. Our attendant, who was of the low class of Arabs, took the boys we met very unceremoniously by the head, calling out: "Here is another Samaritan!" He then conducted us to their synagogue, to see the celebrated Pentateuch, which is there preserved. We were taken to a small, open court, shaded by an apricot-tree, where the priest, an old man in a green robe and white turban, was seated in meditation. He had a long grey beard, and black eyes, that lighted up with a sudden expression of eager greed when we promised him backsheesh for a sight of the sacred book. He arose and took us into a sort of chapel, followed by a number of Samaritan boys. Kneeling down at a niche in the wall, he produced from behind a wooden case a piece of ragged parchment, written with Hebrew characters. But the guide was familiar with this deception, and rated him so soundly that, after a little hesitation, he laid the fragment away, and produced a large tin cylinder, covered with a piece of green satin embroidered in gold. The boys stooped down and reverently kissed the blazoned cover, before it was removed. The cylinder, sliding open by two rows of hinges, opened at the same time the parchment scroll, which was rolled at both ends. It was, indeed, a very ancient manuscript, and in remarkable preservation. The rents have been carefully repaired and the scroll neatly stitched upon another piece of parchment, covered on the outside with violet satin. The priest informed me that it was written by the son of Aaron; but this does not coincide with the fact that the Samaritan Pentateuch is different from that of the Jews. It is, however, no doubt one of the oldest parchment records in the world, and the Samaritans look upon it with unbounded faith and reverence. The Pentateuch, according to their version, contains their only form of religion. They reject everything else which the Old Testament contains. Three or four days ago was their grand feast of sacrifice, when they made a burnt offering of a lamb, on the top of Mount Gerizim. Within a short time, it is said they have shown some curiosity to become acquainted with the New Testament, and the High Priest sent to Jerusalem to procure Arabic copies.

I asked one of the wild-eyed boys whether he could read the sacred book. "Oh, yes," said the priest, "all these boys can read it;" and the one I addressed immediately pulled a volume from his breast, and commenced reading in fluent Hebrew. It appeared to be a part of their church service, for both the priest and boab, or door-keeper, kept up a running series of responses, and occasionally the whole crowd shouted out some deep-mouthed word in chorus. The old man leaned forward with an expression as fixed and intense as if the text had become incarnate in him, following with his lips the sound of the boy's voice. It was a strange picture of religious enthusiasm, and was of itself sufficient to convince me of the legitimacy of the Samaritan's descent. When I rose to leave I gave him the promised fee, and a smaller one to the boy who read the service. This was the signal for a general attack from the door-keeper and all the boys who were present. They surrounded me with eyes sparkling with the desire of gain, kissed the border of my jacket, stroked my beard coaxingly with their hands, which they then kissed, and, crowding up with a boisterous show of affection, were about to fall on my neck in a heap, after the old Hebrew fashion. The priest, clamorous for more, followed with glowing face, and the whole group had a riotous and bacchanalian character, which I should never have imagined could spring from such a passion as avarice.

On returning to our camp, we found Mentor and Telemachus arrived, but not on such friendly terms as their Greek prototypes. We were kept awake for a long time that night by their high words, and the first sound I heard the next morning came from their tent. Telemachus, I suspect, had found some island of Calypso, and did not relish the cold shock of the plunge into the sea, by which Mentor had forced him away. He insisted on returning to Jerusalem, but as Mentor would not allow him a horse, he had not the courage to try it on foot. After a series of altercations, in which he took a pistol to shoot the dragoman, and applied very profane terms to everybody in the company, his wrath dissolved into tears, and when we left, Mentor had decided to rest a day at Nablous, and let him recover from the effects of the storm.

We rode down the beautiful valley, taking the road to Sebaste (Samaria), while our luggage-mules kept directly over the mountains to Jenin. Our path at first followed the course of the stream, between turfy banks and through luxuriant orchards. The whole country we overlooked was planted with olive-trees, and, except the very summits of the mountains, covered with grain-fields. For two hours our course was north-east, leading over the hills, and now and then dipping into beautiful dells. In one of these a large stream gushes from the earth in a full fountain, at the foot of a great olive-tree. The hill-side above it was a complete mass of foliage, crowned with the white walls of a Syrian village. Descending the valley, which is very deep, we came in sight of Samaria, situated on the summit of an isolated hill. The sanctuary of the ancient Christian church of St. John towers high above the mud walls of the modern village. Riding between olive-orchards and wheat-fields of glorious richness and beauty, we passed the remains of an acqueduct, and ascended the hill The ruins of the church occupy the eastern summit. Part of them have been converted into a mosque, which the Christian foot is not allowed to profane. The church, which is in the Byzantine style, is apparently of the time

453

of the Crusaders. It had originally a central and two side-aisles, covered with groined Gothic vaults. The sanctuary is semi-circular, with a row of small arches, supported by double pillars. The church rests on the foundations of some much more ancient building--probably a temple belonging to the Roman city.

Behind the modern village, the hill terminates in a long, elliptical mound, about one-third of a mile in length. We made the tour of it, and were surprised at finding a large number of columns, each of a single piece of marble. They had once formed a double colonnade, extending from the church to a gate on the western side of the summit. Our native guide said they had been covered with an arch, and constituted a long market or bazaar--a supposition in which he may be correct. From the gate, which is still distinctly marked, we overlooked several deep valleys to the west, and over them all, the blue horizon of the Mediterranean, south of Cæsarea. On the northern side of the hill there are upwards of twenty more pillars standing, besides a number hurled down, and the remains of a quadrangular colonnade, on the side of the hill below. The total number of pillars on the summit cannot be less than one hundred, from twelve to eighteen feet in height. The hill is strewn, even to its base, with large hewn blocks and fragments of sculptured stone. The present name of the city was given to it by Herod, and it must have been at that time a most stately and beautiful place.

We descended to a valley on the east, climbed a long ascent, and after crossing the broad shoulder of a mountain beyond, saw below us a landscape even more magnificent than that of Nablous. It was a great winding valley, its bottom rolling in waves of wheat and barley, while every hill-side, up to the bare rock, was mantled with groves of olive. The very summits which looked into this garden of Israel, were green with fragrant plants--wild thyme and sage, gnaphalium and camomile. Away to the west was the sea, and in the north-west the mountain chain of Carmel. We went down to the gardens and pasture-land, and stopped to rest at the Village of Geba, which hangs on the side of the mountain. A spring of whitish but delicious water gushed out of the soil, in the midst of a fig orchard. The women passed us, going back and forth with tall water-jars on their heads. Some herd-boys brought down a flock of black goats, and they were all given drink in a large wooden bowl. They were beautiful animals, with thick curved horns, white eyes, and ears a foot long. It was a truly Biblical picture in every feature.

Beyond this valley we passed a circular basin, which has no outlet, so that in winter the bottom of it must be a lake. After winding among the hills an hour more, we came out upon the town of Jenin, a Turkish village, with a tall white minaret, at the head of the great plain of Esdraelon. It is supposed to be the ancient Jezreel, where the termagant Jezebel was thrown out of the window. We pitched our tent in a garden near the town, under a beautiful mulberry tree, and, as the place is in very bad repute, engaged a man to keep guard at night. An English family was robbed there two or three weeks ago. Our guard did his duty well, pacing back and forth, and occasionally grounding his musket to keep up his courage by the sound. In the evening, François caught a chameleon, a droll-looking little creature, which changed color in a marvellous manner.

Our road, next day, lay directly across the Plain of Esdraelon, one of the richest districts in the world. It is now a green sea, covered with fields of wheat and barley, or great grazing tracts, on which multitudes of sheep and goats are wandering. In some respects it reminded me of the Valley of San José, and if I were to liken Palestine to any other country I have seen, it would be California. The climate and succession of the seasons are the same, the soil is very similar in quality, and the landscapes present the same general features. Here, in spring, the plains are covered with that deluge of floral bloom, which makes California seem a paradise. Here there are the same picturesque groves, the same rank fields of wild oats clothing the mountainsides, the same aromatic herbs impregnating the air with balm, and above all, the same blue, cloudless days and dewless nights. While travelling here, I am constantly reminded of our new Syria on the Pacific.

Towards noon, Mount Tabor separated itself from the chain of hills before us, and stood out singly, at the extremity of the plain. We watered our horses at a spring in a swamp, were some women were collected, beating with sticks the rushes they had gathered to make mats. After reaching the mountains on the northern side of the plain, an ascent of an hour and a-half, through a narrow glen, brought us to Nazareth, which is situated in a cul-de-sac, under the highest peaks of the range. As we were passing a rocky part of the road, Mr. Harrison's horse fell with him and severely injured his leg. We were fortunately near our destination, and on reaching the Latin Convent, Fra Joachim, to whose surgical abilities the traveller's book bore witness, took him in charge. Many others besides ourselves have had reason to be thankful for the good offices of the Latin monks in Palestine. I have never met with a class more kind, cordial, and genial. All the convents are bound to take in and entertain all applicants--of whatever creed or nation--for the space of three days.

In the afternoon, Fra Joachim accompanied me to the Church of the Virgin, which is inclosed within the walls of the convent. It is built over the supposed site of the house in which the mother of Christ was living, at the time of the angelic annunciation. Under the high altar, a flight of steps leads down to the shrine of the Virgin, on the threshold of the house, where the Angel Gabriel's foot rested, as he stood, with a lily in his hand, announcing the miraculous conception. The shrine, of white marble and gold, gleaming in the light of golden lamps, stands under a rough arch of the natural rock, from the side of which hangs a heavy fragment of a granite pillar, suspended, as the devout believe, by divine power. Fra Joachim informed me that, when the Moslems attempted to obliterate all tokens of the holy place, this pillar was preserved by a miracle, that the locality might not be lost to the Christians. At the same time, he said, the angels of God carried away the wooden house which stood at the entrance of the grotto; and, after letting it drop in Marseilles, while they rested, picked it up again and set it down in Loretto, where it still remains. As he said this, there was such entire, absolute belief in the good monk's eyes, and such happiness in that belief, that not for ten times the gold on the shrine would I have expressed a doubt of the story. He then bade me kneel, that I might see the spot where the angel stood, and devoutly repeated a paternoster while I contemplated the pure plate of snowy marble, surrounded with vases of fragrant flowers, between which hung cressets of gold, wherein perfumed oils were burning. All the decorations of the place conveyed the idea of transcendent purity and sweetness; and, for the first time in Palestine, I wished for perfect faith in the spot. Behind the shrine, there are two or three chambers in the rock, which served as habitations for the family of the Virgin.

A young Christian Nazarene afterwards conducted me to the House of Joseph, the Carpenter, which is now inclosed in a little chapel. It is merely a fragment of wall, undoubtedly as old as the time of Christ, and I felt willing to consider it a genuine relic. There was an honest roughness about the large stones, inclosing a small room called the carpenter's shop, which I could not find it in my heart to doubt. Besides, in a quiet country town like Nazareth, which has never knows such vicissitudes as Jerusalem, much more dependence can be placed on popular tradition. For the same reason, I looked with reverence on the Table of Christ, also inclosed within a chapel. This is a large, natural rock, about nine feet by twelve, nearly square, and quite flat on the top. It is said that it once served as a table for Christ and his Disciples. The building called the School of Christ, where he went with other children of his age, is now a church of the Syrian Christians, who were performing a doleful mass, in Arabic, at the time of my visit. It is a vaulted apartment, about forty feet long, and only the lower part of the wall is ancient. At each of these places, the Nazarene put into my hand a piece of pasteboard, on which was printed a prayer in Latin, Italian, and Arabic, with the information that whoever visited the place, and made the prayer, would be entitled to seven years' indulgence. I duly read all the prayers, and, accordingly, my conscience ought to be at rest for twenty-one years.

Chapter VII. The Country of Galilee.

Departure from Nazareth--A Christian Guide--Ascent of Mount Tabor--Wallachian Hermits--The Panorama of Tabor--Ride to Tiberias--A Bath in Genesareth--The Flowers of Galilee--The Mount of Beatitude--Magdala--Joseph's Well--Meeting with a Turk--The Fountain of the Salt-Works--The Upper Valley of the Jordan--Summer Scenery--The Rivers of Lebanon--Tell el-Kadi--An Arcadian Region--The Fountains of Banias.

"Beyond are Bethulia's mountains of green,

And the desolate hills of the wild Gadarene;

And I pause on the goat-crags of Tabor to see

The gleam of thy waters, O dark Galilee!"--Whittier.

Banias (Cæsarea Philippi), *May* 10, 1852.

We left Nazareth on the morning of the 8th inst. My companion had done so well under the care of Fra Joachim that he was able to ride, and our journey was not delayed by his accident. The benedictions of the good Franciscans accompanied us as we rode away from the Convent, past the Fountain of the Virgin, and out of the pleasant little valley where the boy Jesus wandered for many peaceful years. The Christian guide we engaged for Mount Tabor had gone ahead, and we did not find him until we had travelled for more than two hours among the hills. As we approached the sacred mountain, we came upon the region of oaks--the first oak I had seen since leaving Europe last autumn. There are three or four varieties, some with evergreen foliage, and in their wild luxuriance and the picturesqueness of their forms and groupings, they resemble those of California. The sea of grass and flowers in which they stood was sprinkled with thick tufts of wild oats--another point of resemblance to the latter country. But here, there is no gold; there, no sacred memories.

The guide was waiting for us beside a spring, among the trees. He was a tall youth of about twenty, with a mild, submissive face, and wore the dark-blue turban, which appears to be the badge of a native Syrian Christian. I found myself involuntarily pitying him for belonging to a despised sect. There is no disguising the fact that one feels much more respect for the Mussulman rulers of the East, than for their oppressed subjects who profess his own faith. The surest way to make a man contemptible is to treat him contemptuously, and the Oriental Christians, who have been despised for centuries, are, with some few exceptions, despicable enough. Now, however, since the East has become a favorite field of travel, and the Frank possesses an equal dignity with the Moslem, the native Christians are beginning to hold up their heads, and the return of self-respect will, in the course of time, make them respectable.

Mount Tabor stands a little in advance of the hill-country, with which it is connected only by a low spur or shoulder, its base being the Plain of Esdraelon. This is probably the reason why it has been fixed upon as the place of the Transfiguration, as it is not mentioned by name in the New Testament. The words are: "an high mountain apart," which some suppose to refer to the position of the mountain, and not to the remoteness of Christ and the three Disciples from men. The sides of the mountain are covered with clumps of oak, hawthorn and other trees, in many places overrun with the white honeysuckle, its fingers dropping with odor of nutmeg and cloves. The ascent, by a steep and winding path, occupied an hour. The summit is nearly level, and resembles some overgrown American field, or "oak opening." The grass is more than knee-deep; the trees grow high and strong, and there are tangled thickets and bowers of vines without end. The eastern and highest end of the mountain is covered with the remains of an old fortress-convent, once a place of great strength, from the thickness of its walls. In a sort of cell formed among the ruins we found two monk-hermits. I addressed them in all languages of which I know a salutation, without effect, but at last made out that they were Wallachians. They were men of thirty-five, with stupid faces, dirty garments, beards run to waste, and fur caps. Their cell was a mere hovel, without furniture, except a horrid caricature of the Virgin and Child, and four books of prayers in the Bulgarian character. One of them walked about knitting a stocking, and paid no attention to us; but the other, after giving us some deliciously cold water, got upon a pile of rubbish, and stood regarding us with open mouth while we took breakfast. So far from this being a cause of annoyance, I felt really glad that our presence had agitated the stagnant waters of his mind.

The day was hazy and sultry, but the panoramic view from Mount Tabor was still very fine. The great Plain of Esdraelon lay below us like a vast mosaic of green and brown--jasper and verd-antique. On the west, Mount Carmel lifted his head above the blue horizon line of the Mediterranean. Turning to the other side, a strip of the Sea of Galilee glimmered deep down among the hills, and the Ghor, or the Valley of the Jordan, stretched like a broad gash through them. Beyond them, the country of Djebel Adjeloun, the ancient Decapolis, which still holds the walls of Gadara and the temples and theatres of Djerash, faded away into vapor, and, still further to the south, the desolate hills of Gilead, the home of Jephthah. Mount Hermon is visible when the atmosphere is clear but we were not able to see it.

From the top of Mount Tabor to Tiberias, on the Sea of Galilee, is a journey of five hours, through a wild country, with but one single miserable village on the road. At first we rode through lonely dells, grown with oak and brilliant with flowers, especially the large purple mallow, and then over broad, treeless tracts of rolling land, but partially cultivated. The heat was very great; I had no thermometer, but should judge the temperature to have been at least 95° in the shade. From the edge of the upland tract, we looked down on the Sea of Galilee--a beautiful sheet of water sunk among the mountains, and more than 300 feet below the level of the Mediterranean. It lay unruffled in the bottom of the basin, reflecting the peaks of the bare red mountains beyond it. Tiberias was at our very feet, a few palm trees alone relieving the nakedness of its dull walls. After taking a welcome drink at the Fountain of Fig-trees, we descended to the town, which has a desolate and forlorn air. Its walls have been partly thrown down by earthquakes, and never repaired. We found our tents already pitched on the bank above the lake, and under one of the tottering towers.

Not a breath of air was stirring; the red hills smouldered in the heat, and the waters of Genesareth at our feet glimmered with an oily smoothness, unbroken by a ripple. We untwisted our turbans, kicked off our baggy trowsers, and speedily releasing ourselves from the barbarous restraints of dress, dipped into the tepid sea and floated lazily out until we could feel the exquisite coldness of the living springs which sent up their jets from the bottom. I was lying on my back, moving my fins just sufficiently to keep afloat, and gazing dreamily through half-closed eyes on the forlorn palms of Tiberias, when a shrill voice hailed me with: "O Howadji, get out of our way!" There, at the old stone gateway below our tent, stood two Galilean damsels, with heavy earthen jars upon their heads. "Go away yourselves, O maidens!" I answered, "if you want us to come out of the water." "But we must fill our pitchers," one of them replied. "Then fill them at once, and be not afraid; or leave them, and we will fill them for you." Thereupon they put the pitchers down, but remained watching us very complacently while we sank the vessels to the bottom of the lake, and let them fill from the colder and purer tide of the springs. In bringing them back through the water to the gate, the one I propelled before me happened to strike against a stone, and its fair owner, on receiving it, immediately pointed to a crack in the side, which she declared I had made, and went off lamenting. After we had resumed our garments, and were enjoying the pipe of indolence and the coffee of contentment, she returned and made such an outcry, that I was fain to purchase peace by the price of a new pitcher. I passed the first hours of-the night in looking out of my tent-door, as I lay, on the stars sparkling in the bosom of Galilee, like the sheen of Assyrian spears, and the glare of the great fires kindled on the opposite shore.

The next day, we travelled northward along the lake, passing through continuous thickets of oleander, fragrant with its heavy pink blossoms. The thistles were more abundant and beautiful than ever. I noticed, in particular, one with a superb globular flower of a bright blue color, which would make a choice ornament for our gardens at home. At the north-western head of the lake, the mountains fall back and leave a large tract of the richest meadow-land, which narrows away into a deep dell, overhung by high mountain headlands, faced with naked cliffs of red rock. The features of the landscape are magnificent. Up the dell, I saw plainly the Mount of Beatitude, beyond which lies the village of Cana of Galilee. In coming up the meadow, we passed a miserable little village of thatched mud huts, almost hidden by the rank weeds which grew around them. A withered old crone sat at one of the doors, sunning herself. "What is the name of this village?" I asked. "It is Mejdel," was her reply. This was the ancient Magdala, the home of that beautiful but sinful Magdalene, whose repentance has made her one of the brightest of the Saints. The crystal waters of the lake here lave a shore of the cleanest pebbles. The path goes winding through oleanders, nebbuks, patches of hollyhock, anise-seed, fennel, and other spicy plants, while, on the west, great fields of barley stand ripe for the cutting. In some places, the Fellahs, men and women, were at work, reaping and binding the sheaves. After crossing this tract, we came to the hill, at the foot of which was a ruined khan, and on the summit, other undistinguishable ruins, supposed by some to be those of Capernaum. The site of that exalted town, however, is still a matter of discussion.

We journeyed on in a most sweltering atmosphere over the ascending hills, the valley of the Upper Jordan lying deep on our right. In a shallow hollow, under one of the highest peaks, there stands a large deserted khan; over a well of very cold; sweet water, called Bir Youssuf by the Arabs. Somewhere near it, according to tradition, is the field where Joseph was sold by his brethren; and the well is, no doubt, looked upon by many as the identical pit into which he was thrown. A stately Turk of Damascus, with four servants behind him, came riding up as we were resting in the gateway of the khan, and, in answer to my question, informed me that the well was so named from Nebbee Youssuf (the Prophet Joseph), and not from Sultan Joseph Saladin. He took us for his countrymen, accosting me first in Turkish, and, even after I had talked with him some time in bad Arabic, asked me whether I had been making a pilgrimage to the tombs of certain holy Moslem saints, in the neighborhood of Jaffa. He joined company with us, however, and shared his pipe with me, as we continued our journey. We rode for two hours more over hills bare of trees, but covered thick with grass and herbs, and finally lost our way. François went ahead, dashing through the fields of barley and lentils, and we reached the path again, as the Waters of Merom came in sight. We then descended into the Valley of the Upper Jordan, and encamped opposite the lake, at Ain el-Mellaha (the Fountain of the Salt-Works), the first source of the sacred river. A stream of water, sufficient to turn half-a-dozen mills, gushes and gurgles up at the foot of the mountain. There are the remains of an ancient dam, by which a large pool was formed for the irrigation of the valley. It still supplies a little Arab mill below the fountain. This is a frontier post, between the jurisdictions of the Pashas of Jerusalem and Damascus, and the mukkairee of the Greek Caloyer, who left us at Tiberias, was obliged to pay a duty of seven and a half piastres on fifteen mats, which he had bought at Jerusalem for one and a half piastres each. The poor man will perhaps make a dozen piastres (about half a dollar) on these mats at Damascus, after carrying them on his mule for more than two hundred miles.

We pitched our tents on the grassy meadow below the mill--a charming spot, with Tell el-Khanzir (the hill of wild boars) just in front, over the Waters of Merom, and the snow-streaked summit of Djebel esh-Shekh--the great Mount Hermon--towering high above the valley. This is the loftiest peak of the Anti-Lebanon, and is 10,000 feet above the sea. The next morning, we rode for three hours before reaching the second spring of the Jordan, at a place which François called Tell el-Kadi, but which did not at all answer with the description given me by Dr. Robinson, at Jerusalem. The upper part of the broad valley, whence the Jordan draws his waters, is flat, moist, and but little cultivated. There are immense herds of sheep, goats, and buffaloes wandering over it. The people are a dark Arab tribe, and live in tents and miserable clay huts. Where the valley begins to slope upward towards the hills, they plant wheat, barley, and lentils. The soil is the fattest brown loam, and the harvests are wonderfully rich. I saw many tracts of wheat, from half a mile to a mile in extent, which would average forty bushels to the acre. Yet the ground is never manured, and the Arab plough scratches up but a few inches of the surface. What a paradise might be made of this country, were it in better hands!

The second spring is not quite so large as Ain el-Mellaha but, like it, pours out a strong stream from a single source The pool was filled with women, washing the heavy fleeces of their sheep, and beating the dirt out of their striped camel's hair abas with long poles. We left it, and entered on a slope of stony ground, forming the head of the valley. The view extended southward, to the mountains closing the northern cove of the Sea of Galilee. It was a grand, rich landscape--so rich that its desolation seems forced and unnatural. High on the summit of a mountain to the west, the ruins of a large

Crusader fortress looked down upon us. The soil, which slowly climbs upward through a long valley between Lebanon and Anti-Lebanon, is cut with deep ravines. The path is very difficult to find; and while we were riding forward at random, looking in all directions for our baggage mules, we started up a beautiful gazelle. At last, about noon, hot, hungry, and thirsty, we reached a swift stream, roaring at the bottom of a deep ravine, through a bed of gorgeous foliage. The odor of the wild grape-blossoms, which came up to us, as we rode along the edge, was overpowering in its sweetness. An old bridge of two arches crossed the stream. There was a pile of rocks against the central pier, and there we sat and took breakfast in the shade of the maples, while the cold green waters foamed at our feet. By all the Naiads and Tritons, what a joy there is in beholding a running stream! The rivers of Lebanon are miracles to me, after my knowledge of the Desert. A company of Arabs, seven in all, were gathered under the bridge; and, from a flute which one of them blew, I judged they were taking a pastoral holiday. We kept our pistols beside us; for we did not like their looks. Before leaving, they told us that the country was full of robbers, and advised us to be on the lookout. We rode more carefully, after this, and kept with our baggage on reaching it, An hour after leaving the bridge, we came to a large circular, or rather annular mound, overgrown with knee-deep grass and clumps of oak-trees. A large stream, of a bright blue color, gushed down the north side, and after half embracing the mound swept off across the meadows to the Waters of Merom. There could be no doubt that this was Tell el-Kadi, the site of Dan, the most northern town of ancient Israel. The mound on which it was built is the crater of an extinct volcano. The Hebrew word Dan signifies "judge," and Tell el-Kadi, in Arabic, is "The Hill of the Judge."

The Anti-Lebanon now rose near us, its northern and western slopes green with trees and grass. The first range, perhaps 5,000 feet in height, shut out the snowy head of Hermon; but still the view was sublime in its large and harmonious outlines. Our road was through a country resembling Arcadia-- the earth hidden by a dense bed of grass and flowers; thickets of blossoming shrubs; old, old oaks, with the most gnarled of trunks, the most picturesque of boughs, and the glossiest of green leaves; olive-trees of amazing antiquity; and, threading and enlivening all, the clear-cold floods of Lebanon. This was the true haunt of Pan, whose altars are now before me, graven on the marble crags of Hermon. Looking on those altars, and on the landscape, lovely as a Grecian dream, I forget that the lament has long been sung:

"Pan, Pan is dead!"

In another hour, we reached this place, the ancient Cæsarea Philippi, now a poor village, embowered in magnificent trees, and washed by glorious waters. There are abundant remains of the old city: fragments of immense walls; broken granite columns; traces of pavements; great blocks of hewn stone; marble pedestals, and the like. In the rock at the foot of the mountain, there are several elegant niches, with Greek inscriptions, besides a large natural grotto. Below them, the water gushes up through the stones, in a hundred streams, forming a flood of considerable size. We have made our camp in an olive grove near the end of the village, beside an immense terebinth tree, which is inclosed in an open court, paved with stone. This is the town-hall of Banias, where the Shekh dispenses justice, and at the same time, the resort of all the idlers of the place. We went up among them, soon after our arrival, and were given seats of honor near the Shekh, who talked with me a long time about America. The people exhibit a very sensible curiosity, desiring to know the extent of our country, the number of inhabitants, the amount of taxation, the price of grain, and other solid information.

The Shekh and the men of the place inform us that the Druses are infesting the road to Damascus. This tribe is in rebellion in Djebel Hauaran, on account of the conscription, and some of them, it appears, have taken refuge in the fastnesses of Hermon, where they are beginning to plunder travellers. While I was talking with the Shekh, a Druse came down from the mountains, and sat for half an hour among the villagers, under the terebinth, and we have just heard that he has gone back the way he came. This fact has given us some anxiety, as he may have been a spy sent down to gather news and, if so, we are almost certain to be waylaid. If we were well armed, we should not fear a dozen, but all our weapons consist of a sword and four pistols. After consulting together, we decided to apply to the Shekh for two armed men, to accompany us. I accordingly went to him again, and exhibited the firman of the Pasha of Jerusalem, which he read, stating that, even without it, he would have felt it his duty to grant our request. This is the graceful way in which the Orientals submit to a peremptory order. He thinks that one man will be sufficient, as we shall probably not meet with any large party.

The day has been, and still is, excessively hot. The atmosphere is sweltering, and all around us, over the thick patches of mallow and wild mustard, the bees are humming with a continuous sultry sound. The Shekh, with a number of lazy villagers, is still seated under the terebinth, in a tent of shade, impervious to the sun. I can hear the rush of the fountains of Banias--the holy springs of Hermon, whence Jordan is born. But what is this? The odor of the velvety weed of Shiraz meets my nostrils; a dark-eyed son of Pan places the narghileh at my feet; and, bubbling more sweetly than the streams of Jordan, the incense most dear to the god dims the crystal censer, and floats from my lips in rhythmic ejaculations. I, too, am in Arcadia!

Chapter VIII. Crossing the Anti-Lebanon.

The Harmless Guard--Cæsarea Philippi--The Valley of the Druses--The Sides of Mount Hermon--An Alarm--Threading a Defile--Distant view of Djebel Hauaran--Another Alarm--Camp at Katana--We Ride into Damascus.

Damascus, *May* 12, 1852.

We rose early, so as to be ready for a long march. The guard came--a mild-looking Arab--without arms; but on our refusing to take him thus, he brought a Turkish musket, terrible to behold, but quite guiltless of any murderous intent. We gave ourselves up to fate, with true Arab-resignation, and began ascending the Anti-Lebanon. Up and up, by stony paths, under the oaks, beside the streams, and between the wheat-fields, we climbed for two hours, and at last reached a comb or dividing ridge, whence we could look into a valley on the other side, or rather inclosed between the main chain and the offshoot named Djebel Heish, which stretches away towards the south-east. About half-way up the ascent, we passed the ruined acropolis of Cæsarea Philippi, crowning the summit of a lower peak. The walls and bastions cover a great extent of ground, and were evidently used as a stronghold in the Middle Ages.

The valley into which we descended lay directly under one of the peaks of Hermon and the rills that watered it were fed from his snow-fields. It was inhabited by Druses, but no men were to be seen, except a few poor husbandmen, ploughing on the mountain-sides. The women, wearing those enormous horns on their heads which distinguish them from the Mohammedan females, were washing at a pool below. We crossed the valley, and slowly ascended the height on the opposite side, taking care to keep with the baggage-mules. Up to this time, we met very few persons; and we forgot the anticipated perils in contemplating the rugged scenery of the Anti-Lebanon. The mountain-sides were brilliant with flowers, and many new and beautiful specimens arrested our attention. The asphodel grew in bunches beside the streams, and the large scarlet anemone outshone even the poppy, whose color here is the quintessence of flame. Five hours after leaving Banias, we reached the highest part of the pass--a dreary volcanic region, covered with fragments of lava. Just at this place, an old Arab met us, and, after scanning us closely, stopped and accosted Dervish. The latter immediately came running ahead, quite excited with the news that the old man had seen a company of about fifty Druses descend from the sides of Mount Hermon, towards the road we were to travel. We immediately ordered the baggage to halt, and Mr. Harrison, François, and myself rode on to reconnoitre. Our guard, the valiant man of Banias, whose teeth already chattered with fear, prudently kept with the baggage. We crossed the ridge and watched the stony mountain-sides for some time; but no spear or glittering gun-barrel could we see. The caravan was then set in motion; and we had not proceeded far before we met a second company of Arabs, who informed us that the road was free.

Leaving the heights, we descended cautiously into a ravine with walls of rough volcanic rock on each side. It was a pass where three men might have stood their ground against a hundred; and we did not feel thoroughly convinced of our safety till we had threaded its many windings and emerged upon a narrow valley. A village called Beit Jenn nestled under the rocks; and below it, a grove of poplar-trees shaded the banks of a rapid stream. We had now fairly crossed the Anti-Lebanon. The dazzling snows of Mount Hermon overhung us on the west; and, from the opening of the valley, we looked across a wild, waste country, to the distant range of Djebel Hauaran, the seat of the present rebellion, and one of the most interesting regions of Syria. I regretted more than ever not being able to reach it. The ruins of Bozrah, Ezra, and other ancient cities, would well repay the arduous character of the journey, while the traveller might succeed in getting some insight into the life and habits of that singular people, the Druses. But now, and perhaps for some time to come, there is no chance of entering the Hauaran.

Towards the middle of the afternoon, we reached a large village, which is usually the end of the first day's journey from Banias. Our men wanted to stop here, but we considered that to halt then would be to increase the risk, and decided to push on to Katana, four hours' journey from Damascus. They yielded with a bad grace; and we jogged on over the stony road, crossing the long hills which form the eastern base of the Anti-Lebanon. Before long, another Arab met us with the news that there was an encampment of Druses on the plain between us and Katana. At this, our guard, who had recovered sufficient spirit to ride a few paces in advance, fell back, and the impassive Dervish became greatly agitated. Where there is an uncertain danger, it is always better to go ahead than to turn back; and we did so. But the guard reined up on the top of the first ridge, trembling as he pointed to a distant hill, and cried out: "Ahò, ahò henàk!" (There they are!) There were, in fact, the shadows of some rocks, which bore a faint resemblance to tents. Before sunset, we reached the last declivity of the mountains, and saw far in the dusky plain, the long green belt of the gardens of Damascus, and here and there the indistinct glimmer of a minaret. Katana, our resting-place for the night, lay below us, buried in orchards of olive and orange. We pitched our tents on the banks of a beautiful stream, enjoyed the pipe of tranquillity, after our long march, and soon forgot the Druses, in a slumber that lasted unbroken till dawn.

In the morning we sent back the man of Banias, left the baggage to take care of itself, and rode on to Damascus, as fast as our tired horses could carry us. The plain, at first barren and stony, became enlivened with vineyards and fields of wheat, as we advanced. Arabs were everywhere at work, ploughing and directing the water-courses. The belt of living green, the bower in which the great city, the Queen of the Orient, hides her beauty, drew nearer and nearer, stretching out a crescent of foliage for miles on either hand, that gradually narrowed and received us into its cool and fragrant heart. We sank into a sea of olive, pomegranate, orange, plum, apricot, walnut, and plane trees, and were lost. The sun sparkled in the rolling surface above; but we swam through the green depths, below his reach, and thus, drifted on through miles of shade, entered the city.

Since our arrival, I find that two other parties of travellers, one of which crossed the Anti-Lebanon on the northern side of Mount Hermon, were obliged to take guards, and saw several Druse spies posted on the heights, as they passed. A Russian gentleman travelling from here to Tiberias, was stopped three times on the road, and only escaped being plundered from the fact of his having a Druse dragoman. The disturbances are more serious than I had anticipated. Four regiments left here yesterday, sent to the aid of a company of cavalry, which is surrounded by the rebels in a valley of Dejebel Hauaran, and unable to get out.

Chapter IX. Pictures of Damascus.

Damascus from the Anti-Lebanon--Entering the City--A Diorama of Bazaars--An Oriental Hotel--Our Chamber--The Bazaars--Pipes and Coffee--The Rivers of Damascus--Palaces of the Jews--Jewish Ladies--A Christian Gentleman--The Sacred Localities--Damascus Blades--The Sword of Haroun Al-Raschid--An Arrival from Palmyra.

"Are not Abana and Pharpar, rivers of Damascus, better than all the waters of Israel?"--2 Kings, v. 12.

Damascus, *Wednesday, May* 19, 1852.

Damascus is considered by many travellers as the best remaining type of an Oriental city. Constantinople is semi-European; Cairo is fast becoming so; but Damascus, away from the highways of commerce, seated alone between the Lebanon and the Syrian Desert, still retains, in its outward aspect and in the character of its inhabitants, all the pride and fancy and fanaticism of the times of the Caliphs. With this judgment, in general terms, I agree; but not to its ascendancy, in every respect, over Cairo. True, when you behold Damascus from the Salahiyeh, the last slope of the Anti-Lebanon, it is the realization of all that you have dreamed of Oriental splendor; the world has no picture more dazzling. It is Beauty carried to the Sublime, as I have felt when overlooking some boundless forest of palms within the tropics. From the hill, whose ridges heave behind you until in the south they rise to the snowy head of Mount Hermon, the great Syrian plain stretches away to the Euphrates, broken at distances of ten and fifteen miles, by two detached mountain chains. In a terrible gorge at your side, the river Barrada, the ancient Pharpar, forces its way to the plain, and its waters, divided into twelve different channels, make all between you and those blue island-hills of the desert, one great garden, the boundaries of which your vision can barely distinguish. Its longest diameter cannot be less than twenty miles. You look down on a world of foliage, and fruit, and blossoms, whose hue, by contrast with the barren mountains and the yellow rim of the desert which incloses it, seems brighter than all other gardens in the world. Through its centre, following the course of the river, lies Damascus; a line of white walls, topped with domes and towers and tall minarets, winding away for miles through the green sea. Nothing less than a city of palaces, whose walls are marble and whose doors are ivory and pearl, could keep up the enchantment of that distant view.

We rode for an hour through the gardens before entering the gate. The fruit-trees, of whatever variety---walnut, olive, apricot, or fig--were the noblest of their kind. Roses and pomegranates in bloom starred the dark foliage, and the scented jasmine overhung the walls. But as we approached the city, the view was obscured by high mud walls on either side of the road, and we only caught glimpses now and then of the fragrant wilderness. The first street we entered was low and mean, the houses of clay. Following this, we came to an uncovered bazaar, with rude shops on either side, protected by mats stretched in front and supported by poles. Here all sorts of common stuns and utensils were sold, and the street was filled with crowds of Fellahs and Desert Arabs. Two large sycamores shaded it, and the Seraglio of the Pasha of Damascus, a plain two-story building, faced the entrance of the main bazaar, which branched off into the city. We turned into this, and after passing through several small bazaars stocked with dried fruits, pipes and pipe-bowls, groceries, and all the primitive wares of the East, reached a large passage, covered with a steep wooden roof, and entirely occupied by venders of silk stuffs. Out of this we passed through another, devoted to saddles and bridles; then another, full of spices, and at last reached the grand bazaar, where all the richest stuffs of Europe and the East were displayed in the shops. We rode slowly along through the cool twilight, crossed here and there by long pencils of white light, falling through apertures in the roof, and illuminating the gay turbans and silk caftans of the lazy merchants. But out of this bazaar, at intervals, opened the grand gate of a khan, giving us a view of its marble court, its fountains, and the dark arches of its storerooms; or the door of a mosque, with its mosaic floor and pillared corridor. The interminable lines of bazaars, with their atmospheres of spice and fruit and fragrant tobacco, the hushed tread of the slippered crowds; the plash of falling fountains and the bubbling of innumerable narghilehs; the picturesque merchants and their customers, no longer in the big trowsers of Egypt, but the long caftans and

472

abas of Syria; the absence of Frank faces and dresses--in all these there was the true spirit of the Orient, and so far, we were charmed with Damascus.

At the hotel in the Soog el-Haràb, or Frank quarter, the illusion was not dissipated. It had once been the house of some rich merchant. The court into which we were ushered is paved with marble, with a great stone basin, surrounded with vases of flowering plants, in the centre. Two large lemon trees shade the entrance, and a vine, climbing to the top of the house, makes a leafy arbor over the flat roof. The walls of the house are painted in horizontal bars of blue, white, orange and white--a gay grotesqueness of style which does not offend the eye under an eastern sun. On the southern side of the court is the liwan, an arrangement for which the houses of Damascus are noted. It is a vaulted apartment, twenty feet high, entirely open towards the court, except a fine pointed arch at the top, decorated with encaustic ornaments of the most brilliant colors. In front, a tesselated pavement of marble leads to the doors of the chambers on each side. Beyond this is a raised floor covered with matting, and along the farther end a divan, whose piled cushions are the most tempting trap ever set to catch a lazy man. Although not naturally indolent, I find it impossible to resist the fascination of this lounge. Leaning back, cross-legged, against the cushions, with the inseparable pipe in one's hand, the view of the court, the water-basin, the flowers and lemon trees, the servants and dragomen going back and forth, or smoking their narghilehs in the shade--all framed in the beautiful arched entrance, is so perfectly Oriental, so true a tableau from the times of good old Haroun Al-Raschid, that one is surprised to find how many hours have slipped away while he has been silently enjoying it.

Opposite the liwan is a large room paved with marble, with a handsome fountain in the centre. It is the finest in the hotel, and now occupied by Lord Dalkeith and his friends. Our own room is on the upper floor, and is so rich in decorations that I have not yet finished the study of them. Along the side, looking down on the court, we have a mosaic floor of white, red, black and yellow marble. Above this is raised a second floor, carpeted and furnished in European style. The walls, for a height of ten feet, are covered with wooden panelling, painted with arabesque devices in the gayest colors, and along the top there is a series of Arabic inscriptions in gold. There are a number of niches or open closets in the walls, whose arched tops are adorned with pendent wooden ornaments, resembling stalactites, and at the corners of the room the heavy gilded and painted cornice drops into similar grotesque incrustations. A space of bare white wall intervenes between this cornice and the ceiling, which is formed of slim poplar logs, laid side by side, and so covered with paint and with scales and stripes and network devices in gold and silver, that one would take them to be clothed with the skins of the magic serpents that guard the Valley of Diamonds. My most satisfactory remembrance of Damascus will be this room.

My walks through the city have been almost wholly confined to the bazaars, which are of immense extent. One can walk for many miles, without going beyond the cover of their peaked wooden roofs, and in all this round will find no two precisely alike. One is devoted entirely to soap; another to tobacco, through which you cough and sneeze your way to the bazaar of spices, and delightedly inhale its perfumed air. Then there is the bazaar of sweetmeats; of vegetables; of red slippers; of shawls; of caftans; of bakers and ovens; of wooden ware; of jewelry---a great stone building, covered with vaulted passages; of Aleppo silks; of Baghdad carpets; of Indian stuffs; of coffee; and so on, through a seemingly endless variety. As I have already remarked, along the line of the bazaars are many khans, the resort of merchants from all parts of Turkey and Persia, and even India. They are large, stately buildings, and some of them have superb gateways of sculptured marble. The interior courts are paved with stone, with fountains in the centre, and many of them are covered with domes resting on massive pillars. The largest has a roof of nine domes, supported by four grand pillars, which inclose a fountain. The mosques, into which no Christian is allowed to enter, are in general inferior to those of Cairo, but their outer courts are always paved with marble, adorned with fountains, and surrounded by light and elegant corridors. The grand mosque is an imposing edifice, and is said to occupy the site of a former Christian church.

Another pleasant feature of the city is its coffee shops, which abound in the bazaars and on the outskirts of the gardens, beside the running streams.

Those in the bazaars are spacious rooms with vaulted ceilings, divans running around the four walls, and fountains in the centre. During the afternoon they are nearly always filled with Turks, Armenians and Persians, smoking the narghileh, or water-pipe, which is the universal custom in Damascus. The Persian tobacco, brought here by the caravans from Baghdad, is renowned for this kind of smoking. The most popular coffee-shop is near the citadel, on the banks and over the surface of the Pharpar. It is a rough wooden building, with a roof of straw mats, but the sight and sound of the rushing waters, as they shoot away with arrowy swiftness under your feet, the shade of the trees that line the banks, and the cool breeze that always visits the spot, beguile you into a second pipe ere you are aware. "El mà, wa el khòdra, wa el widj el hassàn--water, verdure and a beautiful face," says an old Arab proverb, "are three things which delight the heart," and the Syrians avow that all three are to be found in Damascus. Not only on the three Sundays of each week, but every day, in the gardens about the city, you may see whole families (and if Jews or Christians, many groups of families) spending the day in the shade, beside the beautiful waters. There are several gardens fitted up purposely for these picnics, with kiosks, fountains and pleasant seats under the trees. You bring your pipes, your provisions and the like with you, but servants are in attendance to furnish fire and water and coffee, for which, on leaving, you give them a small gratuity. Of all the Damascenes I have yet seen, there is not one but declares his city to be the Garden of the World, the Pearl of the Orient, and thanks God and the Prophet for having permitted him to be born and to live in it. But, except the bazaars, the khans and the baths, of which there are several most luxurious establishments, the city itself is neither so rich nor so purely Saracenic in its architecture as Cairo. The streets are narrow and dirty, and the houses, which are never more than two low stories in height, are built of sun-dried bricks, coated with plaster. I miss the solid piles of stone, the elegant doorways, and, above all, the exquisite hanging balconies of carved wood, which meet one in the old streets of Cairo. Damascus is the representative of all that is gay, brilliant, and picturesque, in Oriental life; but for stately magnificence, Cairo, and, I suspect, Baghdad, is its superior.

We visited the other day the houses of some of the richest Jews and Christians. Old Abou-Ibrahim, the Jewish servant of the hotel, accompanied and introduced us. It is customary for travellers to make these visits, and the families, far from being annoyed, are flattered by it. The exteriors of the houses are mean; but after threading a narrow passage, we emerged into a court, rivalling in profusion of ornament and rich contrast of colors one's early idea of the Palace of Aladdin. The floors and fountains are all of marble mosaic; the arches of the liwan glitter with gold, and the walls bewilder the eye with the intricacy of their adornments. In the first house, we were received by the family in a room of precious marbles, with niches in the walls, resembling grottoes of silver stalactites. The cushions of the divan were of the richest silk, and a chandelier of Bohemian crystal hung from the ceiling. Silver narghilehs were brought to us, and coffee was served in heavy silver zerfs. The lady of the house was a rather corpulent lady of about thirty-five, and wore a semi-European robe of embroidered silk and lace, with full trowsers gathered at the ankles, and yellow slippers. Her black hair was braided, and fastened at the end with golden ornaments, and the light scarf twisted around her head blazed with diamonds. The lids of her large eyes were stained with kohl, and her eyebrows were plucked out and shaved away so as to leave only a thin, arched line, as if drawn with a pencil, above each eye. Her daughter, a girl of fifteen, who bore the genuine Hebrew name of Rachel, had even bigger and blacker eyes than her mother; but her forehead was low, her mouth large, and the expression of her face exceedingly stupid. The father of the family was a middle-aged man, with a well-bred air, and talked with an Oriental politeness which was very refreshing. An English lady, who was of our party, said to him, through me, that if she possessed such a house she should be willing to remain in Damascus. "Why does she leave, then?" he immediately answered: "this is her house, and everything that is in it." Speaking of visiting Jerusalem, he asked me whether it was not a more beautiful city than Damascus. "It is not more beautiful," I said, "but it is more holy," an expression which the whole company received with great satisfaction.

The second house we visited was even larger and richer than the first, but had an air of neglect and decay. The slabs of rich marble were loose and broken, about the edges of the fountains; the rich painting of the wood-work was beginning to fade; and the balustrades leading to the upper chambers were broken off in places. We were ushered into a room, the walls and ceilings of which were composed entirely of gilded arabesque frame-work, set with small mirrors. When new, it must have had a gorgeous effect; but the gold is now tarnished, and the glasses dim. The mistress of the house was seated on the cushions, dividing her time between her pipe and her needle-work. She merely made a slight inclination of her head as we entered, and went on with her occupation. Presently her two daughters and an Abyssinian slave appeared, and took their places on the cushions at her feet, the whole forming a charming group, which I regretted some of my artist friends at home could not see. The mistress was so exceedingly dignified, that she bestowed but few words on us. She seemed to resent our admiration of the slave, who was a most graceful creature; yet her jealousy, it afterwards appeared, had reference to her own husband, for we had scarcely left, when a servant followed to inform the English lady that if she was willing to buy the Abyssinian, the mistress would sell her at once for two thousand piastres.

The last visit we paid was to the dwelling of a Maronite, the richest Christian in Damascus. The house resembled those we had already seen, except that, having been recently built, it was in better condition, and exhibited better taste in the ornaments. No one but the lady was allowed to enter the female apartments, the rest of us being entertained by the proprietor, a man of fifty, and without exception the handsomest and most dignified person of that age I have ever seen. He was a king without a throne, and fascinated me completely by the noble elegance of his manner. In any country but the Orient, I should have pronounced him incapable of an unworthy thought: here, he may be exactly the reverse.

Although Damascus is considered the oldest city in the world, the date of its foundation going beyond tradition, there are very few relics of antiquity in or near it. In the bazaar are three large pillars, supporting half the pediment, which are said to have belonged to the Christian Church of St. John, but, if so, that church must have been originally a Roman temple. Part of the Roman walls and one of the city gates remain; and we saw the spot where, according to tradition, Saul was let down from the wall in a basket. There are two localities pointed out as the scene of his conversion, which, from his own account, occurred near the city. I visited a subterranean chapel claimed by the Latin monks to be the cellar of the house of Ananias, in which the Apostle was concealed. The cellar is, undoubtedly, of great antiquity; but as the whole quarter was for many centuries inhabited wholly by Turks, it would be curious to know how the monks ascertained which was the house of Ananias. As for the "street called Straight," it would be difficult at present to find any in Damascus corresponding to that epithet.

The famous Damascus blades, so renowned in the time of the Crusaders, are made here no longer. The art has been lost for three or four centuries. Yet genuine old swords, of the true steel, are occasionally to be found. They are readily distinguished from modern imitations by their clear and silvery ring when struck, and by the finely watered appearance of the blade, produced by its having been first made of woven wire, and then worked over and over again until it attained the requisite temper. A droll Turk, who is the shekh ed-dellàl, or Chief of the Auctioneers, and is nicknamed Abou-Anteeka (the Father of the Antiques), has a large collection of sabres, daggers, pieces of mail, shields, pipes, rings, seals, and other ancient articles. He demands enormous prices, but generally takes about one-third of what he first asks. I have spent several hours in his curiosity shop, bargaining for turquoise rings, carbuncles, Persian amulets, and Circassian daggers. While looking over some old swords the other day, I noticed one of exquisite temper, but with a shorter blade than usual. The point had apparently been snapped off in fight, but owing to the excellence of the sword, or the owner's affection for it, the steel had been carefully shaped into a new point. Abou-Anteeka asked five hundred piastres, and I, who had taken a particular fancy to possess it, offered him two hundred in an indifferent way, and then laid it aside to examine other articles. After his refusal to accept my offer, I said nothing more, and was leaving the shop, when the old fellow called me back, saying: "You have forgotten your sword,"--which I thereupon took at my own price. I have shown it to Mr. Wood, the British Consul, who pronounced it an extremely fine specimen of Damascus steel; and, on reading the inscription enamelled upon the blade, ascertains that it was made in the year of the Hegira, 181, which corresponds to A.D. 798. This was during the Caliphate of Haroun Al-Raschid, and who knows but the sword may have once flashed in the presence of that great and glorious sovereign--nay, been drawn by his own hand! Who knows but that

478

the Milan armor of the Crusaders may have shivered its point, on the field of Askalon! I kiss the veined azure of thy blade, O Sword of Haroun! I hang the crimson cords of thy scabbard upon my shoulder, and thou shalt henceforth clank in silver music at my side, singing to my ear, and mine alone, thy chants of battle, thy rejoicing songs of slaughter!

Yesterday evening, three gentlemen of Lord Dalkeith's party arrived from a trip to Palmyra. The road thither lies through a part of the Syrian Desert belonging to the Aneyzeh tribe, who are now supposed to be in league with the Druses, against the Government. Including this party, only six persons have succeeded in reaching Palmyra within a year, and two of them, Messrs. Noel and Cathcart, were imprisoned four days by the Arabs, and only escaped by the accidental departure of a caravan for Damascus. The present party was obliged to travel almost wholly by night, running the gauntlet of a dozen Arab encampments, and was only allowed a day's stay at Palmyra. They were all disguised as Bedouins, and took nothing with them but the necessary provisions. They made their appearance here last evening, in long, white abas, with the Bedouin keffie bound over their heads, their faces burnt, their eyes inflamed, and their frames feverish with seven days and nights of travel. The shekh who conducted them was not an Aneyzeh, and would have lost his life had they fallen in with any of that tribe.

Chapter X. The Visions of Hasheesh.

"Exulting, trembling, raging, fainting,

Possessed beyond the Muse's painting."

Collins.

During my stay in Damascus, that insatiable curiosity which leads me to prefer the acquisition of all lawful knowledge through the channels of my own personal experience, rather than in less satisfactory and less laborious ways, induced me to make a trial of the celebrated Hasheesh--that remarkable drug which supplies the luxurious Syrian with dreams more alluring and more gorgeous than the Chinese extracts from his darling opium pipe. The use of Hasheesh--which is a preparation of the dried leaves of the cannabis indica--has been familiar to the East for many centuries. During the Crusades, it was frequently used by the Saracen warriors to stimulate them to the work of slaughter, and from the Arabic term of "Hashasheën," or Eaters of Hasheesh, as applied to them, the word "assassin" has been naturally derived. An infusion of the same plant gives to the drink called "bhang," which is in common use throughout India and Malaysia, its peculiar properties. Thus prepared, it is a more fierce and fatal stimulant than the paste of sugar and spices to which the Turk resorts, as the food of his voluptuous evening reveries. While its immediate effects seem to be more potent than those of opium, its habitual use, though attended with ultimate and permanent injury to the system, rarely results in such utter wreck of mind and body as that to which the votaries of the latter drug inevitably condemn themselves.

A previous experience of the effects of hasheesh--which I took once, and in a very mild form, while in Egypt--was so peculiar in its character, that my curiosity, instead of being satisfied, only prompted me the more to throw myself, for once, wholly under its influence. The sensations it then produced were those, physically, of exquisite lightness and airiness--of a wonderfully keen perception of the ludicrous, in the most simple and familiar objects. During the half hour in which it lasted, I was at no time so far under its control, that I could not, with the clearest perception, study the changes through which I passed. I noted, with careful attention, the fine sensations which spread throughout the whole tissue of my nervous fibre, each thrill helping to divest my frame of its earthy and material nature, until my substance appeared to me no grosser than the vapors of the atmosphere, and while sitting in the calm of the Egyptian twilight, I expected to be lifted up and carried away by the first breeze that should ruffle the Nile. While this process was going on, the objects by which I was surrounded assumed a strange and whimsical expression. My pipe, the oars which my boatmen plied, the turban worn by the captain, the water-jars and culinary implements, became in themselves so inexpressibly absurd and comical, that I was provoked into a long fit of laughter. The hallucination died away as gradually as it came, leaving me overcome with a soft and pleasant drowsiness, from which I sank into a deep, refreshing sleep.

My companion and an English gentleman, who, with his wife, was also residing in Antonio's pleasant caravanserai--agreed to join me in the experiment. The dragoman of the latter was deputed to procure a sufficient quantity of the drug. He was a dark Egyptian, speaking only the lingua franca of the East, and asked me, as he took the money and departed on his mission, whether he should get hasheesh "per ridere, a per dormire?" "Oh, per ridere, of course," I answered; "and see that it be strong and fresh." It is customary with the Syrians to take a small portion immediately before the evening meal, as it is thus diffused through the stomach and acts more gradually, as well as more gently, upon the system. As our dinner-hour was at sunset, I proposed taking hasheesh at that time, but my friends, fearing that its operation might be more speedy upon fresh subjects, and thus betray them into some absurdity in the presence of the other travellers, preferred waiting until after the meal. It was then agreed that we should retire to our room, which, as it rose like a tower one story higher than the rest of the building, was in a manner isolated, and would screen us from observation.

We commenced by taking a tea-spoonful each of the mixture which Abdallah had procured. This was about the quantity I had taken in Egypt,

481

and as the effect then had been so slight, I judged that we ran no risk of taking an over-dose. The strength of the drug, however, must have been far greater in this instance, for whereas I could in the former case distinguish no flavor but that of sugar and rose leaves, I now found the taste intensely bitter and repulsive to the palate. We allowed the paste to dissolve slowly on our tongues, and sat some time, quietly waiting the result. But, having been taken upon a full stomach, its operation was hindered, and after the lapse of nearly an hour, we could not detect the least change in our feelings. My friends loudly expressed their conviction of the humbug of hasheesh, but I, unwilling to give up the experiment at this point, proposed that we should take an additional half spoonful, and follow it with a cup of hot tea, which, if there were really any virtue in the preparation, could not fail to call it into action. This was done, though not without some misgivings, as we were all ignorant of the precise quantity which constituted a dose, and the limits within which the drug could be taken with safety. It was now ten o'clock; the streets of Damascus were gradually becoming silent, and the fair city was bathed in the yellow lustre of the Syrian moon. Only in the marble court-yard below us, a few dragomen and mukkairee lingered under the lemon-trees, and beside the fountain in the centre.

I was seated alone, nearly in the middle of the room, talking with my friends, who were lounging upon a sofa placed in a sort of alcove, at the farther end, when the same fine nervous thrill, of which I have spoken, suddenly shot through me. But this time it was accompanied with a burning sensation at the pit of the stomach; and, instead of growing upon me with the gradual pace of healthy slumber, and resolving me, as before, into air, it came with the intensity of a pang, and shot throbbing along the nerves to the extremities of my body. The sense of limitation---of the confinement of our senses within the bounds of our own flesh and blood--instantly fell away. The walls of my frame were burst outward and tumbled into ruin; and, without thinking what form I wore--losing sight even of all idea of form--I felt that I existed throughout a vast extent of space. The blood, pulsed from my heart, sped through uncounted leagues before it reached my extremities; the air drawn into my lungs expanded into seas of limpid ether, and the arch of my skull was broader than the vault of heaven. Within the concave that held my brain, were the fathomless deeps of blue; clouds floated there, and the winds of heaven rolled them together, and there shone the orb of the sun. It was--though I thought not of that at the time--like a revelation of the mystery of omnipresence. It is difficult to describe this sensation, or the rapidity with which it mastered me. In the state of mental exaltation in which I was then plunged, all sensations, as they rose, suggested more or less coherent images. They presented themselves to me in a double form: one physical, and therefore to a certain extent tangible; the other spiritual, and revealing itself in a succession of splendid metaphors. The physical feeling of extended being was accompanied by the image of an exploding meteor, not subsiding into darkness, but continuing to shoot from its centre or nucleus-- which corresponded to the burning spot at the pit of my stomach--incessant adumbrations of light that finally lost themselves in the infinity of space. To my mind, even now, this image is still the best illustration of my sensations, as I recall them; but I greatly doubt whether the reader will find it equally clear.

My curiosity was now in a way of being satisfied; the Spirit (demon, shall I not rather say?) of Hasheesh had entire possession of me. I was cast upon the flood of his illusions, and drifted helplessly whithersoever they might choose to bear me. The thrills which ran through my nervous system became more rapid and fierce, accompanied with sensations that steeped my whole being in unutterable rapture. I was encompassed by a sea of light, through which played the pure, harmonious colors that are born of light. While endeavoring, in broken expressions, to describe my feelings to my friends, who sat looking upon me incredulously--not yet having been affected by the drug--I suddenly found myself at the foot of the great Pyramid of Cheops. The tapering courses of yellow limestone gleamed like gold in the sun, and the pile rose so high that it seemed to lean for support upon the blue arch of the sky. I wished to ascend it, and the wish alone placed me immediately upon its apex, lifted thousands of feet above the wheat-fields and palm-groves of Egypt. I cast my eyes downward, and, to my astonishment, saw that it was built, not of limestone, but of huge square plugs of Cavendish tobacco! Words cannot paint the overwhelming sense of the ludicrous which I then experienced. I writhed on my chair in an agony of laughter, which was only relieved by the vision melting away like a dissolving view; till, out of my confusion of indistinct images and fragments of images, another and more wonderful vision arose.

The more vividly I recall the scene which followed, the more carefully I restore its different features, and separate the many threads of sensation which it wove into one gorgeous web, the more I despair of representing its exceeding glory. I was moving over the Desert, not upon the rocking dromedary, but seated in a barque made of mother-of-pearl, and studded with jewels of surpassing lustre. The sand was of grains of gold, and my keel slid through them without jar or sound. The air was radiant with excess of light, though no sun was to be seen. I inhaled the most delicious perfumes; and harmonies, such as Beethoven may have heard in dreams, but never wrote, floated around me. The atmosphere itself was light, odor, music; and each and all sublimated beyond anything the sober senses are capable of receiving. Before me--for a thousand leagues, as it seemed--stretched a vista of rainbows, whose colors gleamed with the splendor of gems--arches of living amethyst, sapphire, emerald, topaz, and ruby. By thousands and tens of thousands, they flew past me, as my dazzling barge sped down the magnificent arcade; yet the vista still stretched as far as ever before me. I revelled in a sensuous elysium, which was perfect, because no sense was left ungratified. But beyond all, my mind was filled with a boundless feeling of triumph. My journey was that of a conqueror--not of a conqueror who subdues his race, either by Love or by Will, for I forgot that Man existed--but one victorious over the grandest as well as the subtlest forces of Nature. The spirits of Light, Color, Odor, Sound, and Motion were my slaves; and, having these, I was master of the universe.

Those who are endowed to any extent with the imaginative faculty, must have at least once in their lives experienced feelings which may give them a clue to the exalted sensuous raptures of my triumphal march. The view of a sublime mountain landscape, the hearing of a grand orchestral symphony, or of a choral upborne by the "full-voiced organ," or even the beauty and luxury of a cloudless summer day, suggests emotions similar in kind, if less intense. They took a warmth and glow from that pure animal joy which degrades not, but spiritualizes and ennobles our material part, and which differs from cold, abstract, intellectual enjoyment, as the flaming diamond of the Orient differs from the icicle of the North. Those finer senses, which occupy a middle ground between our animal and intellectual appetites, were suddenly developed to a pitch beyond what I had ever dreamed, and being thus at one and the same time gratified to the fullest extent of their preternatural capacity, the result was a single harmonious sensation, to describe which human language has no epithet. Mahomet's Paradise, with its palaces of ruby and emerald, its airs of musk and cassia, and its rivers colder than snow and sweeter than honey, would have been a poor and mean terminus for my arcade of rainbows. Yet in the character of this paradise, in the gorgeous fancies of the Arabian Nights, in the glow and luxury of all Oriental poetry, I now recognize more or less of the agency of hasheesh.

The fulness of my rapture expanded the sense of time; and though the whole vision was probably not more than five minutes in passing through my mind, years seemed to have elapsed while I shot under the dazzling myriads of rainbow arches. By and by, the rainbows, the barque of pearl and jewels, and the desert of golden sand, vanished; and, still bathed in light and perfume, I found myself in a land of green and flowery lawns, divided by hills of gently undulating outline. But, although the vegetation was the richest of earth, there were neither streams nor fountains to be seen; and the people who came from the hills, with brilliant garments that shone in the sun, besought me to give them the blessing of water. Their hands were full of branches of the coral honeysuckle, in bloom. These I took; and, breaking off the flowers one by one, set them in the earth. The slender, trumpet-like tubes immediately became shafts of masonry, and sank deep into the earth; the lip of the flower changed into a circular mouth of rose-colored marble, and the people, leaning over its brink, lowered their pitchers to the bottom with cords, and drew them up again, filled to the brim, and dripping with honey.

The most remarkable feature of these illusions was, that at the time when I was most completely under their influence, I knew myself to be seated in the tower of Antonio's hotel in Damascus, knew that I had taken hasheesh, and that the strange, gorgeous and ludicrous fancies which possessed me, were the effect of it. At the very same instant that I looked upon the Valley of the Nile from the pyramid, slid over the Desert, or created my marvellous wells in that beautiful pastoral country, I saw the furniture of my room, its mosaic pavement, the quaint Saracenic niches in the walls, the painted and gilded beams of the ceiling, and the couch in the recess before me, with my two companions watching me. Both sensations were simultaneous, and equally palpable. While I was most given up to the magnificent delusion, I saw its cause and felt its absurdity most clearly. Metaphysicians say that the mind is incapable of performing two operations at the same time, and may attempt to explain this phenomenon by supposing a rapid and incessant vibration of the perceptions between the two states. This explanation, however, is not satisfactory to me; for not more clearly does a skilful musician with the same breath blow two distinct musical notes from a bugle, than I was conscious of two distinct conditions of being in the same moment. Yet, singular as it may seem, neither conflicted with the other. My enjoyment of the visions was complete and absolute, undisturbed by the faintest doubt of their reality, while, in some other chamber of my brain, Reason sat coolly watching them, and heaping the liveliest ridicule on their fantastic features. One set of nerves was thrilled with the bliss of the gods, while another was convulsed with unquenchable laughter at that very bliss. My highest ecstacies could not bear down and silence the weight of my ridicule, which, in its turn, was powerless to prevent me from running into other and more gorgeous absurdities. I was double, not "swan and shadow," but rather, Sphinx-like, human and beast. A true Sphinx, I was a riddle and a mystery to myself.

The drug, which had been retarded in its operation on account of having been taken after a meal, now began to make itself more powerfully felt. The visions were more grotesque than ever, but less agreeable; and there was a painful tension throughout my nervous system--the effect of over-stimulus. I was a mass of transparent jelly, and a confectioner poured me into a twisted mould. I threw my chair aside, and writhed and tortured myself for some time to force my loose substance into the mould. At last, when I had so far succeeded that only one foot remained outside, it was lifted off, and another mould, of still more crooked and intricate shape, substituted. I have no doubt that the contortions through which I went, to accomplish the end of my gelatinous destiny, would have been extremely ludicrous to a spectator, but to me they were painful and disagreeable. The sober half of me went into fits of laughter over them, and through that laughter, my vision shifted into another scene. I had laughed until my eyes overflowed profusely. Every drop that fell, immediately became a large loaf of bread, and tumbled upon the shop-board of a baker in the bazaar at Damascus. The more I laughed, the faster the loaves fell, until such a pile was raised about the baker, that I could hardly see the top of his head. "The man will be suffocated," I cried, "but if he were to die, I cannot stop!"

My perceptions now became more dim and confused. I felt that I was in the grasp of some giant force; and, in the glimmering of my fading reason, grew earnestly alarmed, for the terrible stress under which my frame labored increased every moment. A fierce and furious heat radiated from my stomach throughout my system; my mouth and throat were as dry and hard as if made of brass, and my tongue, it seemed to me, was a bar of rusty iron. I seized a pitcher of water, and drank long and deeply; but I might as well have drunk so much air, for not only did it impart no moisture, but my palate and throat gave me no intelligence of having drunk at all. I stood in the centre of the room, brandishing my arms convulsively, an heaving sighs that seemed to shatter my whole being. "Will no one," I cried in distress, "cast out this devil that has possession of me?" I no longer saw the room nor my friends, but I heard one of them saying, "It must be real; he could not counterfeit such an expression as that. But it don't look much like pleasure." Immediately afterwards there was a scream of the wildest laughter, and my countryman sprang upon the floor, exclaiming, "O, ye gods! I am a locomotive!" This was his ruling hallucination; and, for the space of two or three hours, he continued to pace to and fro with a measured stride, exhaling his breath in violent jets, and when he spoke, dividing his words into syllables, each of which he brought out with a jerk, at the same time turning his hands at his sides, as if they were the cranks of imaginary wheels, The Englishman, as soon as he felt the dose beginning to take effect, prudently retreated to his own room, and what the nature of his visions was, we never learned, for he refused to tell, and, moreover, enjoined the strictest silence on his wife.

By this time it was nearly midnight. I had passed through the Paradise of Hasheesh, and was plunged at once into its fiercest Hell. In my ignorance I had taken what, I have since learned, would have been a sufficient portion for six men, and was now paying a frightful penalty for my curiosity. The excited blood rushed through my frame with a sound like the roaring of mighty waters. It was projected into my eyes until I could no longer see; it beat thickly in my ears, and so throbbed in my heart, that I feared the ribs would give way under its blows. I tore open my vest, placed my hand over the spot, and tried to count the pulsations; but there were two hearts, one beating at the rate of a thousand beats a minute, and the other with a slow, dull motion. My throat, I thought, was filled to the brim with blood, and streams of blood were pouring from my ears. I felt them gushing warm down my cheeks and neck. With a maddened, desperate feeling, I fled from the room, and walked over the flat, terraced roof of the house. My body seemed to shrink and grow rigid as I wrestled with the demon, and my face to become wild, lean and haggard. Some lines which had struck me, years before, in reading Mrs. Browning's "Rhyme of the Duchess May," flashed into my mind:--

"And the horse, in stark despair, with his front hoofs poised in air,

On the last verge, rears amain;

And he hangs, he rocks between--and his nostrils curdle in--

And he shivers, head and hoof, and the flakes of foam fall off;

And his face grows fierce and thin."

That picture of animal terror and agony was mine. I was the horse, hanging poised on the verge of the giddy tower, the next moment to be borne sheer down to destruction. Involuntarily, I raised my hand to feel the leanness and sharpness of my face. Oh horror! the flesh had fallen from my bones, and it was a skeleton head that I carried on my shoulders! With one bound I sprang to the parapet, and looked down into the silent courtyard, then filled with the shadows thrown into it by the sinking moon. Shall I cast myself down headlong? was the question I proposed to myself; but though the horror of that skeleton delusion was greater than my fear of death, there was an invisible hand at my breast which pushed me away from the brink.

I made my way back to the room, in a state of the keenest suffering.

488

My companion was still a locomotive, rushing to and fro, and jerking out his syllables with the disjointed accent peculiar to a steam-engine. His mouth had turned to brass, like mine, and he raised the pitcher to his lips in the attempt to moisten it, but before he had taken a mouthful, set the pitcher down again with a yell of laughter, crying out: "How can I take water into my boiler, while I am letting off steam?"

But I was now too far gone to feel the absurdity of this, or his other exclamations. I was sinking deeper and deeper into a pit of unutterable agony and despair. For, although I was not conscious of real pain in any part of my body, the cruel tension to which my nerves had been subjected filled me through and through with a sensation of distress which was far more severe than pain itself. In addition to this, the remnant of will with which I struggled against the demon, became gradually weaker, and I felt that I should soon be powerless in his hands. Every effort to preserve my reason was accompanied by a pang of mortal fear, lest what I now experienced was insanity, and would hold mastery over me for ever. The thought of death, which also haunted me, was far less bitter than this dread. I knew that in the struggle which was going on in my frame, I was borne fearfully near the dark gulf, and the thought that, at such a time, both reason and will were leaving my brain, filled me with an agony, the depth and blackness of which I should vainly attempt to portray. I threw myself on my bed, with the excited blood still roaring wildly in my ears, my heart throbbing with a force that seemed to be rapidly wearing away my life, my throat dry as a pot-sherd, and my stiffened tongue cleaving to the roof of my mouth--resisting no longer, but awaiting my fate with the apathy of despair.

My companion was now approaching the same condition, but as the effect of the drug on him had been less violent, so his stage of suffering was more clamorous. He cried out to me that he was dying, implored me to help him, and reproached me vehemently, because I lay there silent, motionless, and apparently careless of his danger. "Why will he disturb me?" I thought; "he thinks he is dying, but what is death to madness? Let him die; a thousand deaths were more easily borne than the pangs I suffer." While I was sufficiently conscious to hear his exclamations, they only provoked my keen anger; but after a time, my senses became clouded, and I sank into a stupor. As near as I can judge, this must have been three o'clock in the morning, rather more than five hours after the hasheesh began to take effect. I lay thus all the following day and night, in a state of gray, blank oblivion, broken only by a single wandering gleam of consciousness. I recollect hearing François' voice. He told me afterwards that I arose, attempted to dress myself, drank two cups of coffee, and then fell back into the same death-like stupor; but of all this, I did not retain the least knowledge. On the morning of the second day, after a sleep of thirty hours, I awoke again to the world, with a system utterly prostrate and unstrung, and a brain clouded with the lingering images of my visions. I knew where I was, and what had happened to me, but all that I saw still remained unreal and shadowy. There was no taste in what I ate, no refreshment in what I drank, and it required a painful effort to comprehend what was said to me and return a coherent answer. Will and Reason had come back, but they still sat unsteadily upon their thrones.

My friend, who was much further advanced in his recovery, accompanied me to the adjoining bath, which I hoped would assist in restoring me. It was with great difficulty that I preserved the outward appearance of consciousness. In spite of myself, a veil now and then fell over my mind, and after wandering for years, as it seemed, in some distant world, I awoke with a shock, to find myself in the steamy halls of the bath, with a brown Syrian polishing my limbs. I suspect that my language must have been rambling and incoherent, and that the menials who had me in charge understood my condition, for as soon as I had stretched myself upon the couch which follows the bath, a glass of very acid sherbet was presented to me, and after drinking it I experienced instant relief. Still the spell was not wholly broken, and for two or three days I continued subject to frequent involuntary fits of absence, which made me insensible, for the time, to all that was passing around me. I walked the streets of Damascus with a strange consciousness that I was in some other place at the same time, and with a constant effort to reunite my divided perceptions.

Previous to the experiment, we had decided on making a bargain with the shekh for the journey to Palmyra. The state, however, in which we now found ourselves, obliged us to relinquish the plan. Perhaps the excitement of

490

a forced march across the desert, and a conflict with the hostile Arabs, which was quite likely to happen, might have assisted us in throwing off the baneful effects of the drug; but all the charm which lay in the name of Palmyra and the romantic interest of the trip, was gone. I was without courage and without energy, and nothing remained for me but to leave Damascus.

Yet, fearful as my rash experiment proved to me, I did not regret having made it. It revealed to me deeps of rapture and of suffering which my natural faculties never could have sounded. It has taught me the majesty of human reason and of human will, even in the weakest, and the awful peril of tampering with that which assails their integrity. I have here faithfully and fully written out my experience, on account of the lesson which it may convey to others. If I have unfortunately failed in my design, and have but awakened that restless curiosity which I have endeavored to forestall, let me beg all who are thereby led to repeat the experiment upon themselves, that they be content to take the portion of hasheesh which is considered sufficient for one man, and not, like me, swallow enough for six.

Chapter XI. A Dissertation on Bathing and Bodies.

"No swan-soft woman, rubbed with lucid oils,

The gift of an enamored god, more fair."

Browning.

We shall not set out from Damascus--we shall not leave the Pearl of the Orient to glimmer through the seas of foliage wherein it lies buried--without consecrating a day to the Bath, that material agent of peace and good-will unto men. We have bathed in the Jordan, like Naaman, and been made clean; let us now see whether Abana and Pharpar, rivers of Damascus, are better than the waters of Israel.

The Bath is the "peculiar institution" of the East. Coffee has become colonized in France and America; the Pipe is a cosmopolite, and his blue, joyous breath congeals under the Arctic Circle, or melts languidly into the soft airs of the Polynesian Isles; but the Bath, that sensuous elysium which cradled the dreams of Plato, and the visions of Zoroaster, and the solemn meditations of Mahomet, is only to be found under an Oriental sky. The naked natives of the Torrid Zone are amphibious; they do not bathe, they live in the water. The European and Anglo-American wash themselves and think they have bathed; they shudder under cold showers and perform laborious antics with coarse towels. As for the Hydropathist, the Genius of the Bath, whose dwelling is in Damascus, would be convulsed with scornful laughter, could he behold that aqueous Diogenes sitting in his tub, or stretched out in his wet wrappings, like a sodden mummy, in a catacomb of blankets and feather beds. As the rose in the East has a rarer perfume than in other lands, so does the Bath bestow a superior purification and impart a more profound enjoyment.

Listen not unto the lamentations of travellers, who complain of the heat, and the steam, and the dislocations of their joints. They belong to the stiff-necked generation, who resist the processes, whereunto the Oriental yields himself body and soul. He who is bathed in Damascus, must be as clay in the hands of a potter. The Syrians marvel how the Franks can walk, so difficult is it to bend their joints. Moreover, they know the difference between him who comes to the Bath out of a mere idle curiosity, and him who has tasted its delight and holds it in due honor. Only the latter is permitted to know all its mysteries. The former is carelessly hurried through the ordinary forms of bathing, and, if any trace of the cockney remain in him, is quite as likely to be disgusted as pleased. Again, there are many second and third-rate baths, whither cheating dragomen conduct their victims, in consideration of a division of spoils with the bath-keeper. Hence it is, that the Bath has received but partial justice at the hands of tourists in the East. If any one doubts this, let him clothe himself with Oriental passiveness and resignation, go to the Hamman el-Khyateën, at Damascus, or the Bath of Mahmoud Pasha, at Constantinople, and demand that he be perfectly bathed.

Come with me, and I will show you the mysteries of the perfect bath. Here is the entrance, a heavy Saracenic arch, opening upon the crowded bazaar. We descend a few steps to the marble pavement of a lofty octagonal hall, lighted by a dome. There is a jet of sparkling water in the centre, falling into a heavy stone basin. A platform about five feet in height runs around the hall, and on this are ranged a number of narrow couches, with their heads to the wall, like the pallets in a hospital ward. The platform is covered with straw matting, and from the wooden gallery which rises above it are suspended towels, with blue and crimson borders. The master of the bath receives us courteously, and conducts us to one of the vacant couches. We kick off our red slippers below, and mount the steps to the platform. Yonder traveller, in Frank dress, who has just entered, goes up with his boots on, and we know, from that fact, what sort of a bath he will get.

As the work of disrobing proceeds, a dark-eyed boy appears with a napkin, which he holds before us, ready to bind it about the waist, as soon as we regain our primitive form. Another attendant throws a napkin over our shoulders and wraps a third around our head, turban-wise. He then thrusts a pair of wooden clogs upon our feet, and, taking us by the arm, steadies our tottering and clattering steps, as we pass through a low door and a warm ante-chamber into the first hall of the bath. The light, falling dimly through a cluster of bull's-eyes in the domed ceiling, shows, first, a silver thread of water, playing in a steamy atmosphere; next, some dark motionless objects, stretched out on a low central platform of marble. The attendant spreads a linen sheet in one of the vacant places, places a pillow at one end, takes off our clogs, deposits us gently on our back, and leaves us. The pavement is warm beneath us, and the first breath we draw gives us a sense of suffocation. But a bit of burning aloe-wood has just been carried through the hall, and the steam is permeated with fragrance. The dark-eyed boy appears with a narghileh, which he places beside us, offering the amber mouth-piece to our submissive lips. The smoke we inhale has an odor of roses; and as the pipe bubbles with our breathing, we feel that the dews of sweat gather heavily upon us. The attendant now reappears, kneels beside us, and gently kneads us with dexterous hands. Although no anatomist, he knows every muscle and sinew whose suppleness gives ease to the body, and so moulds and manipulates them that we lose the rigidity of our mechanism, and become plastic in his hands. He turns us upon our face, repeats the same process upon the back, and leaves us a little longer to lie there passively, glistening in our own dew.

We are aroused from a reverie about nothing by a dark-brown shape, who replaces the clogs, puts his arm around our waist and leads us into an inner hall, with a steaming tank in the centre. Here he slips us off the brink, and we collapse over head and ears in the fiery fluid. Once--twice--we dip into the delicious heat, and then are led into a marble alcove, and seated flat upon the floor. The attendant stands behind us, and we now perceive that his hands are encased in dark hair-gloves. He pounces upon an arm, which he rubs until, like a serpent, we slough the worn-out skin, and resume our infantile smoothness and fairness. No man can be called clean until he has bathed in the East. Let him walk directly from his accustomed bath and self-friction with towels, to the Hammam el-Khyateën, and the attendant will exclaim, as he shakes out his hair-gloves: "O Frank! it is a long time since you have bathed." The other arm follows, the back, the breast, the legs, until the work is complete, and we know precisely how a horse feels after he has been curried.

Now the attendant turns two cocks at the back of the alcove, and holding a basin alternately under the cold and hot streams, floods us at first with a fiery dash, that sends a delicious warm shiver through every nerve; then, with milder applications, lessening the temperature of the water by semi-tones, until, from the highest key of heat which we can bear, we glide rapturously down the gamut until we reach the lowest bass of coolness. The skin has by this time attained an exquisite sensibility, and answers to these changes of temperature with thrills of the purest physical pleasure. In fact, the whole frame seems purged of its earthy nature and transformed into something of a finer and more delicate texture.

After a pause, the attendant makes his appearance with a large wooden bowl, a piece of soap, and a bunch of palm-fibres. He squats down beside the bowl, and speedily creates a mass of snowy lather, which grows up to a pyramid and topples over the edge. Seizing us by the crown-tuft of hair upon our shaven head, he plants the foamy bunch of fibres full in our face. The world vanishes; sight, hearing, smell, taste (unless we open our mouth), and breathing, are cut off; we have become nebulous. Although our eyes are shut, we seem to see a blank whiteness; and, feeling nothing but a soft fleeciness, we doubt whether we be not the Olympian cloud which visited Io. But the cloud clears away before strangulation begins, and the velvety mass descends upon the body. Twice we are thus "slushed" from head to foot, and made more slippery than the anointed wrestlers of the Greek games. Then the basin comes again into play, and we glide once more musically through the scale of temperature.

The brown sculptor has now nearly completed his task. The figure of clay which entered the bath is transformed into polished marble. He turns the body from side to side, and lifts the limbs to see whether the workmanship is adequate to his conception. His satisfied gaze proclaims his success. A skilful bath-attendant has a certain aesthetic pleasure in his occupation. The bodies he polishes become to some extent his own workmanship, and he feels responsible for their symmetry or deformity. He experiences a degree of triumph in contemplating a beautiful form, which has grown more airily light and beautiful under his hands. He is a great connoisseur of bodies, and could pick you out the finest specimens with as ready an eye as an artist.

495

I envy those old Greek bathers, into whose hands were delivered Pericles, and Alcibiades, and the perfect models of Phidias. They had daily before their eyes the highest types of Beauty which the world has ever produced; for of all things that are beautiful, the human body is the crown. Now, since the delusion of artists has been overthrown, and we know that Grecian Art is but the simple reflex of Nature--that the old masterpieces of sculpture were no miraculous embodiments of a beau ideal, but copies of living forms--we must admit that in no other age of the world has the physical Man been so perfectly developed. The nearest approach I have ever seen to the symmetry of ancient sculpture was among the Arab tribes of Ethiopia. Our Saxon race can supply the athlete, but not the Apollo.

Oriental life is too full of repose, and the Ottoman race has become too degenerate through indulgence, to exhibit many striking specimens of physical beauty. The face is generally fine, but the body is apt to be lank, and with imperfect muscular development. The best forms I saw in the baths were those of laborers, who, with a good deal of rugged strength, showed some grace and harmony of proportion. It may be received as a general rule, that the physical development of the European is superior to that of the Oriental, with the exception of the Circassians and Georgians, whose beauty well entitles them to the distinction of giving their name to our race.

So far as female beauty is concerned, the Circassian women have no superiors. They have preserved in their mountain home the purity of the Grecian models, and still display the perfect physical loveliness, whose type has descended to us in the Venus de Medici. The Frank who is addicted to wandering about the streets of Oriental cities can hardly fail to be favored with a sight of the faces of these beauties. More than once it has happened to me, in meeting a veiled lady, sailing along in her balloon-like feridjee, that she has allowed the veil to drop by a skilful accident, as she passed, and has startled me with the vision of her beauty, recalling the line of the Persian poet: "Astonishment! is this the dawn of the glorious sun, or is it the full moon?" The Circassian face is a pure oval; the forehead is low and fair, "an excellent thing in woman," and the skin of an ivory whiteness, except the faint pink of the cheeks and the ripe, roseate stain of the lips. The hair is dark, glossy, and luxuriant, exquisitely outlined on the temples; the eyebrows slightly arched, and drawn with a delicate pencil; while lashes like "rays of darkness" shade the large, dark, humid orbs below them. The alabaster of the face, so pure as scarcely to show the blue branching of the veins on the temples, is lighted by those superb eyes--

"Shining eyes, like antique jewels set in Parian statue-stone,"

--whose wells are so dark and deep, that you are cheated into the belief that a glorious soul looks out of them.

Once, by an unforeseen chance, I beheld the Circassian form, in its most perfect development. I was on board an Austrian steamer in the harbor of Smyrna, when the harem of a Turkish pasha came out in a boat to embark for Alexandria. The sea was rather rough, and nearly all the officers of the steamer were ashore. There were six veiled and swaddled women, with a black eunuch as guard, in the boat, which lay tossing for some time at the foot of the gangway ladder, before the frightened passengers could summon courage to step out. At last the youngest of them--a Circassian girl of not more than fifteen or sixteen years of age--ventured upon the ladder, clasping the hand-rail with one hand, while with the other she held together the folds of her cumbrous feridjee. I was standing in the gangway, watching her, when a slight lurch of the steamer caused her to loose her hold of the garment, which, fastened at the neck, was blown back from her shoulders, leaving her body screened but by a single robe of-light, gauzy silk. Through this, the marble whiteness of her skin, the roundness, the glorious symmetry of her form, flashed upon me, as a vision of Aphrodite, seen

"Through leagues of shimmering water, like a star."

It was but a momentary glimpse; yet that moment convinced me that forms of Phidian perfection are still nurtured in the vales of Caucasus.

The necessary disguise of dress hides from us much of the beauty and dignity of Humanity, I have seen men who appeared heroic in the freedom of nakedness, shrink almost into absolute vulgarity, when clothed. The soul not only sits at the windows of the eyes, and hangs upon the gateway of the lips;

she speaks as well in the intricate, yet harmonious lines of the body, and the ever-varying play of the limbs. Look at the torso of Ilioneus, the son of Niobe, and see what an agony of terror and supplication cries out from that headless and limbless trunk! Decapitate Laocoön, and his knotted muscles will still express the same dreadful suffering and resistance. None knew this better than the ancient sculptors; and hence it was that we find many of their statues of distinguished men wholly or partly undraped. Such a view of Art would be considered transcendental now-a-days, when our dress, our costumes, and our modes of speech either ignore the existence of our bodies, or treat them with little of that reverence which is their due.

But, while we have been thinking these thoughts, the attendant has been waiting to give us a final plunge into the seething tank. Again we slide down to the eyes in the fluid heat, which wraps us closely about until we tingle with exquisite hot shiverings. Now comes the graceful boy, with clean, cool, lavendered napkins, which he folds around our waist and wraps softly about the head. The pattens are put upon our feet, and the brown arm steadies us gently through the sweating-room and ante-chamber into the outer hall, where we mount to our couch. We sink gently upon the cool linen, and the boy covers us with a perfumed sheet. Then, kneeling beside the couch, he presses the folds of the sheet around us, that it may absorb the lingering moisture and the limpid perspiration shed by the departing heat. As fast as the linen becomes damp, he replaces it with fresh, pressing the folds about us as tenderly as a mother arranges the drapery of her sleeping babe; for we, though of the stature of a man, are now infantile in our helpless happiness. Then he takes our passive hand and warms its palm by the soft friction of his own; after which, moving to the end of the couch, he lifts our feet upon his lap, and repeats the friction upon their soles, until the blood comes back to the surface of the body with a misty glow, like that which steeps the clouds of a summer afternoon.

We have but one more process to undergo, and the attendant already stands at the head of our couch. This is the course of passive gymnastics, which excites so much alarm and resistance in the ignorant Franks. It is only resistance that is dangerous, completely neutralizing the enjoyment of the process. Give yourself with a blind submission into the arms of the brown Fate, and he will lead you to new chambers of delight. He lifts us to a sitting posture, places himself behind us, and folds his arms around our body, alternately tightening and relaxing his clasp, as if to test the elasticity of the ribs. Then seizing one arm, he draws it across the opposite shoulder, until the joint cracks like a percussion-cap. The shoulder-blades, the elbows, the wrists, and the finger-joints are all made to fire off their muffled volleys; and then, placing one knee between our shoulders, and clasping both hands upon our forehead, he draws our head back until we feel a great snap of the vertebral column. Now he descends to the hip-joints, knees, ankles, and feet, forcing each and all to discharge a salvo de joie. The slight languor left from the bath is gone, and an airy, delicate exhilaration, befitting the winged Mercury, takes its place.

The boy, kneeling, presents us with finjan of foamy coffee, followed by a glass of sherbet cooled with the snows of Lebanon. He presently returns with a narghileh, which we smoke by the effortless inhalation of the lungs. Thus we lie in perfect repose, soothed by the fragrant weed, and idly watching the silent Orientals, who are undressing for the bath or reposing like ourselves. Through the arched entrance, we see a picture of the bazaars: a shadowy painting of merchants seated amid their silks and spices, dotted here and there with golden drops and splashes of sunshine, which have trickled through the roof. The scene paints itself upon our eyes, yet wakes no slightest stir of thought. The brain is a becalmed sea, without a ripple on its shores. Mind and body are drowned in delicious rest; and we no longer remember what we are. We only know that there is an Existence somewhere in the air, and that wherever it is, and whatever it may be, it is happy.

More and more dim grows the picture. The colors fade and blend into each other, and finally merge into a bed of rosy clouds, flooded with the radiance of some unseen sun. Gentlier than "tired eyelids upon tired eyes," sleep lies upon our senses: a half-conscious sleep, wherein we know that we behold light and inhale fragrance. As gently, the clouds dissipate into air, and we are born again into the world. The Bath is at an end. We arise and put on our garments, and walk forth into the sunny streets of Damascus. But as we go homewards, we involuntarily look down to see whether we are really treading upon the earth, wondering, perhaps, that we should be content to do so, when it would be so easy to soar above the house-tops.

Chapter XII. Baalbec and Lebanon.

Departure from Damascus--The Fountains of the Pharpar--Pass of the Anti-Lebanon--Adventure with the Druses--The Range of Lebanon--The Demon of Hasheesh departs--Impressions of Baalbec--The Temple of the Sun--Titanic Masonry--The Ruined Mosque--Camp on Lebanon--Rascality of the Guide--The Summit of Lebanon--The Sacred Cedars--The Christians of Lebanon--An Afternoon in Eden--Rugged Travel--We Reach the Coast--Return to Beyrout.

"Peor and Baälim

Forsake their temples dim."

Milton.

"The cedars wave on Lebanon,

But Judah's statelier maids are gone."

Byron.

Beyrout, *Thursday, May* 27, 1852.

After a stay of eight days in Damascus, we called our men, Dervish and Mustapha, again into requisition, loaded our enthusiastic mules, and mounted our despairing horses. There were two other parties on the way to Baalbec--an English gentleman and lady, and a solitary Englishman, so that our united forces made an imposing caravan. There is always a custom-house examination, not on entering, but on issuing from an Oriental city, but travellers can avoid it by procuring the company of a Consular Janissary as far as the gate. Mr. Wood, the British Consul, lent us one of his officers for the occasion, whom we found waiting, outside of the wall, to receive his private fee for the service. We mounted the long, barren hill west of the plain, and at the summit, near the tomb of a Moslem shekh, turned to take a last long look at the bowery plain, and the minarets of the city, glittering through the blue morning vapor. A few paces further on the rocky road, a different scene presented itself to us. There lay, to the westward, a long stretch of naked yellow mountains, basking in the hot glare of the sun, and through the centre, deep down in the heart of the arid landscape, a winding line of living green showed the course of the Barrada. We followed the river, until the path reached an impassable gorge, which occasioned a detour of two or three hours. We then descended to the bed of the dell, where the vegetation, owing to the radiated heat from the mountains and the fertilizing stimulus of the water below, was even richer than on the plain of Damascus. The trees were plethoric with an overplus of life. The boughs of the mulberries were weighed down with the burden of the leaves; pomegranates were in a violent eruption of blossoms; and the foliage of the fig and poplar was of so deep a hue that it shone black in the sun.

Passing through a gateway of rock, so narrow that we were often obliged to ride in the bed of the stream, we reached a little meadow, beyond which was a small hamlet, almost hidden in the leaves. Here the mountains again approached each other, and from the side of that on the right hand, the main body of the Barrada, or Pharpar, gushed forth in one full stream. The fountain is nearly double the volume of that of the Jordan at Banias, and much more beautiful. The foundations of an ancient building, probably a temple, overhang it, and tall poplars and sycamores cover it with impenetrable shade. From the low aperture, where it bursts into the light, its waters, white with foam, bound away flashing in the chance rays of sunshine, until they are lost to sight in the dense, dark foliage. We sat an hour on the ruined walls, listening to the roar and rush of the flood, and enjoying the shade of the walnuts and sycamores. Soon after leaving, our path crossed a small stream, which comes down to the Barrada from the upper valleys of the Anti-Lebanon, and entered a wild pass, faced with cliffs of perpendicular rock. An old bridge, of one arch, spanned the chasm, out of which we climbed to a tract of high meadow land. In the pass there were some fragments of ancient columns, traces of an aqueduct, and inscriptions on the rocks, among which Mr. H. found the name of Antoninus. The place is not mentioned in any book of travel I have seen, as it is not on the usual road from Damascus to Baalbec.

As we were emerging from the pass, we saw a company of twelve armed men seated in the grass, near the roadside. They were wild-looking characters, and eyed us somewhat sharply as we passed. We greeted them with the usual "salaam aleikoom!" which they did not return. The same evening, as we encamped at the village of Zebdeni, about three hours further up the valley, we were startled by a great noise and outcry, with the firing of pistols. It happened, as we learned on inquiring the cause of all this confusion, that the men we saw in the pass were rebel Druses, who were then lying in wait for the Shekh of Zebdeni, whom, with his son, they had taken captive soon after we passed. The news had by some means been conveyed to the village, and a company of about two hundred persons was then marching out to the rescue. The noise they made was probably to give the Druses intimation of their coming, and thus avoid a fight. I do not believe that any of the mountaineers of Lebanon would willingly take part against the Druses, who, in fact, are not fighting so much against the institution of the conscription law, as its abuse. The law ordains that the conscript shall serve for five years; but since its establishment, as I have been informed, there has not been a single instance of discharge. It amounts, therefore, to lifelong servitude, and there is little wonder that these independent sons of the mountains, as well as the tribes inhabiting the Syrian Desert, should rebel rather than submit.

The next day, we crossed a pass in the Anti-Lebanon beyond Zebdeni, descended a beautiful valley on the western side, under a ridge which was still dotted with patches of snow, and after travelling for some hours over a wide, barren height, the last of the range, saw below us the plain of Baalbec. The grand ridge of Lebanon opposite, crowned with glittering fields of snow, shone out clearly through the pure air, and the hoary head of Hermon, far in the south, lost something of its grandeur by the comparison. Though there is a "divide," or watershed, between Husbeiya, at the foot of Mount Hermon, and Baalbec, whose springs join the Orontes, which flows northward to Antioch, the great natural separation of the two chains continues unbroken to the Gulf of Akaba, in the Red Sea. A little beyond Baalbec, the Anti-Lebanon terminates, sinking into the Syrian plain, while the Lebanon, though its name and general features are lost, about twenty miles further to the north is succeeded by other ranges, which, though broken at intervals, form a regular series, connecting with the Taurus, in Asia Minor.

On leaving Damascus, the Demon of Hasheesh still maintained a partial control over me. I was weak in body and at times confused in my perceptions, wandering away from the scenes about me to some unknown sphere beyond the moon. But the healing balm of my sleep at Zebdeni, and the purity of the morning air among the mountains, completed my cure. As I rode along the valley, with the towering, snow-sprinkled ridge of the Anti-Lebanon on my right, a cloudless heaven above my head, and meads enamelled with the asphodel and scarlet anemone stretching before me, I felt that the last shadow had rolled away from my brain. My mind was now as clear as that sky--my heart as free and joyful as the elastic morning air. The sun never shone so brightly to my eyes; the fair forms of Nature were never penetrated with so perfect a spirit of beauty. I was again master of myself, and the world glowed as if new-created in the light of my joy and gratitude. I thanked God, who had led me out of a darkness more terrible than that of the Valley of the Shadow of Death, and while my feet strayed among the flowery meadows of Lebanon, my heart walked on the Delectable Hills of His Mercy.

By the middle of the afternoon, we reached Baalbec. The distant view of the temple, on descending the last slope of the Anti-Lebanon, is not calculated to raise one's expectations. On the green plain at the foot of the mountain, you see a large square platform of masonry, upon which stand six columns, the body of the temple, and a quantity of ruined walls. As a feature in the landscape, it has a fine effect, but you find yourself pronouncing the speedy judgment, that "Baalbec, without Lebanon, would be rather a poor show." Having come to this conclusion, you ride down the hill with comfortable feelings of indifference. There are a number of quarries on the left hand; you glance at them with an expression which merely says: "Ah! I suppose they got the stones here," and so you saunter on, cross a little stream that flows down from the modern village, pass a mill, return the stare of the quaint Arab miller who comes to the door to see you, and your horse is climbing a difficult path among the broken columns and friezes, before you think it worth while to lift your eyes to the pile above you. Now re-assert your judgment, if you dare! This is Baalbec: what have you to say? Nothing; but you amazedly measure the torsos of great columns which lie piled across one another in magnificent wreck; vast pieces which have dropped from the

504

entablature, beautiful Corinthian capitals, bereft of the last graceful curves of their acanthus leaves, and blocks whose edges are so worn away that they resemble enormous natural boulders left by the Deluge, till at last you look up to the six glorious pillars, towering nigh a hundred feet above your head, and there is a sensation in your brain which would be a shout, if you could give it utterance, of faultless symmetry and majesty, such as no conception of yours and no other creation of art, can surpass.

I know of nothing so beautiful in all remains of ancient Art as these six columns, except the colonnade of the Memnonium, at Thebes, which is of much smaller proportions. From every position, and with all lights of the day or night, they are equally perfect, and carry your eyes continually away from the peristyle of the smaller temple, which is better preserved, and from the exquisite architecture of the outer courts and pavilions. The two temples of Baalbec stand on an artificial platform of masonry, a thousand feet in length, and from fifteen to thirty feet (according to the depression of the soil) in height, The larger one, which is supposed to have been a Pantheon, occupies the whole length of this platform. The entrance was at the north, by a grand flight of steps, now broken away, between two lofty and elegant pavilions which are still nearly entire. Then followed a spacious hexagonal court, and three grand halls, parts of which, with niches for statues, adorned with cornices and pediments of elaborate design, still remain entire to the roof. This magnificent series of chambers was terminated at the southern extremity of the platform by the main temple, which had originally twenty columns on a side, similar to the six now standing.

The Temple of the Sun stands on a smaller and lower platform, which appears to have been subsequently added to the greater one. The cella, or body of the temple, is complete except the roof, and of the colonnade surrounding it, nearly one-half of its pillars are still standing, upholding the frieze, entablature, and cornice, which altogether form probably the most ornate specimen of the Corinthian order of architecture now extant. Only four pillars of the superb portico remain, and the Saracens have nearly ruined these by building a sort of watch-tower upon the architrave. The same unscrupulous race completely shut up the portal of the temple with a blank wall, formed of the fragments they had hurled down, and one is obliged to creep through a narrow hole in order to reach the interior. Here the original doorway faces you--and I know not how to describe the wonderful design of its elaborate sculptured mouldings and cornices. The genius of Greek art seems to have exhausted itself in inventing ornaments, which, while they should heighten the gorgeous effect of the work, must yet harmonize with the grand design of the temple. The enormous keystone over the entrance has slipped down, no doubt from the shock of an earthquake, and hangs within six inches of the bottom of the two blocks which uphold it on either side. When it falls, the whole entablature of the portal will be destroyed. On its lower side is an eagle with outspread wings, and on the side-stones a genius with garlands of flowers, exquisitely sculptured in bas relief. Hidden among the wreaths of vines which adorn the jambs are the laughing heads of fauns. This portal was a continual study to me, every visit revealing new refinements of ornament, which I had not before observed. The interior of the temple, with its rich Corinthian pilasters, its niches for statues, surmounted by pediments of elegant design, and its elaborate cornice, needs little aid of the imagination to restore it to its original perfection. Like that of Dendera, in Egypt, the Temple of the Sun leaves upon the mind an impression of completeness which makes you forget far grander remains.

But the most wonderful thing at Baalbec is the foundation platform upon which the temples stand. Even the colossal fabrics of Ancient Egypt dwindle before this superhuman masonry. The platform itself, 1,000 feet long, and averaging twenty feet in height, suggests a vast mass of stones, but when you come to examine the single blocks of which it is composed, you are crushed with their incredible bulk. On the western side is a row of eleven foundation stones, each of which is thirty-two feet in length, twelve in height, and ten in thickness, forming a wall three hundred and fifty-two feet long! But while you are walking on, thinking of the art which cut and raised these enormous blocks, you turn the southern corner and come upon three stones, the united length of which is one hundred and eighty-seven feet--two of them being sixty-two and the other sixty-three feet in length! There they are, cut with faultless exactness, and so smoothly joined to each other, that you cannot force a cambric needle into the crevice. There is one joint so perfect that it can only be discerned by the minutest search; it is not even so perceptible as the junction of two pieces of paper which have been pasted together. In the quarry, there still lies a finished block, ready for transportation, which is sixty-seven feet in length. The weight of one of these masses has been reckoned at near 9,000 tons, yet they do not form the base of the foundation, but are raised upon other courses, fifteen feet from the ground. It is considered by some antiquarians that they are of a date greatly anterior to that of the temples, and were intended as the basement of a different edifice.

In the village of Baalbec there is a small circular Corinthian temple of very elegant design. It is not more than thirty feet in diameter, and may have been intended as a tomb. A spacious mosque, now roofless and deserted, was constructed almost entirely out of the remains of the temples. Adjoining the court-yard and fountain are five rows of ancient pillars, forty (the sacred number) in all, supporting light Saracenic arches. Some of them are marble, with Corinthian capitals, and eighteen are single shafts of red Egyptian granite. Beside the fountain lies a small broken pillar of porphyry, of a dark violet hue, and of so fine a grain that the stone has the soft rich lustre of velvet. This fragment is the only thing I would carry away if I had the power.

After a day's sojourn, we left Baalbec at noon, and took the road for the Cedars, which lie on the other side of Lebanon, in the direction of Tripoli. Our English fellow-travellers chose the direct road to Beyrout. We crossed the plain in three hours; to the village of Dayr el-Ahmar, and then commenced ascending the lowest slopes of the great range, whose topmost ridge, a dazzling parapet of snow, rose high above us. For several hours, our path led up and down stony ridges, covered with thickets of oak and holly, and with wild cherry, pear, and olive-trees. Just as the sun threw the shadows of the highest Lebanon over us, we came upon a narrow, rocky glen at his very base. Streams that still kept the color and the coolness of the snow-fields from which they oozed, foamed over the stones into the chasm at the bottom. The glen descended into a mountain basin, in which lay the lake of Yemouni, cold and green under the evening shadows. But just opposite us, on a little shelf of soil, there was a rude mill, and a group of superb walnut-trees, overhanging the brink of the largest torrent. We had sent our baggage before us, and the men, with an eye to the picturesque which I should not have suspected in Arabs, had pitched our tents under those trees, where the stream poured its snow-cold beakers beside us, and the tent-door looked down on the plain of Baalbec and across to the Anti-Lebanon. The miller and two or three peasants, who were living in this lonely spot, were Christians.

The next morning we commenced ascending the Lebanon. We had slept just below the snow-line, for the long hollows with which the ridge is cloven were filled up to within a short distance of the glen, out of which we came. The path was very steep, continually ascending, now around the barren shoulder of the mountain, now up some ravine, where the holly and olive still flourished, and the wild rhubarb-plant spread its large, succulent leaves over the soil. We had taken a guide, the day before, at the village of Dayr el-Ahmar, but as the way was plain before us, and he demanded an exorbitant sum, we dismissed him, We had not climbed far, however, before he returned, professing to be content with whatever we might give him, and took us into another road, the first, he said, being impracticable. Up and up we toiled, and the long hollows of snow lay below us, and the wind came cold from the topmost peaks, which began to show near at hand. But now the road, as we had surmised, turned towards that we had first taken, and on reaching the next height we saw the latter at a short distance from us. It was not only a better, but a shorter road, the rascal of a guide having led us out of it in order to give the greater effect to his services. In order to return to it, as was necessary, there were several dangerous snow-fields to be passed. The angle of their descent was so great that a single false step would have hurled our animals, baggage and all, many hundred feet below. The snow was melting, and the crust frozen over the streams below was so thin in places that the animals broke through and sank to their bellies.

It were needless to state the number and character of the anathemas bestowed upon the guide. The impassive Dervish raved; Mustapha stormed; François broke out in a frightful eruption of Greek and Turkish oaths, and the two travellers, though not (as I hope and believe) profanely inclined, could not avoid using a few terse Saxon expressions. When the general indignation had found vent, the men went to work, and by taking each animal separately, succeeded, at imminent hazard, in getting them all over the snow. We then dismissed the guide, who, far from being abashed by the discovery of his trickery, had the impudence to follow us for some time, claiming his pay. A few more steep pulls, over deep beds of snow and patches of barren stone, and at length the summit ridge--a sharp, white wall, shining against the intense black-blue of the zenith--stood before us. We climbed a toilsome zig-zag through the snow, hurried over the stones cumbering the top, and all at once the mountains fell away, ridge below ridge, gashed with tremendous chasms, whose bottoms were lost in blue vapor, till the last heights, crowned with white Maronite convents, hung above the sea, whose misty round bounded the vision. I have seen many grander mountain views, but few so sublimely rugged and broken in their features. The sides of the ridges dropped off in all directions into sheer precipices, and the few villages we could see were built like eagles' nests on the brinks. In a little hollow at our feet was the sacred Forest of Cedars, appearing like a patch of stunted junipers. It is the highest speck of vegetation on Lebanon, and in winter cannot be visited, on account of the snow. The summit on which we stood was about nine thousand feet above the sea, but there were peaks on each side at least a thousand feet higher.

We descended by a very steep path, over occasional beds of snow, and reached the Cedars in an hour and a half. Not until we were within a hundred yards of the trees, and below their level, was I at all impressed with their size and venerable aspect. But, once entered into the heart of the little wood, walking over its miniature hills and valleys, and breathing the pure, balsamic exhalations of the trees, all the disappointment rising to my mind was charmed away in an instant There are about three hundred trees, in all, many of which are of the last century's growth, but at least fifty of them would be considered grand in any forest. The patriarchs are five in number, and are undoubtedly as old as the Christian Era, if not the Age of Solomon. The cypresses in the Garden of Montezuma, at Chapultepec, are even older and grander trees, but they are as entire and shapely as ever, whereas these are gnarled and twisted into wonderful forms by the storms of twenty centuries, and shivered in some places by lightning. The hoary father of them all, nine feet in diameter, stands in the centre of the grove, on a little knoll, and spreads his ponderous arms, each a tree in itself, over the heads of the many generations that have grown up below, as if giving his last benediction before decay. He is scarred less with storm and lightning, than with the knives of travellers, and the marble crags of Lebanon do not more firmly retain their inscriptions than his stony trunk. Dates of the last century are abundant, and I recollect a tablet inscribed: "Souard, 1670," around which the newer wood has grown to the height of three or four inches. The seclusion of the grove, shut in by peaks of barren snow, is complete. Only the voice of the nightingale, singing here by daylight in the solemn shadows, breaks the silence. The Maronite monk, who has charge of a little stone chapel standing in the midst, moves about like a shade, and, not before you are ready to leave, brings his book for you to register your name therein, I was surprised to find how few of the crowd that annually overrun Syria reach the Cedars, which, after Baalbec, are the finest remains of antiquity in the whole country.

After a stay of three hours, we rode on to Eden, whither our men had already gone with the baggage. Our road led along the brink of a tremendous gorge, a thousand feet deep, the bottom of which was only accessible here and there by hazardous foot-paths. On either side, a long shelf of cultivated land sloped down to the top, and the mountain streams, after watering a multitude of orchards and grain-fields, tumbled over the cliffs in long, sparkling cascades, to join the roaring flood below. This is the Christian region of Lebanon, inhabited almost wholly by Maronites, who still retain a portion of their former independence, and are the most thrifty, industrious, honest, and happy people in Syria. Their villages are not concrete masses of picturesque filth, as are those of the Moslems, but are loosely scattered among orchards of mulberry, poplar, and vine, washed by fresh rills, and have an air of comparative neatness and comfort. Each has its two or three chapels, with their little belfries, which toll the hours of prayer. Sad and poetic as is the call from the minaret, it never touched me as when I heard the sweet tongues of those Christian bells, chiming vespers far and near on the sides of Lebanon.

Eden merits its name. It is a mountain paradise, inhabited by people so kind and simple-hearted, that assuredly no vengeful angel will ever drive them out with his flaming sword. It hangs above the gorge, which is here nearly two thousand feet deep, and overlooks a grand wilderness of mountain-

510

piles, crowded on and over each other, from the sea that gleams below, to the topmost heights that keep off the morning sun. The houses are all built of hewn stone, and grouped in clusters under the shade of large walnut-trees. In walking among them, we received kind greetings everywhere, and every one who was seated rose and remained standing as we passed. The women are beautiful, with sprightly, intelligent faces, quite different from the stupid Mahometan females.

The children were charming creatures, and some of the girls of ten or twelve years were lovely as angels. They came timidly to our tent (which the men had pitched as before, under two superb trees, beside a fountain), and offered us roses and branches of fragrant white jasmine. They expected some return, of course, but did not ask it, and the delicate grace with which the offering was made was beyond all pay. It was Sunday, and the men and boys, having nothing better to do, all came to see and talk with us. I shall not soon forget the circle of gay and laughing villagers, in which we sat that evening, while the dark purple shadows gradually filled up the gorges, and broad golden lights poured over the shoulders of the hills. The men had much sport in inducing the smaller boys to come up and salute us. There was one whom they called "the Consul," who eluded them for some time, but was finally caught and placed in the ring before us. "Peace be with you, O Consul," I said, making him a profound inclination, "may your days be propitious! may your shadow be increased!" but I then saw, from the vacant expression on the boy's face, that he was one of those harmless, witless creatures, whom yet one cannot quite call idiots. "He is an unfortunate; he knows nothing; he has no protector but God," said the men, crossing themselves devoutly. The boy took off his cap, crept up and kissed my hand, as I gave him some money, which he no sooner grasped, than he sprang up like a startled gazelle, and was out of sight in an instant.

In descending from Eden to the sea-coast, we were obliged to cross the great gorge of which I spoke. Further down, its sides are less steep, and clothed even to the very bottom with magnificent orchards of mulberry, fig, olive, orange, and pomegranate trees. We were three hours in reaching the opposite side, although the breadth across the top is not more than a mile.

The path was exceedingly perilous; we walked down, leading our horses, and once were obliged to unload our mules to get them past a tree, which would have forced them off the brink of a chasm several hundred feet deep. The view from the bottom was wonderful. We were shut in by steeps of foliage and blossoms from two to three thousand feet high, broken by crags of white marble, and towering almost precipitously to the very clouds. I doubt if Melville saw anything grander in the tropical gorges of Typee. After reaching the other side, we had still a journey of eight hours to the sea, through a wild and broken, yet highly cultivated country.

Beyrout was now thirteen hours distant, but by making a forced march we reached it in a day, travelling along the shore, past the towns of Jebeil, the ancient Byblus, and Joonieh. The hills about Jebeil produce the celebrated tobacco known in Egypt as the Jebelee, or "mountain" tobacco, which is even superior to the Latakiyeh.

Near Beyrout, the mulberry and olive are in the ascendant. The latter tree bears the finest fruit in all the Levant, and might drive all other oils out of the market, if any one had enterprise enough to erect proper manufactories. Instead of this the oil of the country is badly prepared, rancid from the skins in which it is kept, and the wealthy natives import from France and Italy in preference to using it. In the bottoms near the sea, I saw several fields of the taro-plant, the cultivation of which I had supposed was exclusively confined to the Islands of the Pacific. There would be no end to the wealth of Syria were the country in proper hands.

Chapter XIII. Pipes and Coffee.

--"the kind nymph to Bacchus born

By Morpheus' daughter, she that seems

Gifted upon her natal morn

By him with fire, by her with dreams--

Nicotia, dearer to the Muse

Than all the grape's bewildering juice." Lowell.

In painting the picture of an Oriental, the pipe and the coffee-cup are indispensable accessories. There is scarce a Turk, or Arab, or Persian--unless he be a Dervish of peculiar sanctity--but breathes his daily incense to the milder Bacchus of the moderns. The custom has become so thoroughly naturalized in the East, that we are apt to forget its comparatively recent introduction, and to wonder that no mention is made of the pipe in the Arabian Nights. The practice of smoking harmonizes so thoroughly with the character of Oriental life, that it is difficult for us to imagine a time when it never existed. It has become a part of that supreme patience, that wonderful repose, which forms so strong a contrast to the over-active life of the New World--the enjoyment of which no one can taste, to whom the pipe is not familiar. Howl, ye Reformers! but I solemnly declare unto you, that he who travels through the East without smoking, does not know the East.

It is strange that our Continent, where the meaning of Rest is unknown, should have given to the world this great agent of Rest. There is nothing more remarkable in history than the colonization of Tobacco over the whole Earth. Not three centuries have elapsed since knightly Raleigh puffed its fumes into the astonished eyes of Spenser and Shakspeare; and now, find me any corner of the world, from Nova Zembla to the Mountains of the Moon, where the use of the plant is unknown! Tarshish (if India was Tarshish) is less distinguished by its "apes, ivory, and peacocks," than by its hookahs; the valleys of Luzon, beyond Ternate and Tidore, send us more cheroots than spices; the Gardens of Shiraz produce more velvety toombek than roses, and the only fountains which bubble in Samarcand are those of the narghilehs: Lebanon is no longer "excellent with the Cedars," as in the days of Solomon, but most excellent with its fields of Jebelee and Latakiyeh. On the unvisited plains of Central Africa, the table-lands of Tartary, and in the valleys of Japan, the wonderful plant has found a home. The naked negro, "panting at the Line," inhales it under the palms, and the Lapp and Samoyed on the shores of the Frozen Sea.

It is idle for those who object to the use of Tobacco to attribute these phenomena wholly to a perverted taste. The fact that the custom was at once adopted by all the races of men, whatever their geographical position and degree of civilization, proves that there must be a reason for it in the physical constitution of man. Its effect, when habitually used, is slightly narcotic and sedative, not stimulating--or if so, at times, it stimulates only the imagination and the social faculties. It lulls to sleep the combative and destructive propensities, and hence--so far as a material agent may operate--it exercises a humanizing and refining influence. A profound student of Man, whose name is well known to the world, once informed me that he saw in the eagerness with which savage tribes adopt the use of Tobacco, a spontaneous movement of Nature towards Civilization.

I will not pursue these speculations further, for the narghileh (bubbling softly at my elbow, as I write) is the promoter of repose and the begetter of agreeable reverie. As I inhale its cool, fragrant breath, and partly yield myself to the sensation of healthy rest which wraps my limbs as with a velvet mantle, I marvel how the poets and artists and scholars of olden times nursed those dreams which the world calls indolence, but which are the seeds that germinate into great achievements. How did Plato philosophize without the pipe? How did gray Homer, sitting on the temple-steps in the Grecian twilights, drive from his heart the bitterness of beggary and blindness? How did Phidias charm the Cerberus of his animal nature to sleep, while his soul entered the Elysian Fields and beheld the forms of heroes? For, in the higher world of Art, Body and Soul are sworn enemies, and the pipe holds an opiate more potent than all the drowsy syrups of the East, to drug the former into

514

submission. Milton knew this, as he smoked his evening pipe at Chalfont, wandering, the while, among the palms of Paradise.

But it is also our loss, that Tobacco was unknown to the Greeks. They would else have given us, in verse and in marble, another divinity in their glorious Pantheon--a god less drowsy than Morpheus and Somnus, less riotous than Bacchus, less radiant than Apollo, but with something of the spirit of each: a figure, beautiful with youth, every muscle in perfect repose, and the vague expression of dreams in his half-closed eyes. His temple would have been built in a grove of Southern pines, on the borders of a land-locked gulf, sheltered from the surges that buffet without, where service would have been rendered him in the late hours of the afternoon, or in the evening twilight. From his oracular tripod words of wisdom would have been spoken, and the fanes of Delphi and Dodona would have been deserted for his.

Oh, non-smoking friends, who read these lines with pain and incredulity--and you, ladies, who turn pale at the thought of a pipe--let me tell you that you are familiar only with the vulgar form of tobacco, and have never passed between the wind and its gentility. The word conveys no idea to you but that of "long nines," and pig-tail, and cavendish. Forget these for a moment, and look upon this dark-brown cake of dried leaves and blossoms, which exhales an odor of pressed flowers. These are the tender tops of the Jebelee, plucked as the buds begin to expand, and carefully dried in the shade. In order to be used, it is moistened with rose-scented water, and cut to the necessary degree of fineness. The test of true Jebelee is, that it burns with a slow, hidden fire, like tinder, and causes no irritation to the eye when held under it. The smoke, drawn through a long cherry-stick pipe and amber mouth-piece, is pure, cool, and sweet, with an aromatic flavor, which is very pleasant in the mouth. It excites no salivation, and leaves behind it no unpleasant, stale odor.

The narghileh (still bubbling beside me) is an institution known only in the East. It requires a peculiar kind of tobacco, which grows to perfection in the southern provinces of Persia. The smoke, after passing through water (rose-flavored, if you choose), is inhaled through a long, flexible tube directly into the lungs. It occasions not the slightest irritation or oppression, but in a few minutes produces a delicious sense of rest, which is felt even in the finger-ends. The pure physical sensation of rest is one of strength also, and of perfect contentment. Many an impatient thought, many an angry word, have I avoided by a resort to the pipe. Among our aborigines the pipe was the emblem of Peace, and I strongly recommend the Peace Society to print their tracts upon papers of smoking tobacco (Turkish, if possible), and distribute pipes with them.

I know of nothing more refreshing, after the fatigue of a long day's journey, than a well-prepared narghileh. That slight feverish and excitable feeling which is the result of fatigue yields at once to its potency. The blood loses its heat and the pulse its rapidity; the muscles relax, the nerves are soothed into quiet, and the frame passes into a condition similar to sleep, except that the mind is awake and active. By the time one has finished his pipe, he is refreshed for the remainder of the day, and his nightly sleep is sound and healthy. Such are some of the physical effects of the pipe, in Eastern lands. Morally and psychologically, it works still greater transformations; but to describe them now, with the mouth-piece at my lips, would require an active self-consciousness which the habit does not allow.

A servant enters with a steamy cup of coffee, seated in a silver zerf, or cup-holder. His thumb and fore-finger are clasped firmly upon the bottom of the zerf, which I inclose near the top with my own thumb and finger, so that the transfer is accomplished without his hand having touched mine.

After draining the thick brown liquid, which must be done with due deliberation and a pause of satisfaction between each sip, I return the zerf, holding it in the middle, while the attendant places a palm of each hand upon the top and bottom and carries it off without contact. The beverage is made of the berries of Mocha, slightly roasted, pulverized in a mortar, and heated to a foam, without the addition of cream or sugar. Sometimes, however, it is flavored with the extract of roses or violets. When skilfully made, each cup is prepared separately, and the quantity of water and coffee carefully measured.

Coffee is a true child of the East, and its original home was among the hills of Yemen, the Arabia Felix of the ancients. Fortunately for Mussulmen, its use was unknown in the days of Mahomet, or it would probably have fallen under the same prohibition as wine. The word Kahweh (whence café) is an old Arabic term for wine. The discovery of the properties of coffee is attributed to a dervish, who, for some misdemeanor, was carried into the mountains of Yemen by his brethren and there left to perish by starvation. In order to appease the pangs of hunger he gathered the ripe berries from the wild coffee-trees, roasted and ate them. The nourishment they contained, with water from the springs, sustained his life, and after two or three months he returned in good condition to his brethren, who considered his preservation as a miracle, and ever afterwards looked upon him as a pattern of holiness. He taught the use of the miraculous fruit, and the demand for it soon became so great as to render the cultivation of the tree necessary. It was a long time, however, before coffee was introduced into Europe. As late as the beginning of the seventeenth century, Sandys, the quaint old traveller, describes the appearance and taste of the beverage, which he calls "Coffa," and sagely asks: "Why not that black broth which the Lacedemonians used?"

On account of the excellence of the material, and the skilful manner of its preparation, the Coffee of the East is the finest in the world. I have found it so grateful and refreshing a drink, that I can readily pardon the pleasant exaggeration of the Arabic poet, Abd-el Kader Anazari Djezeri Hanbali, the son of Mahomet, who thus celebrates its virtues. After such an exalted eulogy, my own praises would sound dull and tame; and I therefore resume my pipe, commending Abd-el Kader to the reader.

"O Coffee! thou dispellest the cares of the great; thou bringest back those who wander from the paths of knowledge. Coffee is the beverage of the people of God, and the cordial of his servants who thirst for wisdom. When coffee is infused into the bowl, it exhales the odor of musk, and is of the color of ink. The truth is not known except to the wise, who drink it from the foaming coffee-cup. God has deprived fools of coffee, who, with invincible obstinacy, condemn it as injurious.

"Coffee is our gold; and in the place of its libations we are in the enjoyment of the best and noblest society. Coffee is even as innocent a drink as the purest milk, from which it is distinguished only by its color. Tarry with thy coffee in the place of its preparation, and the good God will hover over thee and participate in his feast. There the graces of the saloon, the luxury of life, the society of friends, all furnish a picture of the abode of happiness.

"Every care vanishes when the cup-bearer presents the delicious chalice. It will circulate fleetly through thy veins, and will not rankle there: if thou doubtest this, contemplate the youth and beauty of those who drink it. Grief cannot exist where it grows; sorrow humbles itself in obedience before its powers.

"Coffee is the drink of God's people; in it is health. Let this be the answer to those who doubt its qualities. In it we will drown our adversities, and in its fire consume our sorrows. Whoever has once seen the blissful chalice, will scorn the wine-cup. Glorious drink! thy color is the seal of purity, and reason proclaims it genuine. Drink with confidence, and regard not the prattle of fools, who condemn without foundation."

Chapter XIV. Journey to Antioch and Aleppo.

Change of Plans--Routes to Baghdad--Asia Minor--We sail from Beyrout--Yachting on the Syrian Coast--Tartus and Latakiyeh--The Coasts of Syria--The Bay of Suediah--The Mouth of the Orontes--Landing--The Garden of Syria--Ride to Antioch--The Modern City--The Plains of the Orontes--Remains of the Greek Empire--The Ancient Road--The Plain of Keftin--Approach to Aleppo.

"The chain is loosed, the sails are spread,

The living breath is fresh behind,

As, with dews and sunrise fed,

Comes the laughing morning wind."

Shelley.

Aleppo, *Friday, June* 4, 1852.

A Traveller in the East, who has not unbounded time and an extensive fortune at his disposal, is never certain where and how far he shall go, until his journey is finished. With but a limited portion of both these necessaries, I have so far carried out my original plan with scarcely a variation; but at present I am obliged to make a material change of route. My farthest East is here at Aleppo. At Damascus, I was told by everybody that it was too late in the season to visit either Baghdad or Mosul, and that, on account of the terrible summer heats and the fevers which prevail along the Tigris, it would be imprudent to undertake it. Notwithstanding this, I should probably have gone (being now so thoroughly acclimated that I have nothing to fear from the heat), had I not met with a friend of Col. Rawlinson, the companion of Layard, and the sharer in his discoveries at Nineveh. This gentleman, who met Col. R. not long since in Constantinople, on his way to Baghdad (where he resides as British Consul), informed me that since the departure of Mr. Layard from Mosul, the most interesting excavations have been filled up, in order to preserve the sculptures. Unless one was able to make a new exhumation, he would be by no means repaid for so long and arduous a journey. The ruins of Nineveh are all below the surface of the earth, and the little of them that is now left exposed, is less complete and interesting than the specimens in the British Museum.

There is a route from Damascus to Baghdad, across the Desert, by way of Palmyra, but it is rarely travelled, even by the natives, except when the caravans are sufficiently strong to withstand the attacks of the Bedouins. The traveller is obliged to go in Arab costume, to leave his baggage behind, except a meagre scrip for the journey, and to pay from $300 to $500 for the camels and escort. The more usual route is to come northward to this city, then cross to Mosul and descend the Tigris--a journey of four or five weeks. After weighing all the advantages and disadvantages of undertaking a tour of such length as it would be necessary to make before reaching Constantinople, I decided at Beyrout to give up the fascinating fields of travel in Media, Assyria and Armenia, and take a rather shorter and-perhaps equally interesting route from Aleppo to Constantinople, by way of Tarsus, Konia (Iconium), and the ancient countries of Phrygia, Bithynia, and Mysia. The interior of Asia Minor is even less known to us than the Persian side of Asiatic Turkey, which has of late received more attention from travellers; and, as I shall traverse it in its whole length, from Syria to the Bosphorus, I may find it replete with "green fields and pastures new," which shall repay me for relinquishing the first and more ambitious undertaking. At least, I have so much reason to be grateful for the uninterrupted good health and good luck I have enjoyed during seven months in Africa and the Orient, that I cannot be otherwise than content with the prospect before me.

I left Beyrout on the night of the 28th of May, with Mr. Harrison, who has decided to keep me company as far as Constantinople. François, our classic dragoman, whose great delight is to recite Homer by the sea-side, is retained for the whole tour, as we have found no reason to doubt his honesty or ability. Our first thought was to proceed to Aleppo by land, by way of Homs and Hamah, whence there might be a chance of reaching Palmyra; but as we found an opportunity of engaging an American yacht for the voyage up the coast, it was thought preferable to take her, and save time. She was a neat little craft, called the "American Eagle," brought out by Mr. Smith, our Consul at Beyrout. So, one fine moonlit night, we slowly crept out of the harbor, and after returning a volley of salutes from our friends at Demetri's Hotel, ran into the heart of a thunder-storm, which poured down more rain than all I had seen for eight months before. But our raïs, Assad (the Lion), was worthy of his name, and had two good Christian sailors at his command, so we lay in the cramped little cabin, and heard the floods washing our deck, without fear.

In the morning, we were off Tripoli, which is even more deeply buried than Beyrout in its orange and mulberry groves, and slowly wafted along the bold mountain-coast, in the afternoon reached Tartus, the Ancient Tortosa. A mile from shore is the rocky island of Aradus, entirely covered by a town. There were a dozen vessels lying in the harbor. The remains of a large fortress and ancient mole prove it to have been a place of considerable importance. Tartus is a small old place on the sea-shore--not so large nor so important in appearance as its island-port. The country behind is green and hilly, though but partially cultivated, and rises into Djebel Ansairiyeh, which divides the valley of the Orontes from the sea. It is a lovely coast, especially under the flying lights and shadows of such a breezy day as we had. The wind fell at sunset; but by the next morning, we had passed the tobacco-fields of Latakiyeh, and were in sight of the southern cape of the Bay of Suediah. The mountains forming this cape culminate in a grand conical peak, about 5,000 feet in height, called Djebel Okrab. At ten o'clock, wafted along by a slow wind, we turned the point and entered the Bay of Suediah, formed by the embouchure of the River Orontes. The mountain headland of Akma Dagh, forming the portal of the Gulf of Scanderoon, loomed grandly in front of us across the bay; and far beyond it, we could just distinguish the coast of Karamania, the snow-capped range of Taurus.

The Coasts of Syria might be divided, like those of Guinea, according to the nature of their productions. The northern division is bold and bare, yet flocks of sheep graze on the slopes of its mountains; and the inland plains behind them are covered with orchards of pistachio-trees. Silk is cultivated in the neighborhood of Suediah, but forms only a small portion of the exports. This region may be called the Wool and Pistachio Coast. Southward, from Latakiyeh to Tartus and the northern limit of Lebanon, extends the Tobacco Coast, whose undulating hills are now clothed with the pale-green leaves of the renowned plant. From Tripoli to Tyre, embracing all the western slope of Lebanon, and the deep, rich valleys lying between his knees, the mulberry predominates, and the land is covered with the houses of thatch and matting which shelter the busy worms. This is the Silk Coast. The palmy plains of Jaffa, and beyond, until Syria meets the African sands between Gaza and El-Arish, constitute the Orange Coast. The vine, the olive, and the fig flourish everywhere.

We were all day getting up the bay, and it seemed as if we should never pass Djebel Okrab, whose pointed top rose high above a long belt of fleecy clouds that girdled his waist. At sunset we made the mouth of the Orontes. Our lion of a Captain tried to run into the river, but the channel was very narrow, and when within three hundred yards of the shore the yacht struck. We had all sail set, and had the wind been a little stronger, we should have capsized in an instant. The lion went manfully to work, and by dint of hard poling, shoved us off, and came to anchor in deep water. Not until the danger was past did he open his batteries on the unlucky helmsman, and then the explosion of Arabic oaths was equal to a broadside of twenty-four pounders. We lay all night rocking on the swells, and the next morning, by firing a number of signal guns, brought out a boat, which took us off. We entered the mouth of the Orontes, and sailed nearly a mile between rich wheat meadows before reaching the landing-place of Suediah--two or three uninhabited stone huts, with three or four small Turkish craft, and a health officer. The town lies a mile or two inland, scattered along the hill-side amid gardens so luxuriant as almost to conceal it from view.

This part of the coast is ignorant of travellers, and we were obliged to wait half a day before we could find a sufficient number of horses to take us to Antioch, twenty miles distant. When they came, they were solid farmers' horses, with the rudest gear imaginable. I was obliged to mount astride of a broad pack-saddle, with my legs suspended in coils of rope. Leaving the meadows, we entered a lane of the wildest, richest and loveliest bloom and foliage. Our way was overhung with hedges of pomegranate, myrtle, oleander, and white rose, in blossom, and occasionally with quince, fig, and carob trees, laced together with grape vines in fragrant bloom. Sometimes this wilderness of color and odor met above our heads and made a twilight; then it opened into long, dazzling, sun-bright vistas, where the hues of the oleander, pomegranate and white rose made the eye wink with their gorgeous profusion. The mountains we crossed were covered with thickets of myrtle, mastic, daphne, and arbutus, and all the valleys and sloping meads waved with fig, mulberry, and olive trees. Looking towards the sea, the valley broadened out between mountain ranges whose summits were lost in the clouds. Though the soil was not so rich as in Palestine, the general aspect of the country was much wilder and more luxuriant.

So, by this glorious lane, over the myrtled hills and down into valleys, whose bed was one hue of rose from the blossoming oleanders, we travelled for five hours, crossing the low ranges of hills through which the Orontes forces his way to the sea. At last we reached a height overlooking the valley of the river, and saw in the east, at the foot of the mountain chain, the long lines of barracks built by Ibrahim Pasha for the defence of Antioch. Behind them the ancient wall of the city clomb the mountains, whose crest it followed to the last peak of the chain, From the next hill we saw the city--a large extent of one-story houses with tiled roofs, surrounded with gardens, and half buried in the foliage of sycamores. It extends from the River Orontes, which washes its walls, up the slope of the mountain to the crags of gray rock which overhang it. We crossed the river by a massive old bridge, and entered the town. Riding along the rills of filth which traverse the streets, forming their central avenues, we passed through several lines of bazaars to a large and dreary-looking khan, the keeper of which gave us the best vacant chamber--a narrow place, full of fleas.

Antioch presents not even a shadow of its former splendor. Except the great walls, ten to fifteen miles in circuit, which the Turks have done their best to destroy, every vestige of the old city has disappeared. The houses are all of one story, on account of earthquakes, from which Antioch has suffered more than any other city in the world. At one time, during the Middle Ages, it lost 120,000 inhabitants in one day. Its situation is magnificent, and the modern town, notwithstanding its filth, wears a bright and busy aspect. Situated at the base of a lofty mountain, it overlooks, towards the east, a plain thirty or forty miles in length, producing the most abundant harvests. A great number of the inhabitants are workers in wood and leather, and very thrifty and cheerful people they appear to be.

We remained until the next day at noon, by which time a gray-bearded scamp, the chief of the mukkairees, or muleteers, succeeded in getting us five miserable beasts for the journey to Aleppo. On leaving the city, we travelled along a former street of Antioch, part of the ancient pavement still remaining, and after two miles came to the old wall of circuit, which we passed by a massive gateway, of Roman time. It is now called Bab Boulos, or St. Paul's Gate. Christianity, it will be remembered, was planted in Antioch by Paul and Barnabas, and the Apostle Peter was the first bishop of the city. We now entered the great plain of the Orontes--a level sea, rioting in the wealth of its ripening harvests. The river, lined with luxuriant thickets, meandered through the centre of this glorious picture. We crossed it during the afternoon, and keeping on our eastward course, encamped at night in a meadow near the tents of some wandering Turcomans, who furnished us with butter and milk from their herds.

Leaving the plain the next morning, we travelled due east all day, over long stony ranges of mountains, inclosing only one valley, which bore evidence of great fertility. It was circular, about ten miles in its greater diameter, and bounded on the north by the broad peak of Djebel Saman, or Mount St. Simon. In the morning we passed a ruined castle, standing in a dry, treeless dell, among the hot hills. The muleteers called it the Maiden's Palace, and said that it was built long ago by a powerful Sultan, as a prison for his daughter. For several hours thereafter, our road was lined with remains of buildings, apparently dating from the time of the Greek Empire. There were tombs, temples of massive masonry, though in a bad style of architecture, and long rows of arched chambers, which resembled store-houses. They were all more or less shattered by earthquakes, but in one place I noticed twenty such arches, each of at least twenty feet span. All-the hills, on either hand, as far as we could see, were covered with the remains of buildings. In the plain of St. Simon, I saw two superb pillars, apparently part of a portico, or gateway, and the village of Dana is formed almost entirely of churches and convents, of the Lower Empire. There were but few inscriptions, and these I could not read; but the whole of this region would, no doubt, richly repay an antiquarian research. I am told here that the entire chain of hills, which extends southward for more than a hundred miles, abounds with similar remains, and that, in many places, whole cities stand almost entire, as if recently deserted by their inhabitants.

During the afternoon, we came upon a portion of the ancient road from Antioch to Aleppo, which is still as perfect as when first constructed. It crossed a very stony ridge, and is much the finest specimen of road-making I ever saw, quite putting to shame the Appian and Flaminian Ways at Rome. It is twenty feet wide, and laid with blocks of white marble, from two to four feet square. It was apparently raised upon a more ancient road, which diverges here and there from the line, showing the deeply-cut traces of the Roman chariot-wheels. In the barren depths of the mountains we found every hour cisterns cut in the rock and filled with water left by the winter rains. Many of them, however, are fast drying up, and a month later this will be a desert road.

Towards night we descended from the hills upon the Plain of Keftin, which stretches south-westward from Aleppo, till the mountain-streams which fertilize it are dried up, when it is merged into the Syrian Desert. Its northern edge, along which we travelled, is covered with fields of wheat, cotton, and castor-beans. We stopped all night at a village called Taireb, planted at the foot of a tumulus, older than tradition. The people were in great dread of the Aneyzeh Arabs, who come in from the Desert to destroy their harvests and carry off their cattle. They wanted us to take a guard, but after our experience on the Anti-Lebanon, we felt safer without one.

Yesterday we travelled for seven hours over a wide, rolling country, now waste and barren, but formerly covered with wealth and supporting an abundant population, evidences of which are found in the buildings everywhere scattered over the hills. On and on we toiled in the heat, over this inhospitable wilderness, and though we knew Aleppo must be very near, yet we could see neither sign of cultivation nor inhabitants. Finally, about three o'clock, the top of a line of shattered wall and the points of some minarets issued out of the earth, several miles in front of us, and on climbing a glaring chalky ridge, the renowned city burst at once upon our view. It filled a wide hollow or basin among the white hills, against which its whiter houses and domes glimmered for miles, in the dead, dreary heat of the afternoon, scarcely relieved by the narrow belt of gardens on the nearer side, or the orchards of pistachio trees beyond. In the centre of the city rose a steep, abrupt mound, crowned with the remains of the ancient citadel, and shining minarets shot up, singly or in clusters, around its base. The prevailing hue of the landscape was a whitish-gray, and the long, stately city and long, monotonous hills, gleamed with equal brilliancy under a sky of cloudless and intense blue. This singular monotony of coloring gave a wonderful effect to the view, which is one of the most remarkable in all the Orient.

Chapter XV. Life in Aleppo.

Our Entry into Aleppo--We are conducted to a House--Our Unexpected Welcome--The Mystery Explained--Aleppo--Its Name--Its Situation--The Trade of Aleppo--The Christians--The Revolt of 1850--Present Appearance of the City--Visit to Osman Pasha--The Citadel--View from the Battlements--Society in Aleppo--Etiquette and Costume--Jewish Marriage Festivities--A Christian Marriage Procession--Ride around the Town--Nightingales--The Aleppo Button--A Hospital for Cats--Ferhat Pasha.

Aleppo, *Tuesday, June* 8, 1852.

Our entry into Aleppo was a fitting preliminary to our experiences during the five days we have spent here. After passing a blackamoor, who acted as an advanced guard of the Custom House, at a ragged tent outside of the city, and bribing him with two piastres, we crossed the narrow line of gardens on the western side, and entered the streets. There were many coffee-houses, filled with smokers, nearly all of whom accosted us in Turkish, though Arabic is the prevailing language here. Ignorance made us discourteous, and we slighted every attempt to open a conversation. Out of the narrow streets of the suburbs, we advanced to the bazaars, in order to find a khan where we could obtain lodgings. All the best khans, however, were filled, and we were about to take a very inferior room, when a respectable individual came up to François and said: "The house is ready for the travellers, and I will show you the way." We were a little surprised at this address, but followed him to a neat, quiet and pleasant street near the bazaars, where we were ushered into a spacious court-yard, with a row of apartments opening upon it, and told to make ourselves at home.

The place had evidently been recently inhabited, for the rooms were well furnished, with not only divans, but beds in the Frank style. A lean kitten was scratching at one of the windows, to the great danger of overturning a pair of narghilehs, a tame sea-gull was walking about the court, and two sheep bleated in a stable at the further end. In the kitchen we not only found a variety of utensils, but eggs, salt, pepper, and other condiments. Our guide had left, and the only information we could get, from a dyeing establishment next door, was that the occupants had gone into the country. "Take the good the gods provide thee," is my rule in such cases, and as we were very hungry, we set François to work at preparing dinner. We arranged a divan in the open air, had a table brought out, and by the aid of the bakers in the bazaar, and the stores which the kitchen supplied, soon rejoiced over a very palatable meal. The romantic character of our reception made the dinner a merry one. It was a chapter out of the Arabian Nights, and be he genie or afrite, caliph or merchant of Bassora, into whose hands we had fallen, we resolved to let the adventure take its course. We were just finishing a nondescript pastry which François found at a baker's, and which, for want of a better name, he called méringues à la Khorassan, when there was a loud knock at the street door. We felt at first some little trepidation, but determined to maintain our places, and gravely invite the real master to join us.

It was a female servant, however, who, to our great amazement, made a profound salutation, and seemed delighted to see us. "My master did not expect your Excellencies to-day; he has gone into the gardens, but will soon return. Will your Excellencies take coffee after your dinner?" and coffee was forthwith served. The old woman was unremitting in her attentions; and her son, a boy of eight years, and the most venerable child I ever saw, entertained us with the description of a horse which his master had just bought--a horse which had cost two thousand piastres, and was ninety years old. Well, this Aleppo is an extraordinary place, was my first impression, and the inhabitants are remarkable people; but I waited the master's arrival, as the only means of solving the mystery. About dusk, there was another rap at the door. A lady dressed in white, with an Indian handkerchief bound over her black hair, arrived. "Pray excuse us," said she; "we thought you would not reach here before to-morrow; but my brother will come directly." In fact, the brother did come soon afterwards, and greeted us with a still warmer welcome. "Before leaving the gardens," he said, "I heard of your arrival, and have come in a full gallop the whole way." In order to put an end to this comedy of errors, I declared at once that he was mistaken; nobody in Aleppo could possibly know of our coming, and we were, perhaps, transgressing on his hospitality.

But no: he would not be convinced. He was a dragoman to the English Consulate; his master had told him we would be here the next day, and he must be prepared to receive us. Besides, the janissary of the Consulate had showed us the way to his house. We, therefore, let the matter rest until next morning, when we called on Mr. Very, the Consul, who informed us that the janissary had mistaken us for two gentlemen we had met in Damascus, the travelling companions of Lord Dalkeith. As they had not arrived, he begged us to remain in the quarters which had been prepared for them. We have every reason to be glad of this mistake, as it has made us acquainted with one of the most courteous and hospitable gentlemen in the East.

Aleppo lies so far out of the usual routes of travel, that it is rarely visited by Europeans. One is not, therefore, as in the case of Damascus, prepared beforehand by volumes of description, which preclude all possibility of mistake or surprise. For my part, I only knew that Aleppo had once been the greatest commercial city of the Orient, though its power had long since passed into other hands. But there were certain stately associations lingering around the name, which drew me towards it, and obliged me to include it, at all hazards, in my Asiatic tour. The scanty description of Captains Irby and Mangles, the only one I had read, gave me no distinct idea of its position or appearance; and when, the other day, I first saw it looming grand and gray among the gray hills, more like a vast natural crystallization than the product of human art, I revelled in the novelty of that startling first impression.

The tradition of the city's name is curious, and worth relating. It is called, in Arabic, Haleb el-Shahba--Aleppo, the Gray--which most persons suppose to refer to the prevailing color of the soil. The legend, however, goes much farther. Haleb, which the Venetians and Genoese softened into Aleppo, means literally: "has milked," According to Arab tradition, the patriarch Abraham once lived here: his tent being pitched near the mound now occupied by the citadel. He had a certain gray cow (el-shahba) which was milked every morning for the benefit of the poor. When, therefore, it was proclaimed: "Ibrahim haleb el-shahba" (Abraham has milked the gray cow), all the poor of the tribe came up to receive their share. The repetition of this morning call attached itself to the spot, and became the name of the city which was afterwards founded.

Aleppo is built on the eastern slope of a shallow upland basin, through which flows the little River Koweik. There are low hills to the north and south, between which the country falls into a wide, monotonous plain, extending unbroken to the Euphrates. The city is from eight to ten miles in circuit, and, though not so thickly populated, covers a greater extent of space than Damascus. The population is estimated at 100,000. In the excellence (not the elegance) of its architecture, it surpasses any Oriental city I have yet seen. The houses are all of hewn stone, frequently three and even four stories in height, and built in a most massive and durable style, on account of the frequency of earthquakes. The streets are well paved, clean, with narrow sidewalks, and less tortuous and intricate than the bewildering alleys of Damascus. A large part of the town is occupied with bazaars, attesting the splendor of its former commerce. These establishments are covered with lofty vaults of stone, lighted from the top; and one may walk for miles beneath the spacious roofs. The shops exhibit all the stuffs of the East, especially of Persia and India. There is also an extensive display of European fabrics, as the eastern provinces of Asiatic Turkey, as far as Baghdad, are supplied entirely from Aleppo and Trebizond.

Within ten years--in fact, since the Allied Powers drove Ibrahim Pasha out of Syria--the trade of Aleppo has increased, at the expense of Damascus. The tribes of the Desert, who were held in check during the Egyptian occupancy, are now so unruly that much of the commerce between the latter place and Baghdad goes northward to Mosul, and thence by a safer road to this city. The khans, of which there are a great number, built on a scale according with the former magnificence of Aleppo, are nearly all filled, and Persian, Georgian, and Armenian merchants again make their appearance in the bazaars. The principal manufactures carried on are the making of shoes (which, indeed, is a prominent branch in every Turkish city), and the weaving of silk and golden tissues. Two long bazaars are entirely occupied with shoe-shops, and there is nearly a quarter of a mile of confectionery, embracing more varieties than I ever saw, or imagined possible. I saw yesterday the operation of weaving silk and gold, which is a very slow process. The warp and the body of the woof were of purple silk. The loom only differed from the old hand-looms in general use in having some thirty or forty contrivances for lifting the threads of the warp, so as to form, by variation, certain patterns. The gold threads by which the pattern was worked were contained in twenty small shuttles, thrust by hand under the different parcels of the warp, as they were raised by a boy trained for that purpose, who sat on the top of the loom. The fabric was very brilliant in its appearance, and sells, as the weavers informed me, at 100 piastres per pik--about $7 per yard.

We had letters to Mr. Ford, an American Missionary established here, and Signor di Picciotto, who acts as American Vice-Consul. Both gentlemen have been very cordial in their offers of service, and by their aid we have been enabled to see something of Aleppo life and society. Mr. Ford, who has been here four years, has a pleasant residence at Jedaida, a Christian suburb of the city. His congregation numbers some fifty or sixty proselytes, who are mostly from the schismatic sects of the Armenians. Dr. Smith, who established the mission at Ain-tab (two days' journey north of this), where he died last year, was very successful among these sects, and the congregation there amounts to nine hundred. The Sultan, a year ago, issued a firman, permitting his Christian subjects to erect houses of worship; but, although this was proclaimed in Constantinople and much lauded in Europe as an act of great generosity and tolerance, there has been no official promulgation of it here. So of the aid which the Turkish Government was said to have afforded to its destitute Christian subjects, whose houses were sacked during the fanatical rebellion of 1850. The world praised the Sultan's charity and love of justice, while the sufferers, to this day, lack the first experience of it. But for the spontaneous relief contributed in Europe and among the Christian communities of the Levant, the amount of misery would have been frightful.

To Feridj Pasha, who is at present the commander of the forces here, is mainly due the credit of having put down the rebels with a strong hand. There were but few troops in the city at the time of the outbreak, and as the insurgents, who were composed of the Turkish and Arab population, were in league with the Aneyzehs of the Desert, the least faltering or delay would have led to a universal massacre of the Christians. Fortunately, the troops were divided into two portions, one occupying the barracks on a hill north of the city, and the other, a mere corporal's guard of a dozen men, posted in the citadel. The leaders of the outbreak went to the latter and offered him a large sum of money (the spoils of Christian houses) to give up the fortress. With a loyalty to his duty truly miraculous among the Turks, he ordered his men to fire upon them, and they beat a hasty retreat. The quarter of the insurgents lay precisely between the barracks and the citadel, and by order of Feridj Pasha a cannonade was immediately opened on it from both points. It was not, however, until many houses had been battered down, and a still larger number destroyed by fire, that the rebels were brought to submission. Their allies, the Aneyzehs, appeared on the hill east of Aleppo, to the number of five or six thousand, but a few well-directed cannon-balls told them what they might expect, and they speedily retreated. Two or three hundred Christian families lost nearly all of their property during the sack, and many were left entirely destitute. The house in which Mr. Ford lives was plundered of jewels and furniture to the amount of 400,000 piastres ($20,000). The robbers, it is said, were amazed at the amount of spoil they found. The Government made some feeble efforts to recover it, but the greater part was already sold and scattered through a thousand hands, and the unfortunate Christians have only received about seven per cent. of their loss.

The burnt quarter has since been rebuilt, and I noticed several Christians occupying shops in various parts of it. But many families, who fled at the time, still remain in various parts of Syria, afraid to return to their homes. The Aneyzehs and other Desert tribes have latterly become more daring than ever. Even in the immediate neighborhood of the city, the inhabitants are so fearful of them that all the grain is brought up to the very walls to be threshed. The burying-grounds on both sides are now turned into threshing-floors, and all day long the Turkish peasants drive their heavy sleds around among the tomb-stones.

On the second day after our arrival, we paid a visit to Osman Pasha, Governor of the City and Province of Aleppo. We went in state, accompanied by the Consul, with two janissaries in front, bearing silver maces, and a dragoman behind. The seraï, or palace, is a large, plain wooden building, and a group of soldiers about the door, with a shabby carriage in the court, were the only tokens of its character. We were ushered at once into the presence of the Pasha, who is a man of about seventy years, with a good-humored, though shrewd face. He was quite cordial in his manners, complimenting us on our Turkish costume, and vaunting his skill in physiognomy, which at once revealed to him that we belonged to the highest class of American nobility. In fact, in the firman which he has since sent us, we are mentioned as "nobles." He invited us to pass a day or two with him, saying that he should derive much benefit from our superior knowledge. We replied that such an intercourse could only benefit ourselves, as his greater experience, and the distinguished wisdom which had made his name long since familiar to our ears, precluded the hope of our being of any service to him. After half an hour's stay, during which we were regaled with jewelled pipes, exquisite Mocha coffee, and sherbet breathing of the gardens of Gülistan, we took our leave.

The Pasha sent an officer to show us the citadel. We passed around the moat to the entrance on the western side, consisting of a bridge and double gateway. The fortress, as I have already stated, occupies the crest of an elliptical mound, about one thousand feet by six hundred, and two hundred feet in height. It is entirely encompassed by the city and forms a prominent and picturesque feature in the distant view thereof. Formerly, it was thickly inhabited, and at the time of the great earthquake of 1822, there were three hundred families living within the walls, nearly all of whom perished. The outer walls were very much shattered on that occasion, but the enormous towers and the gateway, the grandest specimen of Saracenic architecture in the East, still remain entire. This gateway, by which we entered, is colossal in its proportions. The outer entrance, through walls ten feet thick, admitted us into a lofty vestibule lined with marble, and containing many ancient inscriptions in mosaic. Over the main portal, which is adorned with sculptured lions' heads, there is a tablet stating that the fortress was built by El Melek el Ashraf (the Holiest of Kings), after which follows: "Prosperity to the True Believers--Death to the Infidels!" A second tablet shows that it was afterwards repaired by Mohammed ebn-Berkook, who, I believe, was one of the Fatimite Caliphs. The shekh of the citadel, who accompanied us, stated the age of the structure at nine hundred years, which, as nearly as I can recollect the Saracenic chronology, is correct. He called our attention to numbers of iron arrow-heads sticking in the solid masonry--the marks of ancient sieges. Before leaving, we were presented with a bundle of arrows from the armory--undoubted relics of Saracen warfare.

The citadel is now a mass of ruins, having been deserted since the earthquake. Grass is growing on the ramparts, and the caper plant, with its white-and-purple blossoms, flourishes among the piles of rubbish. Since the late rebellion, however, a small military barrack has been built, and two companies of soldiers are stationed there, We walked around the walls, which command a magnificent view of the city and the wide plains to the south and east. It well deserves to rank with the panorama of Cairo from the citadel, and that of Damascus from the Anti-Lebanon, in extent, picturesqueness and rich oriental character. Out of the gray ring of the city, which incloses the mound, rise the great white domes and the whiter minarets of its numerous mosques, many of which are grand and imposing structures. The course of the river through the centre of the picture is marked by a belt of the greenest verdure, beyond which, to the west, rises a chain of naked red hills, and still further, fading on the horizon, the blue summit of Mt. St. Simon, and the coast range of Akma Dagh. Eastward, over vast orchards of pistachio trees, the barren plain of the Euphrates fades away to a glimmering, hot horizon. Looking downwards on the heart of the city, I was surprised to see a number of open, grassy tracts, out of which, here and there, small trees were growing. But, perceiving what appeared to be subterranean entrances at various points, I found that these tracts were upon the roofs of the houses and bazaars, verifying what I had frequently heard, that in Aleppo the inhabitants visit their friends in different parts of the city, by passing over the roofs of the houses. Previous to the earthquake of 1822, these vast roof-plains were cultivated as gardens, and presented an extent of airy bowers as large, if not as magnificent, as the renowned Hanging Gardens of ancient Babylon.

Accompanied by Signor di Picciotto, we spent two or three days in visiting the houses of the principal Jewish and Christian families in Aleppo. We found, it is true, no such splendor as in Damascus, but more solid and durable architecture, and a more chastened elegance of taste. The buildings are all of hewn stone, the court-yards paved with marble, and the walls rich with gilding and carved wood. Some of the larger dwellings have small but beautiful gardens attached to them. We were everywhere received with the greatest hospitality, and the visits were considered as a favor rather than an intrusion. Indeed, I was frequently obliged to run the risk of giving offence, by declining the refreshments which were offered us. Each round of visits was a feat of strength, and we were obliged to desist from sheer inability to support more coffee, rose-water, pipes, and aromatic sweetmeats. The character of society in Aleppo is singular; its very life and essence is etiquette. The laws which govern it are more inviolable than those of the Medes and Persians. The question of precedence among the different families is adjusted by the most delicate scale, and rigorously adhered to in the most trifling matters. Even we, humble voyagers as we are, have been obliged to regulate our conduct according to it. After our having visited certain families, certain others would have been deeply mortified had we neglected to call upon them. Formerly, when a traveller arrived here, he was expected to call upon the different Consuls, in the order of their established precedence: the Austrian first, English second, French third, &c. After this, he was obliged to stay at home several days, to give the Consuls an opportunity of returning the visits, which they made in the same order. There was a diplomatic importance about all his movements, and the least violation of etiquette, through ignorance or neglect, was the town talk for days.

This peculiarity in society is evidently a relic of the formal times, when Aleppo was a semi-Venetian city, and the opulent seat of Eastern commerce. Many of the inhabitants are descended from the traders of those times, and they all speak the lingua franca, or Levantine Italian. The women wear a costume partly Turkish and partly European, combining the graces of both; it is, in my eyes, the most beautiful dress in the world. They wear a rich scarf of some dark color on the head, which, on festive occasions, is almost concealed by their jewels, and the heavy scarlet pomegranate blossoms which adorn their dark hair. A Turkish vest and sleeves of embroidered silk, open in front, and a skirt of white or some light color, completes the costume. The Jewesses wear in addition a short Turkish caftan, and full trousers gathered at the ankles. At a ball given by Mr. Very, the English Consul, which we attended, all the Christian beauties of Aleppo were present. There was a fine display of diamonds, many of the ladies wearing several thousand dollars' worth on their heads. The peculiar etiquette of the place was again illustrated on this occasion. The custom is, that the music must be heard for at least one hour before the guests come. The hour appointed was eight, but when we went there, at nine, nobody had arrived. As it was generally supposed that the ball was given on our account, several of the families had servants in the neighborhood to watch our arrival; and, accordingly, we had not been there five minutes before the guests crowded through the door in large numbers. When the first dance (an Arab dance, performed by two ladies at a time) was proposed, the wives of the French and Spanish Consuls were first led, or rather dragged, out. When a lady is asked to dance, she invariably refuses. She is asked a second and a third time; and if the gentleman does not solicit most earnestly, and use some gentle force in getting her upon the floor, she never forgives him.

At one of the Jewish houses which we visited, the wedding festivities of one of the daughters were being celebrated. We were welcomed with great cordiality, and immediately ushered into the room of state, an elegant apartment, overlooking the gardens below the city wall. Half the room was occupied by a raised platform, with a divan of blue silk cushions. Here the ladies reclined, in superb dresses of blue, pink, and gold, while the gentlemen were ranged on the floor below. They all rose at our entrance, and we were conducted to seats among the ladies. Pipes and perfumed drinks were served, and the bridal cake, made of twenty-six different fruits, was presented on a golden salver. Our fair neighbors, some of whom literally blazed with jewels, were strikingly beautiful. Presently the bride appeared at the door, and we all rose and remained standing, as she advanced, supported on each side by the two shebeeniyeh, or bridesmaids. She was about sixteen, slight and graceful in appearance, though not decidedly beautiful, and was attired with the utmost elegance. Her dress was a pale blue silk, heavy with gold embroidery; and over her long dark hair, her neck, bosom, and wrists, played a thousand rainbow gleams from the jewels which covered them. The Jewish musicians, seated at the bottom of the hall, struck up a loud, rejoicing harmony on their violins, guitars, and dulcimers, and the women servants, grouped at the door, uttered in chorus that wild, shrill cry, which accompanies all such festivals in the East. The bride was careful to preserve the decorum expected of her, by speaking no word, nor losing the sad, resigned expression of her countenance. She ascended to the divan, bowed to each of us with a low, reverential inclination, and seated herself on the cushions. The music and dances lasted some time, accompanied by the zughàreet, or cry of the women, which was repeated with double force when we rose to take leave. The whole company waited on us to the street door, and one of the servants, stationed in the court, shouted some long, sing-song phrases after us as we passed out. I could not learn the words, but was told that it was an invocation of prosperity upon us, in return for the honor which our visit had conferred.

In the evening I went to view a Christian marriage procession, which, about midnight, conveyed the bride to the house of the bridegroom. The house, it appeared, was too small to receive all the friends of the family, and I joined a large number of them, who repaired to the terrace of the English Consulate, to greet the procession as it passed. The first persons who appeared were a company of buffoons; after them four janissaries, carrying silver maces; then the male friends, bearing colored lanterns and perfumed torches, raised on gilded poles; then the females, among whom I saw some beautiful Madonna faces in the torchlight; and finally the bride herself, covered from head to foot with a veil of cloth of gold, and urged along by two maidens: for it is the etiquette of such occasions that the bride should resist being taken, and must be forced every step of the way, so that she is frequently three hours in going the distance of a mile. We watched the procession a long time, winding away through the streets--a line of torches, and songs, and incense, and noisy jubilee--under the sweet starlit heaven.

The other evening, Signor di Picciotto mounted us from his fine Arabian stud, and we rode around the city, outside of the suburbs. The sun was low, and a pale yellow lustre touched the clusters of minarets that rose out of the stately masses of buildings, and the bare, chalky hills to the north. After leaving the gardens on the banks of the Koweik, we came upon a dreary waste of ruins, among which the antiquarian finds traces of the ancient Aleppo of the Greeks, the Mongolian conquerors of the Middle Ages, and the Saracens who succeeded them. There are many mosques and tombs, which were once imposing specimens of Saracenic art; but now, split and shivered by wars and earthquakes, are slowly tumbling into utter decay. On the south-eastern side of the city, its chalk foundations have been hollowed into vast, arched caverns, which extend deep into the earth. Pillars have been left at regular intervals, to support the masses above, and their huge, dim labyrinths resemble the crypts of some great cathedral. They are now used as rope-walks, and filled with cheerful workmen.

Our last excursion was to a country-house of Signor di Picciotto, in the Gardens of Babala, about four miles from Aleppo. We set out in the afternoon on our Arabians, with our host's son on a large white donkey of the Baghdad breed. Passing the Turkish cemetery, where we stopped to view the tomb of General Bem, we loosened rein and sped away at full gallop over the hot, white hills. In dashing down a stony rise, the ambitious donkey, who was doing his best to keep up with the horses, fell, hurling Master Picciotto over his head. The boy was bruised a little, but set his teeth together and showed no sign of pain, mounted again, and followed us. The Gardens of Babala are a wilderness of fruit-trees, like those of Damascus. Signor P.'s country-house is buried in a wild grove of apricot, fig, orange, and pomegranate-trees. A large marble tank, in front of the open, arched liwan, supplies it with water. We mounted to the flat roof, and watched the sunset fade from the beautiful landscape. Beyond the bowers of dazzling greenness which surrounded us, stretched the wide, gray hills; the minarets of Aleppo, and the walls of its castled mount shone rosily in the last rays of the sun; an old palace of the Pashas, with the long, low barracks of the soldiery, crowned the top of a hill to the north; dark, spiry cypresses betrayed the place of tombs; and, to the west, beyond the bare red peak of Mount St. Simon, rose the faint blue outline of Giaour Dagh, whose mural chain divides Syria from the plains of Cilicia. As the twilight deepened over the scene, there came a long, melodious cry of passion and of sorrow from the heart of a starry-flowered pomegranate tree in the garden. Other voices answered it from the gardens around, until not one, but fifty nightingales charmed the repose of the hour. They vied with each other in their bursts of passionate music. Each strain soared over the

538

last, or united with others, near and far, in a chorus of the divinest pathos--an expression of sweet, unutterable, unquenchable longing. It was an ecstasy, yet a pain, to listen. "Away!" said Jean Paul to Music: "thou tellest me of that which I have not, and never can have--which I forever seek, and never find!"

But space fails me to describe half the incidents of our stay in Aleppo. There are two things peculiar to the city, however, which I must not omit mentioning. One is the Aleppo Button, a singular ulcer, which attacks every person born in the city, and every stranger who spends more than a month there. It can neither be prevented nor cured, and always lasts for a year. The inhabitants almost invariably have it on the face--either on the cheek, forehead, or tip of the nose--where it often leaves an indelible and disfiguring scar. Strangers, on the contrary, have it on one of the joints; either the elbow, wrist, knee, or ankle. So strictly is its visitation confined to the city proper, that in none of the neighboring villages, nor even in a distant suburb, is it known. Physicians have vainly attempted to prevent it by inoculation, and are at a loss to what cause to ascribe it. We are liable to have it, even after five days' stay; but I hope it will postpone its appearance until after I reach home.

The other remarkable thing here is the Hospital for Cats. This was founded long ago by a rich, cat-loving Mussulman, and is one of the best endowed institutions in the city. An old mosque is appropriated to the purpose, under the charge of several directors; and here sick cats are nursed, homeless cats find shelter, and decrepit cats gratefully purr away their declining years. The whole category embraces several hundreds, and it is quite a sight to behold the court, the corridors, and terraces of the mosque swarming with them. Here, one with a bruised limb is receiving a cataplasm; there, a cataleptic patient is tenderly cared for; and so on, through the long concatenation of feline diseases. Aleppo, moreover, rejoices in a greater number of cats than even Jerusalem. At a rough guess, I should thus state the population of the city: Turks and Arabs, 70,000; Christians of all denominations, 15,000; Jews, 10,000; dogs, 12,000; and cats, 8,000.

Among other persons whom I have met here, is Ferhat Pasha, formerly General Stein, Hungarian Minister of War, and Governor of Transylvania. He accepted Moslemism with Bem and others, and now rejoices in his circumcision and 7,000 piastres a month. He is a fat, companionable sort of man; who, by his own confession, never labored very zealously for the independence of Hungary, being an Austrian by birth. He conversed with me for several hours on the scenes in which he had participated, and attributed the failure of the Hungarians to the want of material means. General Bem, who died here, is spoken of with the utmost respect, both by Turks and Christians. The former have honored him with a large tomb, or mausoleum, covered with a dome.

But I must close, leaving half unsaid. Suffice it to say that no Oriental city has interested me so profoundly as Aleppo, and in none have I received such universal and cordial hospitality. We leave to-morrow for Asia Minor, having engaged men and horses for the whole route to Constantinople.

Chapter XVI. Through the Syrian Gates.

An Inauspicious Departure--The Ruined Church of St. Simon--The Plain of Antioch--A Turcoman Encampment--Climbing Akma Dagh--The Syrian Gates--Scanderoon--An American Captain--Revolt of the Koords--We take a Guard--The Field of Issus--The Robber-Chief, Kutchuk Ali--A Deserted Town--A Land of Gardens.

"Mountains, on whose barren breast

The lab'ring clouds do often rest."

Milton.

In Quarantine (Adana, Asia Minor), *Tuesday, June* 15, 1852.

We left Aleppo on the morning of the 9th, under circumstances not the most promising for the harmony of our journey. We had engaged horses and baggage-mules from the capidji, or chief of the muleteers, and in order to be certain of having animals that would not break down on the way, made a particular selection from a number that were brought us. When about leaving the city, however, we discovered that one of the horses had been changed. Signor di Picciotto, who accompanied us past the Custom-House barriers, immediately dispatched the delinquent muleteer to bring back the true horse, and the latter made a farce of trying to find him, leading the Consul and the capidji (who, I believe, was at the bottom of the cheat) a wild-goose chase over the hills around Aleppo, where of course, the animal was not to be seen. When, at length, we had waited three hours, and had wandered about four miles from the city, we gave up the search, took leave of the Consul and went on with the new horse. Our proper plan would have been to pitch the tent and refuse to move till the matter was settled. The animal, as we discovered during the first day's journey, was hopelessly lame, and we only added to the difficulty by taking him.

We rode westward all day over barren and stony hills, meeting with abundant traces of the power and prosperity of this region during the times of the Greek Emperors. The nevastation wrought by earthquakes has been terrible; there is scarcely a wall or arch standing, which does not bear marks of having been violently shaken. The walls inclosing the fig-orchards near the villages contain many stones with Greek inscriptions, and fragments of cornices. We encamped the first night on the plain at the foot of Mount St. Simon, and not far from the ruins of the celebrated Church of the same name. The building stands in a stony wilderness at the foot of the mountain. It is about a hundred feet long and thirty in height, with two lofty square towers in front. The pavement of the interior is entirely concealed by the masses of pillars, capitals, and hewn blocks that lie heaped upon it. The windows, which are of the tall, narrow, arched form, common in Byzantine Churches, have a common moulding which falls like a mantle over and between them. The general effect of the Church is very fine, though there is much inelegance in the sculptured details. At the extremity is a half-dome of massive stone, over the place of the altar, and just in front of this formerly stood the pedestal whereon, according to tradition, St. Simeon Stylites commenced his pillar-life. I found a recent excavation at the spot, but no pedestal, which has probably been carried off by the Greek monks. Beside the Church stands a large building, with an upper and lower balcony, supported by square stone pillars, around three sides. There is also a paved court-yard, a large cistern cut in the rock and numerous out-buildings, all going to confirm the supposition of its having been a monastery. The main building is three stories high, with pointed gables, and bears a strong resemblance to an American summer hotel, with verandas. Several ancient fig and walnut trees are growing among the ruins, and add to their picturesque appearance.

The next day we crossed a broad chain of hills to the Plain of Antioch, which we reached near its northern extremity. In one of the valleys through which the road lay, we saw a number of hot sulphur springs, some of them of a considerable volume of water. Not far from them was a beautiful fountain of fresh and cold water gushing from the foot of a high rock. Soon after reaching the plain, we crossed the stream of Kara Su, which feeds the Lake of Antioch. This part of the plain is low and swampy, and the streams are literally alive with fish. While passing over the bridge I saw many hundreds, from one to two feet in length. We wandered through the marshy meadows for two or three hours, and towards sunset reached a Turcoman encampment, where the ground was dry enough to pitch our tents. The rude tribe received us hospitably, and sent us milk and cheese in abundance. I visited the tent of the Shekh, who was very courteous, but as he knew no language but Turkish, our conversation was restricted to signs. The tent was of camel's-hair cloth, spacious, and open at the sides. A rug was spread for me, and the Shekh's wife brought me a pipe of tolerable tobacco. The household were seated upon the ground, chatting pleasantly with one another, and apparently not in the least disturbed by my presence. One of the Shekh's sons, who was deaf and dumb, came and sat before me, and described by very expressive signs the character of the road to Scanderoon. He gave me to understand that there were robbers in the mountains, with many grim gestures descriptive of stabbing and firing muskets.

The mosquitoes were so thick during the night that we were obliged to fill the tent with smoke in order to sleep. When morning came, we fancied there would be a relief for us, but it only brought a worse pest, in the shape of swarms of black gnats, similar to those which so tormented me in Nubia. I know of no infliction so terrible as these gnats, which you cannot drive away, and which assail ears, eyes, and nostrils in such quantities that you become mad and desperate in your efforts to eject them. Through glens filled with oleander, we ascended the first slopes of Akma Dagh, the mountain range which divides the Gulf of Scanderoon from the Plain of Antioch. Then, passing a natural terrace, covered with groves of oak, our road took the mountain side, climbing upwards in the shadow of pine and wild olive trees, and between banks of blooming lavender and myrtle. We saw two or three companies of armed guards, stationed by the road-side, for the mountain is infested with robbers, and a caravan had been plundered only three days before. The view, looking backward, took in the whole plain, with the Lake of Antioch glittering in the centre, the valley of the Orontes in the south, and the lofty cone of Djebel-Okrab far to the west. As we approached the summit, violent gusts of wind blew through the pass with such force as almost to overturn our horses. Here the road from Antioch joins that from Aleppo, and both for some distance retain the ancient pavement.

From the western side we saw the sea once more, and went down through the Pylæ Syriæ, or Syrian Gates, as this defile was called by the Romans. It is very narrow and rugged, with an abrupt descent. In an hour from the summit we came upon an aqueduct of a triple row of arches, crossing the gorge. It is still used to carry water to the town of Beilan, which hangs over the mouth of the pass, half a mile below. This is one of the most picturesque spots in Syria. The houses cling to the sides and cluster on the summits of precipitous crags, and every shelf of soil, every crevice where a tree can thrust its roots, upholds a mass of brilliant vegetation. Water is the life of the place. It gushes into the street from exhaustless fountains; it trickles from the terraces in showers of misty drops; it tumbles into the gorge in sparkling streams; and everywhere it nourishes a life as bright and beautiful as its own. The fruit trees are of enormous size, and the crags are curtained with a magnificent drapery of vines. This green gateway opens suddenly upon another, cut through a glittering mass of micaceous rock, whence one looks down on the town and Gulf of Scanderoon, the coast of Karamania beyond, and the distant snows of the Taurus. We descended through groves of pine and oak, and in three hours more reached the shore.

Scanderoon is the most unhealthy place on the Syrian Coast, owing to the malaria from a marsh behind it. The inhabitants are a wretched pallid set, who are visited every year with devastating fevers. The marsh was partly drained some forty years ago by the Turkish government, and a few thousand dollars would be sufficient to remove it entirely, and make the place--which is of some importance as the seaport of Aleppo--healthy and habitable. At present, there are not five hundred inhabitants, and half of these consist of the Turkish garrison and the persons attached to the different Vice-Consulates. The streets are depositories of filth, and pools of stagnant water, on all sides, exhale the most fetid odors. Near the town are the ruins of a castle built by Godfrey of Bouillon. We marched directly down to the sea-shore, and pitched our tent close beside the waves, as the place most free from malaria. There were a dozen vessels at anchor in the road, and one of them proved to be the American bark Columbia, Capt. Taylor. We took a skiff and went on board, where we were cordially welcomed by the mate. In the evening, the captain came to our tent, quite surprised to find two wandering Americans in such a lonely corner of the world. Soon afterwards, with true seaman-

544

like generosity, he returned, bringing a jar of fine Spanish olives and a large bottle of pickles, which he insisted on adding to our supplies. The olives have the choicest Andalusian flavor, and the pickles lose none of their relish from having been put up in New York.

The road from Scanderoon to this place lies mostly along the shore of the gulf, at the foot of Akma Dagh, and is reckoned dangerous on account of the marauding bands of Koords who infest the mountains. These people, like the Druses, have rebelled against the conscription, and will probably hold their ground with equal success, though the Turks talk loudly of invading their strongholds. Two weeks ago, the post was robbed, about ten miles from Scanderoon, and a government vessel, now lying at anchor in the bay, opened a cannonade on the plunderers, before they could be secured. In consequence of the warnings of danger in everybody's mouth, we decided to take an escort, and therefore waited upon the commander of the forces, with the firman of the Pasha of Aleppo. A convoy of two soldiers was at once promised us; and at sunrise, next morning, they took the lead of our caravan.

In order to appear more formidable, in case we should meet with robbers, we put on our Frank pantaloons, which had no other effect than to make the heat more intolerable. But we formed rather a fierce cavalcade, six armed men in all. Our road followed the shore of the bay, having a narrow, uninhabited flat, covered with thickets of myrtle and mastic, between us and the mountains. The two soldiers, more valiant than the guard of Banias, rode in advance, and showed no signs of fear as we approached the suspicious places. The morning was delightfully clear, and the snow-crowned range of Taurus shone through the soft vapors hanging over the gulf. In one place, we skirted the shore for some distance, under a bank twenty feet in height, and so completely mantled with shrubbery, that a small army might have hidden in it. There were gulleys at intervals, opening suddenly on our path, and we looked up them, expecting every moment to see the gleam of a Koordish gun-barrel, or a Turcoman spear, above the tops of the myrtles.

Crossing a promontory which makes out from the mountains, we came upon the renowned plain of Issus, where Darius lost his kingdom to Alexander. On a low cliff overhanging the sea, there are the remains of a single tower of gray stone. The people in Scanderoon call it "Jonah's Pillar," and say that it marks the spot where the Ninevite was cast ashore by the whale. [This makes three places on the Syrian coast where Jonah was vomited forth.] The plain of Issus is from two to three miles long, but not more than half a mile wide, It is traversed by a little river, supposed to be the Pinarus, which comes down through a tremendous cleft in the Akma Dagh. The ground seems too small for the battle-field of such armies as were engaged on the occasion. It is bounded on the north by a low hill, separating it from the plain of Baïas, and it is possible that Alexander may have made choice of this position, leaving the unwieldy forces of Darius to attack him from the plain. His advantage would be greater, on account of the long, narrow form of the ground, which would prevent him from being engaged with more than a small portion of the Persian army, at one time. The plain is now roseate with blooming oleanders, but almost entirely uncultivated. About midway there are the remains of an ancient quay jutting into the sea.

Soon after leaving the field of Issus, we reached the town of Baïas, which is pleasantly situated on the shore, at the mouth of a river whose course through the plain is marked with rows of tall poplar trees. The walls of the town, and the white dome and minaret of its mosque, rose dazzlingly against the dark blue of the sea, and the purple stretch of the mountains of Karamania. A single palm lifted its crest in the foreground. We dismounted for breakfast under the shade of an old bridge which crosses the river. It was a charming spot, the banks above and below being overhung with oleander, white rose, honeysuckle and clematis. The two guardsmen finished the remaining half of our Turcoman cheese, and almost exhausted our supply of bread. I gave one of them a cigar, which he was at a loss how to smoke, until our muleteer showed him.

Baïas was celebrated fifty years ago, as the residence of the robber chief, Kutchuk Ali, who, for a long time, braved the authority of the Porte itself. He was in the habit of levying a yearly tribute on the caravan to Mecca, and the better to enforce his claims, often suspended two or three of his captives at the gates of the town, a day or two before the caravan arrived. Several expeditions were sent against him, but he always succeeded in bribing the commanders, who, on their return to Constantinople, made such representations that Kutchuk Ali, instead of being punished, received one dignity after another, until finally he attained the rank of a Pasha of two tails. This emboldened him to commit enormities too great to be overlooked, and in 1812 Baïas was taken, and the atrocious nest of land-pirates broken up.

I knew that the town had been sacked on this occasion, but was not prepared to find such a complete picture of desolation. The place is surrounded with a substantial wall, with two gateways, on the north and south. A bazaar, covered with a lofty vaulted roof of stone, runs directly through from gate to gate; and there was still a smell of spices in the air, on entering. The massive shops on either hand, with their open doors, invited possession, and might readily be made habitable again. The great iron gates leading from the bazaar into the khans and courts, still swing on their rusty hinges. We rode into the court of the mosque, which is surrounded with a light and elegant corridor, supported by pillars. The grass has as yet but partially invaded the marble pavement, and a stone drinking-trough still stands in the centre. I urged my horse up the steps and into the door of the mosque. It is in the form of a Greek cross, with a dome in the centre, resting on four very elegant pointed arches. There is an elaborately gilded and painted gallery of wood over the entrance, and the pulpit opposite is as well preserved as if the mollah had just left it. Out of the mosque we passed into a second court, and then over a narrow bridge into the fortress. The moat is perfect, and the walls as complete as if just erected. Only the bottom is dry, and now covered with a thicket of wild pomegranate trees. The heavy iron doors of the fortress swung half open, as we entered unchallenged. The interior is almost entire, and some of the cannon still lie buried in the springing grass. The plan of the little town, which appears to have been all built at one time, is most admirable. The walls of circuit, including the fortress, cannot be more than 300 yards square, and yet none of the characteristics of a large Oriental city are omitted.

Leaving Baïas, we travelled northward, over a waste, though fertile plain. The mountains on our right made a grand appearance, with their feet mantled in myrtle, and their tops plumed with pine. They rise from the sea with a long, bold sweep, but each peak falls off in a precipice on the opposite side, as if the chain were the barrier of the world and there was nothing but space beyond. In the afternoon we left the plain for a belt of glorious garden land, made by streams that came down from the mountains. We entered a lane embowered in pomegranate, white rose, clematis, and other flowering vines and shrubs, and overarched by superb plane, lime, and beech trees, chained together with giant grape vines. On either side were fields of ripe wheat and barley, mulberry orchards and groves of fruit trees, under the shade of which the Turkish families sat or slept during the hot hours of the day. Birds sang in the boughs, and the gurgling of water made a cool undertone to their music. Out of fairyland where shall I see again such lovely bowers? We were glad when the soldiers announced that it was necessary to encamp there; as we should find no other habitations for more than twenty miles.

Our tent was pitched under a grand sycamore, beside a swift mountain stream which almost made the circuit of our camp. Beyond the tops of the elm, beech, and fig groves, we saw the picturesque green summits of the lower ranges of Giaour Dagh, in the north-east, while over the southern meadows a golden gleam of sunshine lay upon the Gulf of Scanderoon. The village near us was Chaya, where there is a military station. The guards we had brought from Scanderoon here left us; but the commanding officer advised us to take others on the morrow, as the road was still considered unsafe.

Chapter XVII. Adana and Tarsus.

The Black Gate--The Plain of Cilicia--A Koord Village--Missis--Cilician Scenery--Arrival at Adana--Three days in Quarantine--We receive Pratique--A Landscape--The Plain of Tarsus--The River Cydnus--A Vision of Cleopatra--Tarsus and its Environs--The Duniktash--The Moon of Ramazan.

"Paul said, I am a man which am a Jew of Tarsus, a city in Cilicia, a citizen of no mean city."--Acts, xxi. 89.

Khan on Mt. Taurus, *Saturday, June* 19, 1852.

We left our camp at Chaya at dawn, with an escort of three soldiers, which we borrowed from the guard stationed at that place. The path led along the shore, through clumps of myrtle beaten inland by the wind, and rounded as smoothly as if they had been clipped by a gardener's shears. As we approached the head of the gulf, the peaked summits of Giaour Dagh, 10,000 feet in height, appeared in the north-east. The streams we forded swarmed with immense trout. A brown hedgehog ran across our road, but when I touched him with the end of my pipe, rolled himself into an impervious ball of prickles. Soon after turning the head of the gulf, the road swerved off to the west, and entered a narrow pass, between hills covered with thick copsewood. Here we came upon an ancient gateway of black lava stone, which bears marks of great antiquity It is now called Kara Kapu, the "Black Gate," and some suppose it to have been one of the ancient gates of Cilicia.

Beyond this, our road led over high, grassy hills, without a sign of human habitation, to the ruined khan of Koord Koolak, We dismounted and unloaded our baggage in the spacious stone archway, and drove our beasts into the dark, vaulted halls behind. The building was originally intended for a magazine of supplies, and from the ruined mosque near it, I suspect it was formerly one of the caravan stations for the pilgrims from Constantinople to Mecca. The weather was intensely hot and sultry, and our animals were almost crazy from the attacks of a large yellow gad-fly. After the noonday heat was over we descended to the first Cilician plain, which is bounded on the west by the range of Durdun Dagh. As we had now passed the most dangerous part of the road, we dismissed the three soldiers and took but a single man with us. The entire plain is covered with wild fennel, six to eight feet in height, and literally blazing with its bloomy yellow tops. Riding through it, I could barely look over them, and far and wide, on all sides, spread a golden sea, out of which the long violet hills rose with the liveliest effect. Brown, shining serpents, from four to six feet in length, frequently slid across our path. The plain, which must be sixty miles in circumference, is wholly uncultivated, though no land could possibly be richer.

Out of the region of fennel we passed into one of red and white clover, timothy grass and wild oats. The thistles were so large as to resemble young palm-trees, and the salsify of our gardens grew rank and wild. At length we dipped into the evening shadow of Durdun Dagh, and reached the village of Koord Keui, on his lower slope. As there was no place for our tent on the rank grass of the plain or the steep side of the hill, we took forcible possession of the winnowing-floor, a flat terrace built up under two sycamores, and still covered with the chaff of the last threshing. The Koords took the whole thing as a matter of course, and even brought us a felt carpet to rest upon. They came and seated themselves around us, chatting sociably, while we lay in the tent-door, smoking the pipe of refreshment. The view over the wide golden plain, and the hills beyond, to the distant, snow-tipped peaks of Akma Dagh, was superb, as the shadow of the mountain behind us slowly lengthened over it, blotting out the mellow lights of sunset. There were many fragments of pillars and capitals of white marble built up in the houses, showing that they occupied the site of some ancient village or temple.

The next morning, we crossed Durdun Dagh, and entered the great plain of Cilicia. The range, after we had passed it, presented a grand, bold, broken outline, blue in the morning vapor, and wreathed with shifting belts of cloud. A stately castle, called the Palace of Serpents, on the summit of an isolated peak to the north, stood out clear and high, in the midst of a circle of fog, like a phantom picture of the air. The River Jyhoon, the ancient Pyramus, which rises on the borders of Armenia, sweeps the western base of the mountains. It is a larger stream than the Orontes, with a deep, rapid current, flowing at the bottom of a bed lower than the level of the plain. In three hours, we reached Missis, the ancient Mopsuestia, on the right bank of the river. There are extensive ruins on the left bank, which were probably those of the former city. The soil for some distance around is scattered with broken pillars, capitals, and hewn stones. The ancient bridge still crosses the river, but the central arch having been broken away, is replaced with a wooden platform. The modern town is a forlorn place, and all the glorious plain around it is uncultivated. The view over this plain was magnificent: unbounded towards the sea, but on the north girdled by the sublime range of Taurus, whose great snow-fields gleamed in the sun. In the afternoon, we reached the old bridge over the Jyhoon, at Adana. The eastern bank is occupied with the graves of the former inhabitants, and there are at least fifteen acres of tombstones, as thickly planted as the graves can be dug. The fields of wheat and barley along the river are very rich, and at present the natives are busily occupied in drawing the sheaves on large sleds to the open threshing-floors.

The city is built over a low eminence, and its four tall minarets, with a number of palm-trees rising from the mass of brown brick walls, reminded me of Egypt. At the end of the bridge, we were met by one of the Quarantine officers, who preceded us, taking care that we touched nobody in the streets, to the Quarantine building. This land quarantine, between Syria and Asia Minor, when the former country is free from any epidemic, seems a most absurd thing. We were detained at Adana three days and a half, to be purified, before proceeding further. Lately, the whole town was placed in quarantine for five days, because a Turkish Bey, who lives near Baïas, entered the gates without being noticed, and was found in the bazaars. The Quarantine building was once a palace of the Pashas of Adana, but is now in a half-ruined condition. The rooms are large and airy, and there is a spacious open divan which affords ample shade and a cool breeze throughout the whole day. Fortunately for us, there were only three persons in Quarantine, who occupied a room distant from ours. The Inspector was a very obliging person, and procured us a table and two chairs. The only table to be had in the whole place--a town of 15,000 inhabitants--belonged to an Italian merchant, who kindly gave it for our use. We employed a messenger to purchase provisions in the bazaars; and our days passed quietly in writing, smoking, and gazing indolently from our windows upon the flowery plains beyond the town. Our nights, however, were tormented by small white gnats, which stung us unmercifully. The physician of Quarantine, Dr. Spagnolo, is a Venetian refugee, and formerly editor of La Lega Italiana, a paper published in Venice during the revolution. He informed us that, except the Princess Belgioioso, who passed through Adana on her way to Jerusalem, we were the only travellers he had seen for eleven months.

After three days and four nights of grateful, because involuntary, indolence, Dr. Spagnolo gave us pratique, and we lost no time in getting under weigh again. We were the only occupants of Quarantine; and as we moved out of the portal of the old seraï, at sunrise, no one was guarding it. The Inspector and Mustapha, the messenger, took their back-sheeshes with silent gratitude. The plain on the west side of the town is well cultivated; and as we rode along towards Tarsus, I was charmed with the rich pastoral air of the scenery. It was like one of the midland landscapes of England, bathed in Southern sunshine. The beautiful level, stretching away to the mountains, stood golden with the fields of wheat which the reapers were cutting. It was no longer bare, but dotted with orange groves, clumps of holly, and a number of magnificent terebinth-trees, whose dark, rounded masses of foliage remind one of the Northern oak. Cattle were grazing in the stubble, and horses, almost buried under loads of fresh grass, met us as they passed to the city. The sheaves were drawn to the threshing-floor on sleds, and we could see the husbandmen in the distance treading out and winnowing the grain. Over these bright, busy scenes, rose the lesser heights of the Taurus, and beyond them, mingled in white clouds, the snows of the crowning range.

The road to Tarsus, which is eight hours distant, lies over an unbroken plain. Towards the sea, there are two tumuli, resembling those on the plains east of Antioch. Stone wells, with troughs for watering horses, occur at intervals of three or four miles; but there is little cultivation after leaving the vicinity of Adana. The sun poured down an intense summer heat, and hundreds of large gad-flies, swarming around us, drove the horses wild with their stings. Towards noon, we stopped at a little village for breakfast. We took possession of a shop, which the good-natured merchant offered us, and were about to spread our provisions upon the counter, when the gnats and mosquitoes fairly drove us away. We at once went forward in search of a better place, which gave occasion to our chief mukkairee, Hadji Youssuf, for a violent remonstrance. The terms of the agreement at Aleppo gave the entire control of the journey into our own hands, and the Hadji now sought to violate it. He protested against our travelling more than six hours a day, and conducted himself so insolently, that we threatened to take him before the Pasha of Tarsus. This silenced him for the time; but we hate him so cordially since then, that I foresee we shall have more trouble. In the afternoon, a gust, sweeping along the sides of Taurus, cooled the air and afforded us a little relief.

By three o'clock we reached the River Cydnus, which is bare of trees on its eastern side, but flows between banks covered with grass and shrubs. It is still spanned by the ancient bridge, and the mules now step in the hollow ruts worn long ago by Roman and Byzantine chariot wheels. The stream is not more than thirty yards broad, but has a very full and rapid current of a bluish-white color, from the snows which feed it. I rode down to the brink and drank a cup of the water. It was exceedingly cold, and I do not wonder that a bath in it should have killed the Emperor Barbarossa. From the top of the bridge, there is a lovely view, down the stream, where it washes a fringe of willows and heavy fruit-trees on its western bank, and then winds away through the grassy plain, to the sea. For once, my fancy ran parallel with the inspiration of the scene. I could think of nothing but the galley of Cleopatra slowly stemming the current of the stream, its silken sails filled with the sea-breeze, its gilded oars keeping time to the flutes, whose voluptuous melodies floated far out over the vernal meadows. Tarsus was probably almost hidden then, as now, by its gardens, except just where it touched the river; and the dazzling vision of the Egyptian Queen, as she came up conquering and to conquer, must have been all the more bewildering, from the lovely bowers through which she sailed.

From the bridge an ancient road still leads to the old Byzantine gate of Tarsus. Part of the town is encompassed by a wall, built by the Caliph Haroun Al-Raschid, and there is a ruined fortress, which is attributed to Sultan Bajazet

Small streams, brought from the Cydnus, traverse the environs, and, with such a fertile soil, the luxuriance of the gardens in which the city lies buried is almost incredible. In our rambles in search of a place to pitch the tent, we entered a superb orange-orchard, the foliage of which made a perpetual twilight. Many of the trunks were two feet in diameter. The houses are mostly of one story, and the materials are almost wholly borrowed from the ancient city. Pillars, capitals, fragments of cornices and entablatures abound. I noticed here, as in Adana, a high wooden frame on the top of every house, raised a few steps above the roof, and covered with light muslin, like a portable bathing-house. Here the people put up their beds in the evening, sleep, and come down to the roofs in the morning--an excellent plan for getting better air in these malarious plains and escaping from fleas and mosquitoes. In our search for the Armenian Church, which is said to have been founded by St. Paul ("Saul of Tarsus"), we came upon a mosque, which had been originally a Christian Church, of Greek times.

From the top of a mound, whereupon stand the remains of an ancient circular edifice, we obtained a fine view of the city and plain of Tarsus. A few houses or clusters of houses stood here and there like reefs amid the billowy green, and the minarets--one of them with a nest of young storks on its very summit--rose like the masts of sunken ships. Some palms lifted their tufted heads from the gardens, beyond which the great plain extended from the mountains to the sea. The tumulus near Mersyn, the port of Tarsus, was plainly visible. Two hours from Mersyn are the ruins of Pompeiopolis, the name given by Pompey to the town of Soli, after his conquest of the Cilician pirates. From Soli, on account of the bad Greek spoken by its inhabitants, came the term "solecism." The ruins of Pompeiopolis consist of a theatre, temples, and a number of houses, still in good preservation. The whole coast, as far as Aleya, three hundred miles west of this, is said to abound with ruined cities, and I regret exceedingly that time will not permit me to explore it.

While searching for the antiquities about Tarsus, I accosted a man in a Frank dress, who proved to be the Neapolitan Consul. He told us that the most remarkable relic was the Duniktash (the Round Stone), and procured us a guide. It lies in a garden near the city, and is certainly one of the most remarkable monuments in the East. It consists of a square inclosure of solid masonry, 350 feet long by 150 feet wide, the walls of which are eighteen feet in thickness and twenty feet high. It appears to have been originally a solid mass, without entrance, but a passage has been broken in one place, and in another there is a split or fissure, evidently produced by an earthquake. The material is rough stone, brick and mortar. Inside of the inclosure are two detached square masses of masonry, of equal height, and probably eighty feet on a side, without opening of any kind. One of them has been pierced at the bottom, a steep passage leading to a pit or well, but the sides of the passage thus broken indicate that the whole structure is one solid mass. It is generally supposed that they were intended as tombs: but of whom? There is no sign by which they may be recognized, and, what is more singular, no tradition concerning them.

The day we reached Tarsus was the first of the Turkish fast-month of Ramazan, the inhabitants having seen the new moon the night before. At Adana, where they did not keep such a close look-out, the fast had not commenced. During its continuance, which is from twenty-eight to twenty-nine days, no Mussulman dares eat, drink, or smoke, from an hour before sunrise till half an hour after sunset. The Mohammedan months are lunar, and each month makes the whole round of the seasons, once in thirty-three years. When, therefore, the Ramazan comes in midsummer, as at present, the fulfilment of this fast is a great trial, even to the strongest and most devout. Eighteen hours without meat or drink, and what is still worse to a genuine Turk, without a pipe, is a rigid test of faith. The rich do the best they can to avoid it, by feasting all night and sleeping all day, but the poor, who must perform their daily avocations, as usual, suffer exceedingly. In walking through Tarsus I saw many wretched faces in the bazaars, and the guide who accompanied us had a painfully famished air. Fortunately the Koran expressly permits invalids, children, and travellers to disregard the fast, so that although we eat and drink when we like, we are none the less looked upon as good Mussulmans. About dark a gun is fired and a rocket sent up from the mosque, announcing the termination of the day's fast. The meals are already prepared, the pipes filled, the coffee smokes in the finjans, and the echoes have not died away nor the last sparks of the rocket become extinct, before half the inhabitants are satisfying their hunger, thirst and smoke-lust.

We left Tarsus this morning, and are now encamped among the pines of Mount Taurus. The last flush of sunset is fading from his eternal snows, and I drop my pen to enjoy the silence of twilight in this mountain solitude.

Chapter XVIII. The Pass of Mount Taurus.

We enter the Taurus--Turcomans--Forest Scenery--the Palace of Pan-- Khan Mezarluk--Morning among the Mountains--The Gorge of the Cydnus- -The Crag of the Fortress--The Cilician Gate--Deserted Forts--A Sublime Landscape--The Gorge of the Sihoon--The Second Gate--Camp in the Defile- -Sunrise--Journey up the Sihoon--A Change of Scenery--A Pastoral Valley-- Kolü Kushla--A Deserted Khan--A Guest in Ramazan--Flowers--The Plain of Karamania--Barren Hills--The Town of Eregli--The Hadji again.

"Lo! where the pass expands

Its stony jaws, the abrupt mountain breaks,

And seems, with its accumulated crags,

To overhang the world." Shelley.

Eregli, in *Karamania, June* 22, 1852.

Striking our tent in the gardens of Tarsus, we again crossed the Cydnus, and took a northern course across the plain. The long line of Taurus rose before us, seemingly divided into four successive ranges, the highest of which was folded in clouds; only the long streaks of snow, filling the ravines, being visible. The outlines of these ranges were very fine, the waving line of the summits cut here and there by precipitous gorges--the gateways of rivers that came down to the plain. In about two hours, we entered the lower hills. They are barren and stony, with a white, chalky soil; but the valleys were filled with myrtle, oleander, and lauristinus in bloom, and lavender grew in great profusion on the hill-sides. The flowers of the oleander gave out a delicate, almond-like fragrance, and grew in such dense clusters as frequently to hide the foliage. I amused myself with finding a derivation of the name of this beautiful plant, which may answer until somebody discovers a better one. Hero, when the corpse of her lover was cast ashore by the waves, buried him under an oleander bush, where she was accustomed to sit daily, and lament over his untimely fate. Now, a foreign horticulturist, happening to pass by when the shrub was in blossom, was much struck with its beauty, and asked Hero what it was called. But she, absorbed in grief, and thinking only of her lover, clasped her hands, and sighed out: "O Leander! O Leander!" which the horticulturist immediately entered in his note-book as the name of the shrub; and by that name it is known, to the present time.

For two or three hours, the scenery was rather tame, the higher summits being obscured with a thunder-cloud. Towards noon, however, we passed the first chain, and saw, across a strip of rolling land intervening, the grand ramparts of the second, looming dark and large under the clouds. A circular watch-tower of white stone, standing on the summit of a promontory at the mouth of a gorge on our right, flashed out boldly against the storm. We stopped under an oak-tree to take breakfast; but there was no water; and two Turks, who were resting while their horses grazed in the meadow, told us we should find a good spring half a mile further. We ascended a long slope, covered with wheat-fields, where numbers of Turcoman reapers were busy at work, passed their black tents, surrounded with droves of sheep and goats, and reached a rude stone fountain of good water, where two companies of these people had stopped to rest, on their way to the mountains. It was the time of noon prayer, and they went through their devotions with great solemnity. We nestled deep in a bed of myrtles, while we breakfasted; for the sky was clouded, and the wind blew cool and fresh from the region of rain above us. Some of the Turcomans asked us for bread, and were very grateful when we gave it to them.

In the afternoon, we came into a higher and wilder region, where the road led through thickets of wild olive, holly, oak, and lauristinus, with occasional groves of pine. What a joy I felt in hearing, once more, the grand song of my favorite tree! Our way was a woodland road; a storm had passed over the region in the morning; the earth was still fresh and moist, and there was an aromatic smell of leaves in the air. We turned westward into the entrance of a deep valley, over which hung a perpendicular cliff of gray and red rock, fashioned by nature so as to resemble a vast fortress, with windows, portals and projecting bastions. François displayed his knowledge of mythology, by declaring it to be the Palace of Pan. While we were carrying out the idea, by making chambers for the Fauns and Nymphs in the basement story of the precipice, the path wound around the shoulder of the mountain, and the glen spread away before us, branching up into loftier ranges, disclosing through its gateway of cliffs, rising out of the steeps of pine forest, a sublime vista of blue mountain peaks, climbing to the topmost snows. It was a magnificent Alpine landscape, more glowing and rich than Switzerland, yet equalling it in all the loftier characteristics of mountain scenery. Another and greater precipice towered over us on the right, and the black eagles which had made their eyries in its niched and caverned vaults, were wheeling around its crest. A branch of the Cydnus foamed along the bottom of the gorge, and soma Turcoman boys were tending their herds on its banks.

Further up the glen, we found a fountain of delicious water, beside the deserted Khan of Mezarluk, and there encamped for the night. Our tent was pitched on the mountain side, near a fountain of the coolest, clearest and sweetest water I have seen in all the East. There was perfect silence among the mountains, and the place was as lonely as it was sublime. The night was cool and fresh; but I could not sleep until towards morning. When I opened my belated eyes, the tall peaks on the opposite side of the glen were girdled below their waists with the flood of a sparkling sunrise. The sky was pure as crystal, except a soft white fleece that veiled the snowy pinnacles of Taurus, folding and unfolding, rising and sinking, as if to make their beauty still more attractive by the partial concealment. The morning air was almost cold, but so pure and bracing--so aromatic with the healthy breath of the pines--that I took it down in the fullest possible draughts.

We rode up the glen, following the course of the Cydnus, through scenery of the wildest and most romantic character. The bases of the mountains were completely enveloped in forests of pine, but their summits rose in precipitous crags, many hundreds of feet in height, hanging above our very heads. Even after the sun was five hours high, their shadows fell upon us from the opposite side of the glen. Mixed with the pine were occasional oaks, an undergrowth of hawthorn in bloom, and shrubs covered with yellow and white flowers. Over these the wild grape threw its rich festoons, filling the air with exquisite fragrance.

Out of this glen, we passed into another, still narrower and wilder. The road was the old Roman way, and in tolerable condition, though it had evidently not been mended for many centuries. In half an hour, the pass opened, disclosing an enormous peak in front of us, crowned with the ruins of an ancient fortress of considerable extent. The position was almost impregnable, the mountain dropping on one side into a precipice five hundred feet in perpendicular height. Under the cliffs of the loftiest ridge, there was a terrace planted with walnut-trees: a charming little hamlet in the wilderness. Wild sycamore-trees, with white trunks and bright green foliage, shaded the foamy twists of the Cydnus, as it plunged down its difficult bed. The pine thrust its roots into the naked precipices, and from their summits hung out over the great abysses below. I thought of Œnone's

--"tall, dark pines, that fringed the craggy ledge

High over the blue gorge, and all between

The snowy peak and snow-white cataract

Fostered the callow eaglet;"

and certainly she had on Mount Ida no more beautiful trees than these.

We had doubled the Crag of the Fortress, when the pass closed before us, shut in by two immense precipices of sheer, barren rock, more than a thousand feet in height. Vast fragments, fallen from above, choked up the entrance, whence the Cydnus, spouting forth in foam, leaped into the defile. The ancient road was completely destroyed, but traces of it were to be seen on the rocks, ten feet above the present bed of the stream, and on the broken masses which had been hurled below. The path wound with difficulty among these wrecks, and then merged into the stream itself, as we entered the gateway. A violent wind blew in our faces as we rode through the strait, which is not ten yards in breadth, while its walls rise to the region of the clouds. In a few minutes we had traversed it, and stood looking back on the enormous gap. There were several Greek tablets cut in the rock above the old road, but so defaced as to be illegible. This is undoubtedly the principal gate of the Taurus, and the pass through which the armies of Cyrus and Alexander entered Cilicia.

Beyond the gate the mountains retreated, and we climbed up a little dell, past two or three Turcoman houses, to the top of a hill, whence opened a view of the principal range, now close at hand. The mountains in front were clothed with dark cedars to their very tops, and the snow-fields behind them seemed dazzlingly bright and near. Our course for several miles now lay through a more open valley, drained by the upper waters of the Cydnus. On two opposing terraces of the mountain chains are two fortresses, built by Ibraham Pasha, but now wholly deserted. They are large and well-constructed works of stone, and surrounded by ruins of stables, ovens, and the rude houses of the soldiery. Passing between these, we ascended to the shelf dividing the waters of the Cydnus and the Sihoon. From the point where the slope descends to the latter river, there opened before me one of the most glorious landscapes I ever beheld. I stood at the extremity of a long hollow or depression between the two ranges of the Taurus--not a valley, for it was divided by deep cloven chasms, hemmed in by steeps overgrown with cedars. On my right rose a sublime chain, soaring far out of the region of trees, and lifting its peaked summits of gray rock into toe sky. Another chain, nearly as lofty, but not so broken, nor with such large, imposing features, overhung me on the left; and far in front, filling up the magnificent vista--filling up all between the lower steeps, crowned with pine, and the round white clouds hanging on the verge of heaven--were the shining snows of the Taurus. Great God, how shall I describe the grandeur of that view! How draw the wonderful outlines of those mountains! How paint the airy hue of violet-gray, the soft white lights, the thousandfold pencillings of mellow shadow, the height, the depth, the far-reaching vastness of the landscape!

In the middle distance, a great blue gorge passed transversely across the two ranges and the region between. This, as I rightly conjectured, was the bed of the Sihoon. Our road led downward through groves of fragrant cedars, and we travelled thus for two hours before reaching the river. Taking a northward course up his banks, we reached the second of the Pylæ Ciliciæ before sunset. It is on a grander scale than the first gate, though not so startling and violent in its features. The bare walls on either side fall sheer to the water, and the road, crossing the Sihoon by a lofty bridge of a single arch, is cut along the face of the rock. Near the bridge a subterranean stream, almost as large as the river, bursts forth from the solid heart of the mountain. On either side gigantic masses of rock, with here and there a pine to adorn their sterility, tower to the height of 6,000 feet, in some places almost perpendicular from summit to base. They are worn and broken into all fantastic forms. There are pyramids, towers, bastions, minarets, and long, sharp spires, splintered and jagged as the turrets of an iceberg. I have seen higher mountains, but I have never seen any which looked so high as these. We camped on a narrow plot of ground, in the very heart of the tremendous gorge. A soldier, passing along at dusk, told us that a merchant and his servant were murdered in the same place last winter, and advised us to keep watch. But we slept safely all night, while the stars sparkled over the chasm, and slips of misty cloud hung low on the thousand pinnacles of rock.

When I awoke, the gorge lay in deep shadow; but high up on the western mountain, above the enormous black pyramids that arose from the river, the topmost pinnacles of rock sparkled like molten silver, in the full gush of sunrise. The great mountain, blocking up the gorge behind us, was bathed almost to its foot in the rays, and, seen through such a dark vista, was glorified beyond all other mountains of Earth. The air was piercingly cold and keen, and I could scarcely bear the water of the Sihoon on my sun-inflamed face. There was a little spring not far off, from which we obtained sufficient water to drink, the river being too muddy. The spring was but a thread oozing from the soil; but the Hadji collected it in handfuls, which he emptied into his water-skin, and then brought to us.

The morning light gave a still finer effect to the manifold forms of the mountains than that of the afternoon sun. The soft gray hue of the rocks shone clearly against the cloudless sky, fretted all over with the shadows thrown by their innumerable spires and jutting points, and by the natural arches scooped out under the cliffs. After travelling less than an hour, we passed the riven walls of the mighty gateway, and rode again under the shade of pine forests. The height of the mountains now gradually diminished, and their sides, covered with pine and cedar, became less broken and abrupt. The

562

summits, nevertheless, still retained the same rocky spine, shooting up into tall, single towers, or long lines of even parapets Occasionally, through gaps between, we caught glimpses of the snow-fields, dazzlingly high and white.

After travelling eight or nine miles, we emerged from the pass, and left the Sihoon at a place called Chiftlik Khan--a stone building, with a small fort adjoining, wherein fifteen splendid bronze cannon lay neglected on their broken and rotting carriages. As we crossed the stone bridge over the river, a valley opened suddenly on the left, disclosing the whole range of the Taurus, which we now saw on its northern side, a vast stretch of rocky spires, with sparkling snow-fields between, and long ravines filled with snow, extending far down between the dark blue cliffs and the dark green plumage of the cedars.

Immediately after passing the central chain of the Taurus, the character of the scenery changed. The heights were rounded, the rocky strata only appearing on the higher peaks, and the slopes of loose soil were deeply cut and scarred by the rains of ages. Both in appearance, especially in the scattered growth of trees dotted over the dark red soil, and in their formation, these mountains strongly resemble the middle ranges of the Californian Sierra Nevada. We climbed a long, winding glen, until we had attained a considerable height, when the road reached a dividing ridge, giving us a view of a deep valley, beyond which a chain of barren mountains rose to the height of some five thousand feet. As we descended the rocky path, a little caravan of asses and mules clambered up to meet us, along the brinks of steep gulfs. The narrow strip of bottom land along the stream was planted with rye, now in head, and rolling in silvery waves before the wind.

After our noonday halt, we went over the hills to another stream, which came from the north-west. Its valley was broader and greener than that we had left, and the hills inclosing it had soft and undulating outlines. They were bare of trees, but colored a pale green by their thin clothing of grass and herbs. In this valley the season was so late, owing to its height above the sea, that the early spring-flowers were yet in bloom. Poppies flamed among the wheat, and the banks of the stream were brilliant with patches of a creeping plant, with a bright purple blossom. The asphodel grew in great profusion, and an ivy-leaved shrub, covered with flakes of white bloom, made the air faint with its fragrance. Still further up, we came to orchards of walnut and plum trees, and vineyards There were no houses, but the innabitants, who were mostly Turcomans, live in villages during the winter, and in summer pitch their tents on the mountains where they pasture their flocks. Directly over this quiet pastoral, vale towered the Taurus, and I looked at once on its secluded loveliness and on the wintry heights, whose bleak and sublime heads were mantled in clouds. From no point is there a more imposing view of the whole snowy range. Near the head of the valley we passed a large Turcoman encampment, surrounded with herds of sheep and cattle.

We halted for the evening at a place called Kolü-Kushla---an immense fortress-village, resembling Baïas, and like it, wholly deserted. Near it there is a small town of very neat houses, which is also deserted, the inhabitants having gone into the mountains with their flocks. I walked through the fortress, which is a massive building of stone, about 500 feet square, erected by Sultan Murad as a resting-place for the caravans to Mecca. It has two spacious portals, in which the iron doors are still hanging, connected by a vaulted passage, twenty feet high and forty wide, with bazaars on each side. Side gateways open into large courts, surrounded with arched chambers. There is a mosque entire, with its pulpit and galleries, and the gilded crescent still glittering over its dome. Behind it is a bath, containing an entrance hall and half a dozen chambers, in which the water-pipes and stone tanks still remain. With a little alteration, the building would make a capital Phalanstery, where the Fourierites might try their experiment without contact with Society. There is no field for them equal to Asia Minor--a glorious region, abounding in natural wealth, almost depopulated, and containing a great number of Phalansteries ready built.

We succeeded in getting some eggs, fowls, and milk from an old Turcoman who had charge of the village. A man who rode by on a donkey sold us a bag of yaourt (sour milk-curds), which was delicious, notwithstanding the suspicious appearance of the bag. It was made before the cream had been removed, and was very rich and nourishing. The old Turcoman sat down and watched us while we ate, but would not join us, as these wandering tribes are very strict in keeping Ramazan. When we had reached our dessert--a plate of fine cherries--another white-bearded and dignified gentleman visited us. We handed him the cherries, expecting that he would take a few and politely return the dish: but no such thing. He coolly produced his handkerchief, emptied everything into it, and marched off. He also did not venture to eat, although we pointed to the Taurus, on whose upper snows the last gleam of daylight was just melting away.

We arose this morning in a dark, cloudy dawn. There was a heavy black storm hanging low in the west, and another was gathering its forces along the mountains behind us. A cold wind blew down the valley, and long peals of thunder rolled grandly among the gorges of Taurus. An isolated hill, crowned with a shattered crag which bore a striking resemblance to a ruined fortress, stood out black and sharp against the far, misty, sunlit peaks. As far as the springs were yet undried, the land was covered with flowers. In one place I saw a large square plot of the most brilliant crimson hue, burning amid the green wheat-fields, as if some Tyrian mantle had been flung there. The long, harmonious slopes and rounded summits of the hills were covered with drifts of a beautiful purple clover, and a diminutive variety of the achillea, or yarrow, with glowing yellow blossoms. The leaves had a pleasant aromatic odor, and filled the air with their refreshing breath, as they were crushed under the hoofs of our horses.

We had now reached the highest ridge of the hilly country along the northern base of Taurus, and saw, far and wide before us, the great central plain of Karamania. Two isolated mountains, at forty or fifty miles distance, broke the monotony of the desert-like level: Kara Dagh in the west, and the snow-capped summits of Hassan Dagh in the north-east. Beyond the latter, we tried to catch a glimpse of the famous Mons Argseus, at the base of which is Kaisariyeh, the ancient Cæsarea of Cappadocia. This mountain, which is 13,000 feet high, is the loftiest peak of Asia Minor. The clouds hung low on the horizon, and the rains were falling, veiling it from our sight.

Our road, for the remainder of the day, was over barren hills, covered with scanty herbage. The sun shone out intensely hot, and the glare of the white soil was exceedingly painful to my eyes. The locality of Eregli was betrayed, some time before we reached it, by its dark-green belt of fruit trees. It stands in the mouth of a narrow valley which winds down from the Taurus, and is watered by a large rapid stream that finally loses itself in the lakes and morasses of the plain. There had been a heavy black thunder-cloud gathering, and as we reached our camping-ground, under some fine walnut-trees near the stream, a sudden blast of cold wind swept over the town, filling the air with dust. We pitched the tent in all haste, expecting a storm, but the rain finally passed to the northward. We then took a walk through the town, which is a forlorn place. A spacious khan, built apparently for the Mecca pilgrims, is in ruins, but the mosque has an exquisite minaret, eighty feet high, and still bearing traces of the devices, in blue tiles, which once covered it. The shops were mostly closed, and in those which were still open the owners lay at full length on their bellies, their faces gaunt with fasting. They seemed annoyed at our troubling them, even with purchases. One would have thought that some fearful pestilence had fallen upon the town. The cobblers only, who somewhat languidly plied their implements, seemed to retain a little life. The few Jews and Armenians smoked their pipes in a tantalizing manner, in the very faces of the poor Mussulmans. We bought an oka of excellent cherries, which we were cruel enough to taste in the streets, before the hungry eyes of the suffering merchants.

This evening the asses belonging to the place were driven in from pasture--four or five hundred in all; and such a show of curious asinine specimens as I never before beheld. A Dervish, who was with us in Quarantine, at Adana, has just arrived. He had lost his teskeré (passport), and on issuing forth purified, was cast into prison. Finally he found some one who knew him, and procured his release. He had come on foot to this place in five days, suffering many privations, having been forty-eight hours without food. He is bound to Konia, on a pilgrimage to the tomb of Hazret Mevlana, the founder of the sect of dancing Dervishes. We gave him food, in return for which he taught me the formula of his prayers. He tells me I should always pronounce the name of Allah when my horse stumbles, or I see a man in danger of his life, as the word has a saving power. Hadji Youssuf, who has just been begging for an advance of twenty piastres to buy grain for his horses, swore "by the pardon of God" that he would sell the lame horse at Konia and get a better one. We have lost all confidence in the old villain's promises, but the poor beasts shall not suffer for his delinquencies.

Our tent is in a charming spot, and, from without, makes a picture to be remembered. The yellow illumination from within strikes on the under sides of the walnut boughs, while the moonlight silvers them from above. Beyond gardens where the nightingales are singing, the tall minaret of Eregli stands revealed in the vapory glow. The night is too sweet and balmy for sleep, and yet I must close my eyes upon it, for the hot plains of Karamania await us to-morrow.

Chapter XIX. The Plains of Karamania.

The Plains of Karamania--Afternoon Heat--A Well--Volcanic Phenomena--Kara-bounar--A Grand Ruined Khan--Moonlight Picture--A Landscape of the Plains-Mirages--A Short Interview--The Village of Ismil---Third Day on the Plains--Approach to Konia.

"A weary waste, expanding to the skies."--Goldsmith.

Konia, Capital of Karamania, *Friday, June* 25, 1854.

François awoke us at the break of day, at Eregli, as we had a journey of twelve hours before us. Passing through the town, we traversed a narrow belt of garden and orchard land, and entered the great plain of Karamania. Our road led at first northward towards a range called Karadja Dagh, and then skirted its base westward. After three hours' travel we passed a village of neat, whitewashed houses, which were entirely deserted, all the inhabitants having gone off to the mountains. There were some herds scattered over the plain, near the village. As the day wore on, the wind, which had been chill in the morning, ceased, and the air became hot and sultry. The glare from the white soil was so painful that I was obliged to close my eyes, and so ran a continual risk of falling asleep and tumbling from my horse. Thus, drowsy and half unconscious of my whereabouts, I rode on in the heat and arid silence of the plain until noon, when we reached a well. It was a shaft, sunk about thirty feet deep, with a long, sloping gallery slanting off to the surface. The well was nearly dry, but by descending the gallery we obtained a sufficient supply of cold, pure water. We breakfasted in the shaded doorway, sharing our provisions with a Turcoman boy, who was accompanying his father to Eregli with a load of salt.

Our road now crossed a long, barren pass, between two parts of Karadja Dagh. Near the northern side there was a salt lake of one hundred yards in diameter, sunk in a deep natural basin. The water was intensely saline. On the other side of the road, and a quarter of a mile distant, is an extinct volcano, the crater of which, near two hundred feet deep, is a salt lake, with a trachytic cone three hundred feet high rising from the centre. From the slope of the mountain we overlooked another and somewhat deeper plain, extending to the north and west. It was bounded by broken peaks, all of which betrayed a volcanic origin. Far before us we saw the tower on the hill of Kara-bounar, our resting-place for the night. The road thither was over a barren plain, cheered here and there by patches of a cushion-like plant, which was covered with pink blossoms. Mr. Harrison scared up some coveys of the frankolin, a large bird resembling the pheasant, and enriched our larder with a dozen starlings.

Kara-bounar is built on the slope of a mound, at the foot of which stands a spacious mosque, visible far over the plain. It has a dome, and two tall, pencil-like towers, similar to those of the Citadel-mosque of Cairo. Near it are the remains of a magnificent khan-fortress, said to have been built by the eunuch of one of the former Sultans. As there was no water in the wells outside of the town, we entered the khan and pitched the tent in its grass-grown court. Six square pillars of hewn stone made an aisle to our door, and the lofty, roofless walls of the court, 100 by 150 feet, inclosed us. Another court, of similar size, communicated with it by a broad portal, and the remains of baths and bazaars lay beyond. A handsome stone fountain, with two streams of running water, stood in front of the khan. We were royally lodged, but almost starved in our splendor, as only two or three Turcomans remained out of two thousand (who had gone off with their herds to the mountains), and they were unable to furnish us with provisions. But for our frankolins and starlings we should have gone fasting.

The mosque was a beautiful structure of white limestone, and the galleries of its minarets were adorned with rich arabesque ornaments. While the muezzin was crying his sunset-call to prayer, I entered the portico and looked into the interior, which was so bare as to appear incomplete. As we sat in our palace-court, after dinner, the moon arose, lighting up the niches in the walls, the clusters of windows in the immense eastern gable, and the rows of massive columns. The large dimensions of the building gave it a truly grand effect, and but for the whine of a distant jackal I could have believed that we were sitting in the aisles of a roofless Gothic cathedral, in the heart of Europe. François was somewhat fearful of thieves, but the peace and repose

569

of the place we've so perfect that I would not allow any such apprehensions to disturb me. In two minutes after I touched my bed I was insensible, and I did not move a limb until sunrise.

Beyond Kara-bounar, there is a low, barren ridge, climbing which, we overlooked an immense plain, uncultivated, apparently unfertile, and without a sign of life as far as the eye could reach. Kara Dagh, in the south, lifted nearer us its cluster of dark summits; to the north, the long ridge of Üsedjik Dagh (the Pigmy Mountain) stretched like a cape into the plain; Hassan Dagh; wrapped in a soft white cloud, receded behind us, and the snows of Taurus seemed almost as distant as when we first beheld them from the Syrian Gates. We rode for four hours over the dead level, the only objects that met our eyes being an occasional herd of camels in the distance. About noon, we reached a well, similar to that of the previous day, but of recent construction. A long, steep gallery led down to the water, which was very cold, but had a villainous taste of lime, salt, and sulphur.

After an hour's halt, we started again. The sun was intensely hot, and for hours we jogged on over the dead level, the bare white soil blinding our eyes with its glare. The distant hills were lifted above the horizon by a mirage. Long sheets of blue water were spread along their bases, islanding the isolated peaks, and turning into ships and boats the black specks of camels far away. But the phenomena were by no means on so grand a scale as I had seen in the Nubian Desert. On the south-western horizon, we discerned the summits of the Karaman range of Taurus, covered with snow. In the middle of the afternoon, we saw a solitary tent upon the plain, from which an individual advanced to meet us. As he drew nearer, we noticed that he wore white Frank pantaloons, similar to the Turkish soldiery, with a jacket of brown cloth, and a heavy sabre. When he was within convenient speaking distance, he cried out: "Stop! why are you running away from me?" "What do you call running away?" rejoined François; "we are going on our journey." "Where do you come from?" he then asked. "From there," said François, pointing behind us "Where are you going?" "There!" and the provoking Greek simply pointed forwards. "You have neither faith nor religion!" said the man, indignantly; then, turning upon his heel, he strode back across the plain.

About four o'clock, we saw a long line of objects rising before us, but so distorted by the mirage that it was impossible to know what they were. After a while, however, we decided that they were houses interspersed with trees; but the trees proved to be stacks of hay and lentils, heaped on the flat roofs. This was Ismil, our halting-place. The houses were miserable mud huts; but the village was large, and, unlike most of those we have seen this side of Taurus, inhabited. The people are Turcomans, and their possessions appear to be almost entirely in their herds. Immense numbers of sheep and goats were pasturing on the plain. There were several wells in the place, provided with buckets attached to long swing-poles; the water was very cold, but brackish. Our tent was pitched on the plain, on a hard, gravelly strip of soil. A crowd of wild-haired Turcoman boys gathered in front, to stare at us, and the shepherds quarrelled at the wells, as to which should take his turn at watering his flocks. In the evening a handsome old Turk visited us, and, finding that we were bound to Constantinople, requested François to take a letter to his son, who was settled there.

François aroused us this morning before the dawn, as we had a journey of thirty-five miles before us. He was in a bad humor; for a man, whom he had requested to keep watch over his tent, while he went into the village, had stolen a fork and spoon. The old Turk, who had returned as soon as we were stirring, went out to hunt the thief, but did not succeed in finding him. The inhabitants of the village were up long before sunrise, and driving away in their wooden-wheeled carts to the meadows where they cut grass. The old Turk accompanied us some distance, in order to show us a nearer way, avoiding a marshy spot. Our road lay over a vast plain, seemingly boundless, for the lofty mountain-ranges that surrounded it on all sides were so distant and cloud-like, and so lifted from the horizon by the deceptive mirage, that the eye did not recognize their connection with it. The wind blew strongly from the north-west, and was so cold that I dismounted and walked ahead for two or three hours.

Before noon, we passed two villages of mud huts, partly inhabited, and with some wheat-fields around them. We breakfasted at another well, which furnished us with a drink that tasted like iced sea-water. Thence we rode

571

forth again into the heat, for the wind had fallen by this time, and the sun shone out with great force. There was ever the same dead level, and we rode directly towards the mountains, which, to my eyes, seemed nearly as distant as ever. At last, there was a dark glimmer through the mirage, at their base, and a half-hour's ride showed it to be a line of trees. In another hour, we could distinguish a minaret or two, and finally, walls and the stately domes of mosques. This was Konia, the ancient Iconium, one of the most renowned cities of Asia Minor.

Chapter XX. Scenes in Konia.

Kpproach to Konia---Tomb of Hazret Mevlana--Lodgings in a Khan--An American Luxury--A Night-Scene in Ramazan--Prayers in the Mosque--Remains of the Ancient City--View from the Mosque--The Interior--A Leaning Minaret--The Diverting History of the Muleteers.

"But they shook off the dust on their feet, and came unto Iconium."--Acts, xiii. 51.

Konia (Ancient Iconium), *June* 27, 1852.

The view of Konia from the plain is not striking until one has approached within a mile of the suburbs, when the group of mosques, with their heavy central domes lifted on clusters of smaller ones, and their tall, light, glittering minarets, rising above the foliage of the gardens, against the background of airy hills, has a very pleasing effect. We approached through a long line of dirty suburbs, which looked still more forlorn on account of the Ramazan. Some Turkish officials, in shabby Frank dresses, followed us to satisfy their curiosity by talking with our Katurjees, or muleteers. Outside the city walls, we passed some very large barracks for cavalry, built by Ibrahim Pasha. On the plain north-east of the city, the battle between him and the forces of the Sultan, resulting in the defeat of the latter, was fought.

We next came upon two magnificent mosques, built of white limestone, with a multitude of leaden domes and lofty minarets, adorned with galleries rich in arabesque ornaments. Attached to one of them is the tomb, of Hazret Mevlana, the founder of the sect of Mevlevi Dervishes, which is reputed one of the most sacred places in the East. The tomb is surmounted by a dome, upon which stands a tall cylindrical tower, reeded, with channels between each projection, and terminating in a long, tapering cone. This tower is made of glazed tiles, of the most brilliant sea-blue color, and sparkles in the sun like a vast pillar of icy spar in some Polar grotto. It is a most striking and fantastic object, surrounded by a cluster of minarets and several cypress-trees, amid which it seems placed as the central ornament and crown of the group.

The aspect of the city was so filthy and uninviting that we preferred pitching our tent; but it was impossible to find a place without going back upon the plain; so we turned into the bazaar, and asked the way to a khan. There was a tolerable crowd in the street, although many of the shops were shut. The first khan we visited was too filthy to enter; but the second, though most unpromising in appearance, turned out to be better than it looked. The oda-bashi (master of the rooms) thoroughly swept and sprinkled the narrow little chamber he gave us, laid clean mats upon the floor, and, when our carpets and beds were placed within, its walls of mud looked somewhat comfortable. Its single window, with an iron grating in lieu of glass, looked upon an oblong court, on the second story, surrounded by the rooms of Armenian merchants. The main court (the gate of which is always closed at sunset) is two stories in height, with a rough wooden balcony running around it, and a well of muddy water in the centre.

The oda-bashi lent us a Turkish table and supplied us with dinner from his own kitchen; kibabs, stewed beans, and cucumber salad. Mr. H. and I, forgetting the Ramazan, went out to hunt for an iced sherbet; but all the coffee-shops were closed until sunset. The people stared at our Egyptian costumes, and a fellow in official dress demanded my teskeré. Soon after we returned, François appeared with a splendid lump of ice in a basin and some lemons. The ice, so the khangee said, is taken from a lake among the mountains, which in winter freezes to the thickness of a foot. Behind the lake is a natural cavern, which the people fill with ice, and then close up. At this season they take it out, day by day, and bring it down to the city. It is very pure and thick, and justifies the Turkish proverb in regard to Konia, which is celebrated for three excellent things: "dooz, booz, küz"--salt, ice, and girls.

Soon after sunset, a cannon announced the close of the fast. We waited an hour or two longer, to allow the people time to eat, and then sallied out into the streets. Every minaret in the city blazed with a crown of lighted lamps around its upper gallery, while the long shafts below, and the tapering cones above, topped with brazen crescents, shone fair in the moonlight. It was a strange, brilliant spectacle. In the square before the principal mosque we found a crowd of persons frolicking around the fountain, in the light of a number of torches on poles planted in the ground. Mats were spread on the stones, and rows of Turks of all classes sat thereon, smoking their pipes. Large earthen water-jars stood here and there, and the people drank so often and so long that they seemed determined to provide against the morrow. The boys were having their amusement in wrestling, shouting and firing off squibs, which they threw into the crowd. We kicked off our slippers, sat down among the Turks, smoked a narghileh, drank a cup of coffee and an iced sherbet of raisin juice, and so enjoyed the Ramazan as well as the best of them.

Numbers of True Believers were drinking and washing themselves at the picturesque fountain, and just as we rose to depart, the voice of a boy-muezzin, on one of the tallest minarets, sent down a musical call to prayer. Immediately the boys left off their sports and started on a run for the great mosque, and the grave, gray-bearded Turks got up from the mats, shoved on their slippers, and marched after them. We followed, getting a glimpse of the illuminated interior of the building, as we passed; but the oda-bashi conducted us still further, to a smaller though more beautiful mosque, surrounded with a garden-court. It was a truly magical picture. We entered the gate, and passed on by a marble pavement, under trees and arbors of vines that almost shut out the moonlight, to a paved space, in the centre whereof was a beautiful fountain, in the purest Saracenic style. Its heavy, projecting cornices and tall pyramidal roof rested on a circle of elegant arches, surrounding a marble structure, whence the water gushed forth in a dozen sparkling streams. On three sides it was inclosed by the moonlit trees and arbors; on the fourth by the outer corridor of the mosque, the door of entrance being exactly opposite.

Large numbers of persons were washing their hands and feet at the fountain, after which they entered and knelt on the floor. We stood unobserved in the corridor, and looked in on the splendidly illuminated interior and the crowd at prayer, all bending their bodies to the earth at regular intervals and murmuring the name of Allah. They resembled a plain, of reeds bending before the gusts of wind which precede a storm. When all had entered and were united in solemn prayer, we returned, passing the grand mosque. I stole up to the door, lifted the heavy carpet that hung before it, and looked in. There was a Mevlevi Dervish standing in the entrance, but his eyes were lifted in heavenly abstraction, and he did not see me. The interior was brilliantly lit by white and colored lamps, suspended from the walls and the great central dome. It was an imposing structure, simple in form, yet grand from its dimensions. The floor was covered with kneeling figures, and a deep voice, coming from the other end of the mosque, was uttering pious phrases in a kind of chant. I satisfied my curiosity quickly, and we then returned to the khan.

Yesterday afternoon I made a more thorough examination of the city. Passing through the bazaars, I reached the Serai, or Pasha's Palace, which stands on the site of that of the Sultans of Iconium. It is a long, wooden building, with no pretensions to architectural beauty. Near it there is a large and ancient mosque, with a minaret of singular elegance. It is about 120 feet high, with two hanging galleries; the whole built of blue and red bricks, the latter projecting so as to form quaint patterns or designs. Several ancient buildings near this mosque are surmounted with pyramidal towers, resembling Pagodas of India. Following the long, crooked lanes between mud buildings, we passed these curious structures and reached the ancient wall of the city. In one of the streets lay a marble lion, badly executed, and apparently of the time of the Lower Empire. In the wall were inserted many similar figures, with fragments of friezes and cornices. This is the work of the Seljook Kings, who, in building the wall, took great pains to exhibit the fragments of the ancient city. The number of altars they have preserved is quite remarkable. On the square towers are sunken tablets, containing long Arabic inscriptions.

The high walls of a ruined building in the southern part of the city attracted us, and on going thither we found it to be an ancient mosque, standing on an eminence formed apparently of the debris of other buildings. Part of the wall was also ancient, and in some places showed the marks of an earthquake. A long flight of steps led up to the door of the mosque, and as we ascended we were rewarded by the most charming view of the city and the grand plain. Konia lay at our feet--a wide, straggling array of low mud dwellings, dotted all over with patches of garden verdure, while its three superb mosques, with the many smaller tombs and places of worship, appeared like buildings left from some former and more magnificent capital. Outside of this circle ran a belt of garden land, adorned with groves and long lines of fruit trees; still further, the plain, a sea of faded green, flecked with the softest cloud-shadows, and beyond all, the beautiful outlines and dreamy tints of the different mountain chains. It was in every respect a lovely landscape, and the city is unworthy such surroundings. The sky, which in this region is of a pale, soft, delicious blue, was dotted with scattered fleeces of white clouds, and there was an exquisite play of light and shade over the hills.

There were half a dozen men and boys about the door, amusing themselves with bursting percussion caps on the stone. They addressed us as "hadji!" (pilgrims), begging for more caps. I told them I was not a Turk, but an Arab, which they believed at once, and requested me to enter the mosque. The interior had a remarkably fine effect. It was a maze of arches, supported by columns of polished black marble, forty in number. In form it was nearly square, and covered with a flat, wooden roof. The floor was covered with a carpet, whereon several persons were lying at full length, while an old man, seated in one of the most remote corners, was reading in a loud, solemn voice. It is a peculiar structure, which I should be glad to examine more in detail.

Not far from this eminence is a remarkable leaning minaret, more than a hundred feet in height, while in diameter it cannot be more than fifteen feet. In design it is light and elegant, and the effect is not injured by its deviation from the perpendicular, which I should judge to be about six feet. From the mosque we walked over the mounds of old Iconium to the eastern wall, passing another mosque, wholly in ruin, but which must have once been more splendid than any now standing. The portal is the richest specimen of Saracenic sculpture I have ever seen: a very labyrinth of intricate ornaments. The artist must have seen the great portal of the Temple of the Sun at Baalbec. The minarets have tumbled down, the roof has fallen in, but the walls are still covered with white and blue tiles, of the finest workmanship, resembling a mosaic of ivory and lapis lazuli. Some of the chambers seem to be inhabited, for two old men with white beards lay in the shade, and were not a little startled by our sudden appearance.

We returned to the great mosque, which we had visited on the evening of our arrival, and listened for some time to the voice of a mollah who was preaching an afternoon sermon to a small and hungry congregation. We then entered the court before the tomb of Hazret Mevlana. It was apparently forbidden ground to Christians, but as the Dervishes did not seem to suspect us we walked about boldly, and were about to enter, when an indiscretion of my companion frustrated our plans. Forgetting his assumed character, he went to the fountain and drank, although it was no later than the asser, or afternoon prayer. The Dervishes were shocked and scandalized by this violation of the fast, in the very court-yard of their holiest mosque, and we judged it best to retire by degrees. We sent this morning to request an interview with the Pasha, but he had gone to pass the day in a country palace, about three hours distant. It is a still, hot, bright afternoon, and the silence of the famished populace disposes us to repose. Our view is bounded by the mud walls of the khan, and I already long for the freedom of the great Karamanian Plain. Here, in the heart of Asia Minor, all life seems to stagnate. There is sleep everywhere, and I feel that a wide barrier separates me from the living world.

We have been detained here a whole day, through a chain of accidents, all resulting from the rascality of our muleteers on leaving Aleppo. The lame horse they palmed upon us was unable to go further, so we obliged them to buy another animal, which they succeeded in getting for 350 piastres. We advanced the money, although they were still in our debt, hoping to work our way through with the new horse, and thus avoid the risk of loss or delay. But this morning at sunrise Hadji Youssuf comes with a woeful face to say that the new horse has been stolen in the night, and we, who are ready to start, must sit down and wait till he is recovered. I suspected another trick, but when, after the lapse of three hours, François found the hadji sitting on the ground, weeping, and Achmet beating his breast, it seemed probable that the story was true. All search for the horse being vain, François went with them to the shekh of the horses, who promised, in case it should hereafter be found, to place it in the general pen, where they would be sure to get it on their return. The man who sold them the horse offered them another for the lame one and 150 piastres, and there was no other alternative but to accept it. But we must advance the 150 piastres, and so, in mid-journey, we have already paid them to the end, with the risk of their horses breaking down, or they, horses and all, absconding from us. But the knavish varlets are hardly bold enough for such a climax of villany.

Chapter XXI. The Heart of Asia Minor.

Scenery of the Hills--Ladik, the Ancient Laodicea--The Plague of Gad-Flies--Camp at Ilgün--A Natural Warm Bath--The Gad-Flies Again--A Summer Landscape--Ak-Sheher--The Base of Sultan Dagh--The Fountain of Midas--A Drowsy Journey--The Town of Bolawadün.

"By the forests, lakes, and fountains,

Though the many-folded mountains." Shelley.

Bolawadün, *July* 1, 1852.

Our men brought all the beasts into the court-yard of the khan at Konia, the evening before our departure, so that no more were stolen during the night. The oda-bashi, indefatigable to the last in his attention to us, not only helped load the mules, but accompanied us some distance on our way. All the merchants in the khan collected in the gallery to see us start, and we made our exit in some state. The morning was clear, fresh, and delightful. Turning away from the city walls, we soon emerged from the lines of fruit-trees and interminable fields of tomb-stones, and came out upon the great bare plain of Karamania. A ride of three hours brought us to a long, sloping hill, which gave us a view of the whole plain, and its circuit of mountains. A dark line in the distance marked the gardens of Konia. On the right, near the centre of the plain, the lake, now contracted to very narrow limits, glimmered in the sun. Notwithstanding the waste and unfertile appearance of the country, the soft, sweet sky that hangs over it, the pure, transparent air, the grand sweep of the plain, and the varied forms of the different mountain chains that encompass it, make our journey an inspiring one. A descent of the hills soon shut out the view; and the rest of the day's journey lay among them, skirting the eastern base of Allah Dagh.

The country improved in character, as we advanced. The bottoms of the dry glens were covered with wheat, and shrubbery began to make its appearance on the mountain-sides In the afternoon, we crossed a watershed, dividing Karamania from the great central plain of Asia Minor, and descended to a village called Ladik, occupying the site of the ancient Laodicea, at the foot of Allah Dagh. The plain upon which we came was greener and more flourishing than that we had left. Trees were scattered here and there in clumps, and the grassy wastes, stretching beyond the grain-fields, were dotted with herds of cattle. Emir Dagh stood in the north-west, blue and distant, while, towards the north and north-east, the plain extended to the horizon--a horizon fifty miles distant--without a break. In that direction lay the great salt lake of Yüzler, and the strings of camels we met on the road, laden with salt, were returning from it. Ladik is surrounded with poppy-fields, brilliant with white and purple blossoms. When the petals have fallen, the natives go carefully over the whole field and make incisions in every stalk, whence the opium exudes.

We pitched our tent under a large walnut tree, which we found standing in a deserted inclosure. The graveyard of the village is studded with relics of the ancient town. There are pillars, cornices, entablatures, jambs, altars, mullions and sculptured tablets, all of white marble, and many of them in an excellent state of preservation. They appear to date from the early time of the Lower Empire, and the cross has not yet been effaced from some which serve as head-stones for the True Believers. I was particularly struck with the abundance of altars, some of which contained entire and legible inscriptions. In the town there is the same abundance of ruins. The lid of a sarcophagus, formed of a single block of marble, now serves as a water-trough, and the fountain is constructed of ancient tablets. The town stands on a mound which appears to be composed entirely of the debris of the former place, and near the summit there are many holes which the inhabitants have dug in their search for rings, seals and other relics.

The next day we made a journey of nine hours over a hilly country lying between the ranges of Allah Dagh and Emir Dagh. There were wells of excellent water along the road, at intervals of an hour or two. The day was excessively hot and sultry during the noon hours, and the flies were so bad as to give great inconvenience to our horses. The animal I bestrode kicked so incessantly that I could scarcely keep my seat. His belly was swollen and covered with clotted blood, from their bites. The hadji's mule began to show symptoms of illness, and we had great difficulty in keeping it on its legs. Mr. Harrison bled it in the mouth, as a last resource, and during the afternoon it partly recovered.

An hour before sunset we reached Ilgün, a town on the plain, at the foot of one of the spurs of Emir Dagh. To the west of it there is a lake of considerable size, which receives the streams that flow through the town and water its fertile gardens. We passed through the town and pitched our tent upon a beautiful grassy meadow. Our customary pipe of refreshment was never more heartily enjoyed than at this place. Behind us was a barren hill, at the foot of which was a natural hot bath, wherein a number of women and children were amusing themselves. The afternoon heat had passed away, the air was calm, sweet, and tempered with the freshness of coming evening, and the long shadows of the hills, creeping over the meadows, had almost reached the town. Beyond the line of sycamore, poplar and fig-trees that shaded the gardens of Ilgün, rose the distant chain of Allah Dagh, and in the pale-blue sky, not far above it, the dim face of the gibbous moon showed like the ghost of a planet. Our horses were feeding on the green meadow; an old Turk sat beside us, silent with fasting, and there was no sound but the shouts of the children in the bath. Such hours as these, after a day's journey made in the drowsy heat of an Eastern summer, are indescribably grateful.

After the women had retired from the bath, we were allowed to enter. The interior consisted of a single chamber, thirty feet high, vaulted and almost dark. In the centre was a large basin of hot water, filled by four streams which poured into it. A ledge ran around the sides, and niches in the wall supplied places for our clothes. The bath-keeper furnished us with towels, and we undressed and plunged in. The water was agreeably warm (about 90°), had a sweet taste, and a very slight sulphury smell. The vaulted hall redoubled the slightest noise, and a shaven Turk, who kept us company, sang in his delight, that he might hear the echo of his own voice. When we went back to the tent we found our visitor lying on the ground, trying to stay his hunger. It was rather too bad in us to light our pipes, make a sherbet and drink and smoke in his face, while we joked him about the Ramazan; and he at last got up and

581

walked off, the picture of distress.

We made an early start the next morning, and rode on briskly over the rolling, grassy hills. A beautiful lake, with an island in it, lay at the foot of Emir Dagh. After two hours we reached a guard-house, where our teskerés were demanded, and the lazy guardsman invited us in to take coffee, that he might establish a right to the backsheesh which he could not demand. He had seen us afar off, and the coffee was smoking in the finjans when we arrived. The sun was already terribly hot, and the large, green gad-flies came in such quantities that I seemed to be riding in the midst of a swarm of bees. My horse suffered very much, and struck out his hind feet so violently, in his endeavors to get rid of them, that he racked every joint in my body. They were not content with sucking his blood, but settling on the small segment of my calf, exposed between the big Tartar boot and the flowing trowsers, bit through my stockings with fierce bills. I killed hundreds of them, to no purpose, and at last, to relieve my horse, tied a bunch of hawthorn to a string, by which I swung it under his belly and against the inner side of his flanks. In this way I gave him some relief--a service which he acknowledged by a grateful motion of his head.

As we descended towards Ak-Sheher the country became exceedingly rich and luxuriant. The range of Sultan Dagh (the Mountain of the Sultan) rose on our left, its sides covered with a thick screen of shrubbery, and its highest peak dotted with patches of snow; opposite, the lower range of Emir Dagh (the Mountain of the Prince) lay blue and bare in the sun shine. The base of Sultan Dagh was girdled with groves of fruit-trees, stretching out in long lines on the plain, with fields of ripening wheat between. In the distance the large lake of Ak-Sheher glittered in the sun. Towards the north-west, the plain stretched away for fifty miles before reaching the hills. It is evidently on a much lower level than the plain of Konia; the heat was not only greater, but the season was further advanced. Wheat was nearly ready for cutting, and the poppy-fields where, the day previous, the men were making their first incisions for opium, here had yielded their harvest and were fast ripening their seed. Ak-Sheher is beautifully situated at the entrance of a deep gorge in the mountains. It is so buried in its embowered gardens that little, except the mosque, is seen as you approach it. It is a large place, and boasts a fine mosque, but contains nothing worth seeing. The bazaar, after that of Konia, was the largest we had seen since leaving Tarsus. The greater part of the shopkeepers lay at full length, dozing, sleeping, or staying their appetites till the sunset gun. We found some superb cherries, and plenty of snow, which is brought down from the mountain. The natives were very friendly and good-humored, but seemed surprised at Mr. Harrison tasting the cherries, although I told them we were upon a journey. Our tent was pitched under a splendid walnut tree, outside of the town. The green mountain rose between us and the fading sunset, and the yellow moon was hanging in the east, as we took our dinner at the tent-door. Turks were riding homewards on donkeys, with loads of grass which they had been cutting in the meadows. The gun was fired, and the shouts of the children announced the close of the day's fast, while the sweet, melancholy voice of a boy muezzin called us to sunset prayer, from the minaret.

Leaving Ak-Sheher this morning, we rode along the base of Sultan Dagh. The plain which we overlooked was magnificent. The wilderness of shrubbery which fringed the slopes of the mountain gave place to great orchards and gardens, interspersed with fields of grain, which extended far out on the plain, to the wild thickets and wastes of reeds surrounding the lake. The sides of Sultan Dagh were terraced and cultivated wherever it was practicable, and I saw some fields of wheat high up on the mountain. There were many, people in the road or laboring in the fields; and during the forenoon we passed several large villages. The country is more thickly inhabited, and has a more thrifty and prosperous air than any part of Asia Minor which I have seen. The people are better clad, have more open, honest, cheerful and intelligent faces, and exhibit a genuine courtesy and good-will in their demeanor towards us. I never felt more perfectly secure, or more certain of being among people whom I could trust.

We passed under the summit of Sultan Dagh, which shone out so clear and distinct in the morning sun, that I could scarcely realize its actual height above the plain. From a tremendous gorge, cleft between the two higher peaks, issued a large stream, which, divided into a hundred channels, fertilizes a wide extent of plain. About two hours from Ak-Sheher we passed a splendid fountain of crystal water, gushing up beside the road. I believe it is the same called by some travellers the Fountain of Midas, but am ignorant wherefore the name is given it. We rode for several hours through a succession of grand, rich landscapes. A smaller lake succeeded to that of Ak-Sheher, Emir Dagh rose higher in the pale-blue sky, and Sultan Dagh showed other peaks, broken and striped with snow; but around us were the same glorious orchards and gardens, the same golden-green wheat and rustling phalanxes of poppies-- armies of vegetable Round-heads, beside the bristling and bearded Cavaliers. The sun was intensely hot during the afternoon, as we crossed the plain, and I became so drowsed that it required an agony of exertion to keep from tumbling off my horse. We here left the great post-road to Constantinople, and took a less frequented track. The plain gradually became a meadow, covered with shrub cypress, flags, reeds, and wild water-plants. There were vast wastes of luxuriant grass, whereon thousands of black buffaloes were feeding. A stone causeway, containing many elegant fragments of ancient sculpture, extended across this part of the plain, but we took a summer path beside it, through beds of iris in bloom--a fragile snowy blossom, with a lip of the clearest golden hue. The causeway led to a bare salt plain, beyond which we came to the town of Bolawadün, and terminated our day's journey of forty miles.

Bolawadün is a collection of mud houses, about a mile long, situated on an eminence at the western base of Emir Dagh. I went into the bazaar, which was a small place, and not very well supplied, though, as it was near sunset, there was quite a crowd of people, and the bakers were shovelling out their fresh bread at a brisk rate. Every one took me for a good Egyptian Mohammedan, and I was jostled right and left among the turbans, in a manner that certainly would not have happened me had I not also worn one. Mr. H., who had fallen behind the caravan, came up after we had encamped, and might have wandered a long time without finding us, but for the good-natured efforts of the inhabitants to set him aright. This evening he knocked over a hedgehog, mistaking it for a cat. The poor creature was severely hurt, and its sobs of distress, precisely like those of a little child, were to painful to hear, that we were obliged to have it removed from the vicinity of the tent

Chapter XXII. The Forests of Phrygia.

The Frontier of Phrygia--Ancient Quarries and Tombs--We Enter the Pine Forests--A Guard-House--Encampments of the Turcomans--Pastoral Scenery--A Summer Village--The Valley of the Tombs--Rock Sepulchres of the Phrygian Kings--The Titan's Camp--The Valley of Kümbeh--A Land of Flowers--Turcoman Hospitality--The Exiled Effendis--The Old Turcoman--A Glimpse of Arcadia--A Landscape--Interested Friendship--The Valley of the Pursek--Arrival at Kiutahya.

"And round us all the thicket rang To many a flute of Arcady." Tennyson.

Kiutahya, *July* 5, 1852.

We had now passed through the ancient provinces of Cilicia, Cappadocia, and Lycaonia, and reached the confines of Phrygia--a rude mountain region, which was never wholly penetrated by the light of Grecian civilization. It is still comparatively a wilderness, pierced but by a single high-road, and almost unvisited by travellers, yet inclosing in its depths many curious relics of antiquity. Leaving Bolawadün in the morning, we ascended a long, treeless mountain-slope, and in three or four hours reached the dividing ridge---the watershed of Asia Minor, dividing the affluents of the Mediterranean and the central lakes from the streams that flow to the Black Sea. Looking back, Sultan Dagh, along whose base we had travelled the previous day, lay high and blue in the background, streaked with shining snow, and far away behind it arose a still higher peak, hoary with the lingering winter. We descended into a grassy plain, shut in by a range of broken mountains, covered to their summits with dark-green shrubbery, through which the strata of marble rock gleamed like patches of snow. The hills in front were scarred with old quarries, once worked for the celebrated Phrygian marble. There was neither a habitation nor a human being to be seen, and the landscape had a singularly wild, lonely, and picturesque air.

Turning westward, we crossed a high rolling tract, and entered a valley entirely covered with dwarf oaks and cedars. In spite of the dusty road, the heat, and the multitude of gad-flies, the journey presented an agreeable contrast to the great plains over which we had been travelling for many days. The opposite side of the glen was crowned with a tall crest of shattered rock, in which were many old Phrygian tombs. They were mostly simple chambers, with square apertures. There were traces of many more, the rock having been blown up or quarried down--the tombs, instead of protecting it, only furnishing one facility the more for destruction. After an hour's rest at a fountain, we threaded the windings of the glen to a lower plain, quite shut in by the hills, whose ribs of marble showed through the forests of oak, holly, cedar, and pine, which dotted them. We were now fully entered into the hill-country, and our road passed over heights and through hollows covered with picturesque clumps of foliage. It resembled some of the wild western downs of America, and, but for the Phrygian tombs, whose doorways stared at us from every rock, seemed as little familiar with the presence of Man.

Hadji Youssuf, in stopping to arrange some of the baggage, lost his hold of his mule, and in spite of every effort to secure her, the provoking beast kept her liberty for the rest of the day. In vain did we head her off, chase her, coax her, set traps for her: she was too cunning to be taken in, and marched along at her ease, running into every field of grain, stopping to crop the choicest bunches of grass, or walking demurely in the caravan, allowing the hadji to come within arm's length before she kicked up her heels and dashed away again. We had a long chase through the clumps of oak and holly, but all to no purpose. The great green gad-flies swarmed around us, biting myself as well as my horse. Hecatombs, crushed by my whip, dropped dead in the dust, but the ranks were immediately filled from some invisible reserve. The soil was no longer bare, but entirely covered with grass and flowers. In one of the valleys I saw a large patch of the crimson larkspur, so thick as to resemble a pool of blood. While crossing a long, hot hill, we came upon a little arbor of stones, covered with pine branches. It inclosed an ancient sarcophagus of marble, nearly filled with water. Beside it stood a square cup, with a handle, rudely hewn out of a piece of pine wood. This was a charitable provision for travellers, and constantly supplied by the Turcomans who lived in the vicinity.

The last two hours of our journey that day were through a glorious forest of pines. The road lay in a winding glen, green and grassy, and covered to the summits on both sides with beautiful pine trees, intermixed with cedar. The air had the true northern aroma, and was more grateful than wine. Every turn of the glen disclosed a charming woodland view. It was a wild valley of the northern hills, filled with the burning lustre of a summer sun, and canopied by the brilliant blue of a summer sky. There were signs of the woodman's axe, and the charred embers of forest camp-fires. I thought of the lovely cañadas in the pine forests behind Monterey, and could really have imagined myself there. Towards evening we reached a solitary guard-house, on the edge of the forest. The glen here opened a little, and a stone fountain of delicious water furnished all that we wanted for a camping-place. The house was inhabited by three soldiers; sturdy, good-humored fellows, who immediately spread a mat in the shade for us and made us some excellent coffee. A Turcoman encampment in the neighborhood supplied us with milk and eggs.

The guardsmen were good Mussulmans, and took us for the same. One of them asked me to let him know when the sun was down, and I prolonged his fast until it was quite dark, when I gave him permission to eat. They all had tolerable stallions for their service, and seemed to live pleasantly enough, in their wild way. The fat, stumpy corporal, with his enormously broad pantaloons and automaton legs, went down to the fountain with his musket, and after taking a rest and sighting full five minutes, fired at a dove without hitting it. He afterwards joined us in a social pipe, and we sat on a carpet at the door of the guard-house, watching the splendid moonrise through the pine boughs. When the pipes had burned out I went to bed, and slept a long, sweet sleep until dawn.

We knew that the tombs of the Phrygian Kings could not be far off, and, on making inquiries of the corporal, found that he knew the place. It was not four hours distant, by a by-road and as it would be impossible to reach it without a guide, he would give us one of his men, in consideration of a fee of twenty piastres. The difficulty was evident, in a hilly, wooded country like this, traversed by a labyrinth of valleys and ravines, and so we accepted the soldier. As we were about leaving, an old Turcoman, whose beard was dyed a bright red, came up, saying that he knew Mr. H. was a physician, and could cure him of his deafness. The morning air was sweet with the breath of cedar and pine, and we rode on through the woods and over the open turfy glades, in high spirits. We were in the heart of a mountainous country, clothed with evergreen forests, except some open upland tracts, which showed a thick green turf, dotted all over with park-like clumps, and single great trees. The pines were noble trunks, often sixty to eighty feet high, and with boughs disposed in all possible picturesqueness of form. The cedar frequently showed a solid white bole, three feet in diameter.

We took a winding footpath, often a mere track, striking across the hills in a northern direction. Everywhere we met the Turks of the plain, who are now encamped in the mountains, to tend their flocks through the summer months. Herds of sheep and goats were scattered over the green pasture-slopes, and the idle herd-boys basked in the morning sun, playing lively airs on a reed flute, resembling the Arabic zumarra. Here and there was a woodman, busy at a recently felled tree, and we met several of the creaking carts of the country, hauling logs. All that we saw had a pleasant rural air, a smack of primitive and unsophisticated life. From the higher ridges over which we passed, we could see, far to the east and west, other ranges of pine-covered mountains, and in the distance the cloudy lines of loftier chains. The trunks of the pines were nearly all charred, and many of the smaller trees dead, from the fires which, later in the year, rage in these forests.

After four hours of varied and most inspiring travel, we reached a district covered for the most part with oak woods--a more open though still mountainous region. There was a summer village of Turks scattered over the nearest slope--probably fifty houses in all, almost perfect counterparts of Western log-cabins. They were built of pine logs, laid crosswise, and covered with rough boards. These, as we were told, were the dwellings of the people who inhabit the village of Khosref Pasha Khan during the winter. Great numbers of sheep and goats were browsing over the hills or lying around the doors of the houses. The latter were beautiful creatures, with heavy, curved horns, and long, white, silky hair, that entirely hid their eyes. We stopped at a house for water, which the man brought out in a little cask. He at first proposed giving us yaourt, and his wife suggested kaïmak (sweet curds), which we agreed to take, but it proved to be only boiled milk.

Leaving the village, we took a path leading westward, mounted a long hill, and again entered the pine forests. Before long, we came to a well-built country-house, somewhat resembling a Swiss cottage. It was two stories high, and there was an upper balcony, with cushioned divans, overlooking a thriving garden-patch and some fruit-trees. Three or four men were weeding in the garden, and the owner came up and welcomed us. A fountain of ice-cold water gushed into a stone trough at the door, making a tempting spot for our breakfast, but we were bent on reaching the tombs. There were convenient out-houses for fowls, sheep, and cattle. The herds were out, grazing along the edges of the forest, and we heard the shrill, joyous melodies of the flutes blown by the herd-boys.

We now reached a ridge, whence we looked down through the forest upon a long valley, nearly half a mile wide, and bordered on the opposite side by ranges of broken sandstone crags. This was the place we sought--the Valley of the Phrygian Tombs. Already we could distinguish the hewn faces of the rocks, and the dark apertures to the chambers within. The bottom of the valley was a bed of glorious grass, blazoned with flowers, and redolent of all vernal smells. Several peasants, finding it too hot to mow, had thrown their scythes along the swarths, and were lying in the shade of an oak. We rode over the new-cut hay, up the opposite side, and dismounted at the face of the crags. As we approached them, the number of chambers hewn in the rock, the doors and niches now open to the day, surmounted by shattered spires and turrets, gave the whole mass the appearance of a grand fortress in ruins. The crags, which are of a very soft, reddish-gray sandstone, rise a hundred and fifty feet from their base, and their summits are worn by the weather into the most remarkable forms.

The principal monument is a broad, projecting cliff, one side of which has been cut so as to resemble the façade of a temple. The sculptured part is about sixty feet high by sixty in breadth, and represents a solid wall with two pilasters at the ends, upholding an architrave and pediment, which is surmounted by two large volutes. The whole face of the wall is covered with ornaments resembling panel-work, not in regular squares, but a labyrinth of intricate designs. In the centre, at the bottom, is a shallow square recess, surrounded by an elegant, though plain moulding, but there is no appearance of an entrance to the sepulchral chamber, which may be hidden in the heart of the rock. There is an inscription in Greek running up one side, but it is of a later date than the work itself. On one of the tombs there is an inscription: "To King Midas." These relics are supposed to date from the period of the Gordian Dynasty, about seven centuries before Christ.

A little in front of a headland, formed by the summit walls of two meeting valleys, rises a mass of rocks one hundred feet high, cut into sepulchral chambers, story above story, with the traces of steps between them, leading to others still higher. The whole rock, which may be a hundred and fifty feet long by fifty feet broad, has been scooped out, leaving but narrow partitions to separate the chambers of the dead. These chambers are all plain, but some are of very elegant proportions, with arched or pyramidal roofs, and arched recesses at the sides, containing sarcophagi hewn in the solid stone. There are also many niches for cinerary urns. The principal tomb had a portico, supported by columns, but the front is now entirely hurled down, and only the elegant panelling and stone joists of the ceiling remain. The entire hill was a succession of tombs. There is not a rock which does not bear traces of them. I might have counted several hundred within a stone's throw. The position of these curious remains in a lonely valley, shut in on all sides by dark, pine-covered mountains---two of which are crowned with a natural acropolis of rock, resembling a fortress--increases the interest with which they inspire the beholder. The valley on the western side, with its bed of ripe wheat in the bottom, its tall walls, towers, and pinnacles of rock, and its distant vista of mountain and forest, is the most picturesque in Phrygia.

The Turcoman reapers, who came up to see us and talk with us, said that there were the remains of walls on the summit of the principal acropolis opposite us, and that, further up the valley, there was a chamber with two columns in front. Mr. Harrison and I saddled and rode off, passing along a wall of fantastic rock-turrets, at the base of which was a natural column, about ten feet high, and five in diameter, almost perfectly round, and upholding an immense rock, shaped like a cocked hat. In crossing the meadow we saw a Turk sitting in the sun beside a spring, and busily engaged in knitting a stocking. After a ride of two miles we found the chamber, hewn like the façade of a temple in an isolated rock, overlooking two valleys of wild meadow-land. The pediment and cornice were simple and beautiful, but the columns had been broken away. The chambers were perfectly plain, but the panel-work on the ceiling of the portico was entire.

After passing three hours in examining these tombs, we took the track which our guide pointed out as the road to Kiutahya. We rode two hours through the forest, and came out upon a wooded height, overlooking a grand, open valley, rich in grain-fields and pasture land. While I was contemplating this lovely view, the road turned a corner of the ridge, and lo! before me there appeared (as I thought), above the tops of the pines, high up on the mountain side, a line of enormous tents. Those snow-white cones, uprearing their sharp spires, and spreading out their broad bases--what could they be but an encampment of monster tents? Yet no; they were pinnacles of white rock--perfect cones, from thirty to one hundred feet in height, twelve in all, and ranged side by side along the edge of the cliff, with the precision of a military camp. They were snow-white, perfectly smooth and full, and their bases touched. What made the spectacle more singular, there was no other appearance of the same rock on the mountain. All around them was the dark-green of the pines, out of which they rose like drifted horns of unbroken snow. I named this singular phenomenon--which seems to have escaped the notice of travellers--The Titan's Camp.

In another hour we reached a fountain near the village of Kümbeh, and pitched our tents for the night. The village, which is half a mile in length, is built upon a singular crag, which shoots up abruptly from the centre of the valley, rising at one extremity to a height of more than a hundred feet. It was entirely deserted, the inhabitants having all gone off to the mountains with their herds. The solitary muezzin, who cried the mughreb at the close of the fast, and lighted the lamps on his minaret, went through with his work in most unclerical haste, now that there was no one to notice him. We sent Achmet, the katurgee, to the mountain camp of the villagers, to procure a supply of fowls and barley. We rose very early yesterday morning, shivering in

591

the cold air of the mountains, and just as the sun, bursting through the pines, looked down the little hollow where our tents were pitched, set the caravan in motion. The ride down the valley was charming. The land was naturally rich and highly cultivated, which made its desertion the more singular. Leagues of wheat, rye and poppies spread around us, left for the summer warmth to do its silent work. The dew sparkled on the fields as we rode through them, and the splendor of the flowers in blossom was equal to that of the plains of Palestine. There were purple, white and scarlet poppies; the rich crimson larkspur; the red anemone; the golden daisy; the pink convolvulus; and a host of smaller blooms, so intensely bright and dazzling in their hues, that the meadows were richer than a pavement of precious jewels. To look towards the sun, over a field of scarlet poppies, was like looking on a bed of live coals; the light, striking through the petals, made them burn as with an inward fire. Out of this wilderness of gorgeous color, rose the tall spires of a larger plant, covered with great yellow flowers, while here and there the snowy blossoms of a clump of hawthorn sweetened the morning air.

A short distance beyond Kümbeh, we passed another group of ancient tombs, one of which was of curious design. An isolated rock, thirty feet in height by twenty in diameter, was cut so as to resemble a triangular tower, with the apex bevelled. A chamber, containing a sarcophagus, was hewn out of the interior. The entrance was ornamented with double columns in bas-relief, and a pediment. There was another arched chamber, cut directly through the base of the triangle, with a niche on each side, hollowed out at the bottom so as to form a sarcophagus.

Leaving these, the last of the Phrygian tombs, we struck across the valley and ascended a high range of hills, covered with pine, to an upland, wooded region. Here we found a summer village of log cabins, scattered over a grassy slope. The people regarded us with some curiosity, and the women hastily concealed their faces. Mr. H. rode up to a large new house, and peeped in between the logs. There were several women inside, who started up in great confusion and threw over their heads whatever article was most convenient. An old man, with a long white beard, neatly dressed in a green jacket and shawl turban, came out and welcomed us. I asked for kaïmak, which he promised, and immediately brought out a carpet and spread it on the ground. Then followed a large basin of kaïmak, with wooden spoons, three loaves of bread, and a plate of cheese. We seated ourselves on the carpet, and delved in with the spoons, while the old man retired lest his appetite should be provoked. The milk was excellent, nor were the bread and cheese to be despised.

While we were eating, the Khowagee, or schoolmaster of the community, a genteel little man in a round white turban, came op to inquire of François who we were. "That effendi in the blue dress," said he, "is the Bey, is he not?" "Yes," said F. "And the other, with the striped shirt and white turban, is a writer?" [Here he was not far wrong.] "But how is it that the effendis do not speak Turkish?" he persisted. "Because," said François, "their fathers were exiled by Sultan Mahmoud when they were small children. They have grown up in Aleppo like Arabs, and have not yet learned Turkish; but God grant that the Sultan may not turn his face away from them, and that they may regain the rank their fathers once had in Stamboul." "God grant it!" replied the Khowagee, greatly interested in the story. By this time we had eaten our full share of the kaïmak, which was finished by François and the katurgees. The old man now came up, mounted on a dun mare, stating that he was bound for Kiutahya, and was delighted with the prospect of travelling in such good company, I gave one of his young children some money, as the kaïmak was tendered out of pure hospitality, and so we rode off.

Our new companion was armed to the teeth, having a long gun with a heavy wooden stock and nondescript lock, and a sword of excellent metal. It was, in fact, a weapon of the old Greek empire, and the cross was still enamelled in gold at the root of the blade, in spite of all his efforts to scratch it out. He was something of a fakeer, having made a pilgrimage to Mecca and Jerusalem. He was very inquisitive, plying François with questions about the government. The latter answered that we were not connected with the government, but the old fellow shrewdly hinted that he knew better--we were persons of rank, travelling incognito. He was very attentive to us, offering us water at every fountain, although he believed us to be good Mussulmans. We found him of some service as a guide, shortening our road by taking by-paths through the woods.

For several hours we traversed a beautifully wooded region of hills. Graceful clumps of pine shaded the grassy knolls, where the sheep and silky-haired goats were basking at rest, and the air was filled with a warm, summer smell, blown from the banks of golden broom. Now and then, from the thickets of laurel and arbutus, a shrill shepherd's reed piped some joyous woodland melody. Was it a Faun, astray among the hills? Green dells, open to the sunshine, and beautiful as dreams of Arcady, divided the groves of pine. The sky overhead was pure and cloudless, clasping the landscape with its belt of peace and silence. Oh, that delightful region, haunted by all the bright spirits of the immortal Grecian Song! Chased away from the rest of the earth, here they have found a home--here secret altars remain to them from the times that are departed!

Out of these woods, we passed into a lonely plain, inclosed by piny hills that brightened in the thin, pure ether. In the distance were some shepherds' tents, and musical goat-bells tinkled along the edges of the woods. From the crest of a lofty ridge beyond this plain, we looked back over the wild solitudes wherein we had been travelling for two days--long ranges of dark hills, fading away behind each other, with a perspective that hinted of the hidden gulfs between. From the western slope, a still more extensive prospect opened before us. Over ridges covered with forests of oak and pine, we saw the valley of the Pursek, the ancient Thymbrius, stretching far away to the misty line of Keshish Dagh, The mountains behind Kintahya loomed up high and grand, making a fine feature in the middle distance. We caught but fleeting glimpses of the view through the trees; and then, plunging into the forest again, descended to a cultivated slope, whereon there was a little village, now deserted. The graveyard beside it was shaded with large cedar-trees, and near it there was a fountain of excellent water. "Here," said the old man, "you can wash and pray, and then rest awhile under the trees." François excused us by saying that, while on a journey, we always bathed before praying; but, not to slight his faith entirely, I washed my hands and face before sitting down to our scanty breakfast of bread and water.

Our path now led down through long, winding glens, over grown with oaks, from which the wild yellow honeysuckles fell in a shower of blossoms.

594

As we drew near the valley, the old man began to hint that his presence had been of great service to us, and deserved recompense. "God knows," said he to François, "in what corner of the mountains you might now be, if I had not accompanied you." "Oh," replied François, "there are always plenty of people among the woods, who would have been equally as kind as yourself in showing us the way." He then spoke of the robbers in the neighborhood, and pointed out some graves by the road-side, as those of persons who had been murdered. "But," he added, "everybody in these parts knows me, and whoever is in company with me is always safe." The Greek assured him that we always depended on ourselves for our safety. Defeated on these tacks, he boldly affirmed that his services were worthy of payment. "But," said François "you told us at the village that you had business in Kiutahya, and would be glad to join us for the sake of having company on the road." "Well, then," rejoined the old fellow, making a last effort, "I leave the matter to your politeness." "Certainly," replied the imperturbable dragoman, "we could not be so impolite as to offer money to a man of your wealth and station; we could not insult you by giving you alms." The old Turcoman thereupon gave a shrug and a grunt, made a sullen good-by salutation, and left us.

It was nearly six o'clock when we reached the Pursek. There was no sign of the city, but we could barely discern an old fortress on the lofty cliff which commands the town. A long stone bridge crossed the river, which here separates into half a dozen channels. The waters are swift and clear, and wind away in devious mazes through the broad green meadows. We hurried on, thinking we saw minarets in the distance, but they proved to be poplars. The sun sank lower and lower, and finally went down before there was any token of our being in the vicinity of the city. Soon, however, a line of tiled roofs appeared along the slope of a hill on our left, and turning its base, we saw the city before us, filling the mouth of a deep valley or gorge, which opened from the mountains.

But the horses are saddled, and François tells me it is time to put up my pen. We are off, over the mountains, to the Greek city of Œzani, in the valley of the Rhyndacus.

Chapter XXIII. Kiutahya and the Ruins of Œzani.

Entrance into Kiutahya--The New Khan--An Unpleasant Discovery--Kiutahya--The Citadel--Panorama from the Walls--The Gorge of the Mountains--Camp in a Meadow--The Valley of the Rhyndacus--Chavdür--The Ruins of Œzani--The Acropolis and Temple--The Theatre and Stadium--Ride down the Valley--Camp at Daghje Köi

"There is a temple in ruin stands,

Fashioned by long-forgotten hands;

Two or three columns and many a stone,

Marble and granite, with grass o'ergrown!

Out upon Time! it will leave no more

Of the things to come than the things before!"

Daghje Köi, on the Rhyndacus, *July* 6, 1852.

On entering Kiutahya, we passed the barracks, which were the residence of Kossuth and his companions in exile. Beyond them, we came to a broad street, down which flowed the vilest stream of filth of which even a Turkish city could ever boast. The houses on either side were two stories high, the upper part of wood, with hanging balconies, over which shot the eaves of the tiled roofs. The welcome cannon had just sounded, announcing the close of the day's fast. The coffee-shops were already crowded with lean and hungry customers, the pipes were filled and lighted, and the coffee smoked in the finjans. In half a minute such whiffs arose on all sides as it would have cheered the heart of a genuine smoker to behold. Out of these cheerful places we passed into other streets which were entirely deserted, the inhabitants being at dinner. It had a weird, uncomfortable effect to ride through streets where the clatter of our horses' hoofs was the only sound of life. At last we reached the entrance to a bazaar, and near it a khan--a new khan, very neatly built, and with a spare room so much better than we expected, that we congratulated ourselves heartily. We unpacked in a hurry, and François ran off to the bazaar, from which he speedily returned with some roast kid, cucumbers, and cherries. We lighted two lamps, I borrowed the oda-bashi's narghileh, and François, learning that it was our national anniversary, procured us a flask of Greek wine, that we might do it honor. The beverage, however, resembled a mixture of vinegar and sealing-wax, and we contented ourselves with drinking patriotic toasts, in two finjans of excellent coffee. But in the midst of our enjoyment, happening to cast my eye on the walls, I saw a sight that turned all our honey into gall. Scores on scores--nay, hundreds on hundreds--of enormous bed-bugs swarmed on the plaster, and were already descending to our beds and baggage. To sleep there was impossible, but we succeeded in getting possession of one of the outside balconies, where we made our beds, after searching them thoroughly.

In the evening a merchant, who spoke a little Arabic, came up to me and asked: "Is not your Excellency's friend the hakim pasha" (chief physician). I did not venture to assent, but replied: "No; he is a sowakh" This was beyond his comprehension, and he went away with the impression that Mr. H. was much greater than a hakim pasha. I slept soundly on my out-doors bed, but was awakened towards morning by two tremendous claps of thunder, echoing in the gorge, and the rattling of rain on the roof of the khan.

I spent two or three hours next morning in taking a survey of Kiutahya. The town is much larger than I had supposed: I should judge it to contain from fifty to sixty thousand inhabitants. The situation is remarkable, and gives a picturesque effect to the place when seen from above, which makes one forget its internal filth. It is built in the mouth of a gorge, and around the bases of the hills on either side. The lofty mountains which rise behind it supply it with perpetual springs of pure water. At every dozen steps you come upon a fountain, and every large street has a brook in the centre. The houses are all two and many of them three stories high, with hanging balconies, which remind me much of Switzerland. The bazaars are very extensive, covering all the base of the hill on which stands the ancient citadel. The goods displayed were mostly European cotton fabrics, quincaillerie, boots and slippers, pipe-sticks and silks. In the parts devoted to the produce of the country, I saw very fine cherries, cucumbers and lettuce, and bundles of magnificent clover, three to four feet high.

We climbed a steep path to the citadel, which covers the summit of an abrupt, isolated hill, connected by a shoulder with the great range. The walls are nearly a mile in circuit, consisting almost wholly of immense circular buttresses, placed so near each other that they almost touch. The connecting walls are broken down on the northern side, so that from below the buttresses have the appearance of enormous shattered columns. They are built of rough stones, with regular layers of flat, burnt bricks. On the highest part of the hill stands the fortress, or stronghold, a place which must have been almost impregnable before the invention of cannon. The structure probably dates from the ninth or tenth century, but is built on the foundations of more ancient edifices. The old Greek city of Cotyaeum (whence Kiutahya) probably stood upon this hill. Within the citadel is an upper town, containing about a hundred houses, the residence, apparently of poor families.

From the circuit of the walls, on every side, there are grand views over the plain, the city, and the gorges of the mountains behind. The valley of the Pursek, freshened by the last night's shower, spread out a sheet of vivid green, to the pine-covered mountains which bounded it on all sides. Around the city it was adorned with groves and gardens, and, in the direction of Brousa, white roads went winding away to other gardens and villages in the distance. The mountains of Phrygia, through which we had passed, were the loftiest in the circle that inclosed the valley. The city at our feet presented a thick array of red-tiled roofs, out of which rose here and there the taper shaft of a minaret, or the dome of a mosque or bath. From the southern side of the citadel, we looked down into the gorge which supplies Kiutahya with water--a wild, desert landscape of white crags and shattered peaks of gray rock, hanging over a narrow winding bed of the greenest foliage.

Instead of taking the direct road to Brousa, we decided to make a detour of two days, in order to visit the ruins of the old Greek city of Œzani, which are thirty-six miles south of Kiutahya. Leaving at noon, we ascended the gorge behind the city, by delightfully embowered paths, at first under the eaves of superb walnut-trees, and then through wild thickets of willow, hazel, privet, and other shrubs, tangled together with the odorous white honeysuckle. Near the city, the mountain-sides were bare white masses of gypsum and other rock, in many places with the purest chrome-yellow hue; but as we advanced they were clothed to the summit with copsewood. The streams that foamed down these perennial heights were led into buried channels, to come to light again in sparkling fountains, pouring into ever-full stone basins. The day was cool and cloudy, and the heavy shadows which hung on the great sides of the mountain gateway, heightened, by contrast, the glory of the sunlit plain seen through them.

After passing the summit ridge, probably 5,000 feet above the sea, we came upon a wooded, hilly region, stretching away in long misty lines to Murad Dagh, whose head was spotted with snow. There were patches of wheat and rye in the hollows, and the bells of distant herds tinkled occasionally among the trees. There was no village on the road, and we were on the way to one which we saw in the distance, when we came upon a meadow of good grass, with a small stream running through it. Here we encamped, sending Achmet, the katurgee, to the village for milk and eggs. The ewes had just been milked for the suppers of their owners, but they went over the flock again, stripping their udders, which greatly improved the quality of the milk. The night was so cold that I could scarcely sleep during the morning hours. There was a chill, heavy dew on the meadow; but when François awoke me at sunrise, the sky was splendidly clear and pure, and the early beams had a little warmth in them. Our coffee, before starting, made with sheep's milk, was the richest I ever drank.

After riding for two hours across broad, wild ridges, covered with cedar, we reached a height overlooking the valley of the Rhyndacus, or rather the plain whence he draws his sources--a circular level, ten or twelve miles in diameter, and contracting towards the west into a narrow dell, through which his waters find outlet; several villages, each embowered in gardens, were scattered along the bases of the hills that inclose it. We took the wrong road, but were set aright by a herdsman, and after threading a lane between thriving grain-fields, were cheered by the sight of the Temple of Œzani, lifted on its acropolis above the orchards of Chavdür, and standing out sharp and clear against the purple of the hills.

Our approach to the city was marked by the blocks of sculptured marble that lined the way: elegant mouldings, cornices, and entablatures, thrown together with common stone to make walls between the fields. The village is built on both sides of the Rhyndacus; it is an ordinary Turkish hamlet, with tiled roofs and chimneys, and exhibits very few of the remains of the old city in its composition. This, I suspect, is owing to the great size of the hewn blocks, especially of the pillars, cornices, and entablatures, nearly all of which are from twelve to fifteen feet long. It is from the size and number of these scattered blocks, rather than from the buildings which still partially exist, that one obtains an idea of the size and splendor of the ancient Œzani. The place is filled with fragments, especially of columns, of which there are several hundred, nearly all finely fluted. The Rhyndacus is still spanned by an ancient bridge of three arches, and both banks are lined with piers of hewn stone. Tall poplars and massy walnuts of the richest green shade the clear waters, and there are many picturesque combinations of foliage and ruin--death and life--which would charm a painter's eye. Near the bridge we stopped to examine a pile of immense fragments which have been thrown together by the Turks--pillars, cornices, altars, pieces of a frieze, with bulls' heads bound together by hanging garlands, and a large square block, with a legible tablet. It resembled an altar in form, and, from the word "Artemidoron" appeared to have belonged to some temple to Diana.

Passing through the village we came to a grand artificial platform on its western side, called the Acropolis. It is of solid masonry, five hundred feet square, and averaging ten feet in height. On the eastern side it is supported on rude though massive arches, resembling Etruscan workmanship. On the top and around the edges of this platform lie great numbers of fluted columns, and immense fragments of cornice and architrave. In the centre, on a foundation platform about eight feet high, stands a beautiful Ionic temple, one hundred feet in length. On approaching, it appeared nearly perfect, except the roof, and so many of the columns remain standing that its ruined condition scarcely injures the effect. There are seventeen columns on the side and eight at the end, Ionic in style, fluted, and fifty feet in height.

About half the cella remains, with an elegant frieze and cornice along the top, and a series of tablets, set in panels of ornamental sculpture, running along the sides. The front of the cella includes a small open peristyle, with two composite Corinthian columns at the entrance, making, with those of the outer colonnade, eighteen columns standing. The tablets contain Greek inscriptions, perfectly legible, where the stone has not been shattered. Under the temple there are large vaults, which we found filled up with young kids, who had gone in there to escape the heat of the sun. The portico was occupied by sheep, which at first refused to make room for us, and gave strong olfactory evidence of their partiality for the temple as a resting-place.

On the side of a hill, about three hundred yards to the north, are the remains of a theatre. Crossing some patches of barley and lentils, we entered a stadium, forming an extension of the theatre---that is, it took the same breadth and direction, so that the two might be considered as one grand work, more than one thousand feet long by nearly four hundred wide. The walls of the stadium are hurled down, except an entrance of five arches of massive masonry, on the western side. We rode up the artificial valley, between high, grassy hills, completely covered with what at a distance resembled loose boards, but which were actually the long marble seats of the stadium. Urging our horses over piles of loose blocks, we reached the base of the theatre, climbed the fragments that cumber the main entrance, and looked on the spacious arena and galleries within. Although greatly ruined, the materials of the whole structure remain, and might be put together again. It is a grand wreck; the colossal fragments which have tumbled from the arched proscenium fill the arena, and the rows of seats, though broken and disjointed, still retain their original order. It is somewhat more than a semicircle, the radius being about one hundred and eighty feet. The original height was upwards of fifty feet, and there were fifty rows of seats in all, each row capable of seating two hundred persons, so that the number of spectators who could be accommodated was eight thousand.

The fragments cumbering the arena were enormous, and highly interesting from their character. There were rich blocks of cornice, ten feet long; fluted and reeded pillars; great arcs of heavily-carved sculpture, which appeared to have served as architraves from pillar to pillar, along the face of the proscenium, where there was every trace of having been a colonnade; and other blocks sculptured with figures of animals in alto-relievo. There were generally two figures on each block, and among those which could be recognized were the dog and the lion. Doors opened from the proscenium into the retiring-rooms of the actors, under which were the vaults where the beasts were kept. A young fox or jackal started from his siesta as we entered the theatre, and took refuge under the loose blocks. Looking backwards through the stadium from the seats of the theatre, we had a lovely view of the temple, standing out clear and bright in the midst of the summer plain, with the snow-streaked summits of Murad Dagh in the distance. It was a picture which I shall long remember. The desolation of the magnificent ruins was made all the more impressive by the silent, solitary air of the region around them.

Leaving Chavdür in the afternoon, we struck northward, down the valley of the Rhyndacus, over tracts of rolling land, interspersed with groves of cedar and pine. There were so many branch roads and crossings that we could not fail to go wrong; and after two or three hours found ourselves in the midst of a forest, on the broad top of a mountain, without any road at all. There were some herdsmen tending their flocks near at hand, but they could give us no satisfactory direction. We thereupon, took our own course, and soon brought up on the brink of a precipice, overhanging a deep valley. Away to the eastward we caught a glimpse of the Rhyndacus, and the wooden minaret of a little village on his banks. Following the edge of the precipice, we came at last to a glen, down which ran a rough footpath that finally conducted us, by a long road through the forests, to the village of Daghje Köi, where we are now encamped.

The place seems to be devoted to the making of flints, and the streets are filled with piles of the chipped fragments. Our tent is pitched on the bank of the river, in a barren meadow. The people tell us that the whole region round about has just been visited by a plague of grasshoppers, which have destroyed their crops. Our beasts have wandered off to the hills, in search for grass, and the disconsolate Hadji is hunting them. Achmet, the *katurgee*, lies near the fire, sick; Mr. Harrison complains of fever, and François moves about languidly, with a dismal countenance. So here we are in the solitudes of Bithynia, but there is no God but God, and that which is destined comes to pass.

Chapter XXIV. The Mysian Olympus.

Journey Down the Valley--The Plague of Grasshoppers--A Defile--The Town of Taushanlü--The Camp of Famine--We leave the Rhyndacus--The Base of Olympus--Primeval Forests--The Guard-House--Scenery of the Summit--Forests of Beech--Saw-Mills--Descent of the Mountain--The View of Olympus--Morning--The Land of Harvest--Aineghiöl--A Showery Ride-- The Plain of Brousa--The Structure of Olympus--We reach Brousa--The Tent is Furled.

"I looked yet farther and higher, and saw in the heavens a silvery cloud that stood fast, and still against the breeze; * * * * and so it was as a sign and a testimony--almost as a call from the neglected gods, that I now saw and acknowledged the snowy crown of the Mysian Olympus!" Kinglake.

Brousa, *July* 9, 1852.

From Daghje Küi, there were two roads to Taushanlü, but the people informed us that the one which led across the mountains was difficult to find, and almost impracticable. We therefore took the river road, which we found picturesque in the highest degree. The narrow dell of the Rhyndacus wound through a labyrinth of mountains, sometimes turning at sharp angles between craggy buttresses, covered with forests, and sometimes broadening out into a sweep of valley, where the villagers were working in companies among the grain and poppy fields. The banks of the stream were lined with oak, willow and sycamore, and forests of pine, descending from the mountains, frequently overhung the road. We met numbers of peasants, going to and from the fields, and once a company of some twenty women, who, on seeing us, clustered together like a flock of frightened sheep, and threw their mantles over their heads. They had curiosity enough, however, to peep at us as we went by, and I made them a salutation, which they returned, and then burst into a chorus of hearty laughter. All this region was ravaged by a plague of grasshoppers. The earth was black with them in many places, and our horses ploughed up a living spray, as they drove forward through the meadows. Every spear of grass was destroyed, and the wheat and rye fields were terribly cut up. We passed a large crag where myriads of starlings had built their nests, and every starling had a grasshopper in his mouth.

We crossed the river, in order to pass a narrow defile, by which it forces its way through the rocky heights of Dumanidj Dagh. Soon after passing the ridge, a broad and beautiful valley expanded before us. It was about ten miles in breadth, nearly level, and surrounded by picturesque ranges of wooded mountains. It was well cultivated, principally in rye and poppies, and more thickly populated than almost any part of Europe. The tinned tops of the minarets of Taushanlü shone over the top of a hill in front, and there was a large town nearly opposite, on the other bank of the Rhyndacus, and seven small villages scattered about in various directions. Most of the latter, however, were merely the winter habitations of the herdsmen, who are now living in tents on the mountain tops. All over the valley, the peasants were at work in the harvest-fields, cutting and binding grain, gathering opium from the poppies, or weeding the young tobacco. In the south, over the rim of the hills that shut in this pastoral solitude, rose the long blue summits of Urus Dagh. We rode into Taushanlü, which is a long town, filling up a hollow between two stony hills. The houses are all of stone, two stories high, with tiled roofs and chimneys, so that, but for the clapboarded and shingled minarets, it would answer for a North-German village.

The streets were nearly deserted, and even in the bazaars, which are of some extent, we found but few persons. Those few, however, showed a laudable curiosity with regard to us, clustering about us whenever we stopped, and staring at us with provoking pertinacity. We had some difficulty in procuring information concerning the road, the directions being so contradictory that we were as much in the dark as ever. We lost half an hour in wandering among the hills; and, after travelling four hours over piny uplands, without finding the village of Kara Köi, encamped on a dry plain, on the western bank of the river. There was not a spear of grass for the beasts, everything being eaten up by the grasshoppers, and there were no Turcomans near who could supply us with food. So we dined on hard bread and black coffee, and our forlorn beasts walked languidly about, cropping the dry stalks of weeds and the juiceless roots of the dead grass.

We crossed the river next morning, and took a road following its course, and shaded with willows and sycamores. The lofty, wooded ranges of the Mysian Olympus lay before us, and our day's work was to pass them. After passing the village of Kara Köi, we left the valley of the Rhyndacus, and commenced ascending one of the long, projecting spurs thrust out from the main chain of Olympus. At first we rode through thickets of scrubby cedar, but soon came to magnificent pine forests, that grew taller and sturdier the higher we clomb. A superb mountain landscape opened behind us. The valleys sank deeper and deeper, and at last disappeared behind the great ridges that heaved themselves out of the wilderness of smaller hills. All these ridges were covered with forests; and as we looked backwards out of the tremendous gulf up the sides of which we were climbing, the scenery was wholly wild and uncultivated. Our path hung on the imminent side of a chasm so steep that one slip might have been destruction to both horse and rider. Far below us, at the bottom of the chasm, roared an invisible torrent. The opposite side, vapory from its depth, rose like an immense wall against Heaven. The pines were even grander than those in the woods of Phrygia. Here they grew taller and more dense, hanging their cloudy boughs over the giddy depths, and clutching with desperate roots to the almost perpendicular sides of the gorges. In many places they were the primeval forests of Olympus, and the Hamadryads were not yet frightened from their haunts.

Thus, slowly toiling up through the sublime wilderness, breathing the cold, pure air of those lofty regions, we came at last to a little stream, slowly trickling down the bed of the gorge. It was shaded, not by the pine, but by the Northern beech, with its white trunk and close, confidential boughs, made for the talks of lovers and the meditations of poets. Here we stopped to breakfast, but there was nothing for the poor beasts to eat, and they waited for us droopingly, with their heads thrust together. While we sat there three camels descended to the stream, and after them a guard with a long gun. He was a well-made man, with a brown face, keen, black eye, and piratical air, and would have made a good hero of modern romance. Higher up we came to a guard house, on a little cleared space, surrounded by beech forests. It was a rough stone hut, with a white flag planted on a pole before it, and a miniature water-wheel, running a miniature saw at a most destructive rate, beside the door.

Continuing our way, we entered on a region such as I had no idea could be found in Asia. The mountains, from the bottoms of the gorges to their topmost summits, were covered with the most superb forests of beech I ever saw--masses of impenetrable foliage, of the most brilliant green, touched here and there by the darker top of a pine. Our road was through a deep, dark shade, and on either side, up and down, we saw but a cool, shadowy solitude, sprinkled with dots of emerald light, and redolent with the odor of damp earth, moss, and dead leaves. It was a forest, the counterpart of which could only be found in America--such primeval magnitude of growth, such wild luxuriance, such complete solitude and silence! Through the shafts of the pines we had caught glorious glimpses of the blue mountain world below us; but now the beech folded us in its arms, and whispered in our ears the legends of our Northern home. There, on the ridges of the Mysian Olympus, sacred to the bright gods of Grecian song, I found the inspiration of our darker and colder clime and age. "O gloriosi spiriti degli boschi!"

I could scarcely contain myself, from surprise and joy. François failed to find French adjectives sufficient for his admiration, and even our cheating katurgees were touched by the spirit of the scene. On either side, whenever a glimpse could be had through the boughs, we looked upon leaning walls of trees, whose tall, rounded tops basked in the sunshine, while their bases were wrapped in the shadows cast by themselves. Thus, folded over each other like scales, or feathers on a falcon's wing, they clad the mountain. The trees were taller, and had a darker and more glossy leaf than the American beech. By and by patches of blue shone between the boughs before us, a sign that the summit was near, and before one o'clock we stood upon the narrow ridge forming the crest of the mountain. Here, although we were between five and six thousand feet above the sea, the woods of beech were a hundred feet in height, and shut out all view. On the northern side the forest scenery is even grander than on the southern. The beeches are magnificent trees, straight as an arrow, and from a hundred to a hundred and fifty feet in height. Only now and then could we get any view beyond the shadowy depths sinking below us, and then it was only to see similar mountain ranges, buried in foliage, and rolling far behind each other into the distance. Twice, in the depth of the gorge, we saw a saw-mill, turned by the snow-cold torrents. Piles of pine and beechen boards were heaped around them, and the sawyers were busily plying their lonely business. The axe of the woodman echoed but rarely through the gulfs, though many large trees lay felled by the roadside. The rock, which occasionally cropped out of the soil, was white marble, and there was a shining precipice of it, three hundred feet high, on the opposite side of the gorge.

After four hours of steady descent, during the last hour of which we passed into a forest entirely of oaks, we reached the first terrace at the base of the mountain. Here, as I was riding in advance of the caravan, I met a company of Turkish officers, who saluted me with an inclination of the most profound reverence. I replied with due Oriental gravity, which seemed to justify their respect, for when they met François, who is everywhere looked upon as a Turkish janissary, they asked: "Is not your master a Shekh el-Islàm?" "You are right: he is," answered the unscrupulous Greek. A Shekh el-Islàm is a sort of high-priest, corresponding in dignity to a Cardinal in the Roman Catholic Church. It is rather singular that I am generally taken for a Secretary of some kind, or a Moslem priest, while my companion, who, by this time, has assumed the Oriental expression, is supposed to be either medical or military.

We had no sooner left the forests and entered the copsewood which followed, than the blue bulk, of Olympus suddenly appeared in the west, towering far into the sky. It is a magnificent mountain, with a broad though broken summit, streaked with snow. Before us, stretching away almost to his base, lay a grand mountain slope, covered with orchards and golden harvest-fields. Through lanes of hawthorn and chestnut trees in blossom, which were overgrown with snowy clematis and made a shady roof above our heads, we reached the little village of Orta Köi, and encamped in a grove of pear-trees. There was grass for our beasts, who were on the brink of starvation, and fowls and cucumbers for ourselves, who had been limited to bread and coffee for two days. But as one necessity was restored, another disappeared. We had smoked the last of our delicious Aleppo tobacco, and that which the villagers gave us was of very inferior quality. Nevertheless, the pipe which we smoked with them in the twilight, beside the marble fountain, promoted that peace of mind which is the sweetest preparative of slumber.

François was determined to finish our journey to-day. He had a presentiment that we should reach Brousa, although I expected nothing of the kind. He called us long before the lovely pastoral valley in which we lay had a suspicion of the sun, but just in time to see the first rays strike the high head of Olympus. The long lines of snow blushed with an opaline radiance against the dark-blue of the morning sky, and all the forests and fields below lay still, and cool, and dewy, lapped in dreams yet unrecalled by the fading moon. I bathed my face in the cold well that perpetually poured over its full brim, drank the coffee which François had already prepared, sprang into the saddle, and began the last day of our long pilgrimage. The tent was folded, alas! for the last time; and now farewell to the freedom of our wandering life! Shall I ever feel it again?

The dew glistened on the chestnuts and the walnuts, on the wild grape-vines and wild roses, that shaded our road, as we followed the course of an Olympian stream through a charming dell, into the great plain below. Everywhere the same bountiful soil, the same superb orchards, the same ripe fields of wheat and barley, and silver rye. The peasants were at work, men and women, cutting the grain with rude scythes, binding it into sheaves, and stacking it in the fields. As we rode over the plain, the boys came running out to us with handfuls of grain, saluting us from afar, bidding us welcome as pilgrims, wishing us as many years of prosperity as there were kernels in their sheaves, and kissing the hands that gave them the harvest-toll. The whole landscape had an air of plenty, peace, and contentment. The people all greeted us cordially; and once a Mevlevi Dervish and a stately Turk, riding in company, saluted me so respectfully, stopping to speak with me, that I quite regretted being obliged to assume an air of dignified reserve, and ride away from them.

Ere long, we saw the two white minarets of Aineghiöl, above the line of orchards in front of us, and, in three hours after starting, reached the place. It is a small town, not particularly clean, but with brisk-looking bazaars. In one of the houses, I saw half-a-dozen pairs of superb antlers, the spoils of Olympian stags. The bazaar is covered with a trellised roof, overgrown with grape-vines, which hang enormous bunches of young grapes over the shop-boards. We were cheered by the news that Brousa was only eight hours distant, and I now began to hope that we might reach it. We jogged on as fast as we could urge our weary horses, passed another belt of orchard land, paid more harvest-tolls to the reapers, and commenced ascending a chain of low hills which divides the plain of Aineghiöl from that of Brousa.

At a fountain called the "mid-day konnàk" we met some travellers coming from Brousa, who informed us that we could get there by the time of asser prayer. Rounding the north-eastern base of Olympus, we now saw before us the long headland which forms his south-western extremity. A storm was arising from the sea of Marmora, and heavy white clouds settled on the topmost summits of the mountain. The wind began to blow fresh and cool, and when we had reached a height overlooking the deep valley, in the bottom of which lies the picturesque village of Ak-su, there were long showery lines coming up from the sea, and a filmy sheet of gray rain descended between us and Olympus, throwing his vast bulk far into the background. At Ak-su, the first shower met us, pouring so fast and thick that we were obliged to put on our capotes, and halt under a walnut-tree for shelter. But it soon passed over, laying the dust, for the time, and making the air sweet and cool.

We pushed forward over heights covered with young forests of oak, which are protected by the government, in order that they may furnish ship-timber. On the right, we looked down into magnificent valleys, opening towards the west into the plain of Brousa; but when, in the middle of the afternoon, we reached the last height, and saw the great plain itself, the climax was attained. It was the crown of all that we had yet seen. This superb plain or valley, thirty miles long, by five in breadth, spread away to the westward, between the mighty mass of Olympus on the one side, and a range of lofty mountains on the other, the sides of which presented a charming mixture of forest and cultivated land. Olympus, covered with woods of beech and oak,

610

towered to the clouds that concealed his snowy head; and far in advance, under the last cape he threw out towards the sea, the hundred minarets of Brousa stretched in a white and glittering line, like the masts of a navy, whose hulls were buried in the leafy sea. No words can describe the beauty of the valley, the blending of the richest cultivation with the wildest natural luxuriance. Here were gardens and orchards; there groves of superb chestnut-trees in blossom; here, fields of golden grain or green pasture-land; there, Arcadian thickets overgrown with clematis and wild rose; here, lofty poplars growing beside the streams; there, spiry cypresses looking down from the slopes: and all blended in one whole, so rich, so grand, so gorgeous, that I scarcely breathed when it first burst upon me.

And now we descended to its level, and rode westward along the base of Olympus, grandest of Asian mountains. This after-storm view, although his head was shrouded, was sublime. His base is a vast sloping terrace, leagues in length, resembling the nights of steps by which the ancient temples were approached. From this foundation rise four mighty pyramids, two thousand feet in height, and completely mantled with forests. They are very nearly regular in their form and size, and are flanked to the east and west by headlands, or abutments, the slopes of which are longer and more gradual, as if to strengthen the great structure. Piled upon the four pyramids are others nearly as large, above whose green pinnacles appear still other and higher ones, bare and bleak, and clustering thickly together, to uphold the great central dome of snow. Between the bases of the lowest, the streams which drain the gorges of the mountain issue forth, cutting their way through the foundation terrace, and widening their beds downwards to the plain, like the throats of bugles, where, in winter rains, they pour forth the hoarse, grand monotone of their Olympian music. These broad beds are now dry and stony tracts, dotted all over with clumps of dwarfed sycamores and threaded by the summer streams, shrunken in bulk, but still swift, cold, and clear as ever.

We reached the city before night, and François is glad to find his presentiment fulfilled. We have safely passed through the untravelled heart of Asia Minor, and are now almost in sight of Europe. The camp-fire is extinguished; the tent is furled. We are no longer happy nomads,

611

masquerading in Moslem garb. We shall soon become prosaic Christians, and meekly hold out our wrists for the handcuffs of Civilization. Ah, prate as we will of the progress of the race, we are but forging additional fetters, unless we preserve that healthy physical development, those pure pleasures of mere animal existence, which are now only to be found among our semi-barbaric brethren. Our progress is nervous, when it should be muscular.

Chapter XXV. Brousa and the Sea of Marmora.

The City of Brousa--Return to Civilization--Storm--The Kalputcha Hammam--A Hot Bath--A Foretaste of Paradise--The Streets and Bazaars of Brousa--The Mosque--The Tombs of the Ottoman Sultans--Disappearance of the Katurgees--We start for Moudania--The Sea of Marmora--Moudania--Passport Difficulties--A Greek Caïque--Breakfast with the Fishermen--A Torrid Voyage--The Princes' Islands--Prinkipo--Distant View of Constantinople--We enter the Golden Horn.

"And we glode fast o'er a pellucid plain

Of waters, azure with the noontide ray.

Ethereal mountains shone around--a fane

Stood in the midst, beyond green isles which lay

On the blue, sunny deep, resplendent far away."

Shelley.

Constantinople, *Monday, July* 12, 1852.

Before entering Brousa, we passed the whole length of the town, which is built on the side of Olympus, and on three bluffs or spurs which project from it. The situation is more picturesque than that of Damascus, and from the remarkable number of its white domes and minarets, shooting upward from the groves of chestnut, walnut, and cypress-trees, the city is even more beautiful. There are large mosques on all the most prominent points, and, near the centre of the city, the ruins of an ancient castle, built upon a crag. The place, as we rode along, presented a shifting diorama of delightful views. The hotel is at the extreme western end of the city, not far from its celebrated hot baths. It is a new building, in European style, and being built high on the slope, commands one of the most glorious prospects I ever enjoyed from windows made with hands. What a comfort it was to go up stairs into a clean, bright, cheerful room; to drop at full length on a broad divan; to eat a Christian meal; to smoke a narghileh of the softest Persian tobacco; and finally, most exquisite of all luxuries, to creep between cool, clean sheets, on a curtained bed, and find it impossible to sleep on account of the delicious novelty of the sensation!

At night, another storm came up from the Sea of Marmora. Tremendous peals of thunder echoed in the gorges of Olympus and sharp, broad flashes of lightning gave us blinding glimpses of the glorious plain below. The rain fell in heavy showers, but our tent-life was just closed, and we sat securely at our windows and enjoyed the sublime scene.

The sun, rising over the distant mountains of Isnik, shone full in my face, awaking me to a morning view of the valley, which, freshened by the night's thunder-storm, shone wonderfully bright and clear. After coffee, we went to see the baths, which are on the side of the mountain, a mile from the hotel. The finest one, called the Kalputcha Hammam, is at the base of the hill. The entrance hall is very large, and covered by two lofty domes. In the centre is a large marble urn-shaped fountain, pouring out an abundant flood of cold water. Out of this, we passed into an immense rotunda, filled with steam and traversed by long pencils of light, falling from holes in the roof. A small but very beautiful marble fountain cast up a jet of cold water in the centre. Beyond this was still another hall, of the same size, but with a circular basin, twenty-five feet in diameter, in the centre. The floor was marble mosaic, and the basin was lined with brilliantly-colored tiles. It was kept constantly full by the natural hot streams of the mountain. There were a number of persons in the pool, but the atmosphere was so hot that we did not long disturb them by our curiosity.

We then ascended to the Armenian bath, which is the neatest of all, but it was given up to the women, and we were therefore obliged to go to a Turkish one adjoining. The room into which we were taken was so hot that a violent perspiration immediately broke out all over my body, and by the time the dellèks were ready to rasp me, I was as limp as a wet towel, and as plastic as a piece of putty. The man who took me was sweated away almost to nothing; his very bones appeared to have become soft and pliable. The water was slightly sulphureous, and the pailfuls which he dashed over my

614

head were so hot that they produced the effect of a chill--a violent nervous shudder. The temperature of the springs is 180° Fahrenheit, and I suppose the tank into which he afterwards plunged me must have been nearly up to the mark. When, at last, I was laid on the couch, my body was so parboiled that I perspired at all pores for full an hour--a feeling too warm and unpleasant at first, but presently merging into a mood which was wholly rapturous and heavenly. I was like a soft white cloud, that rests all of a summer afternoon on the peak of a distant mountain. I felt the couch on which I lay no more than the cloud might feel the cliffs on which it lingers so airily. I saw nothing but peaceful, glorious sights; spaces of clear blue sky; stretches of quiet lawns; lovely valleys threaded by the gentlest of streams; azure lakes, unruffled by a breath; calms far out on mid-ocean, and Alpine peaks bathed in the flush of an autumnal sunset. My mind retraced all our journey from Aleppo, and there was a halo over every spot I had visited. I dwelt with rapture on the piny hills of Phrygia, on the gorges of Taurus, on the beechen solitudes of Olympus. Would to heaven that I might describe those scenes as I then felt them! All was revealed to me: the heart of Nature lay bare, and I read the meaning and knew the inspiration of her every mood. Then, as my frame grew cooler, and the fragrant clouds of the narghileh, which had helped my dreams, diminished, I was like that same summer cloud, when it feels a gentle breeze and is lifted above the hills, floating along independent of Earth, but for its shadow.

Brousa is a very long, straggling place, extending for three or four miles along the side of the mountain, but presenting a very picturesque appearance from every point. The houses are nearly all three stories high, built of wood and unburnt bricks, and each story projects over the other, after the manner of German towns of the Middle Ages. They have not the hanging balconies which I have found so quaint and pleasing in Kiutahya. But, especially in the Greek quarter, many of them are plastered and painted of some bright color, which gives a gay, cheerful appearance to the streets. Besides, Brousa is the cleanest Turkish town I have seen. The mountain streams traverse most of the streets, and every heavy rain washes them out thoroughly. The whole city has a brisk, active air, and the workmen appear both more skilful and more industrious than in the other parts of Asia Minor. I noticed a great

615

many workers in copper, iron, and wood, and an extensive manufactory of shoes and saddles. Brousa, however, is principally noted for its silks, which are produced in this valley, and others to the South and East. The manufactories are near the city. I looked over some of the fabrics in the bazaars, but found them nearly all imitations of European stuffs, woven in mixed silk and cotton, and even more costly than the silks of Damascus.

We passed the whole length of the bazaars, and then, turning up one of the side streets on our right, crossed a deep ravine by a high stone bridge. Above and below us there were other bridges, under which a stream flowed down from the mountains. Thence we ascended the height, whereon stands the largest and one of the oldest mosques in Brousa. The position is remarkably fine, commanding a view of nearly the whole city and the plain below it. We entered the court-yard boldly, François taking the precaution to speak to me only in Arabic, as there was a Turk within. Mr. H. went to the fountain, washed his hands and face, but did not dare to swallow a drop, putting on a most dolorous expression of countenance, as if perishing with thirst. The mosque was a plain, square building, with a large dome and two minarets. The door was a rich and curious specimen of the stalactitic style, so frequent in Saracenic buildings. We peeped into the windows, and, although the mosque, which does not appear to be in common use, was darkened, saw enough to show that the interior was quite plain.

Just above this edifice stands a large octagonal tomb, surmounted by a dome, and richly adorned with arabesque cornices and coatings of green and blue tiles. It stood in a small garden inclosure, and there was a sort of porter's lodge at the entrance. As we approached, an old gray-bearded man in a green turban came out, and, on François requesting entrance for us, took a key and conducted us to the building. He had not the slightest idea of our being Christians. We took off our slippers before touching the lintel of the door, as the place was particularly holy. Then, throwing open the door, the old man lingered a few moments after we entered, so as not to disturb our prayers--a mark of great respect. We advanced to the edge of the parapet, turned our faces towards Mecca, and imitated the usual Mohammedan prayer on entering a mosque, by holding both arms outspread for a few moments, then bringing the hands together and bowing the face upon them. This done, we leisurely examined the building, and the old man was ready enough to satisfy our curiosity. It was a rich and elegant structure, lighted from the dome. The walls were lined with brilliant tiles, and had an elaborate cornice, with Arabic inscriptions in gold. The floor was covered with a carpet, whereon stood eight or ten ancient coffins, surrounding a larger one which occupied a raised platform in the centre. They were all of wood, heavily carved, and many of them entirely covered with gilded inscriptions. These, according to the old man, were the coffins of the Ottoman Sultans, who had reigned at Brousa previous to the taking of Constantinople, with some members of their families. There were four Sultans, among whom were Mahomet I., and a certain Achmet. Orchan, the founder of the Ottoman dynasty, is buried somewhere in Brousa, and the great central coffin may have been his. François and I talked entirely in Arabic, and the old man asked: "Who are these Hadjis?" whereupon F. immediately answered: "They are Effendis from Baghdad."

We had intended making the ascent of Olympus, but the summit was too thickly covered with clouds. On the morning of the second day, therefore, we determined to take up the line of march for Constantinople. The last scene of our strange, eventful history with the katurgees had just transpired, by their deserting us, being two hundred piastres in our debt. They left their khan on the afternoon after our arrival, ostensibly for the purpose of taking their beasts out to pasture, and were never heard of more. We let them go, thankful that they had not played the trick sooner. We engaged fresh horses for Moudania, on the Sea of Marmora, and dispatched François in advance, to procure a caïque for Constantinople, while we waited to have our passports signed. But after waiting an hour, as there was no appearance of the precious documents, we started the baggage also, under the charge of a surroudjee, and remained alone. Another hour passed by, and yet another, and the Bey was still occupied in sleeping off his hunger. Mr. Harrison, in desperation, went to the office, and after some delay, received the passports with a visè, but not, as we afterwards discovered, the necessary one.

It was four o'clock by the time we left Brousa. Our horses were stiff, clumsy pack-beasts; but, by dint of whips and the sharp shovel-stirrups, we forced them into a trot and made them keep it. The road was well travelled, and by asking everybody we met: "Bou yôl Moudania yedermi?" ("Is this the way to Moudania?"), we had no difficulty in finding it. The plain in many places is marshy, and traversed by several streams. A low range of hills stretches across, and nearly closes it, the united waters finding their outlet by a narrow valley to the north. From the top of the hill we had a grand view, looking back over the plain, with the long line of Brousa's minarets glittering through the interminable groves at the foot of the mountain Olympus now showed a superb outline; the clouds hung about his shoulders, but his snowy head was bare. Before us lay a broad, rich valley, extending in front to the mountains of Moudania. The country was well cultivated, with large farming establishments here and there.

The sun was setting as we reached the summit ridge, where stood a little guard-house. As we rode over the crest, Olympus disappeared, and the Sea of Marmora lay before us, spreading out from the Gulf of Moudania, which was deep and blue among the hills, to an open line against the sunset. Beyond that misty line lay Europe, which I had not seen for nearly nine months, and the gulf below me was the bound of my tent and saddle life. But one hour more, old horse! Have patience with my Ethiopian thong, and the sharp corners of my Turkish stirrups: but one hour more, and I promise never to molest you again! Our path was downward, and I marvel that the poor brute did not sometimes tumble headlong with me. He had been too long used to the pack, however, and his habits were as settled as a Turk's. We passed a beautiful village in a valley on the right, and came into olive groves and vineyards, as the dusk was creeping on. It was a lovely country of orchards and gardens, with fountains spouting by the wayside, and country houses perched on the steeps. In another hour, we reached the sea-shore. It was now nearly dark, but we could see the tower of Moudania some distance to the west.

Still in a continual trot, we rode on; and as we drew near, Mr. H. fired his gun to announce our approach. At the entrance of the town, we found the sourrudjee waiting to conduct us. We clattered through the rough streets for what seemed an endless length of time. The Ramazan gun had just fired, the minarets were illuminated, and the coffee-houses were filled with people. Finally, François, who had been almost in despair at our non-appearance, hailed us with the welcome news that he had engaged a caïque, and that our baggage was already embarked. We only needed the visès of the authorities, in order to leave. He took our teskerés to get them, and we went upon the balcony of a coffee-house overhanging the sea, and smoked a narghileh.

But here there was another history. The teskerés had not been properly visèd at Brousa, and the Governor at first decided to send us back. Taking François, however, for a Turk, and finding that we had regularly passed quarantine, he signed them after a delay of an hour and a half, and we left the shore, weary, impatient, and wolfish with twelve hours' fasting. A cup of Brousan beer and a piece of bread brought us into a better mood, and I, who began to feel sick from the rolling of the caïque, lay down on my bed, which was spread at the bottom, and found a kind of uneasy sleep. The sail was hoisted at first, to get us across the mouth of the Gulf, but soon the Greeks took to their oars. They were silent, however, and though I only slept by fits, the night wore away rapidly. As the dawn was deepening, we ran into a little bight in the northern side of a promontory, where a picturesque Greek village stood at the foot of the mountains. The houses were of wood, with balconies overgrown with grape-vines, and there was a fountain of cold, excellent water on the very beach. Some Greek boatmen were smoking in the portico of a café on shore, and two fishermen, who had been out before dawn to catch sardines, were emptying their nets of the spoil. Our men kindled a fire on the sand, and roasted us a dish of the fish. Some of the last night's hunger remained, and the meal had enough of that seasoning to be delicious.

After giving our men an hour's rest, we set off for the Princes' Islands, which now appeared to the north, over the glassy plain of the sea. The Gulf of Iskmid, or Nicomedia, opened away to the east, between two mountain headlands. The morning was intensely hot and sultry, and but for the protection of an umbrella, we should have suffered greatly. There was a fiery blue vapor on the sea, and a thunder-cloud hid the shores of Thrace. Now and then came a light puff of wind, whereupon the men would ship the little mast, and crowd on an enormous quantity of sail. So, sailing and rowing, we neared the islands with the storm, but it advanced slowly enough to allow a sight of the mosques of St. Sophia and Sultan Achmed, gleaming far and white, like icebergs astray on a torrid sea. Another cloud was pouring its rain over the Asian shore, and we made haste to get to the landing at Prinkipo before it could reach us. From the south, the group of islands is not remarkable for beauty. Only four of them--Prinkipo, Chalki, Prote, and Antigone--are inhabited, the other five being merely barren rocks.

There is an ancient convent on the summit of Prinkipo, where the Empress Irene--the contemporary of Charlemagne--is buried. The town is on the northern side of the island, and consists mostly of the summer residences of Greek and Armenian merchants. Many of these are large and stately houses, surrounded with handsome gardens. The streets are shaded with sycamores, and the number of coffee-houses shows that the place is much frequented on festal days. A company of drunken Greeks were singing in violation of all metre and harmony--a discord the more remarkable, since nothing could be more affectionate than their conduct towards each other. Nearly everybody was in Frank costume, and our Oriental habits, especially the red Tartar boots, attracted much observation. I began to feel awkward and absurd, and longed to show myself a Christian once more.

Leaving Prinkipo, we made for Constantinople, whose long array of marble domes and gilded spires gleamed like a far mirage over the waveless sea. It was too faint and distant and dazzling to be substantial. It was like one of those imaginary cities which we build in a cloud fused in the light of the setting sun. But as we neared the point of Chalcedon, running along the Asian shore, those airy piles gathered form and substance. The pinnacles of the Seraglio shot up from the midst of cypress groves; fantastic kiosks lined the shore; the minarets of St. Sophia and Sultan Achmed rose more clearly against the sky; and a fleet of steamers and men-of-war, gay with flags, marked the entrance of the Golden Horn. We passed the little bay where St. Chrysostom was buried, the point of Chalcedon, and now, looking up the renowned Bosphorus, saw the Maiden's Tower, opposite Scutari. An enormous pile, the barracks of the Anatolian soldiery, hangs over the high bank, and, as we row abreast of it, a fresh breeze comes up from the Sea of Marmora. The prow of the caïque is turned across the stream, the sail is set, and we glide rapidly and noiselessly over the Bosphorus and into the Golden Horn, between the banks of the Frank and Moslem--Pera and Stamboul. Where on the earth shall we find a panorama more magnificent?

The air was filled with the shouts and noises of the great Oriental metropolis; the water was alive with caïques and little steamers; and all the world of work and trade, which had grown almost to be a fable, welcomed us back to its restless heart. We threaded our rather perilous way over the populous waves, and landed in a throng of Custom-House officers and porters, on the wharf at Galata.

Chapter XXVI. The Night of Predestination.

Constantinople in Ramazan--The Origin of the Fast--Nightly Illuminations--The Night of Predestination--The Golden Horn at Night--Illumination of the Shores--The Cannon of Constantinople--A Fiery Panorama--The Sultan's Caïque--Close of the Celebration--A Turkish Mob--The Dancing Dervishes.

"Skies full of splendid moons and shooting stars,

And spouting exhalations, diamond fires." Keats.

Constantinople, *Wednesday, July* 14, 1862.

Constantinople, during the month of Ramazan, presents a very different aspect from Constantinople at other times. The city, it is true, is much more stern and serious during the day; there is none of that gay, careless life of the Orient which you see in Smyrna, Cairo, and Damascus; but when once the sunset gun has fired, and the painful fast is at an end, the picture changes as if by magic. In all the outward symbols of their religion, the Mussulmans show their joy at being relieved from what they consider a sacred duty. During the day, it is quite a science to keep the appetite dormant, and the people not only abstain from eating and drinking, but as much as possible from the sight of food. In the bazaars, you see the famished merchants either sitting, propped back against their cushions, with the shawl about their stomachs, tightened so as to prevent the void under it from being so sensibly felt, or lying at full length in the vain attempt to sleep. It is whispered here that many of the Turks will both eat and smoke, when there is no chance of detection, but no one would dare infringe the fast in public. Most of the mechanics and porters are Armenians, and the boatmen are Greeks.

I have endeavored to ascertain the origin of this fast month. The Syrian Christians say that it is a mere imitation of an incident which happened to Mahomet. The Prophet, having lost his camels, went day after day seeking them in the Desert, taking no nourishment from the time of his departure in the morning until his return at sunset. After having sought them thus daily, for the period of one entire moon, he found them, and in token of joy, gave a three days' feast to the tribe, now imitated in the festival of Bairam, which lasts for three days after the close of Ramazan. This reason, however, seems too trifling for such a rigid fast, and the Turkish tradition, that the Koran was sent down from heaven during this month, offers a more probable explanation. During the fast, the Mussulmans, as is quite natural, are much more fanatical than at other times. They are obliged to attend prayers at the mosque every night, or to have a mollah read the Koran to them at their own houses. All the prominent features of their religion are kept constantly before their eyes, and their natural aversion to the Giaour, or Infidel, is increased tenfold. I have heard of several recent instances in which strangers have been exposed to insults and indignities.

At dusk the minarets are illuminated; a peal of cannon from the Arsenal, echoed by others from the forts along the Bosphorus, relieves the suffering followers of the Prophet, and after an hour of silence, during which they are all at home, feasting, the streets are filled with noisy crowds, and every coffee-shop is thronged. Every night there are illuminations along the water, which, added to the crowns of light sparkling on the hundred minarets and domes, give a magical effect to the night view of the city. Towards midnight there is again a season of comparative quiet, most of the inhabitants having retired to rest; but, about two hours afterwards a watchman comes along with a big drum, which he beats lustily before the doors of the Faithful, in order to arouse them in time to eat again before the daylight-gun, which announces the commencement of another day's fast.

Last night was the holiest night of Islam, being the twenty-fifth of the fast. It is called the Leilet-el-Kadr, or Night of the Predestination, the anniversary of that on which the Koran was miraculously communicated to the Prophet. On this night the Sultan, accompanied by his whole suite, attends service at the mosque, and on his return to the Seraglio, the Sultana Valide, or Sultana-Mother, presents him with a virgin from one of the noble families of Constantinople. Formerly, St. Sophia was the theatre of this celebration, but this year the Sultan chose the Mosque of Tophaneh, which stands on the shore--probably as being nearer to his imperial palace at Beshiktashe, on the Bosphorus. I consider myself fortunate in having reached Constantinople in season to witness this ceremony, and the illumination of the Golden Horn, which accompanies it.

After sunset the mosques crowning the hills of Stamboul, the mosque of Tophaneh, on this side of the water, and the Turkish men-of-war and steamers afloat at the mouth of the Golden Horn, began to blaze with more than their usual brilliance. The outlines of the minarets and domes were drawn in light on the deepening gloom, and the masts and yards of the vessel were hung with colored lanterns. From the battery in front of the mosque and arsenal of Tophaneh a blaze of intense light streamed out over the water, illuminating the gliding forms of a thousand caïques, and the dark hulls of the vessels lying at anchor. The water is the best place from which to view the illumination, and a party of us descended to the landing-place. The streets of Tophaneh were crowded with swarms of Turks, Greeks and Armenians. The square around the fountain was brilliantly lighted, and venders of sherbet and kaïmak were ranged along the sidewalks. In the neighborhood of the mosque the crowd was so dense that we could with difficulty make our way through. All the open space next the water was filled up with the clumsy arabas, or carriages of the Turks, in which sat the wives of the Pashas and other dignitaries.

We took a caïque, and were soon pulled out into the midst of a multitude of other caïques, swarming all over the surface of the Golden Horn. The view from this point was strange, fantastic, yet inconceivably gorgeous. In front, three or four large Turkish frigates lay in the Bosphorus, their hulls and spars outlined in fire against the dark hills and distant twinkling lights of Asia. Looking to the west, the shores of the Golden Horn were equally traced by the multitude of lamps that covered them, and on either side, the hills on which the city is built rose from the water--masses of dark buildings, dotted all over with shafts and domes of the most brilliant light. The gateway on Seraglio Point was illuminated, as well as the quay in front of the mosque of Tophaneh, all the cannons of the battery being covered with lamps. The commonest objects shared in the splendor, even a large lever used for hoisting goods being hung with lanterns from top to bottom. The mosque was a mass of light, and between the tall minarets flanking it, burned the inscription, in Arabic characters, "Long life to you, O our Sovereign!"

The discharge of a cannon announced the Sultan's departure from his palace, and immediately the guns on the frigates and the batteries on both shores took up the salute, till the grand echoes, filling the hollow throat of the Golden Horn, crashed from side to side, striking the hills of Scutari and the point of Chalcedon, and finally dying away among the summits of the Princes' Islands, out on the Sea of Marmora. The hulls of the frigates were now lighted up with intense chemical fires, and an abundance of rockets were spouted from their decks. A large Drummond light on Seraglio Point, and another at the Battery of Tophaneh, poured their rival streams across the Golden Horn, revealing the thousands of caïques jostling each other from shore to shore, and the endless variety of gay costumes with which they were filled. The smoke of the cannon hanging in the air, increased the effect of this illumination, and became a screen of auroral brightness, through which the superb spectacle loomed with large and unreal features. It was a picture of air--a phantasmagoric spectacle, built of luminous vapor and meteoric fires, and hanging in the dark round of space. In spite of ourselves, we became eager and excited, half fearing that the whole pageant would dissolve the next moment, and leave no trace behind.

Meanwhile, the cannon thundered from a dozen batteries, and the rockets burst into glittering rain over our heads. Grander discharges I never heard; the earth shook and trembled under the mighty bursts of sound, and the reverberation which rattled along the hill of Galata, broken by the scattered buildings into innumerable fragments of sound, resembled the crash of a thousand falling houses. The distant echoes from Asia and the islands in the sea filled up the pauses between the nearer peals, and we seemed to be in the midst of some great naval engagement. But now the caïque of the Sultan is discerned, approaching from the Bosphorus. A signal is given, and a sunrise of intense rosy and golden radiance suddenly lights up the long arsenal and stately mosque of Tophaneh, plays over the tall buildings on the hill of Pera, and falls with a fainter lustre on the Genoese watch-tower that overlooks Galata. It is impossible to describe the effect of this magical illumination. The mosque, with its taper minarets, its airy galleries, and its great central dome, is built of compact, transparent flame, and in the shifting of the red and yellow fires, seems to flicker and waver in the air. It is as lofty, and gorgeous, and unsubstantial as the cloudy palace in Cole's picture of "Youth." The long white front of the arsenal is fused in crimson heat, and burns against the dark as if it were one mass of living coal. And over all hangs the luminous canopy of smoke, redoubling its lustre on the waters of the Golden Horn, and mingling with the phosphorescent gleams that play around the oars of the caïques.

A long barge, propelled by sixteen oars, glides around the dark corner of Tophaneh, and shoots into the clear, brilliant space in front of the mosque. It is not lighted, and passes with great swiftness towards the brilliant landing-place. There are several persons seated under a canopy in the stern, and we are trying to decide which is the Sultan, when a second boat, driven by twenty-four oarsmen, comes in sight. The men rise up at each stroke, and the long, sharp craft flies over the surface of the water, rather than forces its way through it. A gilded crown surmounts the long, curved prow, and a light though superb canopy covers the stern. Under this, we catch a glimpse of the Sultan and Grand Vizier, as they appear for an instant like black silhouettes against the burst of light on shore.

After the Sultan had entered the mosque, the fires diminished and the cannon ceased, though the illuminated masts, minarets and gateways still threw a brilliant gleam over the scene. After more than an hour spent in devotion, he again entered his caïque and sped away to greet his new wife, amid a fresh discharge from the frigates and the batteries on both shores, and a new dawn of auroral splendor. We made haste to reach the landing-place, in order to avoid the crowd of caïques; but, although we were among the first, we came near being precipitated into the water, in the struggle to get ashore. The market-place at Tophaneh was so crowded that nothing but main force brought us through, and some of our party had their pockets picked. A number of Turkish soldiers and police-men were mixed up in the melee, and they were not sparing of blows when they came in contact with a Giaour. In making my way through, I found that a collision with one of the soldiers was inevitable, but I managed to plump against him with such force as to take the breath out of his body, and was out of his reach before he had recovered himself. I saw several Turkish women striking right and left in their endeavors to escape, and place their hands against the faces of those who opposed them, pushing them aside. This crowd was contrived by thieves, for the purpose of plunder, and, from what I have since learned, must have been very successful.

I visited to-day the College of the Mevlevi Dervishes at Pera, and witnessed their peculiar ceremonies. They assemble in a large hall, where they take their seats in a semi-circle, facing the shekh. After going through several times with the usual Moslem prayer, they move in slow march around the room, while a choir in the gallery chants Arabic phrases in a manner very similar to the mass in Catholic churches. I could distinguish the sentences "God is great," "Praise be to God," and other similar ejaculations. The chant was accompanied with a drum and flute, and had not lasted long before the Dervishes set themselves in a rotary motion, spinning slowly around the shekh, who stood in the centre. They stretched both arms out, dropped their heads on one side, and glided around with a steady, regular motion, their long white gowns spread out and floating on the air. Their steps were very similar to those of the modern waltz, which, it is possible, may have been derived from the dance of the Mevlevis. Baron Von Hammer finds in this ceremony an imitation of the dance of the spheres, in the ancient Samothracian Mysteries; but I see no reason to go so far back for its origin. The dance lasted for about twenty minutes, and the Dervishes appeared very much exhausted at the close, as they are obliged to observe the fast very strictly.

Chapter XXVII. The Solemnities of Bairam.

The Appearance of the New Moon--The Festival of Bairam--The Interior of the Seraglio--The Pomp of the Sultan's Court--Rescind Pasha--The Sultan's Dwarf--Arabian Stallions--The Imperial Guard--Appearance of the Sultan--The Inner Court--Return of the Procession--The Sultan on his Throne--The Homage of the Pashas--An Oriental Picture--Kissing the Scarf--The Shekh el-Islàm--The Descendant of the Caliphs--Bairam Commences.

Constantinople, *Monday, July* 19, 1852.

Saturday was the last day of the fast-month of Ramazan, and yesterday the celebration of the solemn festival of Bairam took place. The moon changed on Friday morning at 11 o'clock, but as the Turks have no faith in astronomy, and do not believe the moon has actually changed until they see it, all good Mussulmen were obliged to fast an additional day. Had Saturday been cloudy, and the new moon invisible, I am not sure but the fast would have been still further prolonged. A good look-out was kept, however, and about four o'clock on Saturday afternoon some sharp eyes saw the young crescent above the sun. There is a hill near Gemlik, on the Gulf of Moudania, about fifty miles from here, whence the Turks believe the new moon can be first seen. The families who live on this hill are exempted from taxation, in consideration of their keeping a watch for the moon, at the close of Ramazan. A series of signals, from hill to hill, is in readiness, and the news is transmitted to Constantinople in a very short time Then, when the muezzin proclaims the asser, or prayer two hours before sunset, he proclaims also the close of Ramazan. All the batteries fire a salute, and the big guns along the water announce the joyful news to all parts of the city. The forts on the Bosphorus take up the tale, and both shores, from the Black Sea to the Propontis, shake with the burden of their rejoicing. At night the mosques are illuminated for the last time, for it is only during Ramazan that they are lighted, or open for night service.

After Ramazan, comes the festival of Bairam, which lasts three days, and is a season of unbounded rejoicing. The bazaars are closed, no Turk does any work, but all, clothed in their best dresses, or in an entire new suit if they can afford it, pass the time in feasting, in paying visits, or in making excursions to the shores of the Bosphorus, or other favorite spots around Constantinople. The festival is inaugurated by a solemn state ceremony, at the Seraglio and the mosque of Sultan Achmed, whither the Sultan goes in procession, accompanied by all the officers of the Government. This is the last remaining pageant which has been spared to the Ottoman monarchs by the rigorous reforming measures of Sultan Mahmoud, and shorn as it is of much of its former splendor, it probably surpasses in brilliant effect any spectacle which any other European Court can present. The ceremonies which take place inside of the Seraglio were, until within three or four years, prohibited to Frank eyes, and travellers were obliged to content themselves with a view of the procession, as it passed to the mosque. Through the kindness of Mr. Brown, of the American Embassy, I was enabled to witness the entire solemnity, in all its details.

As the procession leaves the Seraglio at sunrise, we rose with the first streak of dawn, descended to Tophaneh, and crossed to Seraglio Point, where the cavass of the Embassy was in waiting for us. He conducted us through the guards, into the garden of the Seraglio, and up the hill to the Palace. The Capudan Pasha, or Lord High Admiral, had just arrived in a splendid caïque, and pranced up the hill before us on a magnificent stallion, whose trappings blazed with jewels and gold lace. The rich uniforms of the different officers of the army and marine glittered far and near under the dense shadows of the cypress trees, and down the dark alleys where the morning twilight had not penetrated. We were ushered into the great outer court-yard of the Seraglio, leading to the Sublime Porte. A double row of marines, in scarlet jackets and white trowsers, extended from one gate to the other, and a very excellent brass band played "Suoni la tromba" with much spirit. The groups of Pashas and other officers of high rank, with their attendants, gave the scene a brilliant character of festivity. The costumes, except those of the secretaries and servants, were after the European model, but covered with a lavish profusion of gold lace. The horses were all of the choicest Eastern breeds, and the broad housings of their saddles of blue, green, purple, and crimson cloth, were enriched with gold lace, rubies, emeralds and turquoises.

The cavass took us into a chamber near the gate, and commanding a view of the whole court. There we found Mr. Brown and his lady, with several officers from the U.S. steamer San Jacinto. At this moment the sun, appearing above the hill of Bulgaria, behind Scutari, threw his earliest rays upon the gilded pinnacles of the Seraglio. The commotion in the long court-yard below increased. The marines were formed into exact line, the horses of the officers clattered on the rough pavement as they dashed about to expedite the arrangements, the crowd pressed closer to the line of the procession, and in five minutes the grand pageant was set in motion. As the first Pasha made his appearance under the dark archway of the interior gate, the band struck up the Marseillaise (which is a favorite air among the Turks), and the soldiers presented arms. The court-yard was near two hundred yards long, and the line of Pashas, each surrounded with the officers of his staff, made a most dazzling show. The lowest in rank came first. I cannot recollect the precise order, nor the names of all of them, which, in fact, are of little consequence, while power and place are such uncertain matters in Turkey.

Each Pasha wore the red fez on his head, a frock-coat of blue cloth, the breast of which was entirely covered with gold lace, while a broad band of the same decorated the skirts, and white pantaloons. One of the Ministers, Mehemet Ali Pasha, the brother-in-law of the Sultan, was formerly a cooper's apprentice, but taken, when a boy, by the late Sultan Mahmoud, to be a playmate for his son, on account of his extraordinary beauty. Rescind Pasha, the Grand Vizier, is a man of about sixty years of age. He is frequently called Giaour, or Infidel, by the Turks, on account of his liberal policy, which has made him many enemies. The expression of his face denotes intelligence, but lacks the energy necessary to accomplish great reforms. His son, a boy of about seventeen, already possesses the rank of Pasha, and is affianced to the Sultan's daughter, a child of ten, or twelve years old. He is a fat, handsome youth, with a sprightly face, and acted his part in the ceremonies with a nonchalance which made him appear graceful beside his stiff, dignified elders.

After the Pashas came the entire household of the Sultan, including even his eunuchs, cooks, and constables. The Kislar Aga, or Chief Eunuch, a tall African in resplendent costume, is one of the most important personages connected with the Court. The Sultan's favorite dwarf, a little man about forty years old and three feet high, bestrode his horse with as consequential an air as any of them. A few years ago, this man took a notion to marry, and applied to the Sultan for a wife. The latter gave him permission to go into his harem and take the one whom he could kiss. The dwarf, like all short men, was ambitious to have a long wife. While the Sultan's five hundred women, who knew the terms according to which the dwarf was permitted to choose, were laughing at the amorous mannikin, he went up to one of the tallest and handsomest of them, and struck her a sudden blow on the stomach. She collapsed with the pain, and before she could recover he caught her by the neck and gave her the dreaded kiss. The Sultan kept his word, and the tall beauty is now the mother of the dwarfs children.

The procession grows more brilliant as it advances, and the profound inclination made by the soldiers at the further end of the court, announces the approach of the Sultan himself. First come three led horses, of the noblest Arabian blood--glorious creatures, worthy to represent

"The horse that guide the golden eye of heaven,

And snort the morning from their nostrils,

Making their fiery gait above the glades."

Their eyes were more keen and lustrous than the diamonds which studded their head-stalls, and the wealth of emeralds, rubies, and sapphires that gleamed on their trappings would have bought the possessions of a German Prince. After them came the Sultan's body-guard, a company of tall, strong men, in crimson tunics and white trousers, with lofty plumes of peacock feathers in their hats. Some of them carried crests of green feathers, fastened upon long staves. These superb horses and showy guards are the only relics of that barbaric pomp which characterized all State processions during the time of the Janissaries. In the centre of a hollow square of plume-bearing guards rode Abdul-Medjid himself, on a snow-white steed. Every one bowed profoundly as he passed along, but he neither looked to the right or left, nor made the slightest acknowledgment of the salutations. Turkish etiquette exacts the most rigid indifference on the part of the Sovereign, who, on all public occasions, never makes a greeting. Formerly, before the change of costume, the Sultan's turbans were carried before him in the processions, and the servants who bore them inclined them to one side and the other, in answer to the salutations of the crowd.

Sultan Abdul-Medjid is a man of about thirty, though he looks older. He has a mild, amiable, weak face, dark eyes, a prominent nose, and short, dark brown mustaches and beard. His face is thin, and wrinkles are already making their appearance about the corners of his mouth and eyes. But for a certain vacancy of expression, he would be called a handsome man. He sits on his horse with much ease and grace, though there is a slight stoop in his shoulders. His legs are crooked, owing to which cause he appears awkward when on his feet, though he wears a long cloak to conceal the deformity. Sensual indulgence has weakened a constitution not naturally strong, and increased that mildness which has now become a defect in his character. He is not stern enough to be just, and his subjects are less fortunate under his easy rule than under the rod of his savage father, Mahmoud. He was dressed in a style of the utmost richness and elegance. He wore a red Turkish fez, with an immense rosette of brilliants, and a long, floating plume of bird-of-paradise feathers. The diamond in the centre of the rosette is of unusual size; it was picked up some years ago in the Hippodrome, and probably belonged to the treasury of the Greek Emperors. The breast and collar of his coat were one mass of diamonds, and sparkled in the early sun with a thousand rainbow gleams. His mantle of dark-blue cloth hung to his knees, concealing the deformity of his legs. He wore white pantaloons, white kid gloves, and patent leather boots, thrust into his golden stirrups.

A few officers of the Imperial household followed behind the Sultan, and the procession then terminated. Including the soldiers, it contained from two to three thousand persons. The marines lined the way to the mosque of Sultan Achmed, and a great crowd of spectators filled up the streets and the square of the Hippodrome. Coffee was served to us, after which we were all conducted into the inner court of the Seraglio, to await the return of the cortège. This court is not more than half the size of the outer one, but is shaded with large sycamores, embellished with fountains, and surrounded with light and elegant galleries, in pure Saracenic style. The picture which it presented was therefore far richer and more characteristic of the Orient than the outer court, where the architecture is almost wholly after Italian models. The portals at either end rested on slender pillars, over which projected broad eaves, decorated with elaborate carved and gilded work, and above all rose a dome, surmounted by the Crescent. On the right, the tall chimneys of the Imperial kitchens towered above the walls. The sycamores threw their broad, cool shadows over the court, and groups of servants, in gala dresses, loitered about the corridors.

After waiting nearly half an hour, the sound of music and the appearance of the Sultan's body-guard proclaimed the return of the procession. It came in reversed order, headed by the Sultan, after whom followed the Grand Vizier and other Ministers of the Imperial Council, and the Pashas, each surrounded by his staff of officers. The Sultan dismounted at the entrance to the Seraglio, and disappeared through the door. He was absent for more than half an hour, during which time he received the congratulations of his family, his wives, and the principal personages of his household, all of whom came to kiss his feet. Meanwhile, the Pashas ranged themselves in a semicircle around the arched and gilded portico. The servants of the Seraglio brought out a large Persian carpet, which they spread on the marble pavement. The throne, a large square seat, richly carved and covered with gilding, was placed in the centre, and a dazzling piece of cloth-of-gold thrown over the back of it. When the Sultan re-appeared, he took his seat thereon, placing his feet on a small footstool. The ceremony of kissing his feet now commenced. The first who had this honor was the Chief of the Emirs, an old man in a green robe, embroidered with pearls. He advanced to the throne, knelt, kissed the Sultan's patent-leather boot, and retired backward from the presence.

The Ministers and Pashas followed in single file, and, after they had made the salutation, took their stations on the right hand of the throne. Most of them were fat, and their glittering frock-coats were buttoned so tightly that they seemed ready to burst. It required a great effort for them to rise from their knees. During all this time, the band was playing operatic airs, and as each Pasha knelt, a marshal, or master of ceremonies, with a silver wand, gave the signal to the Imperial Guard, who shouted at the top of their voices: "Prosperity to our Sovereign! May he live a thousand years!" This part of the ceremony was really grand and imposing. All the adjuncts were in keeping: the portico, wrought in rich arabesque designs; the swelling domes and sunlit crescents above; the sycamores and cypresses shading the court; the red tunics and peacock plumes of the guard; the monarch himself, radiant with jewels, as he sat in his chair of gold--all these features combined to form a stately picture of the lost Orient, and for the time Abdul-Medjid seemed the true representative of Caliph Haroun Al-Raschid.

After the Pashas had finished, the inferior officers of the Army, Navy, and Civil Service followed, to the number of at least a thousand. They were not considered worthy to touch the Sultan's person, but kissed his golden scarf, which was held out to them by a Pasha, who stood on the left of the throne. The Grand Vizier had his place on the right, and the Chief of the Eunuchs stood behind him. The kissing of the scarf occupied an hour. The Sultan sat quietly during all this time, his face expressing a total indifference to all that was going on. The most skilful physiognomist could not have found in it the shadow of an expression. If this was the etiquette prescribed for him, he certainly acted it with marvellous skill and success.

The long line of officers at length came to an end, and I fancied that the solemnities were now over; but after a pause appeared the Shekh el-Islàm, or High Priest of the Mahometan religion. His authority in religious matters transcends that of the Sultan, and is final and irrevocable. He was a very venerable man, of perhaps seventy-five years of age, and his tottering steps were supported by two mollahs. He was dressed in a long green robe, embroidered with gold and pearls, over which his white beard flowed below his waist. In his turban of white cambric was twisted a scarf of cloth-of-gold. He kissed the border of the Sultan's mantle, which salutation was also made by a long line of the chief priests of the mosques of Constantinople, who followed him. These priests were dressed in long robes of white, green, blue, and violet, many of them with collars of pearls and golden scarfs wound about their turbans, the rich fringes falling on their shoulders. They were grave, stately men, with long gray beards, and the wisdom of age and study in their deep-set eyes.

Among the last who came was the most important personage of all. This was the Governor of Mecca (as I believe he is called), the nearest descendant of the Prophet, and the successor to the Caliphate, in case the family of Othman becomes extinct. Sultan Mahmoud, on his accession to the throne, was the last descendant of Orchan, the founder of the Ottoman Dynasty, the throne being inherited only by the male heirs. He left two sons, who are both living, Abdul-Medjid having departed from the practice of his predecessors, each of whom slew his brothers, in order to make his own sovereignty secure. He has one son, Muzad, who is about ten years old, so that there are now three males of the family of Orchan. In case of their death, the Governor of Mecca would become Caliph, and the sovereignty would be established in his family. He is a swarthy Arab, of about fifty, with a bold, fierce face. He wore a superb dress of green, the sacred color, and was followed by his two sons, young men of twenty and twenty-two. As he advanced to the throne, and was about to kneel and kiss the Sultan's robe, the latter prevented him, and asked politely after his health--the highest mark of respect in his power to show. The old Arab's face gleamed with such a sudden gush of pride and satisfaction, that no flash of lightning could have illumined it more vividly.

The sacred writers, or transcribers of the Koran, closed the procession, after which the Sultan rose and entered the Seraglio. The crowd slowly dispersed, and in a few minutes the grand reports of the cannon on Seraglio Point announced the departure of the Sultan for his palace on the Bosphorus. The festival of Bairam was now fairly inaugurated, and all Stamboul was given up to festivity. There was no Turk so poor that he did not in some sort share in the rejoicing. Our Fourth could scarcely show more flags, let off more big guns or send forth greater crowds of excursionists than this Moslem holiday.

Chapter XXVIII. The Mosques of Constantinople.

Sojourn at Constantinople--Semi-European Character of the City--The Mosque--Procuring a Firman--The Seraglio--The Library--The Ancient Throne-Room--Admittance to St. Sophia--Magnificence of the Interior--The Marvellous Dome--The Mosque of Sultan Achmed--The Sulemanye--Great Conflagrations--Political Meaning of the Fires--Turkish Progress--Decay of the Ottoman Power.

"Is that indeed Sophia's far-famed dome,

Where first the Faith was led in triumph home,

Like some high bride, with banner and bright sign,

And melody, and flowers?" Audrey de Vere.

Constantinople, *Tuesday, August* 8, 1852.

The length of my stay in Constantinople has enabled me to visit many interesting spots in its vicinity, as well as to familiarize myself with the peculiar features of the great capital. I have seen the beautiful Bosphorus from steamers and caïques; ridden up the valley of Buyukdere, and through the chestnut woods of Belgrade; bathed in the Black Sea, under the lee of the Symplegades, where the marble altar to Apollo still invites an oblation from passing mariners; walked over the flowery meadows beside the "Heavenly Waters of Asia;" galloped around the ivy-grown walls where Dandolo and Mahomet II. conquered, and the last of the Palæologi fell; and dreamed away many an afternoon-hour under the funereal cypresses of Pera, and beside the Delphian tripod in the Hippodrome. The historic interest of these spots is familiar to all, nor; with one exception, have their natural beauties been exaggerated by travellers. This exception is the village of Belgrade, over which Mary Montague went into raptures, and set the fashion for tourists ever since. I must confess to having been wofully disappointed. The village is a miserable cluster of rickety houses, on an open piece of barren land, surrounded by the forests, or rather thickets, which keep alive the springs that supply

Constantinople with water. We reached there with appetites sharpened by our morning's ride, expecting to find at least a vender of kibabs (bits of fried meat) in so renowned a place; but the only things to be had were raw salt mackerel, and bread which belonged to the primitive geological formation.

The general features of Constantinople and the Bosphorus are so well known, that I am spared the dangerous task of painting scenes which have been colored by abler pencils. Von Hammer, Lamartine, Willis, Miss Pardoe, Albert Smith, and thou, most inimitable Thackeray! have made Pera and Scutari, the Bazaars and Baths, the Seraglio and the Golden Horn, as familiar to our ears as Cornhill and Wall street. Besides, Constantinople is not the true Orient, which is to be found rather in Cairo, in Aleppo, and brightest and most vital, in Damascus. Here, we tread European soil; the Franks are fast crowding out the followers of the Prophet, and Stamboul itself, were its mosques and Seraglio removed, would differ little in outward appearance from a third-rate Italian town. The Sultan lives in a palace with a Grecian portico; the pointed Saracenic arch, the arabesque sculptures, the latticed balconies, give place to clumsy imitations of Palladio, and every fire that sweeps away a recollection of the palmy times of Ottoman rule, sweeps it away forever.

But the Mosque--that blossom of Oriental architecture, with its crowning domes, like the inverted bells of the lotus, and its reed-like minarets, its fountains and marble courts--can only perish with the faith it typifies. I, for one, rejoice that, so long as the religion of Islam exists (and yet, may its time be short!), no Christian model can shape its houses of worship. The minaret must still lift its airy tower for the muezzin; the dome must rise like a gilded heaven above the prayers of the Faithful, with its starry lamps and emblazoned phrases; the fountain must continue to pour its waters of purification. A reformation of the Moslem faith is impossible. When it begins to give way, the whole fabric must fall. Its ceremonies, as well as its creed, rest entirely on the recognition of Mahomet as the Prophet of God. However the Turks may change in other respects, in all that concerns their religion they must continue the same.

Until within a few years, a visit to the mosques, especially the more sacred ones of St. Sophia and Sultan Achmed, was attended with much difficulty.

Miss Pardoe, according to her own account, risked her life in order to see the interior of St. Sophia, which she effected in the disguise of a Turkish Effendi. I accomplished the same thing, a few days since, but without recourse to any such romantic expedient. Mr. Brown, the interpreter of the Legation, procured a firman from the Grand Vizier, on behalf of the officers of the San Jacinto, and kindly invited me, with several other American and English travellers, to join the party. During the month of Ramazan, no firmans are given, and as at this time there are few travellers in Constantinople, we should otherwise have been subjected to a heavy expense. The cost of a firman, including backsheesh to the priests and doorkeepers, is 700 piastres (about $33).

We crossed the Golden Horn in caïques, and first visited the gardens and palaces on Seraglio Point. The Sultan at present resides in his summer palace of Beshiktashe, on the Bosphorus, and only occupies the Serai Bornou, as it is called, during the winter months. The Seraglio covers the extremity of the promontory on which Constantinople is built, and is nearly three miles in circuit. The scattered buildings erected by different Sultans form in themselves a small city, whose domes and pointed turrets rise from amid groves of cypress and pine. The sea-wall is lined with kiosks, from whose cushioned windows there are the loveliest views of the European and Asian shores. The newer portion of the palace, where the Sultan now receives the ambassadors of foreign nations, shows the influence of European taste in its plan and decorations. It is by no means remarkable for splendor, and suffers by contrast with many of the private houses in Damascus and Aleppo. The building is of wood, the walls ornamented with detestable frescoes by modern Greek artists, and except a small but splendid collection of arms, and some wonderful specimens of Arabic chirography, there is nothing to interest the visitor.

In ascending to the ancient Seraglio, which was founded by Mahomet II., on the site of the palace of the Palæologi, we passed the Column of Theodosius, a plain Corinthian shaft, about fifty feet high. The Seraglio is now occupied entirely by the servants and guards, and the greater part of it shows a neglect amounting almost to dilapidation. The Saracenic corridors surrounding its courts are supported by pillars of marble, granite, and porphyry, the spoils of the Christian capital. We were allowed to walk about at leisure, and inspect the different compartments, except the library, which unfortunately was locked. This library was for a long time supposed to contain many lost treasures of ancient literature--among other things, the missing books of Livy--but the recent researches of Logothetos, the Prince of Samos, prove that there is little of value, among its manuscripts. Before the door hangs a wooden globe, which is supposed to be efficacious in neutralizing the influence of the Evil Eye. There are many ancient altars and fragments of pillars scattered about the courts, and the Turks have even commenced making a collection of antiquities, which, with the exception of two immense sarcophagi of red porphyry, contains nothing of value. They show, however, one of the brazen heads of the Delphian tripod in the Hippodrome, which, they say, Mahomet the Conqueror struck off with a single blow of his sword, on entering Constantinople.

The most interesting portion of the Seraglio is the ancient throne-room, now no longer used, but still guarded by a company of white eunuchs. The throne is an immense, heavy bedstead, the posts of which are thickly incrusted with rubies, turquoises, emeralds, and sapphires. There is a funnel-shaped chimney-piece in the room, a master-work of Benevenuto Cellini. There, half a century ago, the foreign ambassadors were presented, after having been bathed, fed, and clothed with a rich mantle in the outer apartments. They were ushered into the imperial presence, supported by a Turkish official on either side, in order that they might show no signs of breaking down under the load of awe and reverence they were supposed to feel. In the outer Court, adjoining the Sublime Porte, is the Chapel of the Empress Irene, now converted into an armory, which, for its size, is the most tasteful and picturesque collection of weapons I have ever seen. It is especially rich in Saracenic armor, and contains many superb casques of inlaid gold. In a large glass case in the chancel, one sees the keys of some thirty or forty cities, with the date of their capture. It is not likely that another will ever be added to the list.

We now passed out through the Sublime Porte, and directed our steps to the famous Aya Sophia--the temple dedicated by Justinian to the Divine Wisdom. The repairs made to the outer walls by the Turks, and the addition of the four minarets, have entirely changed the character of the building, without injuring its effect. As a Christian Church, it must have been less imposing than in its present form. A priest met us at the entrance, and after reading the firman with a very discontented face, informed us that we could not enter until the mid-day prayers were concluded. After taking off our shoes, however, we were allowed to ascend to the galleries, whence we looked down on the bowing worshippers. Here the majesty of the renowned edifice, despoiled as it now is, bursts at once upon the eye. The wonderful flat dome, glittering with its golden mosaics, and the sacred phrase from the Koran: "God is the Light of the Heavens and the Earth," swims in the air, one hundred and eighty feet above the marble pavement. On the eastern and western sides, it rests on two half domes; which again rise from or rest upon a group of three small half-domes, so that the entire roof of the mosque, unsupported by a pillar, seems to have been dropped from above on the walls, rather than to have been built up from them. Around the edifice run an upper and a lower gallery, which alone preserve the peculiarities of the Byzantine style. These galleries are supported by the most precious columns which ancient art could afford: among them eight shafts of green marble, from the Temple of Diana, at Ephesus; eight of porphyry, from the Temple of the Sun, at Baalbek; besides Egyptian granite from the shrines of Isis and Osiris, and Pentelican marble from the sanctuary of Pallas Athena. Almost the whole of the interior has been covered with gilding, but time has softened its brilliancy, and the rich, subdued gleam of the walls is in perfect harmony with the varied coloring of the ancient marbles.

Under the dome, four Christian seraphim, executed in mosaic, have been allowed to remain, but the names of the four archangels of the Moslem faith are inscribed underneath. The bronze doors are still the same, the Turks having taken great pains to obliterate the crosses with which they were adorned. Around the centre of the dome, as on that of Sultan Achmed, may be read, in golden letters, and in all the intricacy of Arabic penmanship, the beautiful verse:--"God is the Light of the Heavens and the Earth. His wisdom is a light on the wall, in which burns a lamp covered with glass. The glass shines like a star, the lamp is lit with the oil of a blessed tree. No Eastern, no Western oil, it shines for whoever wills." After the prayers were over, and we had descended to the floor of the mosque, I spent the rest of my time under the dome, fascinated by its marvellous lightness and beauty. The worshippers present looked at us with curiosity, but without ill-will; and before we left, one of the priests came slyly with some fragments of the ancient gilded mosaic, which, he was heathen enough to sell, and we to buy.

From St. Sophia we went to Sultan Achmed, which faces the Hippodrome, and is one of the stateliest piles of Constantinople. It is avowedly an imitation of St. Sophia, and the Turks consider it a more wonderful work, because the dome is seven feet higher. It has six minarets, exceeding in this respect all the mosques of Asia. The dome rests on four immense pillars, the bulk of which quite oppresses the light galleries running around the walls. This, and the uniform white color of the interior, impairs the effect which its bold style and imposing dimensions would otherwise produce. The outside view, with the group of domes swelling grandly above the rows of broad-armed sycamores, is much more satisfactory. In the tomb of Sultan Achmed, in one corner of the court, we saw his coffin, turban, sword, and jewelled harness. I had just been reading old Sandys' account of his visit to Constantinople, in 1610, during this Sultan's reign, and could only think of him as Sandys represents him, in the title-page to his book, as a fat man, with bloated cheeks, in a long gown and big turban, and the words underneath:-- "Achmed, sive Tyrannus."

The other noted mosques of Constantinople are the Yeni Djami, or Mosque of the Sultana Valide, on the shore of the Golden Horn, at the end of the bridge to Galata; that of Sultan Bajazet; of Mahomet II., the Conqueror, and of his son, Suleyman the Magnificent, whose superb mosque well deserves this title. I regret exceedingly that our time did not allow us to view the interior, for outwardly it not only surpasses St. Sophia, and all other mosques in the city, but is undoubtedly one of the purest specimens of Oriental architecture extant. It stands on a broad terrace, on one of the seven hills of Stamboul, and its exquisitely proportioned domes and minarets shine as if crystalized in the blue of the air. It is a type of Oriental, as the Parthenon is of Grecian, and the Cologne Cathedral of Gothic art. As I saw it the other night, lit by the flames of a conflagration, standing out red and clear against the darkness, I felt inclined to place it on a level with either of those renowned structures. It is a product of the rich fancy of the East, splendidly ornate, and not without a high degree of symmetry--yet here the symmetry is that of ornament alone, and not the pure, absolute proportion of forms, which we find in Grecian Art. It requires a certain degree of enthusiasm--nay, a slight inebriation of the imaginative faculties--in order to feel the sentiment of this Oriental Architecture. If I rightly express all that it says to me, I touch the verge of rapsody. The East, in almost all its aspects, is so essentially poetic, that a true picture of it must be poetic in spirit, if not in form.

Constantinople has been terribly ravaged by fires, no less than fifteen having occurred during the past two weeks. Almost every night the sky has been reddened by burning houses, and the minarets of the seven hills lighted with an illumination brighter than that of the Bairam. All the space from the Hippodrome to the Sea of Marmora has been swept away; the lard, honey, and oil magazines on the Golden Horn, with the bazaars adjoining; several large blocks on the hill of Galata, with the College of the Dancing Dervishes; a part of Scutari, and the College of the Howling Dervishes, all have disappeared; and to-day, the ruins of 3,700 houses, which were destroyed last night, stand smoking in the Greek quarter, behind the aqueduct of Valens. The entire amount of buildings consumed in these two weeks is estimated at between five and six thousand! The fire on the hill of Galata threatened to destroy a great part of the suburb of Pera. It came, sweeping over the brow of the hill, towards my hotel, turning the tall cypresses in the burial ground into shafts of angry flame, and eating away the crackling dwellings of hordes of hapless Turks. I was in bed; from a sudden attack of fever, but seeing the other guests packing up their effects and preparing to leave, I was obliged to do the same; and this, in my weak state, brought on such a perspiration that the ailment left me, The officers of the United States steamer San Jacinto, and the French frigate Charlemagne, came to the rescue with their men and fire-engines, and the flames were finally quelled. The proceedings of the Americans, who cut holes in the roofs and played through them upon the fires within, were watched by the Turks with stupid amazement. "Máshallah!" said a fat Bimbashi, as he stood sweltering in the heat; "The Franks are a wonderful people."

To those initiated into the mysteries of Turkish politics, these fires are more than accidental; they have a most weighty significance. They indicate either a general discontent with the existing state of affairs, or else a powerful plot against the Sultan and his Ministry. Setting fire to houses is, in fact, the Turkish method of holding an "indignation meeting," and from the rate with which they are increasing, the political crisis must be near at hand. The Sultan, with his usual kindness of heart, has sent large quantities of tents and other supplies to the guiltless sufferers; but no amount of kindness can soften the rancor of these Turkish intrigues. Reschid Pasha, the present Grand Vizier, and the leader of the party of Progress, is the person against whom this storm of opposition is now gathering.

In spite of all efforts, the Ottoman Power is rapidly wasting away. The life of the Orient is nerveless and effete; the native strength of the race has died out, and all attempts to resuscitate it by the adoption of European institutions produce mere galvanic spasms, which leave it more exhausted than before. The rosy-colored accounts we have had of Turkish Progress are for the most part mere delusions. The Sultan is a well-meaning but weak man, and tyrannical through his very weakness. Had he strength enough to break through the meshes of falsehood and venality which are woven so close about him, he might accomplish some solid good. But Turkish rule, from his ministers down to the lowest cadi, is a monstrous system of deceit and corruption. These people have not the most remote conception of the true aims of government; they only seek to enrich themselves and their parasites, at the expense of the people and the national treasury. When we add to this the conscript system, which is draining the provinces of their best Moslem subjects, to the advantage of the Christians and Jews, and the blindness of the Revenue Laws, which impose on domestic manufactures double the duty levied on foreign products, it will easily be foreseen that the next half-century, or less, will completely drain the Turkish Empire of its last lingering energies.

Already, in effect, Turkey exists only through the jealousy of the European nations. The treaty of Unkiar-iskelessi, in 1833, threw her into the hands of Russia, although the influence of England has of late years reigned almost exclusively in her councils. These are the two powers who are lowering at each other with sleepless eyes, in the Dardanelles and the Bosphorus. The people, and most probably the government, is strongly preposessed in favor of the English; but the Russian Bear has a heavy paw, and when he puts it into the scale, all other weights kick the beam. It will be a long and wary struggle, and no man can prophecy the result. The Turks are a people easy to govern, were even the imperfect laws, now in existence, fairly administered. They would thrive and improve under a better state of things; but I cannot avoid the conviction that the regeneration of the East will never be effected at their hands.

Chapter XXIX. Farewell to the Orient--Malta.

Embarcation--Farewell to the Orient--Leaving Constantinople--A Wreck--The Dardanelles--Homeric Scenery--Smyrna Revisited--The Grecian Isles--Voyage to Malta--Detention--La Valetta--The Maltese--The Climate--A Boat for Sicily.

"Farewell, ye mountains,

By glory crowned

Ye sacred fountains

Of Gods renowned;

Ye woods and highlands,

Where heroes dwell;

Ye seas and islands,

Farewell! Farewell!"

Frithiof's Saga.

In The Dardanelles, *Saturday, August* 7, 1852.

At last, behold me fairly embarked for Christian Europe, to which I bade adieu in October last, eager for the unknown wonders of the Orient. Since then, nearly ten months have passed away, and those wonders are now familiar as every-day experiences. I set out, determined to be satisfied with no slight taste of Eastern life, but to drain to the bottom its beaker of mingled sunshine and sleep. All this has been accomplished; and if I have not wandered so far, nor enriched myself with such varied knowledge of the relics of ancient history, as I might have purposed or wished, I have at least learned to know the Turk and the Arab, been soothed by the patience inspired by their fatalism, and warmed by the gorgeous gleams of fancy that animate their poetry and religion. These ten months of my life form an episode which seems to belong to a separate existence. Just refined enough to be poetic, and just barbaric enough to be freed from all conventional fetters, it is as grateful to brain and soul, as an Eastern bath to the body. While I look forward, not without pleasure, to the luxuries and conveniences of Europe, I relinquish with a sigh the refreshing indolence of Asia.

We have passed between the Castles of the two Continents, guarding the mouth of the Dardanelles, and are now entering the Grecian Sea. To-morrow, we shall touch, for a few hours, at Smyrna, and then turn westward, on the track of Ulysses and St. Paul. Farewell, then, perhaps forever, to the bright Orient! Farewell to the gay gardens, the spicy bazaars, to the plash of fountains and the gleam of golden-tipped minarets! Farewell to the perfect morn's, the balmy twilights, the still heat of the blue noons, the splendor of moon and stars! Farewell to the glare of the white crags, the tawny wastes of dead sand, the valleys of oleander, the hills of myrtle and spices! Farewell to the bath, agent of purity and peace, and parent of delicious dreams--to the shebook, whose fragrant fumes are breathed from the lips of patience and contentment--to the narghileh, crowned with that blessed plant which grows in the gardens of Shiraz, while a fountain more delightful than those of Samarcand bubbles in its crystal bosom I Farewell to the red cap and slippers, to the big turban, the flowing trousers, and the gaudy shawl--to squatting on broad divans, to sipping black coffee in acorn cups, to grave faces and salaam aleikooms, and to aching of the lips and forehead! Farewell to the evening meal in the tent door, to the couch on the friendly earth, to the yells of the muleteers, to the deliberate marches of the plodding horse, and the endless rocking of the dromedary that knoweth his master! Farewell, finally, to annoyance without anger, delay without vexation, indolence without ennui, endurance without fatigue, appetite without intemperance, enjoyment without pall!

La Valetta, Malta, Saturday, August 14, 1852.

My last view of Stamboul was that of the mosques of St. Sophia and Sultan Achmed, shining faintly in the moonlight, as we steamed down the Sea of Marmora. The Caire left at nine o'clock, freighted with the news of Reschid Pasha's deposition, and there were no signs of conflagration in all the long miles of the city that lay behind us. So we speculated no more on the exciting topics of the day, but went below and took a vapor bath in our berths; for I need not assure you that the nights on the Mediterranean at this season are anything but chilly. And here I must note the fact, that the French steamers, while dearer than the Austrian, are more cramped in their accommodations, and filled with a set of most uncivil servants. The table is good, and this is the only thing to be commended. In all other respects, I prefer the Lloyd vessels.

Early next morning, we passed the promontory of Cyzicus, and the Island of Marmora, the marble quarries of which give name to the sea. As we were approaching the entrance to the Dardanelles, we noticed an Austrian brig drifting in the current, the whiff of her flag indicating distress. Her rudder was entirely gone, and she was floating helplessly towards the Thracian coast. A boat was immediately lowered and a hawser carried to her bows, by which we towed her a short distance; but our steam engine did not like this drudgery, and snapped the rope repeatedly, so that at last we were obliged to leave her to her fate. The lift we gave, however, had its effect, and by dexterous maneuvering with the sails, the captain brought her safely into the harbor of Gallipoli, where she dropped anchor beside us.

Beyond Gallipoli, the Dardanelles contract, and the opposing continents rise into lofty and barren hills. In point of natural beauty, this strait is greatly inferior to the Bosphorus. It lacks the streams and wooded valleys which open upon the latter. The country is but partially cultivated, except around the town of Dardanelles, near the mouth of the strait. The site of the bridge of Xerxes is easily recognized, the conformation of the different shores seconding the decision of antiquarians. Here, too, are Sestos and Abydos, of passionate and poetic memory. But as the sun dipped towards the sea, we passed out of the narrow gateway. On our left lay the plain of Troy, backed by the blue range of Mount Ida. The tamulus of Patroclus crowned a low bluff looking on the sea. On the right appeared the long, irregular island of Imbros, and the peaks of misty Samothrace over and beyond it. Tenedos was before us. The red flush of sunset tinged the grand Homeric landscape, and lingered and lingered on the summit of Ida, as if loth to depart. I paced the deck until long after it was too dark to distinguish it any more.

The next morning we dropped anchor in the harbor of Smyrna, where we remained five hours. I engaged a donkey, and rode out to the Caravan Bridge, where the Greek driver and I smoked narghilehs and drank coffee in the shade of the acacias. I contrasted my impressions with those of my first visit to Smyrna last October--my first glimpse of Oriental ground. Then, every dog barked at me, and all the horde of human creatures who prey upon innocent travellers ran at my heels, but now, with my brown face and Turkish aspect of grave indifference, I was suffered to pass as quietly as my donkey-driver himself. Nor did the latter, nor the ready cafidji, who filled our pipes on the banks of the Meles, attempt to overcharge me--a sure sign that the Orient had left its seal on my face. Returning through the city, the same mishap befel me which travellers usually experience on their first arrival. My donkey, while dashing at full speed through a crowd of Smyrniotes in their Sunday dresses, slipped up in a little pool of black mud, and came down with a crash. I flew over his head and alighted firmly on my feet, but the spruce young Greeks, whose snowy fustanelles were terribly bespattered, came off much worse. The donkey shied back, levelled his ears and twisted his head on one side, awaiting a beating, but his bleeding legs saved him.

We left at two o'clock, touched at Scio in the evening, and the next morning at sunrise lay-to in the harbor of Syra. The Piræus was only twelve hours distant; but after my visitation of fever in Constantinople, I feared to encounter the pestilential summer heats of Athens. Besides, I had reasons for hastening with all speed to Italy and Germany. At ten o'clock we weighed anchor again and steered southwards, between the groups of the Cyclades, under a cloudless sky and over a sea of the brightest blue. The days were endurable under the canvas awning of our quarter-deck, but the nights in our berths were sweat-baths, which left us so limp and exhausted that we were almost fit to vanish, like ghosts, at daybreak.

Our last glimpse of the Morea--Cape Matapan--faded away in the moonlight, and for two days we travelled westward over the burning sea. On the evening of the 11th, the long, low outline of Malta rose gradually against the last flush of sunset, and in two hours thereafter, we came to anchor in Quarantine Harbor. The quarantine for travellers returning from the East, which formerly varied from fourteen to twenty-one days, is now reduced to one day for those arriving from Greece or Turkey, and three days for those from Egypt and Syria. In our case, it was reduced to sixteen hours, by an official courtesy. I had intended proceeding directly to Naples; but by the contemptible trickery of the agents of the French steamers--a long history, which it is unnecessary to recapitulate--am left here to wait ten days for another steamer. It is enough to say that there are six other travellers at the same hotel, some coming from Constantinople, and some from Alexandria, in the same predicament. Because a single ticket to Naples costs some thirty or forty francs less than by dividing the trip into two parts, the agents in those cities refuse to give tickets further than Malta to those who are not keen enough to see through the deception. I made every effort to obtain a second ticket in time to leave by the branch steamer for Italy, but in vain.

La Valetta is, to my eyes, the most beautiful small city in the world. It is a jewel of a place; not a street but is full of picturesque effects, and all the look-outs, which you catch at every turn, let your eyes rest either upon one of the beautiful harbors on each side, or the distant horizon of the sea. The streets are so clean that you might eat your dinner off the pavement; the white balconies and cornices of the houses, all cleanly cut in the soft Maltese stone, stand out in intense relief against the sky, and from the manifold reflections and counter reflections, the shadows (where there are any) become a sort of milder light. The steep sides of the promontory, on which the city is built, are turned into staircases, and it is an inexhaustible pastime to watch the groups, composed of all nations who inhabit the shores of the Mediterranean, ascending and descending. The Auberges of the old Knights, the Palace of the Grand Master, the Church of St. John, and other relics of past time, but more especially the fortifications, invest the place with a romantic interest, and I suspect that, after Venice and Granada, there are few cities where the Middle Ages have left more impressive traces of their history.

The Maltese are contented, and appear to thrive under the English administration. They are a peculiar people, reminding me of the Arab even more than the Italian, while a certain rudeness in their build and motions suggests their Punic ancestry. Their language is a curious compound of Arabic and Italian, the former being the basis. I find that I can understand more than half that is said, the Arabic terminations being applied to Italian words. I believe it has never been successfully reduced to writing, and the restoration of pure Arabic has been proposed, with much reason, as preferable to an attempt to improve or refine it. Italian is the language used in the courts of justice and polite society, and is spoken here with much more purity than either in Naples or Sicily.

The heat has been so great since I landed that I have not ventured outside of the city, except last evening to an amateur theatre, got up by the non-commissioned officers and privates in the garrison. The performances were quite tolerable, except a love-sick young damsel who spoke with a rough masculine voice, and made long strides across the stage when she rushed into her lover's arms. I am at a loss to account for the exhausting character of the heat. The thermometer shows 90° by day, and 80° to 85° by night--a much lower temperature than I have found quite comfortable in Africa and Syria. In the Desert 100° in the shade is rather bracing than otherwise; here, 90° renders all exercise, more severe than smoking a pipe, impossible. Even in a state of complete inertia, a shirt-collar will fall starchless in five minutes.

Rather than waste eight more days in this glimmering half-existence, I have taken passage in a Maltese speronara, which sails this evening for Catania, in Sicily, where the grand festival of St. Agatha, which takes place once in a hundred years, will be celebrated next week. The trip promises a new experience, and I shall get a taste, slight though it be, of the golden Trinacria of the ancients. Perhaps, after all, this delay which so vexes me (bear in mind, I am no longer in the Orient!) may be meant solely for my good. At least, Mr. Winthrop, our Consul here, who has been exceedingly kind and courteous to me, thinks it a rare good fortune that I shall see the Catanian festa.

Chapter XXX. The Festival of St. Agatha.

Departure from Malta--The Speronara--Our Fellow-Passengers--The First Night on Board--Sicily--Scarcity of Provisions--Beating in the Calabrian Channel--The Fourth Morning--The Gulf of Catania--A Sicilian Landscape--The Anchorage--The Suspected List--The Streets of Catania--Biography of St. Agatha--The Illuminations--The Procession of the Veil--The Biscari Palace--The Antiquities of Catania--The Convent of St. Nicola.

"The morn is full of holiday, loud bells

With rival clamors ring from every spire;

Cunningly-stationed music dies and swells

In echoing places; when the winds respire,

Light flags stream out like gauzy tongues of fire."--Keats.

Catania, Sicily, *Friday, August* 20, 1852.

I went on board the speronara in the harbor of La Valetta at the appointed hour (5 P.M.), and found the remaining sixteen passengers already embarked. The captain made his appearance an hour later, with our bill of health and passports, and as the sun went down behind the brown hills of the island, we passed the wave-worn rocks of the promontory, dividing the two harbors, and slowly moved off towards Sicily.

The Maltese speronara resembles the ancient Roman galley more than any modern craft. It has the same high, curved poop and stern, the same short masts and broad, square sails. The hull is too broad for speed, but this adds to the security of the vessel in a gale. With a fair wind, it rarely makes more than eight knots an hour, and in a calm, the sailors (if not too lazy) propel it forward with six long oars. The hull is painted in a fanciful style, generally blue, red, green and white, with bright red masts. The bulwarks are low, and the deck of such a convexity that it is quite impossible to walk it in a heavy sea. Such was the vessel to which I found myself consigned. It was not more than fifty feet long, and of less capacity than a Nile dahabiyeh. There was a sort of deck cabin, or crib, with two berths, but most of the passengers slept in the hold. For a passage to Catania I was obliged to pay forty francs, the owner swearing that this was the regular price; but, as I afterwards discovered, the Maltese only paid thirty-six francs for the whole trip. However, the Captain tried to make up the money's worth in civilities, and was incessant in his attentions to "your Lordships," as he styled myself and my companion, Cæsar di Cagnola, a young Milanese.

The Maltese were tailors and clerks, who were taking a holiday trip to witness the great festival of St. Agatha. With two exceptions, they were a wild and senseless, though good-natured set, and in spite of sea-sickness, which exercised them terribly for the first two days, kept up a constant jabber in their bastard Arabic from morning till night. As is usual in such a company, one of them was obliged to serve as a butt for the rest, and "Maestro Paolo," as they termed him, wore such a profoundly serious face all the while, from his sea-sickness, that the fun never came to an end. As they were going to a religious festival, some of them had brought their breviaries along with them; but I am obliged to testify that, after the first day, prayers were totally forgotten. The sailors, however, wore linen bags, printed with a figure of the Madonna, around their necks.

The sea was rather rough, but Cæsar and I fortified our stomachs with a bottle of English ale, and as it was dark by this time, sought our resting-places for the night. As we had paid double, places were assured us in the coop on deck, but beds were not included in the bargain. The Maltese, who had brought mattresses and spread a large Phalansteriau bed in the hold, fared much better. I took one of my carpet bags for a pillow and lay down on the planks, where I succeeded in getting a little sleep between the groans of the helpless land-lubbers. We had the ponente, or west-wind, all night, but the speronara moved sluggishly, and in the morning it changed to the greco-levante, or north-east. No land was in sight; but towards noon, the sky became clearer, and we saw the southern coast of Sicily--a bold mountain-shore, looming phantom-like in the distance. Cape Passaro was to the east, and the rest of the day was spent in beating up to it. At sunset, we were near

652

enough to see the villages and olive-groves of the beautiful shore, and, far behind the nearer mountains, ninety miles distant, the solitary cone of Etna.

The second night passed like the first, except that our bruised limbs were rather more sensitive to the texture of the planks. We crawled out of our coop at dawn, expecting to behold Catania in the distance; but there was Cape Passaro still staring us in the face. The Maltese were patient, and we did not complain, though Cæsar and I began to make nice calculations as to the probable duration of our two cold fowls and three loaves of bread. The promontory of Syracuse was barely visible forty miles ahead; but the wind was against us, and so another day passed in beating up the eastern coast. At dusk, we overtook another speronara which had left Malta two hours before us, and this was quite a triumph to our captain, All the oars were shipped, the sailors and some of the more courageous passengers took hold, and we shot ahead, scudding rapidly along the dark shores, to the sound of the wild Maltese songs. At length, the promontory was gained, and the restless current, rolling down from Scylla and Charybdis, tossed our little bark from wave to wave with a recklessness that would have made any one nervous but an old sailor like myself.

"To-morrow morning," said the Captain, "we shall sail into Catania;" but after a third night on the planks, which were now a little softer, we rose to find ourselves abreast of Syracuse, with Etna as distant as ever. The wind was light, and what little we made by tacking was swept away by the current, so that, after wasting the whole forenoon, we kept a straight course across the mouth of the channel, and at sunset saw the Calabrian Mountains. This move only lost us more ground, as it happened. Cæsar and I mournfully and silently consumed our last fragment of beef, with the remaining dry crusts of bread, and then sat down doggedly to smoke and see whether the captain would discover our situation. But no; while we were supplied, the whole vessel was at our Lordships' command, and now that we were destitute, he took care to make no rash offers. Cæsar, at last, with an imperial dignity becoming his name, commanded dinner. It came, and the pork and maccaroni, moistened with red Sicilian wine, gave us patience for another day.

The fourth morning dawned, and--Great Neptune be praised!--we were actually within the Gulf of Catania. Etna loomed up in all his sublime bulk, unobscured by cloud or mist, while a slender jet of smoke, rising from his crater, was slowly curling its wreaths in the clear air, as if happy to receive the first beam of the sun. The towers of Syracuse, which had mocked us all the preceding day, were no longer visible; the land-locked little port of Augusta lay behind us; and, as the wind continued favorable, ere long we saw a faint white mark at the foot of the mountain. This was Catania. The shores of the bay were enlivened with olive-groves and the gleam of the villages, while here and there a single palm dreamed of its brothers across the sea. Etna, of course, had the monarch's place in the landscape, but even his large, magnificent outlines could not usurp all my feeling. The purple peaks to the westward and farther inland, had a beauty of their own, and in the gentle curves with which they leaned towards each other, there was a promise of the flowery meadows of Enna. The smooth blue water was speckled with fishing-boats. We hailed one, inquiring when the festa was to commence; but, mistaking our question, they answered: "Anchovies." Thereupon, a waggish Maltese informed them that Maestro Paolo thanked them heartily. All the other boats were hailed in the name of Maestro Paolo, who, having recovered from his sea-sickness, took his bantering good-humoredly.

Catania presented a lovely picture, as we drew near the harbor. Planted at the very foot of Etna, it has a background such as neither Naples nor Genoa can boast. The hills next the sea are covered with gardens and orchards, sprinkled with little villages and the country palaces of the nobles--a rich, cultured landscape, which gradually merges into the forests of oak and chestnut that girdle the waist of the great volcano. But all the wealth of southern vegetation cannot hide the footsteps of that Ruin, which from time to time visits the soil. Half-way up, the mountain-side is dotted with cones of ashes and cinders, some covered with the scanty shrubbery which centuries have called forth, some barren and recent; while two dark, winding streams of sterile lava descend to the very shore, where they stand congealed in ragged needles and pyramids. Part of one of these black floods has swept the town, and, tumbling into the sea, walls one side of the port.

We glided slowly past the mole, and dropped anchor a few yards from the shore. There was a sort of open promenade planted with trees, in front of us, surrounded with high white houses, above which rose the dome of the Cathedral and the spires of other churches. The magnificent palace of Prince Biscari was on our right, and at its foot the Customs and Revenue offices. Every roof, portico, and window was lined with lamps, a triumphal arch spanned the street before the palace, and the landing-place at the offices was festooned with crimson and white drapery, spangled with gold. While we were waiting permission to land, a scene presented itself which recalled the pagan days of Sicily to my mind. A procession came in sight from under the trees, and passed along the shore. In the centre was borne a stately shrine, hung with garlands, and containing an image of St. Agatha. The sound of flutes and cymbals accompanied it, and a band of children, bearing orange and palm branches, danced riotously before. Had the image been Pan instead of St. Agatha, the ceremonies would have been quite as appropriate.

The speronara's boat at last took us to the gorgeous landing place, where we were carefully counted by a fat Sicilian official, and declared free from quarantine. We were then called into the Passport Office where the Maltese underwent a searching examination. One of the officers sat with the Black Book, or list of suspected persons of all nations, open before him, and looked for each name as it was called out. Another scanned the faces of the frightened tailors, as if comparing them with certain revolutionary visages in his mind. Terrible was the keen, detective glance of his eye, and it went straight through the poor Maltese, who vanished with great rapidity when they were declared free to enter the city. At last, they all passed the ordeal, but Cæsar and I remained, looking in at the door. "There are still these two Frenchmen," said the captain. "I am no Frenchman," I protested; "I am an American." "And I," said Cæsar, "am an Austrian subject." Thereupon we received a polite invitation to enter; the terrible glance softened into a benign, respectful smile; he of the Black Book ran lightly over the C's and T's, and said, with a courteous inclination: "There is nothing against the signori." I felt quite relieved by this; for, in the Mediterranean, one is never safe from spies, and no person is too insignificant to escape the ban, if once suspected.

Calabria was filled to overflowing with strangers from all parts of the Two

Sicilies, and we had some difficulty in finding very bad and dear lodgings. It was the first day of the festa, and the streets were filled with peasants, the men in black velvet jackets and breeches, with stockings, and long white cotton caps hanging on the shoulders, and the women with gay silk shawls on their heads, after the manner of the Mexican reboza. In all the public squares, the market scene in Masaniello was acted to the life. The Sicilian dialect is harsh and barbarous, and the original Italian is so disguised by the admixture of Arabic, Spanish, French, and Greek words, that even my imperial friend, who was a born Italian, had great difficulty in understanding the people.

I purchased a guide to the festa, which, among other things, contained a biography of St. Agatha. It is a beautiful specimen of pious writing, and I regret that I have not space to translate the whole of it. Agatha was a beautiful Catanian virgin, who secretly embraced Christianity during the reign of Nero. Catania was then governed by a prætor named Quintianus, who, becoming enamored of Agatha, used the most brutal means to compel her to submit to his desires, but without effect. At last, driven to the cruelest extremes, he cut off her breasts, and threw her into prison. But at midnight, St. Peter, accompanied by an angel, appeared to her, restored the maimed parts, and left her more beautiful than ever. Quintianus then ordered a furnace to be heated, and cast her therein. A terrible earthquake shook the city; the sun was eclipsed; the sea rolled backwards, and left its bottom dry; the prætor's palace fell in ruins, and he, pursued by the vengeance of the populace, fled till he reached the river Simeto, where he was drowned in attempting to cross. "The thunders of the vengeance of God," says the biography, "struck him down into the profoundest Hell." This was in the year 252.

The body was carried to Constantinople in 1040, "although the Catanians wept incessantly at their loss;" but in 1126, two French knights, named Gilisbert and Goselin, were moved by angelic influences to restore it to its native town, which they accomplished, "and the eyes of the Catanians again burned with joy." The miracles effected by the saint are numberless, and her power is especially efficacious in preventing earthquakes and eruptions of Mount Etna. Nevertheless, Catania has suffered more from these causes than any other town in Sicily. But I would that all saints had as good a claim to canonization as St. Agatha. The honors of such a festival as this are not out of place, when paid to such youth, beauty, and "heavenly chastity," as she typifies.

The guide, which I have already consulted, gives a full account of the festa, in advance, with a description of Catania. The author says: "If thy heart is not inspired by gazing on this lovely city, it is a fatal sign--thou wert not born to feel the sweet impulses of the Beautiful!" Then, in announcing the illuminations and pyrotechnic displays, he exclaims: "Oh, the amazing spectacle! Oh, how happy art thou, that thou beholdest it! I What pyramids of lamps! What myriads of rockets! What wonderful temples of flame! The Mountain himself is astonished at such a display." And truly, except the illumination of the Golden Horn on the Night of Predestination, I have seen nothing equal to the spectacle presented by Catania, during the past three nights. The city, which has been built up from her ruins more stately than ever, was in a blaze of light--all her domes, towers, and the long lines of her beautiful palaces revealed in the varying red and golden flames of a hundred thousand lamps and torches. Pyramids of fire, transparencies, and illuminated triumphal arches filled the four principal streets, and the fountain in the Cathedral square gleamed like a jet of molten silver, spinning up from one of the pores of Etna. At ten o'clock, a gorgeous display of fireworks closed the day's festivities, but the lamps remained burning nearly all night.

On the second night, the grand Procession of the Veil took place. I witnessed this imposing spectacle from the balcony of Prince Gessina's palace. Long lines of waxen torches led the way, followed by a military band, and then a company of the highest prelates, in their most brilliant costumes, surrounding the Bishop, who walked under a canopy of silk and gold, bearing the miraculous veil of St. Agatha. I was blessed with a distant view of it, but could see no traces of the rosy hue left upon it by the flames of the Saint's martyrdom. Behind the priests came the Intendente of Sicily, Gen. Filangieri, the same who, three years ago, gave up Catania to sack and slaughter. He was followed by the Senate of the City, who have just had the cringing cowardice to offer him a ball on next Sunday night. If ever a man deserved the vengeance of an outraged people, it is this Filangieri, who was first a Liberal, when the cause promised success, and then made himself the scourge of the vilest of kings. As he passed me last night in his carriage of State, while the music pealed in rich rejoicing strains, that solemn chant with which the monks break upon the revellers, in "Lucrezia Borgia," came into my mind:

"La gioja del profani

'E un fumo passagier'--"

[the rejoicing of the profane is a transitory mist.] I heard, under the din of all these festivities, the voice of that Retribution which even now lies in wait, and will not long be delayed.

To-night Signor Scavo, the American Vice-Consul, took me to the palace of Prince Biscari, overlooking the harbor, in order to behold the grand display of fireworks from the end of the mole. The showers of rockets and colored stars, and the temples of blue and silver fire, were repeated in the dark, quiet bosom of the sea, producing the most dazzling and startling effects. There was a large number of the Catanese nobility present, and among them a Marchesa Gioveni, the descendant of the bloody house of Anjou. Prince Biscari is a benign, courtly old man, and greatly esteemed here. His son is at present in exile, on account of the part he took in the late revolution. During the sack of the city under Filangieri, the palace was plundered of property to the amount of ten thousand dollars. The museum of Greek and Roman antiquities attached to it, and which the house of Biscari has been collecting for many years, is probably the finest in Sicily. The state apartments were thrown open this evening, and when I left, an hour ago, the greater portion of the guests were going through mazy quadrilles on the mosaic pavements.

Among the antiquities of Catania which I have visited, are the Amphitheatre, capable of holding 15,000 persons, the old Greek Theatre, the same in which Alcibiades made his noted harangue to the Catanians, the Odeon, and the ancient Baths. The theatre, which is in tolerable preservation, is built of lava, like many of the modern edifices in the city. The Baths proved to me, what I had supposed, that the Oriental Bath of the present day is identical with that of the Ancients. Why so admirable an institution has never been introduced into Europe (except in the Bains Chinois of Paris) is more than I can tell. From the pavement of these baths, which is nearly twenty feet below the surface of the earth, the lava of later eruptions has burst up, in places, in hard black jets. The most wonderful token of that flood which whelmed Catania two hundred years ago, is to be seen at the Grand Benedictine Convent of San Nicola, in the upper part of the city. Here the stream of lava divides itself just before the Convent, and flows past on both sides, leaving the building and gardens untouched. The marble courts, the fountains, the splendid galleries, and the gardens of richest southern bloom and fragrance, stand like an epicurean island in the midst of the terrible stony waves, whose edges bristle with the thorny aloe and cactus. The monks of San Nicola are all chosen from the Sicilian nobility, and live a comfortable life of luxury and vice. Each one has his own carriage, horses, and servants, and each his private chambers outside of the convent walls and his kept concubines. These facts are known and acknowledged by the Catanians, to whom they are a lasting scandal.

It is past midnight, and I must close. Cæsar started this afternoon, alone, for the ascent of Etna. I would have accompanied him, but my only chance of reaching Messina in time for the next steamer to Naples is the diligence which leaves here to-morrow. The mountain has been covered with clouds for the last two days, and I have had no view at all comparable to that of the morning of my arrival. To-morrow the grand procession of the Body of St. Agatha takes place, but I am quite satisfied with three days of processions and horse races, and three nights of illuminations.

I leave in the morning, with a Sicilian passport, my own availing me nothing, after landing.

Chapter XXXI. The Eruption of Mount Etna.

The Mountain Threatens--The Signs Increase--We Leave Catania--Gardens Among the Lava--Etna Labors--Aci Reale--The Groans of Etna--The Eruption--Gigantic Tree of Smoke--Formation of the New Crater--We Lose Sight of the Mountain--Arrival at Messina--Etna is Obscured--Departure.

-------"the shattered side

Of thundering Ætna, whose combustible

And fuel'd entrails thence conceiving fire,

Sublimed with mineral fury, aid the winds,

And leave a singed bottom." Milton.

Messina, Sicily, *Monday, August* 23, 1852.

The noises of the festival had not ceased when I closed my letter at midnight, on Friday last. I slept soundly through the night, but was awakened before sunrise by my Sicilian landlord. "O, Excellenza! have you heard the Mountain? He is going to break out again; may the holy Santa Agatha protect us!" It is rather ill-timed on the part of the Mountain, was my involuntary first thought, that he should choose for a new eruption precisely the centennial festival of the only Saint who is supposed to have any power over him. It shows a disregard of female influence not at all suited to the present day, and I scarcely believe that he seriously means it. Next came along the jabbering landlady: "I don't like his looks. It was just so the last time. Come, Excellenza, you can see him from the back terrace." The sun was not yet risen, but the east was bright with his coming, and there was not a cloud in the sky. All the features of Etna were sharply sculptured in the clear air. From the topmost cone, a thick stream of white smoke was slowly puffed out at short intervals, and rolled lazily down the eastern side. It had a heavy, languid character, and I should have thought nothing of the appearance but for the alarm of my hosts. It was like the slow fire of Earth's incense, burning on that grand mountain altar.

I hurried off to the Post Office, to await the arrival of the diligence from Palermo. The office is in the Strada Etnea, the main street of Catania, which runs straight through the city, from the sea to the base of the mountain, whose peak closes the long vista. The diligence was an hour later than usual, and I passed the time in watching the smoke which continued to increase in volume, and was mingled, from time to time, with jets of inky blackness. The postilion said he had seen fires and heard loud noises during the night. According to his account, the disturbances commenced about midnight. I could not but envy my friend Cæsar, who was probably at that moment on the summit, looking down into the seething fires of the crater.

At last, we rolled out of Catania. There were in the diligence, besides myself, two men and a woman, Sicilians of the secondary class. The road followed the shore, over rugged tracts of lava, the different epochs of which could be distinctly traced in the character of the vegetation. The last great flow (of 1679) stood piled in long ridges of terrible sterility, barely allowing the aloe and cactus to take root in the hollows between. The older deposits were sufficiently decomposed to nourish the olive and vine; but even here, the orchards were studded with pyramids of the harder fragments, which are laboriously collected by the husbandmen. In the few favored spots which have been untouched for so many ages that a tolerable depth of soil has accumulated, the vegetation has all the richness and brilliancy of tropical lands. The palm, orange, and pomegranate thrive luxuriantly, and the vines almost break under their heavy clusters. The villages are frequent and well built, and the hills are studded, far and near, with the villas of rich proprietors, mostly buildings of one story, with verandahs extending their whole length. Looking up towards Etna, whose base the road encircles, the views are gloriously rich and beautiful. On the other hand is the blue Mediterranean and the irregular outline of the shore, here and there sending forth promontories of lava, cooled by the waves into the most fantastic forms.

We had sot proceeded far before a new sign called my attention to the mountain. Not only was there a perceptible jar or vibration in the earth, but a dull, groaning sound, like the muttering of distant thunder, began to be heard. The smoke increased in volume, and, as we advanced further to the eastward, and much nearer to the great cone, I perceived that it consisted of two jets, issuing from different mouths. A broad stream of very dense white smoke still flowed over the lip of the topmost crater and down the eastern side. As its breadth did not vary, and the edges were distinctly defined, it was no doubt the sulphureous vapor rising from a river of molten lava. Perhaps a thousand yards below, a much stronger column of mingled black and white smoke gushed up, in regular beats or pants, from a depression in the mountain side, between two small, extinct cones. All this part of Etna was scarred with deep chasms, and in the bottoms of those nearest the opening, I could see the red gleam of fire. The air was perfectly still, and as yet there was no cloud in the sky.

When we stopped to change horses at the town of Aci Reale, I first felt the violence of the tremor and the awful sternness of the sound. The smoke by this time seemed to be gathering on the side towards Catania, and hung in a dark mass about half-way down the mountain. Groups of the villagers were gathered in the streets which looked upwards to Etna, and discussing the chances of an eruption. "Ah," said an old peasant, "the Mountain knows how to make himself respected. When he talks, everybody listens." The sound was the most awful that ever met my ears. It was a hard, painful moan, now and then fluttering like a suppressed sob, and had, at the same time, an expression of threatening and of agony. It did not come from Etna alone. It had no fixed location; it pervaded all space. It was in the air, in the depths of the sea, in the earth under my feet--everywhere, in fact; and as it continued to increase in violence, I experienced a sensation of positive pain. The people looked anxious and alarmed, although they said it was a good thing for all Sicily; that last year they had been in constant fear from earthquakes, and that an eruption invariably left the island quiet for several years. It is true that, during the past year, parts of Sicily and Calabria have been visited with severe shocks, occasioning much damage to property. A merchant of this city informed me yesterday that his whole family had slept for two months in the vaults of his warehouse, fearing that their residence might be shaken down in the night.

As we rode along from Aci Reale to Taormina, all the rattling of the diligence over the rough road could not drown the awful noise. There was a strong smell of sulphur in the air, and the thick pants of smoke from the lower crater continued to increase in strength. The sun was fierce and hot, and the edges of the sulphureous clouds shone with a dazzling whiteness. A mounted soldier overtook us, and rode beside the diligence, talking with the postillion. He had been up to the mountain, and was taking his report to the Governor of the district. The heat of the day and the continued tremor of the air lulled me into a sort of doze, when I was suddenly aroused by a cry from the soldier and the stopping of the diligence. At the same time, there was a terrific peal of sound, followed by a jar which must have shaken the whole island. We looked up to Etna, which was fortunately in full view before us. An immense mass of snow-white smoke had burst up from the crater and was rising perpendicularly into the air, its rounded volumes rapidly whirling one over the other, yet urged with such impetus that they only rolled outwards after they had ascended to an immense height. It might have been one minute or five--for I was so entranced by this wonderful spectacle that I lost the sense of time--but it seemed instantaneous (so rapid and violent were the effects of the explosion), when there stood in the air, based on the summit of the mountain, a mass of smoke four or five miles high, and shaped precisely like the Italian pine tree.

Words cannot paint the grandeur of this mighty tree. Its trunk of columned smoke, one side of which was silvered by the sun, while the other, in shadow, was lurid with red flame, rose for more than a mile before it sent out its cloudy boughs. Then parting into a thousand streams, each of which again threw out its branching tufts of smoke, rolling and waving in the air, it stood in intense relief against the dark blue of the sky. Its rounded masses of foliage were dazzlingly white on one side, while, in the shadowy depths of the branches, there was a constant play of brown, yellow, and crimson tints, revealing the central shaft of fire. It was like the tree celebrated in the Scandinavian sagas, as seen by the mother of Harold Hardrada--that tree, whose roots pierced through the earth, whose trunk was of the color of blood, and whose branches filled the uttermost corners of the heavens.

This outburst seemed to have relieved the mountain, for the tremors were now less violent, though the terrible noise still droned in the air, and earth, and sea. And now, from the base of the tree, three white streams slowly crept into as many separate chasms, against the walls of which played the flickering glow of the burning lava. The column of smoke and flame was still hurled upwards, and the tree, after standing about ten minutes--a new and awful revelation of the active forces of Nature--gradually rose and spread, lost its form, and, slowly moved by a light wind (the first that disturbed the dead calm of the day), bent over to the eastward. We resumed our course. The vast belt of smoke at last arched over the strait, here about twenty miles wide, and sank towards the distant Calabrian shore. As we drove under it, for some miles of our way, the sun was totally obscured, and the sky presented the singular spectacle of two hemispheres of clear blue, with a broad belt of darkness drawn between them. There was a hot, sulphureous vapor in the air, and showers of white ashes fell, from time to time. We were distant about twelve miles, in a straight line, from the crater; but the air was so clear, even under the shadow of the smoke, that I could distinctly trace the downward movement of the rivers of lava.

This was the eruption, at last, to which all the phenomena of the morning had been only preparatory. For the first time in ten years the depths of Etna had been stirred, and I thanked God for my detention at Malta, and the singular hazard of travel which had brought me here, to his very base, to witness a scene, the impression of which I shall never lose, to my dying day. Although the eruption may continue and the mountain pour forth fiercer fires and broader tides of lava, I cannot but think that the first upheaval, which lets out the long-imprisoned forces, will not be equalled in grandeur by any later spectacle. After passing Taormina, our road led us under the hills of the coast, and although I occasionally caught glimpses of Etna, and saw the reflection of fires from the lava which was filling up his savage ravines, the smoke at last encircled his waist, and he was then shut out of sight by the intervening mountains. We lost a bolt in a deep valley opening on the sea, and during our stoppage I could still hear the groans of the Mountain, though farther off and less painful to the ear. As evening came on, the beautiful hills of Calabria, with white towns and villages on their sides, gleamed in the purple light of the setting sun. We drove around headland after headland, till the strait opened, and we looked over the harbor of Messina to Capo Faro, and the distant islands of the Tyrrhene Sea.

I leave this afternoon for Naples and Leghorn. I have lost already so much time between Constantinople and this place, that I cannot give up ten days more to Etna. Besides, I am so thoroughly satisfied with what I have seen, that I fear no second view of the eruption could equal it. Etna cannot be seen from here, nor from a nearer point than a mountain six or eight miles distant. I tried last evening to get a horse and ride out to it, in order to see the appearance of the eruption by night; but every horse, mule and donkey in the place was engaged, except a miserable lame mule, for which five dollars was demanded. However, the night happened to be cloudy so that I could have seen nothing.

My passport is finally en règle. It has cost the labors of myself and an able-bodied valet-de-place since yesterday morning, and the expenditure of five dollars and a half, to accomplish this great work. I have just been righteously abusing the Neapolitan Government to a native merchant whom, from his name, I took to be a Frenchman, but as I am off in an hour or two, hope to escape arrest. Perdition to all Tyranny!

Chapter XXXII. Gibraltar.

Unwritten Links of Travel--Departure from Southampton--The Bay of Biscay--Cintra--Trafalgar--Gibraltar at Midnight--Landing--Search for a Palm-Tree--A Brilliant Morning--The Convexity of the Earth--Sun-Worship--The Rock.

------"to the north-west, Cape St. Vincent died away,

Sunset ran, a burning blood-red, blushing into Cadiz Bay.

In the dimmest north-east distance dawned Gibraltar, grand and gray."

Browning.

Gibraltar, *Saturday, November* 6, 1852.

I leave unrecorded the links of travel which connected Messina and Gibraltar. They were over the well-trodden fields of Europe, where little ground is left that is not familiar. In leaving Sicily I lost the Saracenic trail, which I had been following through the East, and first find it again here, on the rock of Calpe, whose name, Djebel el-Tarik (the Mountain of Tarik), still speaks of the fiery race whose rule extended from the unknown ocean of the West to "Ganges and Hydaspes, Indian streams." In Malta and Sicily, I saw their decaying watch-towers, and recognized their sign-manual in the deep, guttural, masculine words and expressions which they have left behind them. I now design following their footsteps through the beautiful Belàd-el-Andaluz, which, to the eye of the Melek Abd-er-rahmàn, was only less lovely than the plains of Damascus.

While in Constantinople, I received letters which opened to me wider and richer fields of travel than I had already traversed. I saw a possibility of exploring the far Indian realms, the shores of farthest Cathay and the famed Zipango of Marco Polo. Before entering on this new sphere of experiences, however, it was necessary for me to visit Italy, Germany, and England. I sailed from Messina to Leghorn, and travelled thence, by way of Florence, Venice, and the Tyrol, to Munich. After three happy weeks at Gotha, and among the valleys of she Thüringian Forest, I went to London, where business and the preparation for my new journeys detained me two or three weeks longer. Although the comforts of European civilization were pleasant, as a change, after the wild life of the Orient, the autumnal rains of England soon made me homesick for the sunshine I had left. The weather was cold, dark, and dreary, and the oppressive, sticky atmosphere of the bituminous metropolis weighed upon me like a nightmare. Heartily tired of looking at a sun that could show nothing brighter than a red copper disk, and of breathing an air that peppered my face with particles of soot, I left on the 28th of October. It was one of the dismalest days of autumn; the meadows of Berkshire were flooded with broad, muddy streams, and the woods on the hills of Hampshire looked brown and sodden, as if slowly rotting away. I reached Southampton at dusk, but there the sky was neither warmer nor clearer, so I spent the evening over a coal fire, all impatience for the bright beloved South, towards which my face was turned once more.

The Madras left on the next day, at 2 P.M., in the midst of a cheerless rain, which half blotted out the pleasant shores of Southampton Water, and the Isle of Wight. The Madras was a singularly appropriate vessel for one bound on such a journey as mine. The surgeon was Dr. Mungo Park, and one of my room-mates was Mr. R. Crusoe. It was a Friday, which boded no good for the voyage; but then my journey commenced with my leaving London the day previous, and Thursday is a lucky day among the Arabs. I caught a watery view of the gray cliffs of the Needles, when dinner was announced, but many were those (and I among them) who commenced that meal, and did not stay to finish it.

Is there any piece of water more unreasonably, distressingly, disgustingly rough and perverse than the British Channel? Yes: there is one, and but one--the Bay of Biscay. And as the latter succeeds the former, without a pause between, and the head-winds never ceased, and the rain continually poured, I leave you to draw the climax of my misery. Four days and four nights in a berth, lying on your back, now dozing dull hour after hour, now making faint endeavors to eat, or reading the feeblest novel ever written, because the mind cannot digest stronger aliment--can there be a greater contrast to the wide-awake life, the fiery inspiration, of the Orient? My blood became so sluggish and my mind so cloudy and befogged, that I despaired of ever thinking clearly or feeling vividly again. "The winds are rude" in Biscay, Byron says. They are, indeed: very rude. They must have been raised in some most disorderly quarter of the globe. They pitched the waves right over our bulwarks, and now and then dashed a bucketful of water down the cabin skylight, swamping the ladies' cabin, and setting scores of bandboxes afloat. Not that there was the least actual danger; but Mrs. ---- would not be persuaded that we were not on the brink of destruction, and wrote to friends at home a voluminous account of her feelings. There was an Irishman on board, bound to Italy, with his sister. It was his first tour, and when asked why he did not go direct, through France, he replied, with brotherly concern, that he was anxious his sister should see the Bay of Biscay.

This youth's perceptions were of such an emerald hue, that a lot of wicked Englishmen had their own fun out of him. The other day, he was trying to shave, to the great danger of slicing off his nose, as the vessel was rolling fearfully. "Why don't you have the ship headed to the wind?" said one of the Englishmen, who heard his complaints; "she will then lie steady, and you can shave beautifully." Thereupon the Irishman sent one of the stewards upon deck with a polite message to the captain, begging him to put the vessel about for five minutes.

Towards noon of the fifth day, we saw the dark, rugged mountains that guard the north-western corner of the Spanish Peninsula. We passed the Bay of Corunna, and rounding the bold headland of Finisterre, left the Biscayan billows behind us. But the sea was still rough and the sky clouded, although the next morning the mildness of the air showed the change in our latitude. About noon that day, we made the Burlings, a cluster of rocks forty miles north of Lisbon, and just before sunset, a transient lifting of the clouds revealed the Rock of Cintra, at the mouth of the Tagus. The tall, perpendicular cliffs, and the mountain slopes behind, covered with gardens, orchards, and scattered villas and hamlets, made a grand though dim picture, which was soon hidden from our view.

On the 4th, we were nearly all day crossing the mouth of the Bay of Cadiz, and only at sunset saw Cape Trafalgar afar off, glimmering through the reddish haze. I remained on deck, as there were patches of starlight in the sky. After passing the light-house at Tarifa, the Spanish shore continued to be visible. In another hour, there was a dim, cloudy outline high above the horizon, on our right. This was the Lesser Atlas, in Morocco. And now, right ahead, distinctly visible, though fifteen miles distant, lay a colossal lion, with his head on his outstretched paws, looking towards Africa. If I had been brought to the spot blindfolded, I should have known what it was. The resemblance is certainly very striking, and the light-house on Europa Point seemed to be a lamp held in his paws. The lights of the city and fortifications rose one by one, glittering along the base, and at midnight we dropped anchor before them on the western side.

I landed yesterday morning. The mists, which had followed me from England, had collected behind the Rock, and the sun, still hidden by its huge bulk, shone upwards through them, making a luminous background, against which the lofty walls and jagged ramparts of this tremendous natural fortification were clearly defined. I announced my name, and the length of time I designed remaining, at a little office on the quay, and was then allowed to pass into the city. A number of familiar white turbans met me on entering, and I could not resist the temptation of cordially saluting the owners in their own language. The town is long and narrow, lying steeply against the Rock. The houses are white, yellow and pink, as in Spanish towns, but the streets are clean and well paved. There is a square, about the size of an ordinary building-lot, where a sort of market of dry goods and small articles is held The "Club-House Hotel" occupies one side of it; and, as I look out of my window upon it, I see the topmost cliffs of the Rock above me, threatening to topple down from a height of 1,500 feet.

My first walk in Gibraltar was in search of a palm-tree. After threading the whole length of the town, I found two small ones in a garden, in the bottom of the old moat. The sun was shining, and his rays seemed to fall with double warmth on their feathery crests. Three brown Spaniards, bare-armed, were drawing water with a pole and bucket, and filling the little channels

669

which conveyed it to the distant vegetables. The sea glittered blue below; an Indian fig-tree shaded me; but, on the rock behind, an aloe lifted its blossoming stem, some twenty feet high, into the sunshine. To describe what a weight was lifted from my heart would seem foolish to those who do not know on what little things the whole tone of our spirits sometimes depends.

But if an even balance was restored yesterday, the opposite scale kicked the beam this morning. Not a speck of vapor blurred the spotless crystal of the sky, as I walked along the hanging paths of the Alameda. The sea was dazzling ultra-marine, with a purple lustre; every crag and notch of the mountains across the bay, every shade of brown or gray, or the green of grassy patches, was drawn and tinted with a pencil so exquisitely delicate as almost to destroy the perspective. The white houses of Algeciras, five miles off, appeared close at hand: a little toy-town, backed by miniature hills. Apes' Hill, the ancient Abyla, in Africa, advanced to meet Calpe, its opposing pillar, and Atlas swept away to the east ward, its blue becoming paler and paler, till the powers of vision finally failed. From the top of the southern point of the Rock, I saw the mountain-shore of Spain, as far as Malaga, and the snowy top of one of the Sierra Nevada. Looking eastward to the horizon line of the Mediterranean, my sight extended so far, in the wonderful clearness of the air, that the convexity of the earth's surface was plainly to be seen. The sea, instead of being a plane, was slightly convex, and the sky, instead of resting upon it at the horizon, curved down beyond it, as the upper side of a horn curves over the lower, when one looks into the mouth. There is none of the many aspects of Nature more grand than this, which is so rarely seen, that I believe the only person who has ever described it is Humboldt, who saw it, looking from the Silla de Caraccas over the Caribbean Sea. It gives you the impression of standing on the edge of the earth, and looking off into space. From the mast-head, the ocean appears either flat or slightly concave, and æronauts declare that this apparent concavity becomes more marked, the higher they ascend. It is only at those rare periods when the air is so miraculously clear as to produce the effect of no air--rendering impossible the slightest optical illusion--that our eyes can see things as they really are. So pure was the atmosphere to-day, that, at meridian, the moon, although a thin sickle, three days distant from the sun, shone perfectly white and clear.

670

As I loitered in the Alameda, between thick hedges of ever-blooming geraniums, clumps of heliotrope three feet high, and luxuriant masses of ivy, around whose warm flowers the bees clustered and hummed, I could only think of the voyage as a hideous dream. The fog and gloom had been in my own eyes and in my own brain, and now the blessed sun, shining full in my face, awoke me. I am a worshipper of the Sun. I took off my hat to him, as I stood there, in a wilderness of white, crimson, and purple flowers, and let him blaze away in my face for a quarter of an hour. And as I walked home with my back to him, I often turned my face from side to side that I might feel his touch on my cheek. How a man can live, who is sentenced to a year's imprisonment, is more than I can understand.

But all this (you will say) gives you no picture of Gibraltar. The Rock is so familiar to all the world, in prints and descriptions, that I find nothing new to say of it, except that it is by no means so barren a rock as the island of Malta, being clothed, in many places, with beautiful groves and the greenest turf; besides, I have not yet seen the rock-galleries, having taken passage for Cadiz this afternoon. When I return--as I hope to do in twenty days, after visiting Seville and Granada--I shall procure permission to view all the fortifications, and likewise to ascend to the summit.

Chapter XXXIII. Cadiz And Seville.

Voyage to Cadiz--Landing--The City--Its Streets--The Women of Cadiz--Embarkation for Seville--Scenery of the Guadalquivir--Custom House Examination--The Guide--The Streets of Seville--The Giralda--The Cathedral of Seville--The Alcazar-Moorish Architecture--Pilate's House--Morning View from the Giralda--Old Wine--Murillos--My Last Evening in Seville.

"The walls of Cadiz front the shore,

And shimmer o'er the sea."

R. H. Stoddard.

"Beautiful Seville!

Of which I've dreamed, until I saw its towers

In every cloud that hid the setting sun."

George H. Boker.

Seville, *November* 10, 1852.

I left Gibraltar on the evening of the 6th, in the steamer Iberia. The passage to Cadiz was made in nine hours, and we came to anchor in the harbor before day-break. It was a cheerful picture that the rising sun presented to us. The long white front of the city, facing the East, glowed with a bright rosy lustre, on a ground of the clearest blue. The tongue of land on which Cadiz stands is low, but the houses are lifted by the heavy sea-wall which encompasses them. The main-land consists of a range of low but graceful hills, while in the south-east the mountains of Ronda rise at some distance. I went immediately on shore, where my carpet-bag was seized upon by a boy, with the rich brown complexion of one Murillo's beggars, who trudged off with it to the gate. After some little detention there, I was conducted to a long, deserted, barn-like building, where I waited half an hour before the proper officer came. When the latter had taken his private toll of my contraband cigars, the brown imp conducted me to Blanco's English Hotel, a neat and comfortable house on the Alameda.

Cadiz is soon seen. Notwithstanding its venerable age of three thousand years--having been founded by Hercules, who figures on its coat-of-arms--it is purely a commercial city, and has neither antiquities, nor historic associations that interest any but Englishmen. It is compactly built, and covers a smaller space than accords with my ideas of its former splendor. I first walked around the sea-ramparts, enjoying the glorious look-off over the blue waters. The city is almost insulated, the triple line of fortifications on the land side being of but trifling length. A rocky ledge stretches out into the sea from the northern point, and at its extremity rises the massive light-house tower, 170 feet high. The walls toward the sea were covered with companies of idle anglers, fishing with cane rods of enormous length. On the open, waste spaces between the bastions, boys had spread their limed cords to catch singing birds, with chirping decoys placed here and there in wicker cages. Numbers of boatmen and peasants, in their brown jackets, studded with tags and bugles, and those round black caps which resemble smashed bandboxes, loitered about the walls or lounged on the grass in the sun.

Except along the Alameda, which fronts the bay, the exterior of the city has an aspect of neglect and desertion. The interior, however, atones for this in the gay and lively air of its streets, which, though narrow, are regular and charmingly clean. The small plazas are neatness itself, and one is too content with this to ask for striking architectural effects. The houses are tall and stately, of the most dazzling whiteness, and though you could point out no one as a pattern of style, the general effect is chaste and harmonious. In fact, there are two or three streets which you would almost pronounce faultless. The numbers of hanging balconies and of court-yards paved with marble and surrounded with elegant corridors, show the influence of Moorish taste. There is not a mean-looking house to be seen, and I have no doubt that Cadiz is the best built city of its size in the world. It lies, white as new-fallen snow, like a cluster of ivory palaces, between sea and sky. Blue and silver are its colors, and, as everybody knows, there can be no more charming contrast.

I visited both the old and new cathedrals, neither of which is particularly interesting. The latter is unfinished, and might have been a fine edifice had the labor and money expended on its construction been directed by taste. The interior, rich as it is in marbles and sculpture, has a heavy, confused effect. The pillars dividing the nave from the side-aisles are enormous composite masses, each one consisting of six Corinthian columns, stuck around and against a central shaft. More satisfactory to me was the Opera-House, which I visited in the evening, and where the dazzling array of dark-eyed Gaditanas put a stop to architectural criticism. The women of Cadiz are noted for their beauty and their graceful gait. Some of them are very beautiful, it is true; but beauty is not the rule among them. Their gait, however, is the most graceful possible, because it is perfectly free and natural. The commonest serving-maid who walks the streets of Cadiz would put to shame a whole score of our mincing and wriggling belles.

Honest old Blanco prepared me a cup of chocolate by sunrise next morning, and accompanied me down to the quay, to embark for Seville. A furious wind was blowing from the south-east, and the large green waves raced and chased one another incessantly over the surface of the bay. I took a heavy craft, which the boatmen pushed along under cover of the pier, until they reached the end, when the sail was dropped in the face of the wind, and away we shot into the watery tumult. The boat rocked and bounced over the agitated surface, running with one gunwale on the waves, and sheets of briny spray broke over me. I felt considerably relieved when I reached the deck of the steamer, but it was then diversion enough to watch those who followed. The crowd of boats pitching tumultuously around the steamer, jostling against each other, their hulls gleaming with wet, as they rose on the beryl-colored waves, striped with long, curded lines of wind-blown foam, would have made a fine subject for the pencil of Achenbach.

At last we pushed off, with a crowd of passengers fore and aft, and a pyramid of luggage piled around the smoke-pipe. There was a party of four Englishmen on board, and, on making their acquaintance, I found one of them to be a friend to some of my friends--Sir John Potter, the progressive ex-Mayor of Manchester. The wind being astern, we ran rapidly along the coast, and in two hours entered the mouth of the Guadalquivir. [This name comes from the Arabic wadi el-kebeer--literally, the Great Valley.] The shores are a dead flat. The right bank is a dreary forest of stunted pines, abounding with deer and other game; on the left is the dilapidated town of San Lucar, whence Magellan set sail on his first voyage around the world. A mile further is Bonanza, the port of Xeres, where we touched and took on board a fresh lot of passengers. Thenceforth, for four hours, the scenery of the Guadalquivir had a most distressing sameness. The banks were as flat as a board, with here and there a straggling growth of marshy thickets. Now and then we passed a herdsman's hut, but there were no human beings to be seen, except the peasants who tended the large flocks of sheep and cattle. A sort of breakfast was served in the cabin, but so great was the number of guests that I had much difficulty in getting anything to eat. The waiters were models of calmness and deliberation.

As we approached Seville, some low hills appeared on the left, near the river. Dazzling white villages were planted at their foot, and all the slopes were covered with olive orchards, while the banks of the stream were bordered with silvery birch trees. This gave the landscape, in spite of the African warmth and brightness of the day, a gray and almost wintry aspect. Soon the graceful Giralda, or famous Tower of Seville, arose in the distance; but, from the windings of the river, we were half an hour in reaching the landing-place. One sees nothing of the far-famed beauty of Seville, on approaching it. The boat stops below the Alameda, where the passengers are received by Custom-House officers, who, in my case, did not verify the stories told of them in Cadiz. I gave my carpet-bag to a boy, who conducted me along the hot and dusty banks to the bridge over the Guadalquivir, where he turned into the city. On passing the gate, two loafer-like guards stopped my baggage, notwithstanding it had already been examined. "What!" said I, "do you examine twice on entering Seville?" "Yes," answered one; "twice, and even three times;" but added in a lower tone, "it depends entirely on yourself." With that he slipped behind me, and let one hand fall beside my pocket. The transfer of a small coin was dexterously made, and I passed on without further stoppage to the Fonda de Madrid.

Sir John Potter engaged Antonio Bailli, the noted guide of Seville, who professes to have been the cicerone of all distinguished travellers, from Lord Byron and Washington Irving down to Owen Jones, and I readily accepted his invitation to join the party. Bailli is recommended by Ford as "fat and good-humored" Fat he certainly is, and very good-humored when speaking of himself, but he has been rather spoiled by popularity, and is much too profuse in his critical remarks on art and architecture. Nevertheless, as my stay in Seville is limited, I have derived no slight advantage from his services.

On the first morning I took an early stroll through the streets. The houses are glaringly white, like those of Cadiz, but are smaller and have not the same stately exteriors. The windows are protected by iron gratings, of florid patterns, and, as many of these are painted green, the general effect is pleasing. Almost every door opens upon a patio, or courtyard, paved with black and white marble and adorned with flowers and fountains. Many of these remain from the time of the Moors, and are still surrounded by the delicate arches and brilliant tile-work of that period. The populace in the streets are entirely Spanish--the jaunty majo in his queer black cap, sash, and embroidered jacket, and the nut-brown, dark-eyed damsel, swimming along in her mantilla, and armed with the irresistible fan.

We went first to the Cathedral, built on the site of the great mosque of Abou Youssuf Yakoub. The tall Giralda beckoned to us over the tops of the intervening buildings, and finally a turn in the street brought us to the ancient Moorish gateway on the northern side. This is an admirable specimen of the horse-shoe arch, and is covered with elaborate tracery. It originally opened into the court, or hàram, of the mosque, which still remains, and is shaded by a grove of orange trees. The Giralda, to my eye, is a more perfect tower than the Campanile of Florence, or that of San Marco, at Venice, which is evidently an idea borrowed from it. The Moorish structure, with a base of fifty feet square, rises to the height of two hundred and fifty feet. It is of a light pink color, and the sides, which are broken here and there by exquisitely proportioned double Saracenic arches, are covered from top to bottom with arabesque tracery, cut in strong relief. Upon this tower, a Spanish architect has placed a tapering spire, one hundred feet high, which fortunately harmonizes with the general design, and gives the crowning grace to the work.

676

The Cathedral of Seville may rank as one of the grandest Gothic piles in Europe. The nave lacks but five feet of being as high as that of St. Peter's, while the length and breadth of the edifice are on a commensurate scale. The ninety-three windows of stained glass fill the interior with a soft and richly-tinted light, mellower and more gentle than the sombre twilight of the Gothic Cathedrals of Europe. The wealth lavished on the smaller chapels and shrines is prodigious, and the high altar, inclosed within a gilded railing fifty feet high, is probably the most enormous mass of wood-carving in existence. The Cathedral, in fact, is encumbered with its riches. While they bewilder you as monuments of human labor and patience, they detract from the grand simplicity of the building. The great nave, on each side of the transept, is quite blocked up, so that the choir and magnificent royal chapel behind it have almost the effect of detached edifices.

We returned again this morning, remaining two hours, and succeeded in making a thorough survey, including a number of trashy pictures and barbarously rich shrines. Murillo's "Guardian Angel" and the "Vision of St. Antonio" are the only gems. The treasury contains a number of sacred vessels of silver, gold and jewels--among other things, the keys of Moorish Seville, a cross made of the first gold brought from the New-World by Columbus, and another from that robbed in Mexico by Cortez. The Cathedral won my admiration more and more. The placing of the numerous windows, and their rich coloring, produce the most glorious effects of light in the lofty aisles, and one is constantly finding new vistas, new combinations of pillar, arch and shrine. The building is in itself a treasury of the grandest Gothic pictures.

From the Cathedral we went to the Alcazar (El-Kasr), or Palace of the Moorish Kings. We entered by a long passage, with round arches on either side, resting on twin pillars, placed at right angles to the line of the arch, as one sees both in Saracenic and Byzantine structures. Finally, old Bailli brought us into a dull, deserted court-yard, where we were surprised by the sight of an entire Moorish façade, with its pointed arches, its projecting roof, its rich sculptured ornaments and its illuminations of red, blue, green and gold. It has been lately restored, and now rivals in freshness and brilliancy any of the rich houses of Damascus. A doorway, entirely too low and mean for the splendor of the walls above it, admitted us into the first court. On each side of the passage are the rooms of the guard and the Moorish nobles. Within, all is pure Saracenic, and absolutely perfect in its grace and richness. It is the realization of an Oriental dream; it is the poetry and luxury of the East in tangible forms. Where so much depends on the proportion and harmony of the different parts--on those correspondences, the union of which creates that nameless soul of the work, which cannot be expressed in words--it is useless to describe details. From first to last--the chambers of state; the fringed arches; the open tracery, light and frail as the frost-stars crystallized on a window-pane; the courts, fit to be vestibules to Paradise; the audience-hall, with its wondrous sculptures, its columns and pavement of marble, and its gilded dome; the garden, gorgeous with its palm, banana, and orange-trees--all were in perfect keeping, all jewels of equal lustre, forming a diadem which still lends a royal dignity to the phantom of Moorish power.

We then passed into the gardens laid out by the Spanish monarchs--trim, mathematical designs, in box and myrtle, with concealed fountains springing up everywhere unawares in the midst of the paven walks; yet still made beautiful by the roses and jessamines that hung in rank clusters over the marble balustrades, and by the clumps of tall orange trees, bending to earth under the weight of their fruitage. We afterward visited Pilate's House, as it is called--a fine Spanish-Moresco palace, now belonging to the Duke of Medina Coeli. It is very rich and elegant, but stands in the same relation to the Alcazar as a good copy does to the original picture. The grand staircase, nevertheless, is a marvel of tile work, unlike anything else in Seville, and exhibits a genius in the invention of elaborate ornamental patterns, which is truly wonderful. A number of workmen were busy in restoring the palace, to fit it for the residence of the young Duke. The Moorish sculptures are reproduced in plaster, which, at least, has a better effect than the fatal whitewash under which the original tints of the Alcazar are hidden. In the courts stand a number of Roman busts--Spanish antiquities, and therefore not of great merit--singularly out of place in niches surrounded by Arabic devices and sentences from the Koran.

This morning, I climbed the Giralda. The sun had just risen, and the clay was fresh and crystal-clear. A little door in the Cathedral, near the foot

678

of the tower, stood open, and I entered. A rather slovenly Sevillaña had just completed her toilet, but two children were still in undress. However, she opened a door in the tower, and I went up without hindrance. The ascent is by easy ramps, and I walked four hundred yards, or nearly a quarter of a mile, before reaching the top of the Moorish part. The panoramic view was superb. To the east and west, the Great Valley made a level line on a far-distant horizon. There were ranges of hills in the north and south, and those rising near the city, clothed in a gray mantle of olive-trees, were picturesquely crowned with villages. The Guadalquivir, winding in the most sinuous mazes, had no longer a turbid hue; he reflected the blue morning sky, and gleamed brightly between his borders of birch and willow. Seville sparkled white and fair under my feet, her painted towers and tiled domes rising thickly out of the mass of buildings. The level sun threw shadows into the numberless courts, permitting the mixture of Spanish and Moorish architecture to be plainly discerned, even at that height. A thin golden vapor softened the features of the landscape, towards the sun, while, on the opposite side, every object stood out in the sharpest and clearest outlines.

On our way to the Muséo, Bailli took us to the house of a friend of his, in order that we might taste real Manzanilla wine. This is a pale, straw-colored vintage, produced in the valley of the Guadalquivir. It is flavored with camomile blossoms, and is said to be a fine tonic for weak stomachs. The master then produced a dark-red wine, which he declared to be thirty years old. It was almost a syrup in consistence, and tasted more of sarsaparilla than grapes. None of us relished it, except Bailli, who was so inspired by the draught, that he sang us two Moorish songs and an Andalusian catch, full of fun and drollery.

The Muséo contains a great amount of bad pictures, but it also contains twenty-three of Murillo's works, many of them of his best period. To those who have only seen his tender, spiritual "Conceptions" and "Assumptions," his "Vision of St. Francis" in this gallery reveals a mastery of the higher walks of his art, which they would not have anticipated. But it is in his "Cherubs" and his "Infant Christs" that he excels. No one ever painted infantile grace and beauty with so true a pencil. There is but one Velasquez in the collection, and the only thing that interested me, in two halls filled with rubbish, was a "Conception" by Murillo's mulatto pupil, said by some to have been his slave. Although an imitation of the great master, it is a picture of much sweetness and beauty. There is no other work of the artist in existence, and this, as the only production of the kind by a painter of mixed African blood, ought to belong to the Republic of Liberia.

Among the other guests at the Fonda de Madrid is Mr. Thomas Hobhouse, brother of Byron's friend. We had a pleasant party in the Court this evening, listening to blind Pépé, who sang to his guitar a medley of merry Andalusian refrains. Singing made the old man courageous, and, at the close, he gave us the radical song of Spain, which is now strictly prohibited. The air is charming, but too gay; one would sooner dance than fight to its measures. It does not bring the hand to the sword, like the glorious Marseillaise.

Adios, beautiful Seville!

Chapter XXXIV. Journey in a Spanish Diligence.

Spanish Diligence Lines--Leaving Seville--An Unlucky Start--Alcalà of the Bakers--Dinner at Carmona--A Dehesa--The Mayoral and his Team--Ecija--Night Journey--Cordova--The Cathedral-Mosque--Moorish Architecture--The Sierra Morena--A Rainy Journey--A Chapter of Accidents--Baylen--The Fascination of Spain--Jaen--The Vega of Granada.

Granada, *November* 14, 1852.

It is an enviable sensation to feel for the first time that you are in Granada. No amount of travelling can weaken the romantic interest which clings about this storied place, or take away aught from the freshness of that emotion with which you first behold it, I sit almost at the foot of the Alhambra, whose walls I can see from my window, quite satisfied for to-day with being here. It has been raining since I arrived, the thunder is crashing overhead, and the mountains are covered with clouds, so I am kept in-doors, with the luxury of knowing that all the wonders of the place are within my reach. And now let me beguile the dull weather by giving you a sketch of my journey from Seville hither.

There are three lines of stages from Seville to Madrid, and their competition has reduced the fare to $12, which, for a ride of 350 miles, is remarkably cheap. The trip is usually made in three days and a half. A branch line from Baylen--nearly half-way--strikes southward to Granada, and as there is no competition on this part of the road, I was charged $15 for a through seat in the coupé. On account of the lateness of the season, and the limited time at my command, this was preferable to taking horses and riding across the country from Seville to Cordova. Accordingly, at an early hour on Thursday morning last, furnished with a travelling ticket inscribed: "Don Valtar de Talor" (myself!), I took leave of my English friends at the Fonda de Madrid, got into an immense, lumbering yellow vehicle, drawn by ten mules, and started, trusting to my good luck and bad Spanish to get safely through. The commencement, however, was unpropitious, and very often a stumble at starting makes the whole journey limp. The near mule in the foremost span was a horse, ridden by our postillion, and nothing could prevent that horse from darting into all sorts of streets and alleys where we had no desire to go. As all mules have implicit faith in horses, of course the rest of the animals followed. We were half an hour in getting out of Seville, and when at last we reached the open road and dashed off at full gallop, one of the mules in the traces fell and was dragged in the dust some twenty or thirty yards before we could stop. My companions in the coupé were a young Spanish officer and his pretty Andalusian bride, who was making her first journey from home, and after these mishaps was in a state of constant fear and anxiety.

The first stage across the valley of the Guadalquivir took us to the town of Alcalà, which lies in the lap of the hills above the beautiful little river Guadaira. It is a picturesque spot; the naked cliffs overhanging the stream have the rich, red hue of cinnabar, and the trees and shrubbery in the meadows, and on the hill-sides are ready grouped to the artist's hand. The town is called Alcalà de los Panadores (of the Bakers) from its hundreds of flour mills and bake-ovens, which supply Seville with those white, fine, delicious twists, of which Spain may be justly proud. They should have been sent to the Exhibition last year, with the Toledo blades and the wooden mosaics. We left the place and its mealy-headed population, and turned eastward into wide, rolling tracts, scattered here and there with gnarled olive trees. The soil was loose and sandy, and hedges of aloes lined the road. The country is thinly populated, and very little of it under cultivation.

About noon we reached Carmona, which was founded by the Romans, as, indeed, were nearly all the towns of Southern Spain. It occupies the crest and northern slope of a high hill, whereon the ancient Moorish castle still stands. The Alcazar, or palace, and the Moorish walls also remain, though in a very ruinous condition. Here we stopped to dinner, for the "Nueva Peninsular," in which I was embarked, has its hotels all along the route, like that of Zurutuza, in Mexico. We were conducted into a small room adjoining the stables, and adorned with colored prints illustrating the history of Don John of Austria. The table-cloths, plates and other appendages were of very ordinary quality, but indisputably clean; we seated ourselves, and presently

682

the dinner appeared. First, a vermicelli pilaff, which I found palatable, then the national olla, a dish of enormous yellow peas, sprinkled with bits of bacon and flavored with oil; then three successive courses of chicken, boiled, stewed and roasted, but in every case done to rags, and without a particle of the original flavor. This was the usual style of our meals on the road, whether breakfast, dinner or supper, except that kid was sometimes substituted for fowl, and that the oil employed, being more or less rancid, gave different flavors to the dishes, A course of melons, grapes or pomegranates wound up the repast, the price of which varied from ten to twelve reals--a real being about a half-dime. In Seville, at the Fonda de Madrid, the cooking is really excellent; but further in the interior, judging from what I have heard, it is even worse than I have described.

Continuing our journey, we passed around the southern brow of the hill, under the Moorish battlements. Here a superb view opened to the south and east over the wide Vega of Carmona, as far as the mountain chain which separates it from the plain of Granada. The city has for a coat of arms a silver star in an azure field, with the pompous motto: "As Lucifer shines in the morning, so shines Carmona in Andalusia." If it shines at all, it is because it is a city set upon a hill; for that is the only splendor I could find about the place. The Vega of Carmona is partially cultivated, and now wears a sombre brown hue, from its tracts of ploughed land.

Cultivation soon ceased, however, and we entered on a dehesa, a boundless plain of waste land, covered with thickets of palmettos. Flocks of goats and sheep, guarded by shepherds in brown cloaks, wandered here and there, and except their huts and an isolated house, with its group of palm-trees, there was no sign of habitation. The road was a deep, red sand, and our mules toiled along slowly and painfully, urged by the incessant cries of the mayoral, or conductor, and his mozo. As the mayoral's whip could only reach the second span, the business of the latter was to jump down every ten minutes, run ahead and belabor the flanks of the foremost mules, uttering at the same time a series of sharp howls, which seemed to strike the poor beasts with quite as much severity as his whip. I defy even a Spanish ear to distinguish the import of these cries, and the great wonder was how they could all come out of one small throat. When it came to a hard pull, they cracked and exploded like volleys of musketry, and flew like hail-stones about the ears of the machos (he-mules). The postillion, having only the care of the foremost span, is a silent man, but he has contracted a habit of sleeping in the saddle, which I mention for the benefit of timid travellers, as it adds to the interest of a journey by night.

The clouds which had been gathering all day, now settled down upon the plain, and night came on with a dull rain. At eight o'clock we reached the City of Ecija, where we had two hours' halt and supper. It was so dark and rainy that I saw nothing, not even the classic Xenil, the river of Granada, which flows through the city on its way to the Guadalquivir, The night wore slowly away, and while the mozo drowsed on his post, I caught snatches of sleep between his cries. As the landscape began to grow distinct in the gray, cloudy dawn, we saw before us Cordova, with the dark range of the Sierra Morena rising behind it. This city, once the glory of Moorish Spain, the capital of the great Abd-er-Rahman, containing, when in its prime, a million of inhabitants, is now a melancholy wreck. It has not a shadow of the art, science, and taste which then distinguished it, and the only interest it now possesses is from these associations, and the despoiled remnant of its renowned Mosque.

We crossed the Guadalquivir on a fine bridge built on Roman foundations, and drove slowly down the one long, rough, crooked street. The diligence stops for an hour, to allow passengers to breakfast, but my first thought was for the Cathedral-mosque, la Mezquita, as it is still called. "It is closed," said the ragged crowd that congregated about us; "you cannot get in until eight o'clock." But I remembered that a silver key will open anything in Spain, and taking a mozo as a guide we hurried off as fast as the rough pavements would permit. We had to retrace the whole length of the city, but on reaching the Cathedral, found it open. The exterior is low, and quite plain, though of great extent. A Moorish gateway admitted me into the original court-yard, or hàram, of the mosque, which is planted with orange trees and contains the fountain, for the ablutions of Moslem worshippers, in the centre. The area of the Mosque proper, exclusive of the court-yard, is about

400 by 350 feet. It was built on the plan of the great Mosque of Damascus, about the end of the eighth century. The materials--including twelve hundred columns of marble, jasper and porphyry, from the ruins of Carthage, and the temples of Asia Minor---belonged to a Christian basilica, of the Gothic domination, which was built upon the foundations of a Roman temple of Janus; so that the three great creeds of the world have here at different times had their seat. The Moors considered this mosque as second in holiness to the Kaaba of Mecca, and made pilgrimages to it from all parts of Moslem Spain and Barbary. Even now, although shorn of much of its glory, it surpasses any Oriental mosque into which I have penetrated, except St. Sophia, which is a Christian edifice.

All the nineteen original entrances--beautiful horse-shoe arches--are closed, except the central one. I entered by a low door, in one corner of the corridor. A wilderness of columns connected by double arches (one springing above the other, with an opening between), spread their dusky aisles before me in the morning twilight. The eight hundred and fifty shafts of this marble forest formed labyrinths and mazes, which at that early hour appeared boundless, for their long vistas disappeared in the shadows. Lamps were burning before distant shrines, and a few worshippers were kneeling silently here and there. The sound of my own footsteps, as I wandered through the ranks of pillars, was all that I heard. In the centre of the wood (for such it seemed) rises the choir, a gaudy and tasteless excrescence added by the Christians. Even Charles V., who laid a merciless hand on the Alhambra, reproved the Bishop of Cordova for this barbarous and unnecessary disfigurement.

The sacristan lighted lamps in order to show me the Moorish chapels. Nothing but the precious materials of which these exquisite structures are composed could have saved them from the holy hands of the Inquisition, which intentionally destroyed all the Roman antiquities of Cordova. Here the fringed arches, the lace-like filigrees, the wreathed inscriptions, and the domes of pendent stalactites which enchant you in the Alcazar of Seville, are repeated, not in stucco, but in purest marble, while the entrance to the "holy of holies" is probably the most glorious piece of mosaic in the world. The pavement of the interior is deeply worn by the knees of the Moslem pilgrims, who compassed it seven times, kneeling, as they now do in the Kaaba, at Mecca. The sides are embroidered with sentences from the Koran, in Cufic characters, and the roof is in the form of a fluted shell, of a single piece of pure white marble, fifteen feet in diameter. The roof of the vestibule is a wonderful piece of workmanship, formed of pointed arches, wreathed and twined through each other, like basket-work. No people ever wrought poetry into stone so perfectly as the Saracens. In looking on these precious relics of an elegant and refined race, I cannot help feeling a strong regret that their kingdom ever passed into other hands.

Leaving Cordova, our road followed the Guadalquivir, along the foot of the Sierra Morena, which rose dark and stern, a barrier to the central table-lands of La Mancha. At Alcolea, we crossed the river on a noble bridge of black marble, out of all keeping with the miserable road. It rained incessantly, and the scenery through which we passed had a wild and gloomy character. The only tree to be seen was the olive, which covered the hills far and near, the profusion of its fruit showing the natural richness of the soil. This part of the road is sometimes infested with robbers, and once, when I saw two individuals waiting for us in a lonely defile, with gun-barrels thrust out from under their black cloaks, I anticipated a recurrence of a former unpleasant experience. But they proved to be members of the guardia civil, and therefore our protectors.

The ruts and quagmires, made by the rain, retarded our progress, and it was dark when we reached Andujar, fourteen leagues from Cordova. To Baylen, where I was to quit the diligence, and take another coming down from Madrid to Granada, was four leagues further. We journeyed on in the dark, in a pouring rain, up and down hill for some hours, when all at once the cries of the mozo ceased, and the diligence came to a dead stop. There was some talk between our conductors, and then the mayoral opened the door and invited us to get out. The postillion had fallen asleep, and the mules had taken us into a wrong road. An attempt was made to turn the diligence, but failed, leaving it standing plump against a high bank of mud. We stood, meanwhile, shivering in the cold and wet, and the fair Andalusian shed abundance of tears. Fortunately, Baylen was close at hand, and, after some delay, two men came with lanterns and escorted us to the posada, or inn, where we arrived at midnight. The diligence from Madrid, which was due six hours before, had not made its appearance, and we passed the rest of the night in a cold room, fasting, for the meal was only to be served when the other passengers came. At day-break, finally, a single dish of oily meat was vouchsafed to us, and, as it was now certain that some accident had happened, the passengers to Madrid requested the Administrador to send them on in an extra conveyance. This he refused, and they began to talk about getting up a pronunciamento, when a messenger arrived with the news that the diligence had broken down at midnight, about two leagues off. Tools were thereupon dispatched, nine hours after the accident happened, and we might hope to be released from our imprisonment in four or five more.

Baylen is a wretched place, celebrated for having the first palm-tree which those see who come from Madrid, and for the victory gained by Castaños over the French forces under Dupont, which occasioned the flight of Joseph Buonaparte from Madrid, and the temporary liberation of Spain from the French yoke. Castaños, who received the title of Duke de Baylen, and is compared by the Spaniards to Wellington, died about three months ago. The battle-field I passed in the night; the palm-tree I found, but it is now a mere stump, the leaves having been stripped off to protect the houses of the inhabitants from lightning. Our posada had one of them hung at the window. At last, the diligence came, and at three P.M., when I ought to have been in sight of Granada, I left the forlorn walls of Baylen. My fellow-passengers were a young sprig of the Spanish nobility and three chubby-faced nuns.

The rest of the journey that afternoon was through a wide, hilly region, entirely bare of trees and habitations, and but partially cultivated. There was something sublime in its very nakedness and loneliness, and I felt attracted to it as I do towards the Desert. In fact, although I have seen little fine scenery since leaving Seville, have had the worst of weather, and no very pleasant travelling experiences, the country has exercised a fascination over me, which I do not quite understand. I find myself constantly on the point of making a vow to return again. Much to my regret, night set in before we reached Jaen, the capital of the Moorish kingdom of that name. We halted for a short time in the large plaza of the town, where the dash of fountains mingled with the sound of the rain, and the black, jagged outline of a mountain overhanging the place was visible through the storm.

All night we journeyed on through the mountains, sometimes splashing through swollen streams, sometimes coming almost to a halt in beds of deep mud. When this morning dawned, we were ascending through wild, stony hills, overgrown with shrubbery, and the driver said we were six leagues from Granada. Still on, through a lonely country, with now and then a large venta, or country inn, by the road-side, and about nine o'clock, as the sky became more clear, I saw in front of us, high up under the clouds, the snow-fields of the Sierra Nevada. An hour afterwards we were riding between gardens, vineyards, and olive orchards, with the magnificent Vega of Granada stretching far away on the right, and the Vermilion Towers of the Alhambra crowning the heights before us.

Chapter XXXV. Granada And The Alhambra.

Mateo Ximenez, the Younger--The Cathedral of Granada--A Monkish Miracle--Catholic Shrines--Military Cherubs--The Royal Chapel--The Tombs of Ferdinand and Isabella--Chapel of San Juan de Dios--The Albaycin--View of the Vega--The Generalife--The Alhambra--Torra de la Vela--The Walls and Towers--A Visit to Old Mateo--The Court of the Fish-pond--The Halls of the Alhambra--Character of the Architecture--Hall of the Abencerrages--Hall of the Two Sisters--The Moorish Dynasty in Spain.

"Who has not in Granada been,

Verily, he has nothing seen."

Andalusian Proverb.

Granada, *Wednesday, Nov.* 17, 1852.

Immediately on reaching here, I was set upon by an old gentleman who wanted to act as guide, but the mozo of the hotel put into my hand a card inscribed "Don Mateo Ximenez, Guide to the celebrated Washington Irving," and I dismissed the other applicant. The next morning, as the mozo brought me my chocolate, he said; "Señor, el chico is waiting for you." The "little one" turned out to be the son of old Mateo, "honest Mateo," who still lives up in the Alhambra, but is now rather too old to continue his business, except on great occasions. I accepted the young Mateo, who spoke with the greatest enthusiasm of Mr. Irving, avowing that the whole family was devoted to him, in life and death. It was still raining furiously, and the golden Darro, which roars in front of the hotel, was a swollen brown flood. I don't wonder that he sometimes threatens, as the old couplet says, to burst up the Zacatin, and bear it down to his bride, the Xenil.

Towards noon, the clouds broke away a little, and we sallied out. Passing through the gate and square of Vivarrambla (may not this name come from the Arabic bob er-raml, the "gate of the sand?"), we soon reached the Cathedral. This massive structure, which makes a good feature in the distant view of

Granada, is not at all imposing, near at hand. The interior is a mixture of Gothic and Roman, glaring with whitewash, and broken, like that of Seville, by a wooden choir and two grand organs, blocking up the nave. Some of the side chapels, nevertheless, are splendid masses of carving and gilding. In one of them, there are two full-length portraits of Ferdinand and Isabella, supposed to be by Alonzo Cano. The Cathedral contains some other good pictures by the same master, but all its former treasures were carried off by the French.

We next went to the Picture Gallery, which is in the Franciscan Convent. There are two small Murillos, much damaged, some tolerable Alonzo Canos, a few common-place pictures by Juan de Sevilla, and a hundred or more by authors whose names I did not inquire, for a more hideous collection of trash never met my eye. One of them represents a miracle performed by two saints, who cut off the diseased leg of a sick white man, and replace it by the sound leg of a dead negro, whose body is seen lying beside the bed. Judging from the ghastly face of the patient, the operation is rather painful, though the story goes that the black leg grew fast, and the man recovered. The picture at least illustrates the absence of "prejudice of color" among the Saints.

We went into the adjoining Church of Santo Domingo, which has several very rich shrines of marble and gold. A sort of priestly sacristan opened the Church of the Madonna del Rosario---a glittering mixture of marble, gold, and looking-glasses, which has rather a rich effect. The beautiful yellow and red veined marbles are from the Sierra Nevada. The sacred Madonna--a big doll with staring eyes and pink cheeks--has a dress of silver, shaped like an extinguisher, and encrusted with rubies and other precious stones. The utter absence of taste in most Catholic shrines is an extraordinary thing. It seems remarkable that a Church which has produced so many glorious artists should so constantly and grossly violate the simplest rules of art. The only shrine which I have seen, which was in keeping with the object adored, is that of the Virgin, at Nazareth, where there is neither picture nor image, but only vases of fragrant flowers, and perfumed oil in golden lamps, burning before a tablet of spotless marble.

Among the decorations of the chapel, there are a host of cherubs frescoed on the ceiling, and one of them is represented in the act of firing off a blunderbuss. "Is it true that the angels carry blunderbusses?" I asked the priest. He shrugged his shoulders with a sort of half-smile, and said nothing. In the Cathedral, on the plinths of the columns in the outer aisles, are several notices to the effect that "whoever speaks to women, either in the nave or the aisles, thereby puts himself in danger of excommunication." I could not help laughing, as I read this monkish and yet most unmonk-like statute. "Oh," said Mateo, "all that was in the despotic times; it is not so now."

A deluge of rain put a stop to my sight-seeing until the next morning, when I set out with Mateo to visit the Royal Chapel. A murder had been committed in the night, near the entrance of the Zacatin, and the paving-stones were still red with the blood of the victim. A funcion of some sort was going on in the Chapel, and we went into the sacristy to wait. The priests and choristers were there, changing their robes; they saluted me good-humoredly, though there was an expression in their faces that plainly said: "a heretic!" When the service was concluded, I went into the chapel and examined the high altar, with its rude wood-carvings, representing the surrender of Granada. The portraits of Ferdinand and Isabella, Cardinal Ximenez, Gonzalvo of Cordova, and King Boabdil, are very curious. Another tablet represents the baptism of the conquered Moors.

In the centre of the chapel stand the monuments erected to Ferdinand and Isabella, and their successors Philip L, and Maria, by Charles V. They are tall catafalques of white marble, superbly sculptured, with the full length effigies of the monarchs upon them. The figures are admirable; that of Isabella, especially, though the features are settled in the repose of death, expresses all the grand and noble traits which belonged to her character. The sacristan removed the matting from a part of the floor, disclosing an iron grating underneath, A damp, mouldly smell, significant of death and decay, came up through the opening. He lighted two long waxen tapers, lifted the grating, and I followed him down the narrow steps into the vault where lie the coffins of the Catholic Sovereigns. They were brought here from the Alhambra, in 1525. The leaden sarcophagi, containing the bodies of Ferdinand and Isabella, lie, side by side, on stone slabs; and as I stood between the two, resting a

691

hand on each, the sacristan placed the tapers in apertures in the stone, at the head and foot. They sleep, as they wished, in their beloved Granada, and no profane hand has ever disturbed the repose of their ashes.

After visiting the Church of San Jeronimo, founded by Gonzalvo of Cordova, I went to the adjoining Church and Hospital of San Juan de Dios. A fat priest, washing his hands in the sacristy, sent a boy to show me the Chapel of San Juan, and the relics. The remains of the Saint rest in a silver chest, standing in the centre of a richly-adorned chapel. Among the relics is a thorn from the crown of Christ, which, as any botanist may see, must have grown on a different plant from the other thorn they show at Seville; and neither kind is found in Palestine. The true spina christi, the nebbuk, has very small thorns; but nothing could be more cruel, as I found when riding through patches of it near Jericho. The boy also showed me a tooth of San Lorenzo, a crooked brown bicuspis, from which I should infer that the saint was rather an ill-favored man. The gilded chapel of San Juan is in singular contrast with one of the garments which he wore when living--a cowl of plaited reeds, looking like an old fish basket--which is kept in a glass case. His portrait is also to be seen--a mild and beautiful face, truly that of one who went about doing good. He was a sort of Spanish John Howard, and deserved canonization, if anybody ever did.

I ascended the street of the Darro to the Albaycin, which we entered by one of the ancient gates. This suburb is still surrounded by the original fortifications, and undermined by the capacious cisterns of the Moors. It looks down on Granada; and from the crumbling parapets there are superb views over the city, the Vega, and its inclosing mountains. The Alhambra rose opposite, against the dark-red and purple background of the Sierra Nevada, and a canopy of heavy rain-clouds rested on all the heights. A fitful gleam of sunshine now and then broke through and wandered over the plain, touching up white towers and olive groves and reaches of the winding Xenil, with a brilliancy which suggested the splendor of the whole picture, if once thus restored to its proper light. I could see Santa Fé in the distance, toward Loxa; nearer, and more eastward, the Sierra de Elvira, of a deep violet color, with the woods of the Soto de Roma, the Duke of Wellington's estate, at its base; and beyond it the Mountain of Parapanda, the weather-guage of Granada, still covered with clouds. There is an old Granadian proverb which says:--"When Parapanda wears his bonnet, it will rain whether God wills it or no." From the chapel of San Miguel, above the Albaycin, there is a very striking view of the deep gorge of the Darro, at one's feet, with the gardens and white walls of the Generalife rising beyond, and the Silla del Moro and the Mountain of the Sun towering above it. The long, irregular lines of the Alhambra, with the huge red towers rising here and there, reminded me somewhat of a distant view of Karnak; and, like Karnak, the Alhambra is picturesque from whatever point it is viewed.

We descended through wastes of cactus to the Darro, in whose turbid stream a group of men were washing for gold. I watched one of them, as he twirled his bowl in precisely the California style, but got nothing for his pains. Mateo says that they often make a dollar a day, each. Passing under the Tower of Comares and along the battlements of the Alhambra, we climbed up to the Generalife. This charming villa is still in good preservation, though its exquisite filigree and scroll-work have been greatly injured by whitewash. The elegant colonnades surround gardens rich in roses, myrtles and cypresses, and the fountains that lulled the Moorish Kings in their summer idleness still pour their fertilizing streams. In one of the rooms is a small and bad portrait gallery, containing a supposed portrait of Boabdil. It is a mild, amiable face, but wholly lacks strength of character.

To-day I devoted to the Alhambra. The storm, which, as the people say, has not been equalled for several years, showed no signs of breaking up, and in the midst of a driving shower I ascended to the Vermilion Towers, which are supposed to be of Phoenician origin. They stand on the extremity of a long, narrow ledge, which stretches out like an arm from the hill of the Alhambra. The paséo lies between, and is shaded by beautiful elms, which the Moors planted.

I entered the Alhambra by the Gate of Justice, which is a fine specimen of Moorish architecture, though of common red brick and mortar. It is singular what a grace the horse-shoe arch gives to the most heavy and lumbering mass of masonry. The round arches of the Christian edifices of Granada seem tame and inelegant, in comparison. Over the arch of the vestibule of this gate is the colossal hand, and over the inner entrance the key, celebrated in the tales of Washington Irving and the superstitions of the people. I first ascended the Torre de la Vela, where the Christian flag was first planted on the 2d of January, 1492. The view of the Vega and City of Granada was even grander than from the Albaycin. Parapanda was still bonneted in clouds, but patches of blue sky began to open above the mountains of Loxa. A little boy accompanied us, to see that I did not pull the bell, the sound of which would call together all the troops in the city. While we stood there, the funeral procession of the man murdered two nights before came up the street of Gomerez, and passed around the hill under the Vermilion Towers.

I made the circuit of the walls before entering the Palace. In the Place of the Cisterns, I stopped to take a drink of the cool water of the Darro, which is brought thither by subterranean channels from the hills. Then, passing the ostentatious pile commenced by Charles V., but which was never finished, and never will be, nor ought to be, we walked along the southern ramparts to the Tower of the Seven Floors, amid the ruins of winch I discerned the top of the arch by which the unfortunate Boabdil quitted Granada, and which was thenceforth closed for ever. In the Tower of the Infantas, a number of workmen were busy restoring the interior, which has been cruelly damaged. The brilliant azulejo, or tile-work, the delicate arches and filigree sculpture of the walls, still attest its former elegance, and give some color to the tradition that it was the residence of the Moorish Princesses.

As we passed through the little village which still exists among the ruins of the fortress, Mateo invited me to step in and see his father, the genuine "honest Mateo," immortalized in the "Tales of the Alhambra." The old man has taken up the trade of silk-weaving, and had a number of gay-colored ribbons on his loom. He is more than sixty years old and now quite gray-headed, but has the same simple manners, the same honest face that attracted his temporary master. He spoke with great enthusiasm of Mr. Irving, and brought out from a place of safety the "Alhambra" and the "Chronicles of the Conquest," which he has carefully preserved. He then produced an Andalusian sash, the work of his own hands, which he insisted on binding around my waist, to see how it would look. I must next take off my coat and hat, and put on his Sunday jacket and jaunty sombrero. "Por Dios!" he exclaimed: "que buen mozo! Senor, you are a legitimate Andalusian!" After this, of course, I could do no less than buy the sash. "You must show it to Washington Irving," said he, "and tell him it was made by Mateo's own hands;" which I promised. I must then go into the kitchen, and eat a pomegranate from his garden--a glorious pomegranate, with kernels of crimson, and so full of blood that you could not touch them but it trickled through your fingers. El Marques, a sprightly dog, and a great slate-colored cat, took possession of my legs, and begged for a share of every mouthful I took, while old Mateo sat beside me, rejoicing in the flavor of a Gibraltar cigar which I gave him. But my time was precious, and so I let the "Son of the Alhambra" go back to his loom, and set out for the Palace of the Moorish Kings.

This palace is so hidden behind the ambitious shell of that of Charles V. that I was at a loss where it could be. I thought I had compassed the hill, and yet had seen no indications of the renowned magnificence of the Alhambra. But a little door in a blank wall ushered me into a true Moorish realm, the Court of the Fishpond, or of the Myrtles, as it is sometimes called. Here I saw again the slender pillars, the fringed and embroidered arches, and the perforated, lace-like tracery of the fairy corridors. Here, hedges of roses and myrtles still bloomed around the ancient tank, wherein hundreds of gold-fish disported. The noises of the hill do not penetrate here, and the solitary porter who admitted me went back to his post, and suffered me to wander at will through the enchanted halls.

I passed out of this court by an opposite door, and saw, through the vistas of marble pillars and the wonderful fret-work which seems a thing of air rather than of earth, the Fountain of the Lions. Thence I entered in succession the Hall of the Abencerrages, the Hall of the Two Sisters, the apartments of the Sultanas, the Mosque, and the Hall of the Ambassadors. These places--all that is left of the renowned palace--are now well kept, and carefully guarded. Restorations are going on, here and there, and the place is scrupulously watched, that no foreign Vandal, may further injure what the native Goths have done their best to destroy. The rubbish has been cleared away; the rents in the walls have been filled up, and, for the first time since it passed into Spanish hands, there seems a hope that the Alhambra will be allowed to stand. What has been already destroyed we can only partially conjecture; but no one sees what remains without completing the picture in his own imagination, and placing it among the most perfect and marvellous creations of human genius.

Nothing can exceed the richness of invention which, in this series of halls, corridors, and courts, never repeats the same ornaments, but, from the simplest primitive forms and colors, produces a thousand combinations, not one of which is in discord with the grand design. It is useless to attempt a detailed description of this architecture; and it is so unlike anything else in the world, that, like Karnak and Baalbec, those only know the Alhambra who see it. When you can weave stone, and hang your halls with marble tapestry, you may rival it. It is nothing to me that these ornaments are stucco; to sculpture them in marble is only the work of the hands. Their great excellence is in the design, which, like all great things, suggests even more than it gives. If I could create all that the Court of Lions suggested to me for its completion, it would fulfil the dream of King Sheddad, and surpass the palaces of the Moslem Paradise.

The pavilions of the Court of Lions, and the halls which open into it, on either side, approach the nearest to their original perfection. The floors are marble, the wainscoting of painted tiles, the walls of embroidery, still gleaming with the softened lustre of their original tints, and the lofty conical domes seem to be huge sparry crystalizations, hung with dropping stalactites, rather than any work of the human hand. Each of these domes is composed of five thousand separate pieces, and the pendent prismatic blocks, colored and gilded, gradually resolve themselves, as you gaze, into the most intricate and elegant designs. But you must study long ere you have won all the secret of their beauty. To comprehend them, one should spend a whole day, lying on his back, under each one. Mateo spread his cloak for me in the fountain in the Hall of the Abencerrages, over the blood-stains made by the decapitation of those gallant chiefs, and I lay half an hour looking upward: and this is what I made out of the dome. From its central pinnacle hung the chalice of a flower with feathery petals, like the "crape myrtle" of our Southern States Outside of this, branched downward the eight rays of a large star, whose points touched the base of the dome; yet the star was itself composed of flowers, while between its rays and around its points fell a shower of blossoms, shells, and sparry drops. From the base of the dome hung a gorgeous pattern of lace, with a fringe of bugles, projecting into eight points so as to form a star of drapery, hanging from the points of the flowery star in the dome. The spaces between the angles were filled with masses of stalactites, dropping one below the other, till they tapered into the plain square sides of the hall.

In the Hall of the Two Sisters, I lay likewise for a considerable time, resolving its misty glories into shape. The dome was still more suggestive of flowers. The highest and central piece was a deep trumpet-flower, whose mouth was cleft into eight petals. It hung in the centre of a superb lotus-cup, the leaves of which were exquisitely veined and chased. Still further below swung a mass of mimosa blossoms, intermixed with pods and lance-like leaves, and around the base of the dome opened the bells of sixteen gorgeous tulips. These pictures may not be very intelligible, but I know not how else to paint the effect of this fairy architecture.

In Granada, as in Seville and Cordova, one's sympathies are wholly with the Moors. The few mutilated traces which still remain of their power, taste, and refinement, surpass any of the monuments erected by the race which conquered them. The Moorish Dynasty in Spain was truly, as Irving observes, a splendid exotic, doomed never to take a lasting root in the soil It was choked to death by the native weeds; and, in place of lands richly cultivated and teeming with plenty, we now have barren and-almost depopulated wastes-- in place of education, industry, and the cultivation of the arts and sciences, an enslaved, ignorant and degenerate race. Andalusia would be far more prosperous at this day, had she remained in Moslem hands. True, she would not have received that Faith which is yet destined to be the redemption of the world, but the doctrines of Mahomet are more acceptable to God, and more beneficial to Man than those of that Inquisition, which, in Spain alone, has shed ten times as much Christian blood as all the Moslem races together for the last six centuries. It is not from a mere romantic interest that I lament the fate of Boabdil, and the extinction of his dynasty. Had he been a king worthy to reign in those wonderful halls, he never would have left them. Had he perished there, fighting to the last, he would have been freed from forty years of weary exile and an obscure death. Well did Charles V. observe, when speaking of him: "Better a tomb in the Alhambra than a palace in the Alpujanas!"

Chapter XXXVI. The Bridle-Roads of Andalusia.

Change of Weather--Napoleon and his Horses--Departure from Granada--My Guide, José Garcia--His Domestic Troubles--The Tragedy of the Umbrella--The Vow against Aguardiente--Crossing the Vega--The Sierra Nevada--The Baths of Alhama--"Woe is Me, Alhama!"--The Valley of the River Vélez--Vélez Malaga--The Coast Road--The Fisherman and his Donkey--Malaga--Summer Scenery--The Story of Don Pedro, without Fear and without Care--The Field of Monda--A Lonely Venta.

Venta de Villalon, *November* 20, 1852.

The clouds broke away before I had been two hours in the Alhambra, and the sunshine fell broad and warm into its courts. They must be roofed with blue sky, in order to give the full impression of their brightness and beauty. Mateo procured me a bottle of vino rancio, and we drank it together in the Court of Lions. Six hours had passed away before I knew it, and I reluctantly prepared to leave. The clouds by this time had disappeared; the Vega slept in brilliant sunshine, and the peaks of the Sierra Nevada shone white and cold against the sky.

On reaching the hotel, I found a little man, nicknamed Napoleon, awaiting me. He was desirous to furnish me with horses, and, having a prophetic knowledge of the weather, promised me a bright sky as far as Gibraltar. "I furnish all the señors," said he; "they know me, and never complain of me or my horses;" but, by way of security, on making the bargain, I threatened to put up a card in the hotel at Gibraltar, warning all travellers against him, in case I was not satisfied. My contract was for two horses and a guide, who were to be ready at sunrise the next morning. Napoleon was as good as his word; and before I had finished an early cup of chocolate, there was a little black Andalusian stallion awaiting me. The alforjas, or saddle-bags, of the guide were strengthened by a stock of cold provisions, the leathern bota hanging beside it was filled with ripe Granada wine; and now behold me ambling over the Vega, accoutred in a gay Andalusian jacket, a sash woven by Mateo

Ximenes, and one of those bandboxy sombreros, which I at first thought so ungainly, but now consider quite picturesque and elegant.

My guide, a short but sinewy and well-knit son of the mountains, named José Garcia, set off at a canter down the banks of the Darro. "Don't ride so fast!" cried Napoleon, who watched our setting out, from the door of the fonda; but José was already out of hearing. This guide is a companion to my liking. Although he is only twenty-seven, he has been for a number of years a correo, or mail-rider, and a guide for travelling parties. His olive complexion is made still darker by exposure to the sun and wind, and his coal-black eyes shine with Southern heat and fire. He has one of those rare mouths which are born with a broad smile in each corner, and which seem to laugh even in the midst of grief. We had not been two hours together, before I knew his history from beginning to end. He had already been married eight years, and his only trouble was a debt of twenty-four dollars, which the illness of his wife had caused him. This money was owing to the pawnbroker, who kept his best clothes in pledge until he could pay it. "Señor," said he, "if I had ten million dollars, I would rather give them all away than have a sick wife." He had a brother in Puerto Principe, Cuba, who sent over money enough to pay the rent of the house, but he found that children were a great expense. "It is most astonishing," he said, "how much children can eat. From morning till night, the bread is never out of their mouths."

José has recently been travelling with some Spaniards, one of whom made him pay two dollars for an umbrella which was lost on the road. This umbrella is a thorn in his side. At every venta where we stop, the story is repeated, and he is not sparing of his maledictions. The ghost of that umbrella is continually raised, and it will be a long time before he can shut it. "One reason why I like to travel with foreign Señors," said he to me, "is, that when I lose anything, they never make me pay for it." "For all that," I answered, "take care you don't lose my umbrella: it cost three dollars." Since then, nothing can exceed José's attention to that article. He is at his wit's end how to secure it best. It appears sometimes before, sometimes behind him, lashed to the saddle with innumerable cords; now he sticks it into the alforja, now carries it in his hand, and I verily believe that he sleeps with it in his arms. Every evening, as he tells his story to the muleteers, around the kitchen fire, he always winds up by triumphantly appealing to me with: "Well, Señor, have I lost your umbrella yet?"

Our bargain is that I shall feed him on the way, and as we travel in the primitive style of the country, we always sit down together to the same dish. To his supervision, the olla is often indebted for an additional flavor, and no "thorough-bred" gentleman could behave at table with more ease and propriety. He is as moderate as a Bedouin in his wants, and never touches the burning aguardiente which the muleteers are accustomed to drink. I asked him the reason of this. "I drink wine. Senor," he replied, "because that, you know, is like meat and bread; but I have made a vow never to drink aguardiente again. Two of us got drunk on it, four or five years ago, in Granada, and we quarrelled. My comrade drew his knife and stabbed me here, in the left shoulder. I was furious and cut him across the breast. We both went to the hospital--I for three months and he for six--and he died in a few days after getting out. It cost my poor father many a thousand reals; and when I was able to go to work, I vowed before the Virgin that I would never touch aguardiente again."

For the first league, our road lay over the rich Vega of Granada, but gradually became wilder and more waste. Passing the long, desert ridge, known as the "Last Sigh of the Moor," we struck across a region of low hills. The road was very deep, from the recent rains, and studded, at short intervals, by rude crosses, erected to persons who had been murdered. José took a grim delight in giving me the history of each. Beyond the village of Lamala, which lies with its salt-pans in a basin of the hills, we ascended the mountain ridge which forms the southern boundary of the Vega. Granada, nearly twenty miles distant, was still visible. The Alhambra was dwindled to a speck, and I took my last view of it and the magnificent landscape which lies spread out before it. The Sierra Nevada, rising to the height of 13,000 feet above the sea, was perfectly free from clouds, and the whole range was visible at one glance. All its chasms were filled with snow, and for nearly half-way down its sides there was not a speck of any other color. Its summits were almost wholly devoid of shadow, and their notched and jagged outlines rested flatly against the sky, like ivory inlaid on a table of lapis-lazuli.

From these waste hills, we descended into the valley of Cacia, whose poplar-fringed river had been so swollen by the rains that the correo from Malaga had only succeeded in passing it that morning. We forded it without accident, and, crossing a loftier and bleaker range, came down into the valley of the Marchan. High on a cliff over the stream stood Alhama, my resting-place for the night. The natural warm baths, on account of which this spot was so beloved by the Moors, are still resorted to in the summer. They lie in the bosom of a deep and rugged gorge, half a mile further down the river. The town occupies the crest of a narrow promontory, bounded, on all sides but one, by tremendous precipices. It is one of the most picturesque spots imaginable, and reminded me--to continue the comparison between Syria and Andalusia, which I find so striking--of the gorge of the Barrada, near Damascus. Alhama is now a poor, insignificant town, only visited by artists and muleteers. The population wear long brown cloaks and slouched hats, like the natives of La Mancha.

I found tolerable quarters in a house on the plaza, and took the remaining hour of daylight to view the town. The people looked at me with curiosity, and some boys, walking on the edge of the tajo, or precipice, threw over stones that I might see how deep it was. The rock, in some places, quite overhung the bed of the Marchan, which half-girdles its base. The close scrutiny to which I was subjected by the crowd in the plaza called to mind all I had heard of Spanish spies and robbers. At the venta, I was well treated, but received such an exorbitant bill in the morning that I was ready to exclaim, with King Boabdil, "Woe is me, Alhama!" On comparing notes with José, I found that he had been obliged to pay, in addition, for what he received--a discovery which so exasperated that worthy that he folded his hands, bowed his head, made three kisses in the air, and cried out: "I swear before the Virgin that I will never again take a traveller to that inn."

We left Alhama an hour before daybreak, for we had a rough journey of more than forty miles before us. The bridle-path was barely visible in the darkness, but we continued ascending to a height of probably 5,000 feet above the sea, and thus met the sunrise half-way. Crossing the llano of Ace faraya, we reached a tremendous natural portal in the mountains, from whence, as from a door, we looked down on all the country lying between us and the sea. The valley of the River Vélez, winding among the hills, pointed out the course of our road. On the left towered over us the barren Sierra Tejeda, an isolated group of peaks, about 8,000 feet in height. For miles, the road was a rocky ladder, which we scrambled down on foot, leading our horses. The vegetation gradually became of a warmer and more luxuriant cast; the southern slopes were planted with the vine that produces the famous Malaga raisins, and the orange groves in the sunny depths of the valleys were as yellow as autumnal beeches, with their enormous loads of fruit. As the bells of Vélez Malaga were ringing noon, we emerged from the mountains, near the mouth of the river, and rode into the town to breakfast.

We halted at a queer old inn, more like a Turkish khan than a Christian hostlery. It was kept by a fat landlady, who made us an olla of kid and garlic, which, with some coarse bread and the red Malaga wine, soon took off the sharp edge of our mountain appetites. While I was washing my hands at a well in the court-yard, the mozo noticed the pilgrim-seal of Jerusalem, which is stamped indelibly on my left arm. His admiration and reverence were so great that he called the fat landlady, who, on learning that it had been made in Jerusalem, and that I had visited the Holy Sepulchre, summoned her children to see it. "Here, my children!" she said; "cross yourselves, kneel down, and kiss this holy seal; for, as long as you live, you may never see the like of it again." Thus I, a Protestant heretic, became a Catholic shrine. The children knelt and kissed my arm with touching simplicity; and the seal will henceforth be more sacred to me than ever.

The remaining twenty miles or more of the road to Malaga follow the line of the coast, passing headlands crowned by the atalayas, or watch-towers, of the Moors. It is a new road, and practicable for carriages, so that, for Spain, it may be considered an important achievement. The late rains have, however, already undermined it in a number of places. Here, as among the mountains, we met crowds of muleteers, all of whom greeted me with: "Vaya usted con Dios, caballero!"--("May you go with God, cavalier!") By this time, all my forgotten Spanish had come back again, and a little experience of the simple ways of the people made me quite at home among them. In almost every instance, I was treated precisely as a Spaniard would have been, and less annoyed by the curiosity of the natives than I have been in Germany, and even America.

We were still two leagues from Malaga, at sunset, The fishermen along the coast were hauling in their nets, and we soon began to overtake companies of them, carrying their fish to the city on donkeys. One stout, strapping fellow, with flesh as hard and yellow as a sturgeon's, was seated sideways on a very small donkey, between two immense panniers of fish, As he trotted before us, shouting, and slapping the flanks of the sturdy little beast, José and I began to laugh, whereupon the fellow broke out into the following monologue, addressed to the donkey: "Who laughs at this burrico? Who says he's not fine gold from head to foot? What is it that he can't do? If there was a mountain ever so high, he would gallop over it. If there was a river ever so deep, he would swim through it If he could but speak, I might send him to market alone with the fish, and not a chavo of the money would he spend on the way home. Who says he can't go as far as that limping horse? Arrrre, burrico! punate--ar-r-r-r-e-e!"

We reached Malaga, at last, our horses sorely fagged. At the Fonda de la Alameda, a new and very elegant hotel, I found a bath and a good dinner, both welcome things to a tired traveller. The winter of Malaga is like spring in other lands and on that account it is much visited by invalids, especially English. It is a lively commercial town of about 80,000 inhabitants, and, if the present scheme of railroad communication with Madrid is carried out, must continue to increase in size and importance. A number of manufacturing establishments have lately been started, and in this department it bids fair to rival Barcelona. The harbor is small, but good, and the country around rich in all the productions of temperate and even tropical climates. The city contains little to interest the tourist. I visited the Cathedral, an immense unfinished mass, without a particle of architectural taste outwardly, though the interior has a fine effect from its large dimensions.

At noon to-day we were again in the saddle, and took the road to the Baths of Caratraca. The tall factory chimneys of Malaga, vomiting forth streams of black smoke, marred the serenity of the sky; but the distant view of the city is very fine. The broad Vega, watered by the Guadaljorce, is rich and well cultivated, and now rejoices in the verdure of spring. The meadows are clothed with fresh grass, butter-cups and daisies are in blossom, and larks sing in the olive-trees. Now and then, we passed a casa del campo, with its front half buried in orange-trees, over which towered two or three sentinel palms. After two leagues of this delightful travel, the country became more hilly, and the groups of mountains which inclosed us assumed the most picturesque and enchanting forms. The soft haze in which the distant peaks were bathed, the lovely violet shadows filling up their chasms and gorges, and the fresh meadows, vineyards, and olive groves below, made the landscape one of the most beautiful I have seen in Spain.

As we were trotting along through the palmetto thickets, José asked me if I should not like to hear an Andalusian story. "Nothing would please me better," I replied. "Ride close beside me, then," said he, "that you may understand every word of it." I complied, and he gave me the following, just as I repeat it: "There was once a very rich man, who had thousands of cattle in the Sierra Nevada, and hundreds of houses in the city. Well: this man put a plate, with his name on it, on the door of the great house in which he lived, and the name was this: Don Pedro, without Fear and without Care. Now, when the King was making his paséo, he happened to ride by this house in his carriage, and saw the plate on the door. 'Read me the name on that plate!' said he to his officer. Then the officer read the name: Don Pedro, without Fear and without Care. 'I will see whether Don Pedro is without Fear and without Care,' said the King. The next day came a messenger to the house, and, when he saw Don Pedro, said he to him; 'Don Pedro, without Fear and without Care, the King wants you!' 'What does the King want with me?' said Don Pedro. 'He sends you four questions which you must answer within four days, or he will have you shot; and the questions are:--How can the Sierra Nevada be cleared of snow? How can the sea be made smaller? How many arrobas does the moon weigh? And: How many leagues from here to the Land of Heavenly Glory?' Then Don Pedro without Fear and without Care began to sweat from fright, and knew not what he should do. He called some of his arrieros and loaded twenty mules with money, and went up into the Sierra

Nevada, where his herdsmen tended his flocks; for, as I said, he had many thousand cattle. 'God keep you, my master!' said the chief herdsman, who was young, and buen mozo, and had as good a head as ever was set on two shoulders. 'Anda, hombre! said Don Pedro, 'I am a dead man;' and so he told the herdsman all that the King had said. 'Oh, is that all?' said the knowing mozo. 'I can get you out of the scrape. Let me go and answer the questions in your name, my master!' 'Ah, you fool! what can you do?' said Don Pedro without Fear and without Care, throwing himself upon the earth, and ready to die.

"But, nevertheless, the herdsman dressed himself up as a caballero, went down to the city, and, on the fourth day, presented himself at the King's palace. 'What do you want?' said the officers. 'I am Don Pedro without Fear and without Care, come to answer the questions which the King sent to me.' 'Well,' said the King, when he was brought before him, 'let me hear your answers, or I will have you shot this day.' 'Your Majesty,' said the herdsman, 'I think I can do it. If you were to set a million of children to playing among the snow of the Sierra Nevada, they would soon clear it all away; and if you were to dig a ditch as wide and as deep as all Spain, you would make the sea that much smaller,' 'But,' said the King, 'that makes only two questions; there are two more yet,' 'I think I can answer those, also,' said the herdsman: 'the moon contains four quarters, and therefore weighs only one arroba; and as for the last question, it is not even a single league to the Land of Heavenly Glory--for, if your Majesty were to die after breakfast, you would get there before you had an appetite for dinner,' 'Well done! said the King; and he then made him Count, and Marquez, and I don't know how many other titles. In the meantime, Don Pedro without Fear and without Care had died of his fright; and, as he left no family, the herdsman took possession of all his estates, and, until the day of his death, was called Don Pedro without Fear and without Care."

I write, sitting by the grated window of this lonely inn, looking out on the meadows of the Guadaljorce. The chain of mountains which rises to the west of Malaga is purpled by the light of the setting sun, and the houses and Castle of Carlama hang on its side, in full view. Further to the right, I see the smoke of Monda, where one of the greatest battles of antiquity was fought--that which overthrew the sons of Pompey, and gave the Roman Empire to Cæsar. The mozo of the venta is busy, preparing my kid and rice, and José is at his elbow, gently suggesting ingredients which may give the dish a richer flavor. The landscape is softened by the hush of coming evening; a few birds are still twittering among the bushes, and the half-moon grows whiter and clearer in mid-heaven. The people about me are humble, but appear honest and peaceful, and nothing indicates that I am in the wild Serrania de Ronda, the country of robbers, contrabandistas, and assassins.

Chapter XXXVII. The Mountains of Ronda.

Orange Valleys--Climbing the Mountains--José's Hospitality--El Burgo--The Gate of the Wind--The Cliff and Cascades of Ronda--The Mountain Region--Traces of the Moors--Haunts of Robbers--A Stormy Ride--The Inn at Gaucin--Bad News--A Boyish Auxiliary--Descent from the Mountains--The Ford of the Guadiaro--Our Fears Relieved--The Cork Woods--Ride from San Roque to Gibraltar--Parting with José--Travelling in Spain--Conclusion.

Gibraltar, *Thursday, November* 25, 1852.

I passed an uncomfortable night at the Venta de Villalon, lying upon a bag stuffed with equal quantities of wool and fleas. Starting before dawn, we followed a path which led into the mountains, where herdsmen and boys were taking out their sheep and goats to pasture; then it descended into the valley of a stream, bordered with rich bottom-lands. I never saw the orange in a more flourishing state. We passed several orchards of trees thirty feet high, and every bough and twig so completely laden with fruit, that the foliage was hardly to be seen.

At the Venta del Vicario, we found a number of soldiers just setting out for Ronda. They appeared to be escorting a convoy of goods, for there were twenty or thirty laden mules gathered at the door. We now ascended a most difficult and stony path, winding through bleak wastes of gray rock, till we reached a lofty pass in the mountain range. The wind swept through the narrow gateway with a force that almost unhorsed us. From the other side, a sublime but most desolate landscape opened to my view. Opposite, at ten miles' distance, rose a lofty ridge of naked rock, overhung with clouds. The country between was a chaotic jumble of stony hills, separated by deep chasms, with just a green patch here and there, to show that it was not entirely forsaken by man. Nevertheless as we descended into it, we found valleys with vineyards and olive groves, which were invisible from above. As we were both getting hungry, José stopped at a ventorillo and ordered two cups of wine, for which he insisted on paying. "If I had as many horses as my master, Napoleon," said he, "I would regale the Señors whenever I travelled with them. I would have puros, and sweetmeats, with plenty of Malaga or Valdepeñas in the bota, and they should never complain of their fare." Part of our road was studded with gray cork-trees, at a distance hardly to be distinguished from olives, and José dismounted to gather the mast, which was as sweet and palatable as chestnuts, with very little of the bitter quercine flavor. At eleven o'clock, we reached El Burgo, so called, probably, from its ancient Moorish fortress. It is a poor, starved village, built on a barren hill, over a stream which is still spanned by a lofty Moorish bridge of a single arch.

The remaining three leagues to Ronda were exceedingly rough and difficult. Climbing a barren ascent of nearly a league in length, we reached the Puerto del Viento, or Gate of the Wind, through which drove such a current that we were obliged to dismount; and even then it required all my strength to move against it. The peaks around, far and near, faced with precipitous cliffs, wore the most savage and forbidding aspect: in fact, this region is almost a counterpart of the wilderness lying between Jerusalem and the Dead Sea, Very soon, we touched the skirt of a cloud, and were enveloped in masses of chill, whirling vapor, through which we travelled for three or four miles to a similar gate on the western side of the chain. Descending again, we emerged into a clearer atmosphere, and saw below us a wide extent of mountain country, but of a more fertile and cheerful character. Olive orchards and wheat-fields now appeared; and, at four o'clock, we rode into the streets of Ronda.

No town can surpass this in the grandeur and picturesqueness of its position. It is built on the edge of a broad shelf of the mountains, which falls away in a sheer precipice of from six to eight hundred feet in height, and, from the windows of many of the houses you can look down the dizzy abyss. This shelf, again, is divided in the centre by a tremendous chasm, three hundred feet wide, and from four to six hundred feet in depth, in the bed of which roars the Guadalvin, boiling in foaming whirlpools or leaping in sparkling cascades, till it reaches the valley below. The town lies on both sides of the chasm, which is spanned by a stone bridge of a single arch, with abutments nearly four hundred feet in height. The view of this wonderful cleft, either from above or below, is one of the finest of its kind in the world.

Honda is as far superior to Tivoli, as Tivoli is to a Dutch village, on the dead levels of Holland. The panorama which it commands is on the grandest scale. The valley below is a garden of fruit and vines; bold yet cultivated hills succeed, and in the distance rise the lofty summits of another chain of the Serrania de Honda. Were these sublime cliffs, these charming cascades of the Guadalvin, and this daring bridge, in Italy instead of in Spain, they would be sketched and painted every day in the year; but I have yet to know where a good picture of Ronda may be found.

In the bottom of the chasm are a number of corn-mills as old as the time of the Moors. The water, gushing out from the arches of one, drives the wheel of that below, so that a single race supplies them all. I descended by a very steep zig-zag path nearly to the bottom. On a little point or promontory overhanging the black depths, there is a Moorish gateway still standing. The sunset threw a lovely glow over the brown cliffs and the airy town above; but they were far grander when the cascades glittered in the moonlight, and the gulf out of which they leap was lost in profound shadow. The window of my bed-room hung over the chasm.

Honda was wrapped in fog, when José awoke me on the morning of the 22d. As we had but about twenty-four miles to ride that day, we did not leave until sunrise. We rode across the bridge, through the old town and down the hill, passing the triple lines of the Moorish walls by the original gateways. The road, stony and rugged beyond measure, now took to the mountains. From the opposite height, there was a fine view of the town, perched like an eagle's nest on the verge of its tremendous cliffs; but a curtain of rain soon fell before it, and the dense dark clouds settled around us, and filled up the gorges on either hand. Hour after hour, we toiled along the slippery paths, scaling the high ridges by rocky ladders, up which our horses climbed with the greatest difficulty. The scenery, whenever I could obtain a misty glimpse of it, was sublime. Lofty mountain ridges rose on either hand; bleak jagged summits of naked rock pierced the clouds, and the deep chasms which separated them sank far below us, dark and indistinct through the rain. Sometimes I caught sight of a little hamlet, hanging on some almost inaccessible ledge, the home of the lawless, semi-Moorish mountaineers who inhabit this wild region. The faces of those we met exhibited marked traces of their Moslem ancestry, especially in the almond-shaped eye and the dusky olive complexion. Their dialect retains many Oriental forms of expression, and I was not a little surprised at finding the Arabic "eiwa" (yes) in general use, instead of the Spanish "si."

About eleven o'clock, we reached the rude village of Atajate, where we procured a very good breakfast of kid, eggs, and white Ronda wine. The wind and rain increased, but I had no time to lose, as every hour swelled the mountain floods and made the journey more difficult. This district is in the worst repute of any in Spain; it is a very nest of robbers and contrabandistas. At the venta in Atajate, they urged us to take a guard, but my valiant José declared that he had never taken one, and yet was never robbed; so I trusted to his good luck. The weather, however, was our best protection. In such a driving rain, we could bid defiance to the flint locks of their escopettes, if, indeed, any could be found, so fond of their trade, as to ply it in a storm

"Wherein the cub-drawn bear would crouch,

The lion and the belly-pinched wolf

Keep their furs dry."

Nevertheless, I noticed that each of the few convoys of laden mules which we met, had one or more of the guardia cicia accompanying it. Besides these, the only persons abroad were some wild-looking individuals, armed to the teeth, and muffled in long cloaks, towards whom, as they passed, José would give his head a slight toss, and whisper to me: "more contrabandistas."

We were soon in a condition to defy the weather. The rain beat furiously in our faces, especially when threading the wind-blown passes between the higher peaks. I raised my umbrella as a defence, but the first blast snapped it in twain. The mountain-sides were veined with rills, roaring downward into the hollows, and smaller rills soon began to trickle down my own sides. During the last part of our way, the path was notched along precipitous steeps, where the storm was so thick that we could see nothing either above or below. It was like riding along the outer edge of the world, When once you are thoroughly wet, it is a great satisfaction to know that you can be no wetter; and so José and I went forward in the best possible humor, finding so much diversion in our plight that the dreary leagues were considerably shortened.

At the venta of Gaucin, where we stopped, the people received us kindly. The house consisted of one room--stable, kitchen, and dining-room all in one. There was a small apartment in a windy loft, where a bed (much too short) was prepared for me. A fire of dry heather was made in the wide fireplace, and the ruddy flames, with a change of clothing and a draught of the amber vintage of Estepona, soon thawed out the chill of the journey. But I received news which caused me a great deal of anxiety. The River Guadiaro was so high that nobody could cross, and two forlorn muleteers had been waiting eight days at the inn, for the waters to subside. Augmented by the rain which had fallen, and which seemed to increase as night came on, how could I hope to cross it on the morrow? In two days, the India steamer would be at Gibraltar; my passage was already taken, and I must be there. The matter was discussed for some time; it was pronounced impossible to travel by the usual road, but the landlord knew a path among the hills which led to a ferry on the Guadiaro, where there was a boat, and from thence we could make our way to San Roque, which is in sight of Gibraltar. He demanded rather a large fee for accompanying me, but there was nothing else to be done. José and I sat down in great tribulation to our accustomed olla, but neither of us could do justice to it, and the greater part gladdened the landlord's two boys--beautiful little imps, with faces like Murillo's cherubs.

Nevertheless, I passed rather a merry evening, chatting with some of the villagers over a brazier of coals; and one of the aforesaid boys, who, although only eight years old, already performed the duties of mozo, lighted me to my loft. When he had put down the lamp, he tried' the door, and asked me: "Have you the key?" "No," said I, "I don't want one; I am not afraid." "But," he rejoined, "perhaps you may get afraid in the night; and if you do, strike on this part of the wall (suiting the action to the word)--I sleep on that side." I willingly promised to call him to my aid, if I should get alarmed. I slept but little, for the wind was howling around the tiles over my head, and I was busy with plans for constructing rafts and swimming currents with a rope

712

around my waist. Finally, I found a little oblivion, but it seemed that I had scarcely closed my eyes, when José pushed open the door. "Thanks be to God, senor!" said he, "it begins to dawn, and the sky is clear: we shall certainly get to Gibraltar to-day."

The landlord was ready, so we took some bread and a basket of olives, and set out at once. Leaving Gaucin, we commenced descending the mountain staircase by which the Serrania of Ronda is scaled, on the side towards Gibraltar. "The road," says Mr. Ford, "seems made by the Evil One in a hanging garden of Eden." After four miles of frightfully rugged descent, we reached an orange grove on the banks of the Xenar, and then took a wild path leading along the hills on the right of the stream. We overtook a few muleteers, who were tempted out by the fine weather, and before long the correo, or mail-rider from Ronda to San Roque, joined us. After eight miles more of toilsome travel we reached the valley of the Guadiaro. The river was not more than twenty yards wide, flowing with a deep, strong current, between high banks. Two ropes were stretched across, and a large, clumsy boat was moored to the shore. We called to the ferrymen, but they hesitated, saying that nobody had yet been able to cross. However, we all got in, with our horses, and two of the men, with much reluctance, drew us over. The current was very powerful, although the river had fallen a little during the night, but we reached the opposite bank without accident.

We had still another river, the Guargante, to pass, but we were cheered by some peasants whom we met, with the news that the ferry-boat had resumed operations. After this current lay behind us, and there was now nothing but firm land all the way to Gibraltar, José declared with much earnestness that he was quite as glad, for my sake, as if somebody had given him a million of dollars. Our horses, too, seemed to feel that something had been achieved, and showed such a fresh spirit that we loosened the reins and let them gallop to their hearts' content over the green meadows. The mountains were now behind us, and the Moorish castle of Gaucin crested a peak blue with the distance. Over hills covered with broom and heather in blossom, and through hollows grown with oleander, arbutus and the mastic shrub, we rode to the cork-wood forests of San Roque, the sporting-ground of Gibraltar officers.

713

The barking of dogs, the cracking of whips, and now and then a distant halloo, announced that a hunt was in progress, and soon we came upon a company of thirty or forty horsemen, in caps, white gloves and top-boots, scattered along the crest of a hill. I had no desire to stop and witness the sport, for the Mediterranean now lay before me, and the huge gray mass of "The Rock" loomed in the distance.

At San Roque, which occupies the summit of a conical hill, about half-way between Gibraltar and Algeciras, the landlord left us, and immediately started on his return. Having now exchanged the rugged bridle-paths of Ronda for a smooth carriage-road, José and I dashed on at full gallop, to the end of our journey. We were both bespattered with mud from head to foot, and our jackets and sombreros had lost something of their spruce air. We met a great many ruddy, cleanly-shaven Englishmen, who reined up on one side to let us pass, with a look of wonder at our Andalusian impudence. Nothing diverted José more than to see one of these Englishmen rising in his stirrups, as he went by on a trot. "Look, look, Señor!" he exclaimed; "did you ever see the like?" and then broke into a fresh explosion of laughter. Passing the Spanish Lines, which stretch across the neck of the sandy little peninsula, connecting Gibraltar with the main land, we rode under the terrible batteries which snarl at Spain from this side of the Rock. Row after row of enormous guns bristle the walls, or look out from the galleries hewn in the sides of inaccessible cliffs An artificial moat is cut along the base of the Rock, and a simple bridge-road leads into the fortress and town. After giving up my passport I was allowed to enter, José having already obtained a permit from the Spanish authorities.

I clattered up the long street of the town to the Club House, where I found a company of English friends. In the evening, José made his appearance, to settle our accounts and take his leave of me. While scrambling down the rocky stair-way of Gaucin, José had said to me: "Look you, Señor, I am very fond of English beer, and if I get you to Gibraltar to day you must give me a glass of it." When, therefore, he came in the evening, his eyes sparkled at the sight of a bottle of Alsop's Ale, and a handful of good Gibraltar cigars. "Ah, Señor," said he, after our books were squared, and he had pocketed his gratification, "I am sorry we are going to part; for we are good friends, are we not, Señor?" "Yes, José," said I; "if I ever come to Granada again, I shall take no other guide than José Garcia; and I will have you for a longer journey than this. We shall go over all Spain together, mi amigo!" "May God grant it!" responded José, crossing himself; "and now, Señor, I must go. I shall travel back to Granada, muy triste, Señor, muy triste" The faithful fellows eyes were full of tears, and, as he lifted my hand twice to his lips, some warm drops fell upon it. God bless his honest heart; wherever he goes!

And now a word as to travelling in Spain, which is not attended with half the difficulties and annoyances I had been led to expect. My experience, of course, is limited to the provinces of Andalusia, but my route included some of the roughest roads and most dangerous robber-districts in the Peninsula. The people with whom I came in contact were invariably friendly and obliging, and I was dealt with much more honestly than I should have been in Italy. With every disposition to serve you, there is nothing like servility among the Spaniards. The native dignity which characterizes their demeanor prepossesses me very strongly in their favor. There is but one dialect of courtesy, and the muleteers and common peasants address each other with the same grave respect as the Dons and Grandees. My friend José was a model of good-breeding.

I had little trouble either with passport-officers or custom-houses. My passport, in fact, was never once demanded, although I took the precaution to have it visèd in all the large cities. In Seville and Malaga, it was signed by the American Consuls, without the usual fee of two dollars--almost the only instances which have come under my observation. The regulations of the American Consular System, which gives the Consuls no salary, but permits them, instead, to get their pay out of travellers, is a disgrace to our government. It amounts, in effect, to a direct tax on travel, and falls heavily on the hundreds of young men of limited means, who annually visit Europe for the purpose of completing their education. Every American citizen who travels in Italy pays a passport tax of ten dollars. In all the ports of the Mediterranean, there is an American Vice-Consul, who does not even get the postage paid on his dispatches, and to whom the advent of a traveller is of course a welcome sight. Misled by a false notion of economy, our government is fast becoming proverbial for its meanness. If those of our own citizens who represent us abroad only worked as they are paid, and if the foreigners who act as Vice-Consuls without pay did not derive some petty trading advantages from their position, we should be almost without protection.

With my departure from Spain closes the record of my journey in the Lands of the Saracen; for, although I afterwards beheld more perfect types of Saracenic Art on the banks of the Jumna and the Ganges, they grew up under the great Empire of the descendants of Tamerlane, and were the creations of artists foreign to the soil. It would, no doubt, be interesting to contrast the remains of Oriental civilization and refinement, as they still exist at the extreme eastern and western limits of the Moslem sway, and to show how that Art, which had its birth in the capitals of the Caliphs--Damascus and Baghdad--attained its most perfect development in Spain and India; but my visit to the latter country connects itself naturally with my voyage to China, Loo-Choo, and Japan, forming a separate and distinct field of travel.

On the 27th of November, the Overland Mail Steamer arrived at Gibraltar, and I embarked in her for Alexandria, entering upon another year of even more varied, strange, and adventurous experiences, than that which had closed. I am almost afraid to ask those patient readers, who have accompanied me thus far, to travel with me through another volume; but next to the pleasure of seeing the world, comes the pleasure of telling of it, and I must needs finish my story.

About Author

Bayard Taylor (January 11, 1825 – December 19, 1878) was an American poet, literary critic, translator, travel author, and diplomat.

Life and work

Taylor was born on January 11, 1825, in Kennett Square in Chester County, Pennsylvania. He was the fourth son, the first to survive to maturity, of the Quaker couple, Joseph and Rebecca (née Way) Taylor. His father was a wealthy farmer. Bayard received his early instruction in an academy at West Chester, Pennsylvania, and later at nearby Unionville. At the age of seventeen, he was apprenticed to a printer in West Chester. The influential critic and editor Rufus Wilmot Griswold encouraged him to write poetry. The volume that resulted, Ximena, or the Battle of the Sierra Morena, and other Poems, was published in 1844 and dedicated to Griswold.

Using the money from his poetry and an advance for travel articles, he visited parts of England, France, Germany and Italy, making largely pedestrian tours for almost two years. He sent accounts of his travels to the Tribune, The Saturday Evening Post, and Gazette of the United States.

In 1846, a collection of his articles was published in two volumes as Views Afoot, or Europe seen with Knapsack and Staff. That publication resulted in an invitation to serve as an editorial assistant for Graham's Magazine for a few months in 1848. That same year, Horace Greeley, editor of the New York Tribune, hired Taylor and sent him to California to report on the gold rush. He returned by way of Mexico and published another two-volume collection of travel essays, El Dorado; or, Adventures in the Path of Empire (1850). Within two weeks of release, the books sold 10,000 copies in the U.S. and 30,000 in Great Britain.

In 1849 Taylor married Mary Agnew, who died of tuberculosis the next year. That same year, Taylor won a popular competition sponsored by P. T. Barnum to write an ode for the "Swedish Nightingale", singer Jenny Lind. His poem "Greetings to America" was set to music by Julius Benedict and performed by the singer at numerous concerts on her tour of the United States.

In 1851 he traveled to Egypt, where he followed the Nile River as far as 12° 30' N. He also traveled in Palestine and Mediterranean countries, writing poetry based on his experiences. Toward the end of 1852, he sailed from England to Calcutta, and then to China, where he joined the expedition of Commodore Matthew Calbraith Perry to Japan. The results of these journeys were published as A Journey to Central Africa; or, Life and Landscapes from Egypt to the Negro Kingdoms of the White Nile (1854); The Lands of the Saracen; or, Pictures of Palestine, Asia Minor, Sicily and Spain (1854); and A Visit to India, China and Japan in the Year 1853 (1855).

He returned to the U.S. on December 20, 1853, and undertook a successful public lecturer tour that extended from Maine to Wisconsin. After two years, he went to northern Europe to study Swedish life, language and literature. The trip inspired his long narrative poem Lars. His series of articles Swedish Letters to the Tribune were republished as Northern Travel: Summer and Winter Pictures (1857).

In Berlin in 1856, Taylor met the great German scientist Alexander von Humboldt, hoping to interview him for the New York Tribune. Humboldt was welcoming, and inquired whether they should speak English or German. Taylor planned to go to central Asia, where Humboldt had traveled in 1829. Taylor informed Humboldt of Washington Irving's death; Humboldt had met him in Paris. Taylor saw Humboldt again in 1857 at Potsdam.

In October 1857, he married Maria Hansen, the daughter of the Danish/German astronomer Peter Hansen. The couple spent the following winter in Greece. In 1859 Taylor returned to the American West and lectured at San Francisco.

In 1862, he was appointed to the U.S. diplomatic service as secretary of legation at St. Petersburg, and acting minister to Russia for a time during 1862-3 after the resignation of Ambassador Simon Cameron.

He published his first novel Hannah Thurston in 1863. The newspaper

The New York Times first praised him for "break new ground with such assured success". A second much longer appreciation in the same newspaper was thoroughly negative, describing "one pointless, aimless situation leading to another of the same stamp, and so on in maddening succession". It concluded: "The platitudes and puerilities which might otherwise only raise a smile, when confronted with such pompous pretensions, excite the contempt of every man who has in him the feeblest instincts of common honesty in literature." It proved successful enough for his publisher to announce another novel from him the next year.

In 1864 Taylor and his wife Maria returned to the U.S. In 1866, Taylor traveled to Colorado and made a large loop through the northern mountains on horseback with a group that included William Byers, editor of the newspaper Rocky Mountain News. His letters describing this adventure were later compiled and published as Colorado: A Summer Trip.

His late novel, Joseph and His Friend: A Story of Pennsylvania (1870), first serialized in the magazine The Atlantic, was described as a story of young man in rural Pennsylvania and "the troubles which arise from the want of a broader education and higher culture". It is believed to be based on the poets Fitz-Greene Halleck and Joseph Rodman Drake, and since the late 20th-century has been called America's first gay novel. Taylor spoke at the dedication of a monument to Halleck in his native town, Guilford, Connecticut. He said that in establishing this monument to an American poet "we symbolize the intellectual growth of the American people.... The life of the poet who sleeps here represents the long period of transition between the appearance of American poetry and the creation of an appreciative and sympathetic audience for it."

Taylor imitated and parodied the writings of various poets in Diversions of the Echo Club (London, 1873; Boston, 1876).In 1874 Taylor traveled to Iceland to report for the Tribune on the one thousandth anniversary of the first European settlement there.

During March 1878, the U.S. Senate confirmed his appointment as United States Minister to Prussia. Mark Twain, who traveled to Europe on the same ship, was envious of Taylor's command of German.

Taylor's travel writings were widely quoted by congressmen seeking to defend racial discrimination. Richard Townshend quoted passages from Taylor such as "the Chinese are morally, the most debased people on the face of the earth" and "A Chinese city is the greatest of all abominations."

A few months after arriving in Berlin, Taylor died there on December 19, 1878. His body was returned to the U.S. and buried in Kennett Square, Pennsylvania. The New York Times published his obituary on its front page, referring to him as "a great traveler, both on land and paper". Shortly after his death, Henry Wadsworth Longfellow wrote a memorial poem in Taylor's memory, at the urging of Oliver Wendell Holmes, Sr.

Legacy and honors

Cedarcroft, Taylor's home from 1859 to 1874, which he built near Kennett Square, is preserved as a National Historic Landmark.

The Bayard Taylor School was added to the National Register of Historic Places in 1988.

The Bayard Taylor Memorial Library is in Kennett Square.

Evaluations

Though he wanted to be known most as a poet, Taylor was mostly recognized as a travel writer during his lifetime. Modern critics have generally accepted him as technically skilled in verse, but lacking imagination and, ultimately, consider his work as a conventional example of 19th-century sentimentalism.

His translation of Faust, however, was recognized for its scholarly skill and remained in print through 1969. According to the 1920 edition of Encyclopedia Americana:

> It is by his translation of Faust, one of the finest attempts of the kind in any literature, that Taylor is generally known; yet as an original poet he stands well up in the second rank of Americans. His Poems of the Orient and his Pennsylvania ballads comprise his best work. His verse is finished and sonorous, but at times over-rhetorical.

According to the 1911 edition of Encyclopædia Britannica:

> Taylor's most ambitious productions in poetry—- his Masque of the Gods (Boston, 1872), Prince Deukalion; a lyrical drama (Boston, 1878), The Picture of St John (Boston, 1866), Lars; a Pastoral of Norway (Boston, 1873), and The Prophet; a tragedy (Boston, 1874)—- are marred by a ceaseless effort to overstrain his power. But he will be remembered by his poetic and excellent translation of Goethe's Faust (2 vols, Boston, 1870-71) in the original metres.
>
> Taylor felt, in all truth, the torment and the ecstasy of verse; but, as a critical friend has written of him, his nature was so ardent, so full-blooded, that slight and common sensations intoxicated him, and he estimated their effect, and his power to transmit it to others, beyond the true value. He had, from the earliest period at which he began to compose, a distinct lyrical faculty: so keen indeed was his ear that he became too insistently haunted by the music of others, pre-eminently of Tennyson. But he had often a true and fine note of his own. His best short poems are The Metempsychosis of the Pine and the well-known Bedouin love-song.
>
> In his critical essays Bayard Taylor had himself in no inconsiderable degree what he wrote of as that pure poetic insight which is the vital spirit of criticism. The most valuable of these prose dissertations are the Studies in German Literature (New York, 1879).

In Appletons' Cyclopædia of American Biography of 1889, Edmund Clarence Stedman gives the following critique:

> His poetry is striking for qualities that appeal to the ear and eye, finished, sonorous in diction and rhythm, at times too rhetorical, but rich in sound, color, and metrical effects. His early models were Byron and Shelley, and his more ambitious lyrics and dramas exhibit the latter's peculiar, often vague, spirituality. Lars, somewhat after the manner of Tennyson, is his longest and most attractive narrative poem. Prince Deukalion was designed for a masterpiece; its blank verse and choric

interludes are noble in spirit and mould. Some of Taylor's songs, oriental idyls, and the true and tender Pennsylvanian ballads, have passed into lasting favor, and show the native quality of his poetic gift. His fame rests securely upon his unequalled rendering of Faust in the original metres, of which the first and second parts appeared in 1870 and 1871. His commentary upon Part II for the first time interpreted the motive and allegory of that unique structure. (source: wikipedia)

NOTABLE WORKS

Ximena, or the Battle of the Sierra Morena, and other Poems (1844)

Views Afoot, or Europe seen with Knapsack and Staff (1846)

Rhymes of Travel: Ballads and Poems (1849)

El Dorado; or, Adventures in the Path of Empire (1850)

Romances, Lyrics, and Songs (1852)

Journey to Central Africa; or, Life and Landscapes from Egypt to the Negro Kingdoms of the White Nile, A (1854)

Lands of the Saracen; or, Pictures of Palestine, Asia Minor, Sicily and Spain, The (1854)

A visit to India, China, and Japan in the year 1853 (1855)

Lands of the Saracen; or, Pictures of Palestine, Asia Minor, Sicily and Spain, The (1855)

Poems of the Orient (Boston: Ticknor and Fields, 1855)

Poems of Home and Travel (1856)

Cyclopedia of Modern Travel (1856)

Northern Travel: Summer and Winter Pictures (1857)

View A-Foot, or Europe Seen with Knapsack and Staff (1859)

Life, Travels And Books Of Alexander Von Humboldt, The (1859)

At Home and Abroad, First Series: A Sketch-book of Life, Scenery, and Men (1859)

Cyclopaedia of Modern Travel Vol I (1861)

Prose Writings: India, China, and Japan (1862)

Travels in Greece and Russia, with an Excursion to Crete (1859)

Poet's Journal (1863)

Hanna Thurston (1863)

John Godfrey's Fortunes Related by Himself: A story of American Life (1864)

"Cruise On Lake Ladoga, A" (1864)

"The Poems of Bayard Taylor" (1865)

John Godrey's Fortunes Related By Himself - A story of American Life (1865)

The Story of Kennett (1866)

Visit To The Balearic Islands, Complete in Two Parts, A (1867)

Picture of St. John, The (1867)

Colorado: A Summer Trip (1867)

"Little Land Of Appenzell, The" (1867)

"Island of Maddalena with a Distant View of Caprera, The" (1868)

"Land Of Paoli, The" (1868)

"Catalonian Bridle-Roads" (1868)

"Kyffhauser And Its Legend, The" (1868)

By-Ways Of Europe (1869)

Joseph and His Friend: A Story of Pennsylvania (1870)

Ballad of Abraham Lincoln, The (1870)

"Sights In And Around Yedo" (1871)

Northern Travel (1871)

Japan in Our Day (1872)

Masque of the Gods, The (1872)

"Heart Of Arabia, The" (1872)

Travels in South Africa (1872)

At Home and Abroad: A Sketch-Book of Life, Scenery and Men (1872)

Diversions of the Echo Club (1873)

Lars: A Pastoral of Norway (1873)

Wonders of the Yellowstone - The Illustrated Library of Travel, Exploration and Adventure (with James Richardson) (1873)

Northern Travel: Summer and Winter Pictures - Sweden, Denmark and Lapland (1873).

Lake Regions of Central Africa (1873)

Prophet: A Tragedy, The. (1874)

Home Pastorals Ballads & Lyrics (1875)

Egypt And Iceland In The Year 1874 (1875)

Boys of Other Countries: Stories for American Boys (1876)

Echo Club and Other Literary Diversions (1876)

Picturesque Europe Part Thirty-Six (1877)

National Ode: The Memorial Freedom Poem, The (1877)

Bismarck: His Authentic Biography (1877)

"Assyrian Night-Song" (August 1877)

Prince Deukalion (1878)

Picturesque Europe (1878)

Studies in German Literature (1879)

Faust: A Tragedy translated in the Original Metres (1890)

Travels in Arabia (1892).

A school history of Germany (1882).

EDITIONS

Collected editions of his Poetical Works and his Dramatic Works were published at Boston in 1888; his Life and Letters (Boston, 2 vols., 1884) were edited by his wife and Horace Scudder.

Marie Hansen Taylor translated into German Bayard's Greece (Leipzig, 1858), Hannah Thurston (Hamburg, 1863), Story of Kennett (Gotha, 1868), Tales of Home (Berlin, 1879), Studies in German Literature (Leipzig, 1880), and notes to Faust, both parts (Leipzig, 1881). After her husband's death, she edited, with notes, his Dramatic Works (1880), and in the same year his Poems in a "Household Edition", and brought together his Critical Essays and Literary Notes. In 1885 she prepared a school edition of Lars, with notes and a sketch of its author's life.

CPSIA information can be obtained
at www.ICGtesting.com
Printed in the USA
LVHW090346140720
660560LV00013B/605

9 789390 194674